# Lost Legends of Nothing

Katherine Tegen Books is an imprint of HarperCollins Publishers.
HarperAlley is an imprint of HarperCollins Publishers.

Lost Legends of Nothing
Copyright © 2023 by Alejandra Green and Fanny Rodriguez
All rights reserved. Manufactured in Bosnia and Herzegovina.
No part of this book may be used or reproduced in any manner whatsoever without
written permission except in the case of brief quotations embodied in critical articles
and reviews. For information address HarperCollins Children's Books, a division of
HarperCollins Publishers, 195 Broadway, New York, NY 10007.
www.harpercollinschildrens.com

ISBN 978-0-06-283950-3 — ISBN 978-0-06-283951-0 (hardcover)

The artists used Adobe Photoshop to create the digital illustrations for this book.
Typography by Fanny Rodriguez
22 23 24 25 26  GPS  10 9 8 7 6 5 4 3 2 1
First Edition

For the one soul I'm lucky enough to share
my life with nothing but love, laughter, and
adventure. For everything and always.
Thank you.

—Ale

For my dearest, the one who always keeps
me from getting lost through sidequests.
Thank you for making nothing so
wonderful.

—Fanny

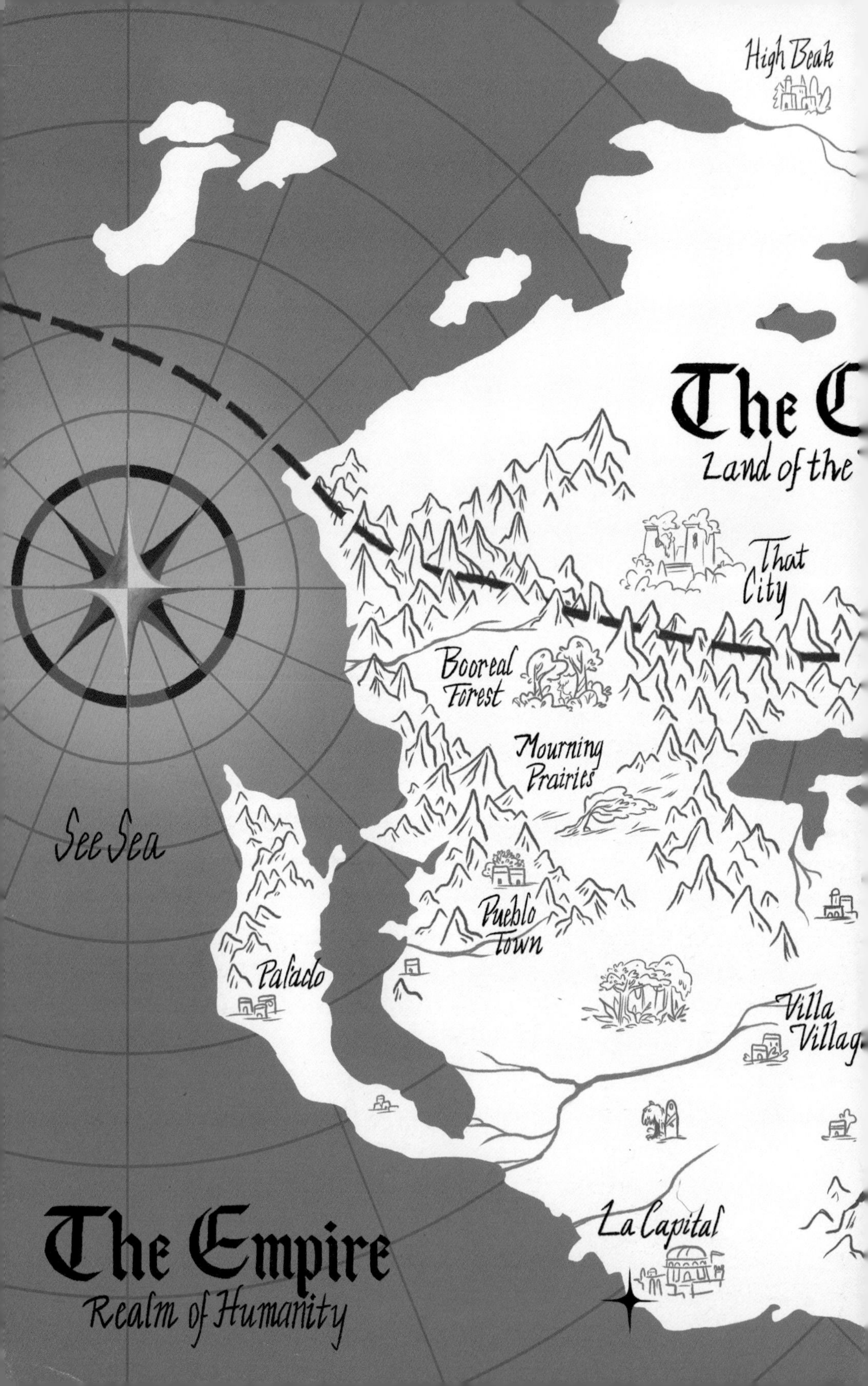
High Beak
The C
Land of the
That City
Booreal Forest
Mourning Prairies
See Sea
Pueblo Town
Palado
Villa Villag
La Capital
The Empire
Realm of Humanity

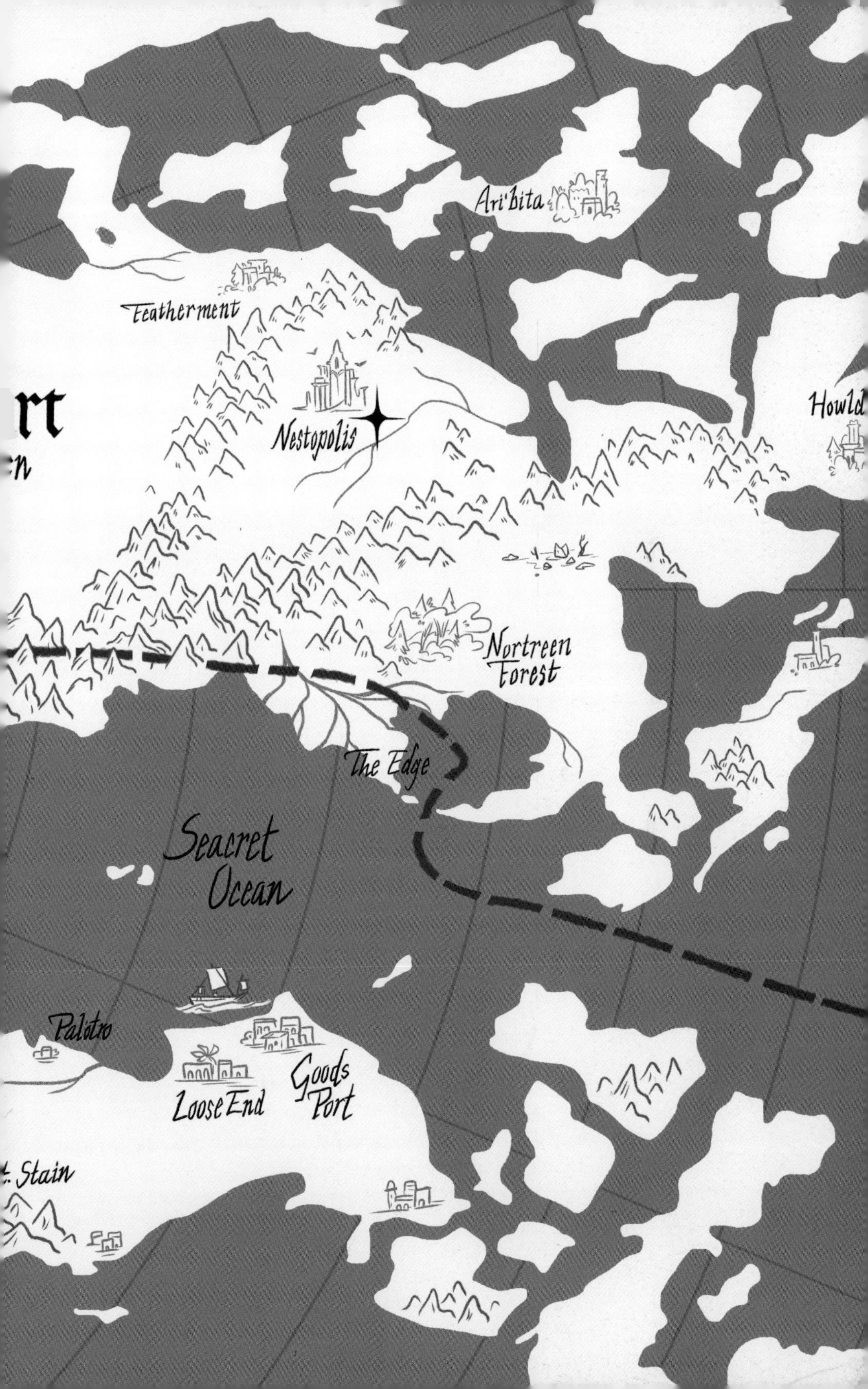
Ari'bita
Featherment
rt
n
Nestopolis
Howld
Nortreen Forest
The Edge
Seacret Ocean
Paldro
Loose End
Goods Port
. Stain

Alejandra Green & Fanny Rodriguez

# Lost Legends of Nothing

KATHERINE TEGEN BOOKS

*An Imprint of HarperCollins Publishers*

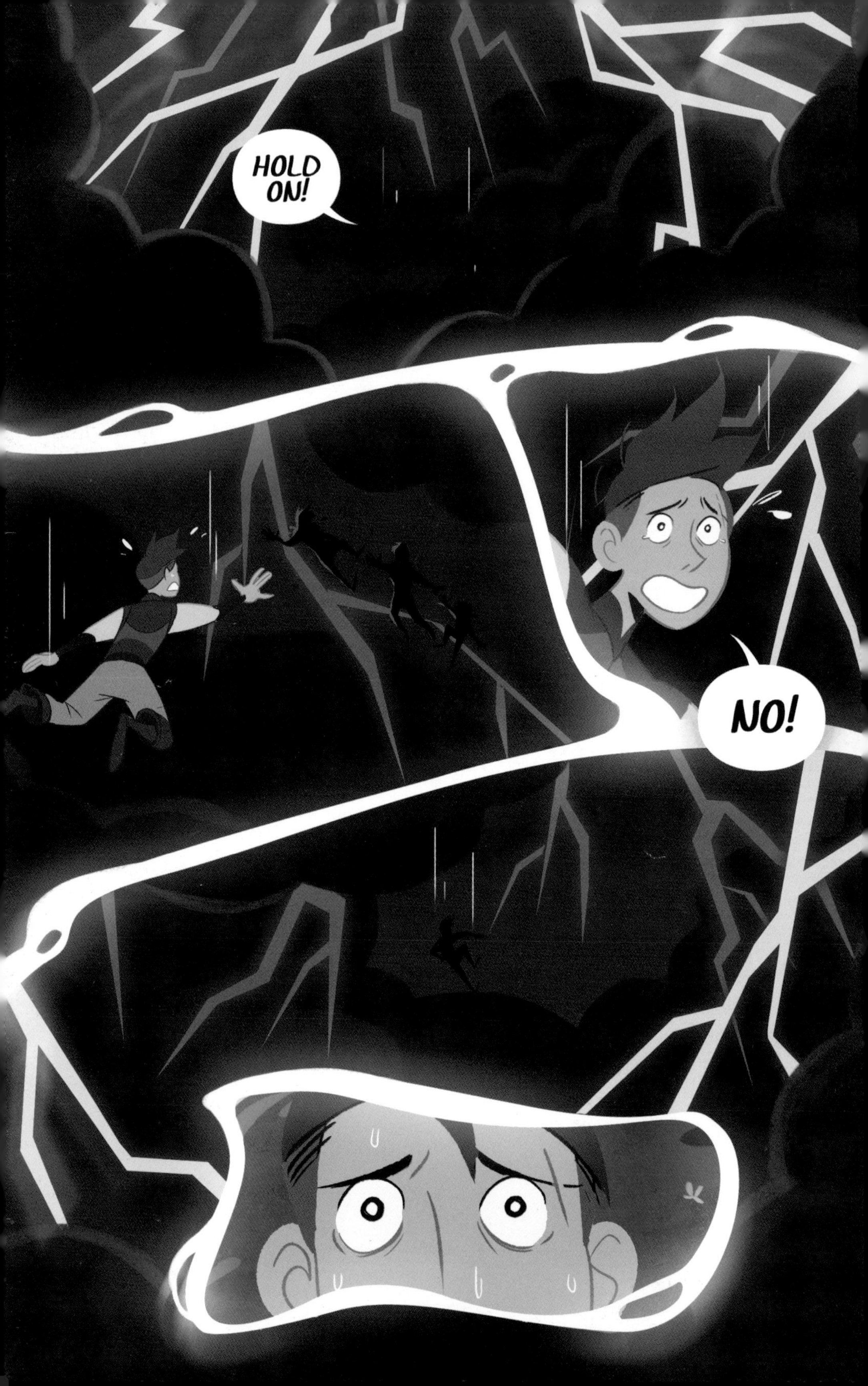
HOLD ON!
NO!

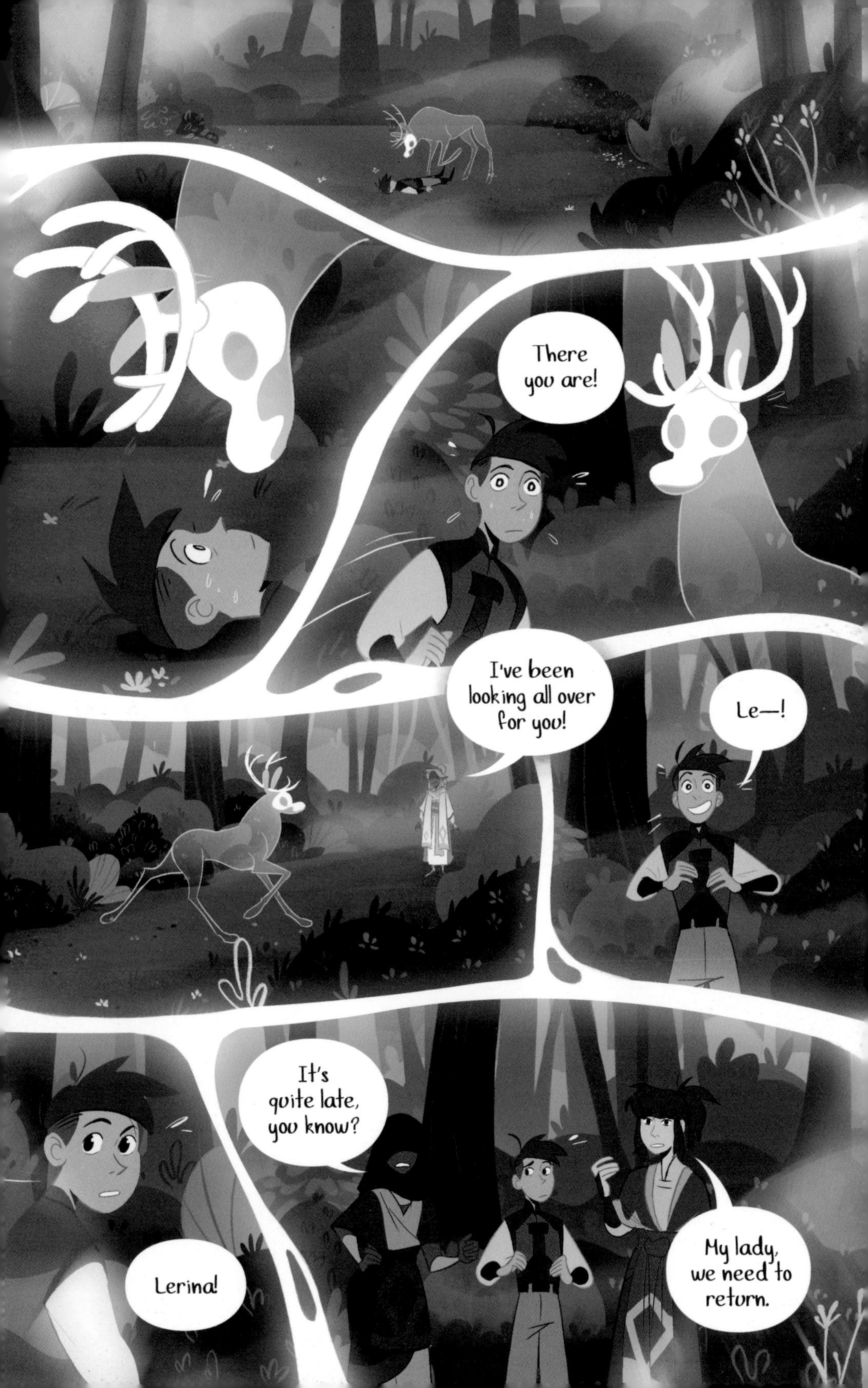
There you are!
I've been looking all over for you!
Le—!
Lerina!
It's quite late, you know?
My lady, we need to return.

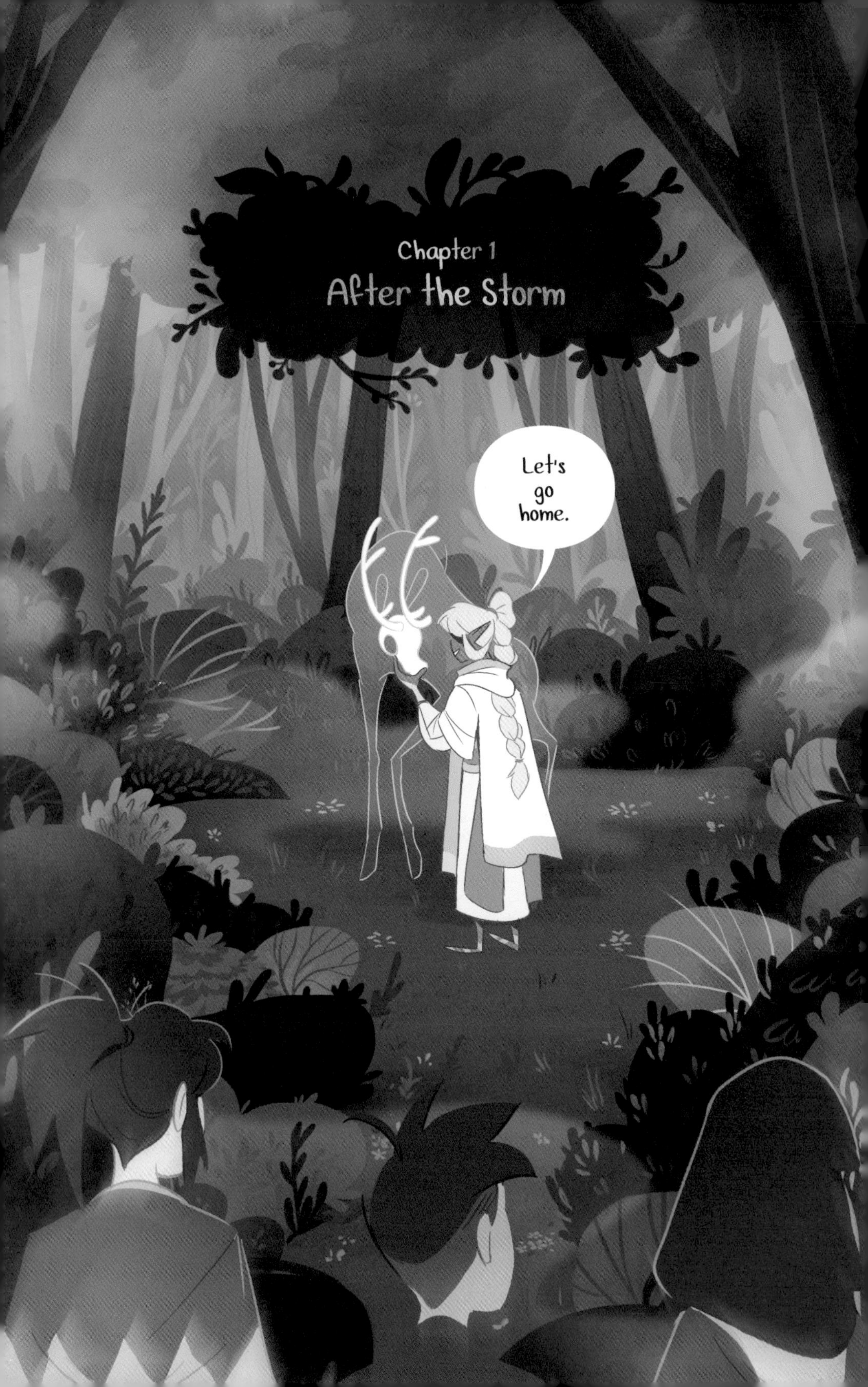

Chapter 1
After the Storm
Let's go home.

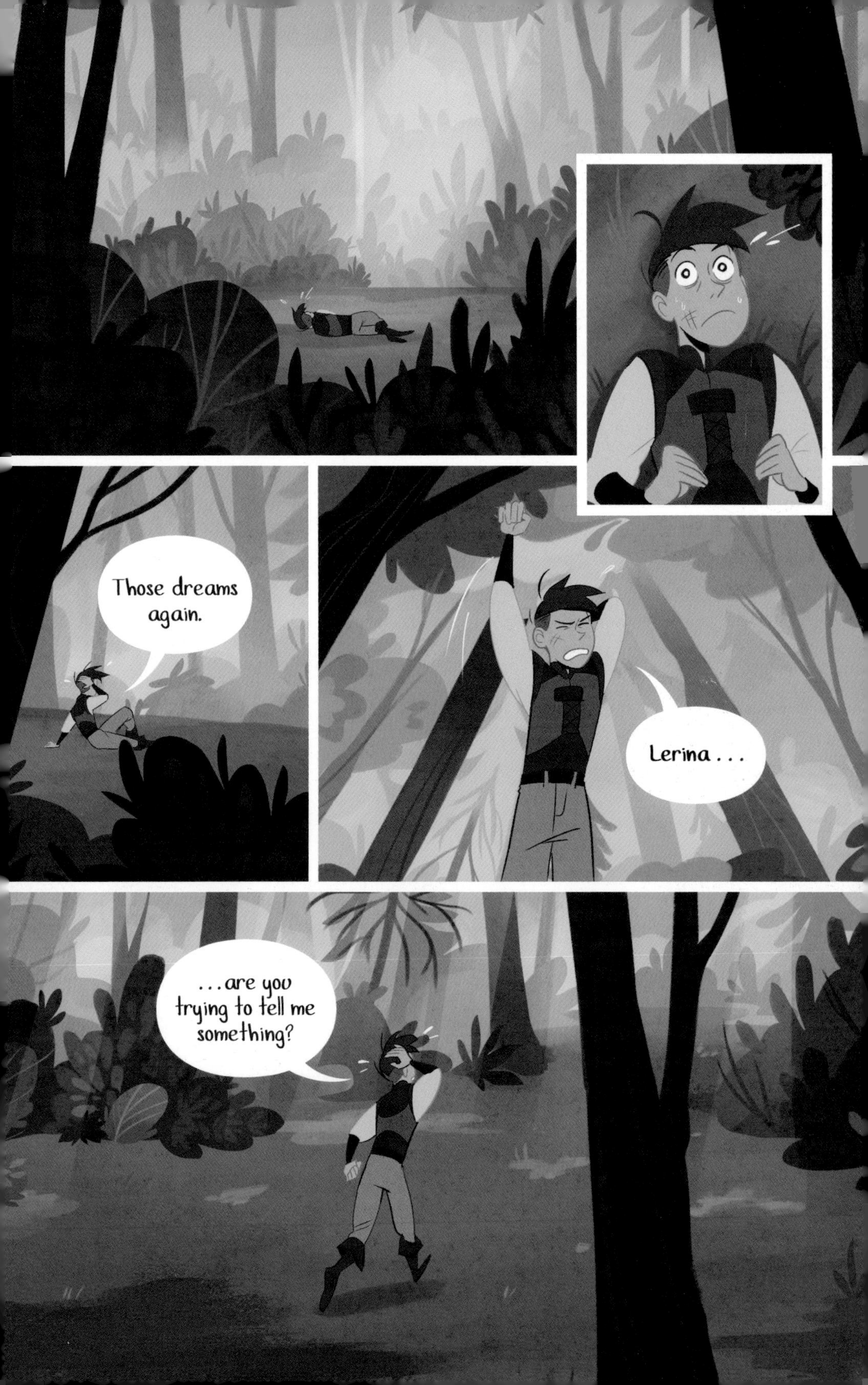
Those dreams again.
Lerina . . .
. . . are you trying to tell me something?

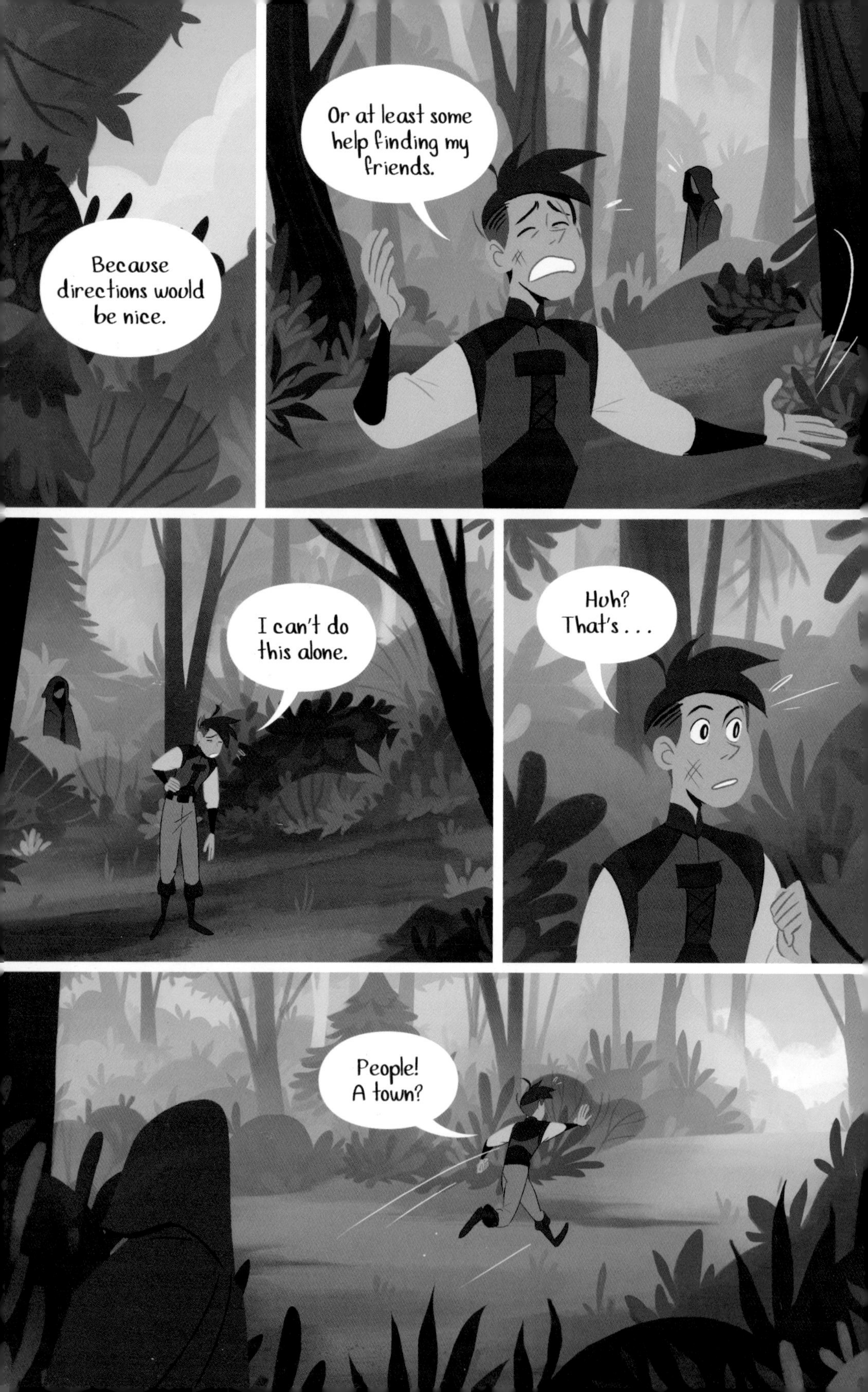
Because directions would be nice.
Or at least some help finding my friends.
I can't do this alone.
Huh? That's . . .
People! A town?

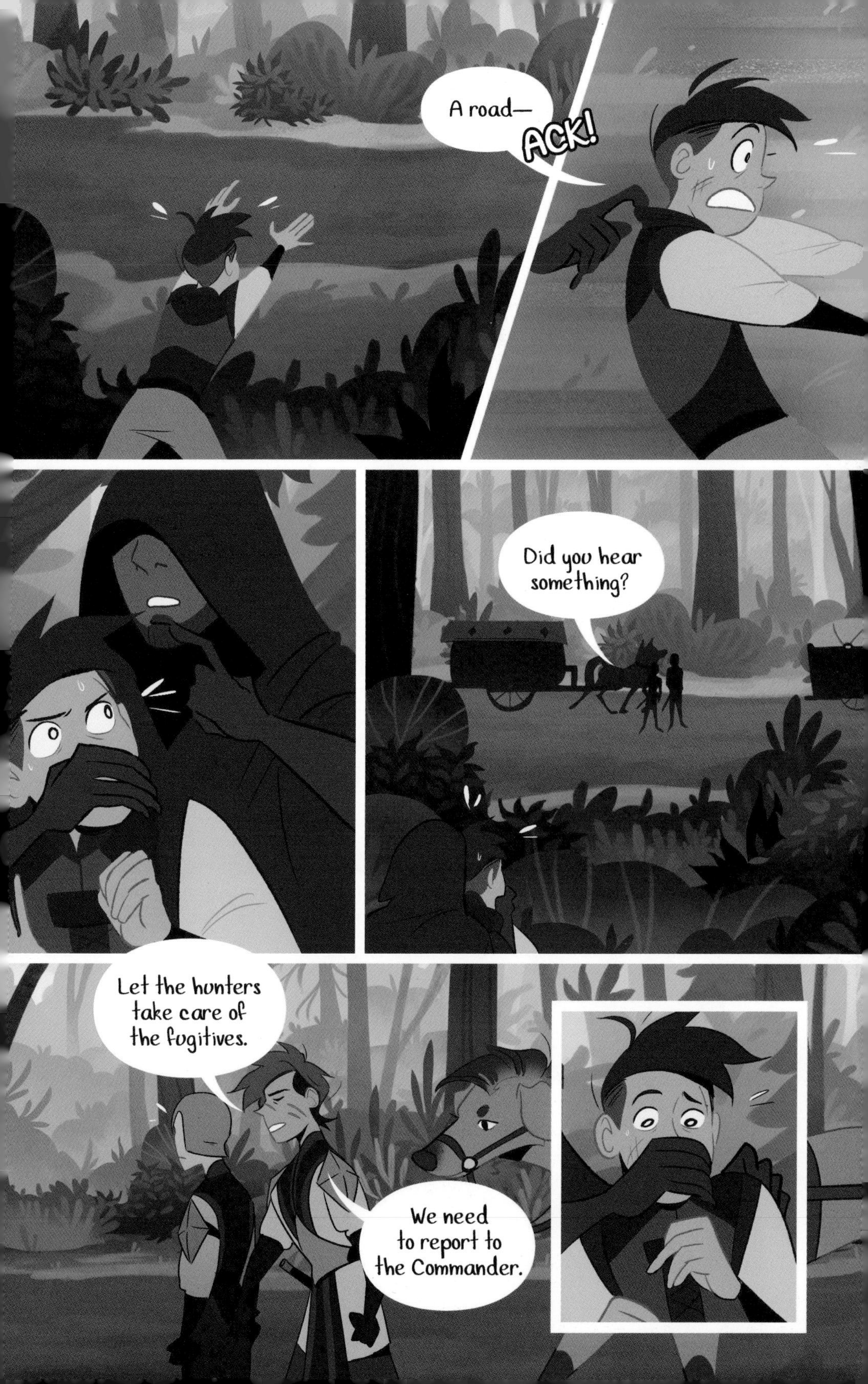
A road—
ACK!
Did you hear something?
Let the hunters take care of the fugitives.
We need to report to the Commander.

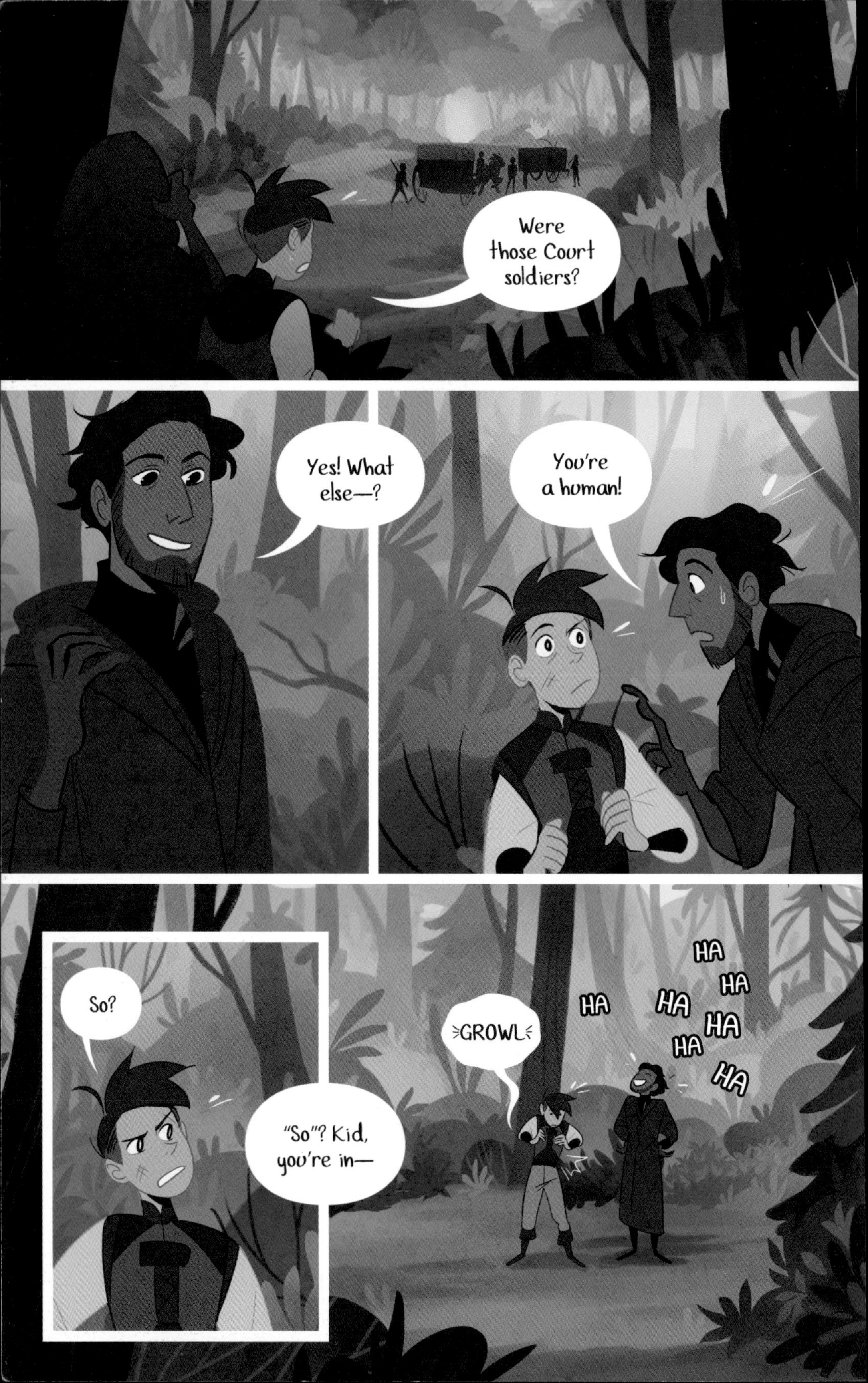
Were those Court soldiers?
Yes! What else—?
You're a human!
So?
"So"? Kid, you're in—
GROWL
HA
HA
HA
HA
HA
HA
HA

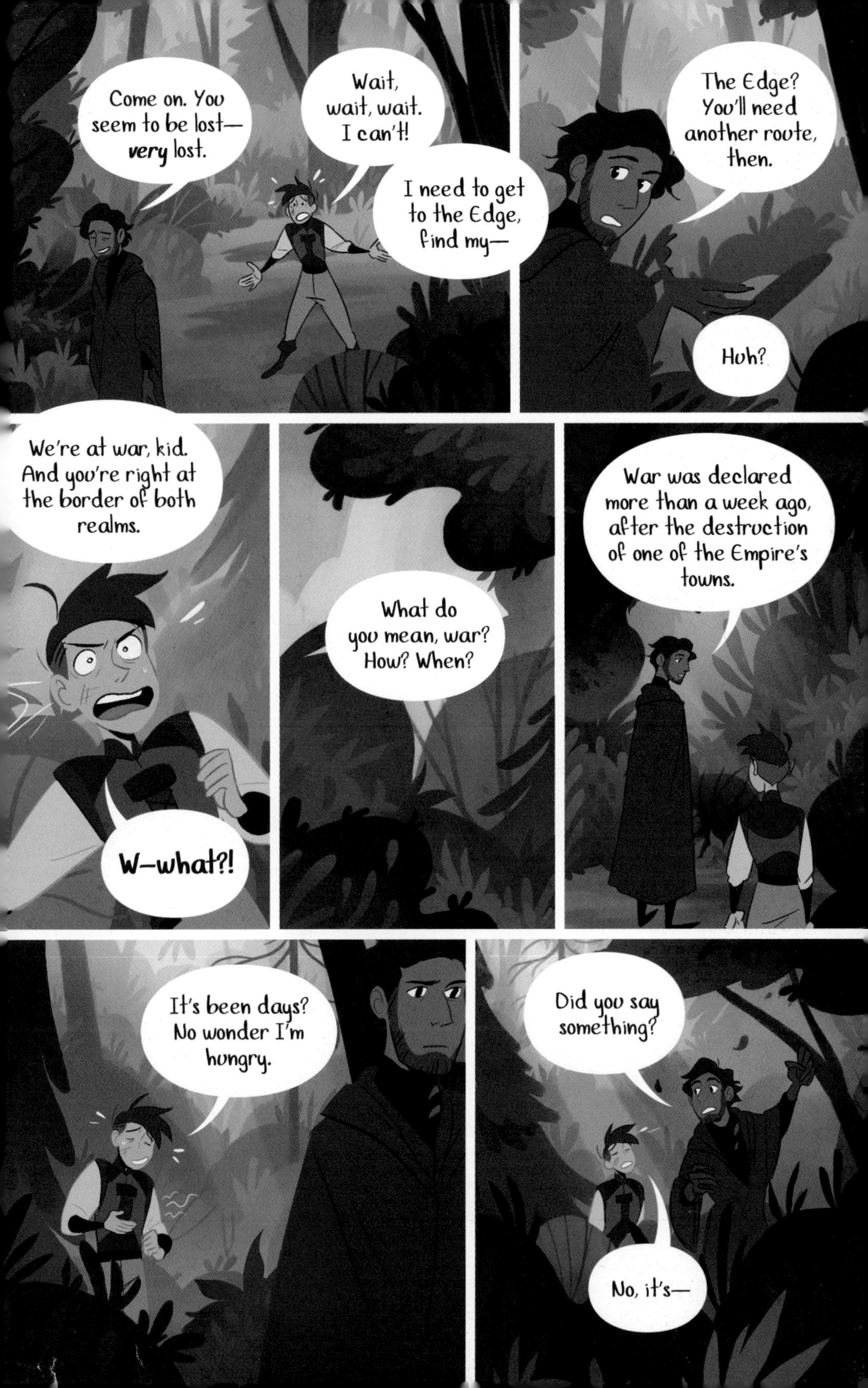
Come on. You seem to be lost—**very** lost.
Wait, wait, wait. I can't!
I need to get to the Edge, find my—
The Edge? You'll need another route, then.
Huh?
We're at war, kid. And you're right at the border of both realms.
W-what?!
What do you mean, war? How? When?
War was declared more than a week ago, after the destruction of one of the Empire's towns.
It's been days? No wonder I'm hungry.
Did you say something?
No, it's—

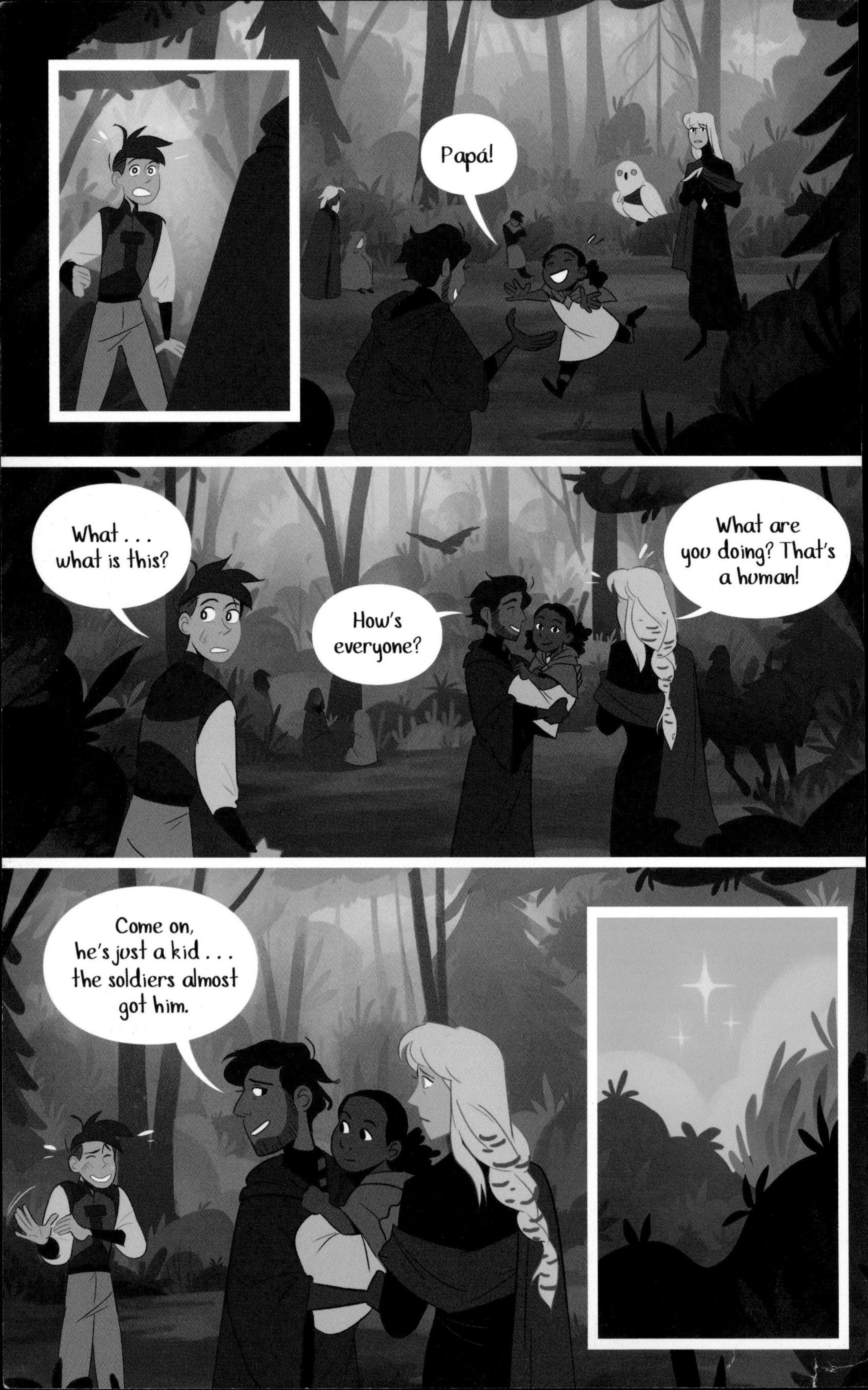
Papá!
What . . . what is this?
How's everyone?
What are you doing? That's a human!
Come on, he's just a kid . . . the soldiers almost got him.

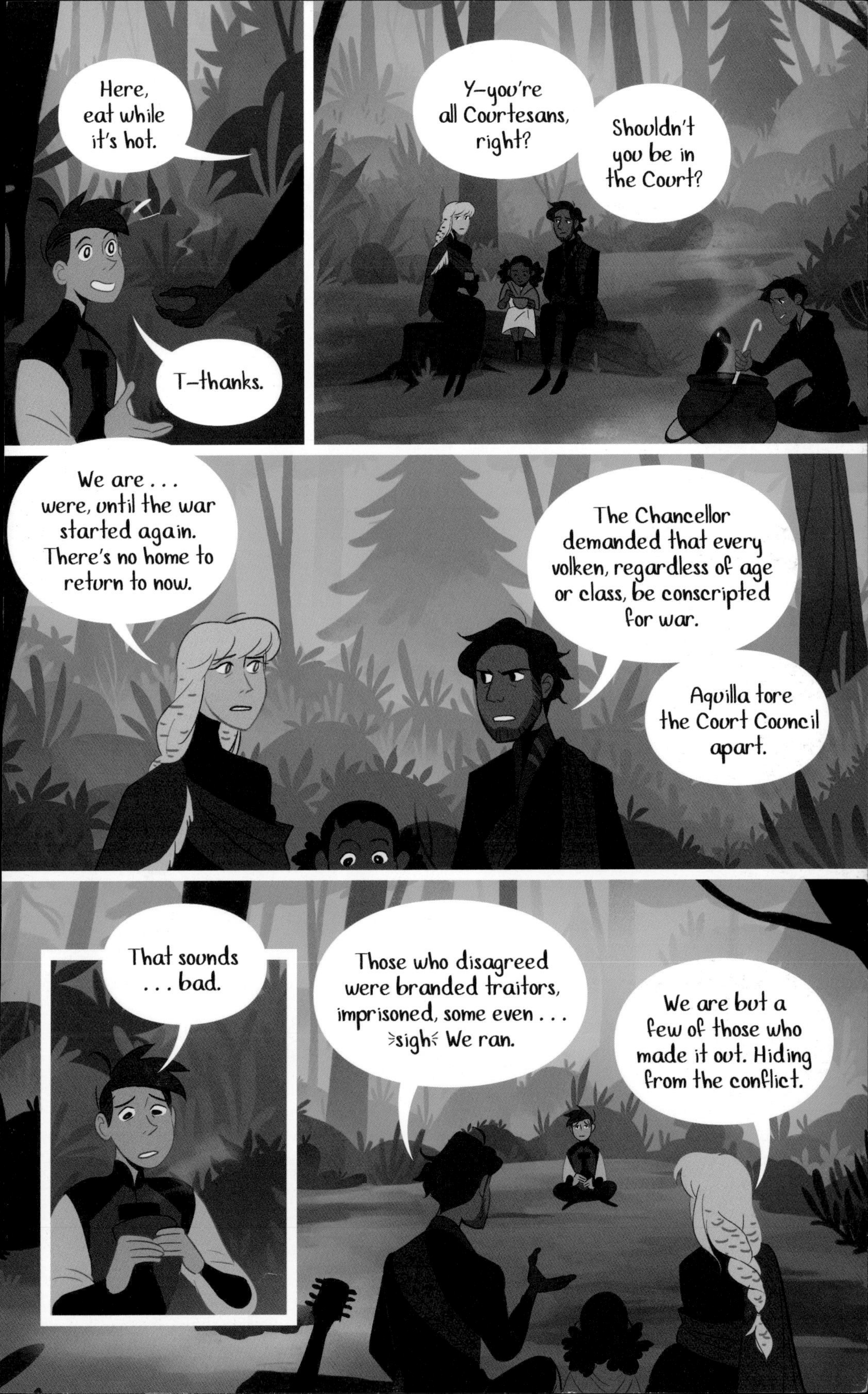
Here, eat while it's hot.
T–thanks.
Y–you're all Courtesans, right?
Shouldn't you be in the Court?
We are . . . were, until the war started again. There's no home to return to now.
The Chancellor demanded that every volken, regardless of age or class, be conscripted for war.
Aquilla tore the Court Council apart.
That sounds . . . bad.
Those who disagreed were branded traitors, imprisoned, some even . . . ⪢sigh⪡ We ran.
We are but a few of those who made it out. Hiding from the conflict.

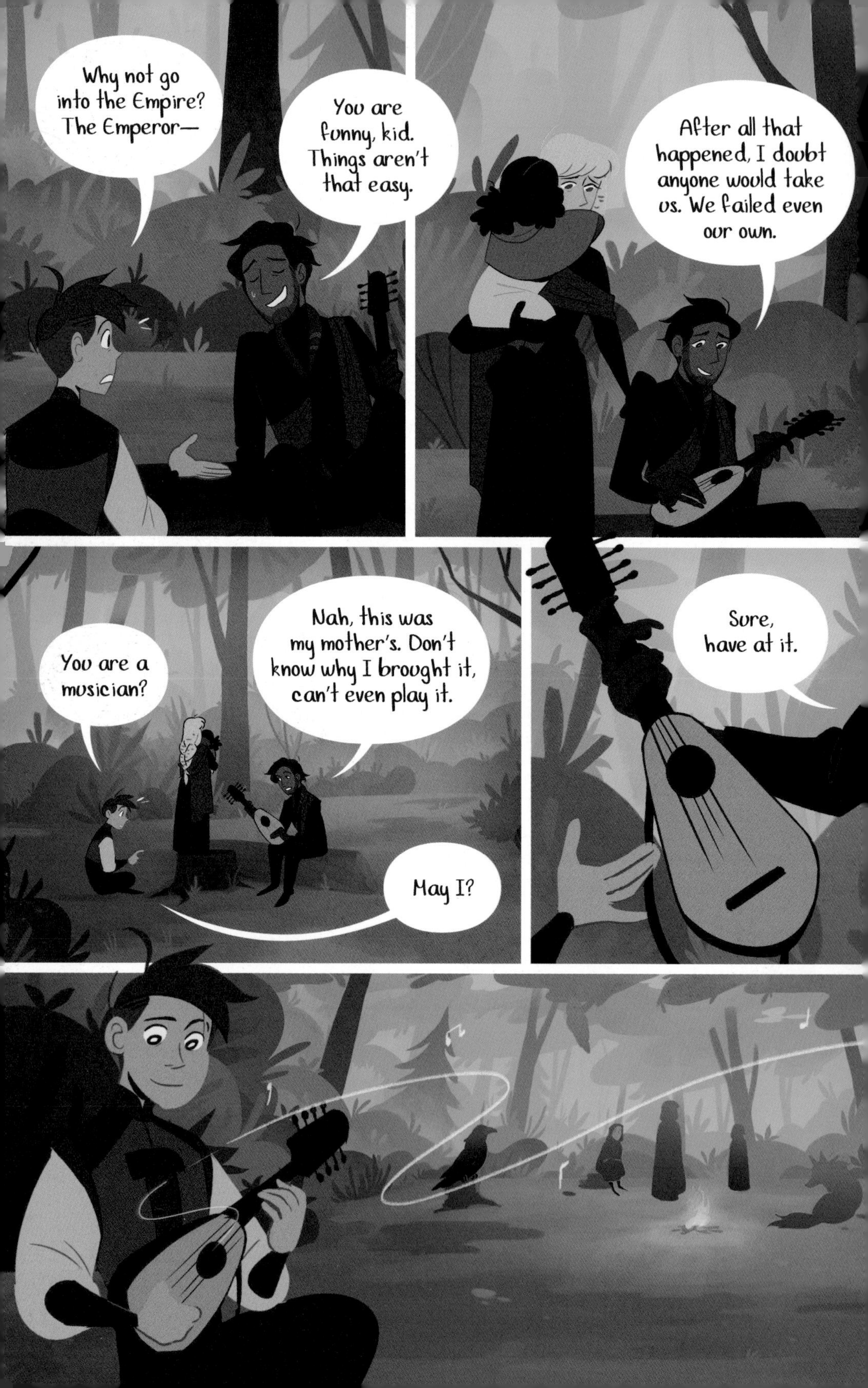
Why not go into the Empire? The Emperor—
You are funny, kid. Things aren't that easy.
After all that happened, I doubt anyone would take us. We failed even our own.
You are a musician?
Nah, this was my mother's. Don't know why I brought it, can't even play it.
May I?
Sure, have at it.

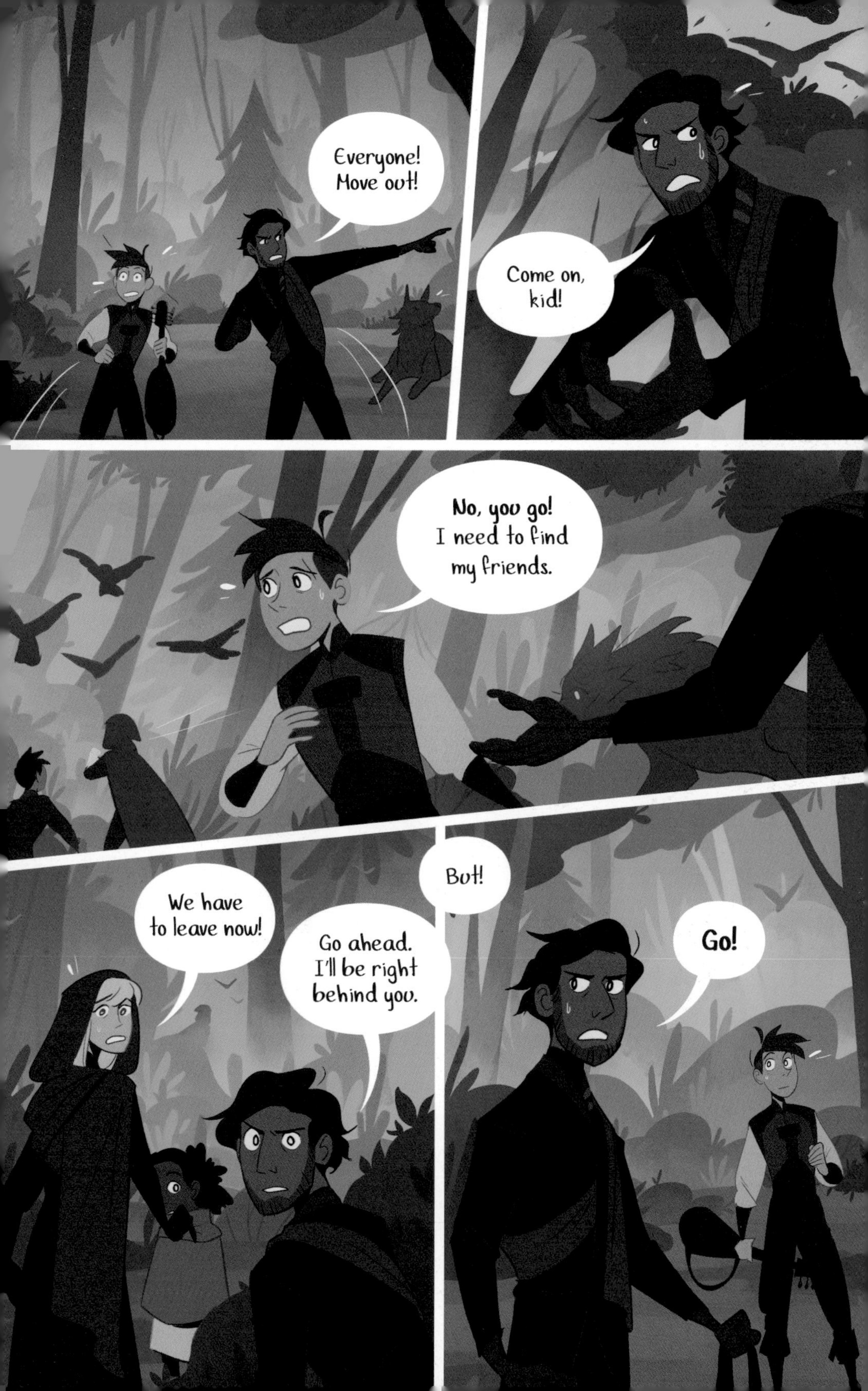
Everyone! Move out!
Come on, kid!
No, you go! I need to find my friends.
We have to leave now!
Go ahead. I'll be right behind you.
But!
Go!

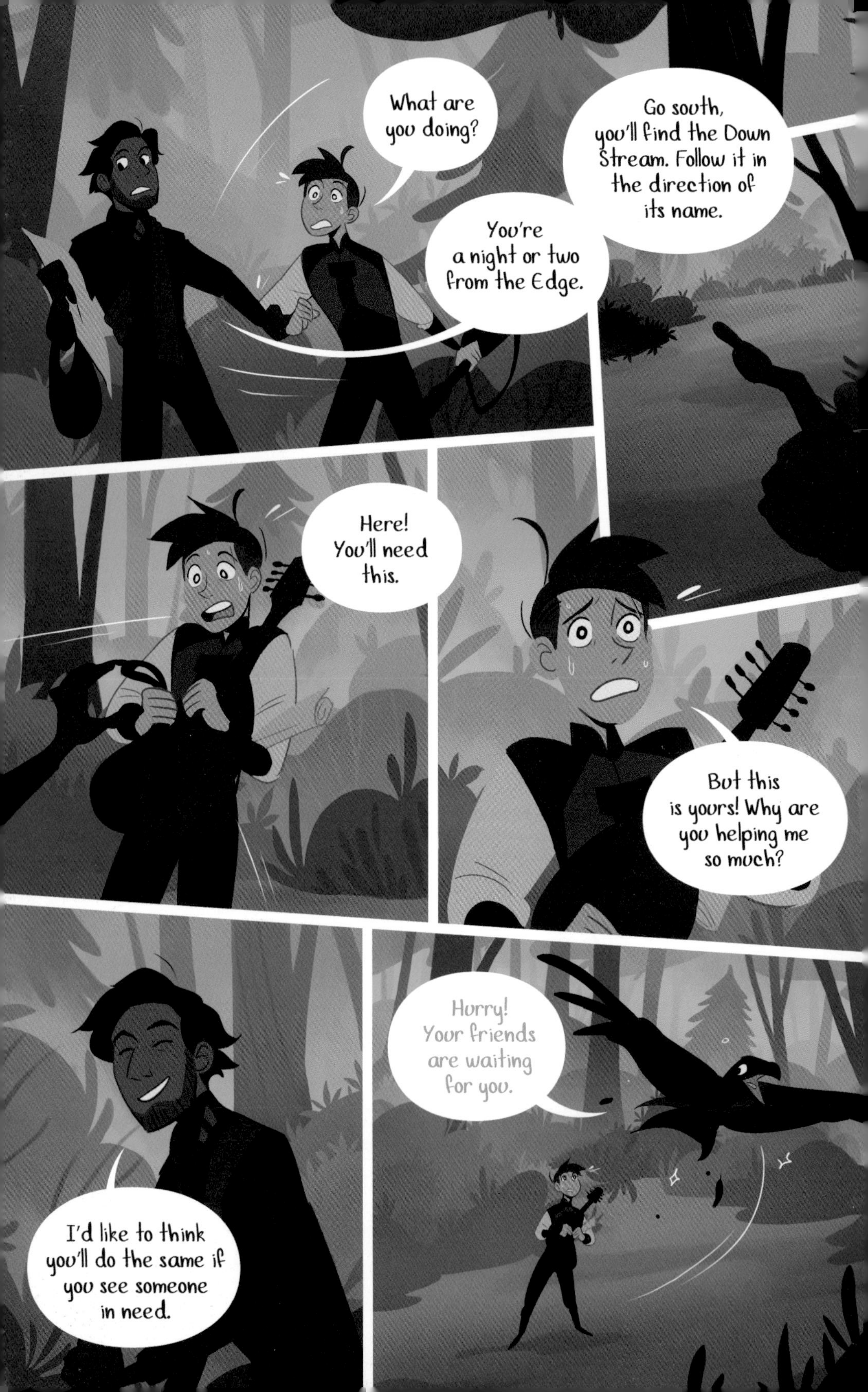
What are you doing?
Go south, you'll find the Down Stream. Follow it in the direction of its name.
You're a night or two from the Edge.
Here! You'll need this.
But this is yours! Why are you helping me so much?
I'd like to think you'll do the same if you see someone in need.
Hurry! Your friends are waiting for you.

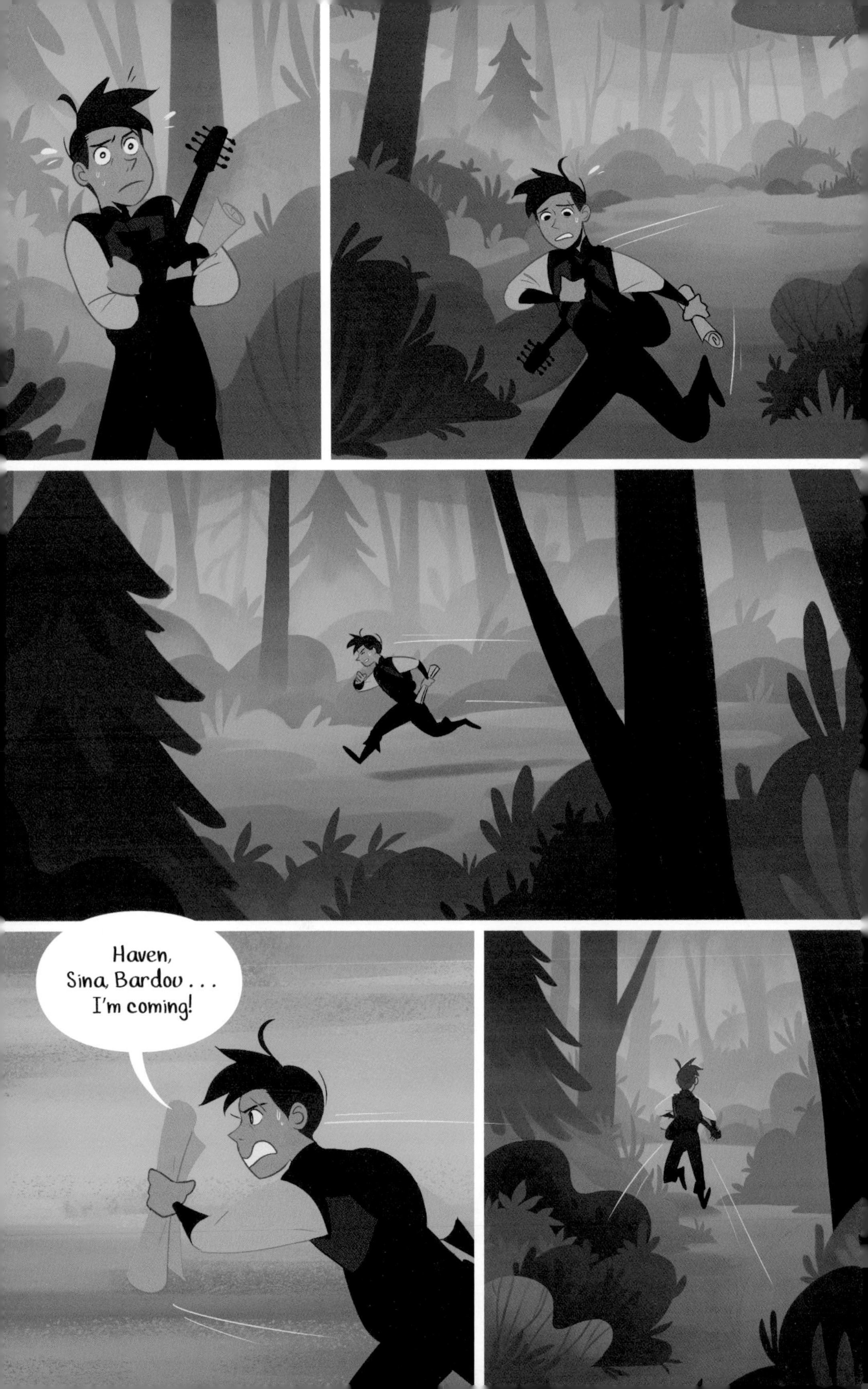
Haven, Sina, Bardou . . . I'm coming!

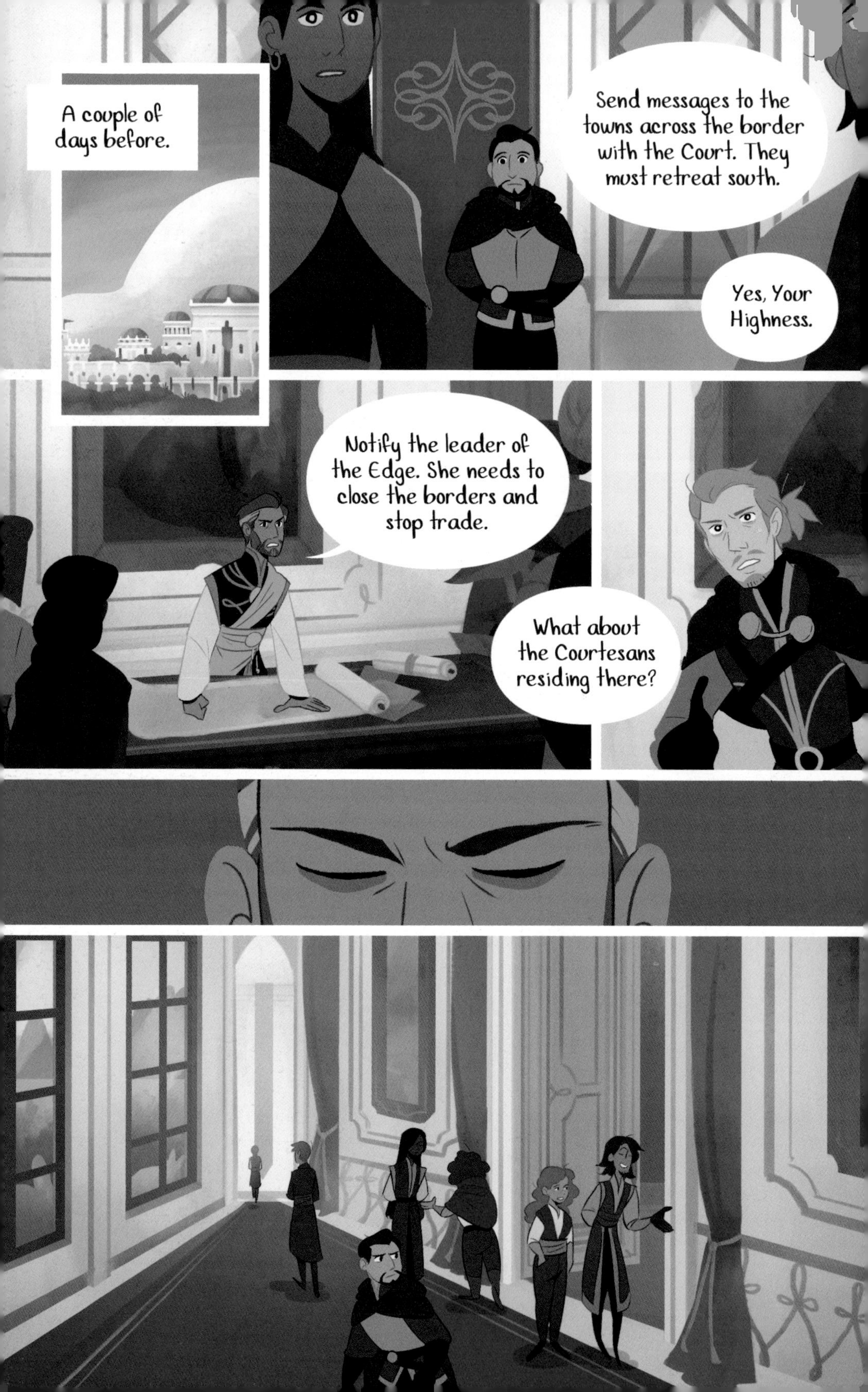
A couple of days before.
Send messages to the towns across the border with the Court. They must retreat south.
Yes, Your Highness.
Notify the leader of the Edge. She needs to close the borders and stop trade.
What about the Courtesans residing there?

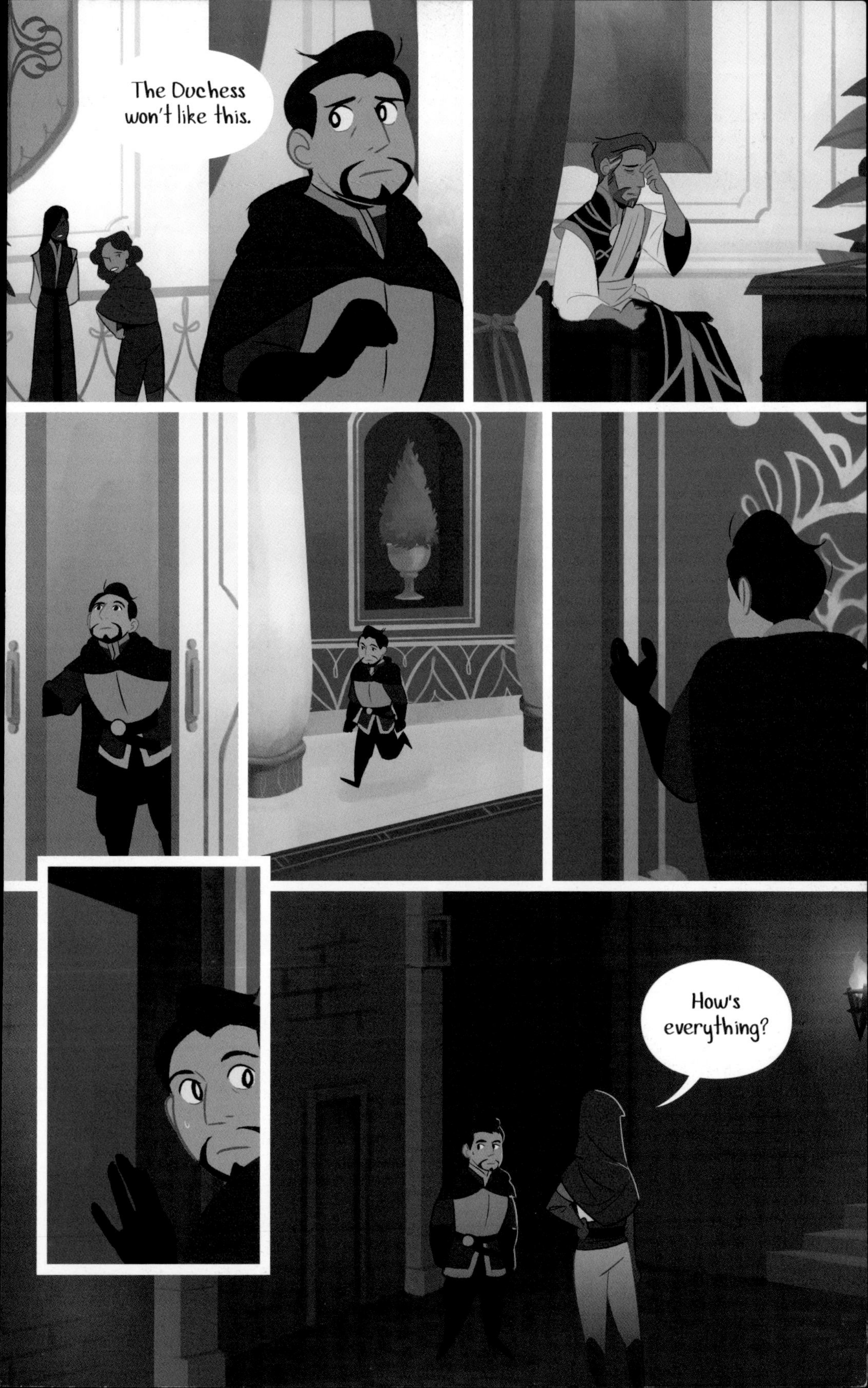
The Duchess won't like this.
How's everything?

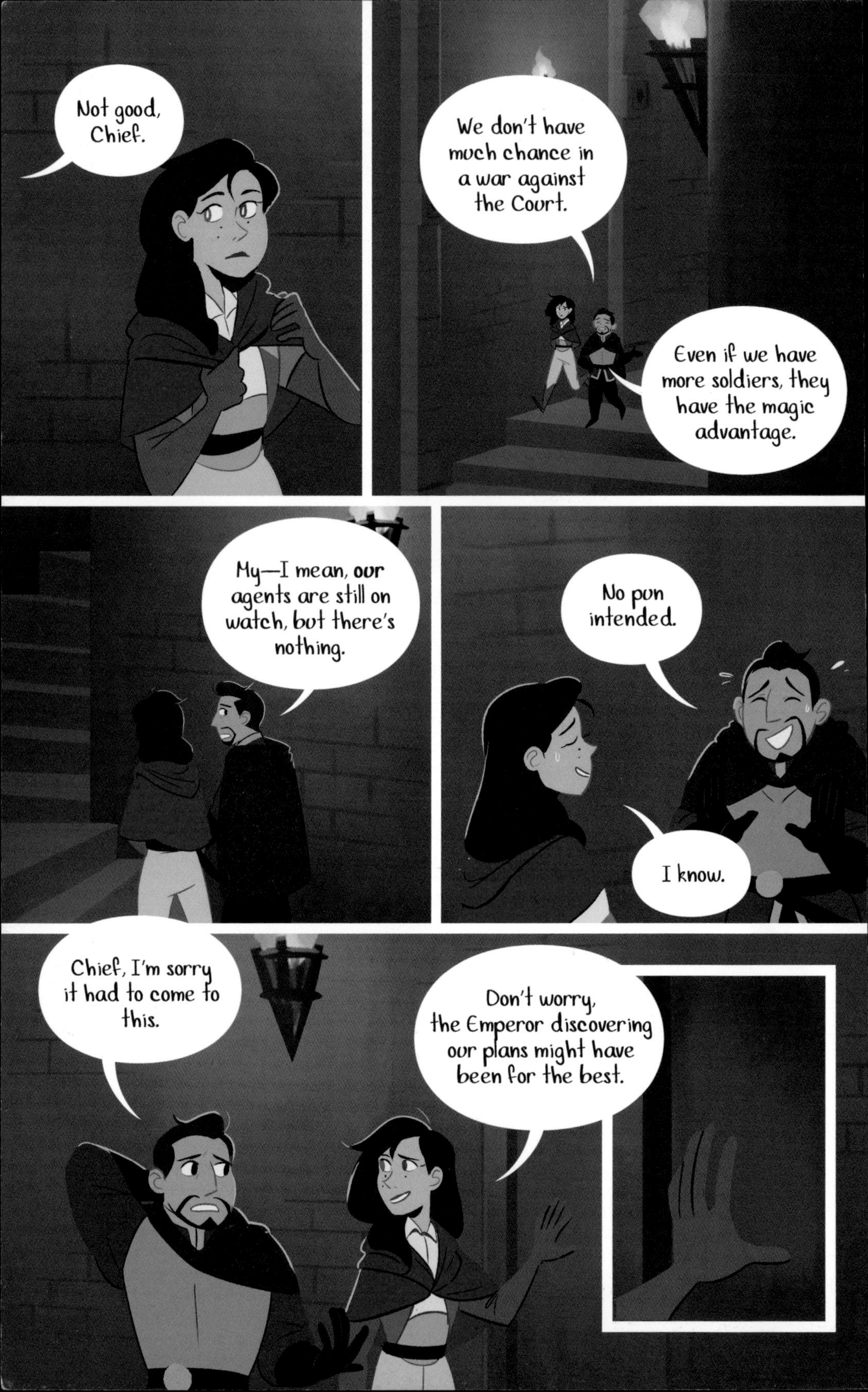
Not good, Chief.
We don't have much chance in a war against the Court.
Even if we have more soldiers, they have the magic advantage.
My—I mean, **our** agents are still on watch, but there's nothing.
No pun intended.
I know.
Chief, I'm sorry it had to come to this.
Don't worry, the Emperor discovering our plans might have been for the best.

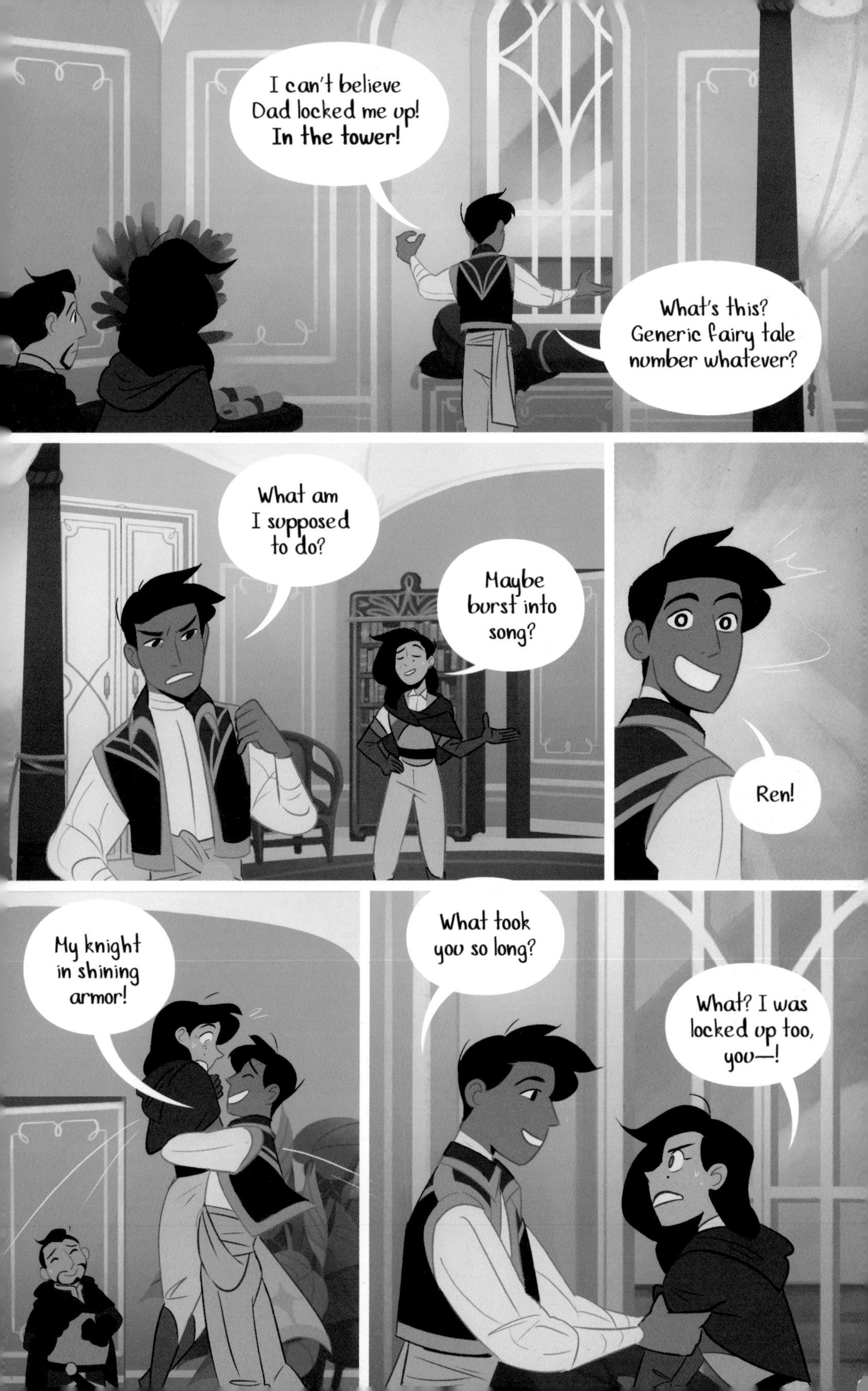
I can't believe Dad locked me up! In the tower!
What's this? Generic fairy tale number whatever?
What am I supposed to do?
Maybe burst into song?
Ren!
My knight in shining armor!
What took you so long?
What? I was locked up too, you—!

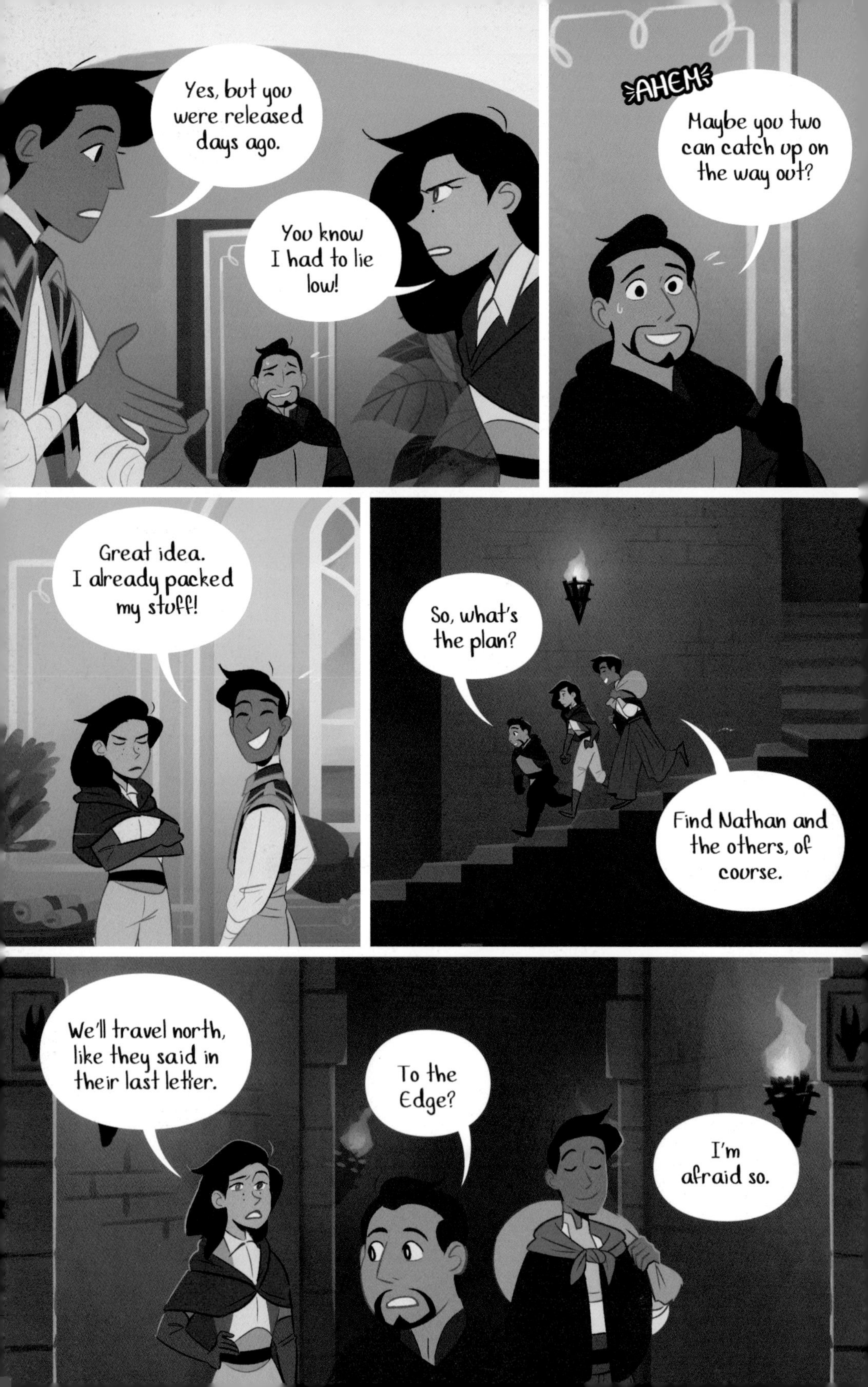
Yes, but you were released days ago.
You know I had to lie low!
AHEM
Maybe you two can catch up on the way out?
Great idea. I already packed my stuff!
So, what's the plan?
Find Nathan and the others, of course.
We'll travel north, like they said in their last letter.
To the Edge?
I'm afraid so.

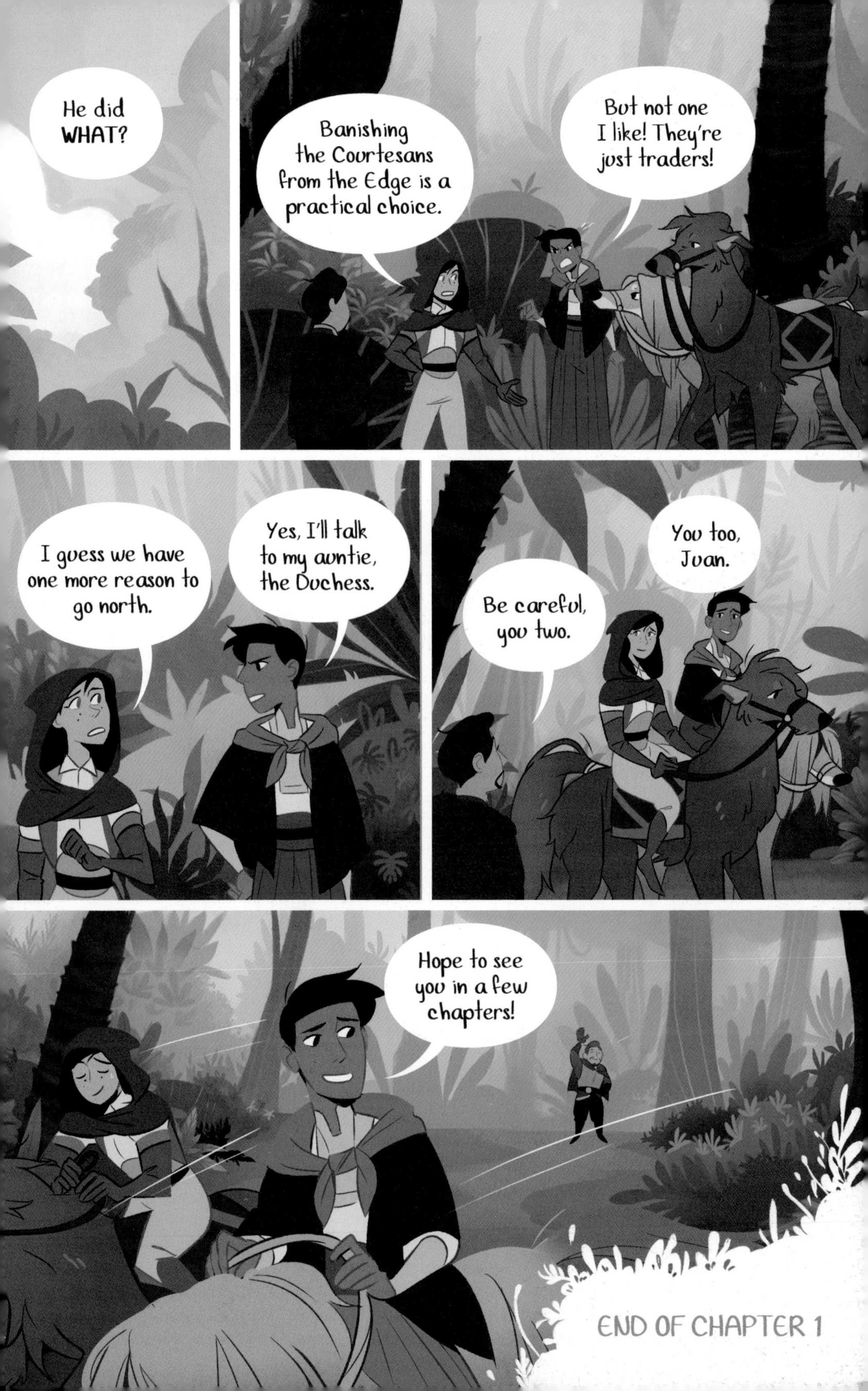
He did WHAT?
Banishing the Courtesans from the Edge is a practical choice.
But not one I like! They're just traders!
I guess we have one more reason to go north.
Yes, I'll talk to my auntie, the Duchess.
Be careful, you two.
You too, Juan.
Hope to see you in a few chapters!
END OF CHAPTER 1

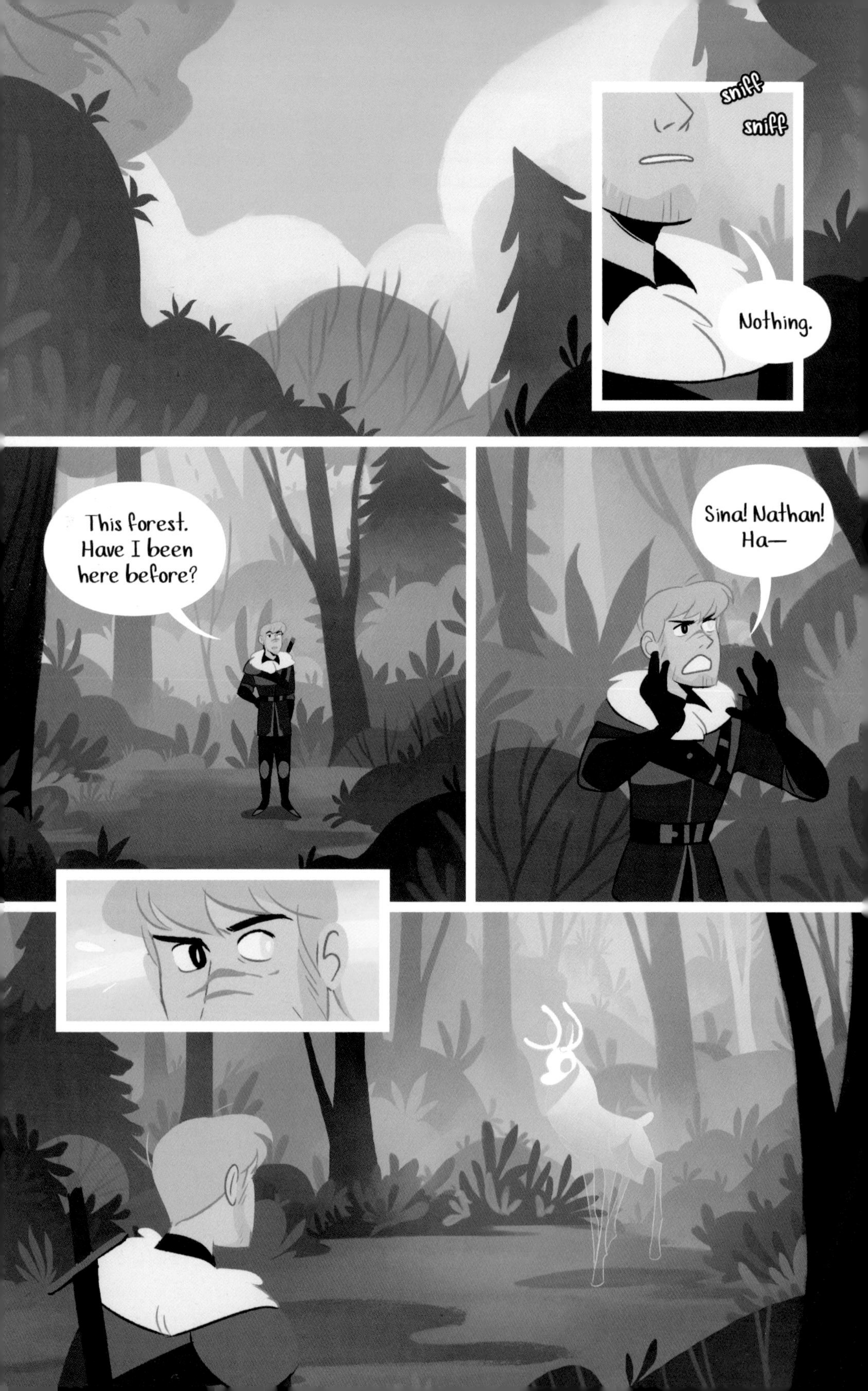
sniff
sniff
Nothing.
This forest. Have I been here before?
Sina! Nathan! Ha—

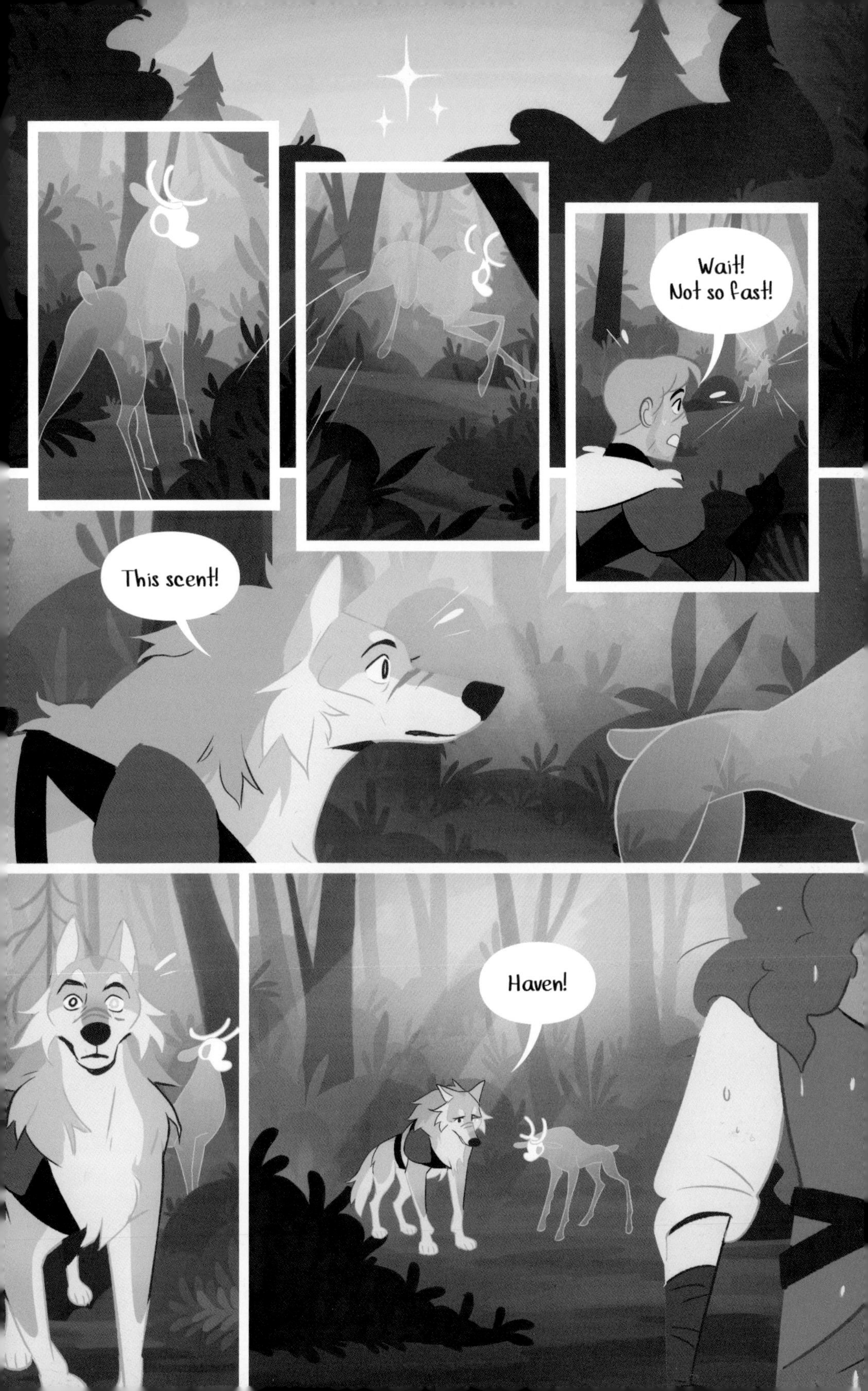
Wait! Not so fast!
This scent!
Haven!

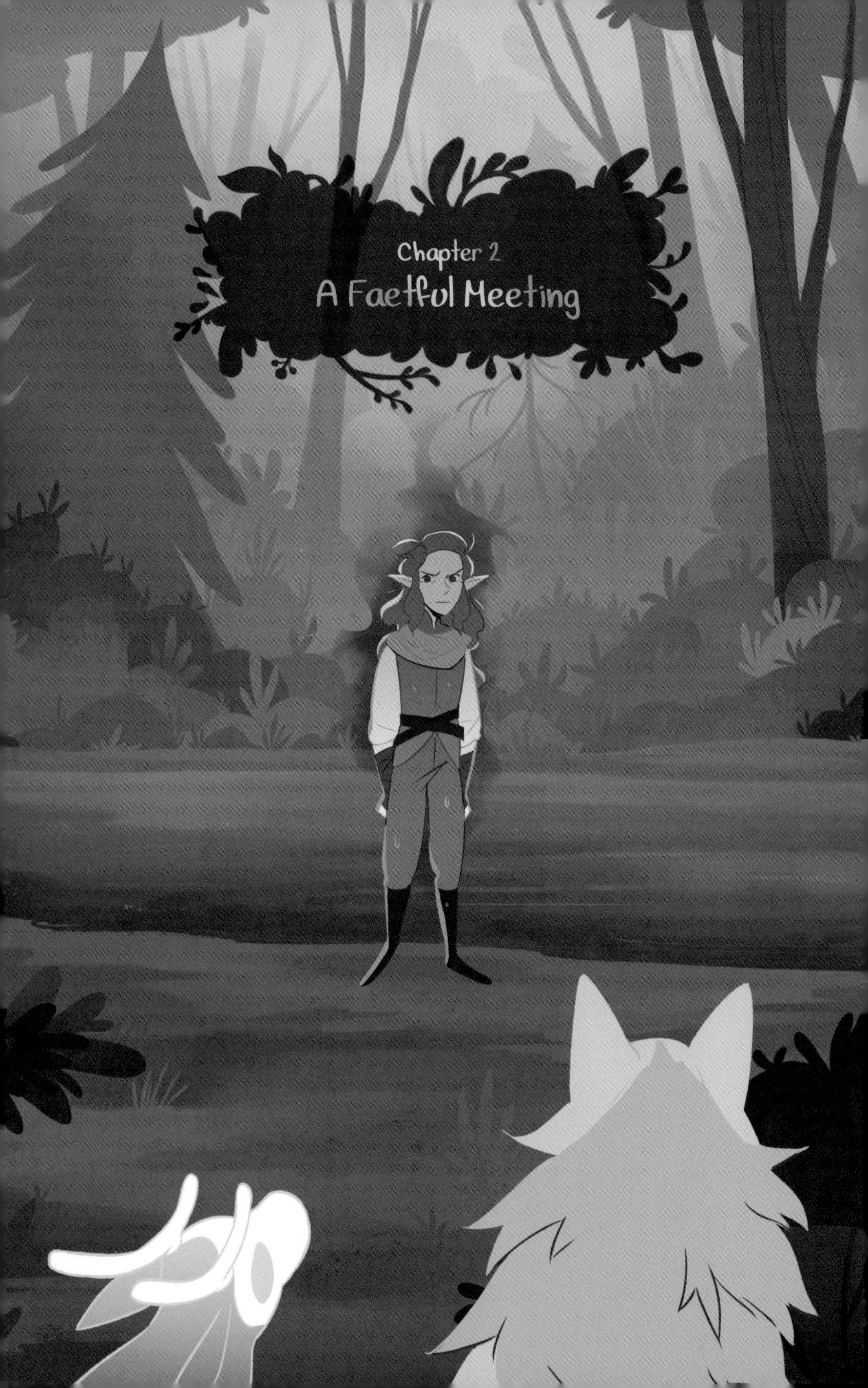
Chapter 2
A Faetful Meeting

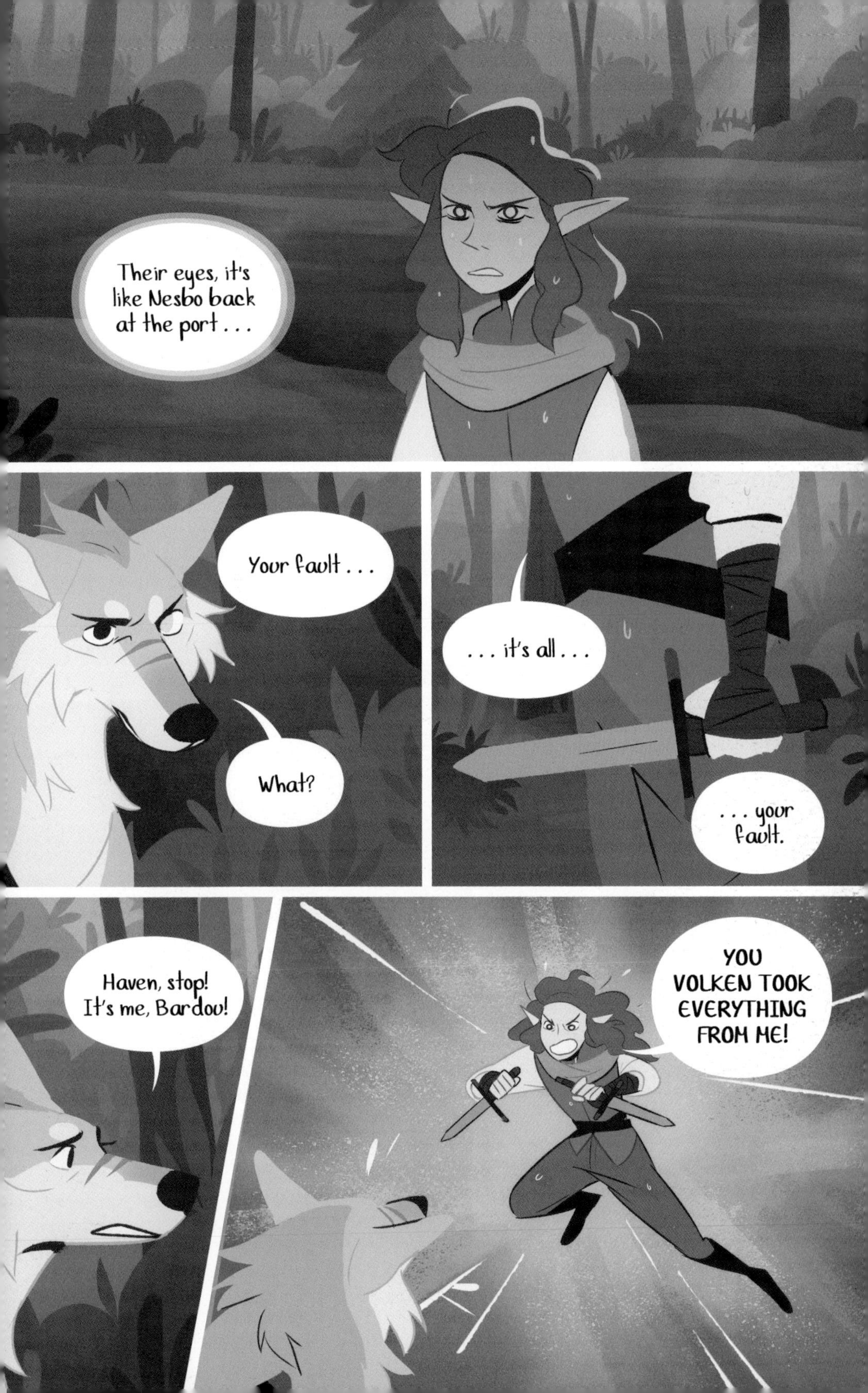
Their eyes, it's like Nesbo back at the port . . .
Your fault . . .
What?
. . . it's all . . .
. . . your fault.
Haven, stop! It's me, Bardou!
YOU VOLKEN TOOK EVERYTHING FROM ME!

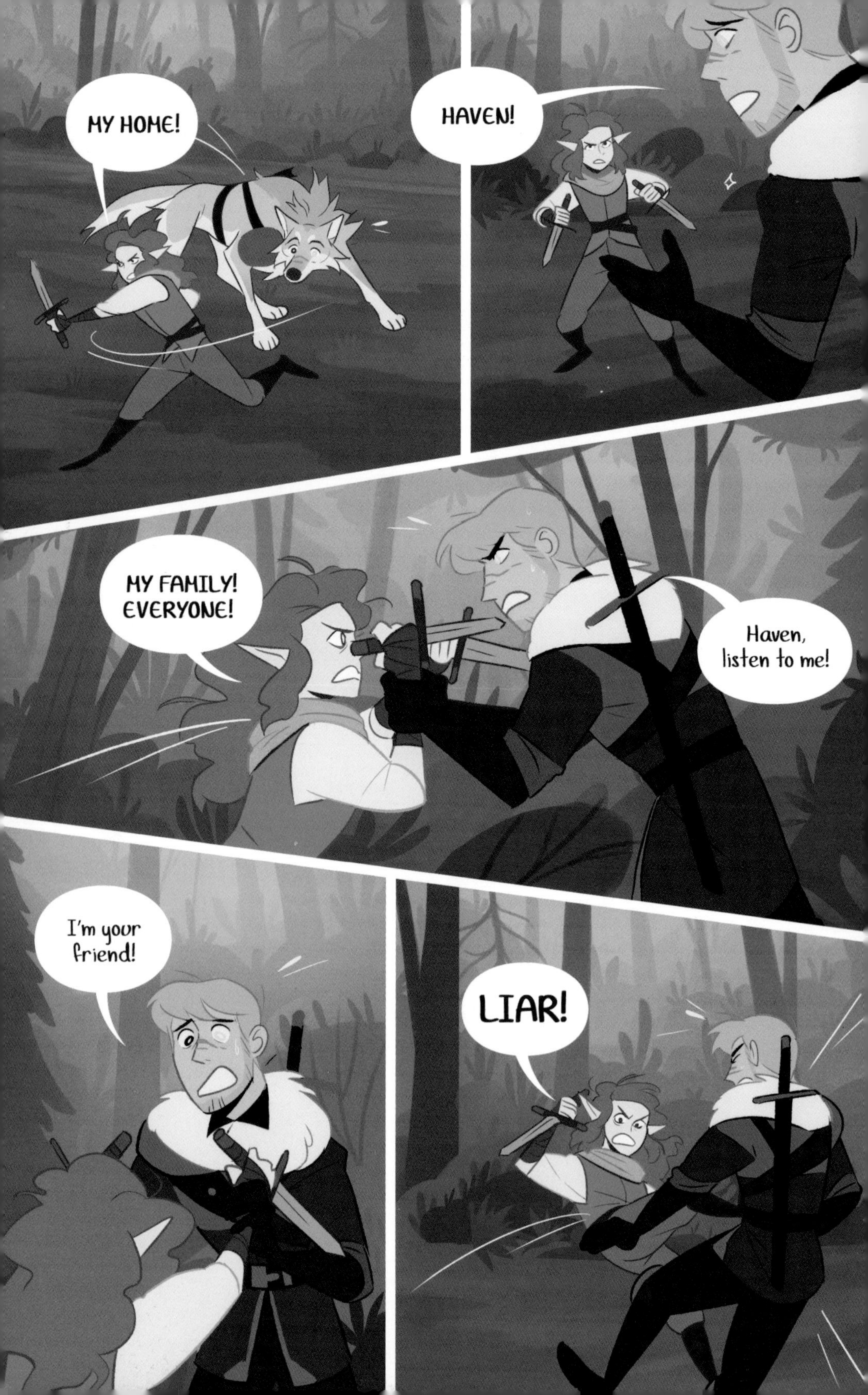
MY HOME!
HAVEN!
MY FAMILY! EVERYONE!
Haven, listen to me!
I'm your friend!
LIAR!

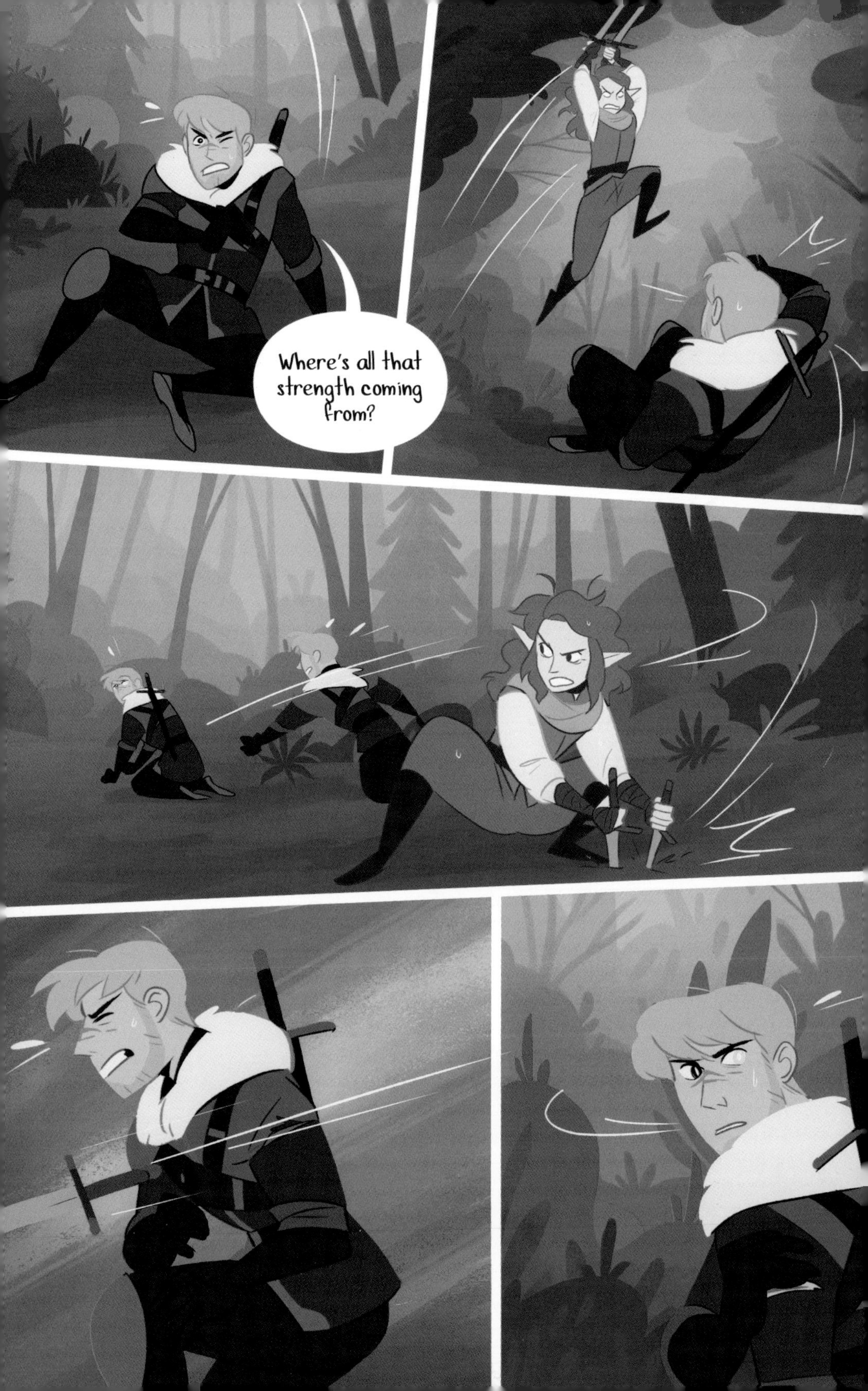
Where's all that strength coming from?

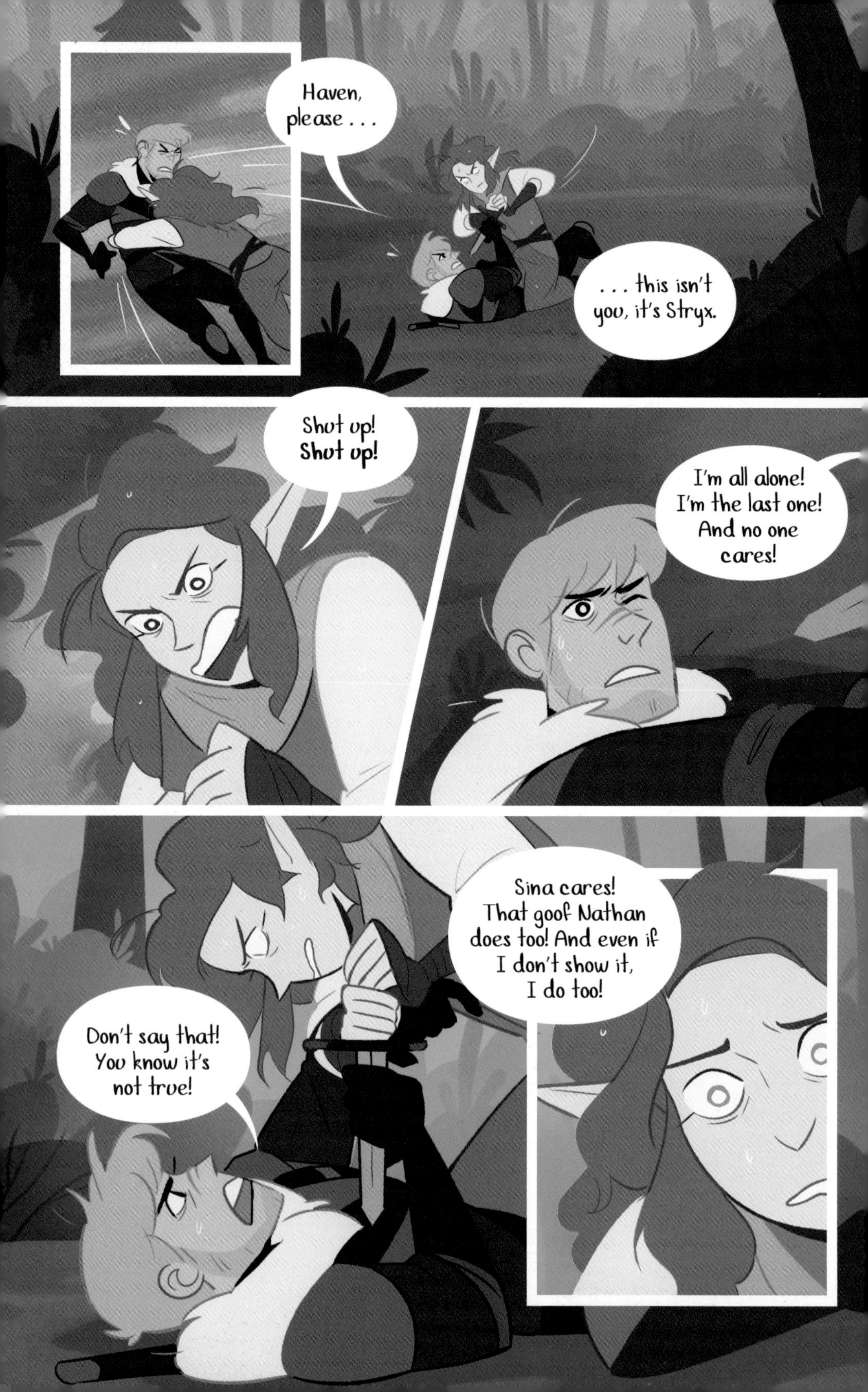
Haven, please . . .
. . . this isn't you, it's Stryx.
Shut up! Shut up!
I'm all alone! I'm the last one! And no one cares!
Sina cares! That goof Nathan does too! And even if I don't show it, I do too!
Don't say that! You know it's not true!

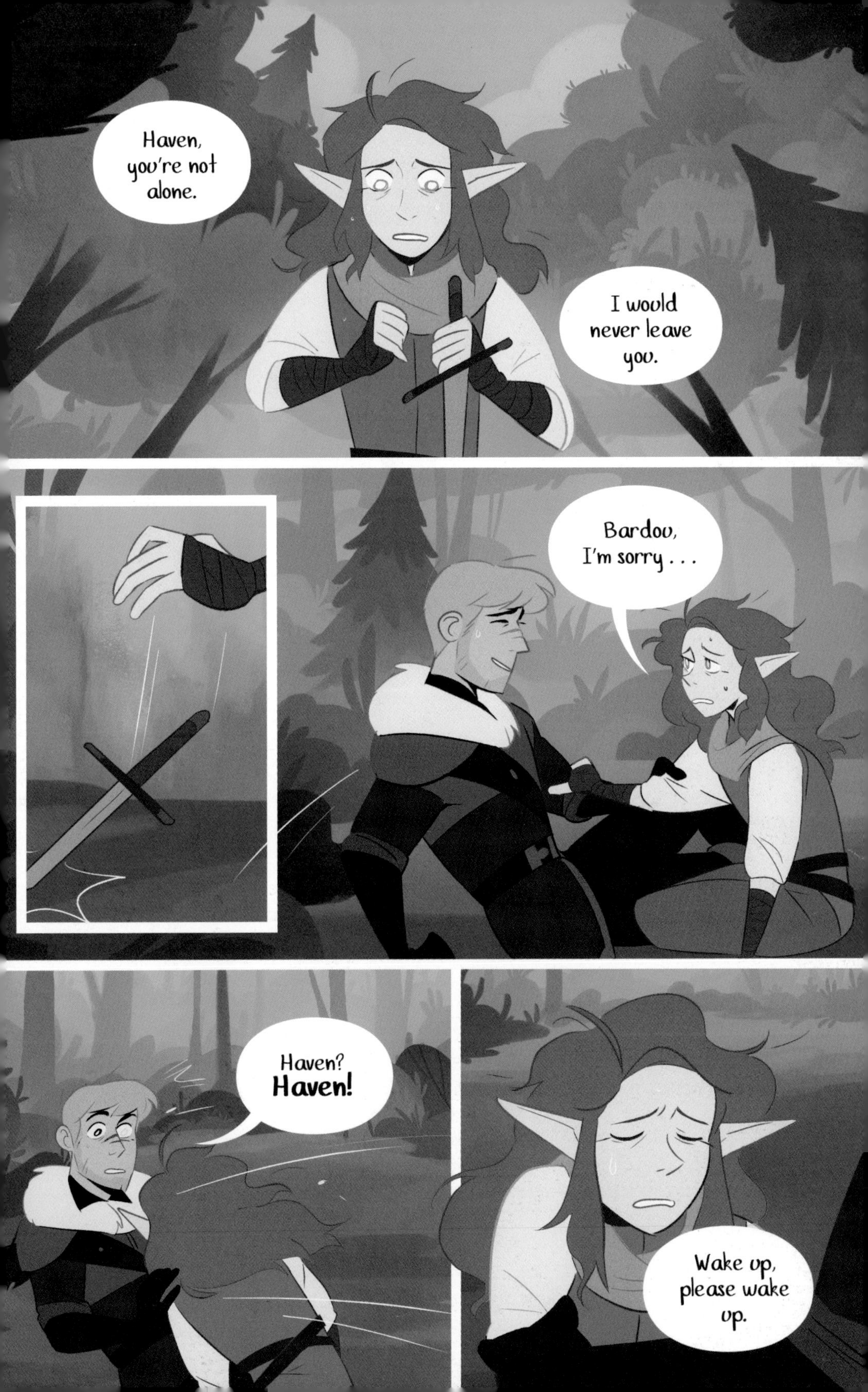
Haven, you're not alone.
I would never leave you.
Bardou, I'm sorry . . .
Haven? **Haven!**
Wake up, please wake up.

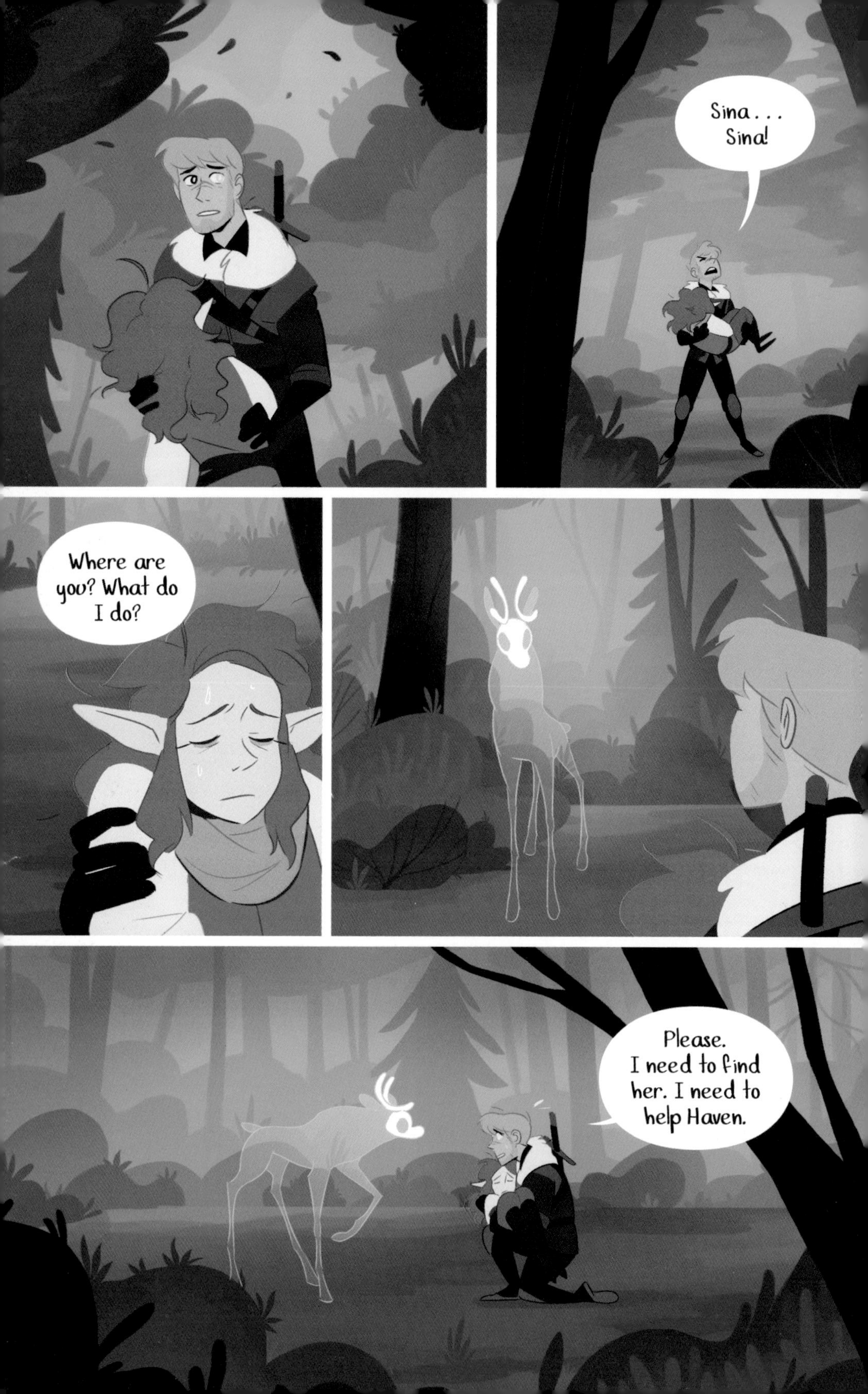
Sina . . .
Sina!
Where are you? What do I do?
Please. I need to find her. I need to help Haven.

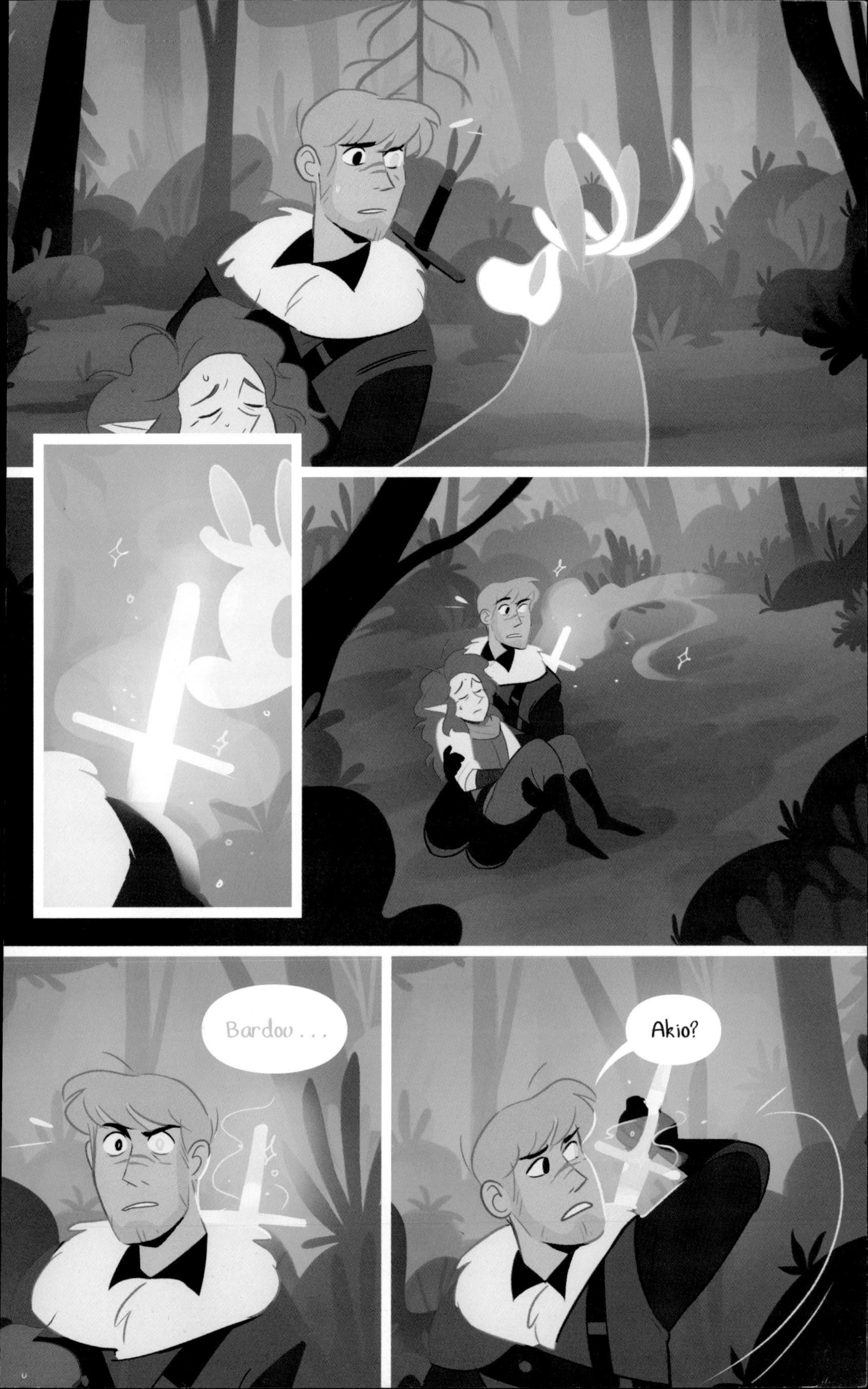
Bardou . . .
Akio?

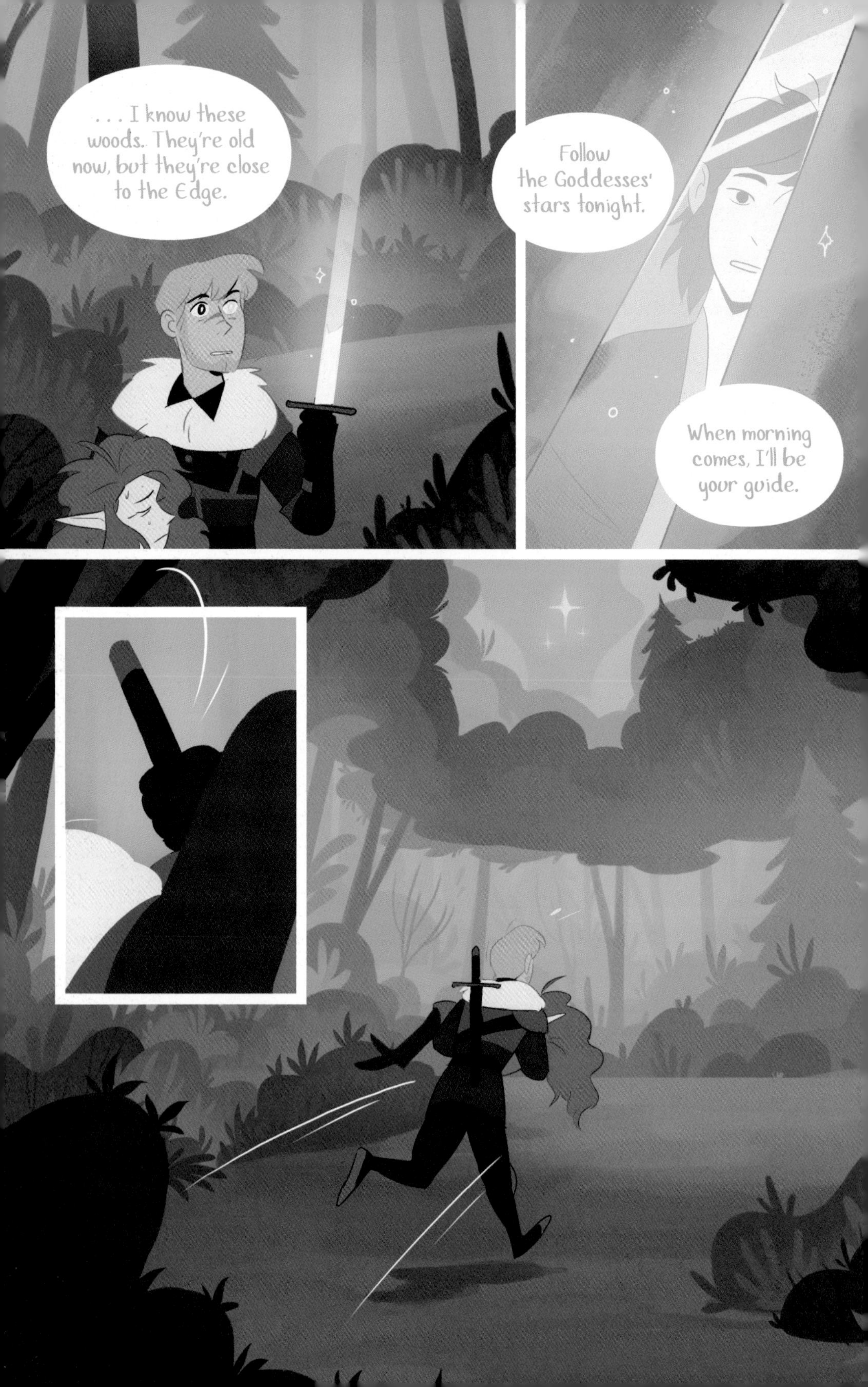
. . . I know these woods. They're old now, but they're close to the Edge.
Follow the Goddesses' stars tonight.
When morning comes, I'll be your guide.

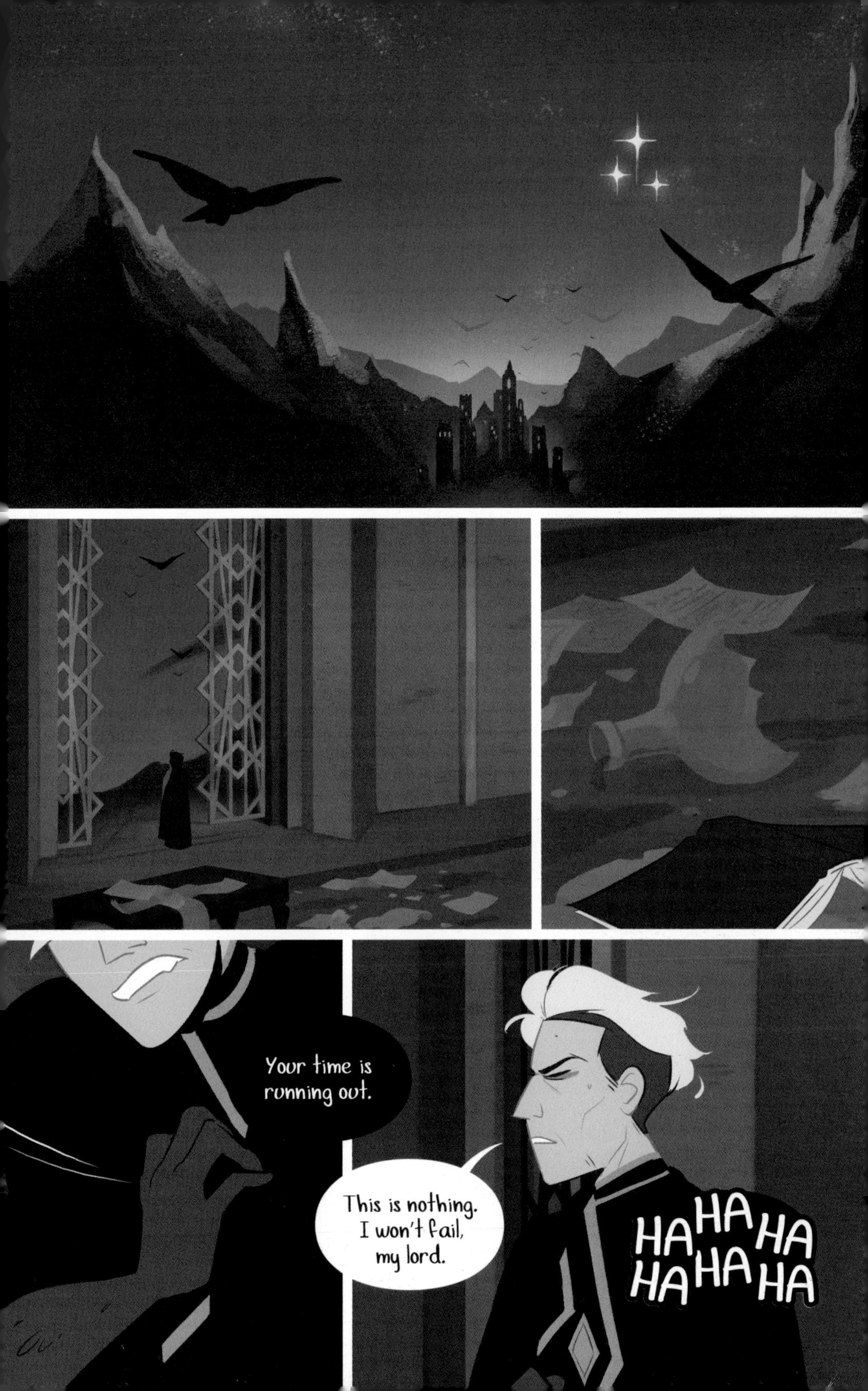
Your time is running out.
This is nothing. I won't fail, my lord.
HA HA HA HA HA HA

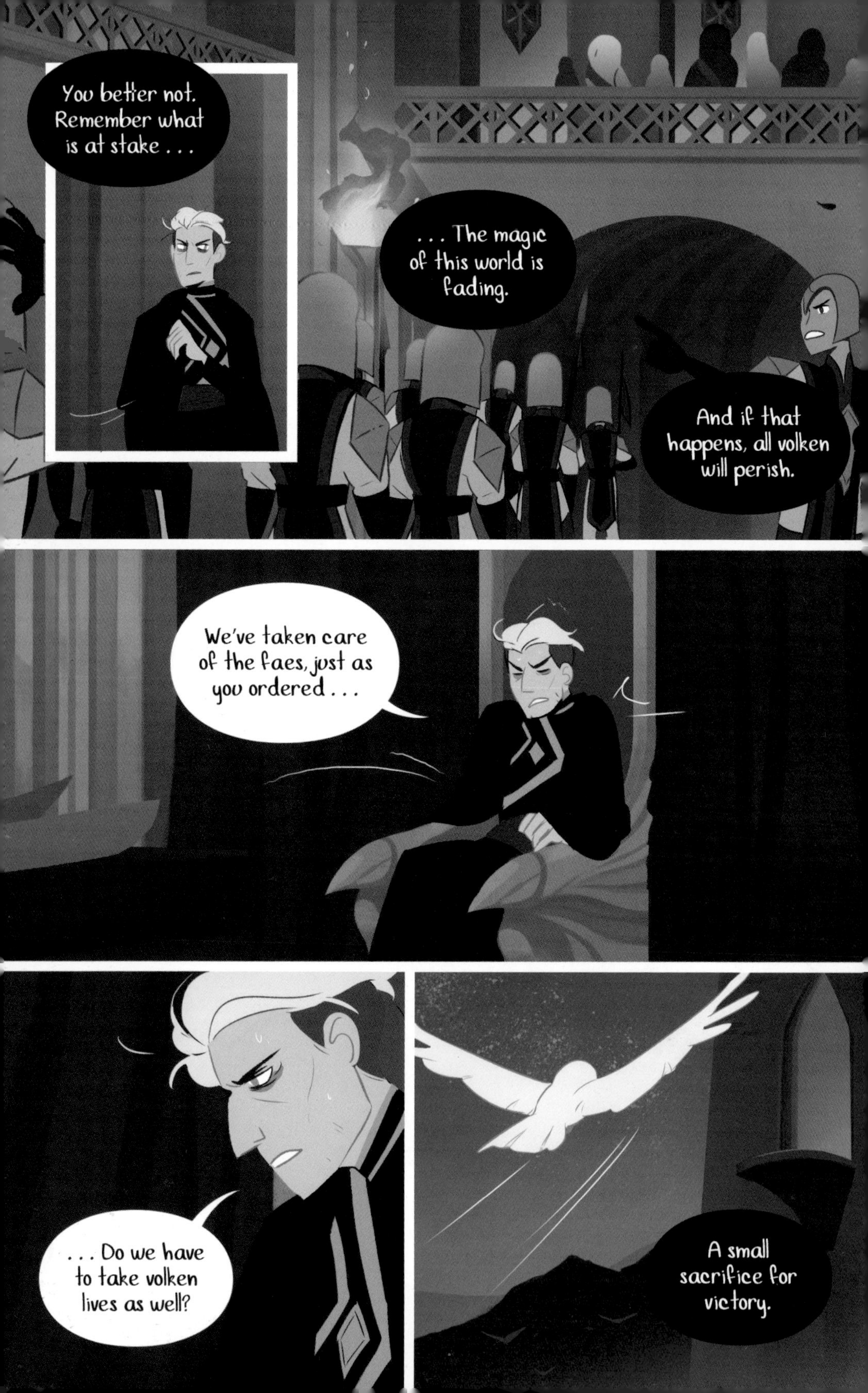
You better not. Remember what is at stake . . .
. . . The magic of this world is fading.
And if that happens, all volken will perish.
We've taken care of the faes, just as you ordered . . .
. . . Do we have to take volken lives as well?
A small sacrifice for victory.

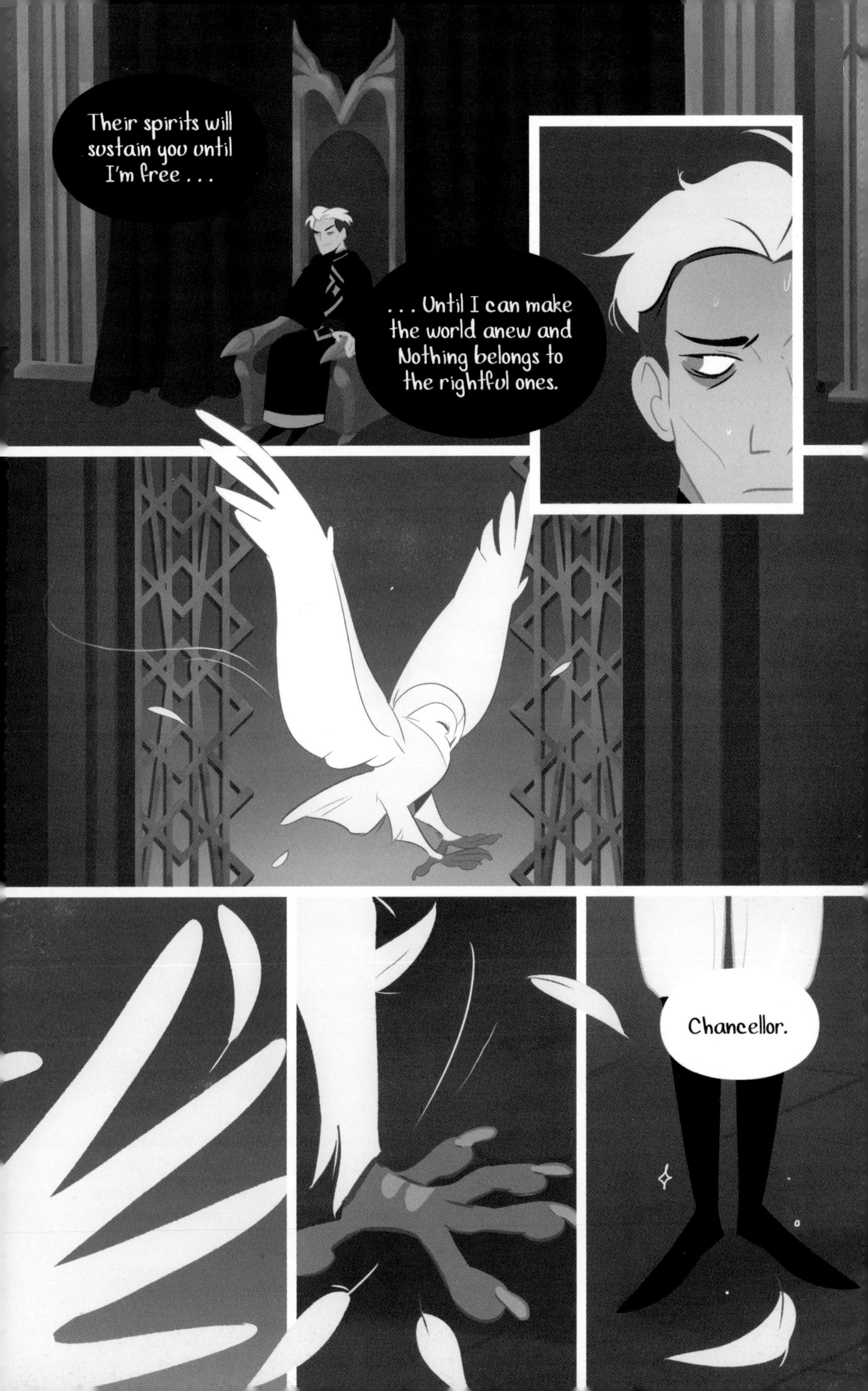
Their spirits will sustain you until I'm free . . .
. . . Until I can make the world anew and Nothing belongs to the rightful ones.
Chancellor.

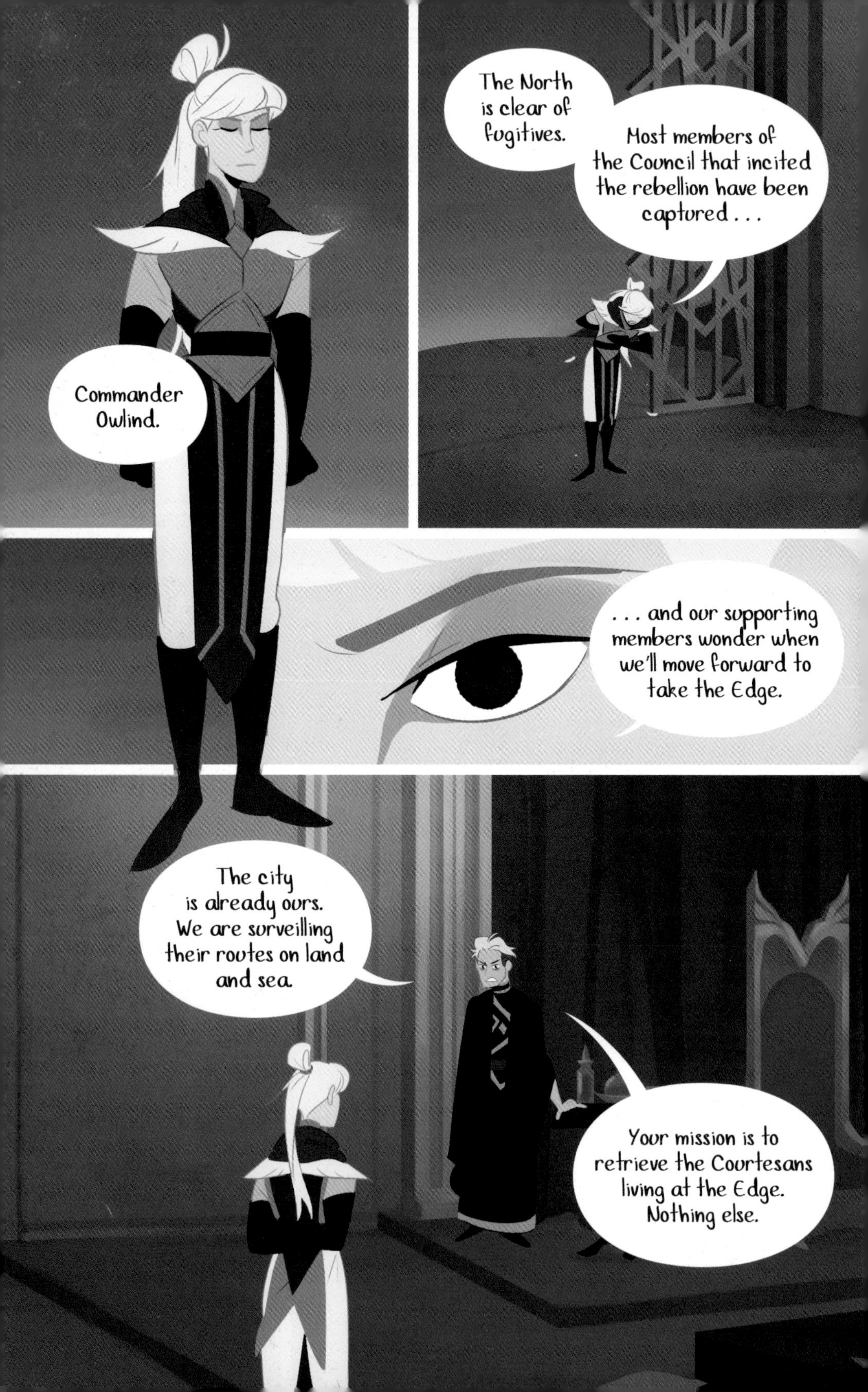
Commander Owlind.
The North is clear of fugitives.
Most members of the Council that incited the rebellion have been captured . . .
. . . and our supporting members wonder when we'll move forward to take the Edge.
The city is already ours. We are surveilling their routes on land and sea.
Your mission is to retrieve the Courtesans living at the Edge. Nothing else.

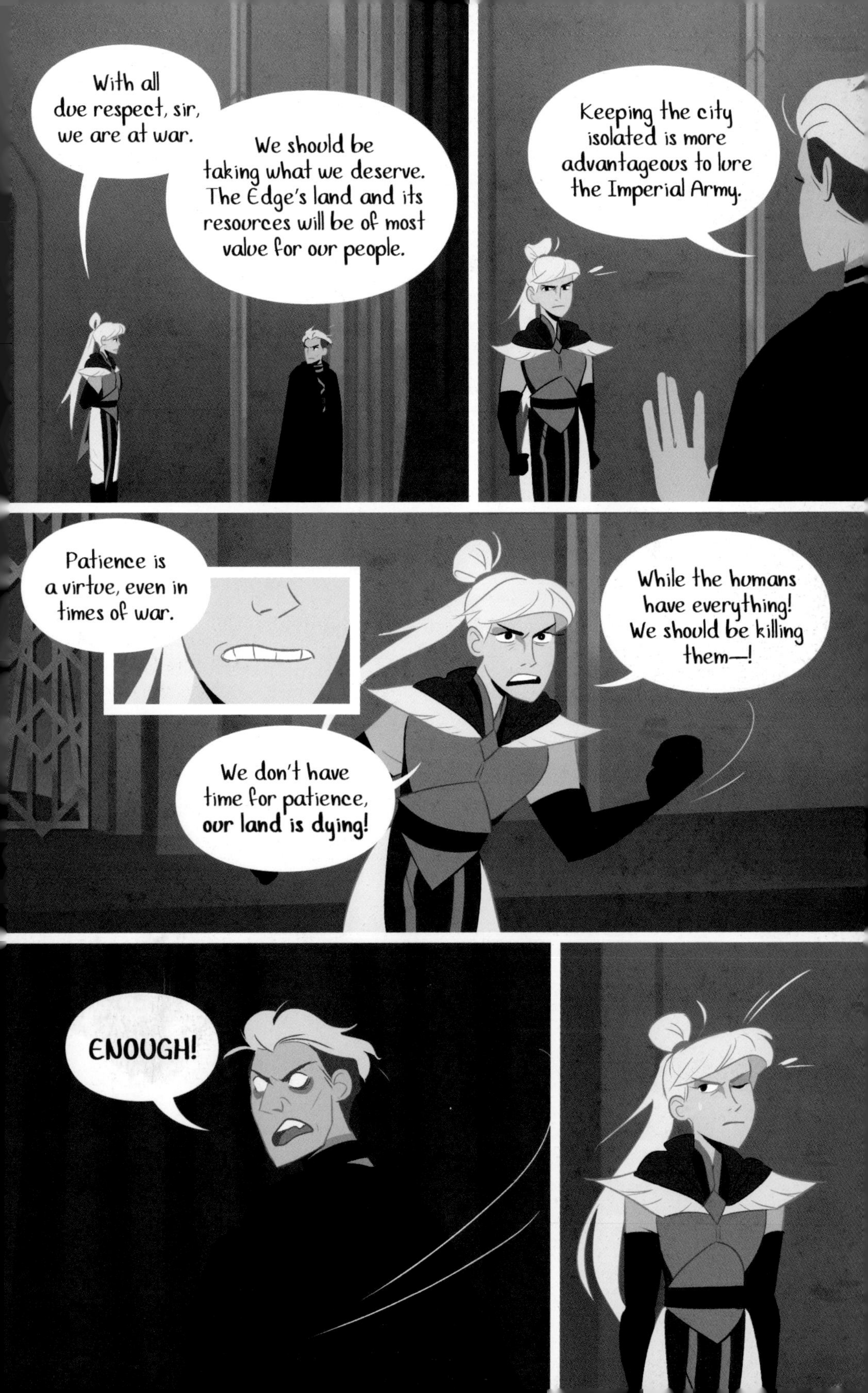

With all due respect, sir, we are at war.
We should be taking what we deserve. The Edge's land and its resources will be of most value for our people.
Keeping the city isolated is more advantageous to lure the Imperial Army.
Patience is a virtue, even in times of war.
While the humans have everything! We should be killing them—!
We don't have time for patience, our land is dying!
ENOUGH!

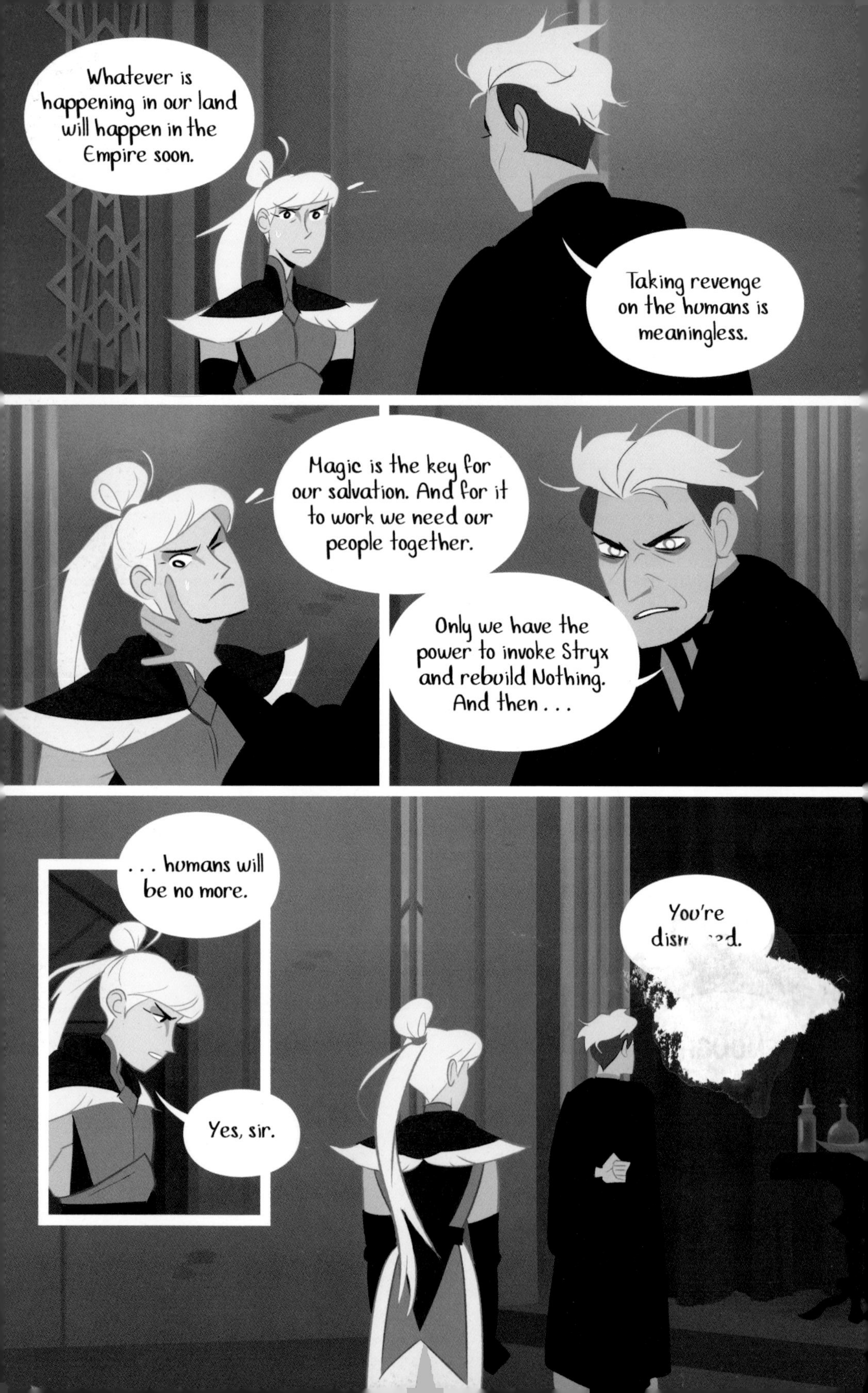
Whatever is happening in our land will happen in the Empire soon.
Taking revenge on the humans is meaningless.
Magic is the key for our salvation. And for it to work we need our people together.
Only we have the power to invoke Stryx and rebuild Nothing. And then . . .
. . . humans will be no more.
Yes, sir.
You're

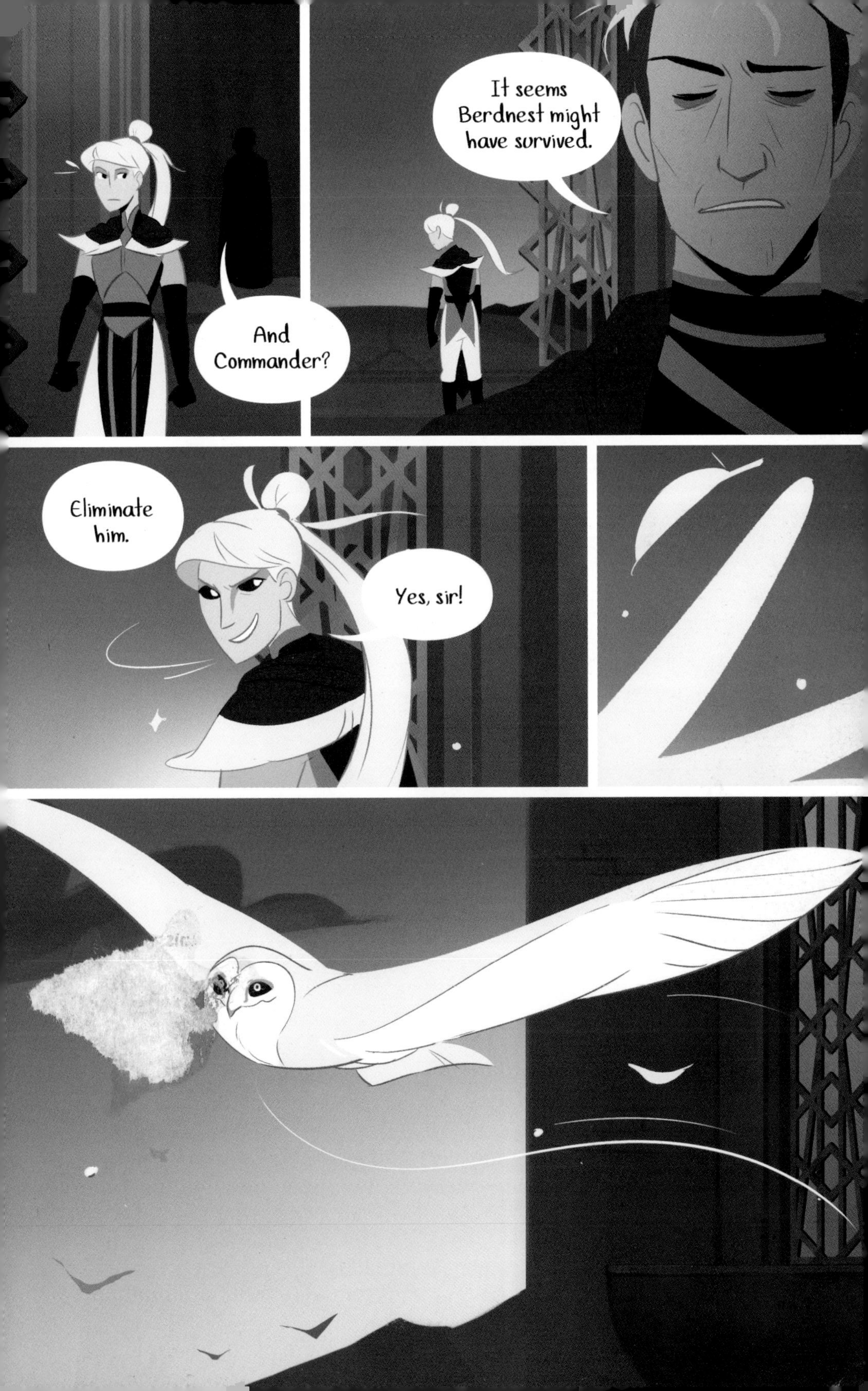
It seems Berdnest might have survived.
And Commander?
Eliminate him.
Yes, sir!

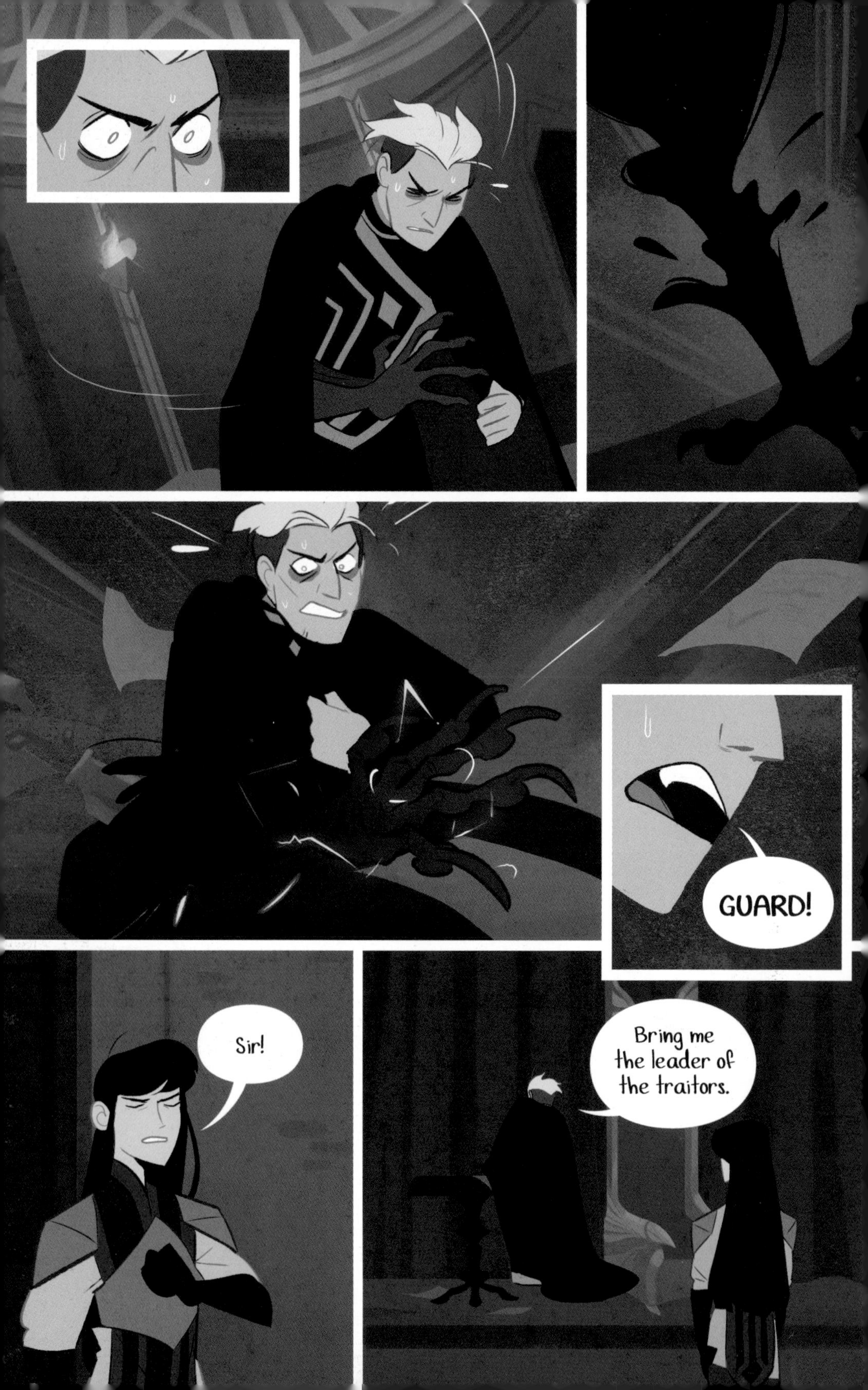
GUARD!
Sir!
Bring me the leader of the traitors.

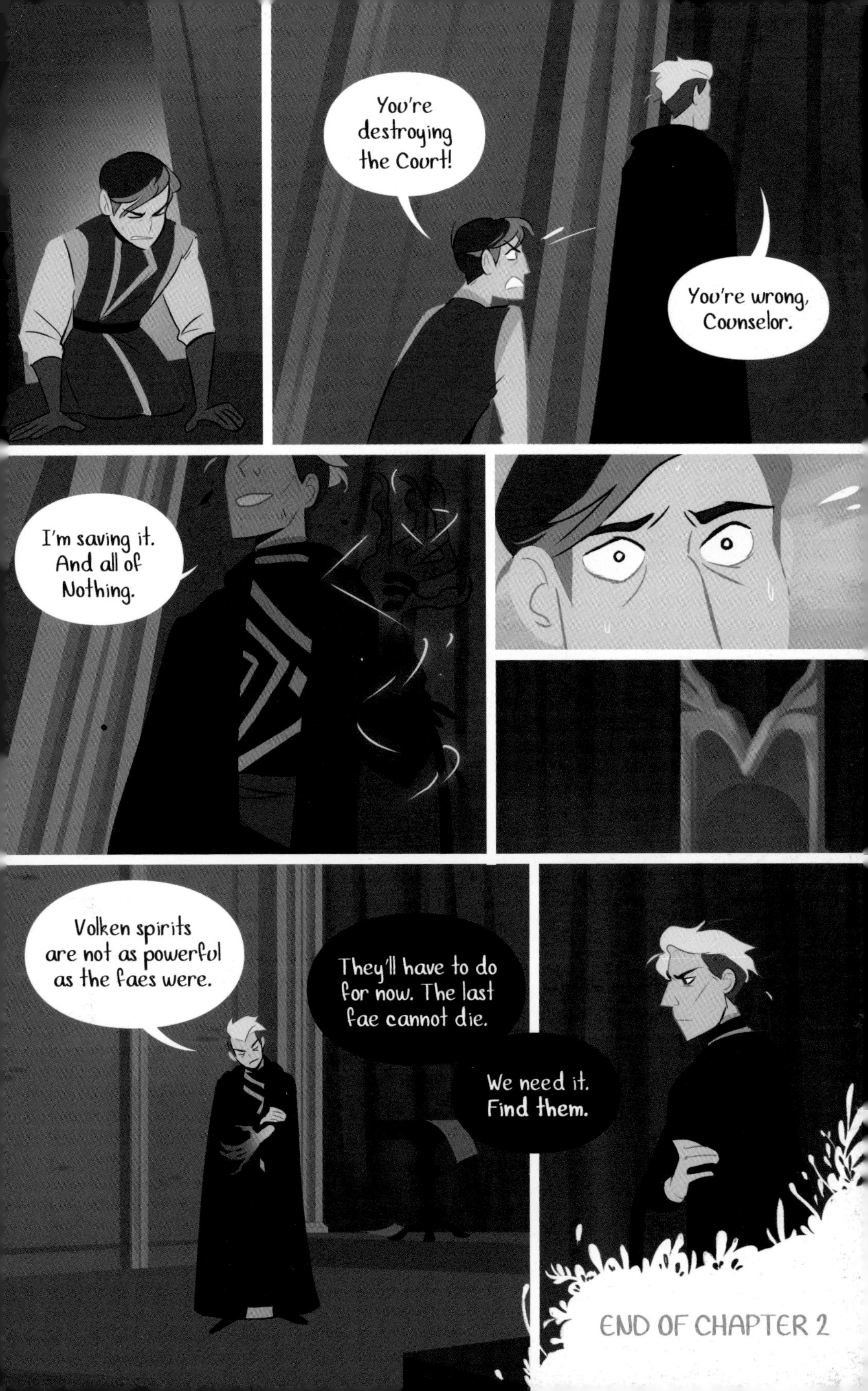
You're destroying the Court!
You're wrong, Counselor.
I'm saving it. And all of Nothing.
Volken spirits are not as powerful as the faes were.
They'll have to do for now. The last fae cannot die.
We need it. Find them.
END OF CHAPTER 2

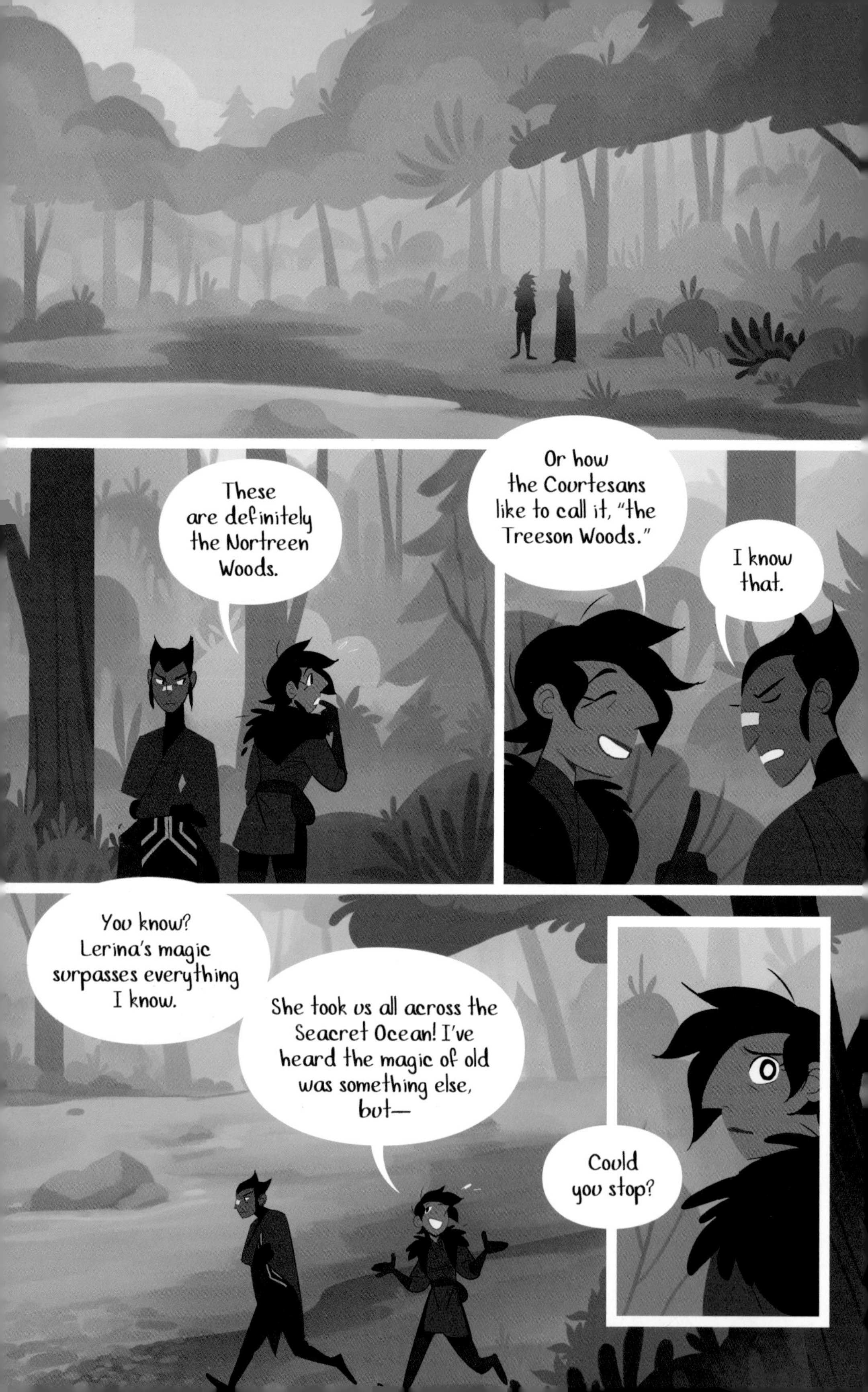
These are definitely the Nortreen Woods.
Or how the Courtesans like to call it, "the Treeson Woods."
I know that.
You know? Lerina's magic surpasses everything I know.
She took us all across the Seacret Ocean! I've heard the magic of old was something else, but—
Could you stop?

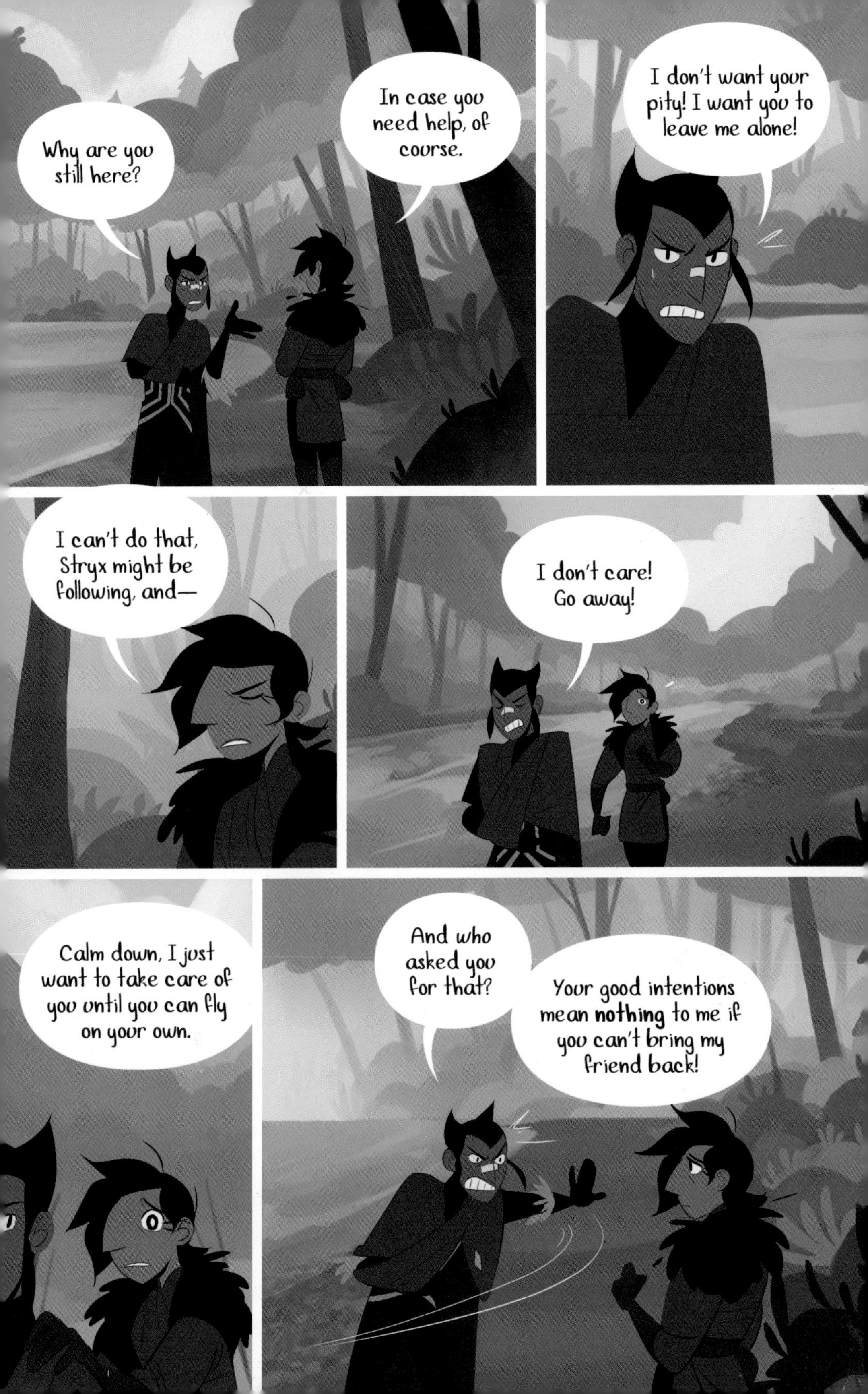
Why are you still here?
In case you need help, of course.
I don't want your pity! I want you to leave me alone!
I can't do that, Stryx might be following, and—
I don't care! Go away!
Calm down, I just want to take care of you until you can fly on your own.
And who asked you for that?
Your good intentions mean **nothing** to me if you can't bring my friend back!

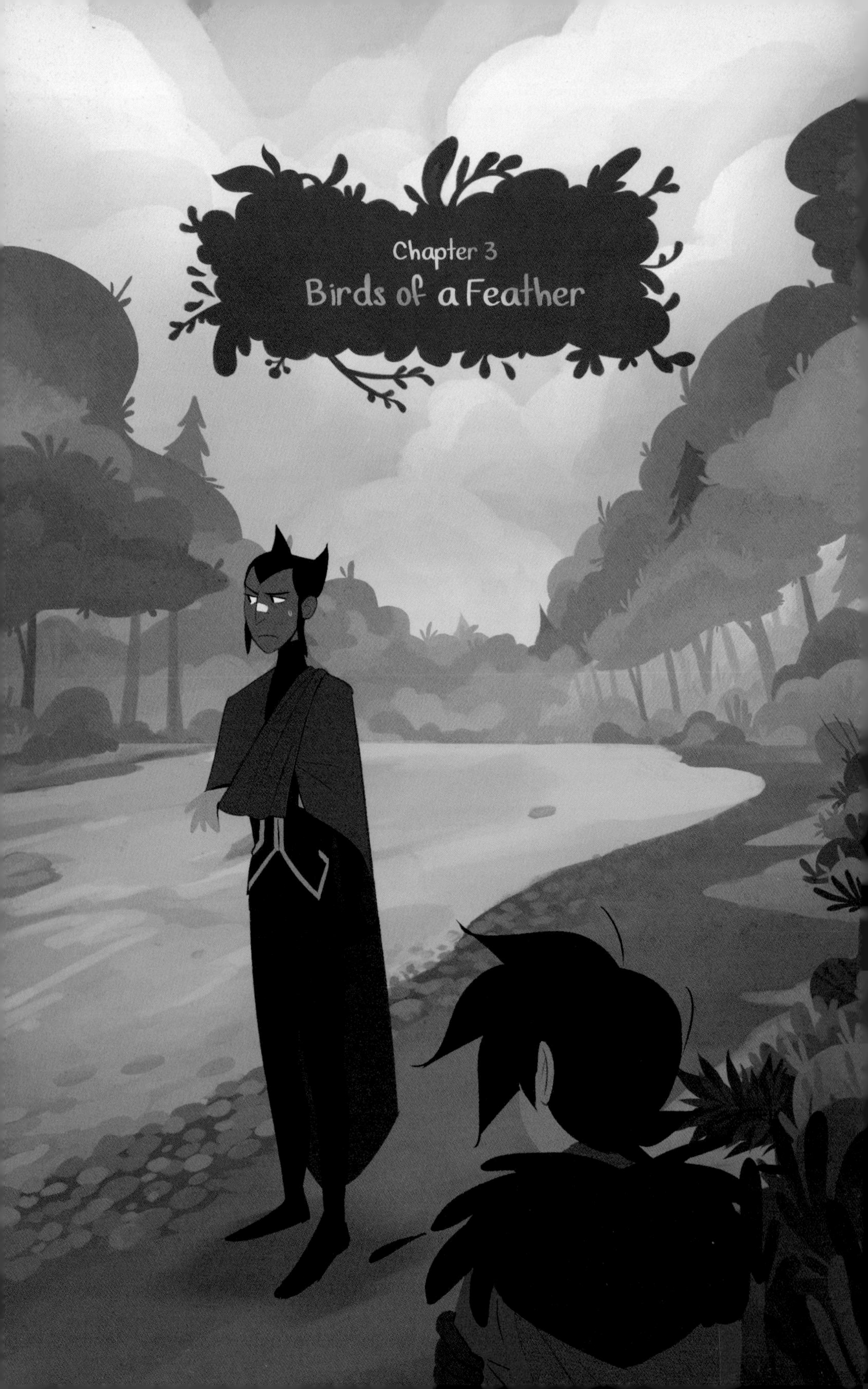
Chapter 3
Birds of a Feather

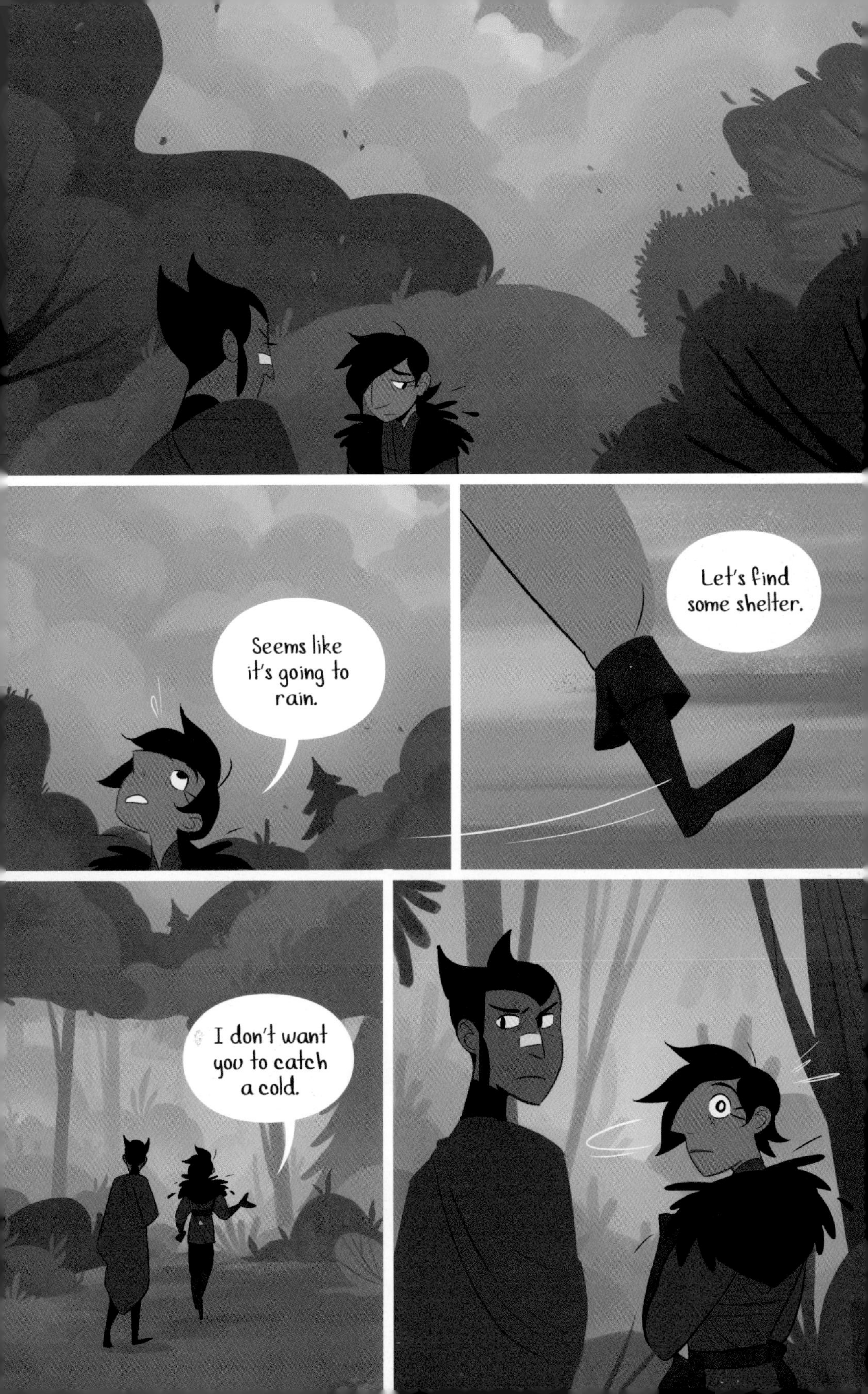
Seems like it's going to rain.
Let's find some shelter.
I don't want you to catch a cold.

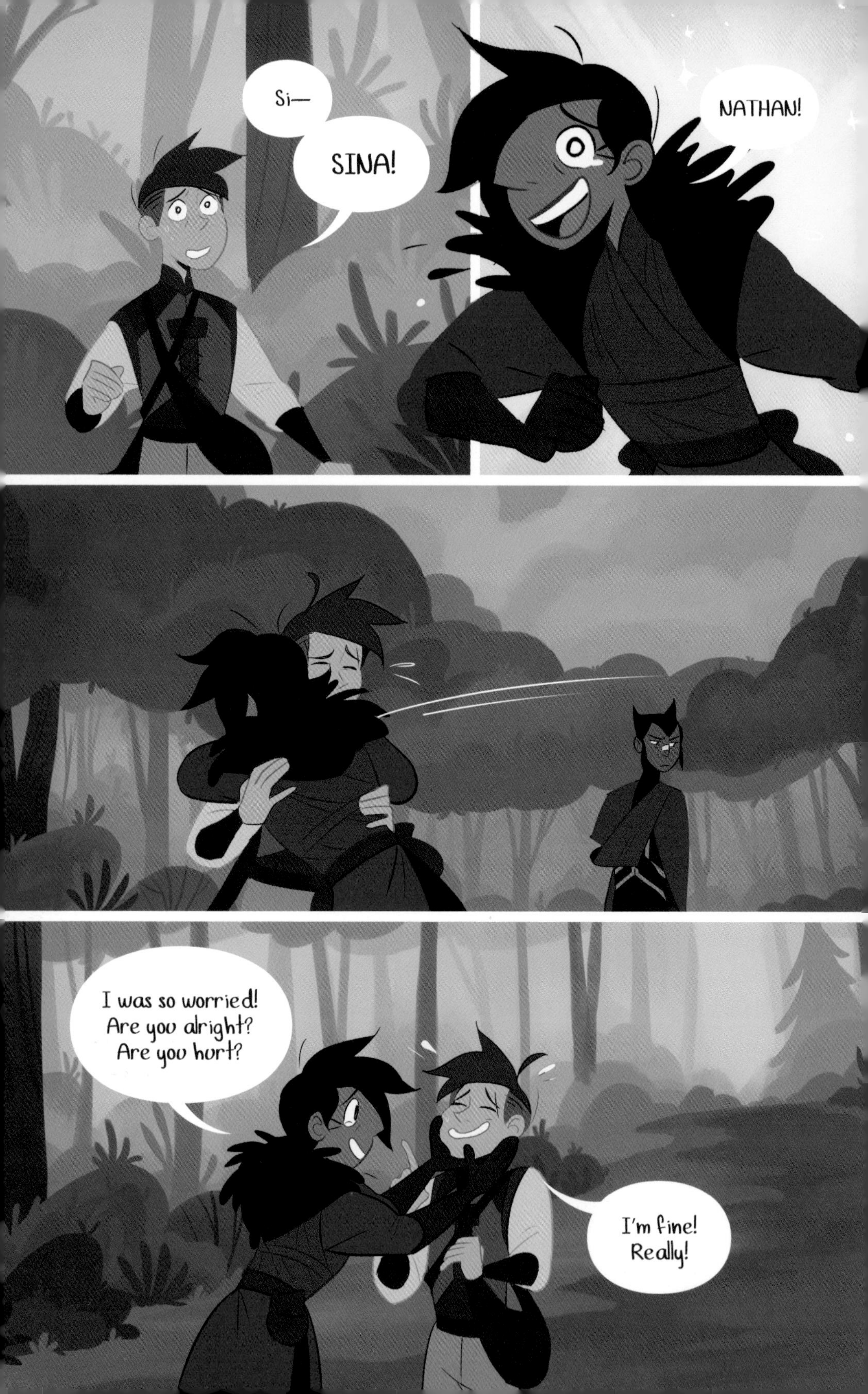
Si—
SINA!
NATHAN!
I was so worried! Are you alright? Are you hurt?
I'm fine! Really!

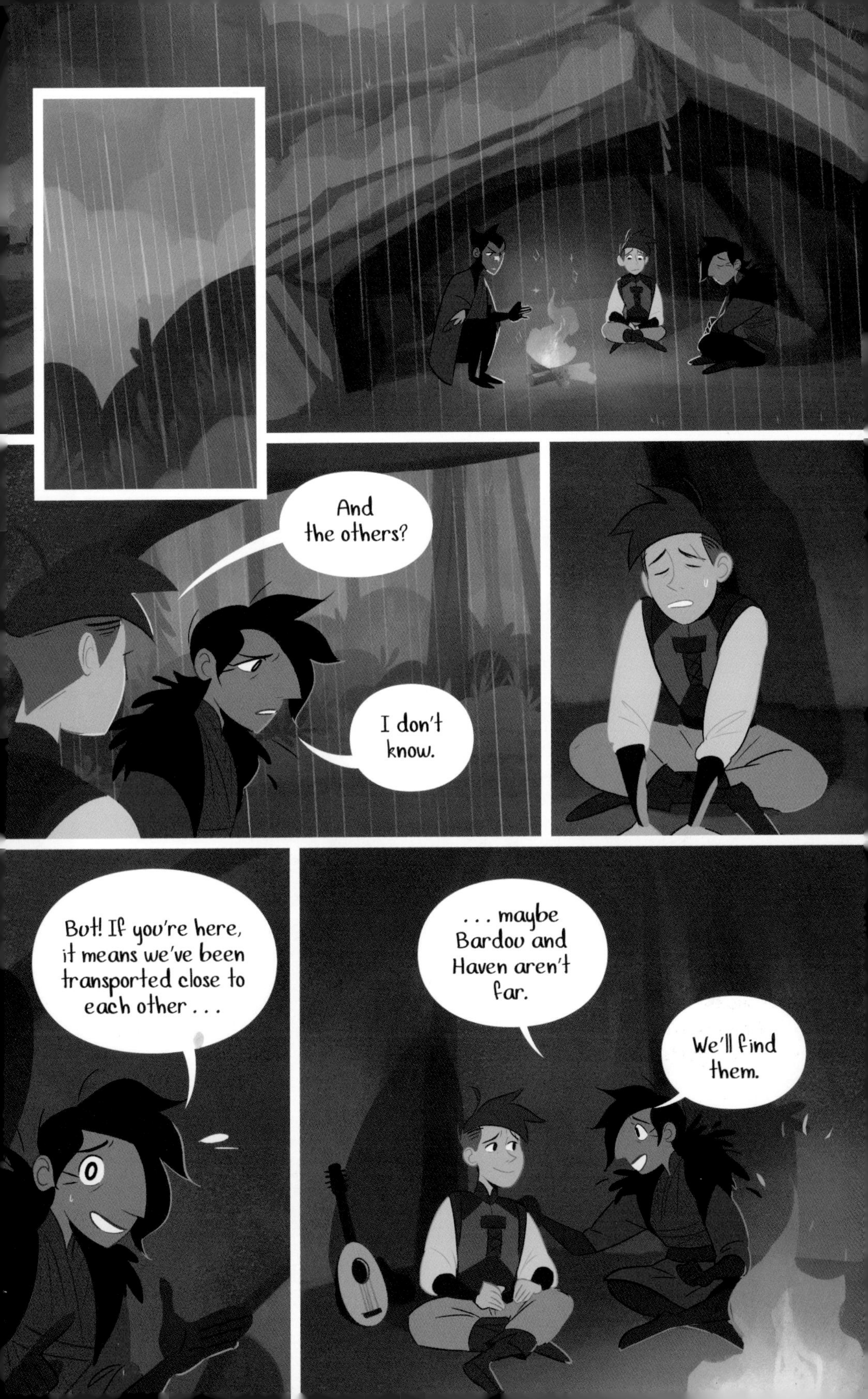
And the others?
I don't know.
But! If you're here, it means we've been transported close to each other . . .
. . . maybe Bardou and Haven aren't far.
We'll find them.

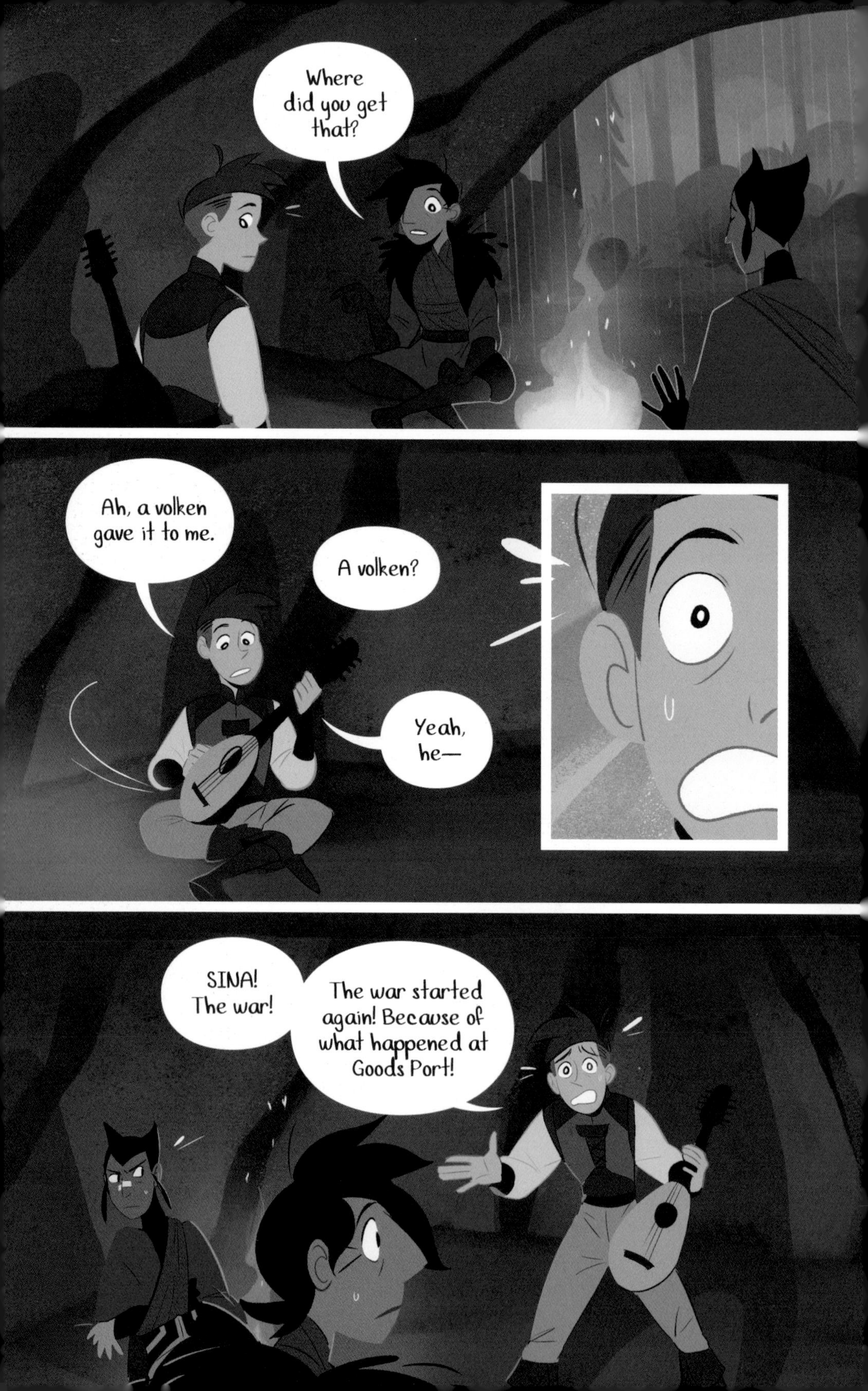
Where did you get that?
Ah, a volken gave it to me.
A volken?
Yeah, he—
SINA! The war!
The war started again! Because of what happened at Goods Port!

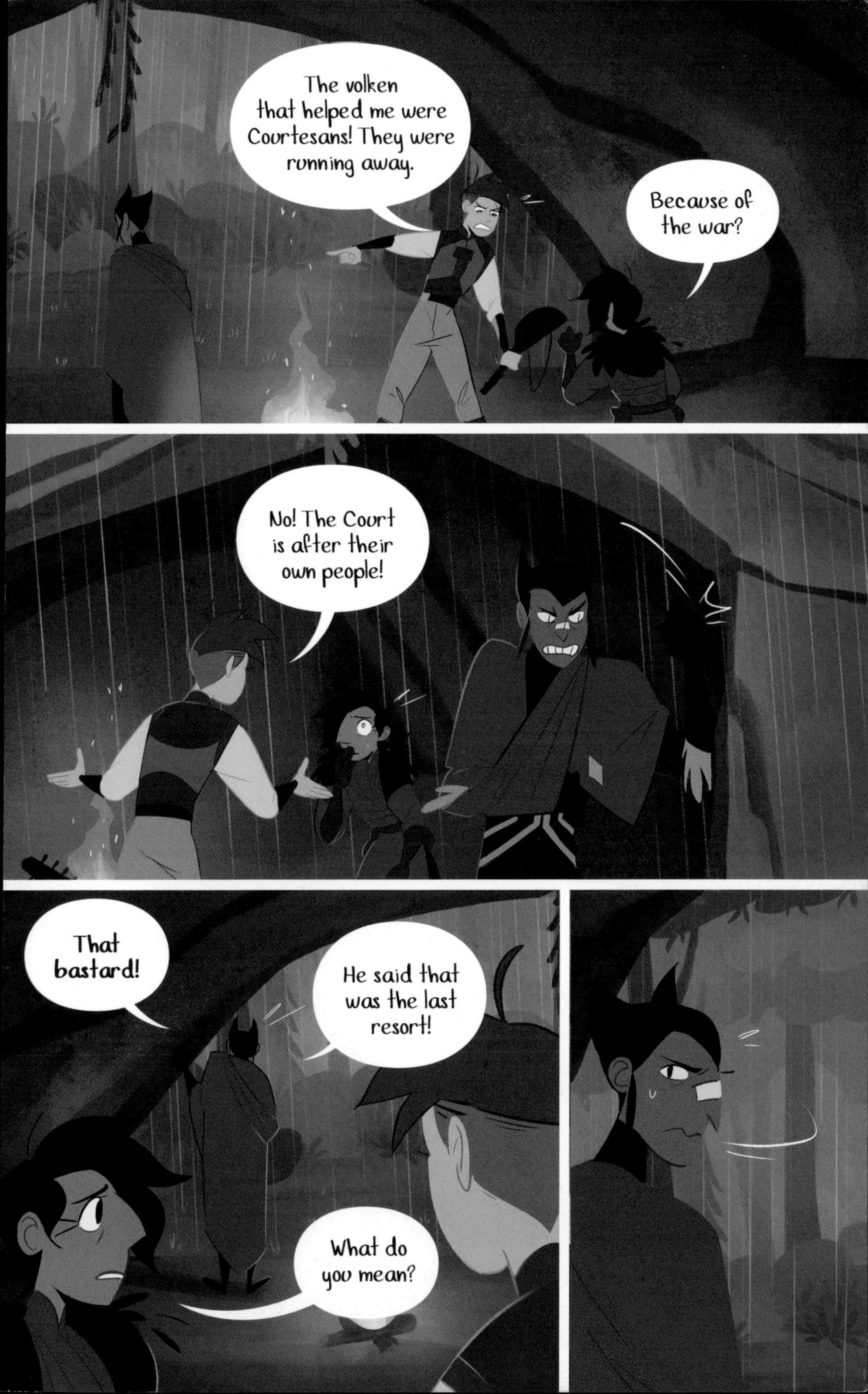
The volken that helped me were Courtesans! They were running away.
Because of the war?
No! The Court is after their own people!
That bastard!
He said that was the last resort!
What do you mean?

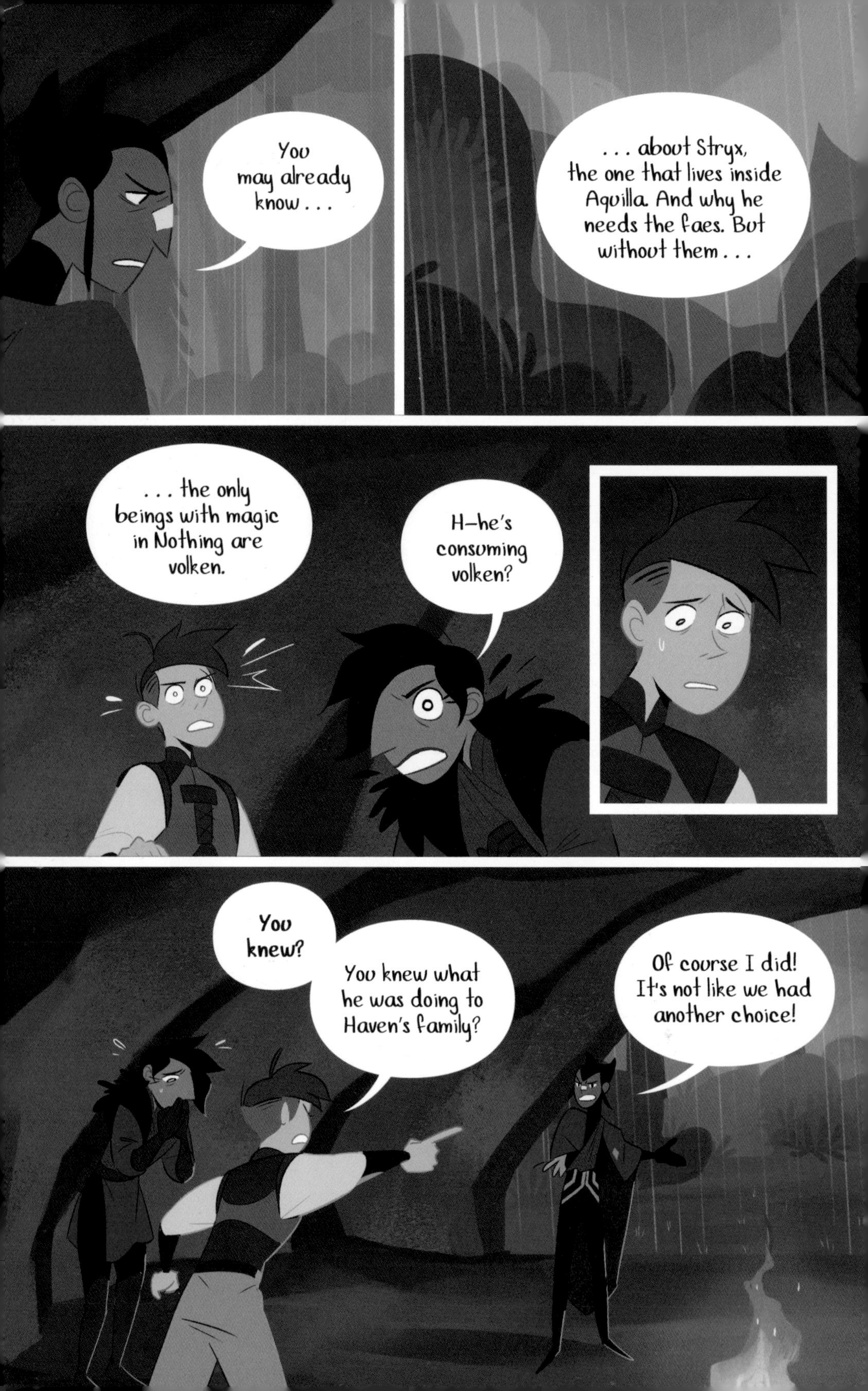
You may already know . . .
. . . about Stryx, the one that lives inside Aquilla. And why he needs the faes. But without them . . .
. . . the only beings with magic in Nothing are volken.
H–he's consuming volken?
You knew?
You knew what he was doing to Haven's family?
Of course I did! It's not like we had another choice!

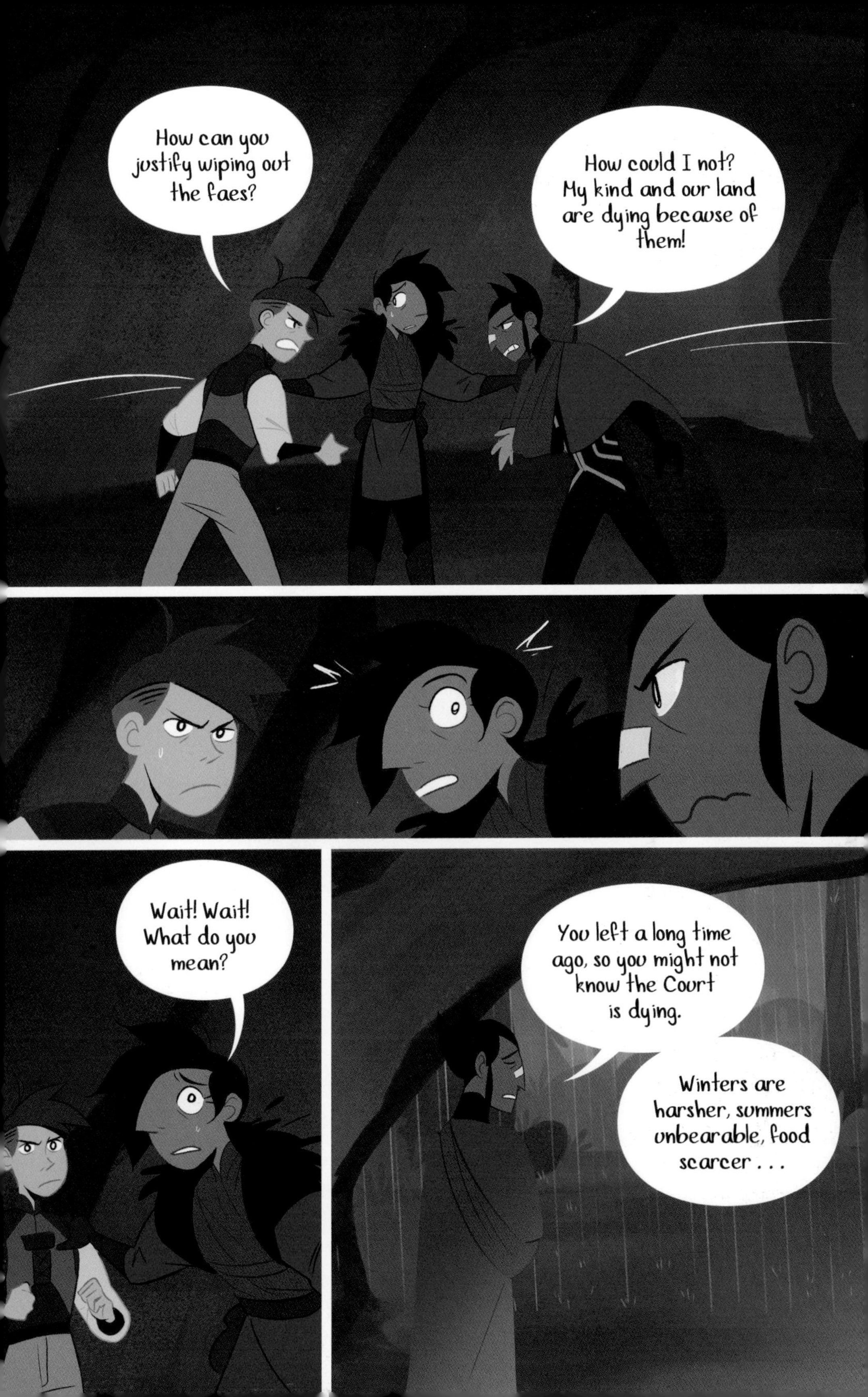
How can you justify wiping out the faes?
How could I not? My kind and our land are dying because of them!
Wait! Wait! What do you mean?
You left a long time ago, so you might not know the Court is dying.
Winters are harsher, summers unbearable, food scarcer . . .

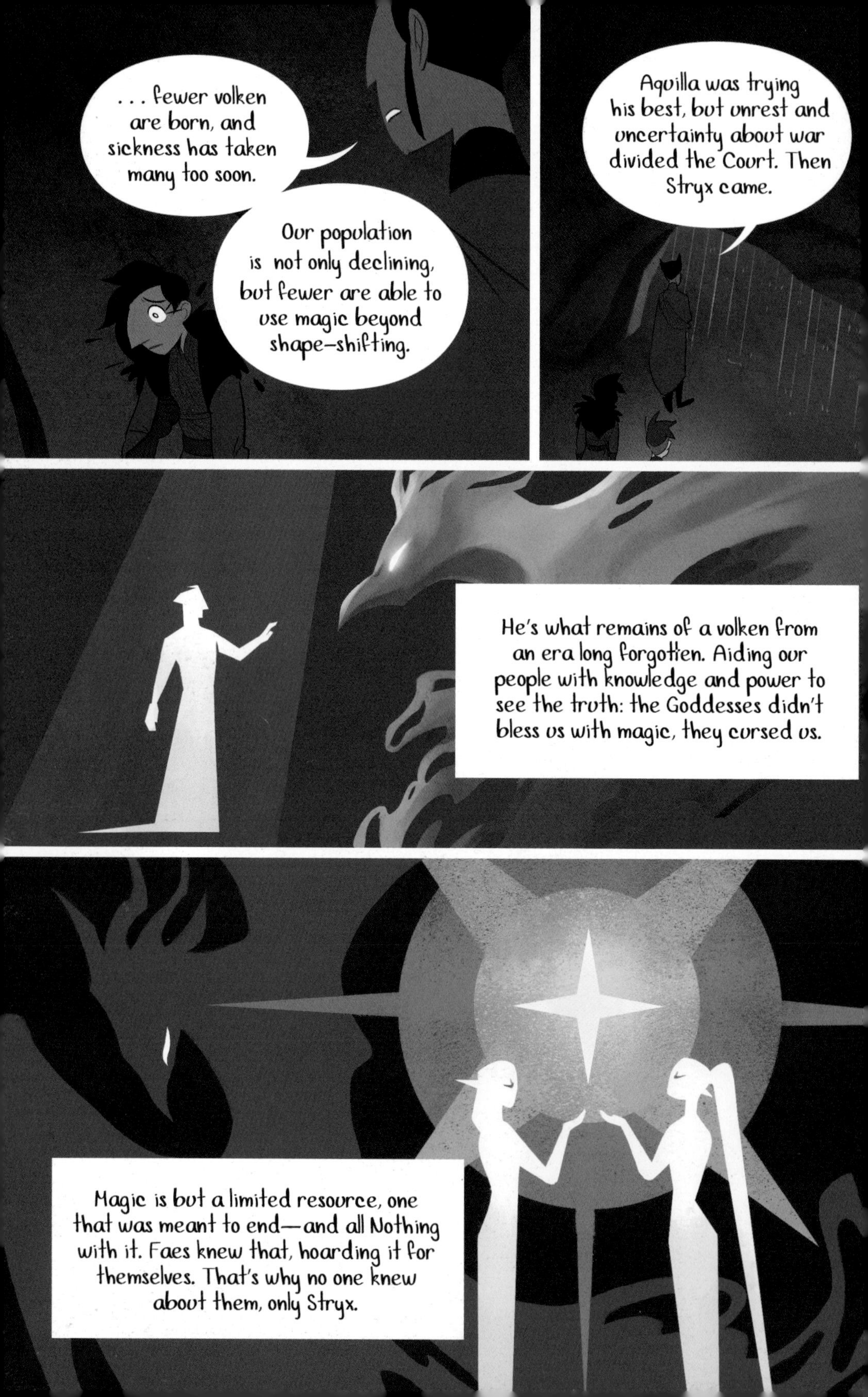
. . . fewer volken are born, and sickness has taken many too soon.
Our population is not only declining, but fewer are able to use magic beyond shape-shifting.
Aquilla was trying his best, but unrest and uncertainty about war divided the Court. Then Stryx came.
He's what remains of a volken from an era long forgotten. Aiding our people with knowledge and power to see the truth: the Goddesses didn't bless us with magic, they cursed us.
Magic is but a limited resource, one that was meant to end—and all Nothing with it. Faes knew that, hoarding it for themselves. That's why no one knew about them, only Stryx.

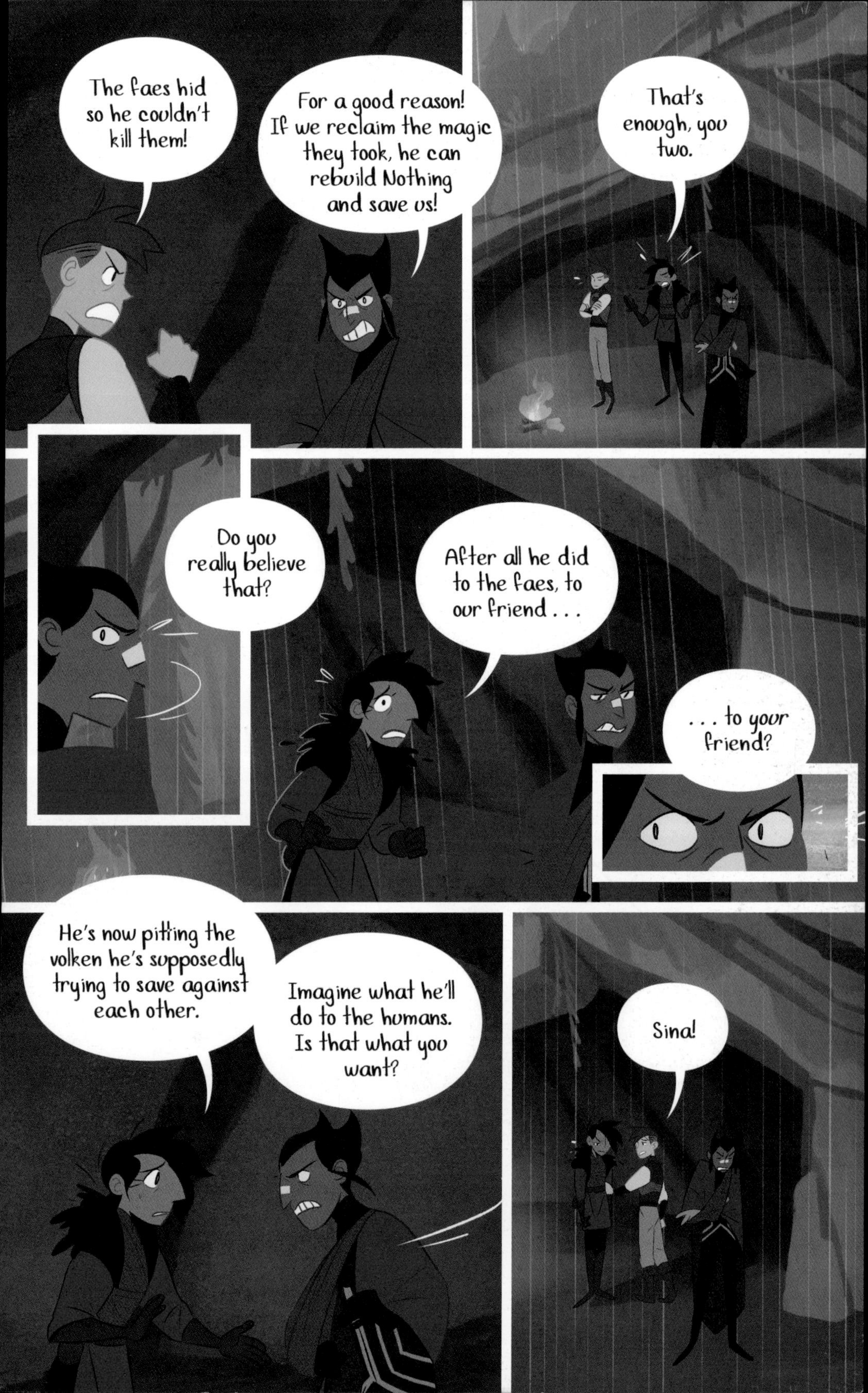
The faes hid so he couldn't kill them!
For a good reason! If we reclaim the magic they took, he can rebuild Nothing and save us!
That's enough, you two.
Do you really believe that?
After all he did to the faes, to our friend . . .
. . . to your friend?
He's now pitting the volken he's supposedly trying to save against each other.
Imagine what he'll do to the humans. Is that what you want?
Sina!

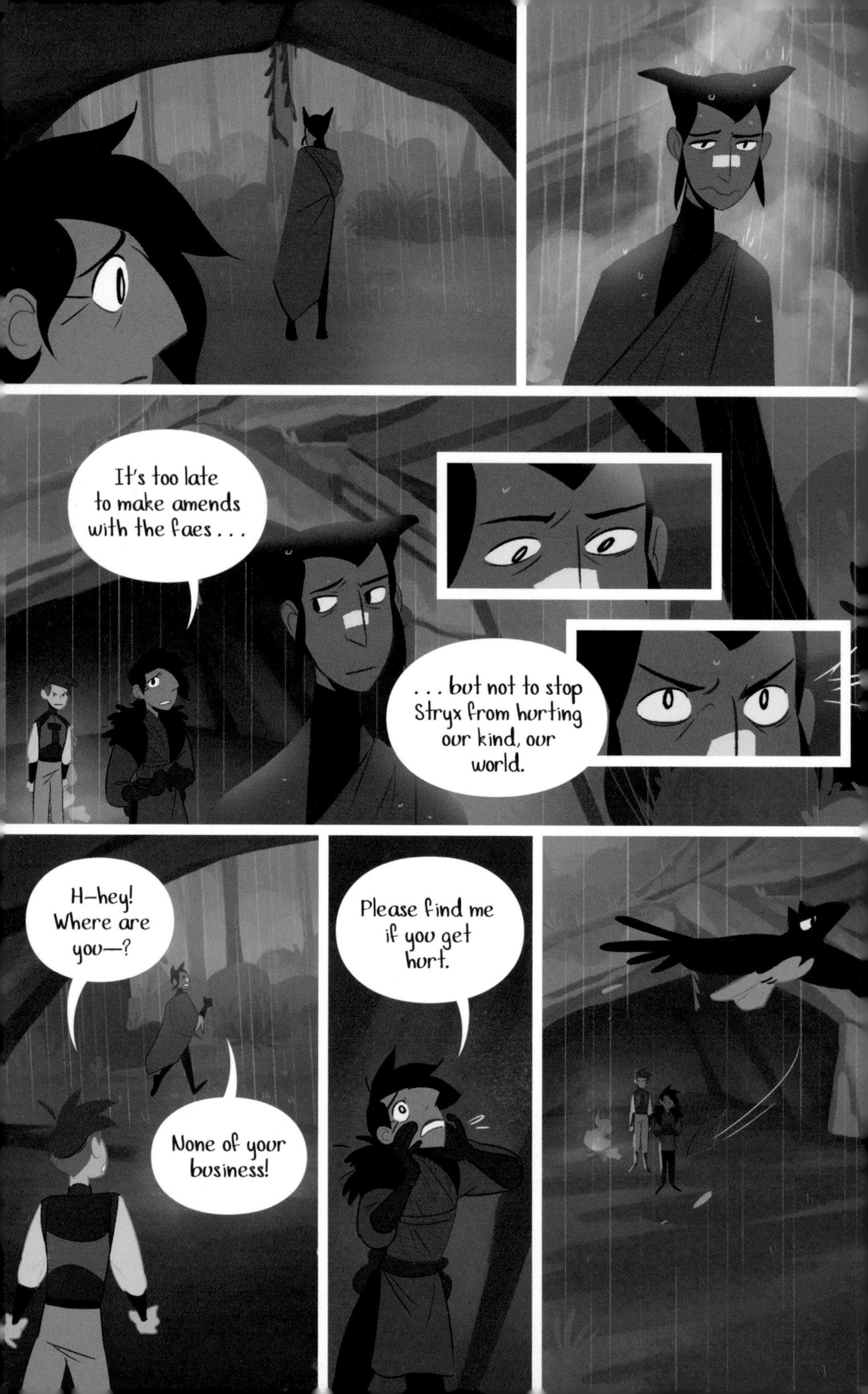
It's too late to make amends with the faes . . .
. . . but not to stop Stryx from hurting our kind, our world.
H—hey! Where are you—?
None of your business!
Please find me if you get hurt.

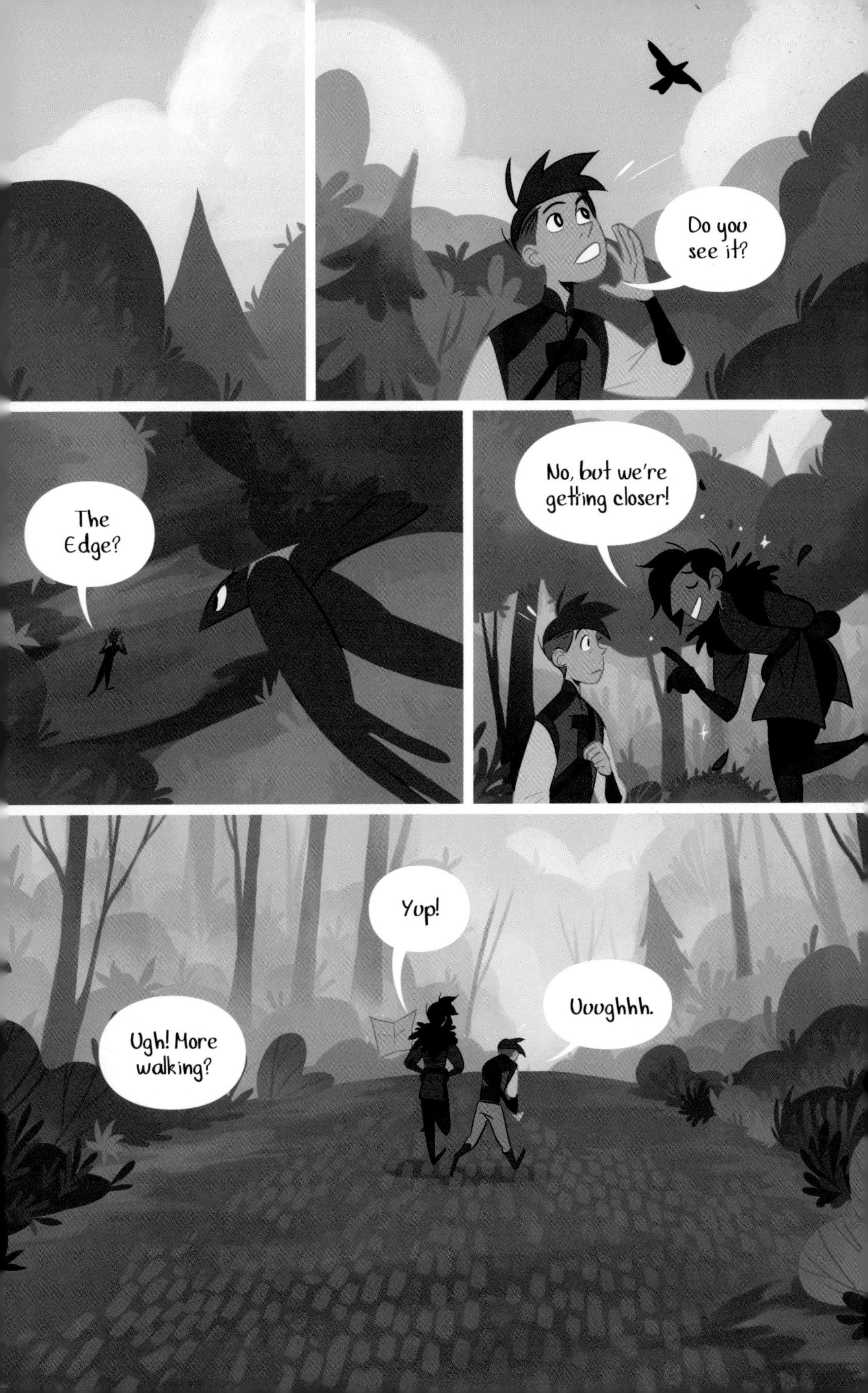
Do you see it?
The Edge?
No, but we're getting closer!
Yup!
Uuughhh.
Ugh! More walking?

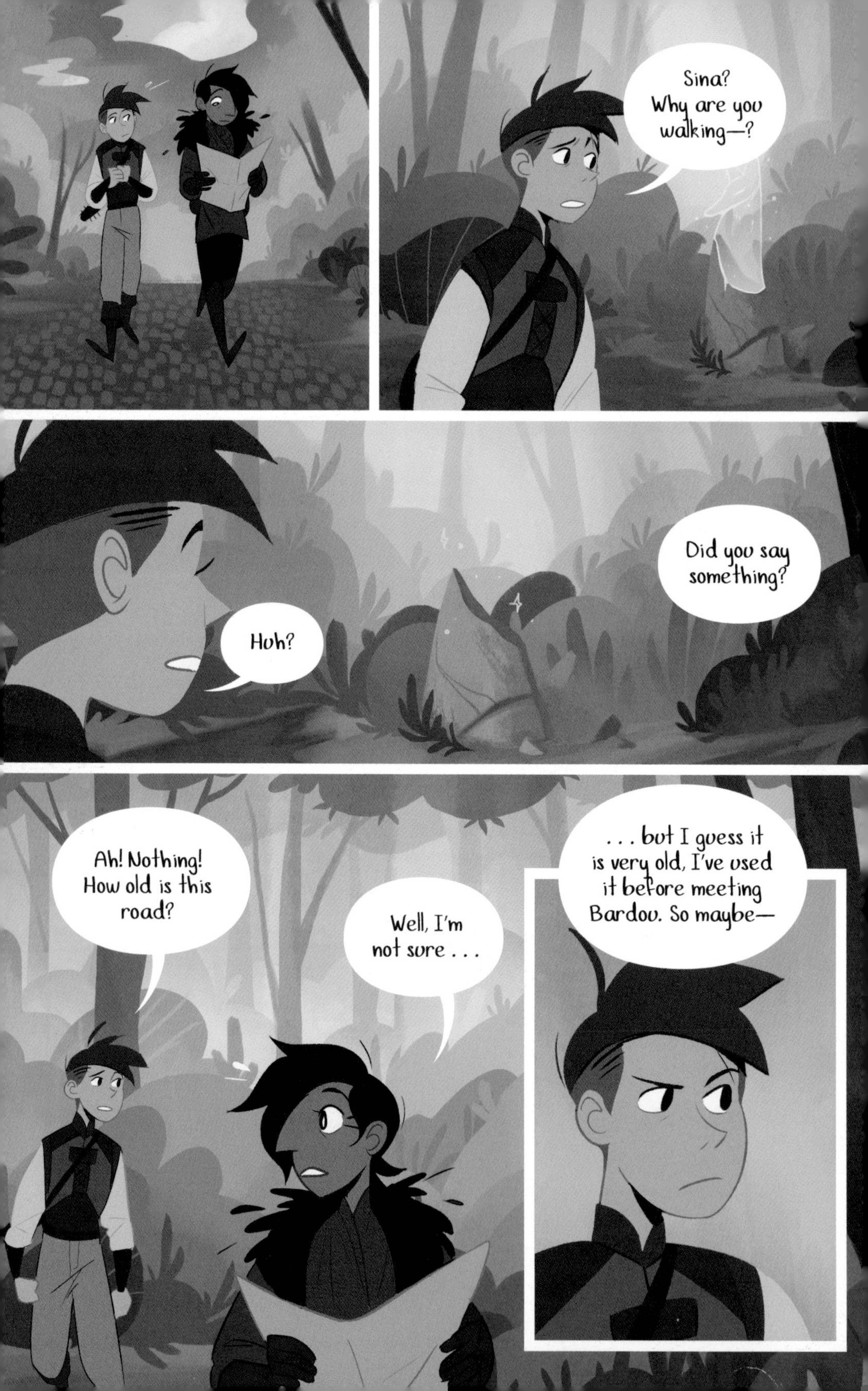
Sina?
Why are you walking—?
Did you say something?
Huh?
Ah! Nothing! How old is this road?
Well, I'm not sure . . .
. . . but I guess it is very old, I've used it before meeting Bardou. So maybe—

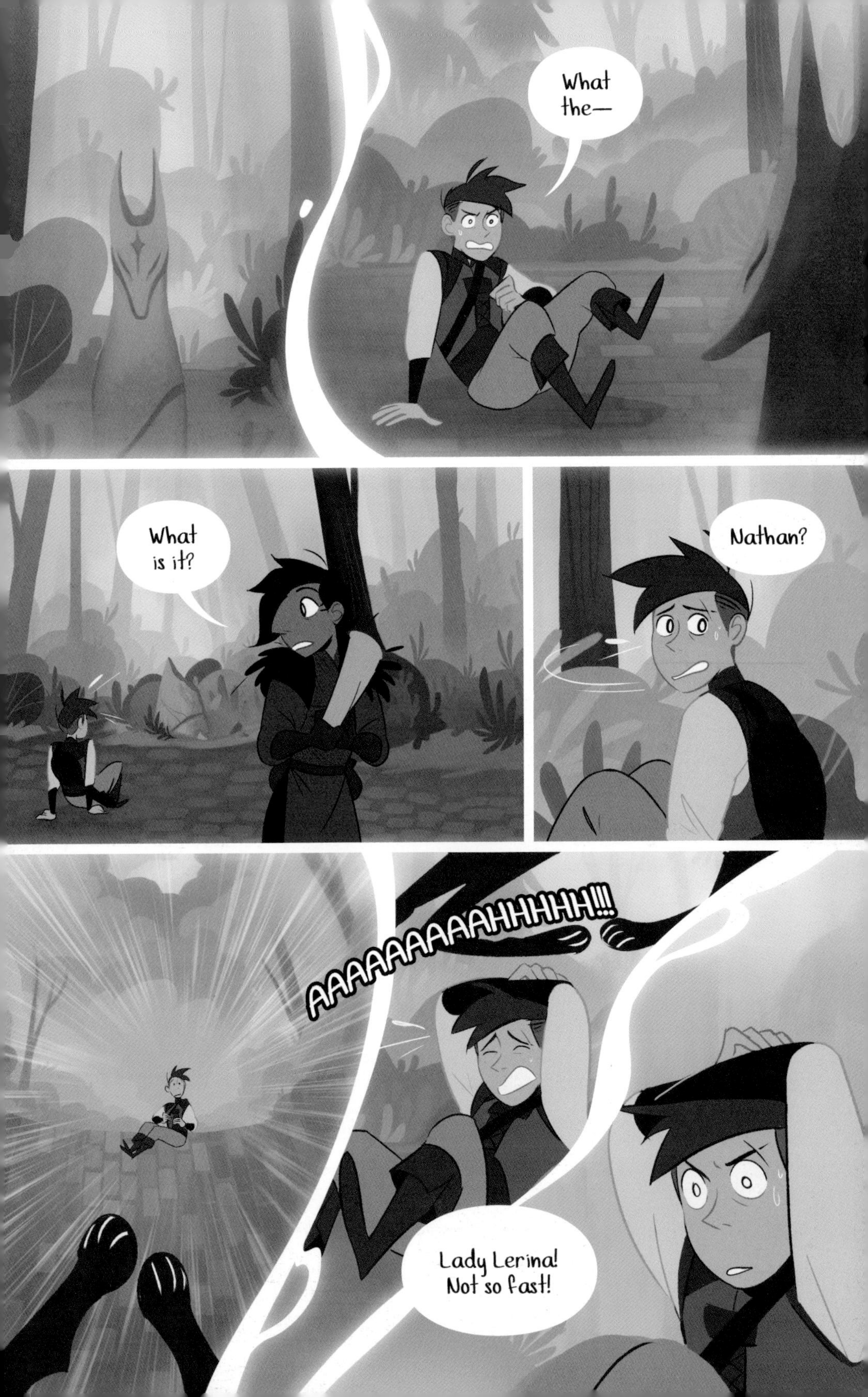
What the—
What is it?
Nathan?
AAAAAAAAAAHHHHHH!!!
Lady Lerina! Not so fast!

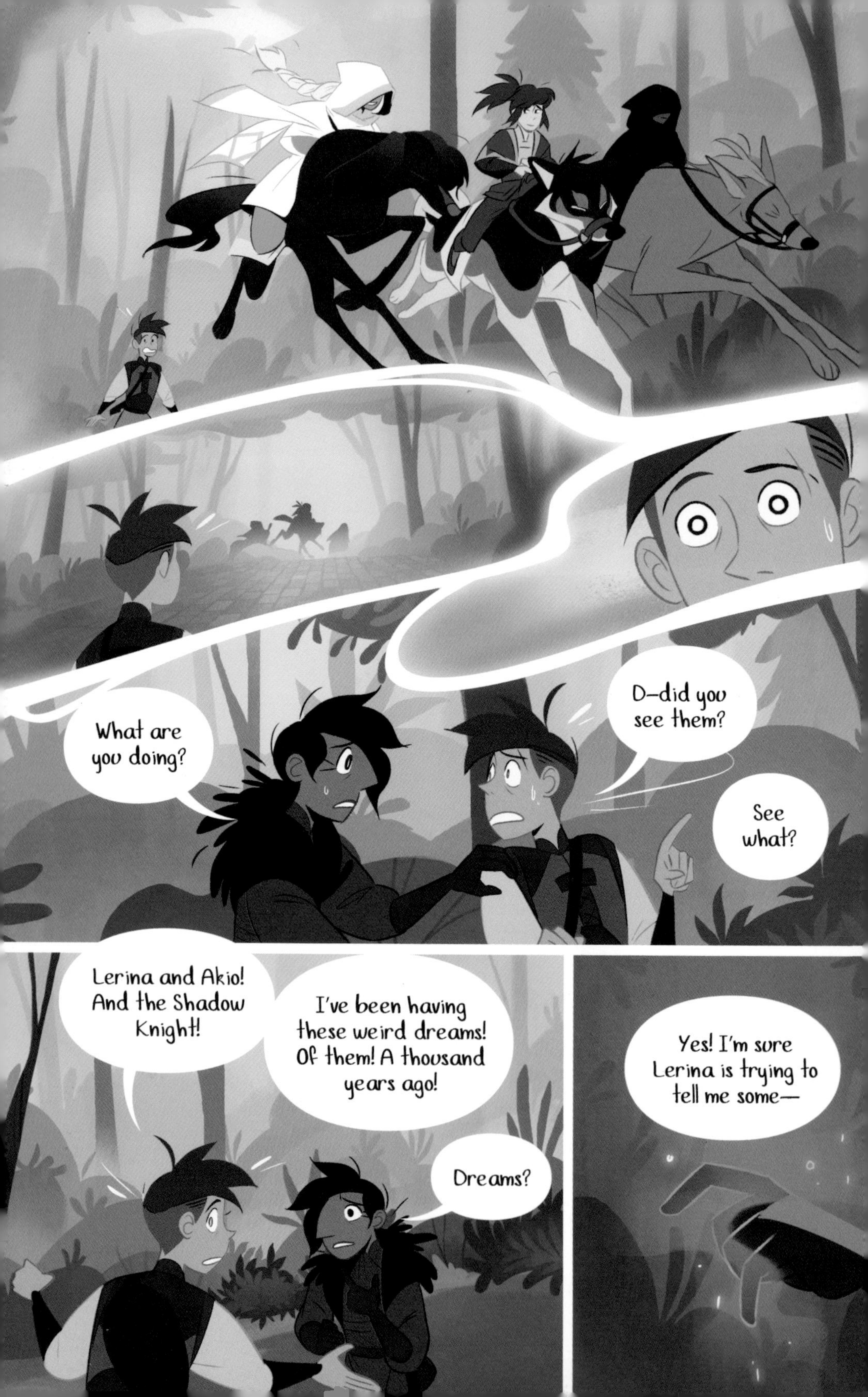
What are you doing?
D-did you see them?
See what?
Lerina and Akio! And the Shadow Knight!
I've been having these weird dreams! Of them! A thousand years ago!
Dreams?
Yes! I'm sure Lerina is trying to tell me some—

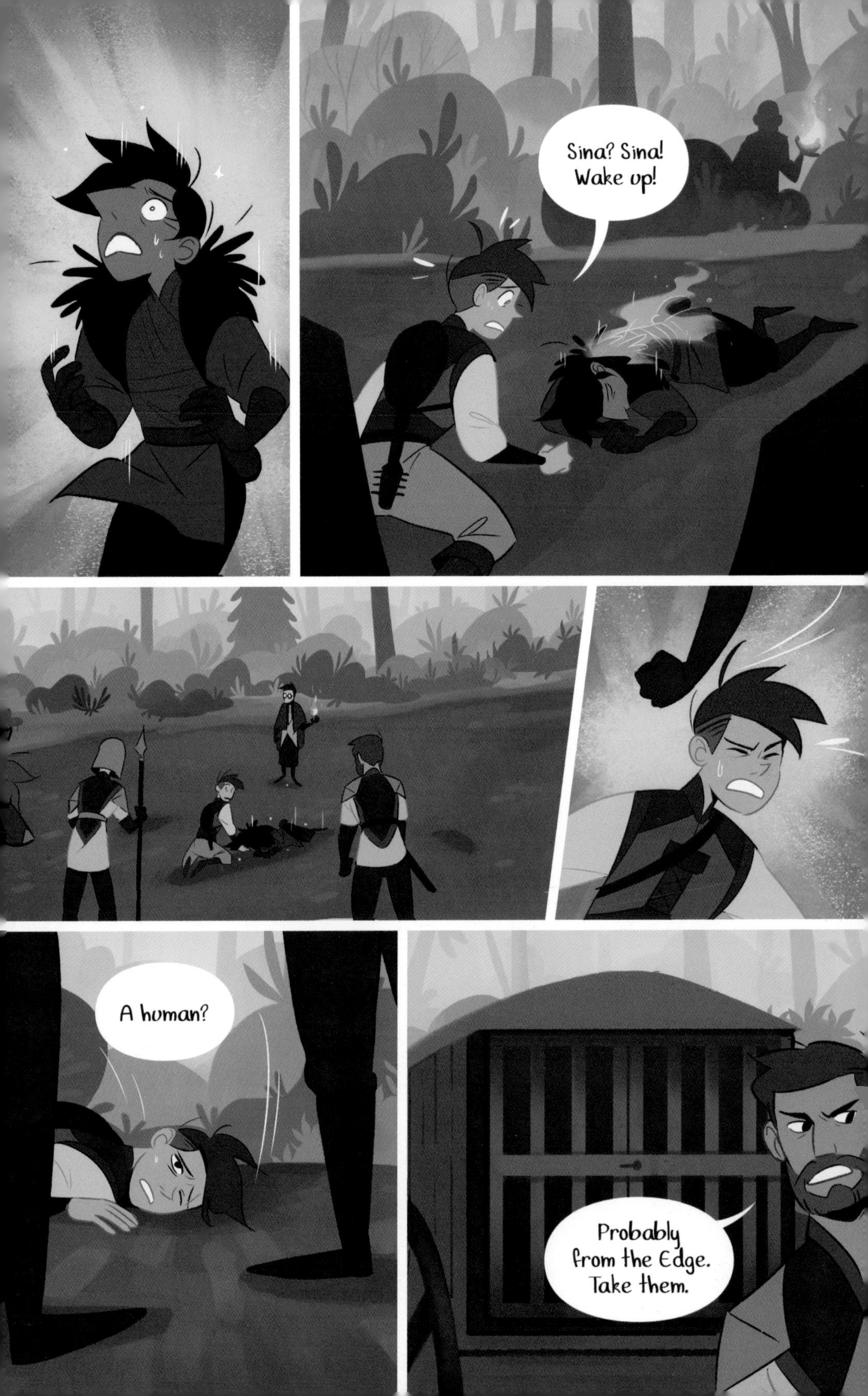
Sina? Sina! Wake up!
A human?
Probably from the Edge. Take them.

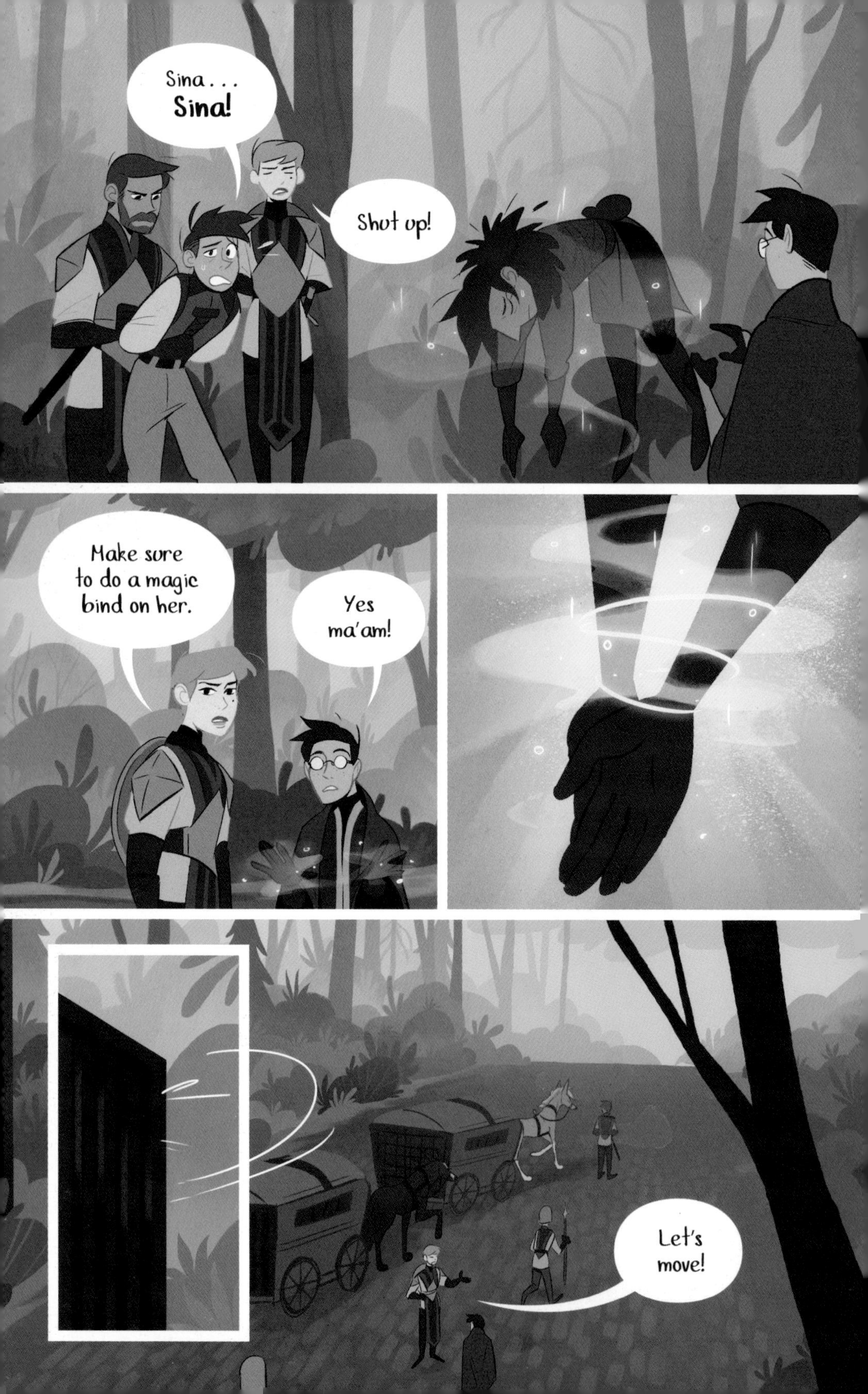
Sina . . .
Sina!
Shut up!
Make sure to do a magic bind on her.
Yes ma'am!
Let's move!

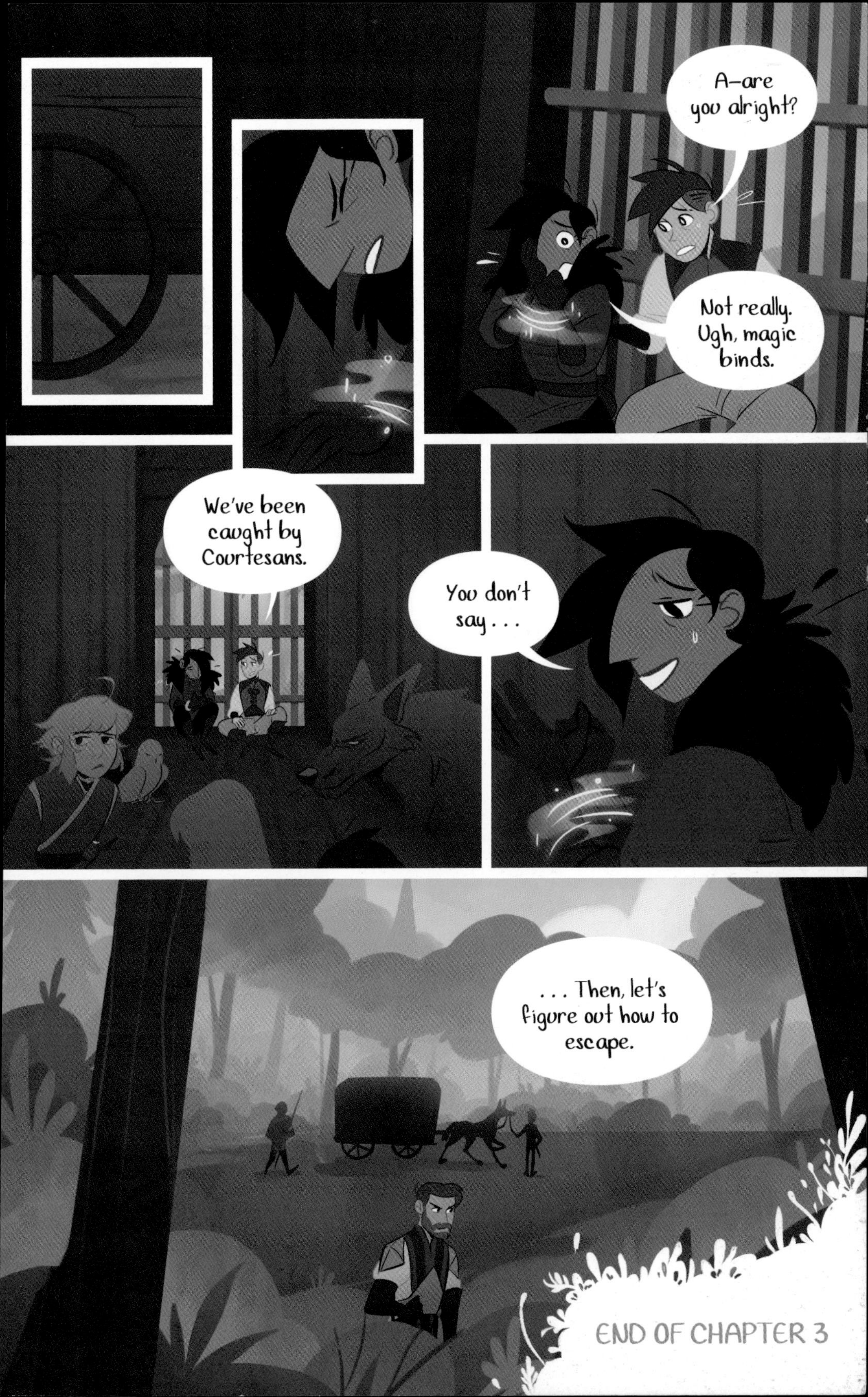
A-are you alright?
Not really. Ugh, magic binds.
We've been caught by Courtesans.
You don't say . . .
. . . Then, let's figure out how to escape.
END OF CHAPTER 3

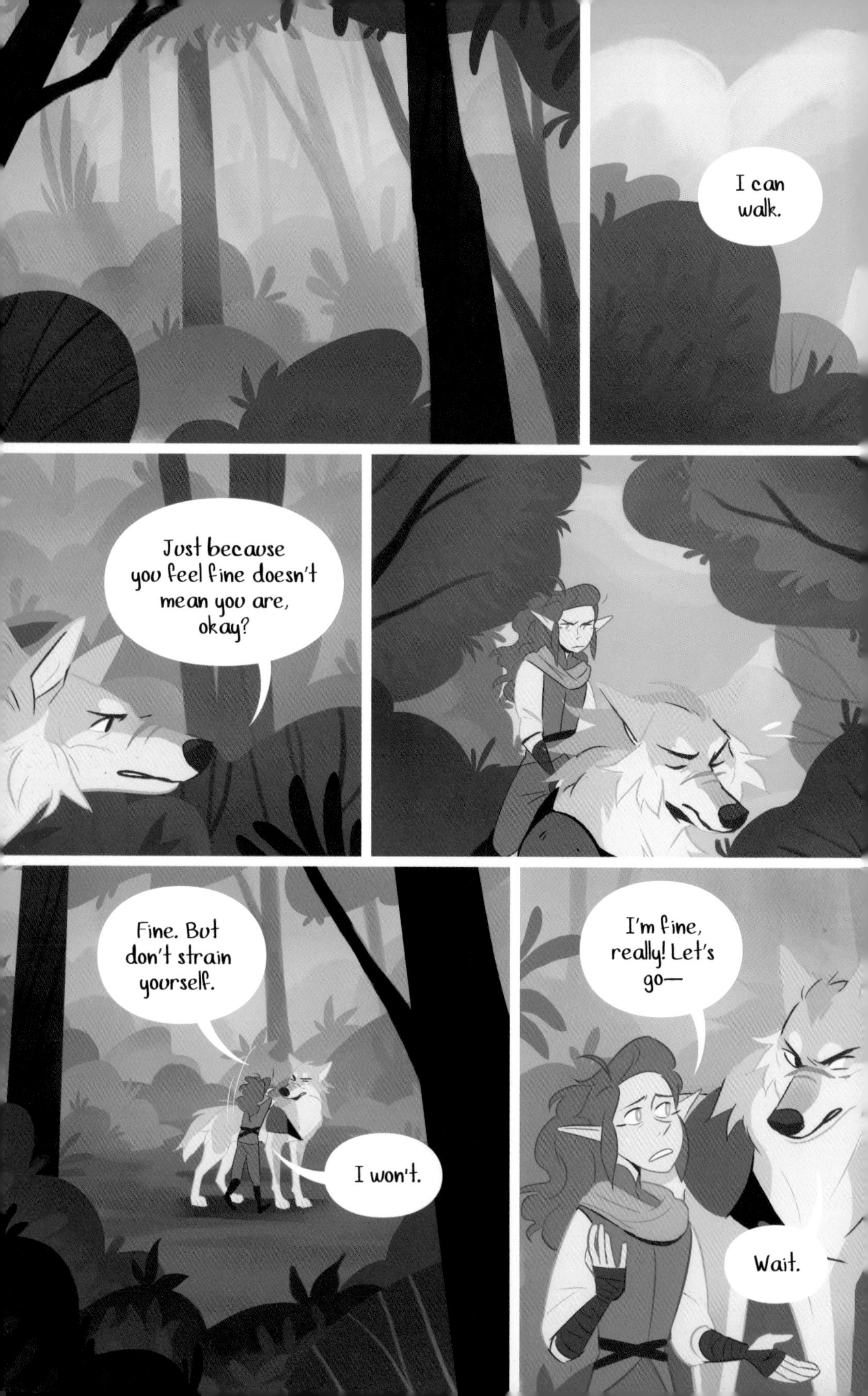
I can walk.
Just because you feel fine doesn't mean you are, okay?
Fine. But don't strain yourself.
I won't.
I'm fine, really! Let's go—
Wait.

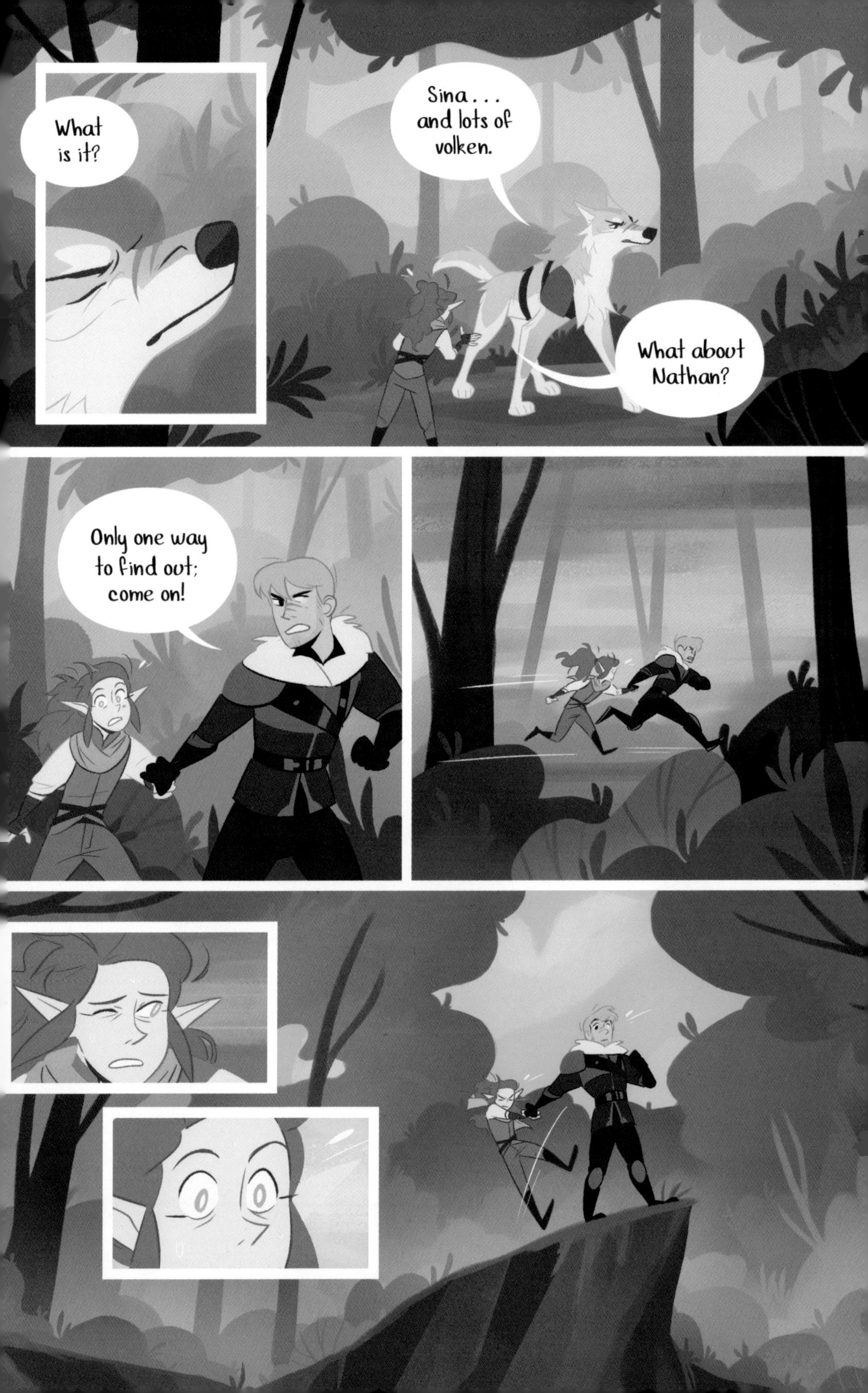
What is it?
Sina . . . and lots of volken.
What about Nathan?
Only one way to find out; come on!

# Chapter 4
# Reunion

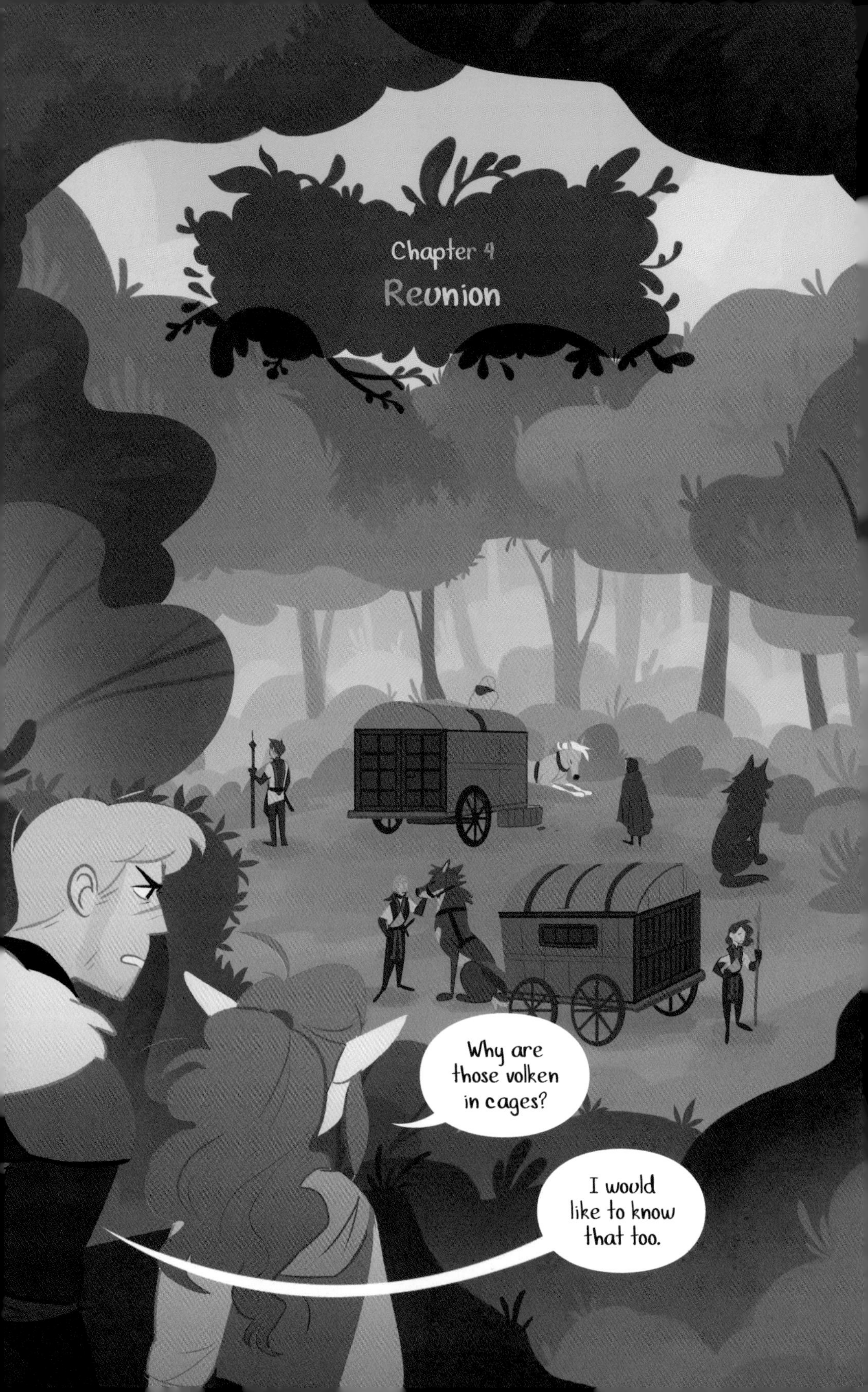
Why are those volken in cages?
I would like to know that too.

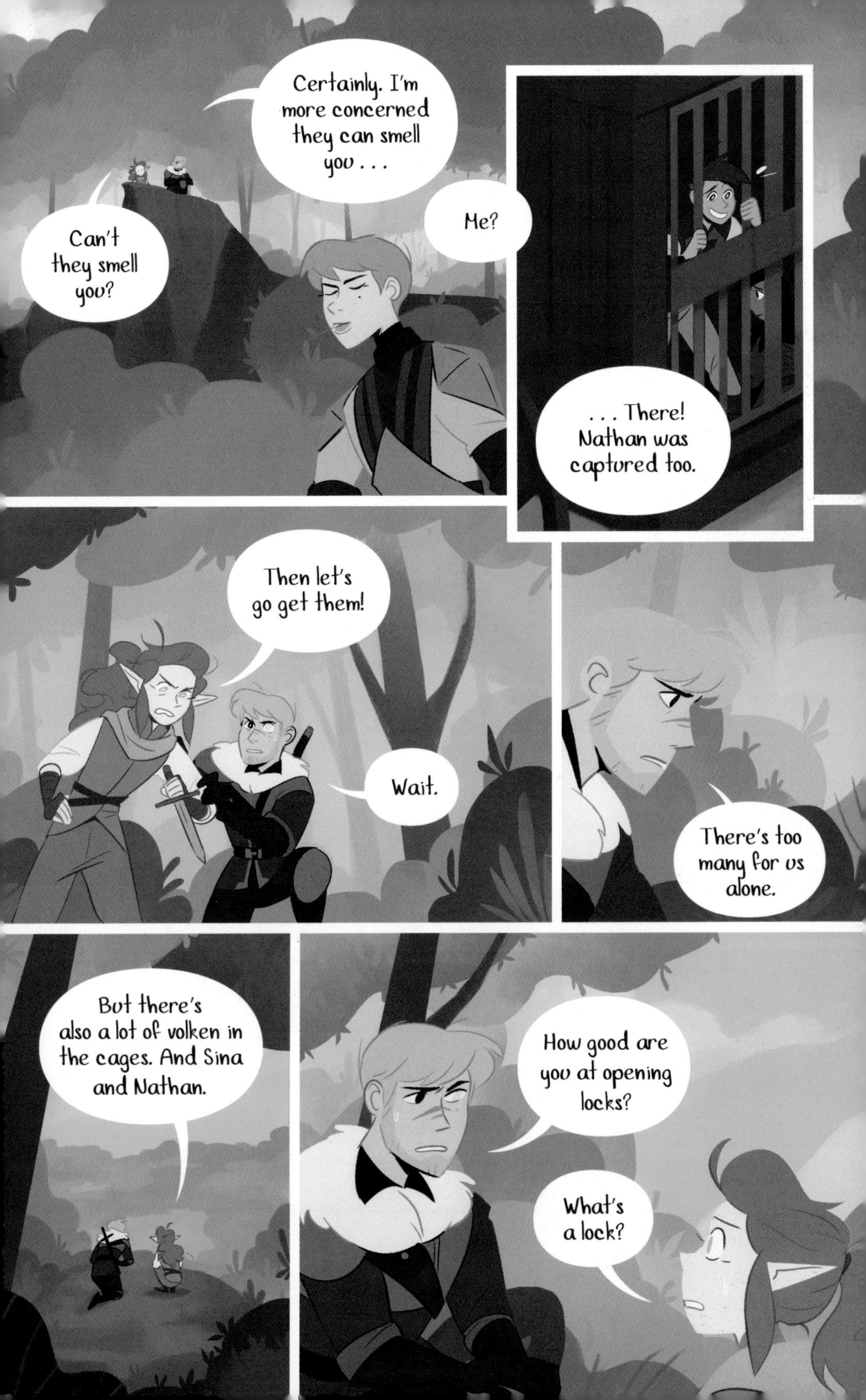
Certainly. I'm more concerned they can smell you . . .
Can't they smell you?
Me?
. . . There! Nathan was captured too.
Then let's go get them!
Wait.
There's too many for us alone.
But there's also a lot of volken in the cages. And Sina and Nathan.
How good are you at opening locks?
What's a lock?

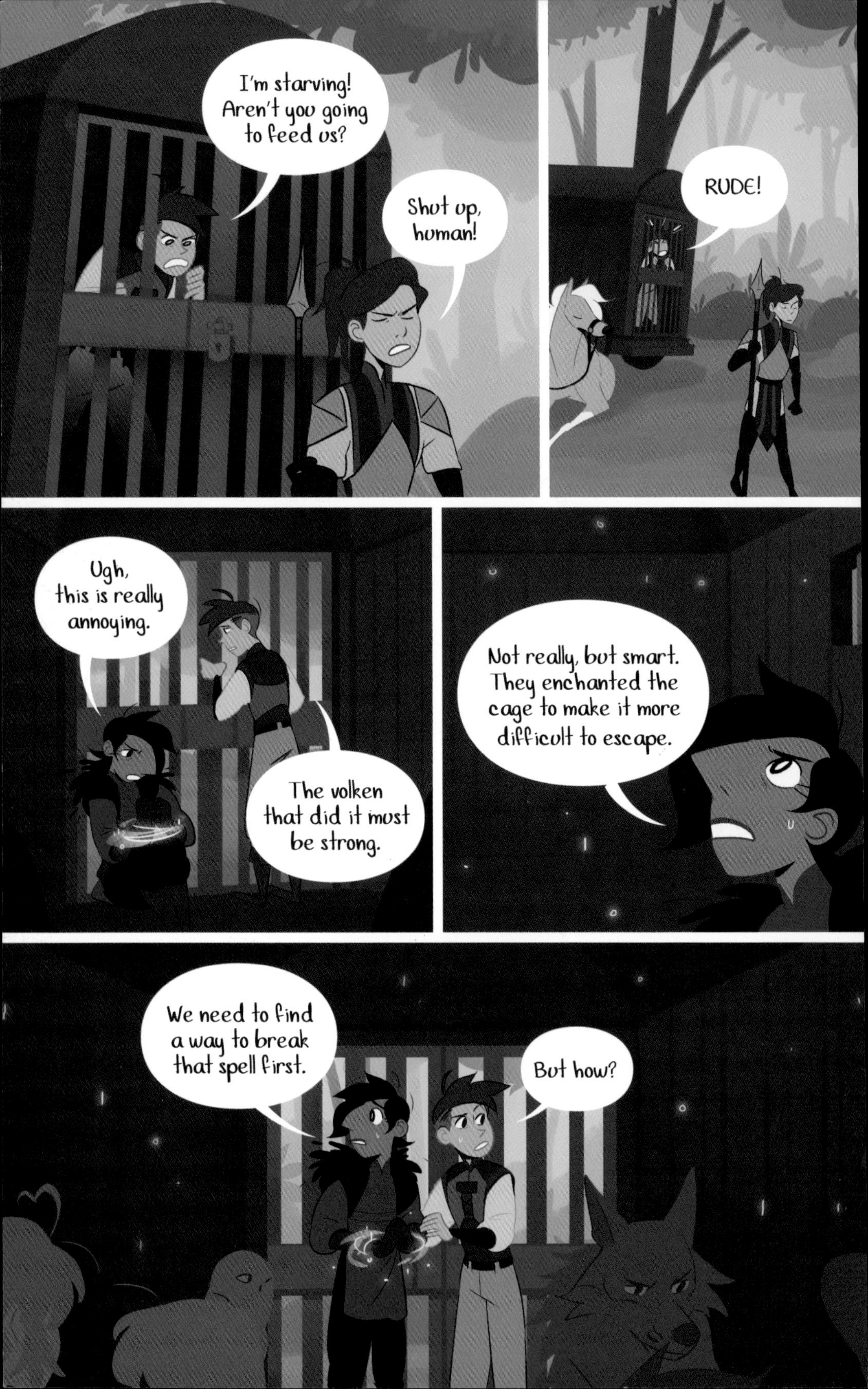
I'm starving! Aren't you going to feed us?
Shut up, human!
RUDE!
Ugh, this is really annoying.
The volken that did it must be strong.
Not really, but smart. They enchanted the cage to make it more difficult to escape.
We need to find a way to break that spell first.
But how?

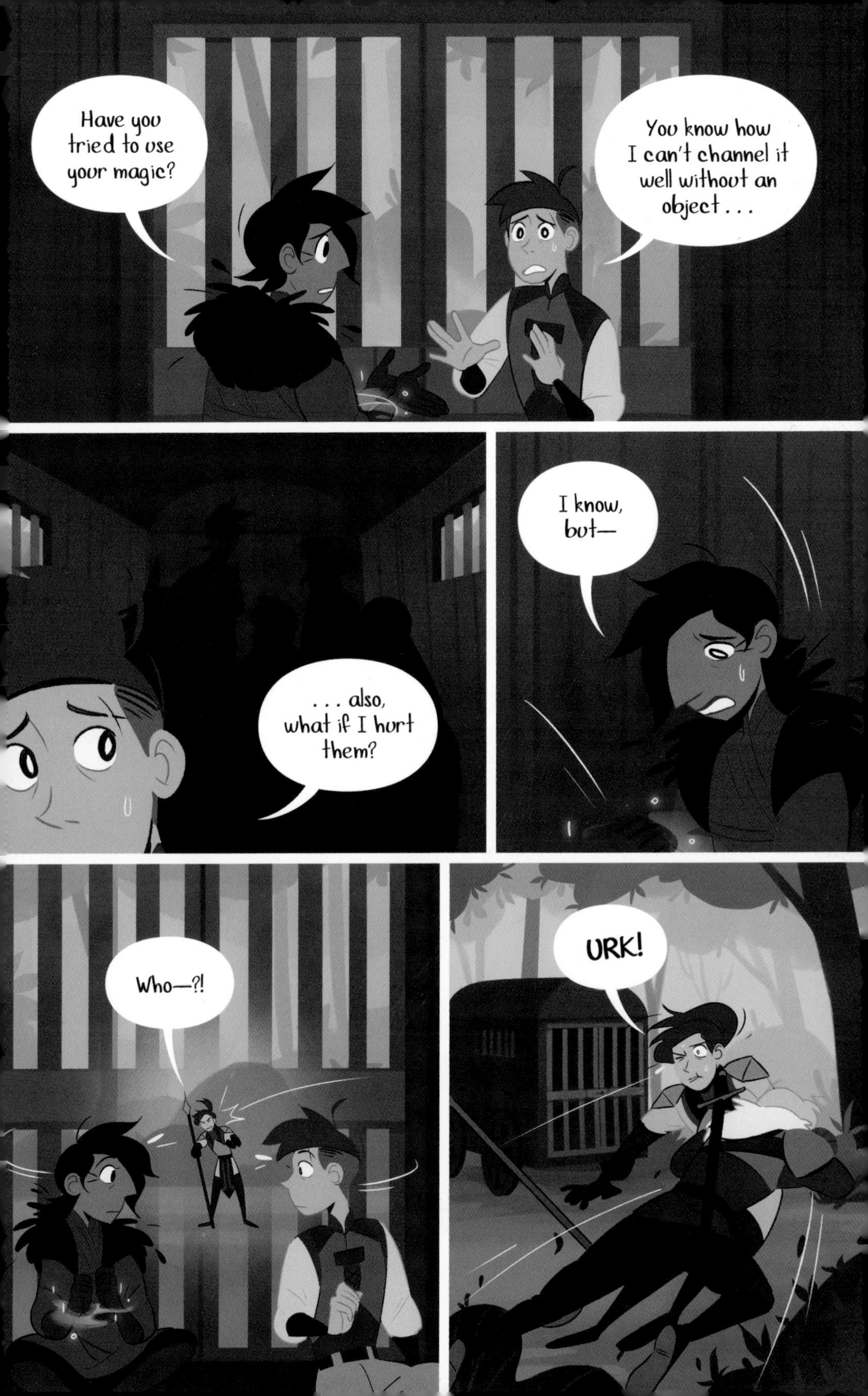
Have you tried to use your magic?
You know how I can't channel it well without an object . . .
. . . also, what if I hurt them?
I know, but—
Who—?!
URK!

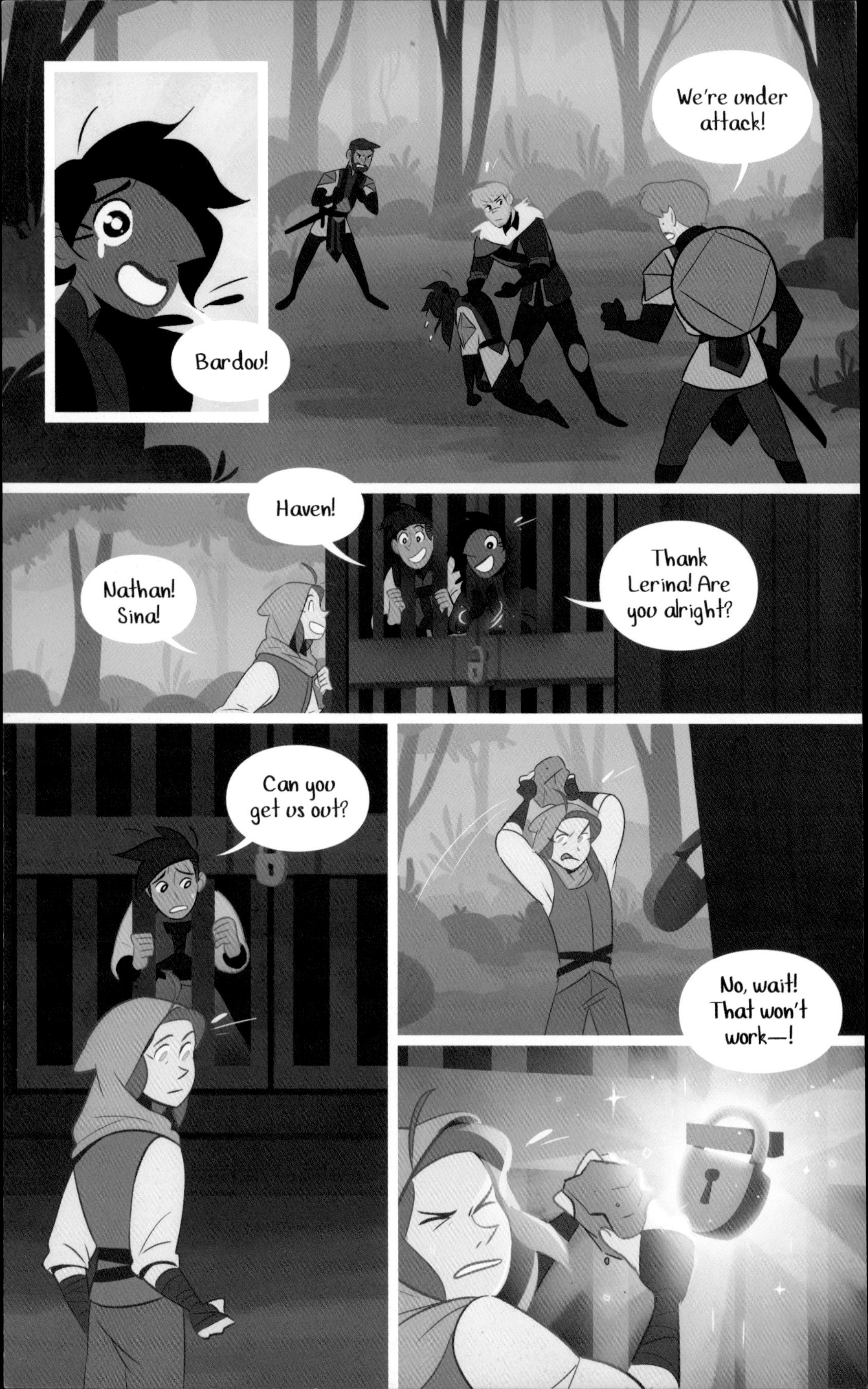
Bardou!
We're under attack!
Haven!
Nathan! Sina!
Thank Lerina! Are you alright?
Can you get us out?
No, wait! That won't work—!

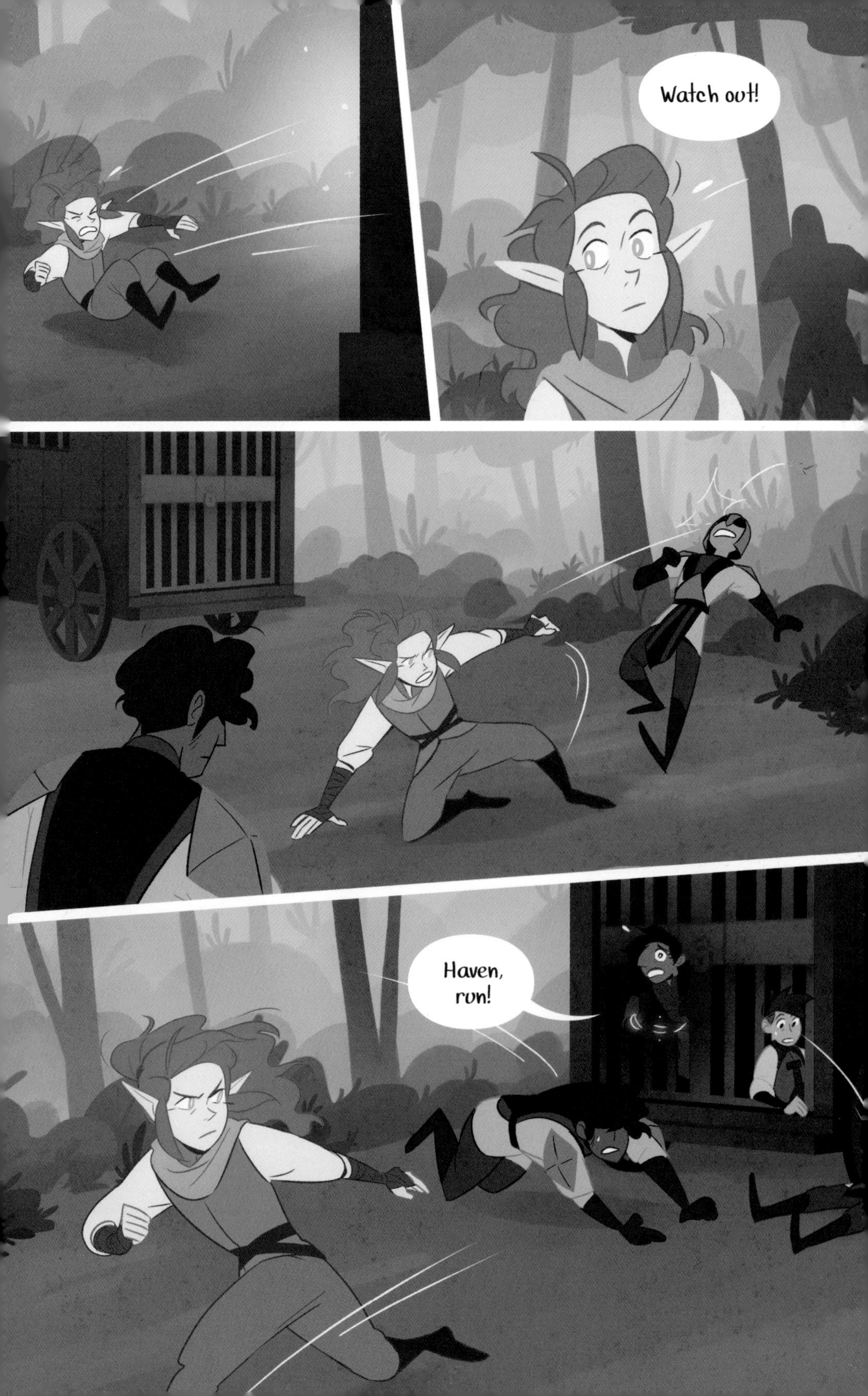
Watch out!
Haven, run!

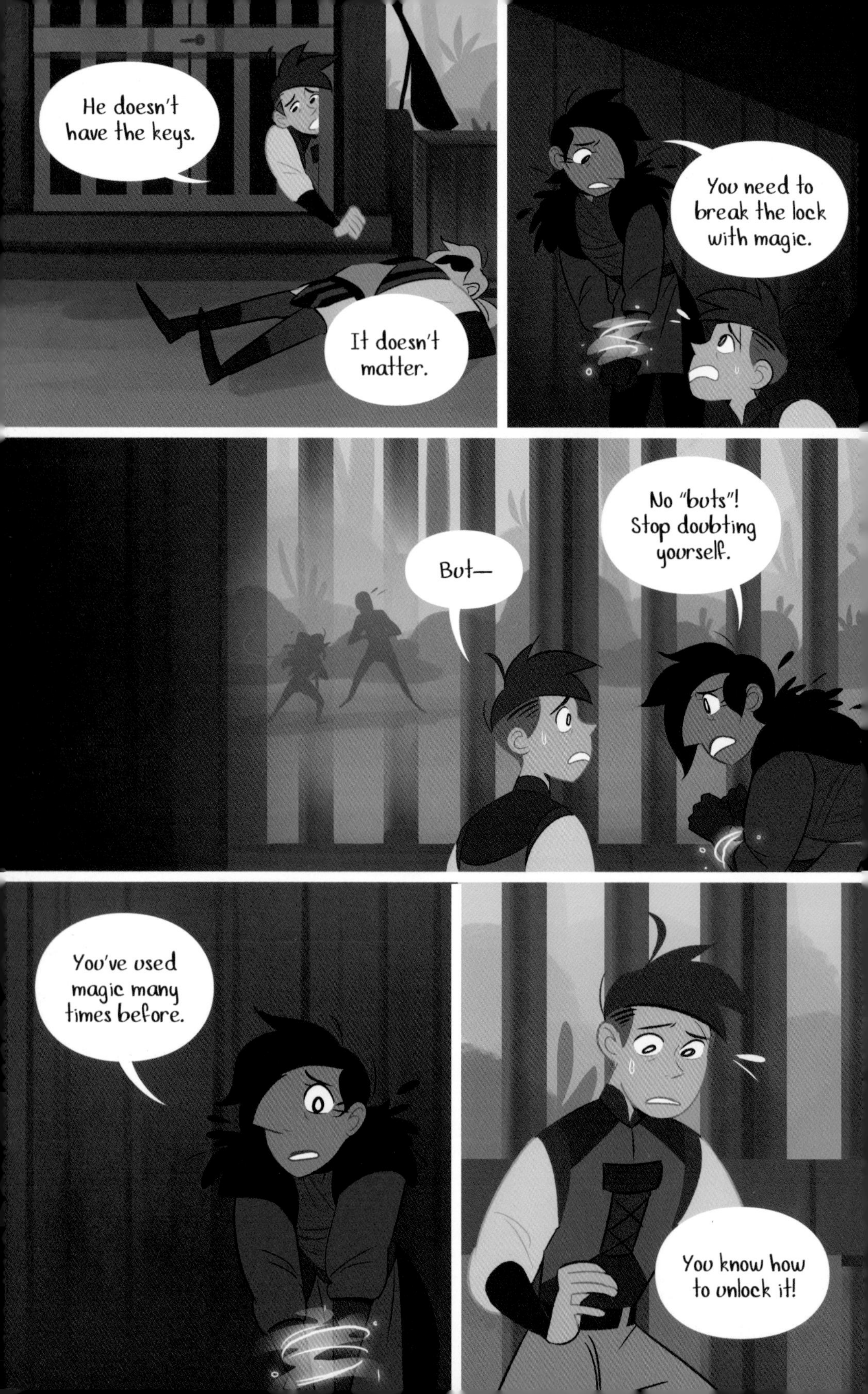
He doesn't have the keys.
It doesn't matter.
You need to break the lock with magic.
But—
No "buts"! Stop doubting yourself.
You've used magic many times before.
You know how to unlock it!

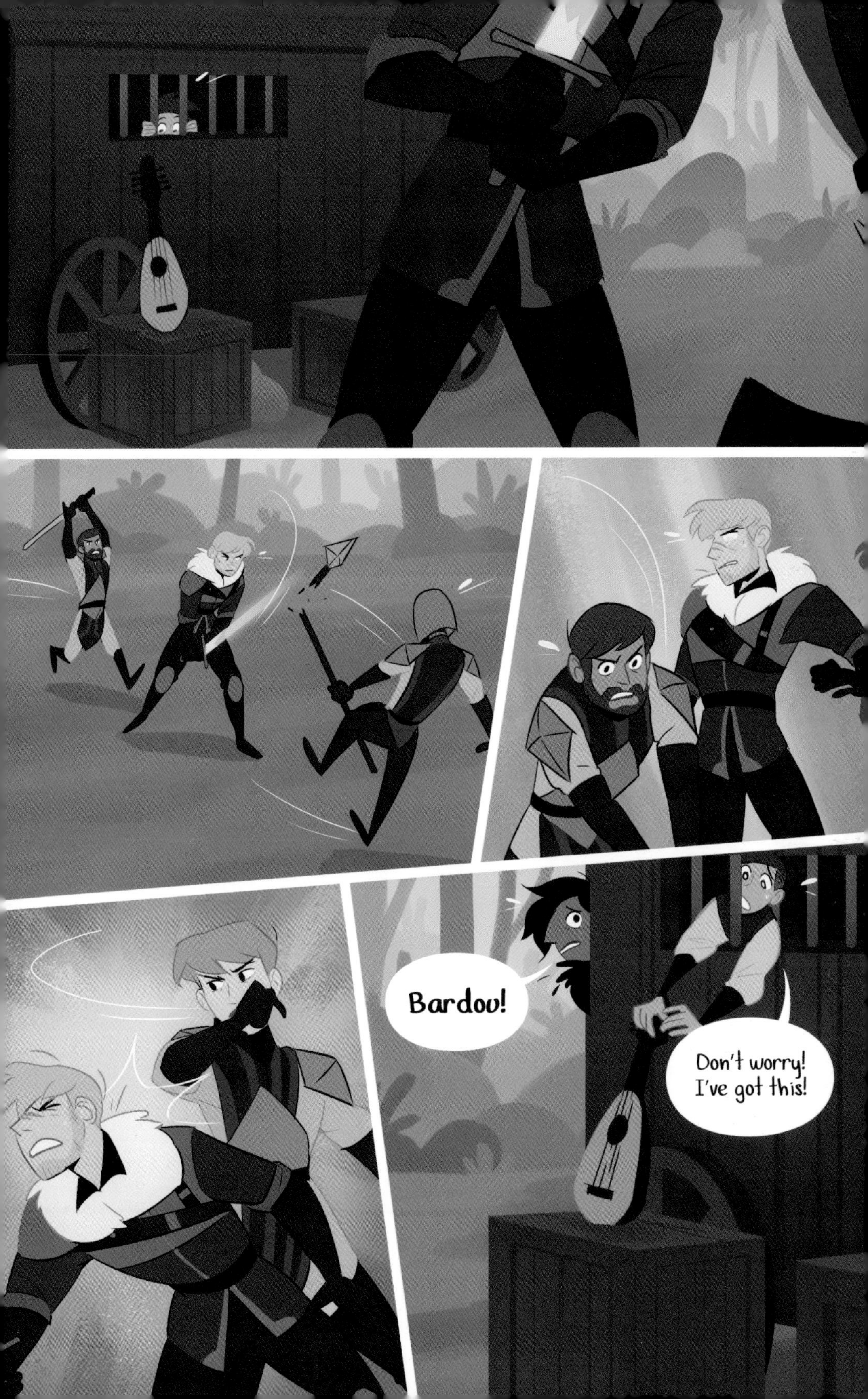
Bardou!
Don't worry! I've got this!

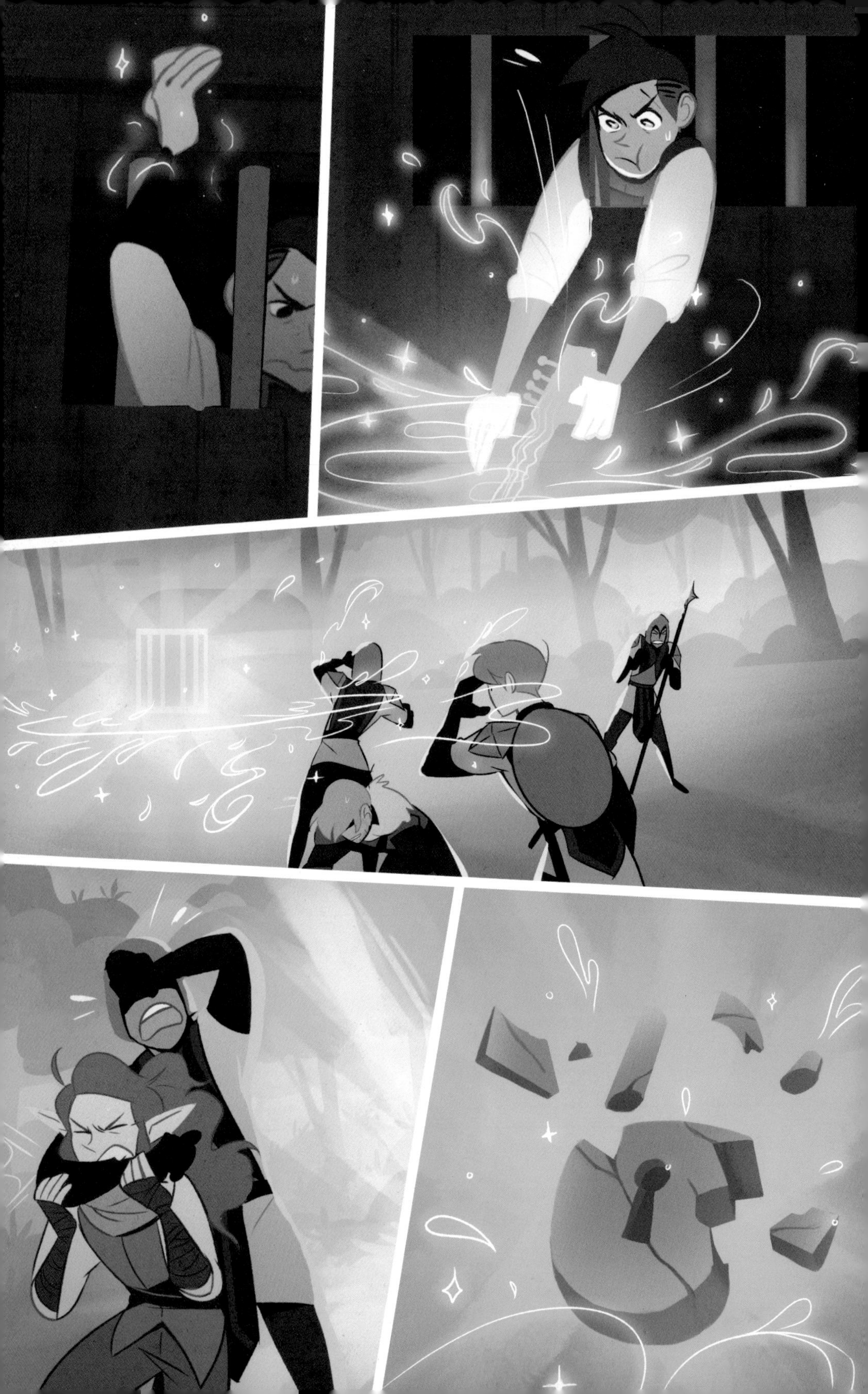

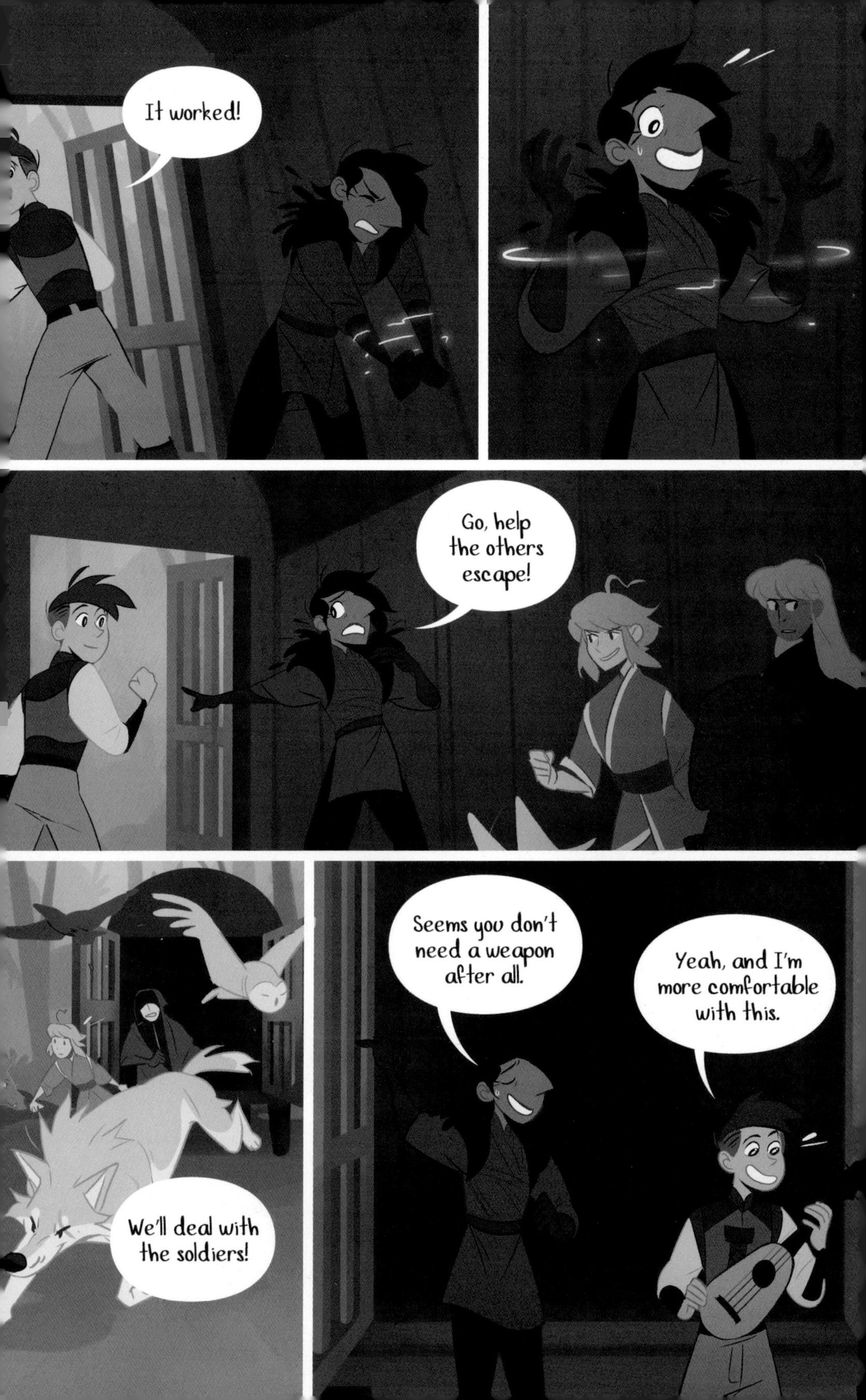
It worked!
Go, help the others escape!
We'll deal with the soldiers!
Seems you don't need a weapon after all.
Yeah, and I'm more comfortable with this.

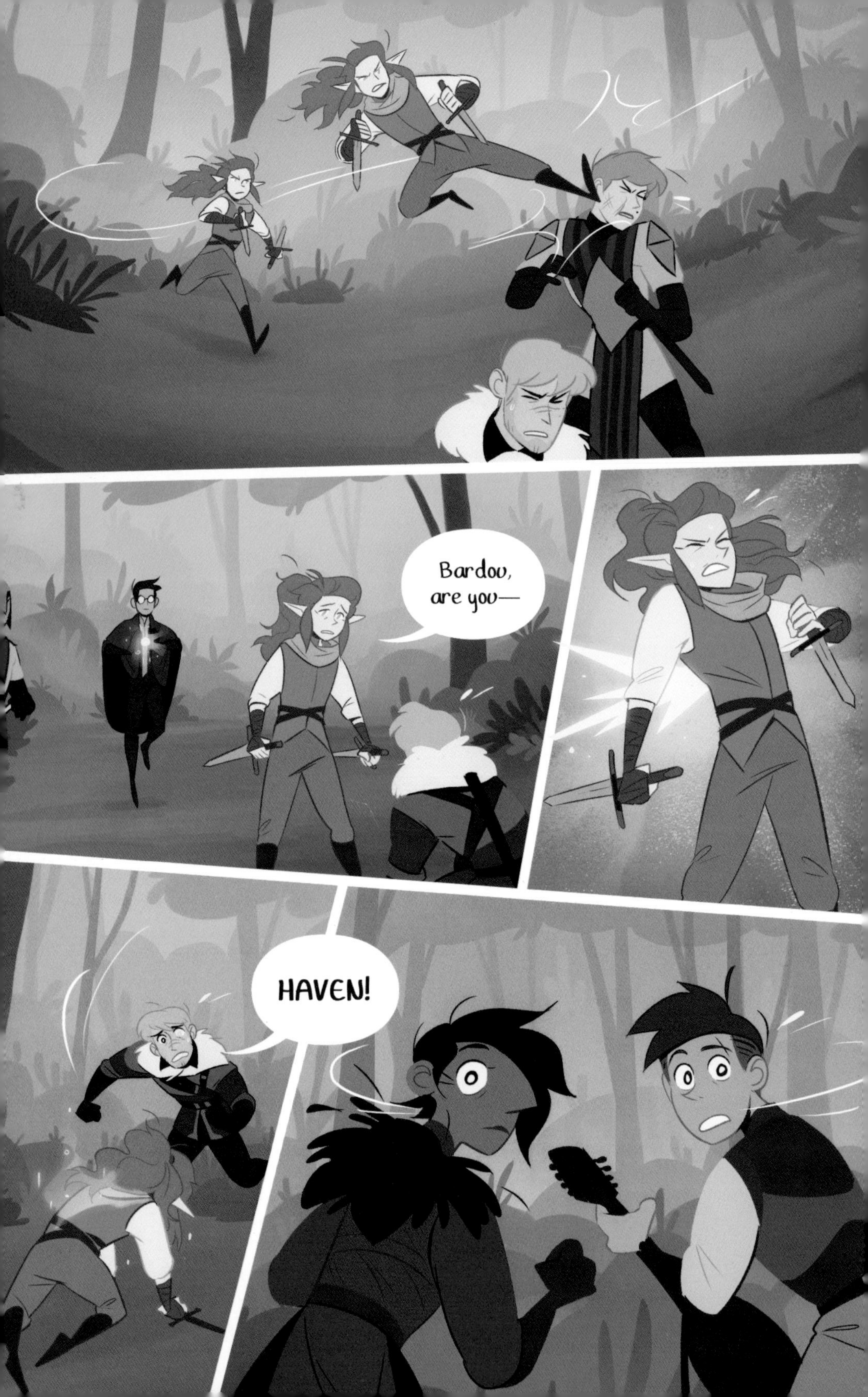
Bardou,
are you—
HAVEN!

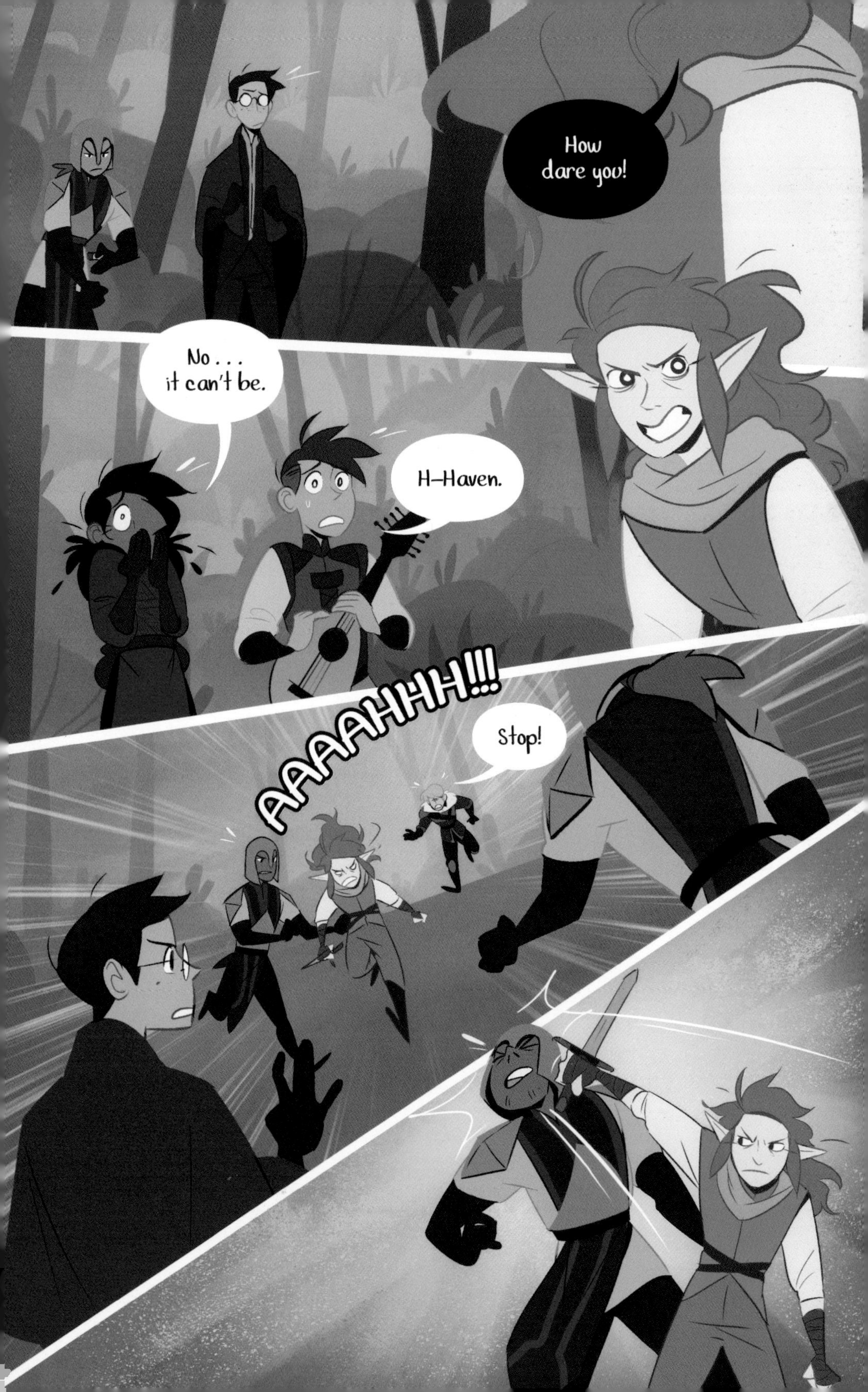
How dare you!
No . . . it can't be.
H-Haven.
AAAAHHH!!!
Stop!

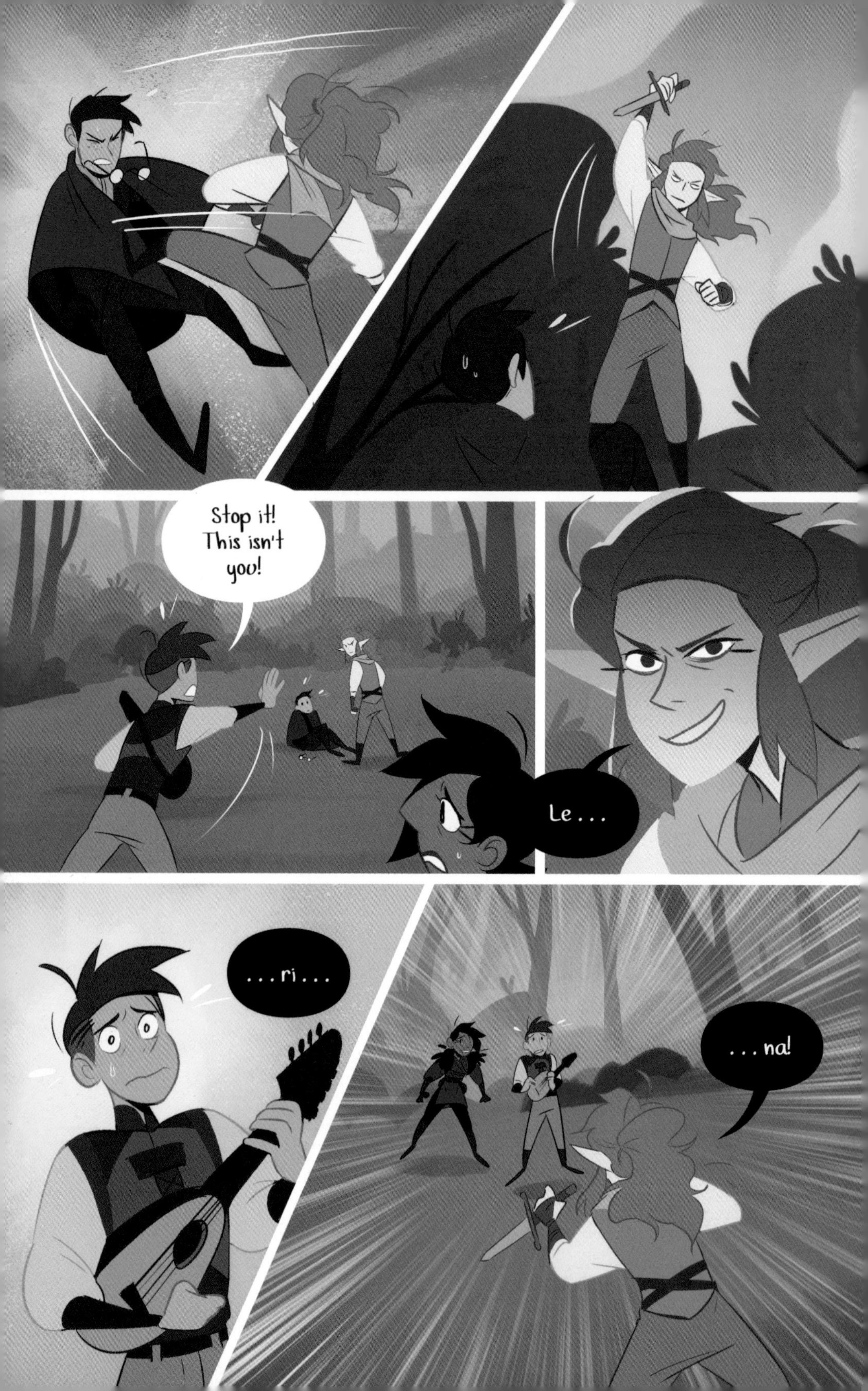
Stop it! This isn't you!
Le . . .
. . . ri . . .
. . . na!

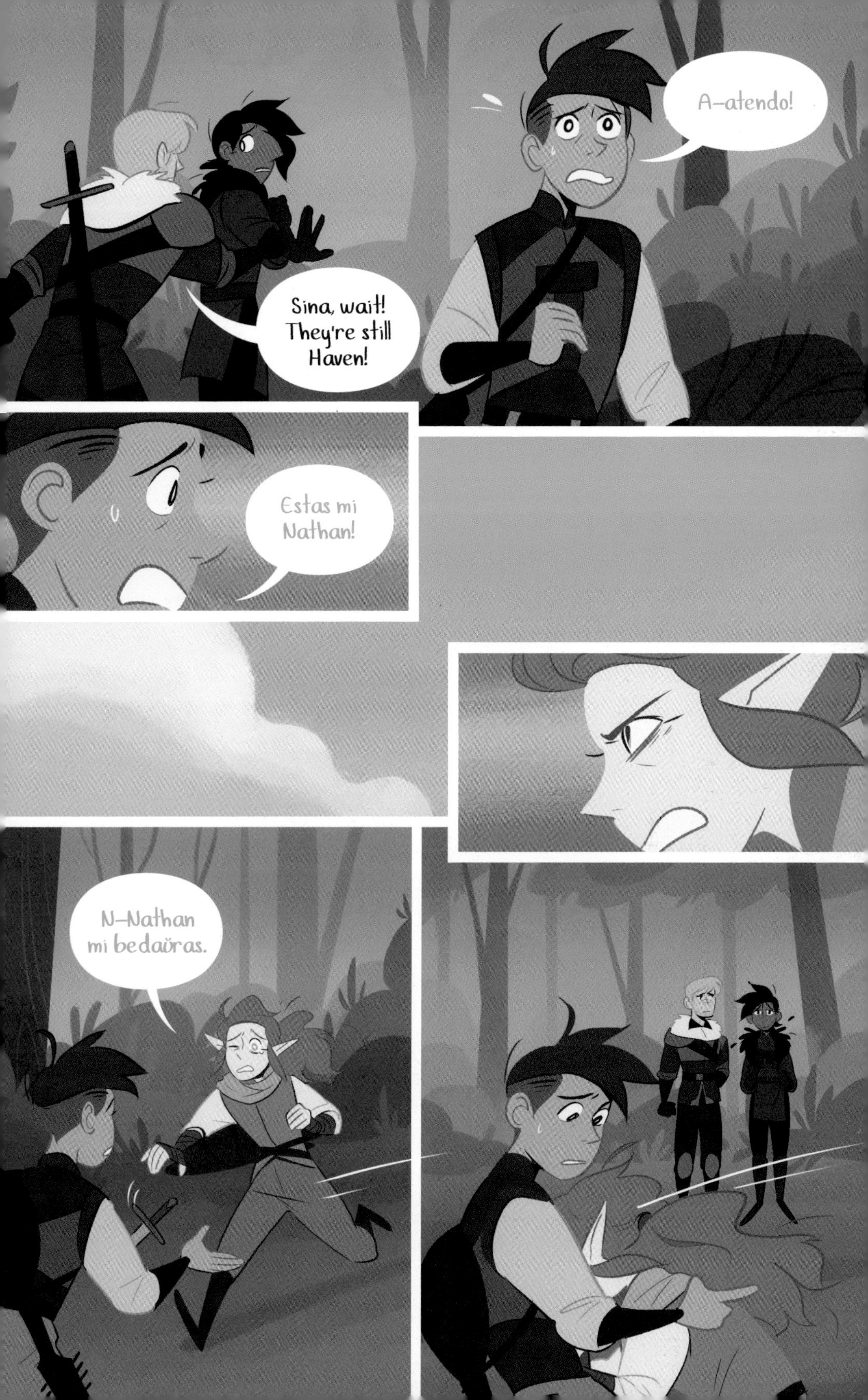

Sina, wait! They're still Haven!
A-atendo!
Estas mi Nathan!
N-Nathan mi bedaüras.

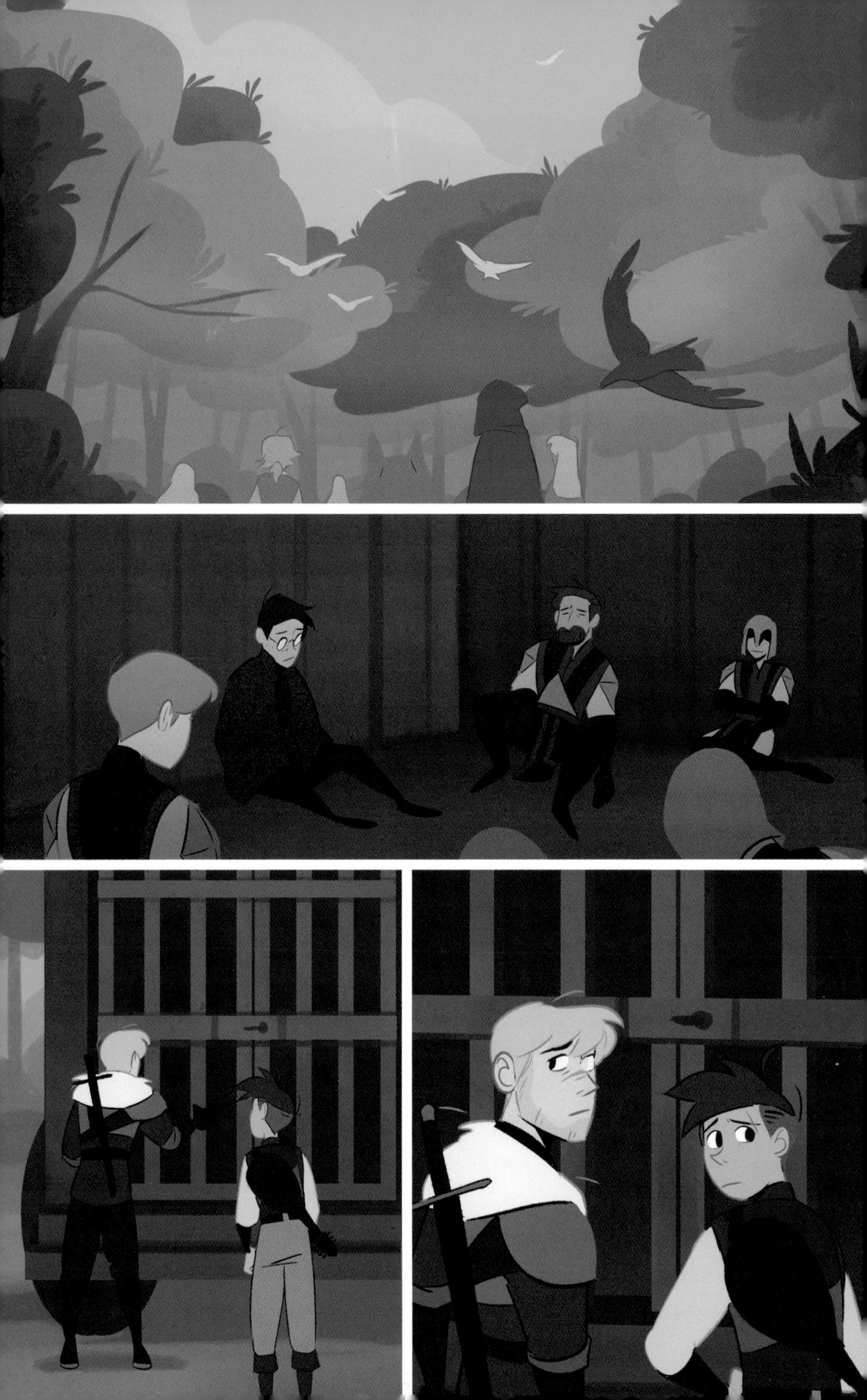

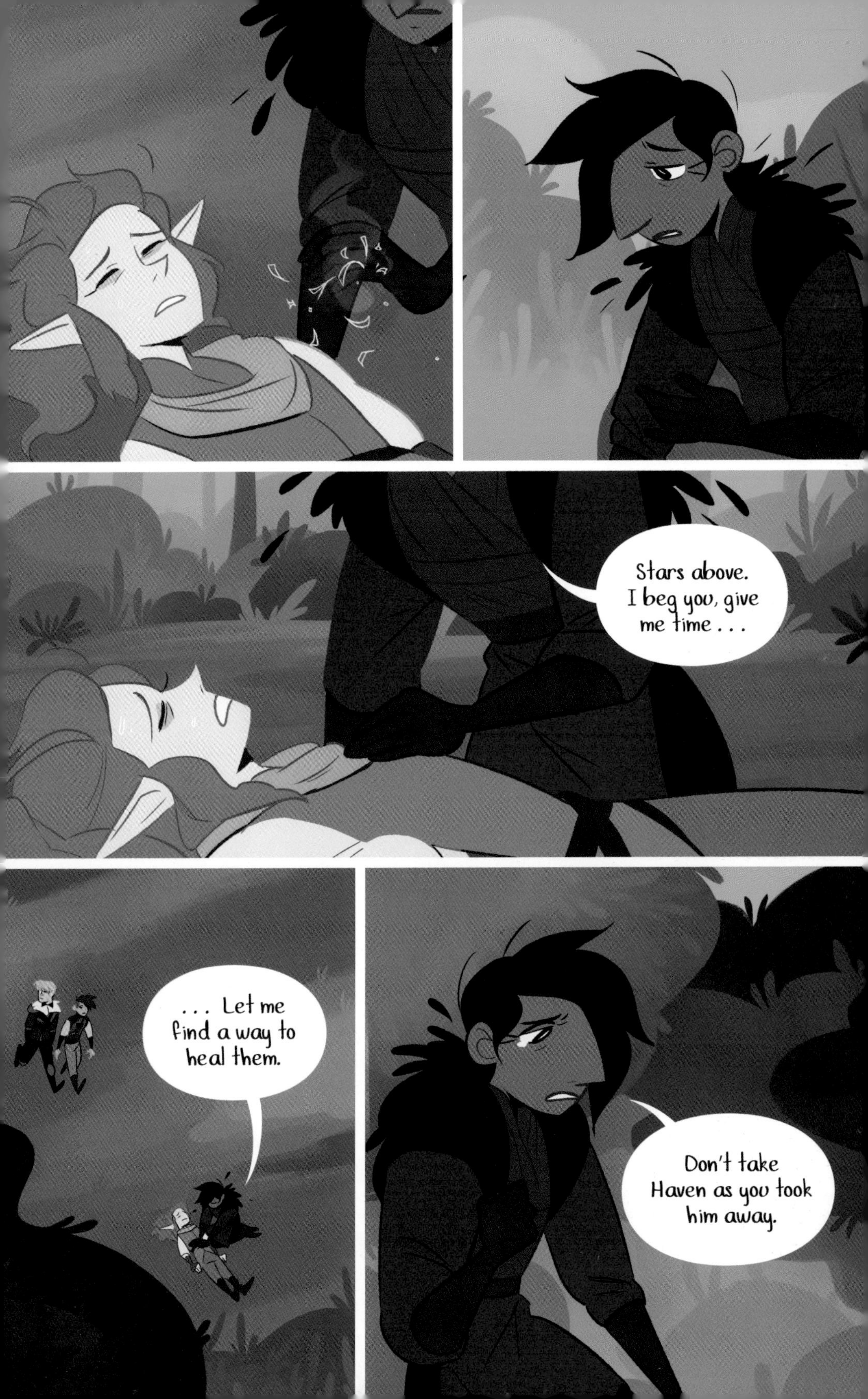
Stars above. I beg you, give me time . . .
. . . Let me find a way to heal them.
Don't take Haven as you took him away.

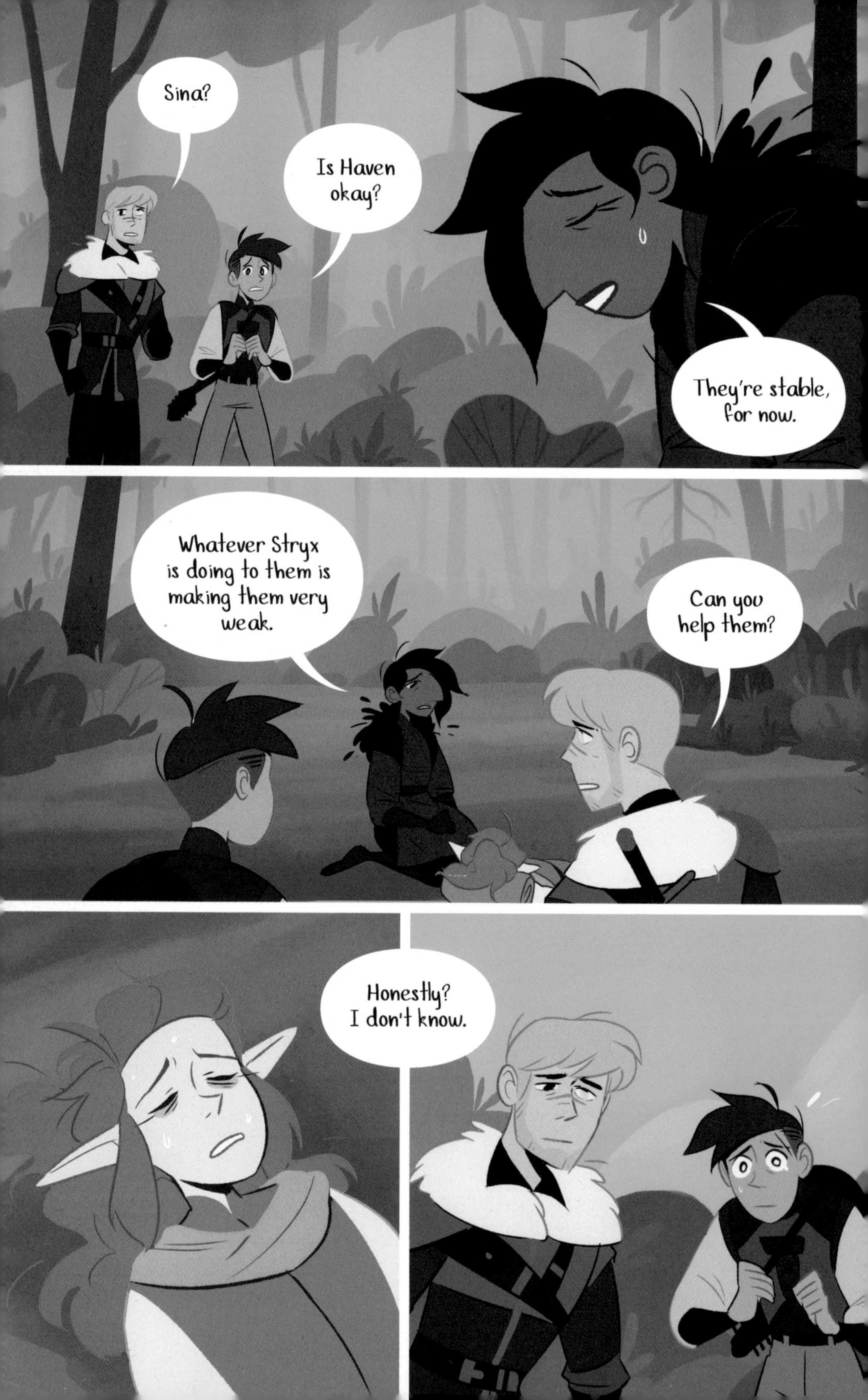
Sina?
Is Haven okay?
They're stable, for now.
Whatever Stryx is doing to them is making them very weak.
Can you help them?
Honestly? I don't know.

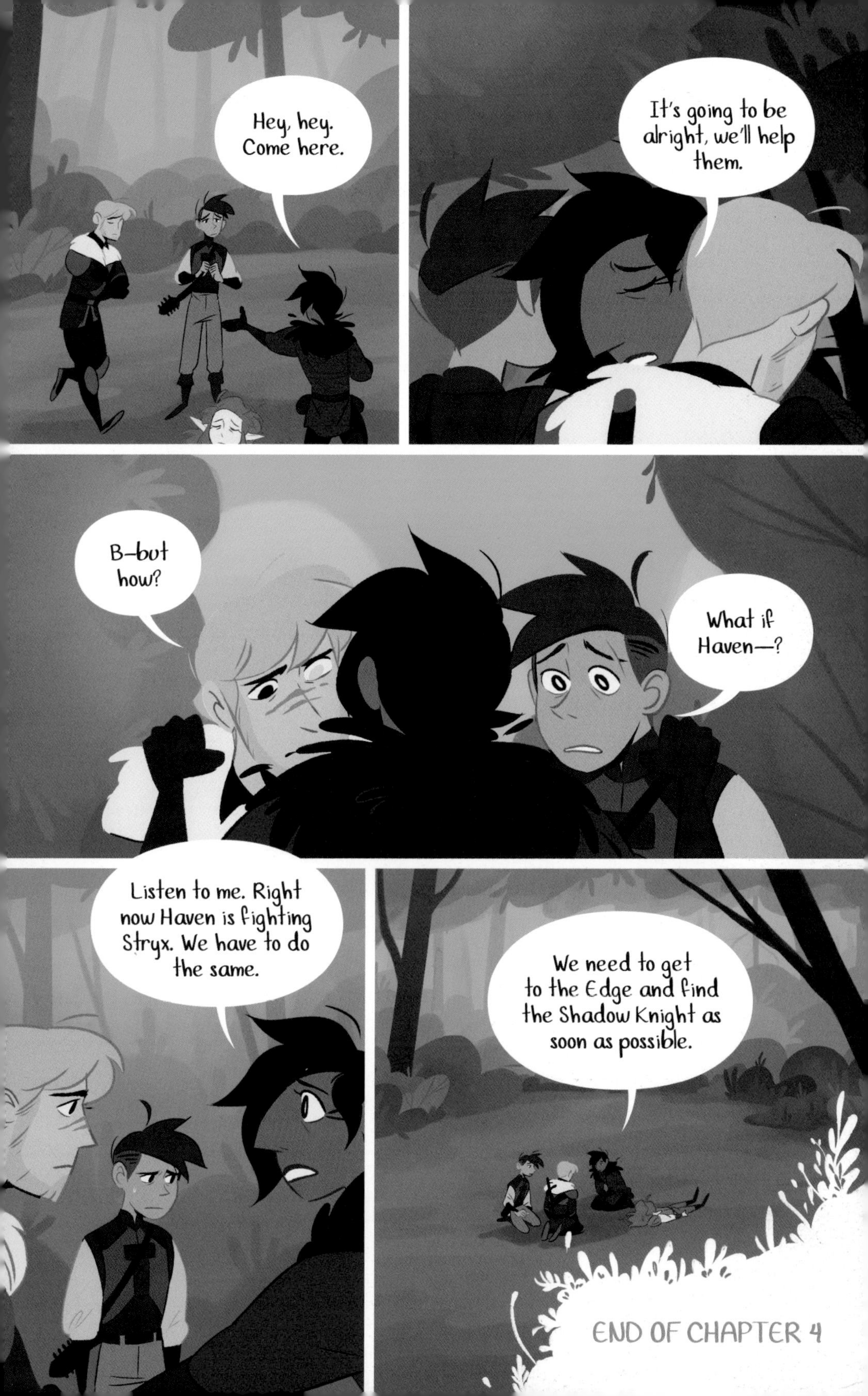

Hey, hey. Come here.
It's going to be alright, we'll help them.
B-but how?
What if Haven—?
Listen to me. Right now Haven is fighting Stryx. We have to do the same.
We need to get to the Edge and find the Shadow Knight as soon as possible.
END OF CHAPTER 4

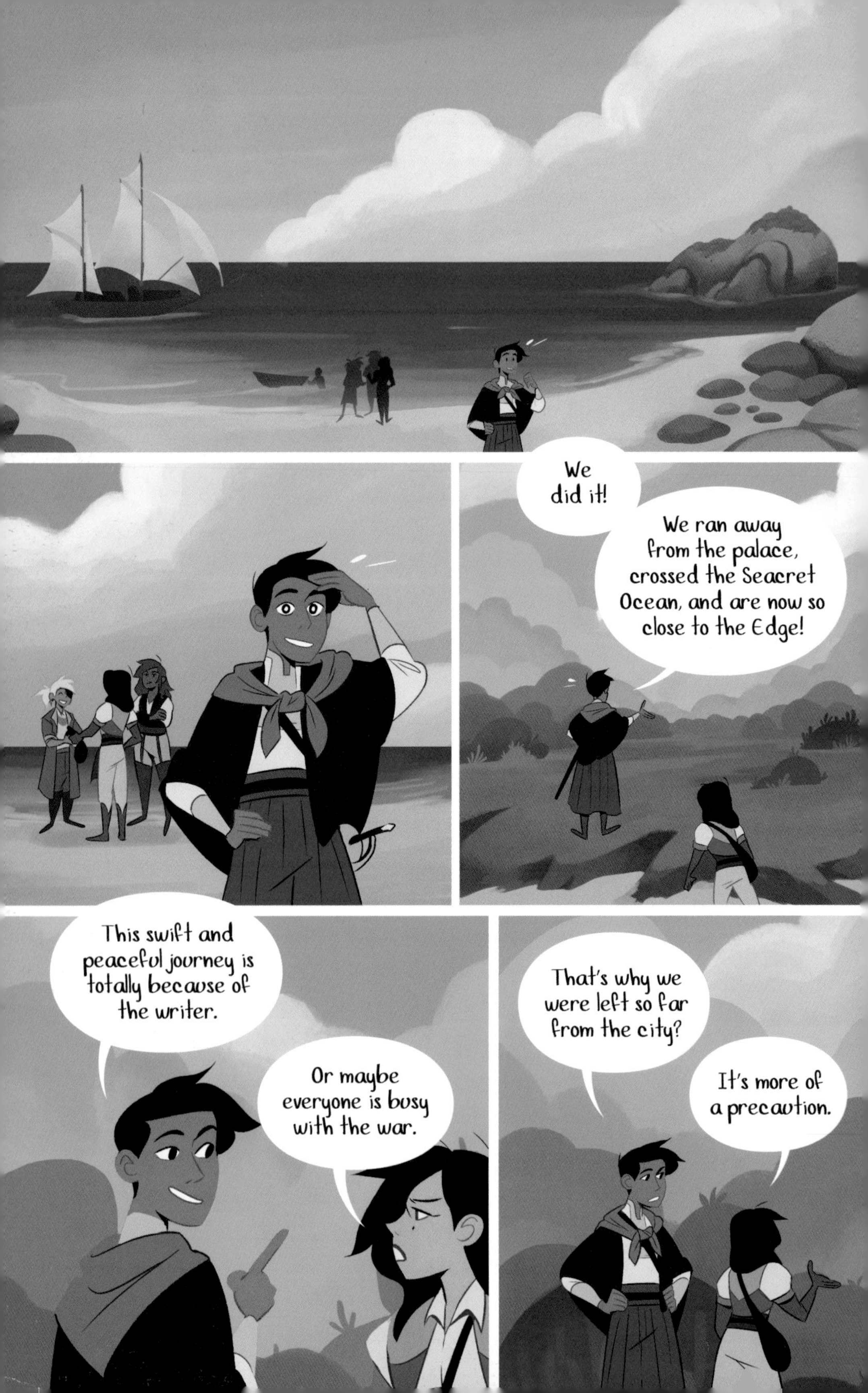
We did it!
We ran away from the palace, crossed the Seacret Ocean, and are now so close to the Edge!
This swift and peaceful journey is totally because of the writer.
Or maybe everyone is busy with the war.
That's why we were left so far from the city?
It's more of a precaution.

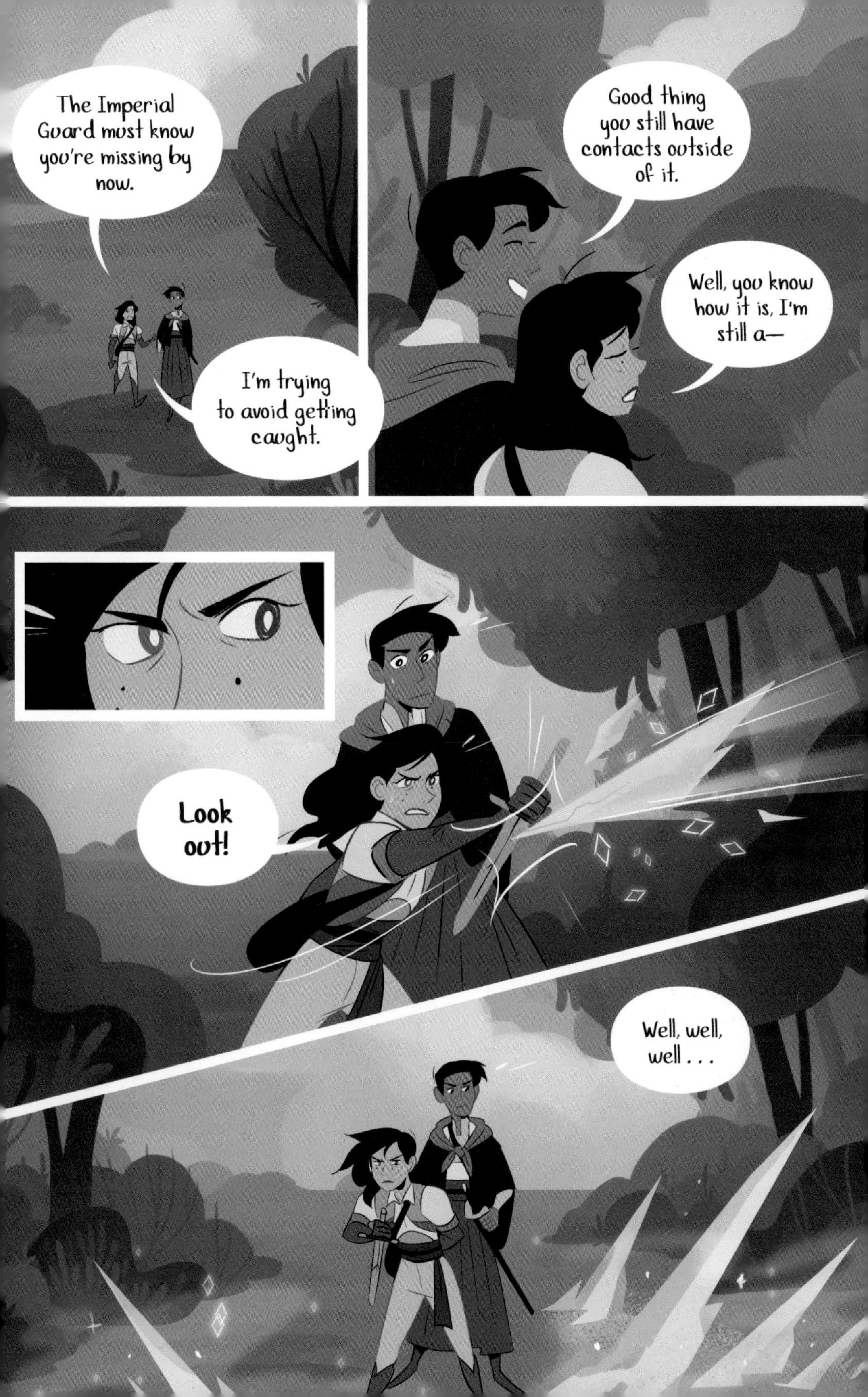
The Imperial Guard must know you're missing by now.
I'm trying to avoid getting caught.
Good thing you still have contacts outside of it.
Well, you know how it is, I'm still a—
Look out!
Well, well, well . . .

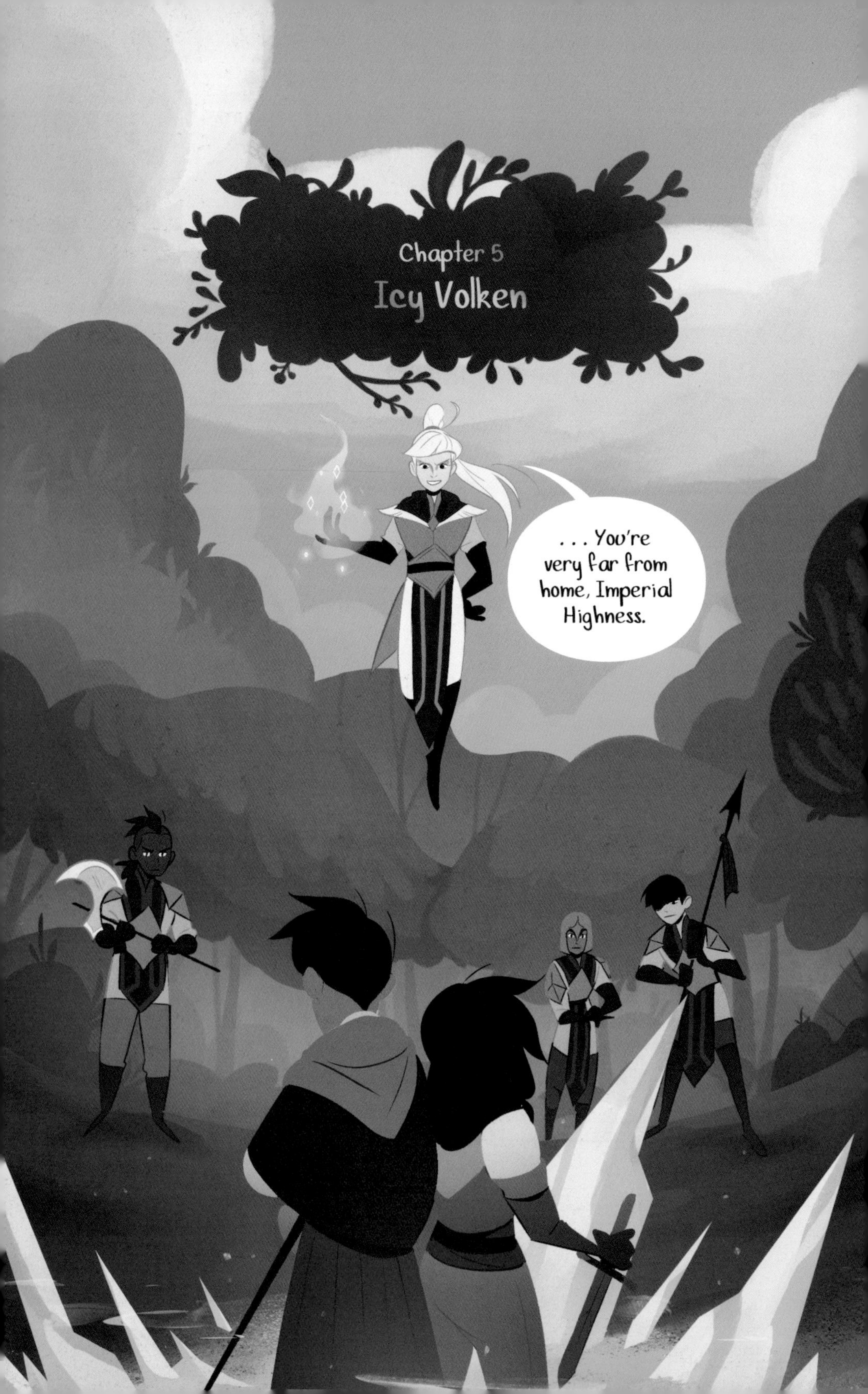
Chapter 5
Icy Volken
. . . You're very far from home, Imperial Highness.

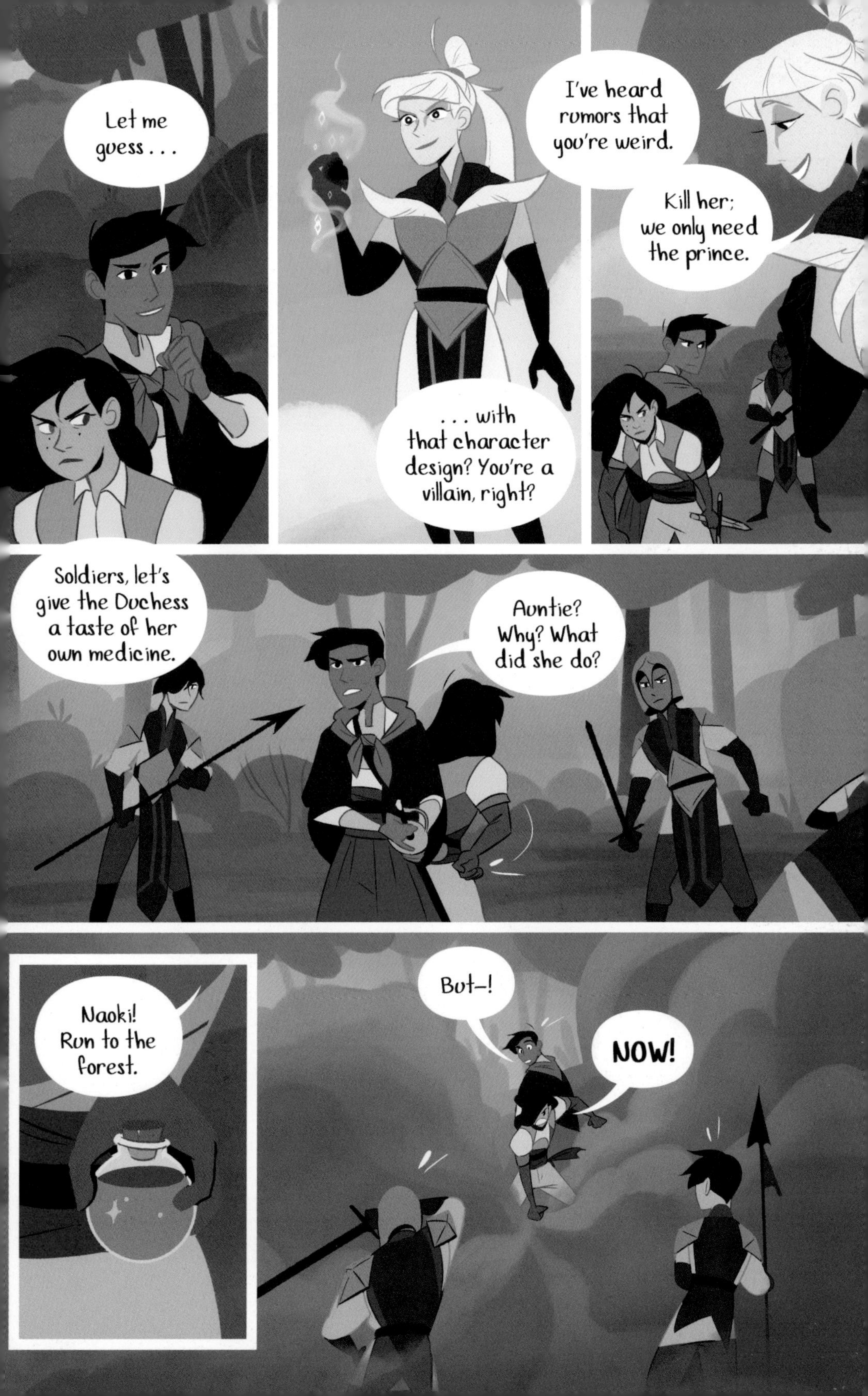
Let me guess . . .
I've heard rumors that you're weird.
. . . with that character design? You're a villain, right?
Kill her; we only need the prince.
Soldiers, let's give the Duchess a taste of her own medicine.
Auntie? Why? What did she do?
Naoki! Run to the forest.
But—!
NOW!

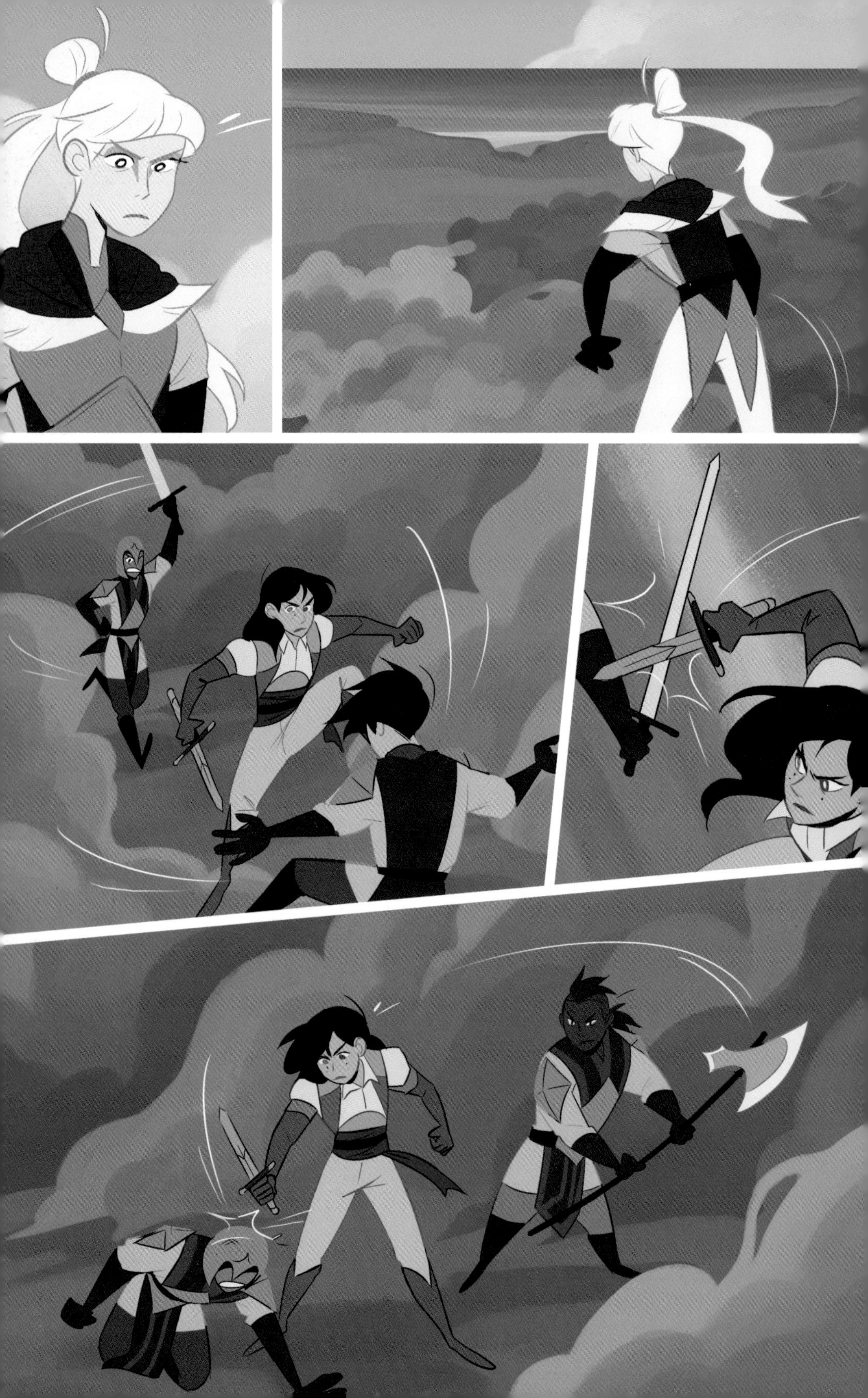

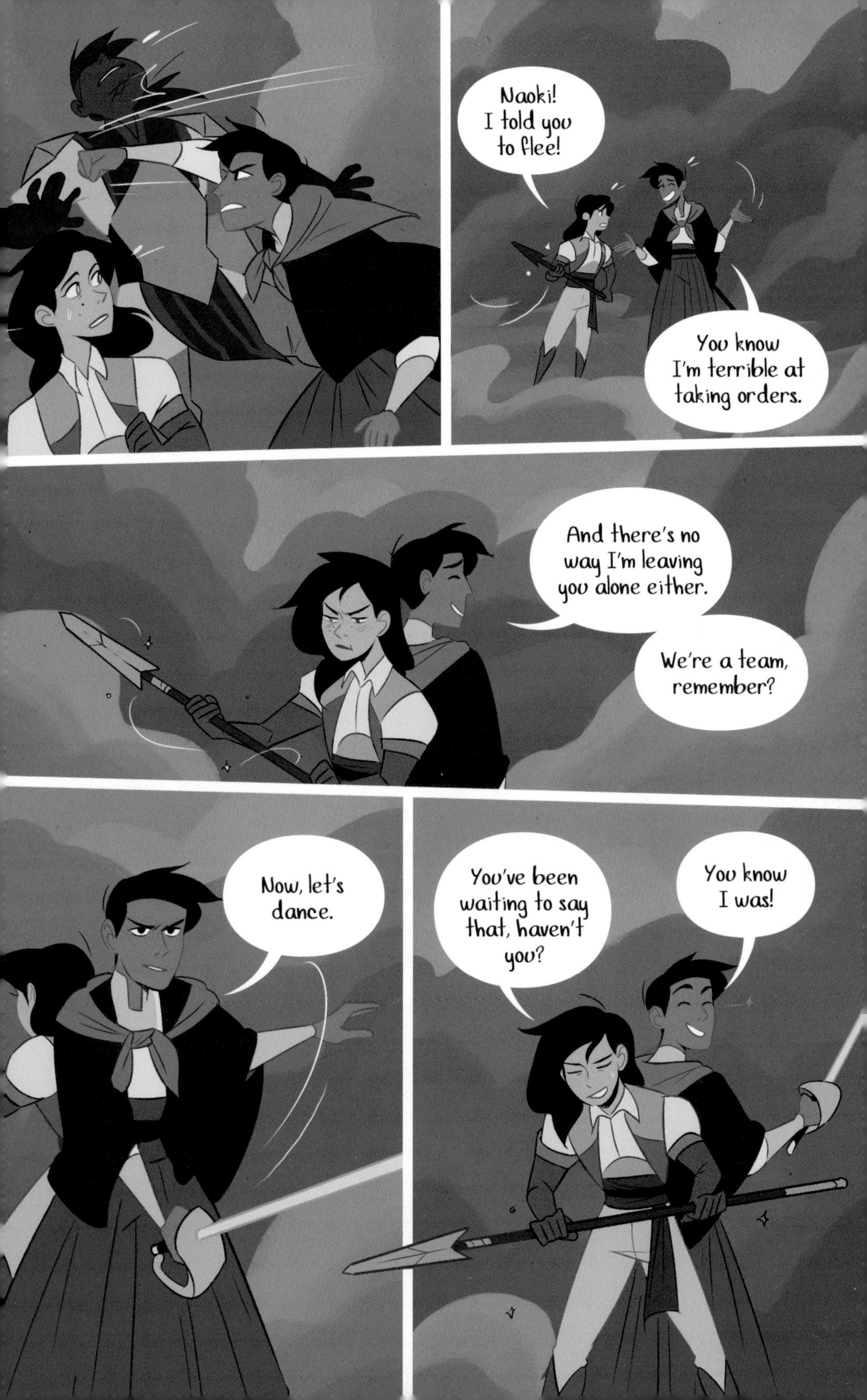
Naoki! I told you to flee!
You know I'm terrible at taking orders.
And there's no way I'm leaving you alone either.
We're a team, remember?
Now, let's dance.
You've been waiting to say that, haven't you?
You know I was!

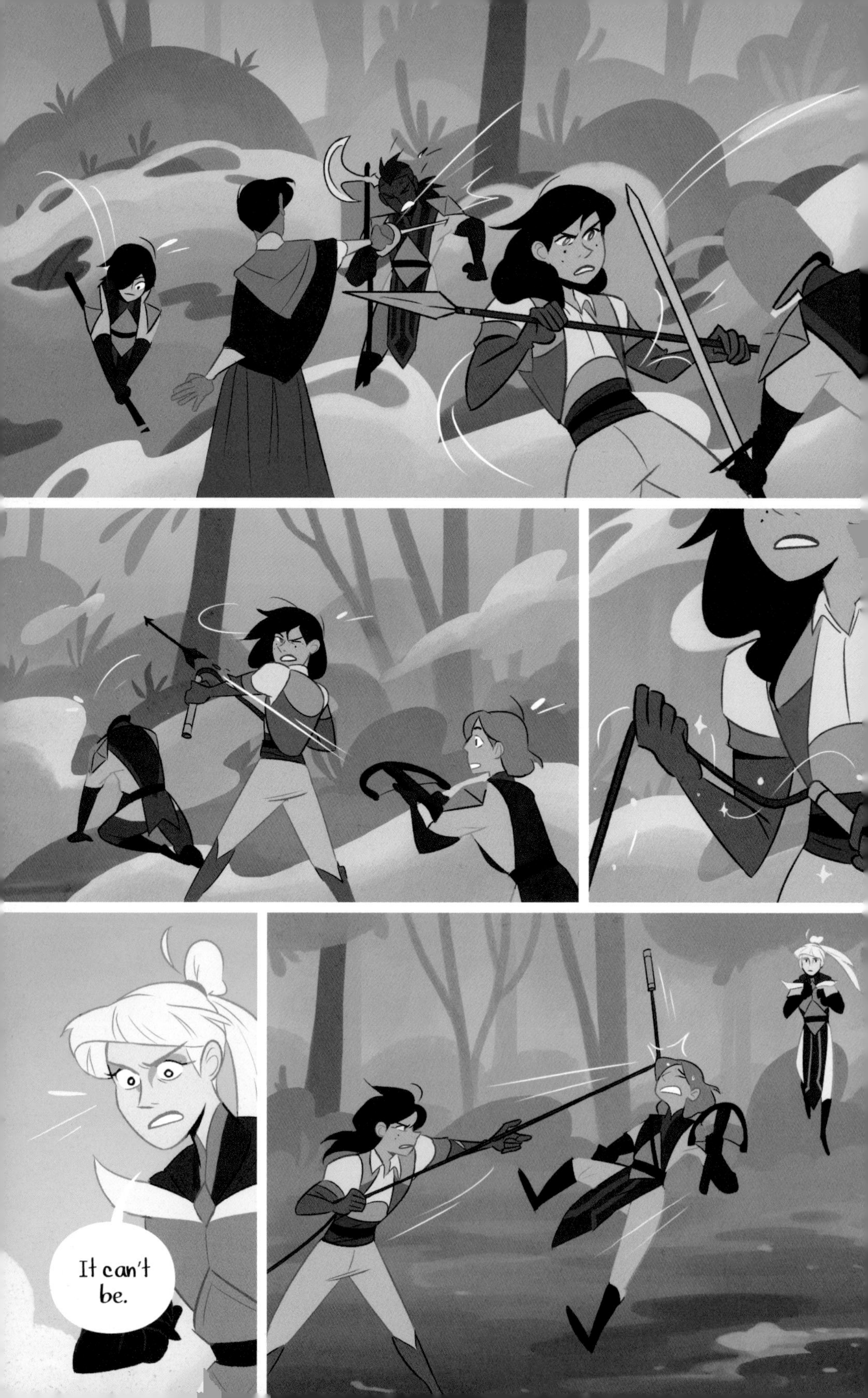
It can't be.

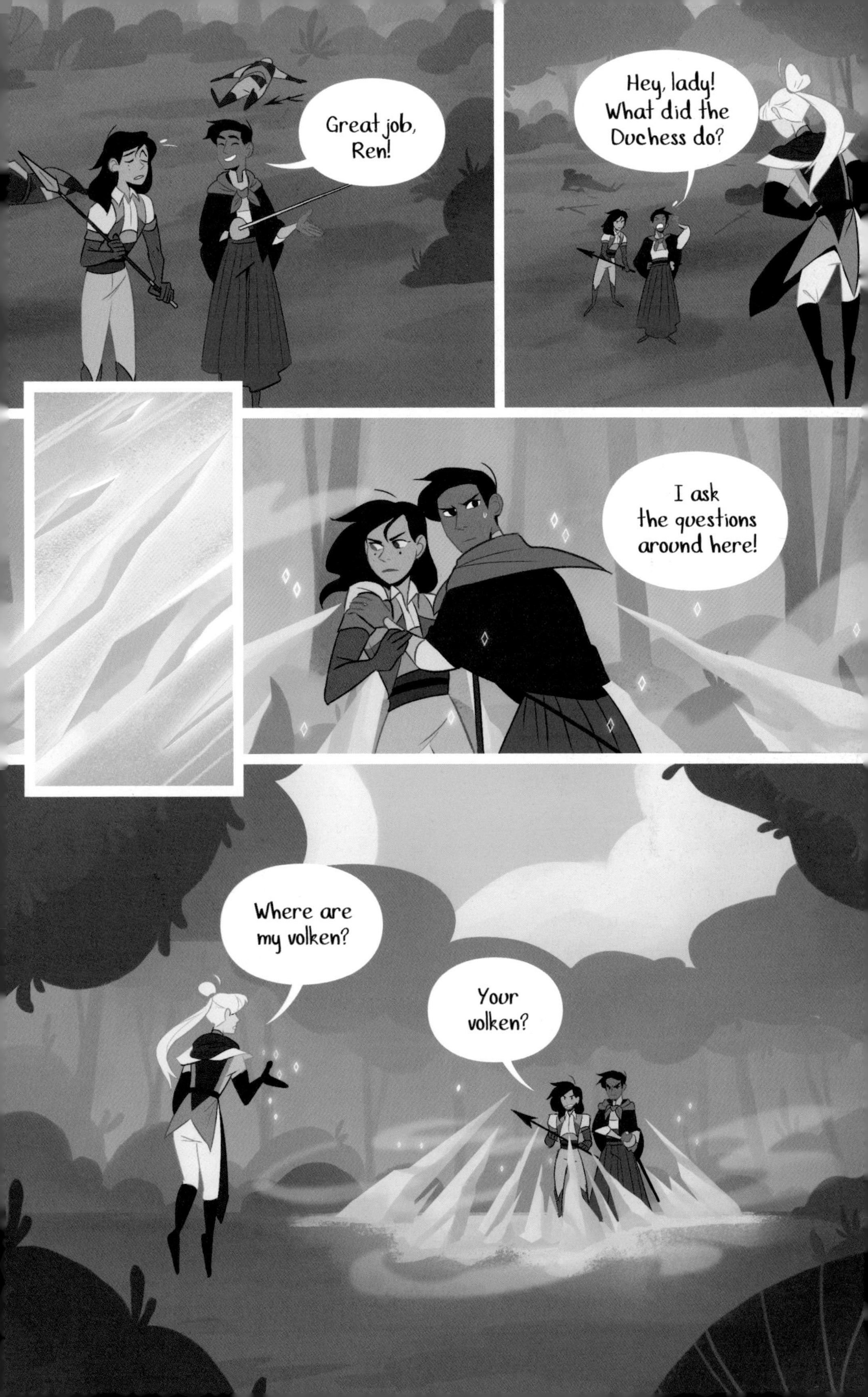
Great job, Ren!
Hey, lady! What did the Duchess do?
I ask the questions around here!
Where are my volken?
Your volken?

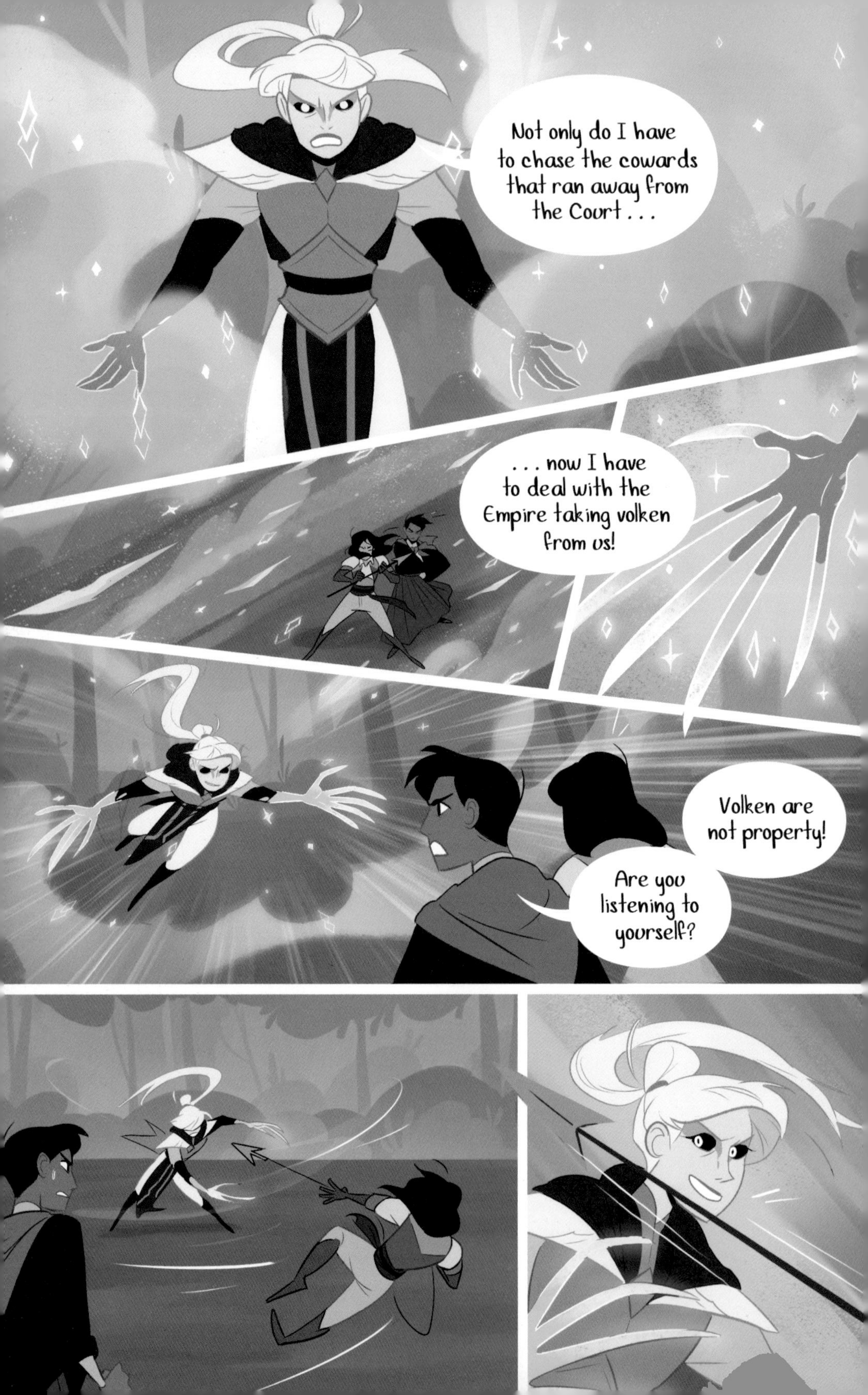
Not only do I have to chase the cowards that ran away from the Court . . .
. . . now I have to deal with the Empire taking volken from us!
Volken are not property!
Are you listening to yourself?

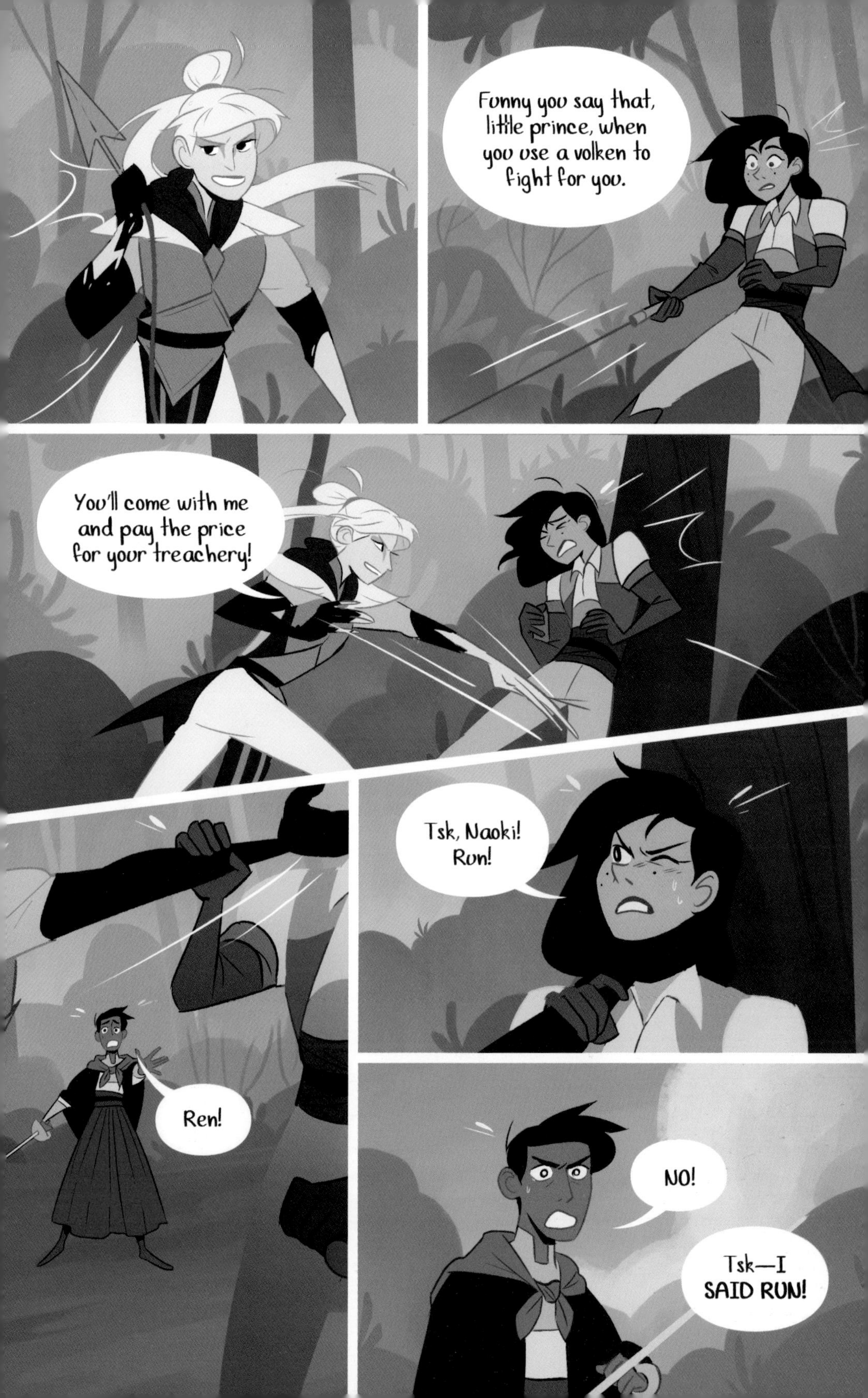
Funny you say that, little prince, when you use a volken to fight for you.
You'll come with me and pay the price for your treachery!
Tsk, Naoki! Run!
Ren!
NO!
Tsk—I SAID RUN!

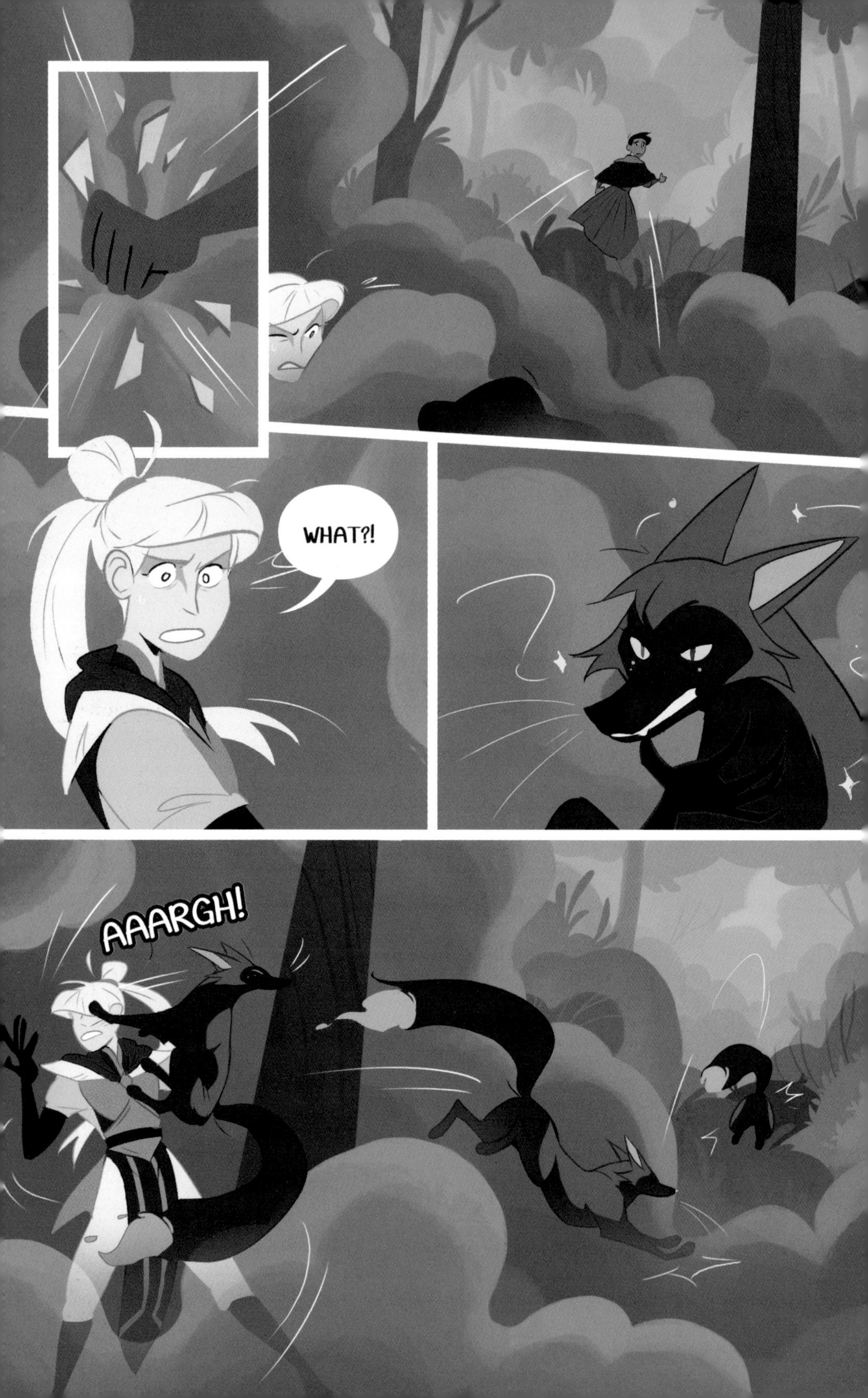
WHAT?!
AAARGH!

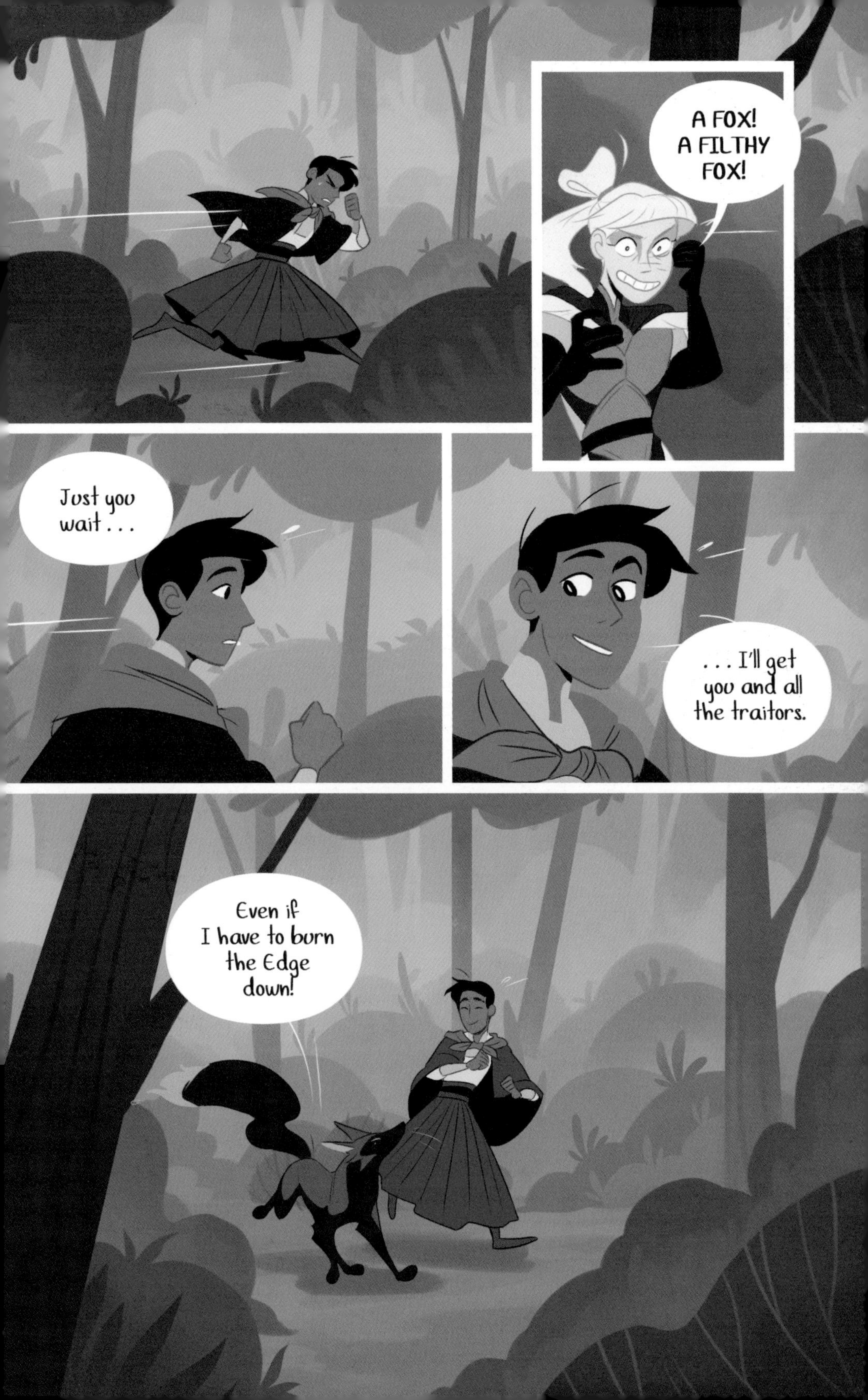
A FOX! A FILTHY FOX!
Just you wait . . .
. . . I'll get you and all the traitors.
Even if I have to burn the Edge down!

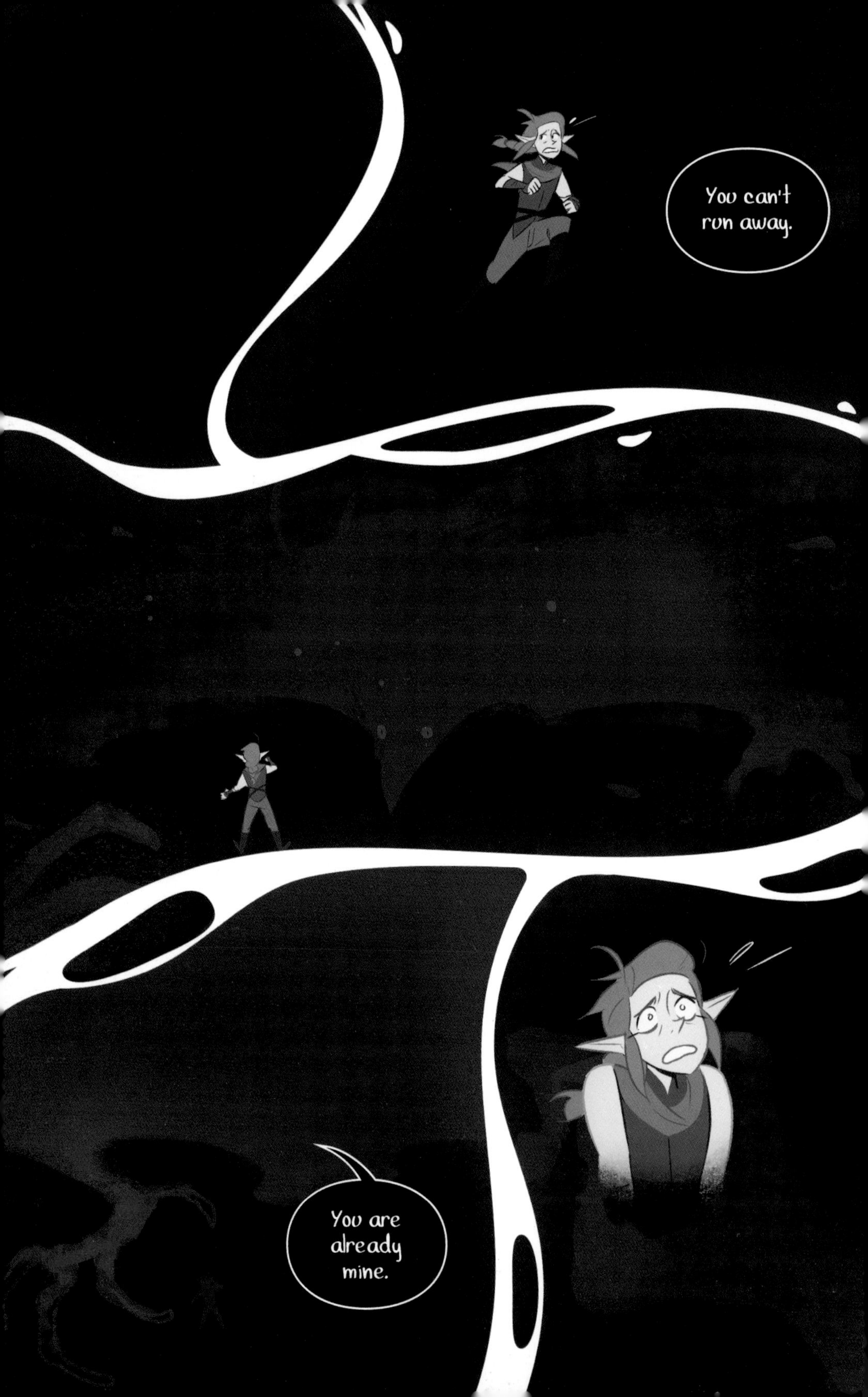
You can't run away.
You are already mine.

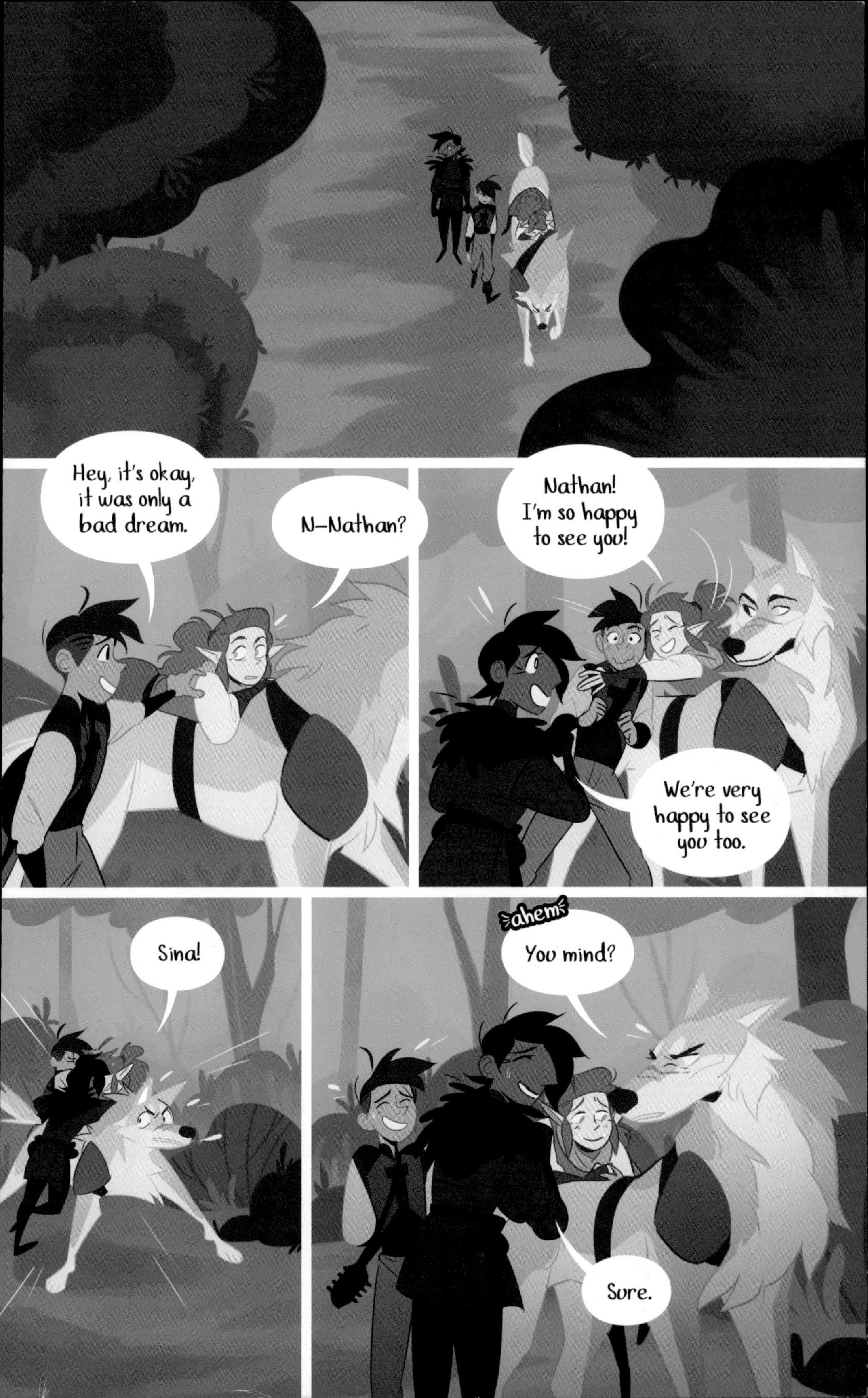
Hey, it's okay, it was only a bad dream.
N-Nathan?
Nathan! I'm so happy to see you!
We're very happy to see you too.
Sina!
ahem
You mind?
Sure.

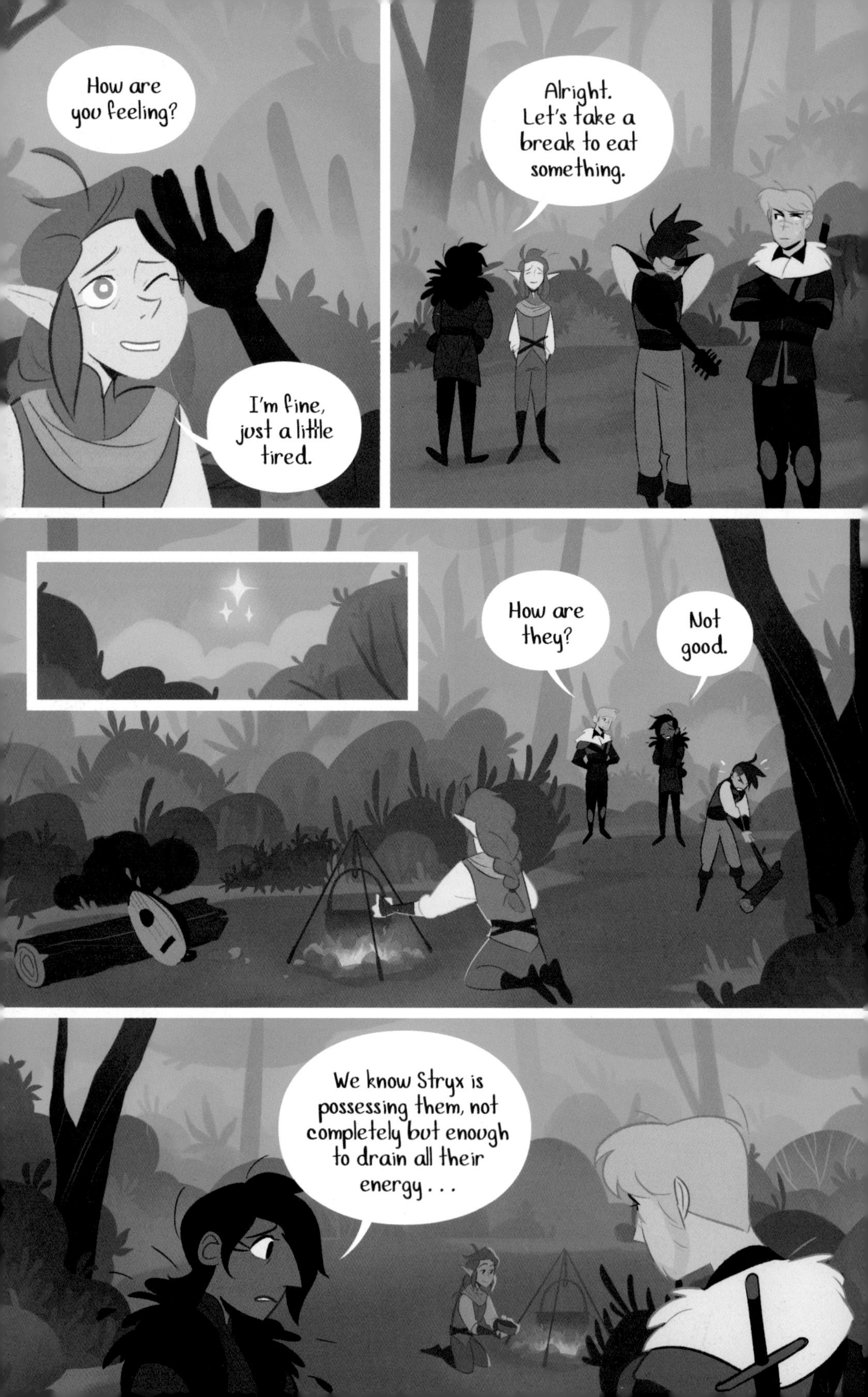
How are you feeling?
I'm fine, just a little tired.
Alright. Let's take a break to eat something.
How are they?
Not good.
We know Stryx is possessing them, not completely but enough to drain all their energy . . .

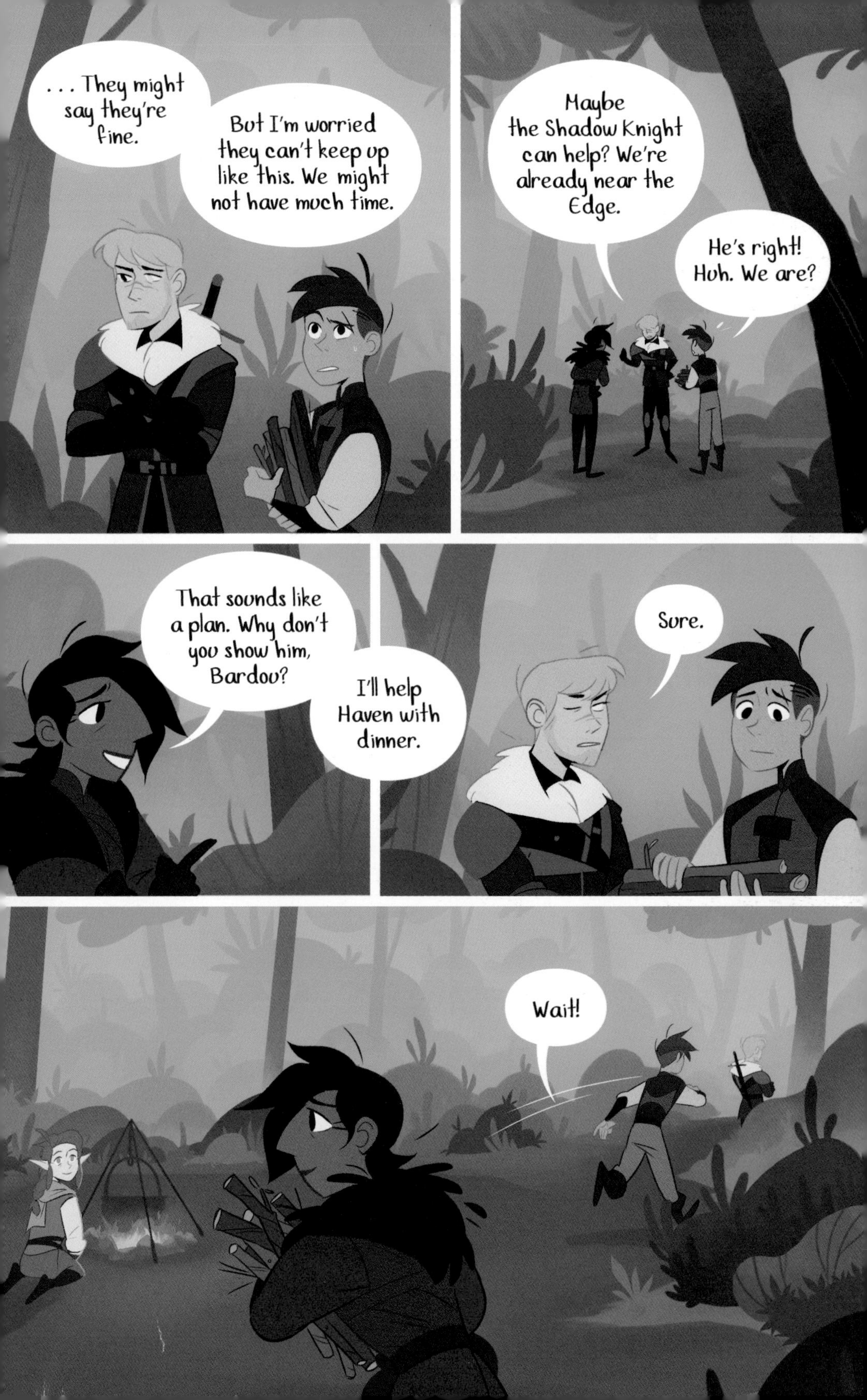

. . . They might say they're fine.
But I'm worried they can't keep up like this. We might not have much time.
Maybe the Shadow Knight can help? We're already near the Edge.
He's right! Huh. We are?
That sounds like a plan. Why don't you show him, Bardou?
I'll help Haven with dinner.
Sure.
Wait!

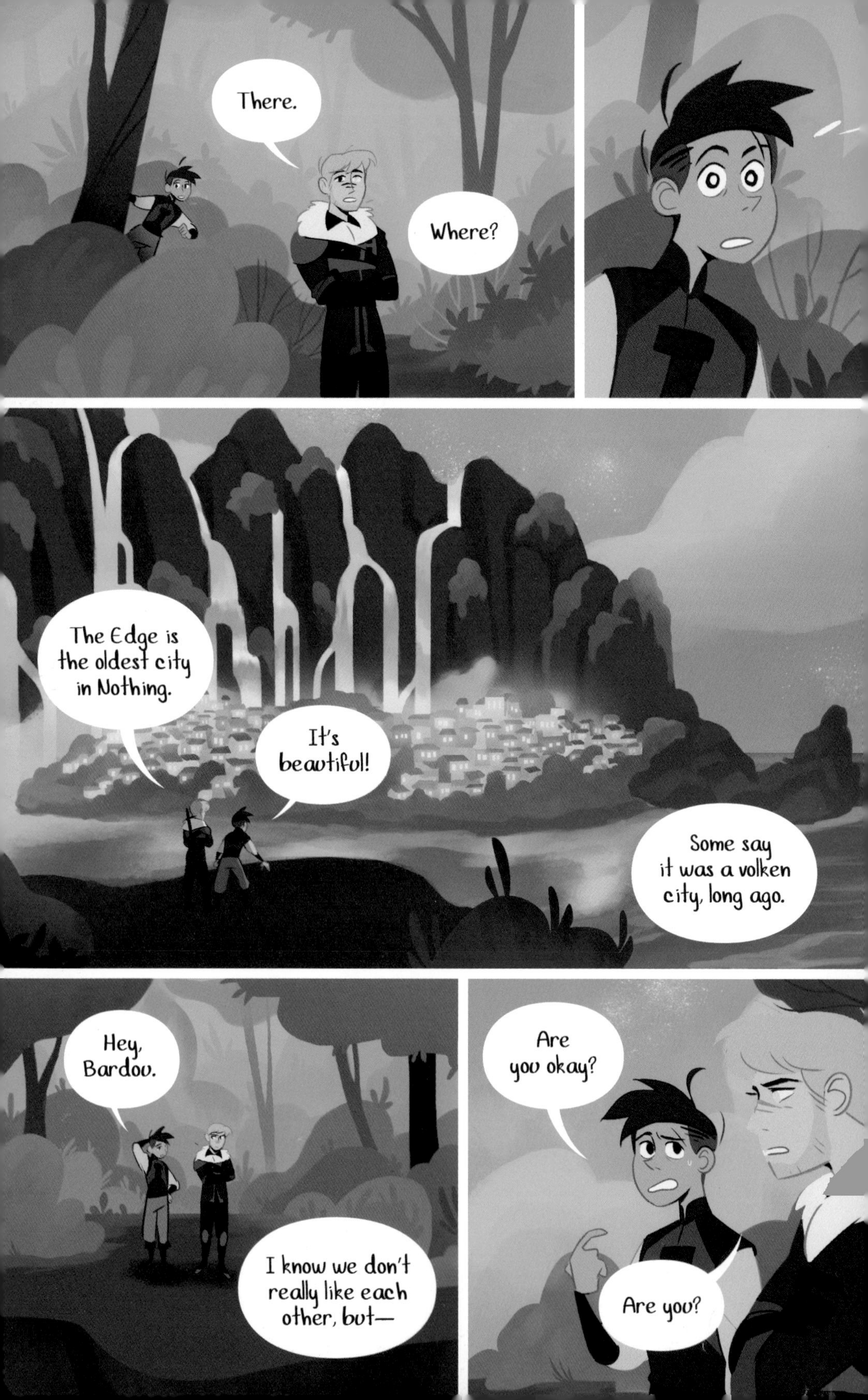
There.
Where?
The Edge is the oldest city in Nothing.
It's beautiful!
Some say it was a volken city, long ago.
Hey, Bardou.
I know we don't really like each other, but—
Are you okay?
Are you?

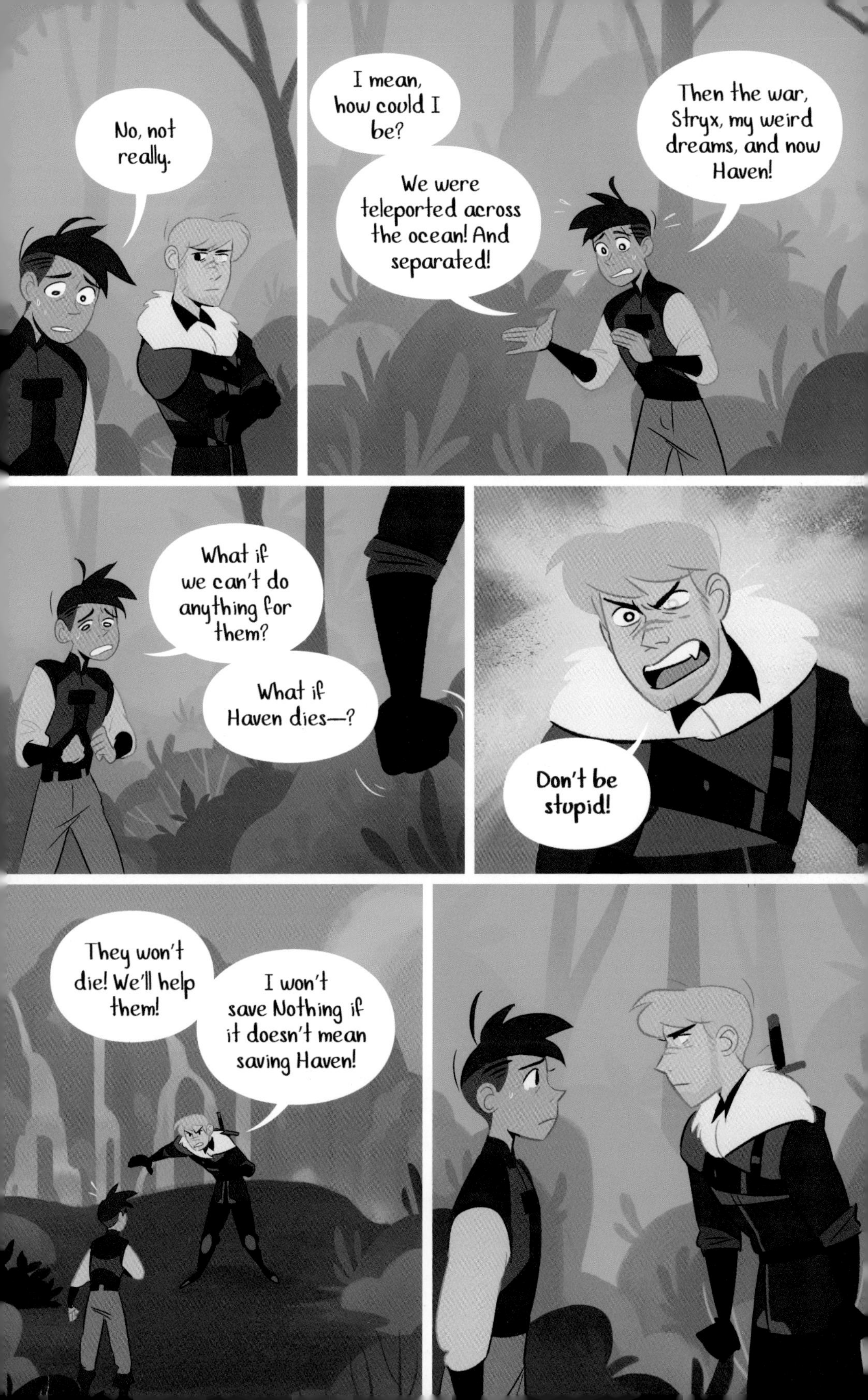
No, not really.
I mean, how could I be?
We were teleported across the ocean! And separated!
Then the war, Stryx, my weird dreams, and now Haven!
What if we can't do anything for them?
What if Haven dies—?
Don't be stupid!
They won't die! We'll help them!
I won't save Nothing if it doesn't mean saving Haven!

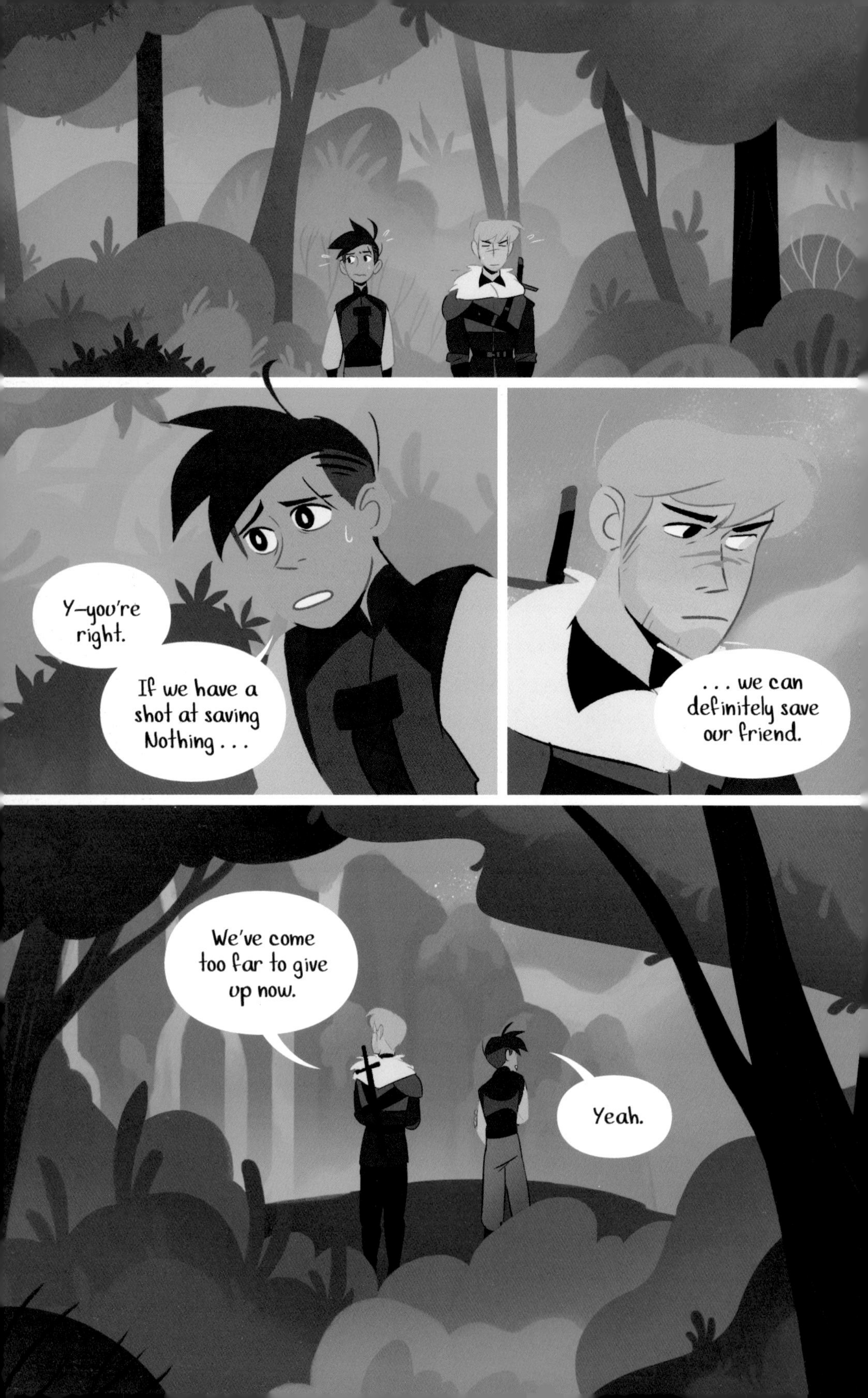
Y—you're right.
If we have a shot at saving Nothing . . .
. . . we can definitely save our friend.
We've come too far to give up now.
Yeah.

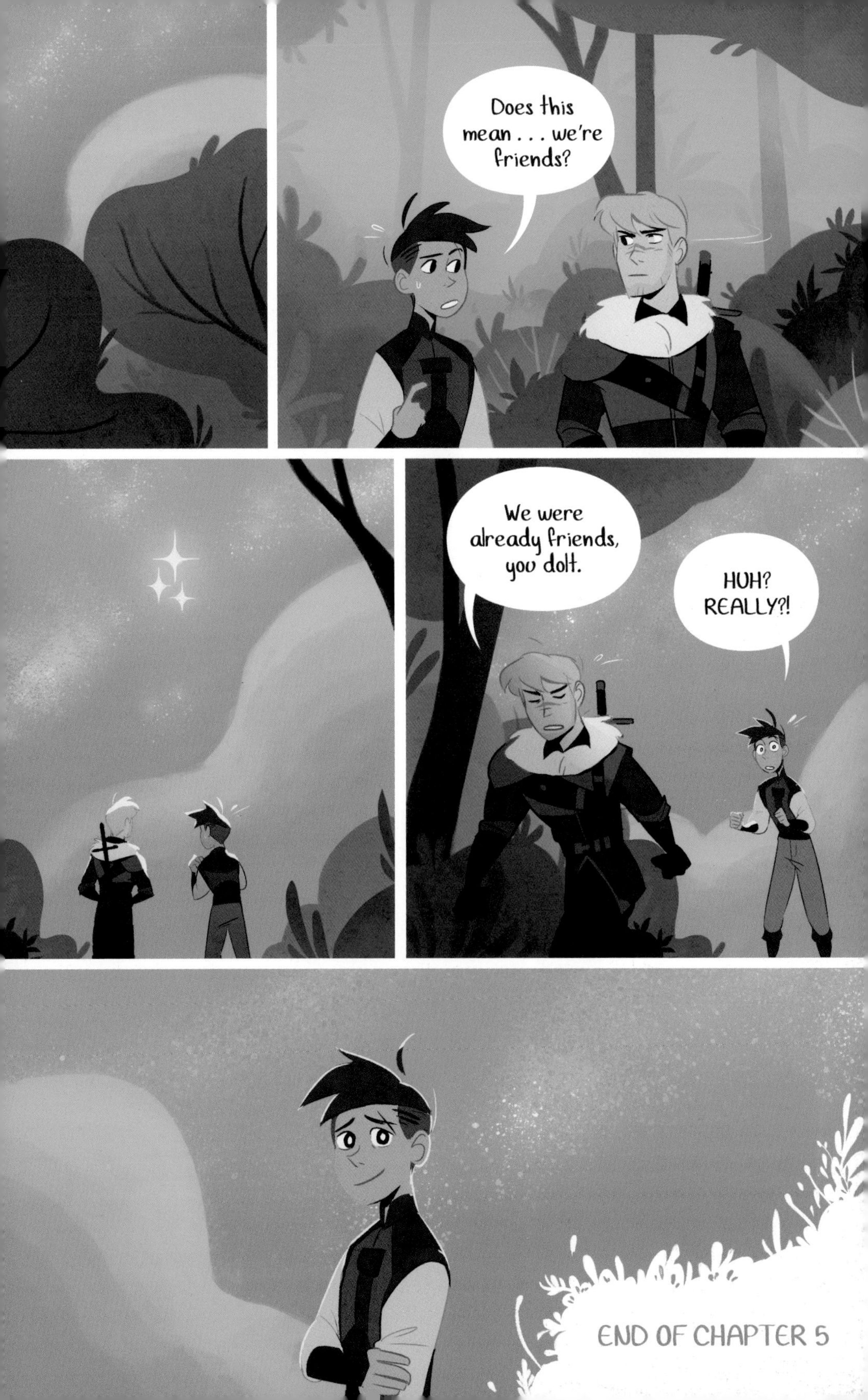
Does this mean . . . we're friends?
We were already friends, you dolt.
HUH? REALLY?!
END OF CHAPTER 5

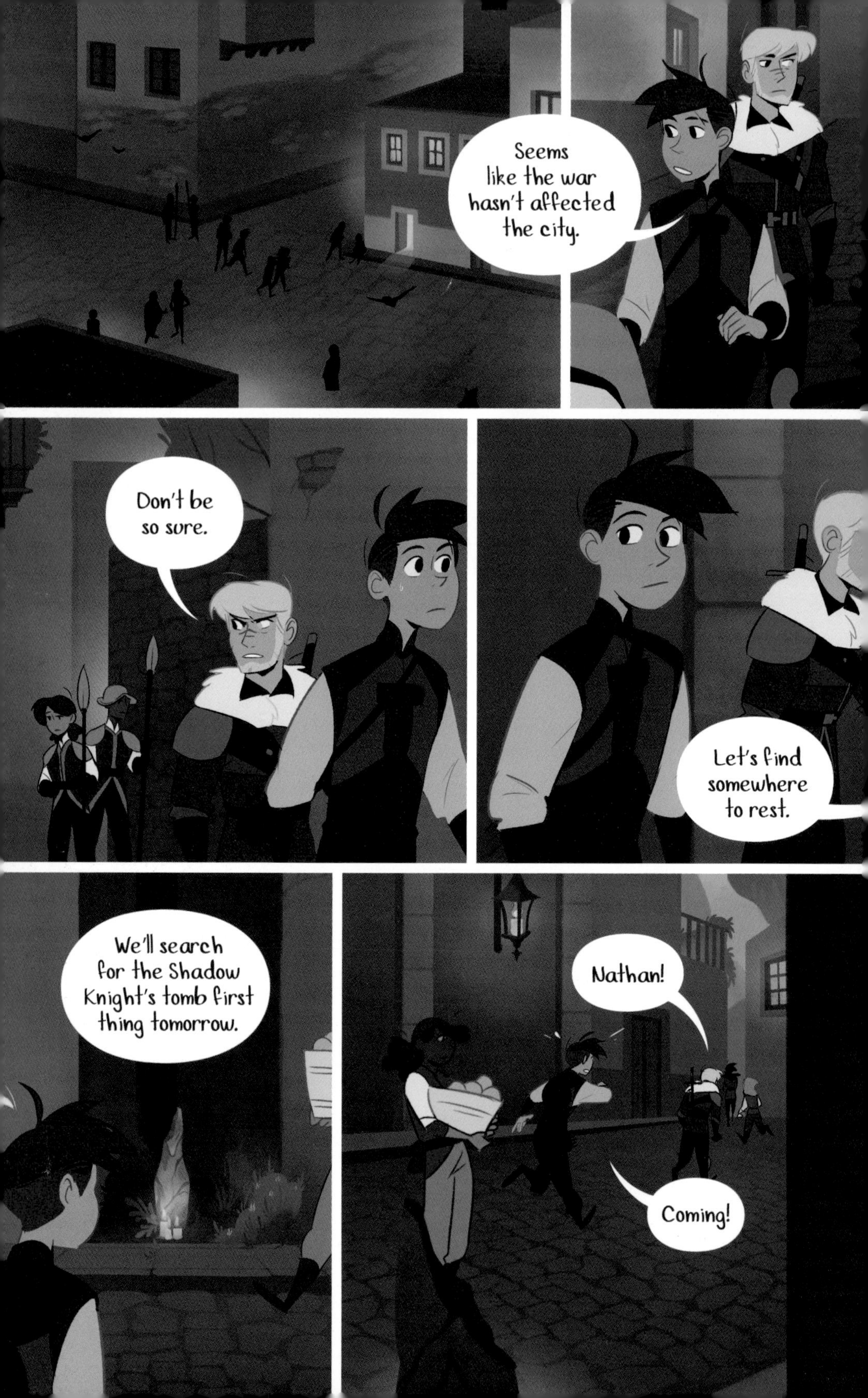
Seems like the war hasn't affected the city.
Don't be so sure.
Let's find somewhere to rest.
We'll search for the Shadow Knight's tomb first thing tomorrow.
Nathan!
Coming!

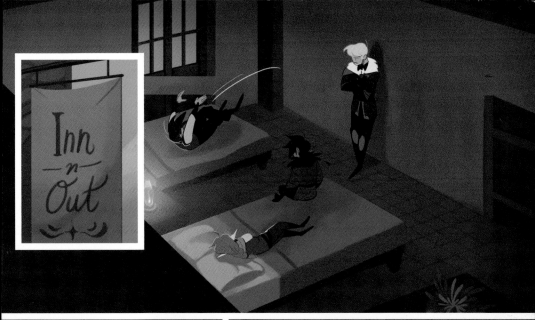

Sina?

It's nothing, I'll watch Haven tonight.

Huh...

No, I will. You need to rest.

But—

# Chapter 6

## Edge of the Empire

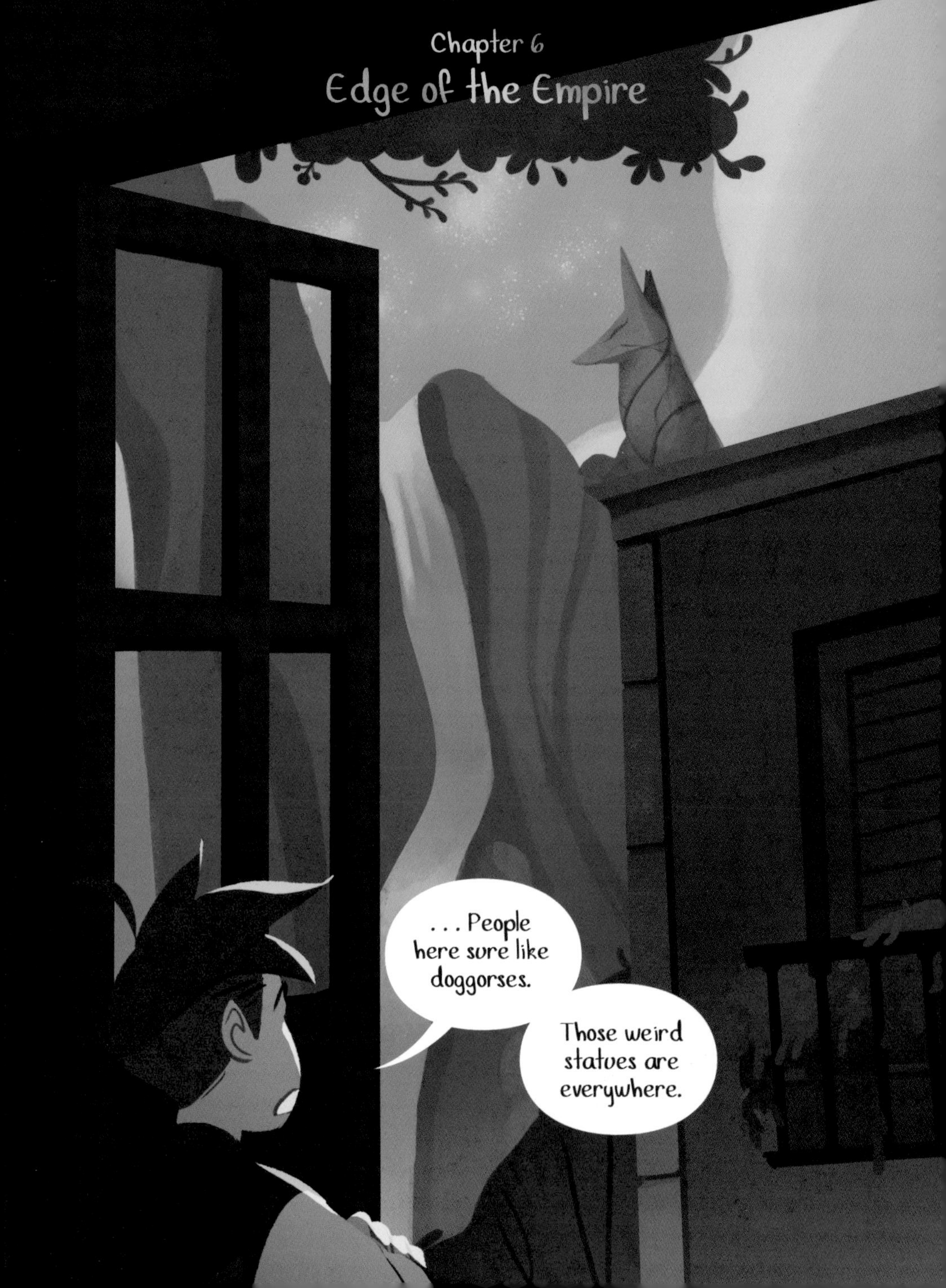
. . . People here sure like doggorses.
Those weird statues are everywhere.

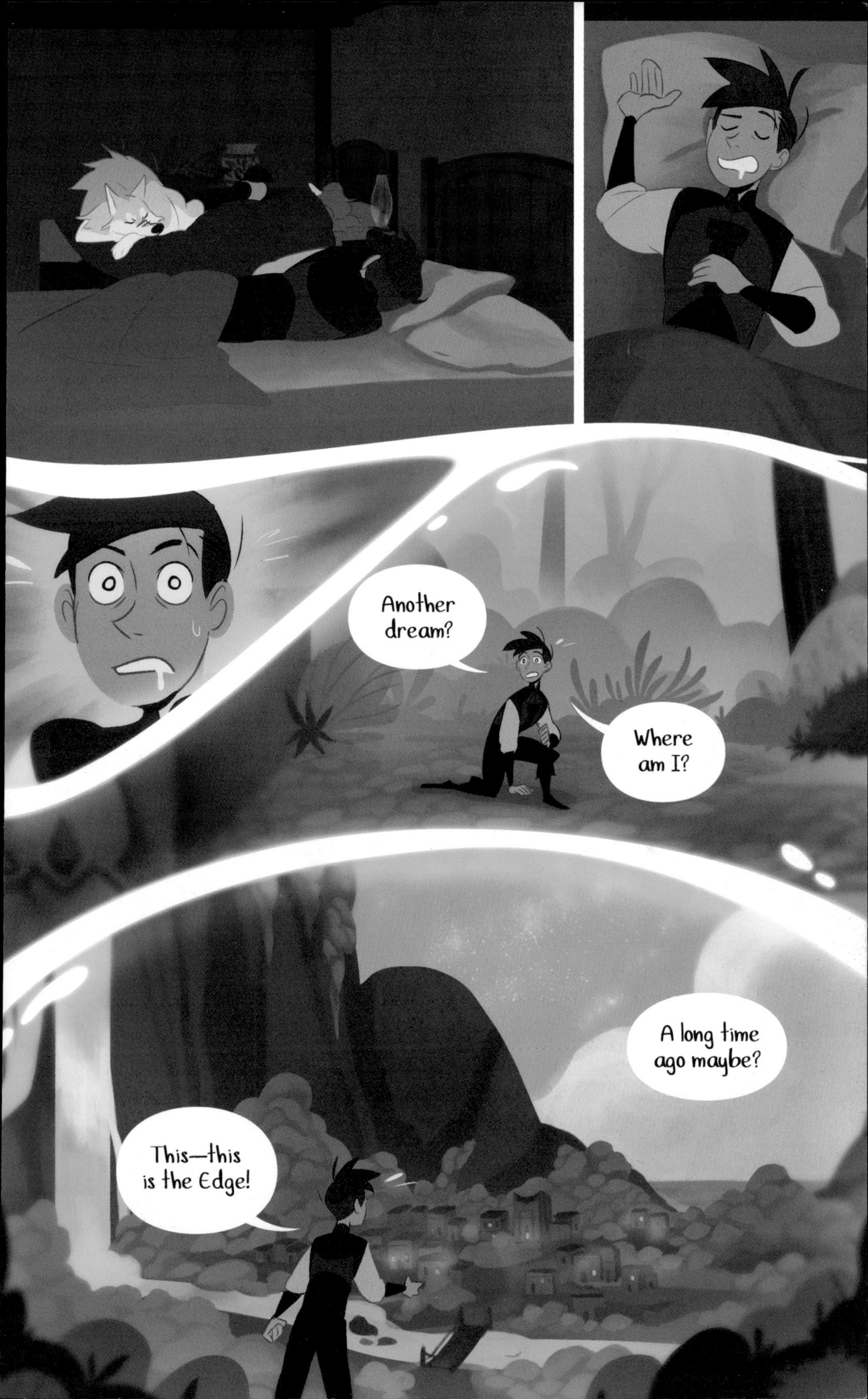
Another dream?
Where am I?
A long time ago maybe?
This—this is the Edge!

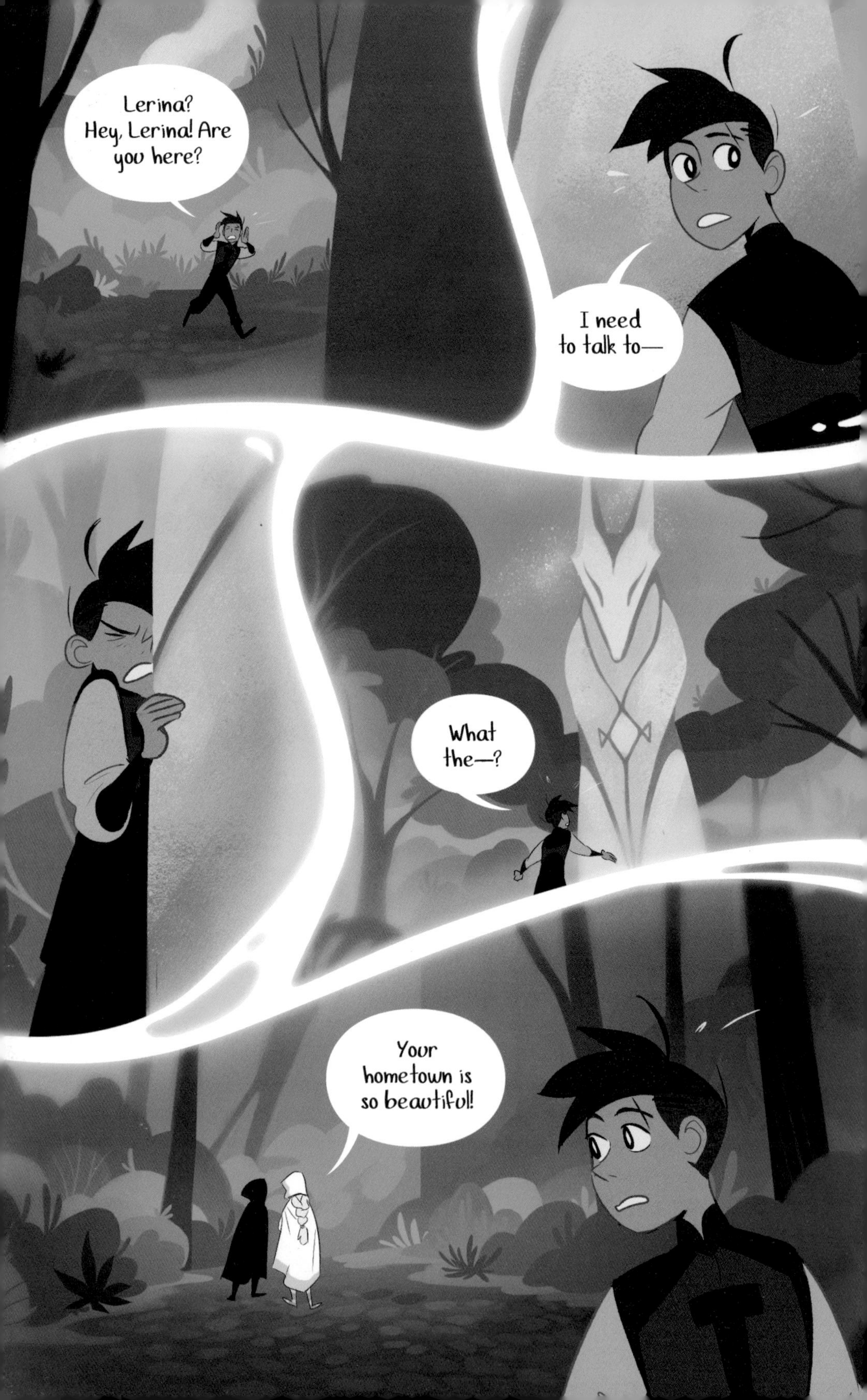
Lerina? Hey, Lerina! Are you here?
I need to talk to—
What the—?
Your hometown is so beautiful!

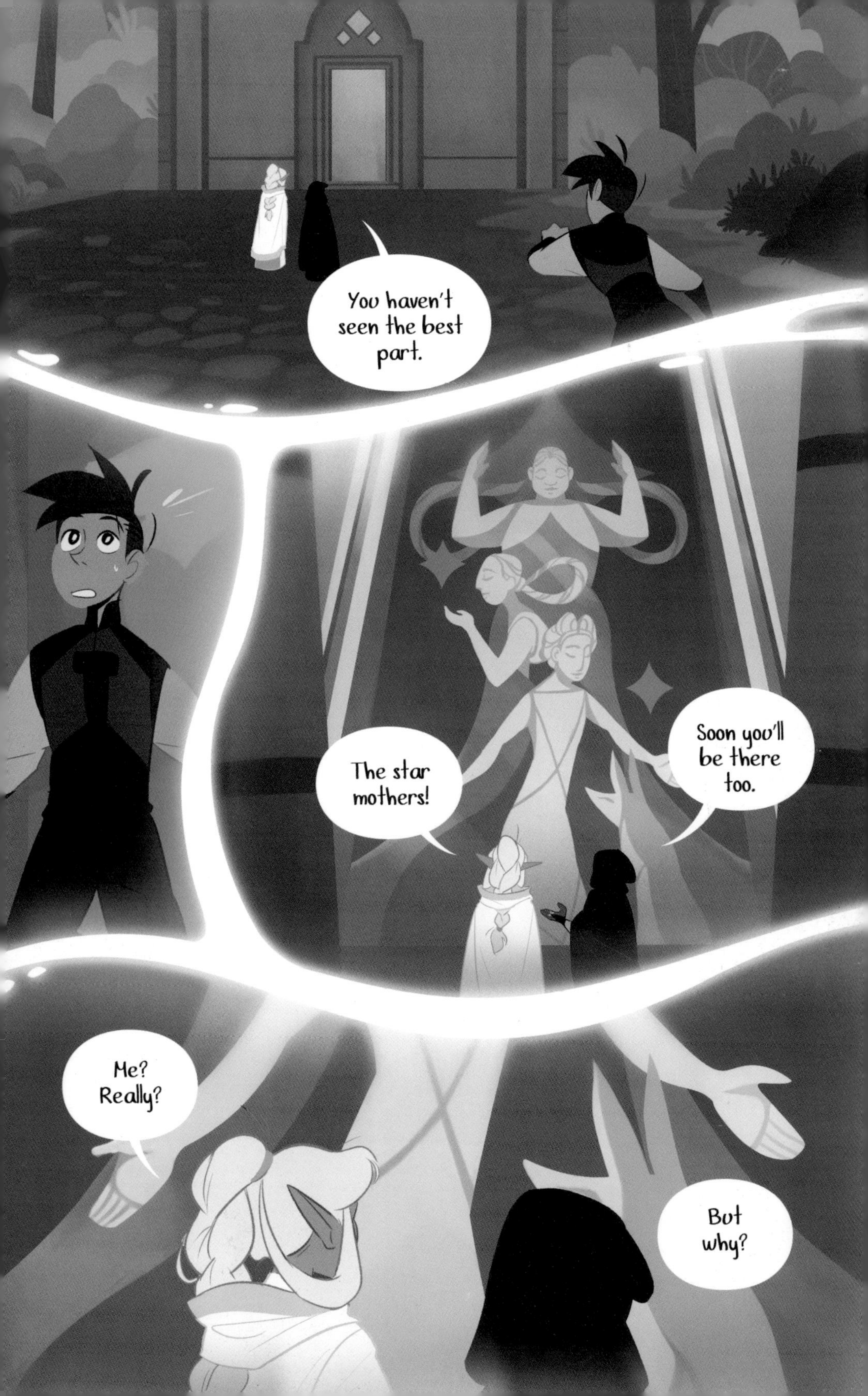
You haven't seen the best part.
The star mothers!
Soon you'll be there too.
Me? Really?
But why?

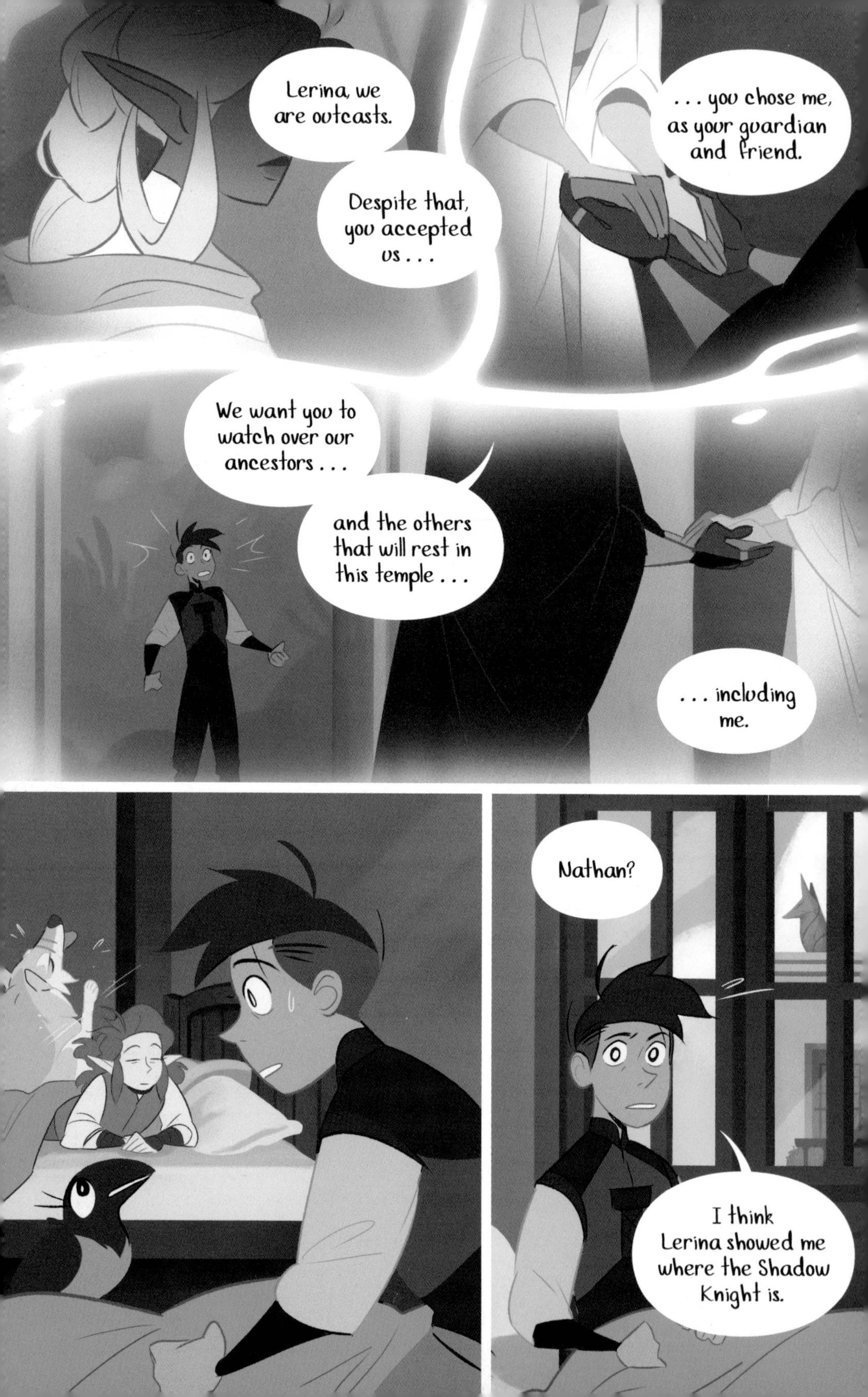
Lerina, we are outcasts.
Despite that, you accepted us . . .
. . . you chose me, as your guardian and friend.
We want you to watch over our ancestors . . .
and the others that will rest in this temple . . .
. . . including me.
Nathan?
I think Lerina showed me where the Shadow Knight is.

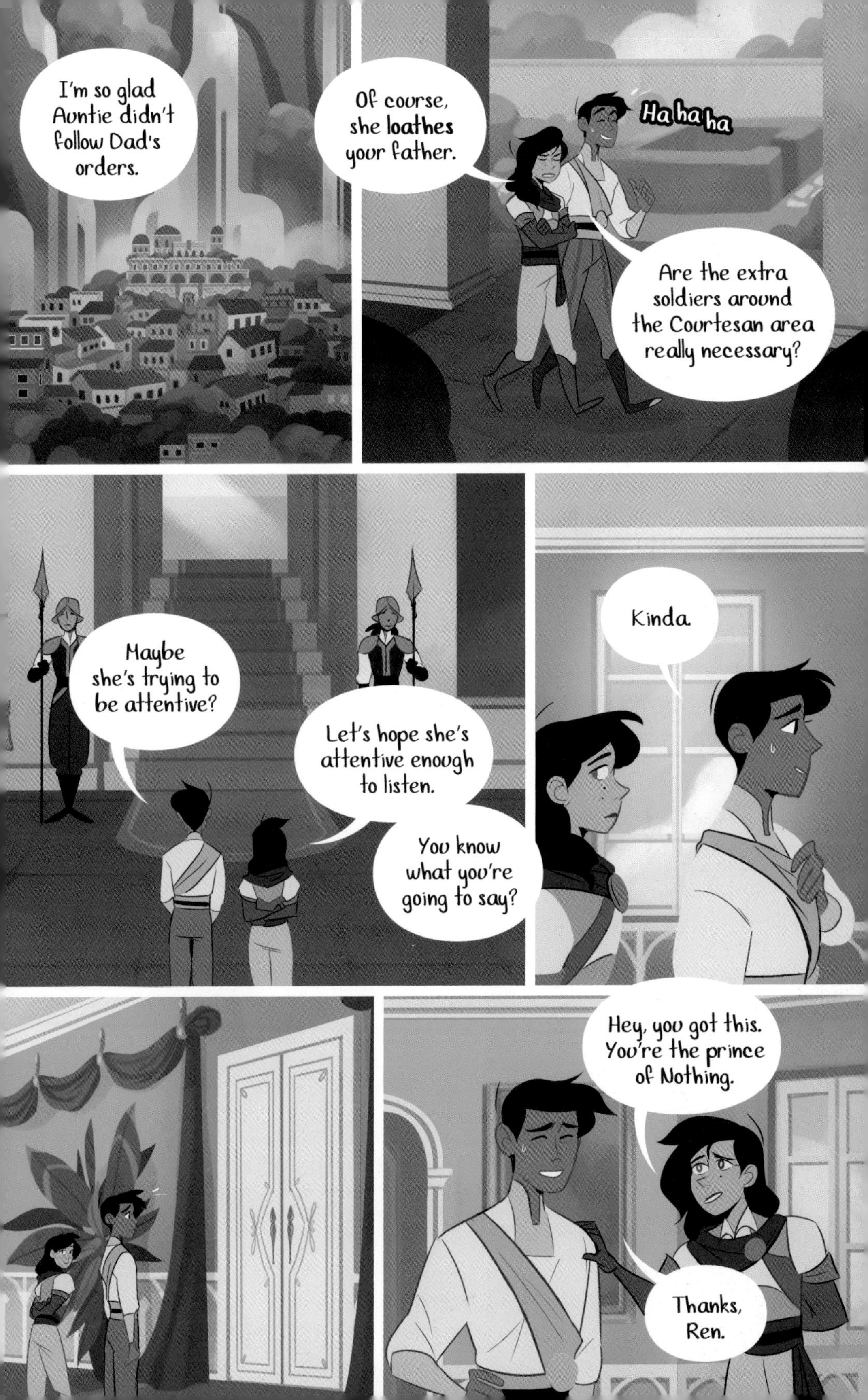
I'm so glad Auntie didn't follow Dad's orders.
Of course, she **loathes** your father.
Ha ha ha
Are the extra soldiers around the Courtesan area really necessary?
Maybe she's trying to be attentive?
Let's hope she's attentive enough to listen.
You know what you're going to say?
Kinda.
Hey, you got this. You're the prince of Nothing.
Thanks, Ren.

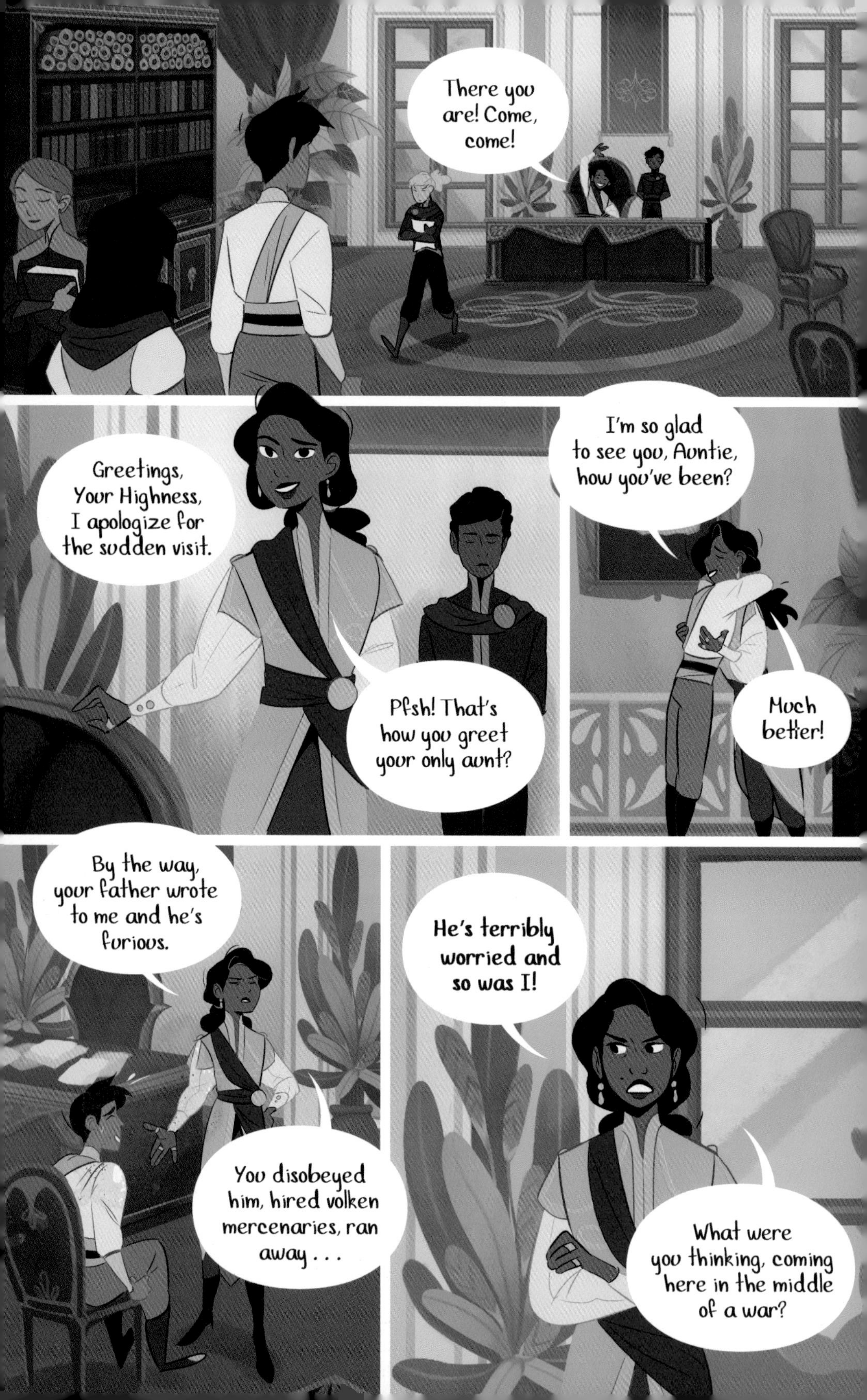
There you are! Come, come!
Greetings, Your Highness, I apologize for the sudden visit.
Pfsh! That's how you greet your only aunt?
I'm so glad to see you, Auntie, how you've been?
Much better!
By the way, your father wrote to me and he's furious.
You disobeyed him, hired volken mercenaries, ran away . . .
He's terribly worried and so was I!
What were you thinking, coming here in the middle of a war?

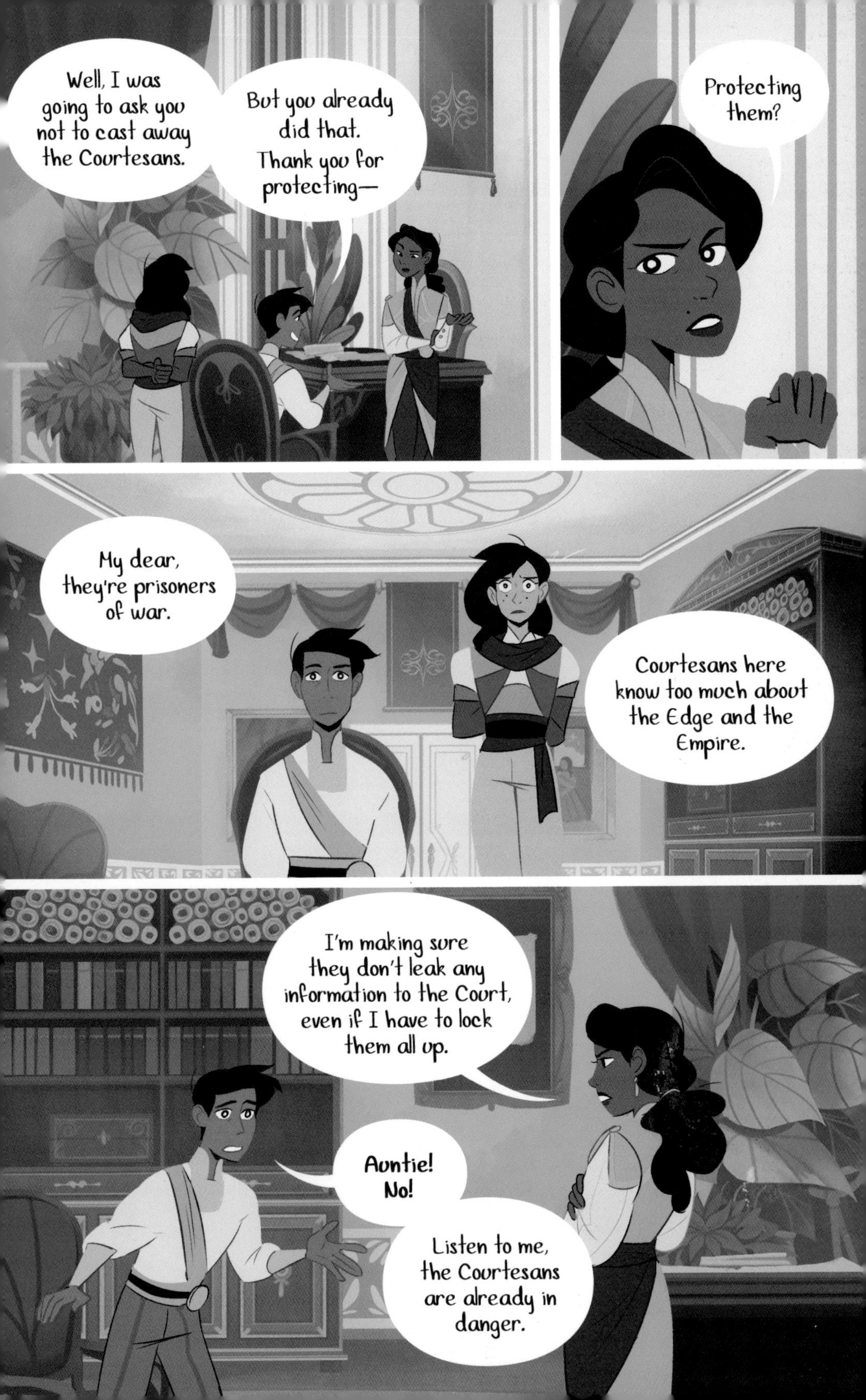
Well, I was going to ask you not to cast away the Courtesans.
But you already did that. Thank you for protecting—
Protecting them?
My dear, they're prisoners of war.
Courtesans here know too much about the Edge and the Empire.
I'm making sure they don't leak any information to the Court, even if I have to lock them all up.
Auntie! No!
Listen to me, the Courtesans are already in danger.

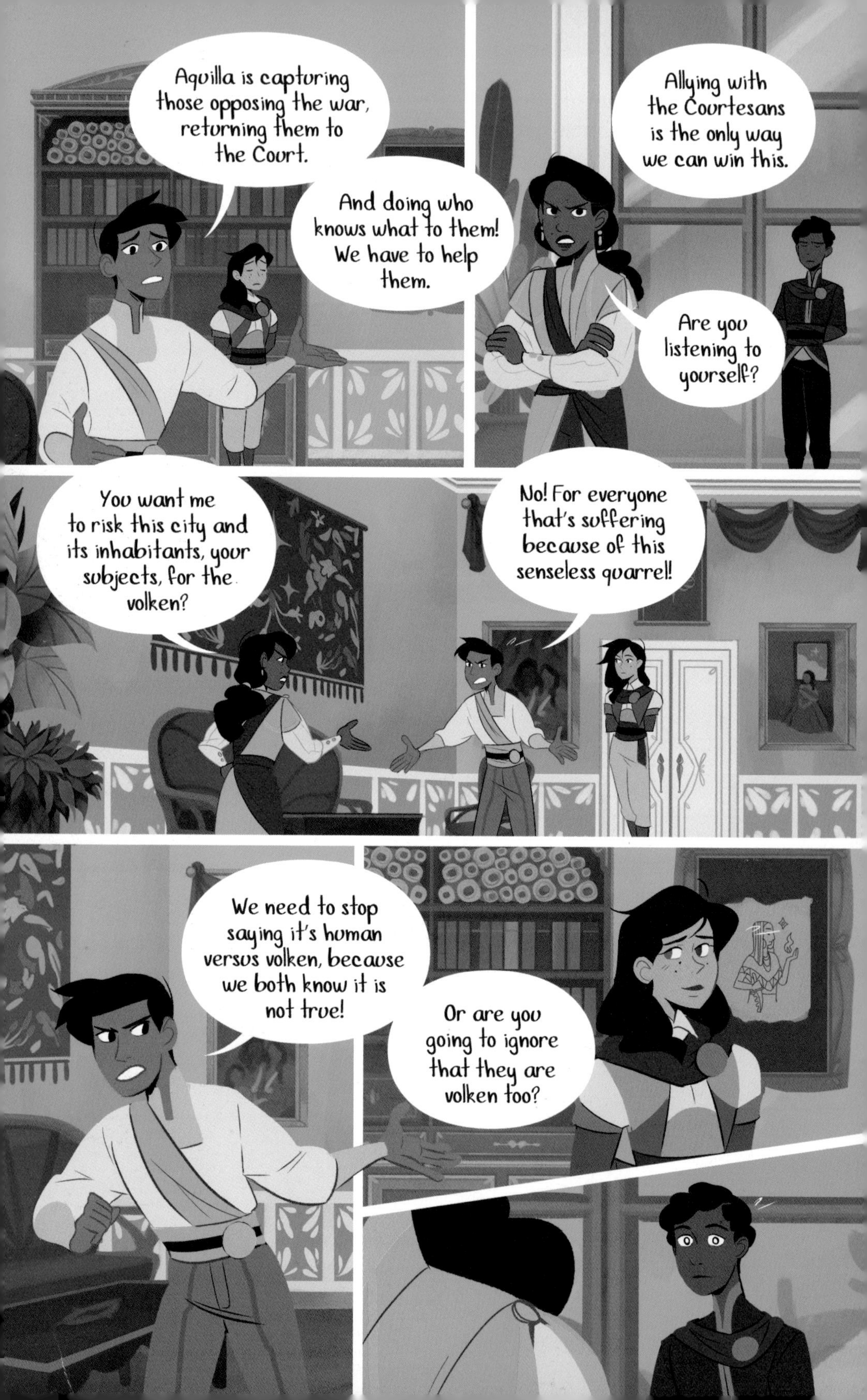
Aquilla is capturing those opposing the war, returning them to the Court.
And doing who knows what to them! We have to help them.
Allying with the Courtesans is the only way we can win this.
Are you listening to yourself?
You want me to risk this city and its inhabitants, your subjects, for the volken?
No! For everyone that's suffering because of this senseless quarrel!
We need to stop saying it's human versus volken, because we both know it is not true!
Or are you going to ignore that they are volken too?

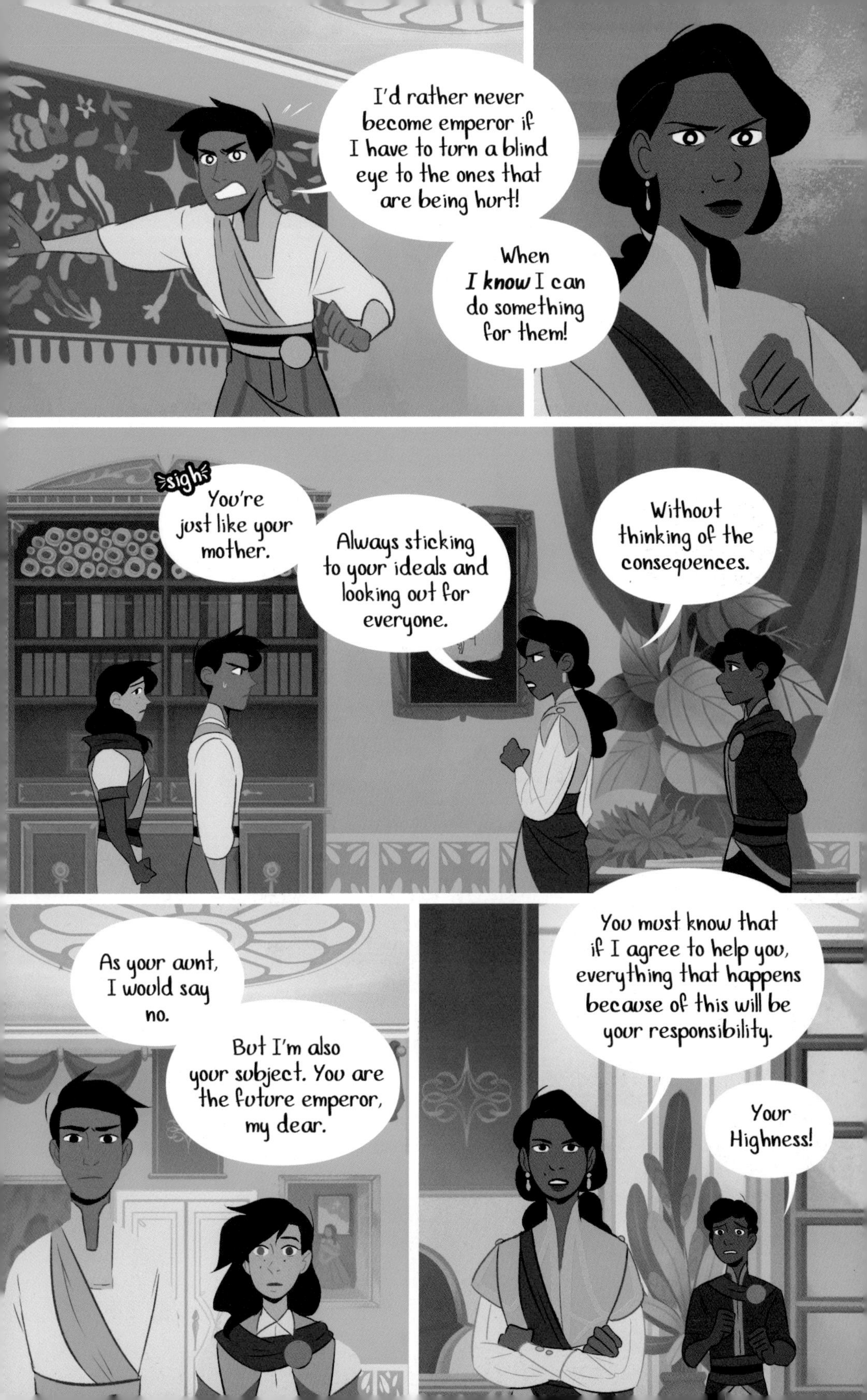
I'd rather never become emperor if I have to turn a blind eye to the ones that are being hurt!
When *I know* I can do something for them!
sigh
You're just like your mother.
Always sticking to your ideals and looking out for everyone.
Without thinking of the consequences.
As your aunt, I would say no.
But I'm also your subject. You are the future emperor, my dear.
You must know that if I agree to help you, everything that happens because of this will be your responsibility.
Your Highness!

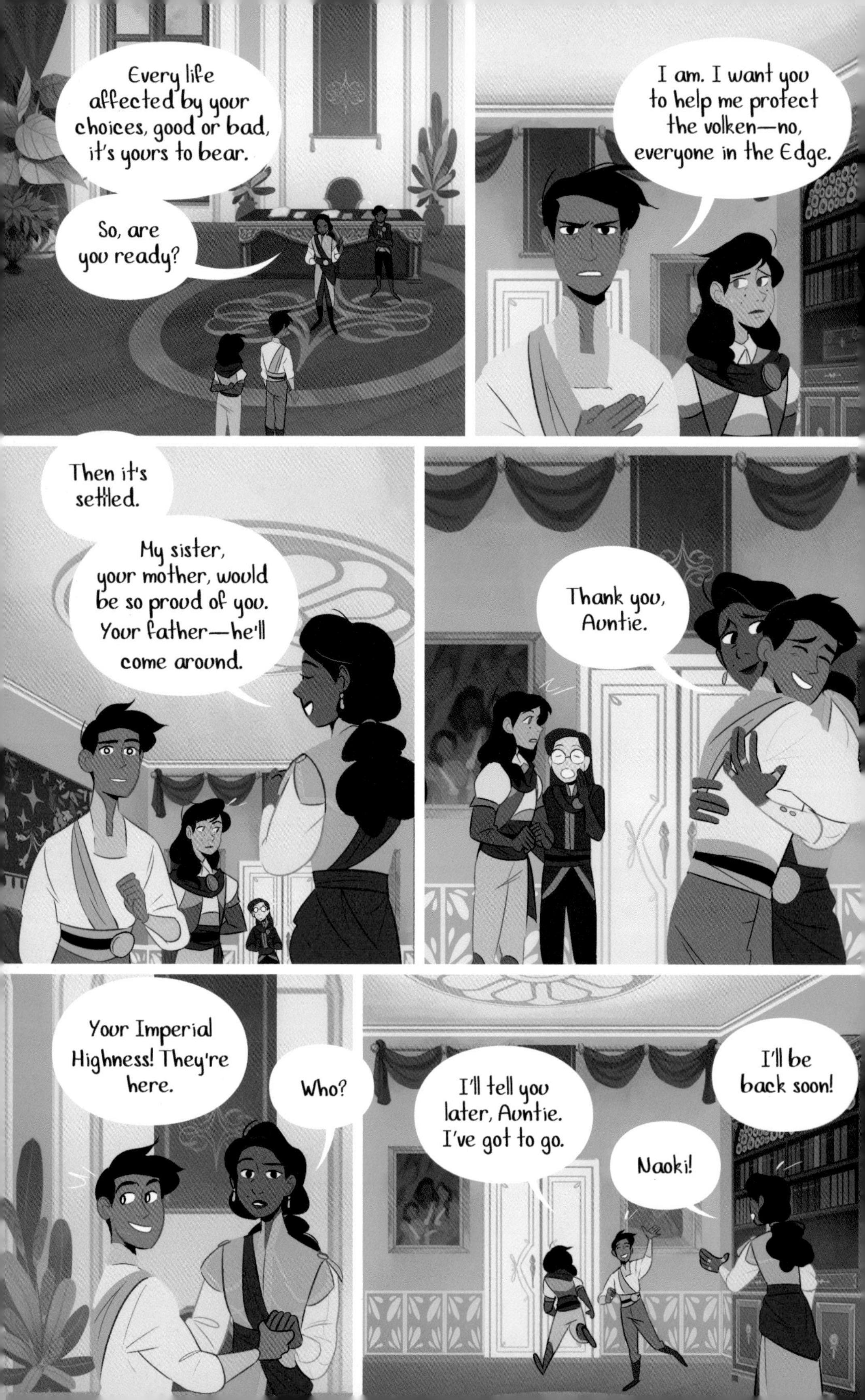
Every life affected by your choices, good or bad, it's yours to bear.
So, are you ready?
I am. I want you to help me protect the volken—no, everyone in the Edge.
Then it's settled.
My sister, your mother, would be so proud of you. Your father—he'll come around.
Thank you, Auntie.
Your Imperial Highness! They're here.
Who?
I'll tell you later, Auntie. I've got to go.
I'll be back soon!
Naoki!

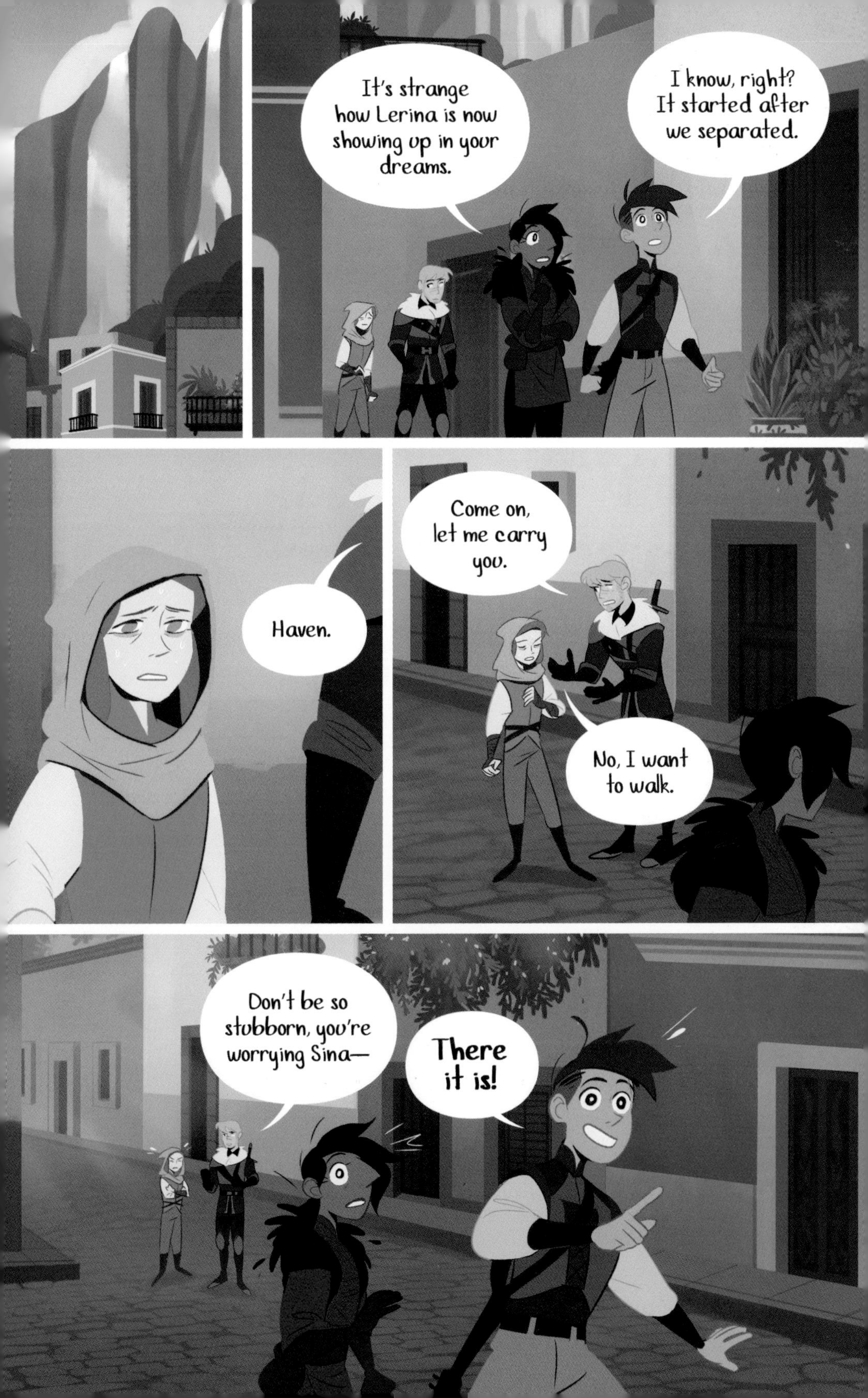
It's strange how Lerina is now showing up in your dreams.
I know, right? It started after we separated.
Haven.
Come on, let me carry you.
No, I want to walk.
Don't be so stubborn, you're worrying Sina—
There it is!

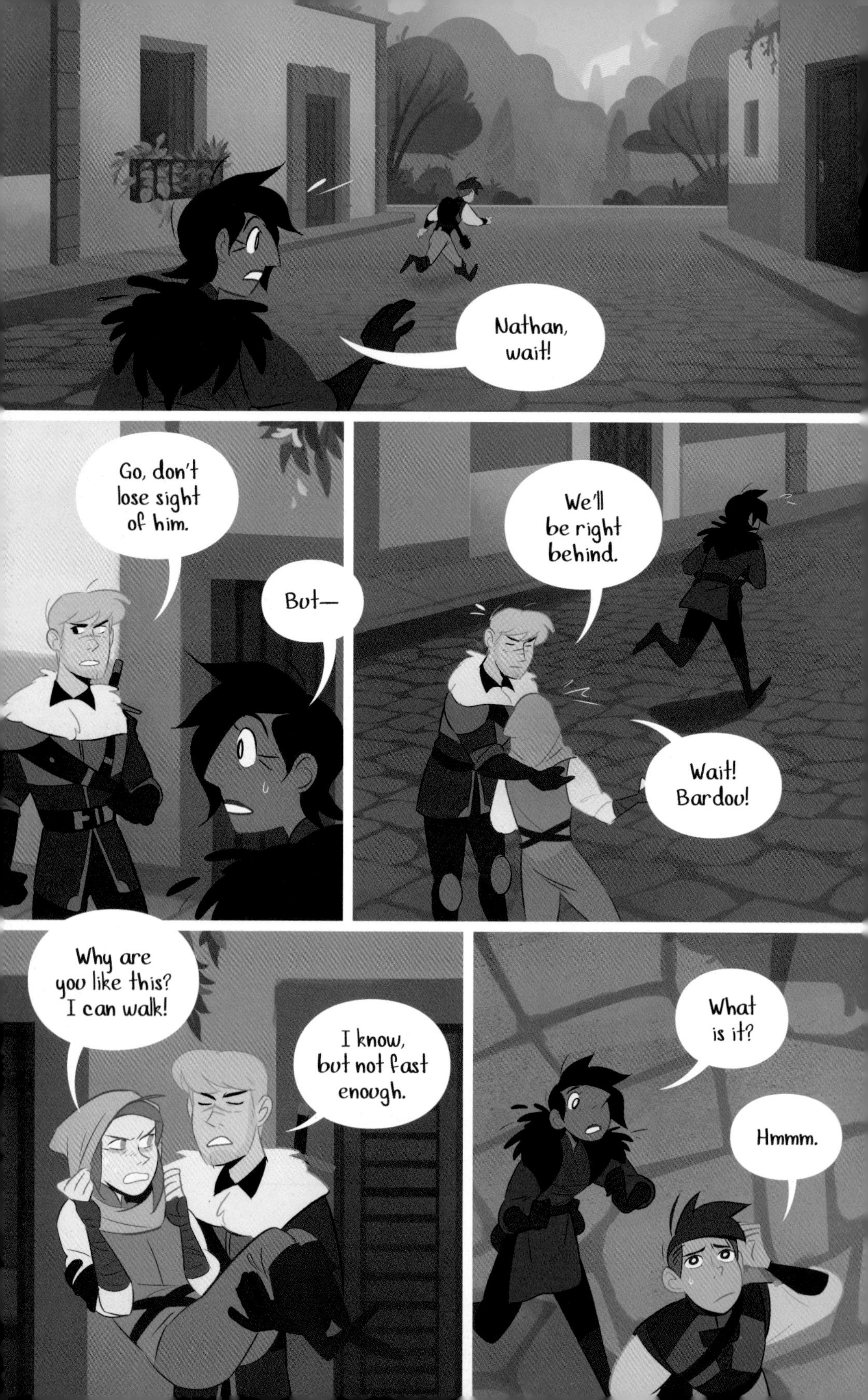
Nathan, wait!
Go, don't lose sight of him.
But—
We'll be right behind.
Wait! Bardou!
Why are you like this? I can walk!
I know, but not fast enough.
What is it?
Hmmm.

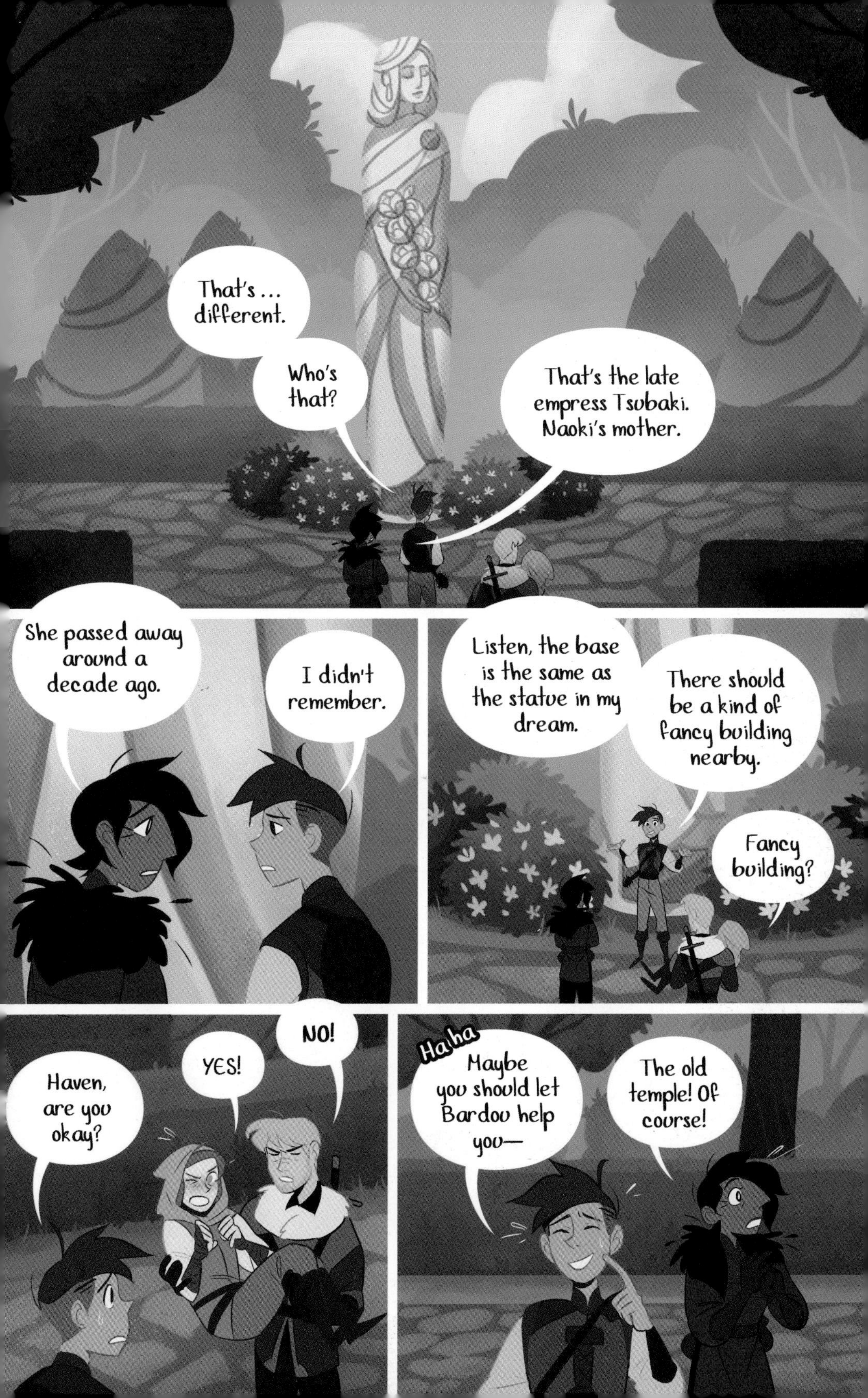
That's ... different.
Who's that?
That's the late empress Tsubaki. Naoki's mother.
She passed away around a decade ago.
I didn't remember.
Listen, the base is the same as the statue in my dream.
There should be a kind of fancy building nearby.
Fancy building?
Haven, are you okay?
YES!
NO!
Ha ha
Maybe you should let Bardou help you—
The old temple! Of course!

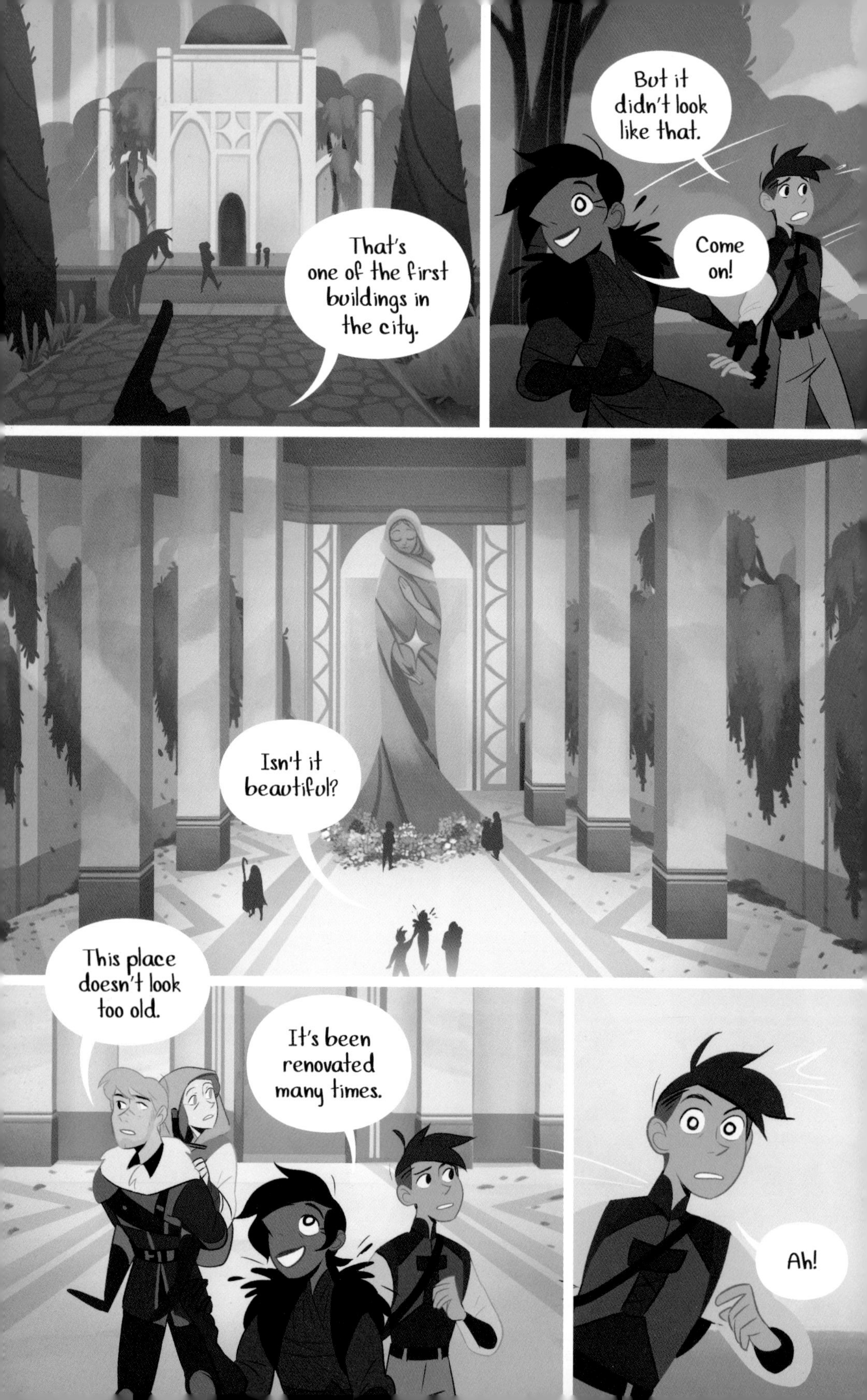
That's one of the first buildings in the city.
But it didn't look like that.
Come on!
Isn't it beautiful?
This place doesn't look too old.
It's been renovated many times.
Ah!

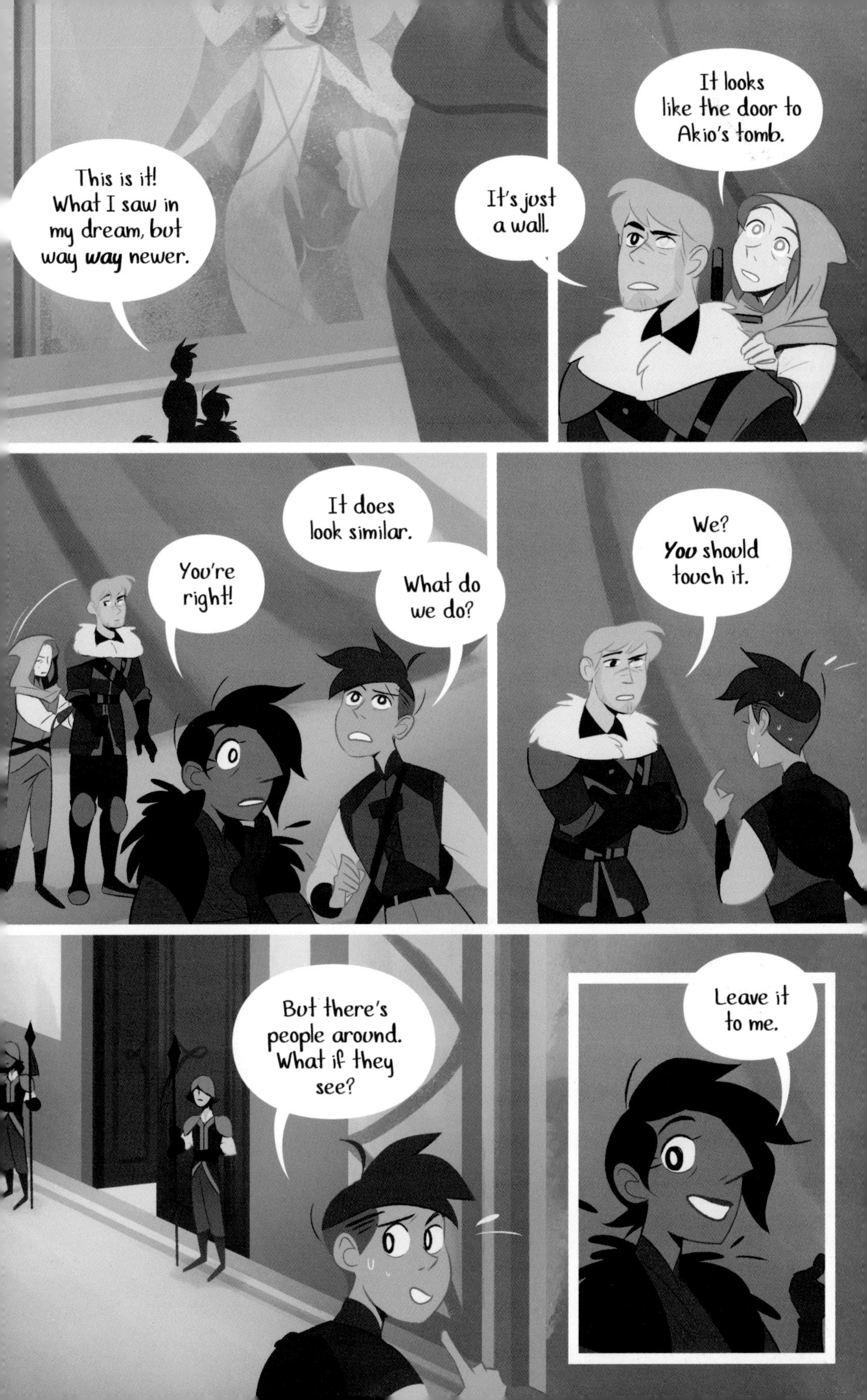

This is it! What I saw in my dream, but way **way** newer.
It's just a wall.
It looks like the door to Akio's tomb.
You're right!
It does look similar.
What do we do?
We? *You* should touch it.
But there's people around. What if they see?
Leave it to me.

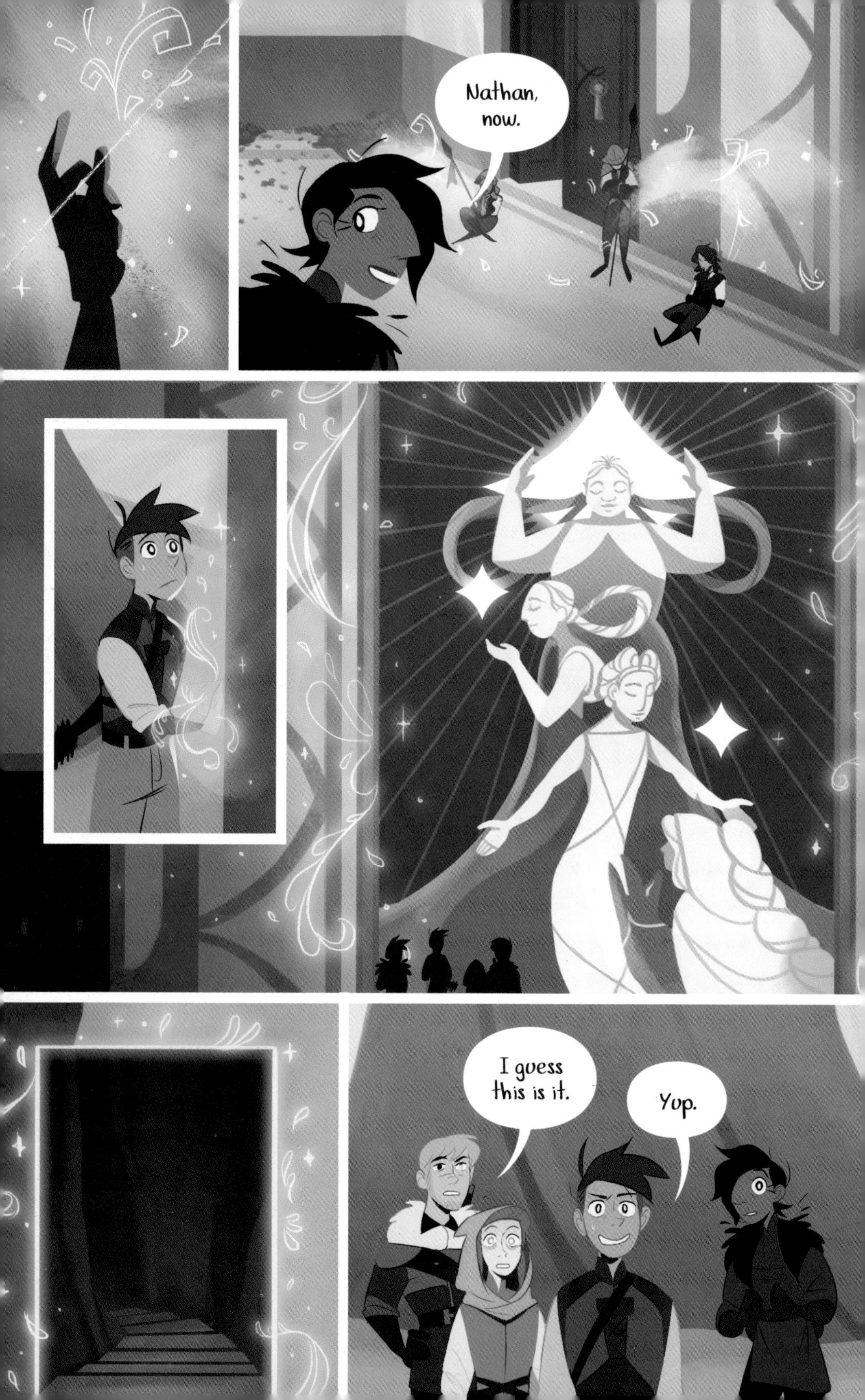
Nathan, now.
I guess this is it.
Yup.

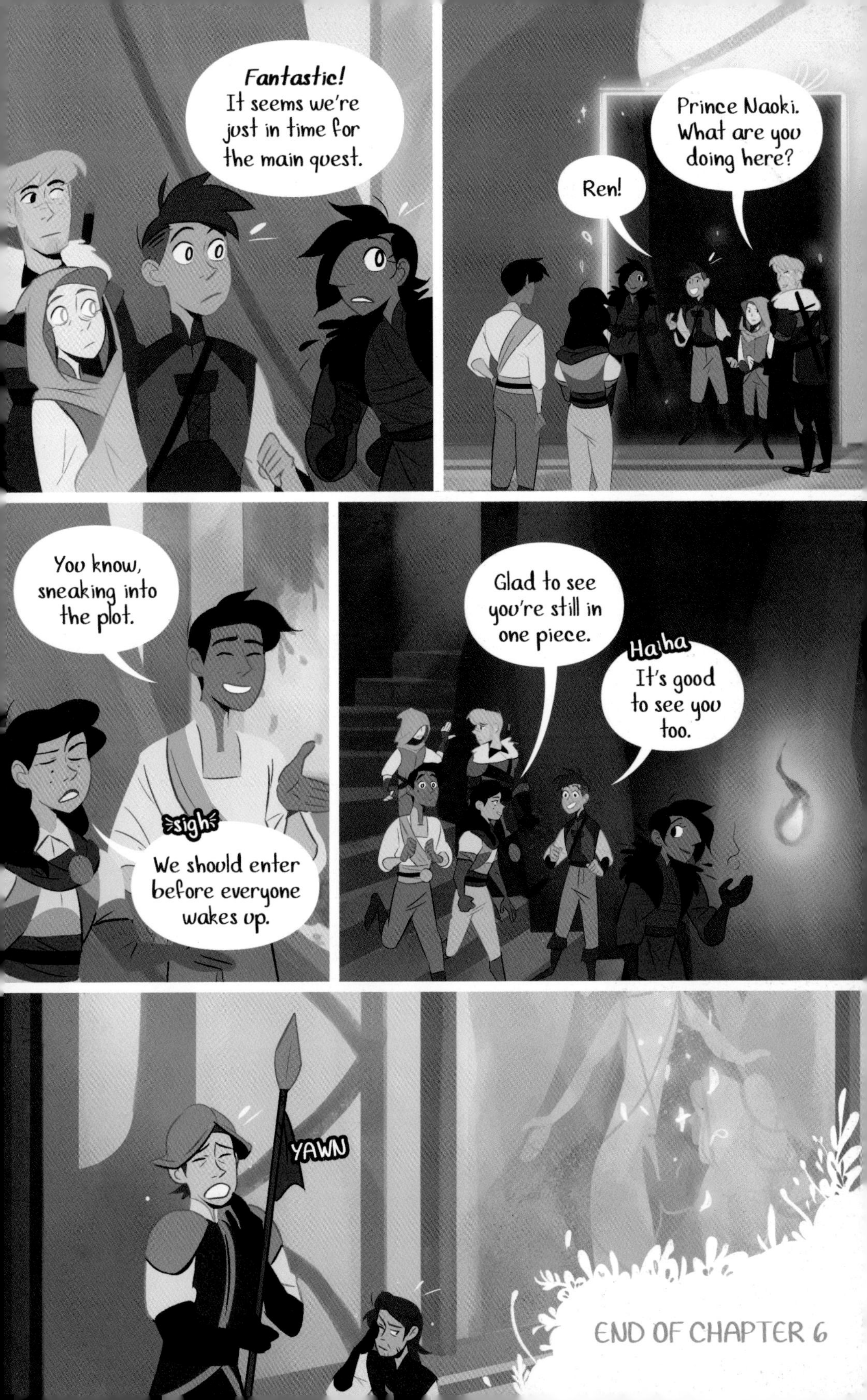
Fantastic!
It seems we're just in time for the main quest.
Prince Naoki. What are you doing here?
Ren!
You know, sneaking into the plot.
sigh
We should enter before everyone wakes up.
Glad to see you're still in one piece.
Haha
It's good to see you too.
YAWN
END OF CHAPTER 6

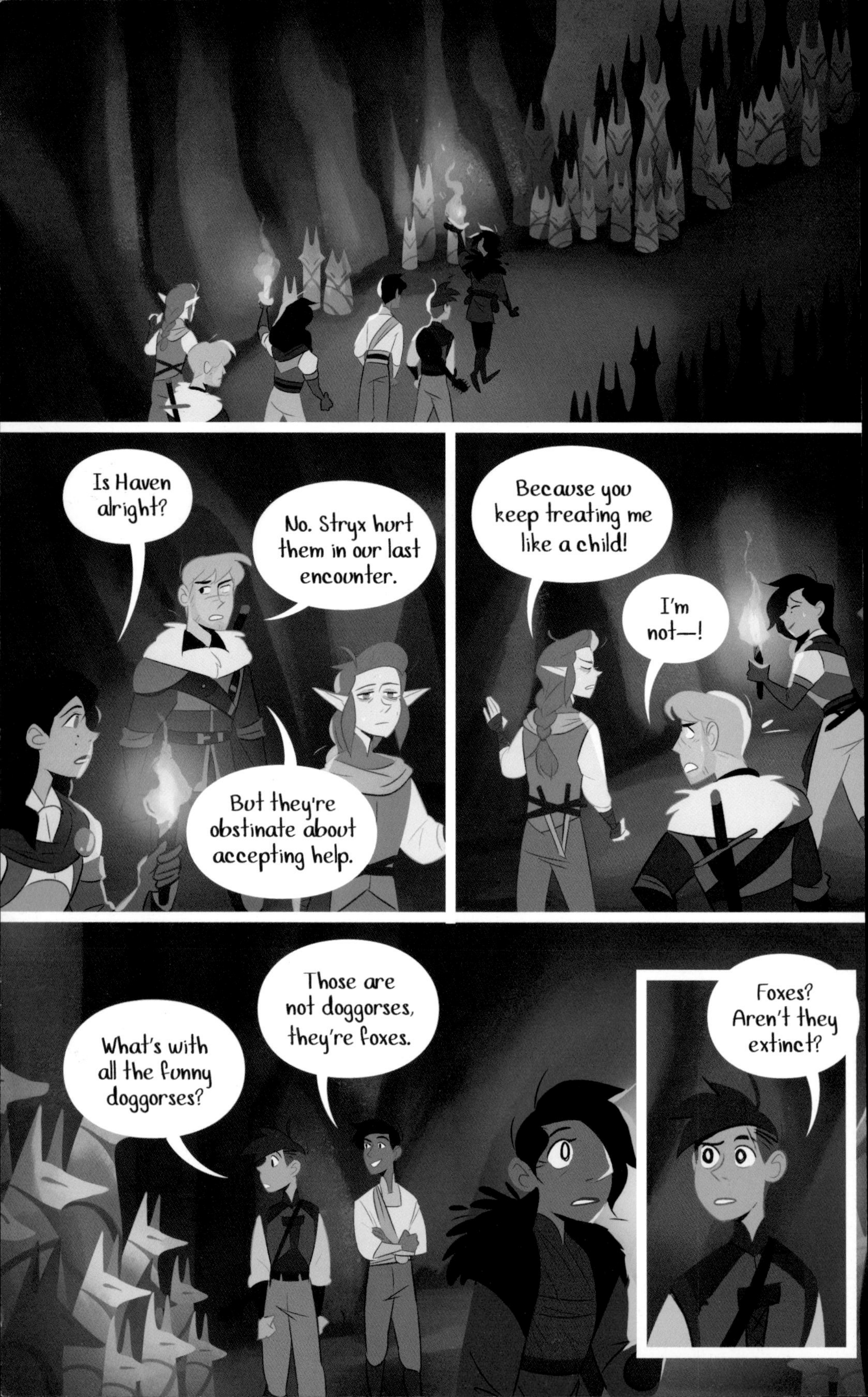
Is Haven alright?
No. Stryx hurt them in our last encounter.
But they're obstinate about accepting help.
Because you keep treating me like a child!
I'm not—!
What's with all the funny doggorses?
Those are not doggorses, they're foxes.
Foxes? Aren't they extinct?

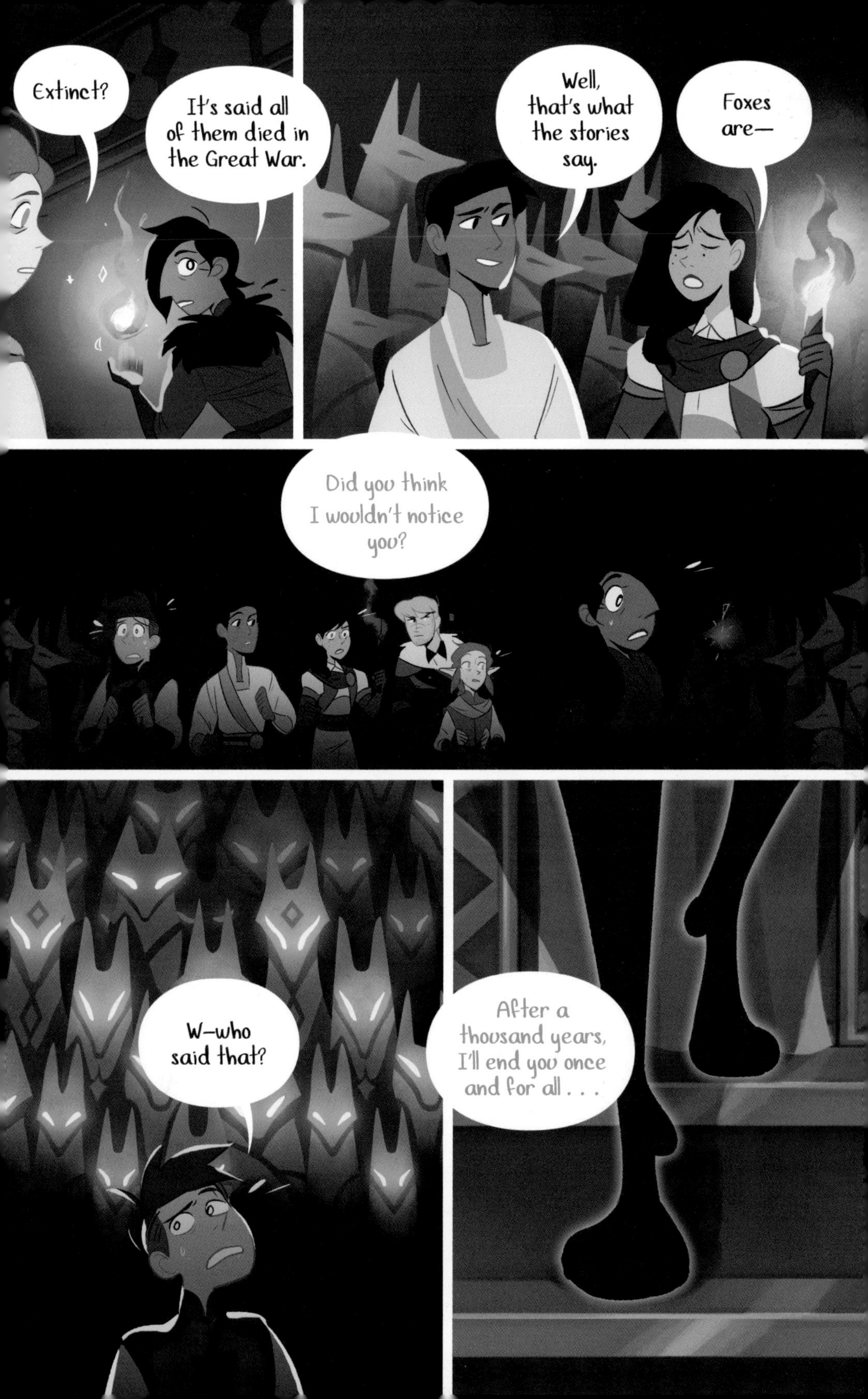
Extinct?
It's said all of them died in the Great War.
Well, that's what the stories say.
Foxes are—
Did you think I wouldn't notice you?
W—who said that?
After a thousand years, I'll end you once and for all . . .

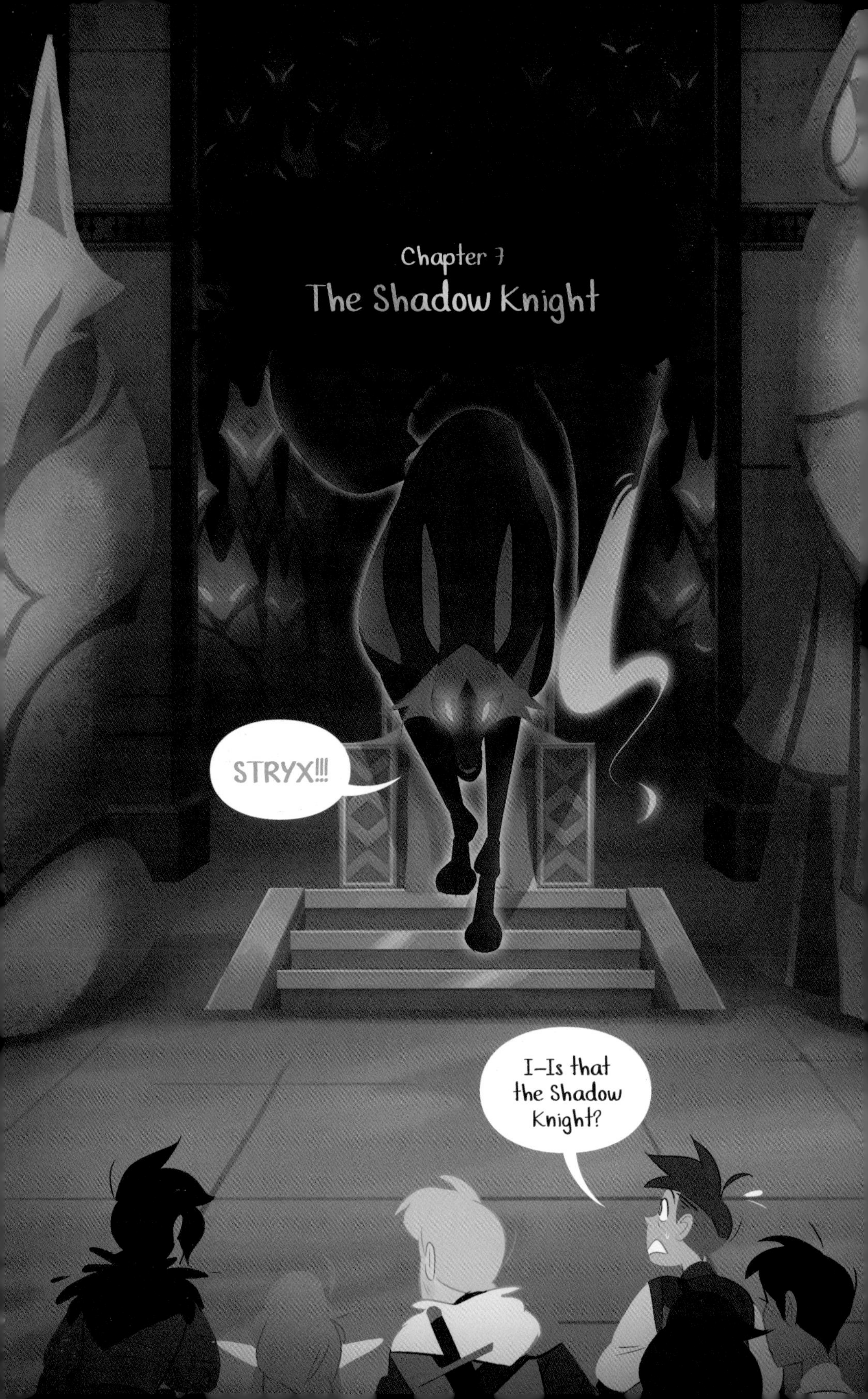
Chapter 7
The Shadow Knight
STRYX!!!
I—Is that the Shadow Knight?

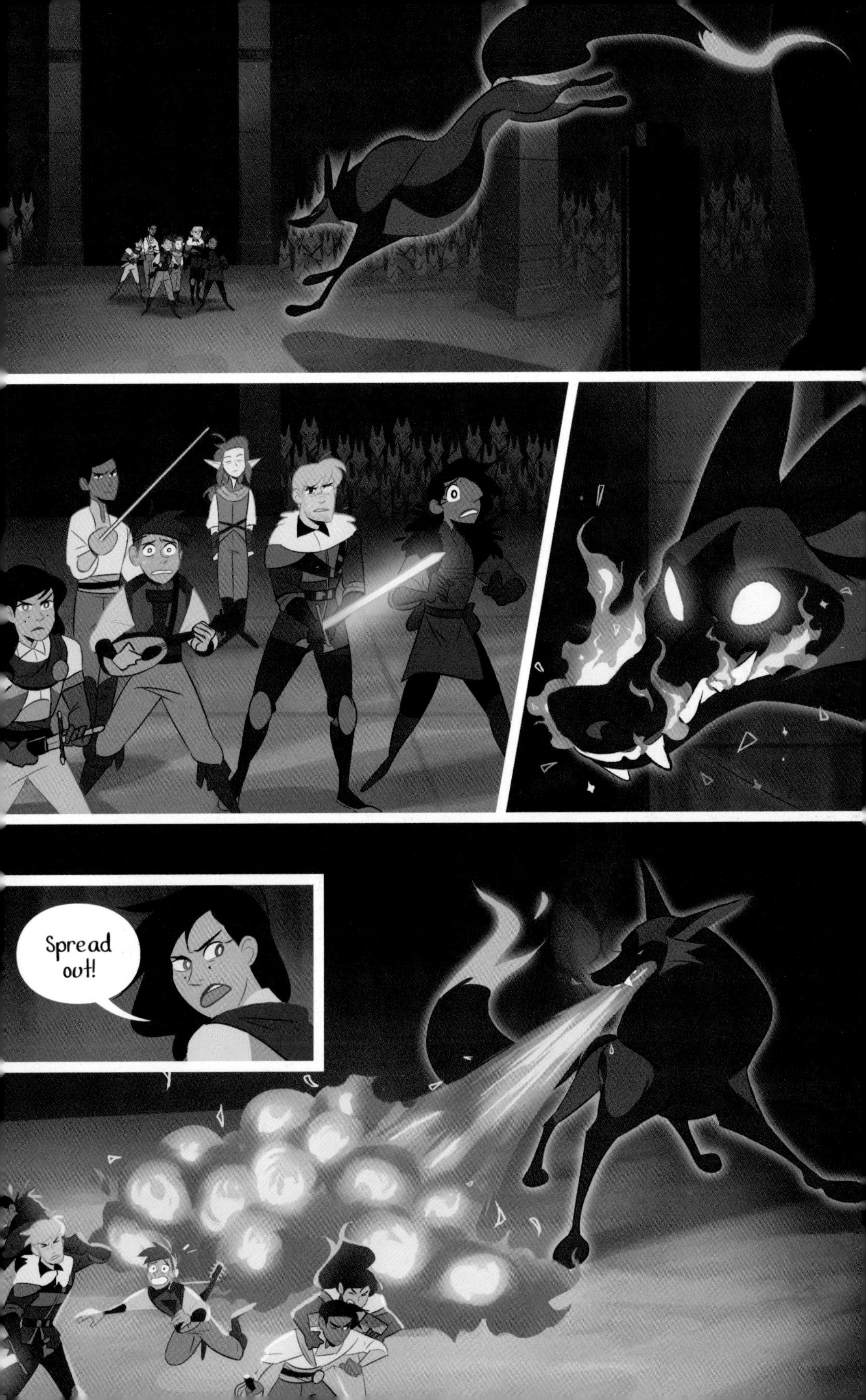
Spread out!

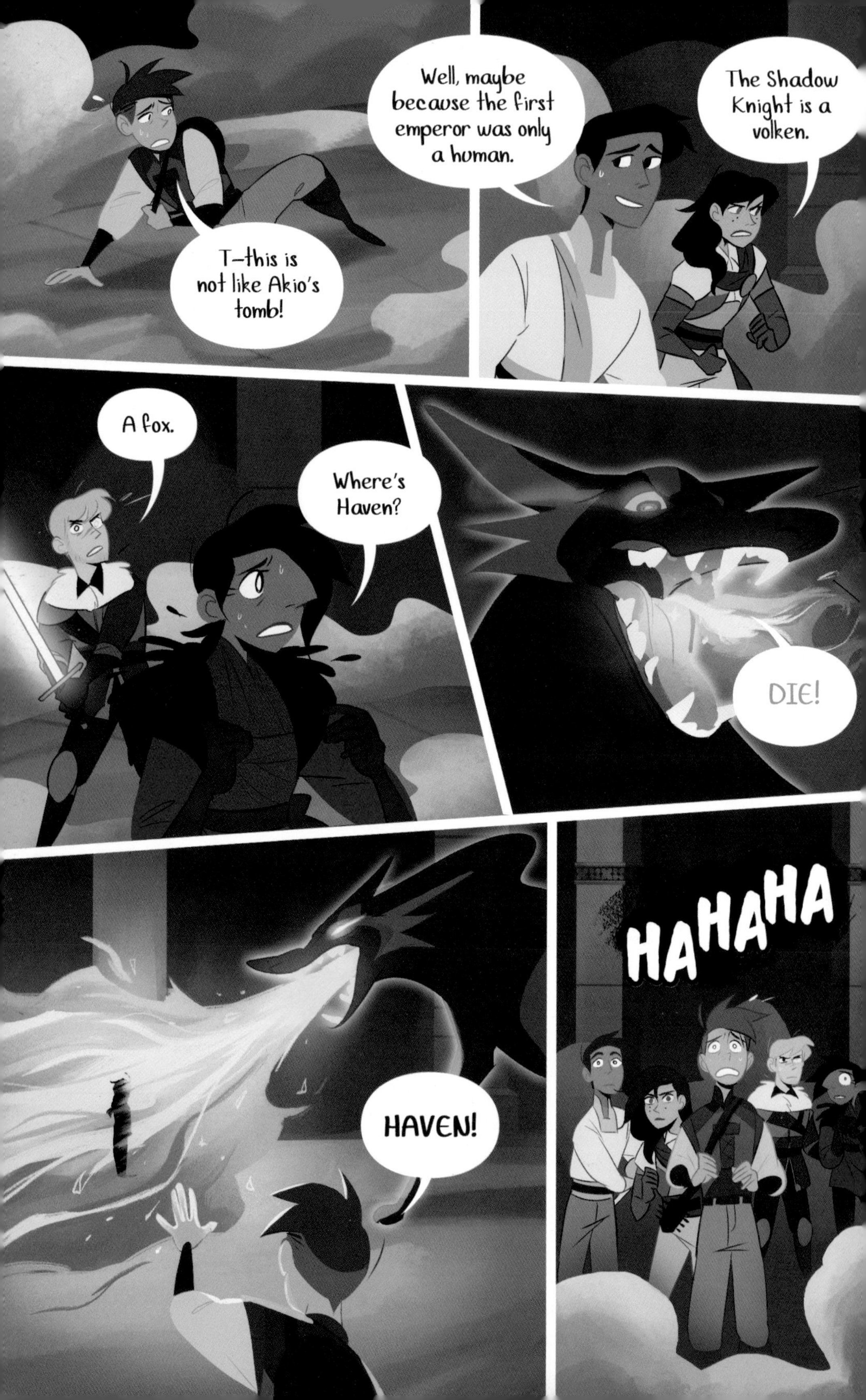

T—this is not like Akio's tomb!
Well, maybe because the first emperor was only a human.
The Shadow Knight is a volken.
A fox.
Where's Haven?
DIE!
HAVEN!
HAHAHA

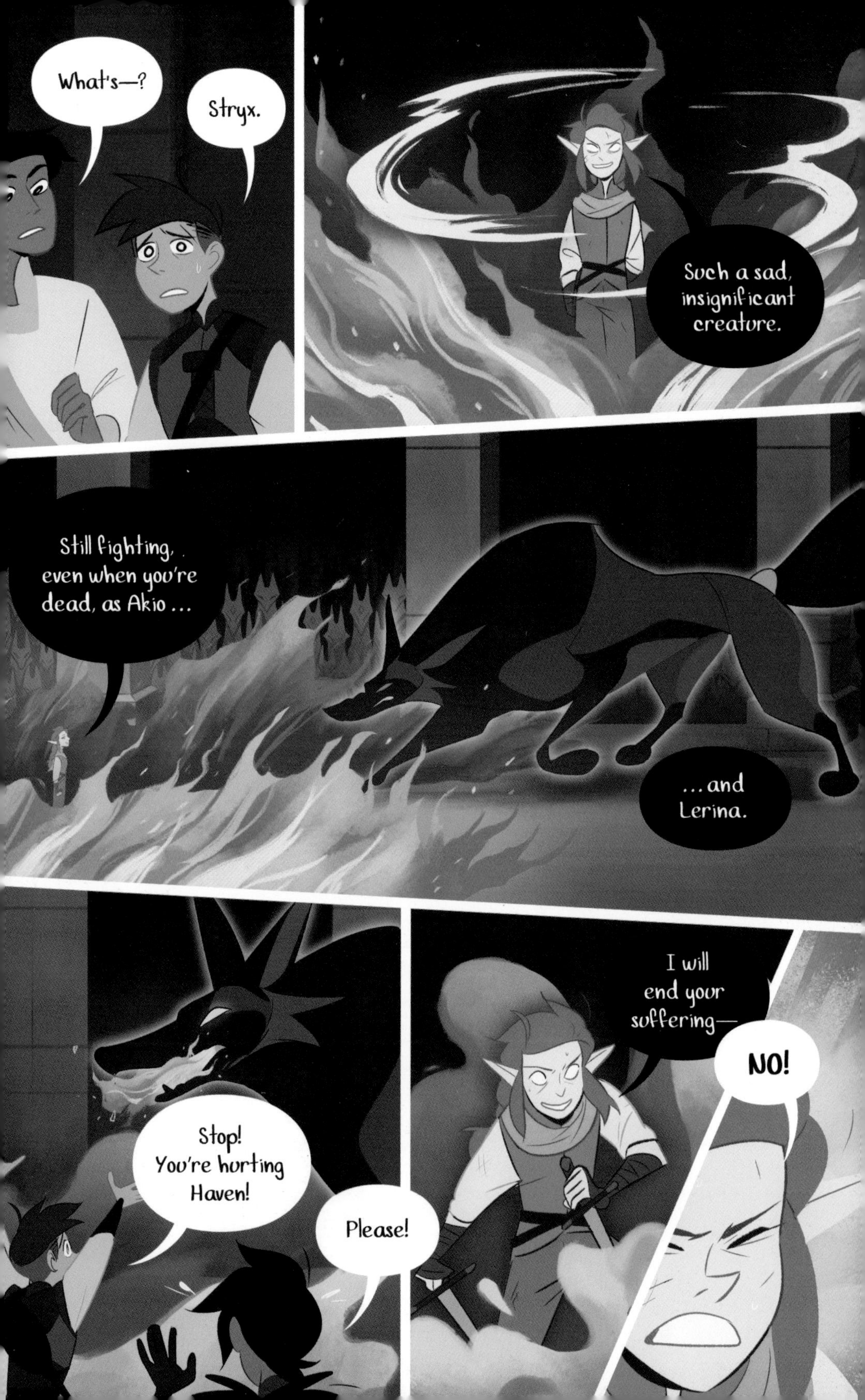
What's—?
Stryx.
Such a sad, insignificant creature.
Still fighting, even when you're dead, as Akio ...
... and Lerina.
Stop! You're hurting Haven!
Please!
I will end your suffering—
NO!

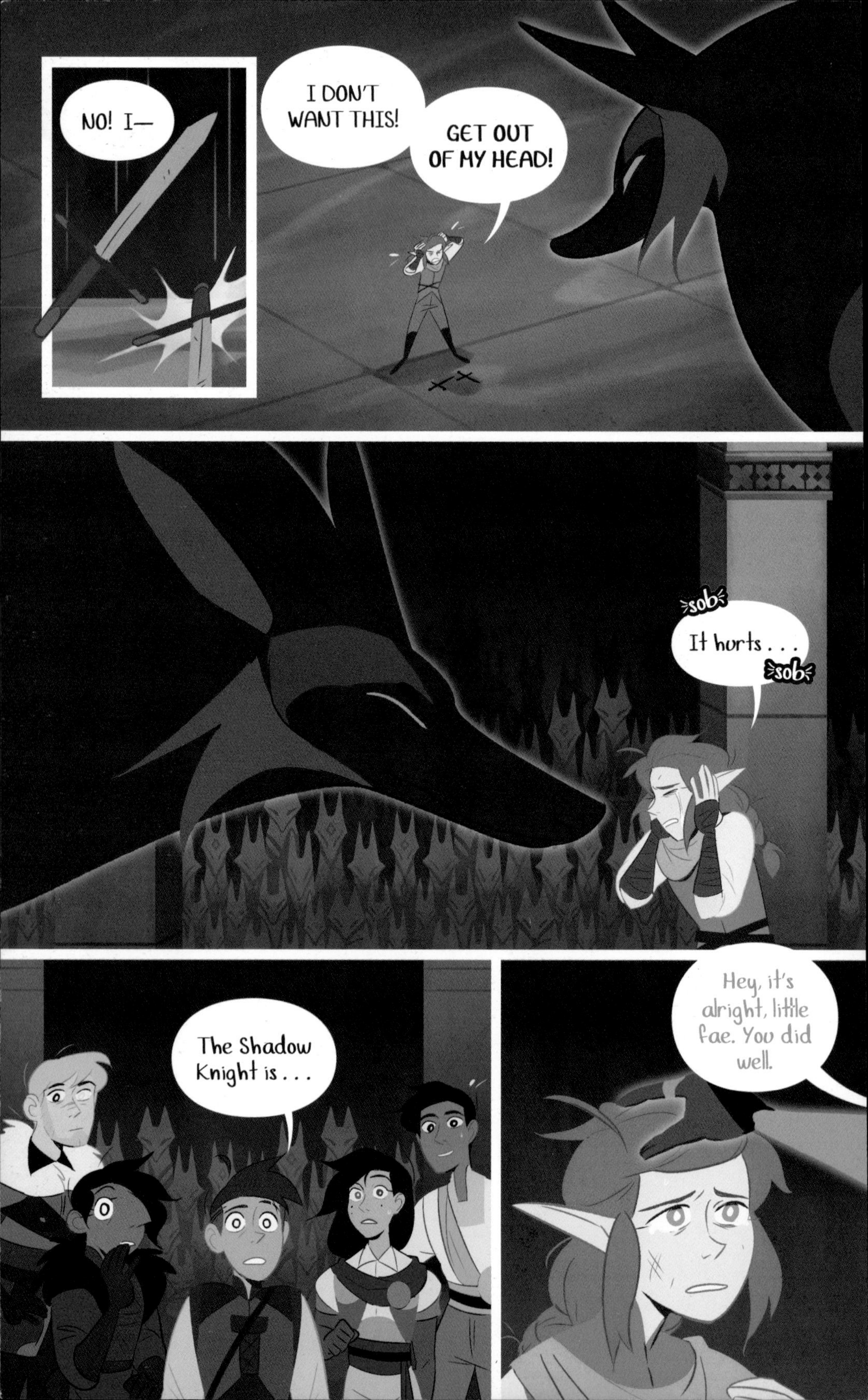
NO! I—
I DON'T WANT THIS!
GET OUT OF MY HEAD!
sob
It hurts . . .
sob
The Shadow Knight is . . .
Hey, it's alright, little fae. You did well.

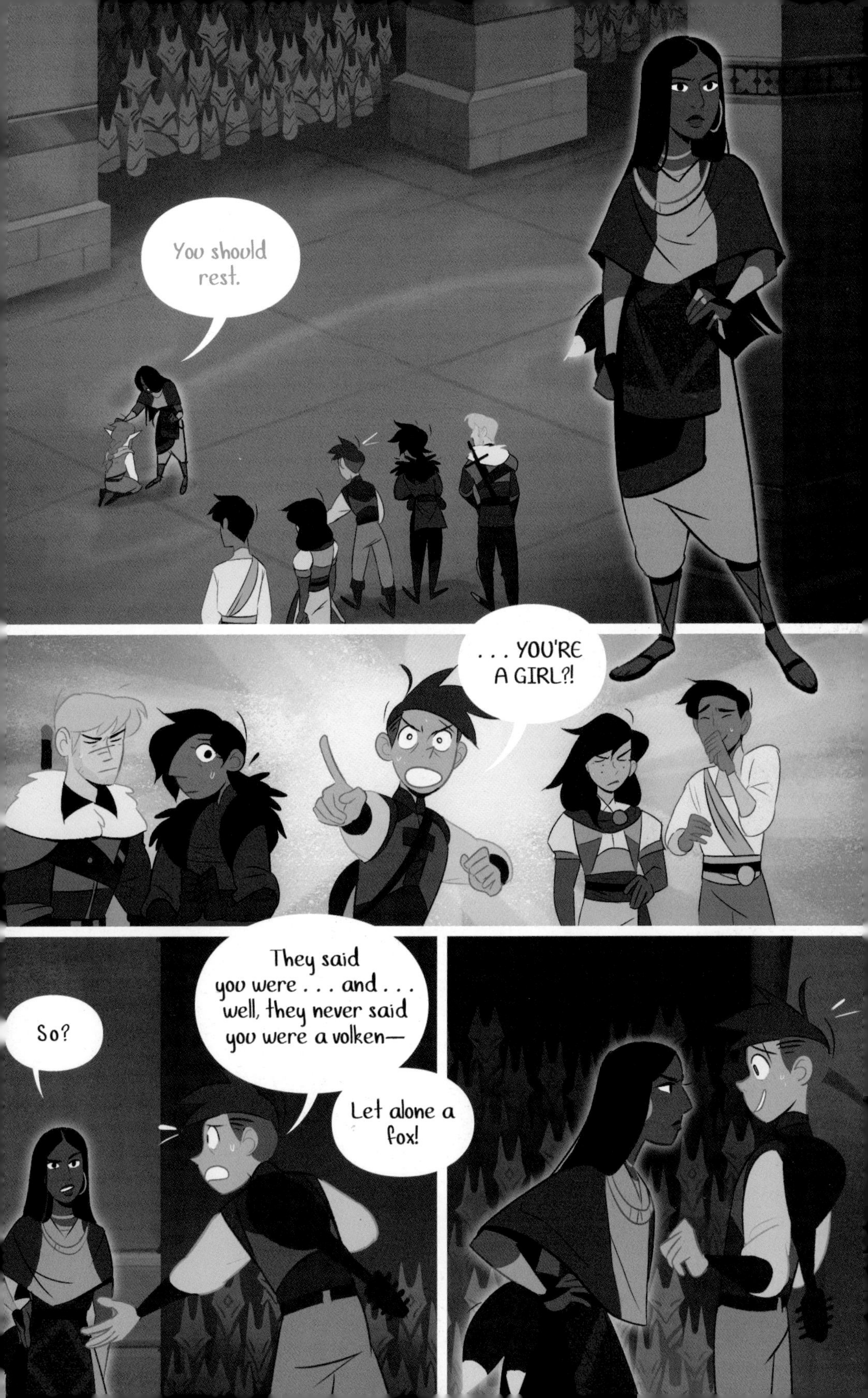
You should rest.
. . . YOU'RE A GIRL?!
So?
They said you were . . . and . . . well, they never said you were a volken—
Let alone a fox!

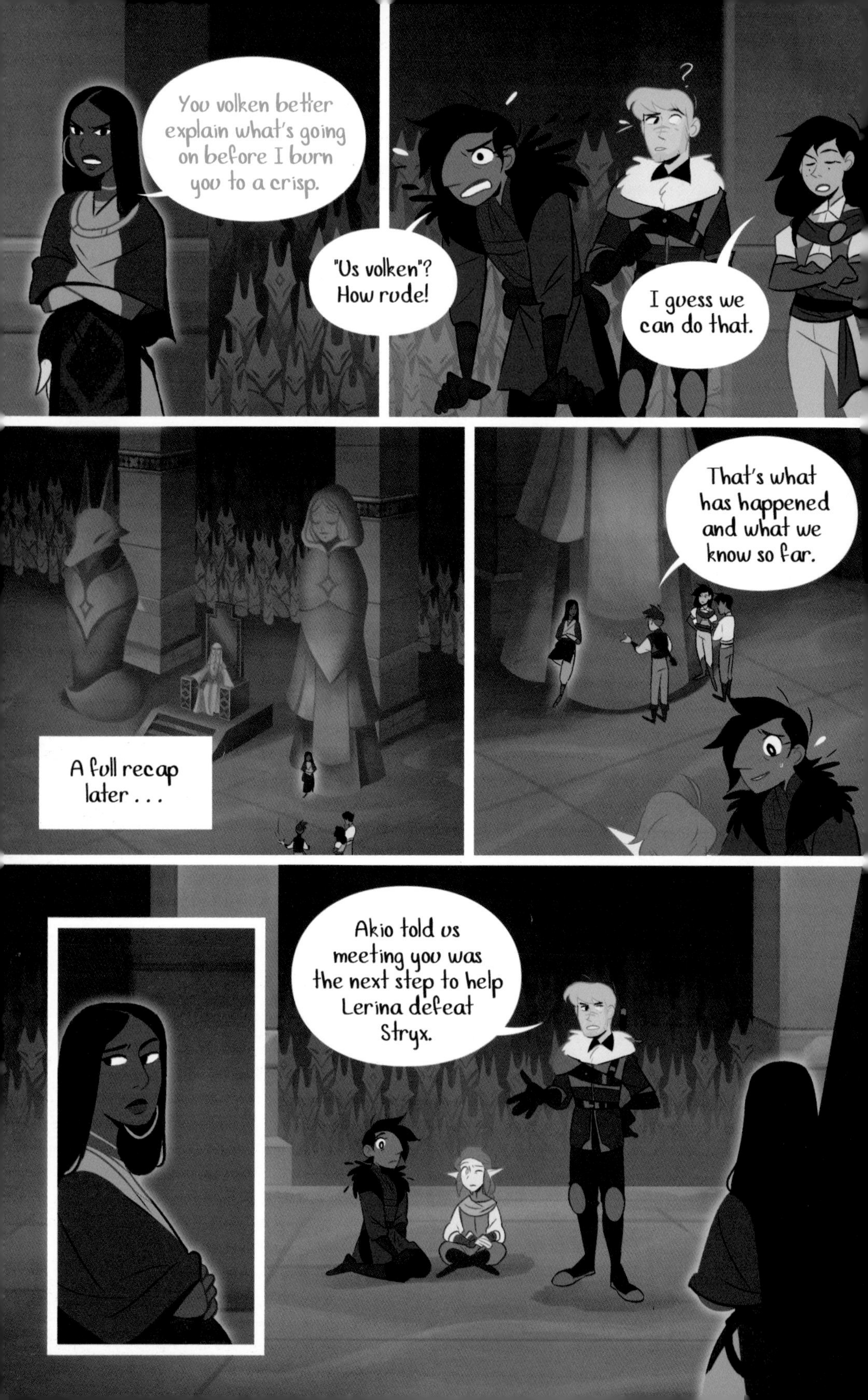
You volken better explain what's going on before I burn you to a crisp.
"Us volken"? How rude!
I guess we can do that.
A full recap later . . .
That's what has happened and what we know so far.
Akio told us meeting you was the next step to help Lerina defeat Stryx.

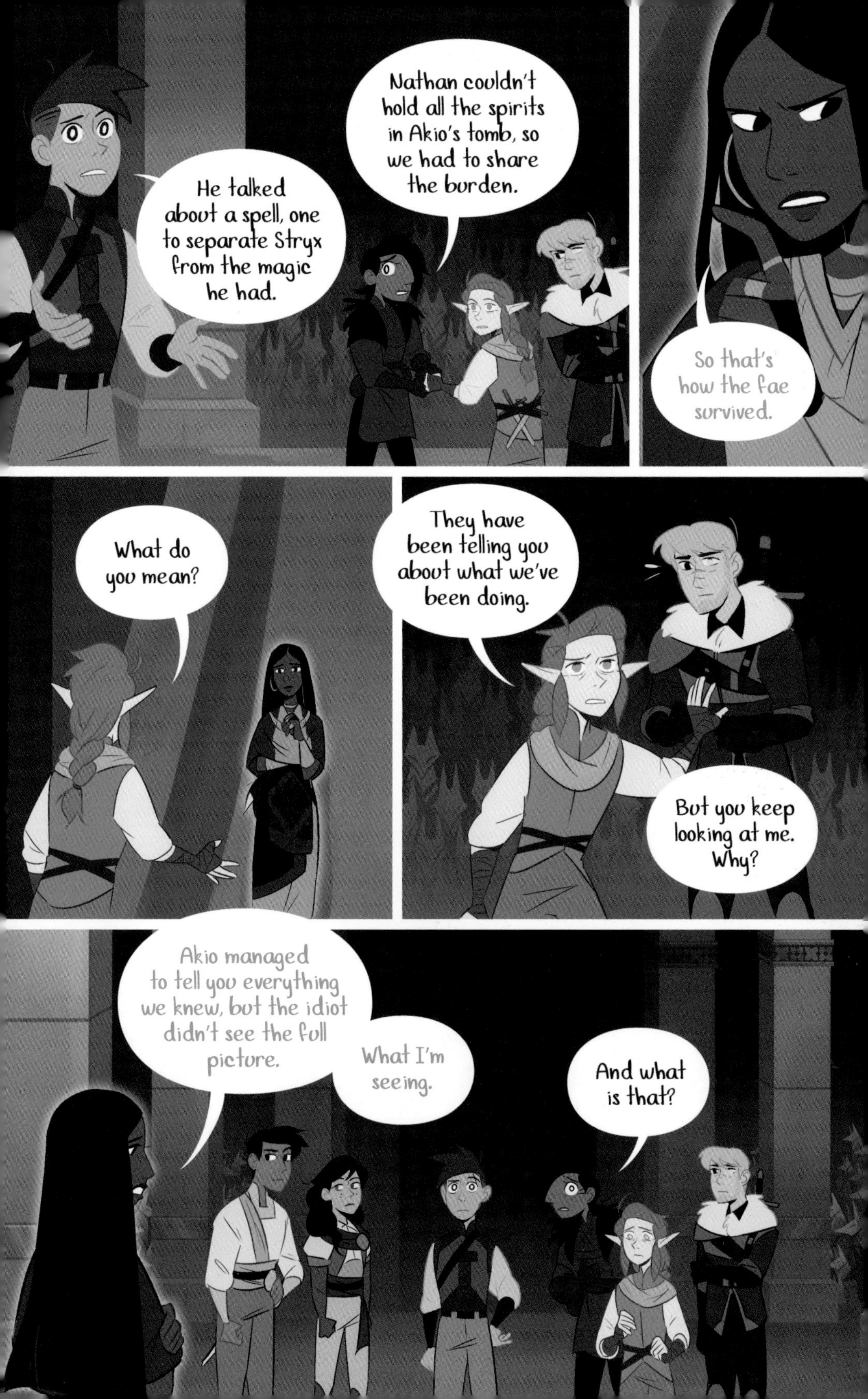
He talked about a spell, one to separate Stryx from the magic he had.
Nathan couldn't hold all the spirits in Akio's tomb, so we had to share the burden.
So that's how the fae survived.
What do you mean?
They have been telling you about what we've been doing.
But you keep looking at me. Why?
Akio managed to tell you everything we knew, but the idiot didn't see the full picture.
What I'm seeing.
And what is that?

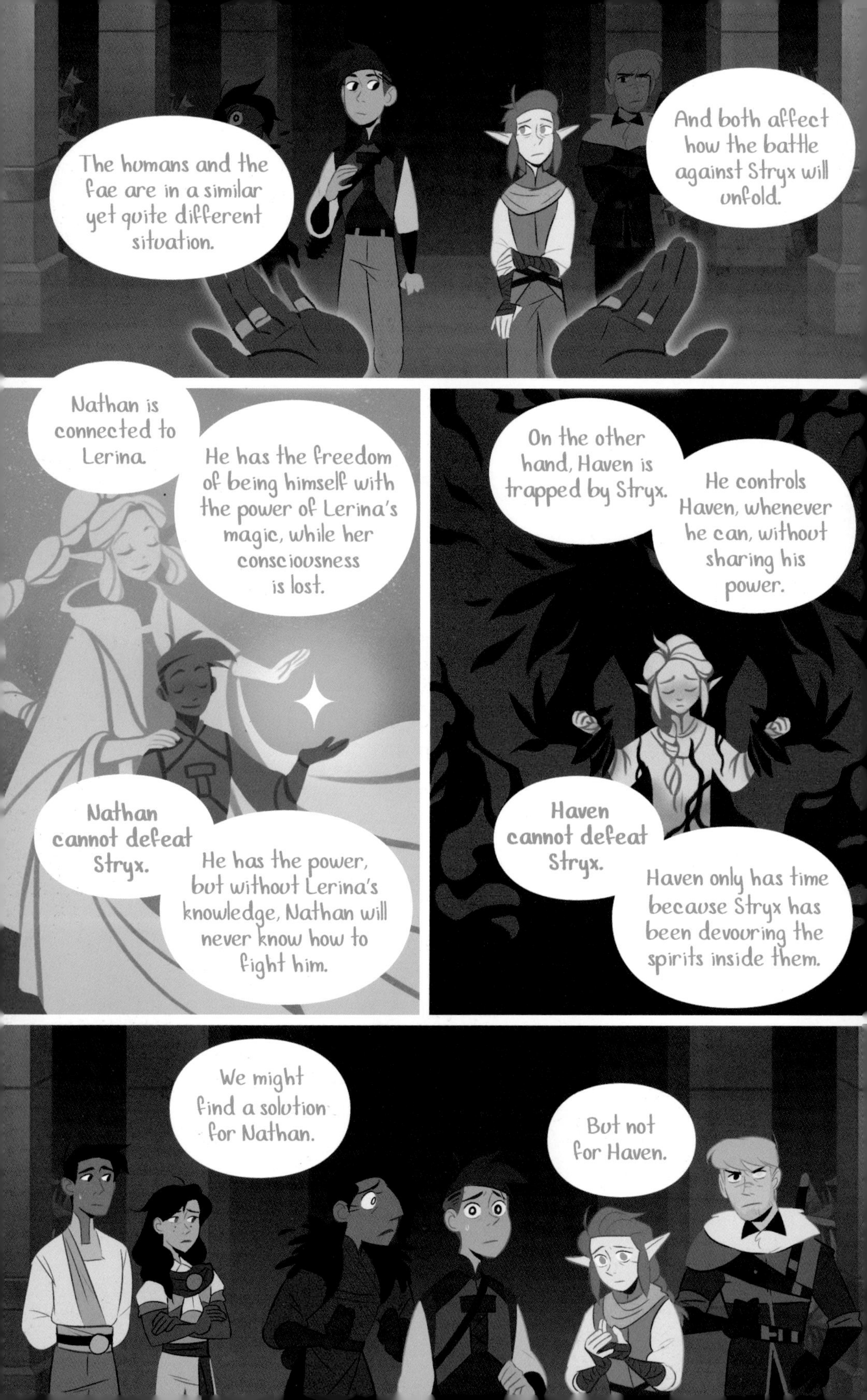
The humans and the fae are in a similar yet quite different situation.
And both affect how the battle against Stryx will unfold.
Nathan is connected to Lerina.
He has the freedom of being himself with the power of Lerina's magic, while her consciousness is lost.
Nathan cannot defeat Stryx.
He has the power, but without Lerina's knowledge, Nathan will never know how to fight him.
On the other hand, Haven is trapped by Stryx.
He controls Haven, whenever he can, without sharing his power.
Haven cannot defeat Stryx.
Haven only has time because Stryx has been devouring the spirits inside them.
We might find a solution for Nathan.
But not for Haven.

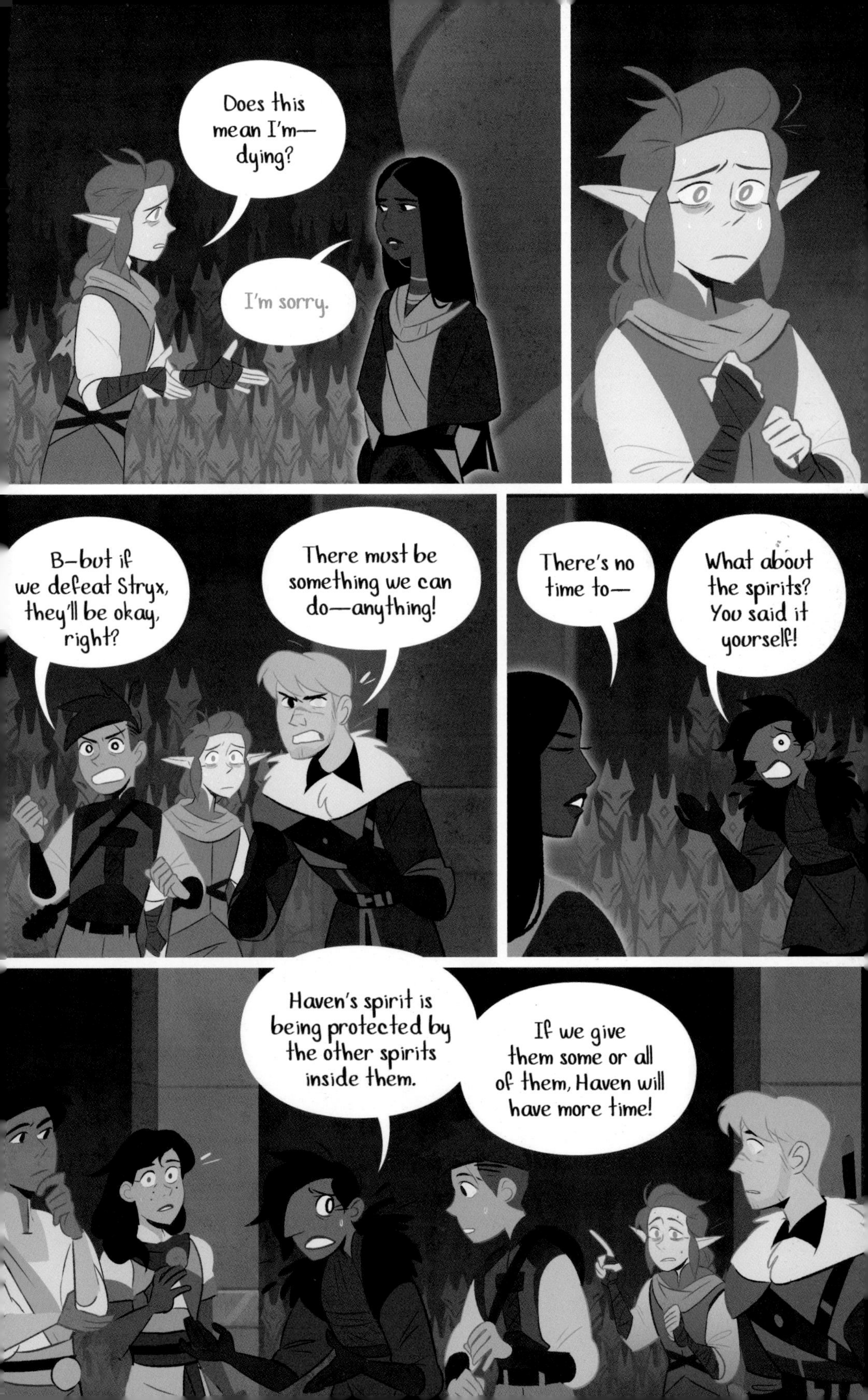
Does this mean I'm—dying?
I'm sorry.
B-but if we defeat Stryx, they'll be okay, right?
There must be something we can do—anything!
There's no time to—
What about the spirits? You said it yourself!
Haven's spirit is being protected by the other spirits inside them.
If we give them some or all of them, Haven will have more time!

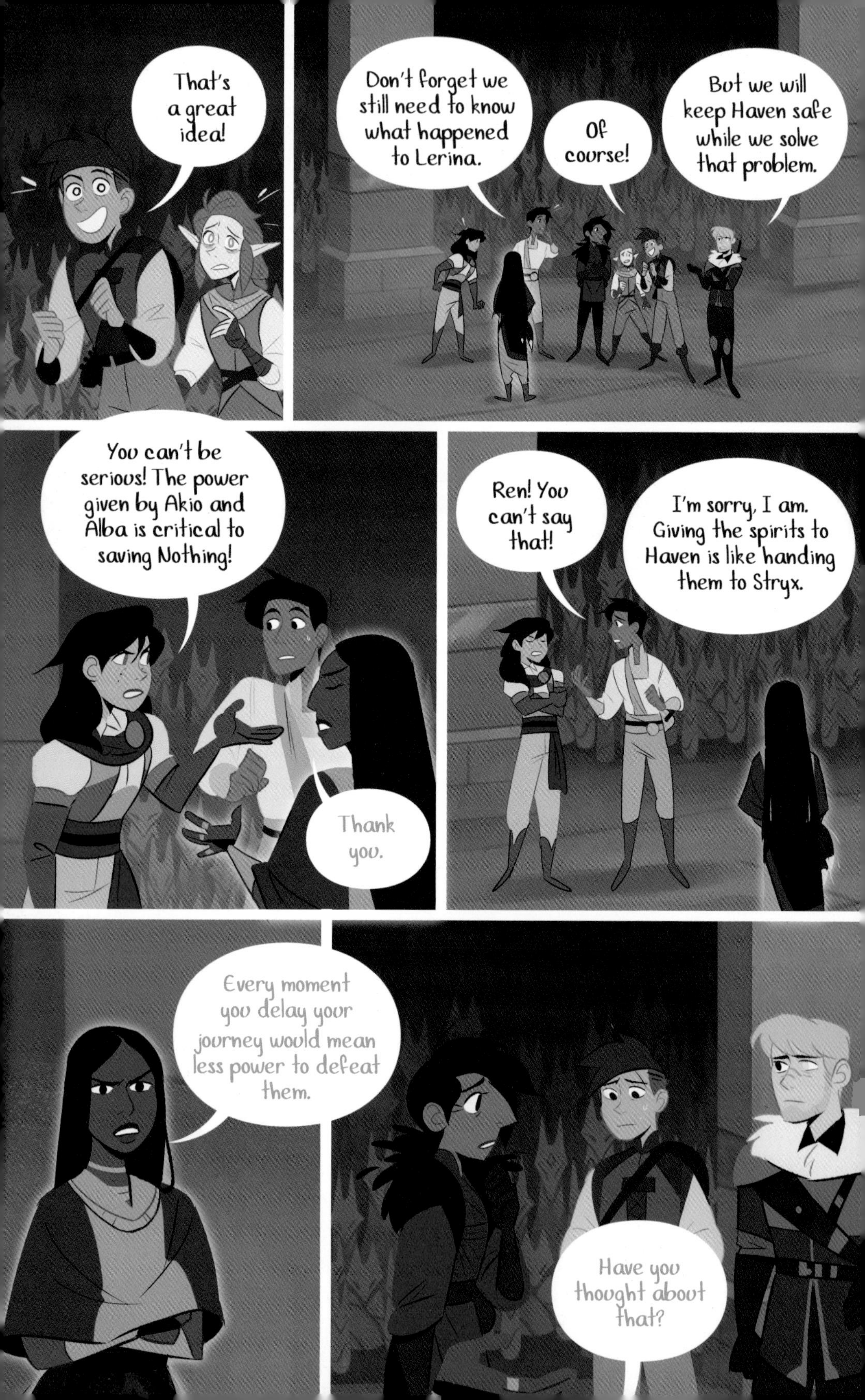
That's a great idea!
Don't forget we still need to know what happened to Lerina.
Of course!
But we will keep Haven safe while we solve that problem.
You can't be serious! The power given by Akio and Alba is critical to saving Nothing!
Thank you.
Ren! You can't say that!
I'm sorry, I am. Giving the spirits to Haven is like handing them to Stryx.
Every moment you delay your journey would mean less power to defeat them.
Have you thought about that?

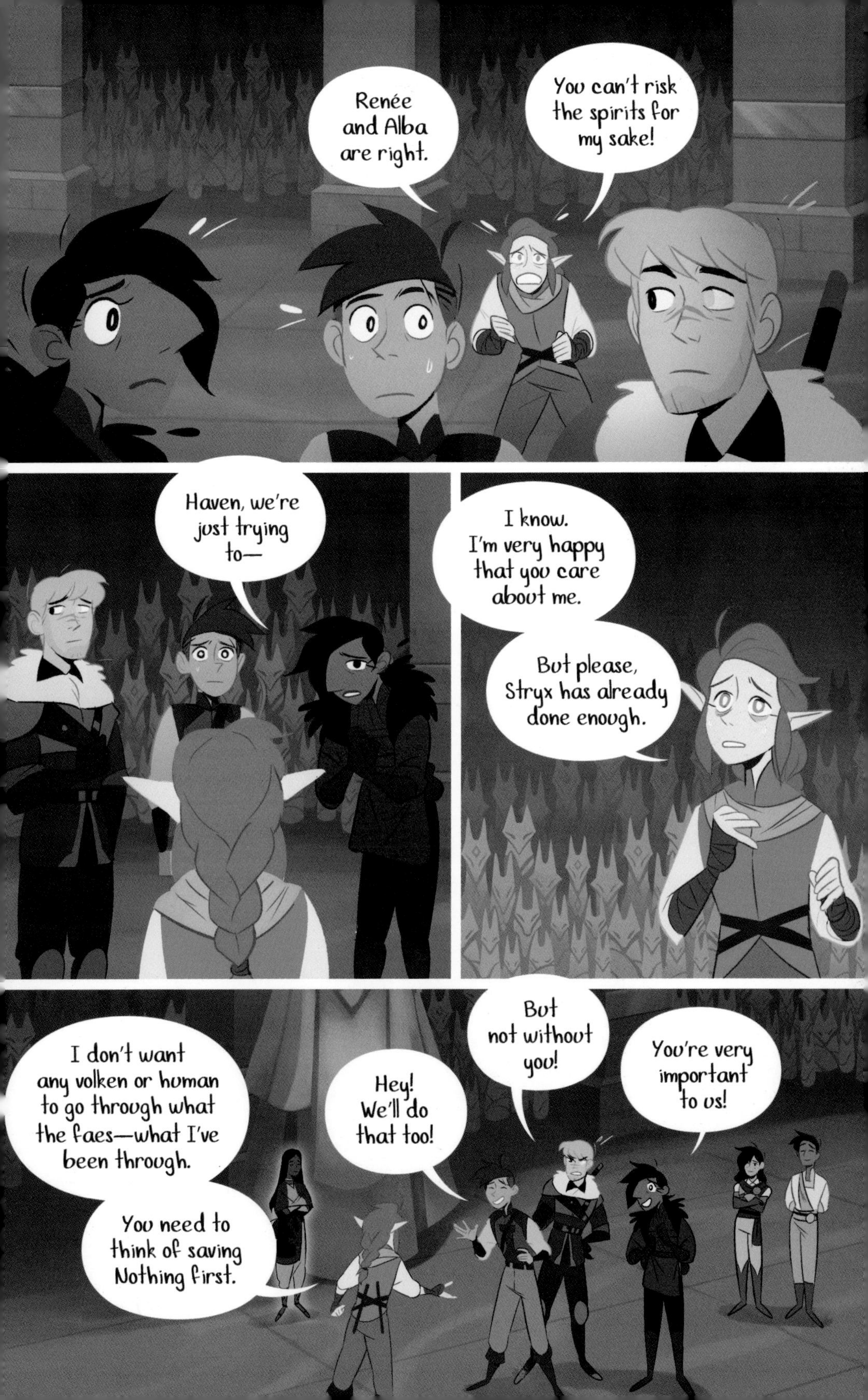
Renée and Alba are right.
You can't risk the spirits for my sake!
Haven, we're just trying to—
I know. I'm very happy that you care about me.
But please, Stryx has already done enough.
I don't want any volken or human to go through what the faes—what I've been through.
You need to think of saving Nothing first.
Hey! We'll do that too!
But not without you!
You're very important to us!

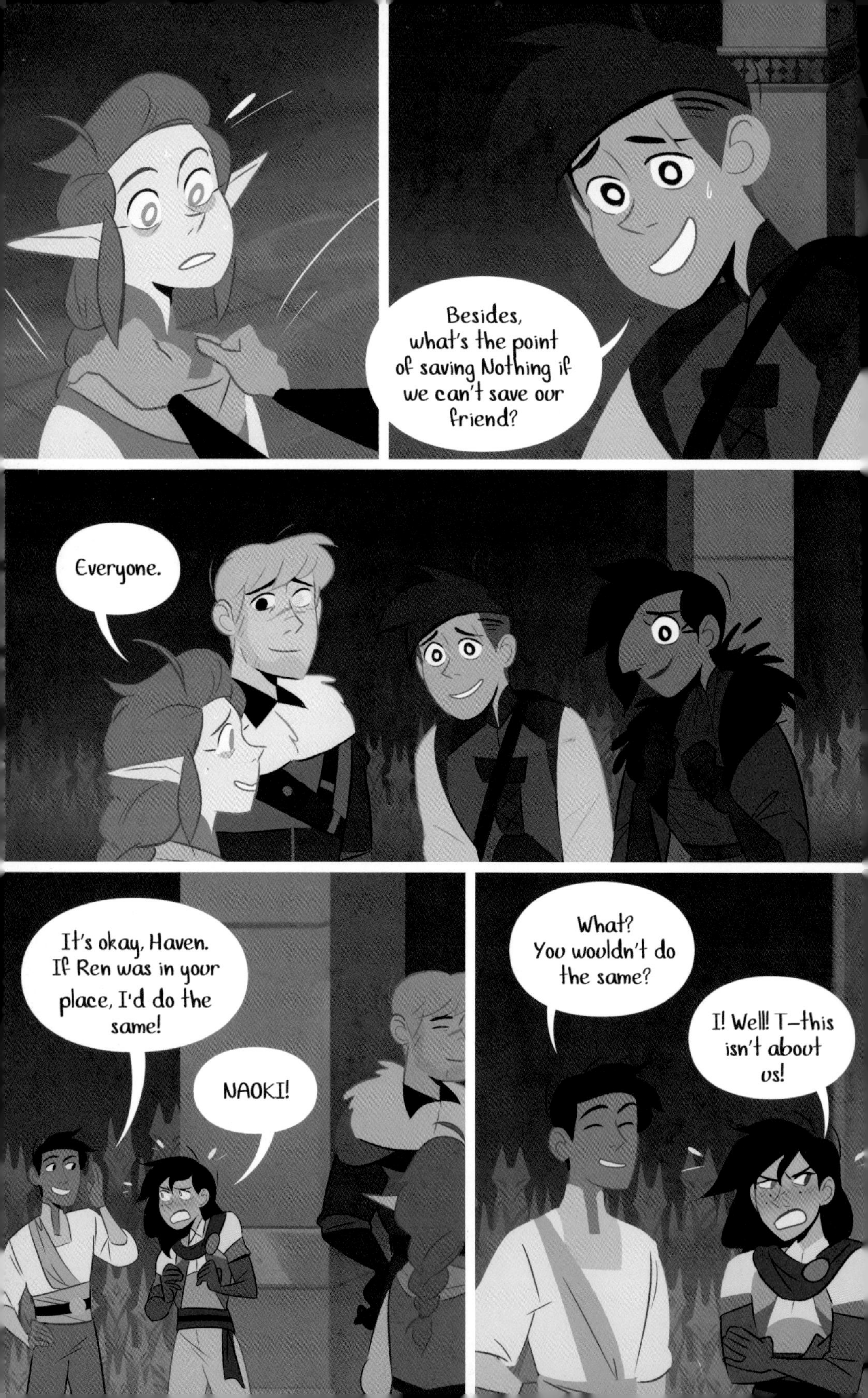
Besides, what's the point of saving Nothing if we can't save our friend?
Everyone.
It's okay, Haven. If Ren was in your place, I'd do the same!
NAOKI!
What? You wouldn't do the same?
I! Well! T—this isn't about us!

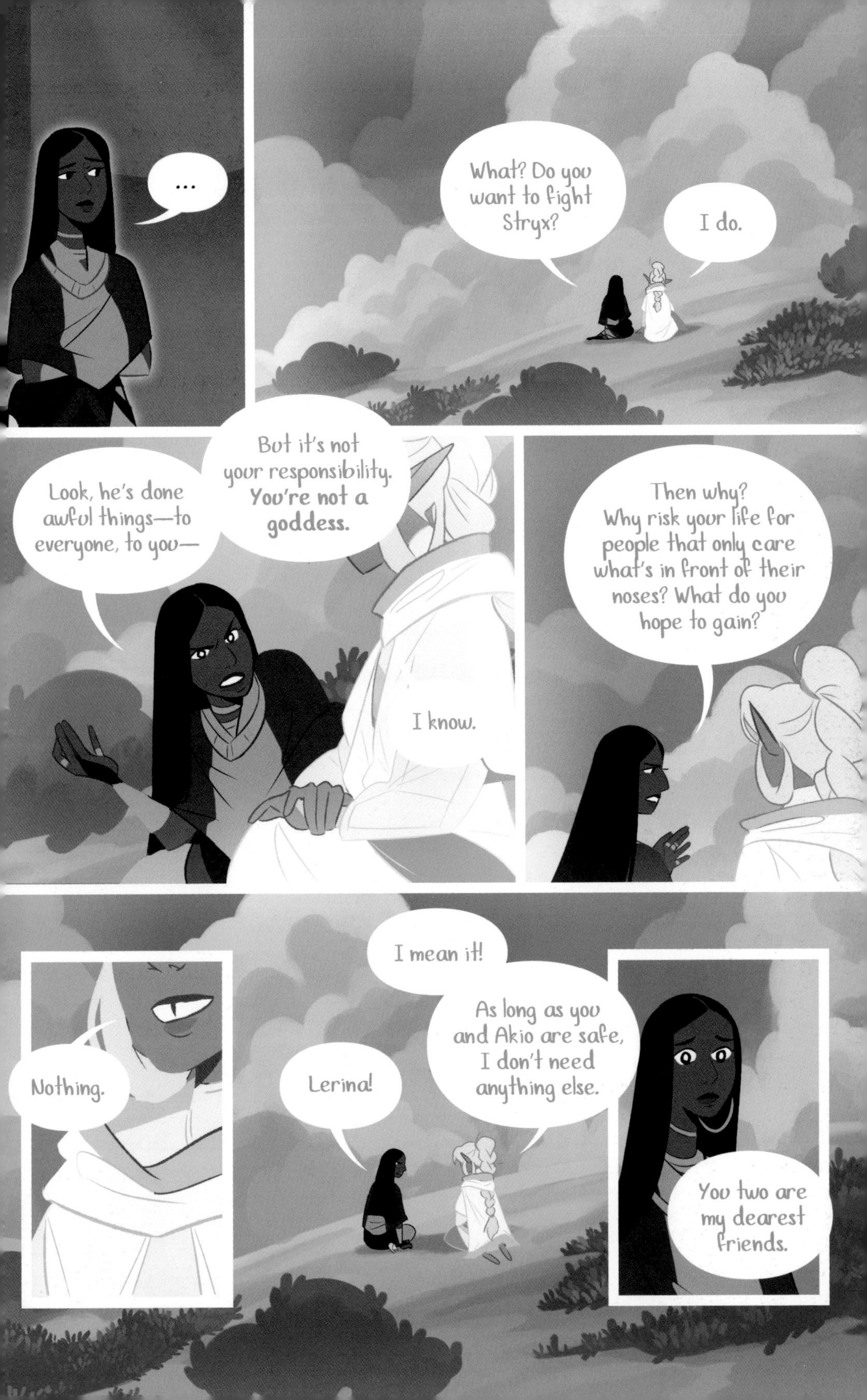
...
What? Do you want to fight Stryx?
I do.
Look, he's done awful things—to everyone, to you—
But it's not your responsibility. You're not a goddess.
I know.
Then why? Why risk your life for people that only care what's in front of their noses? What do you hope to gain?
Nothing.
I mean it!
Lerina!
As long as you and Akio are safe, I don't need anything else.
You two are my dearest friends.

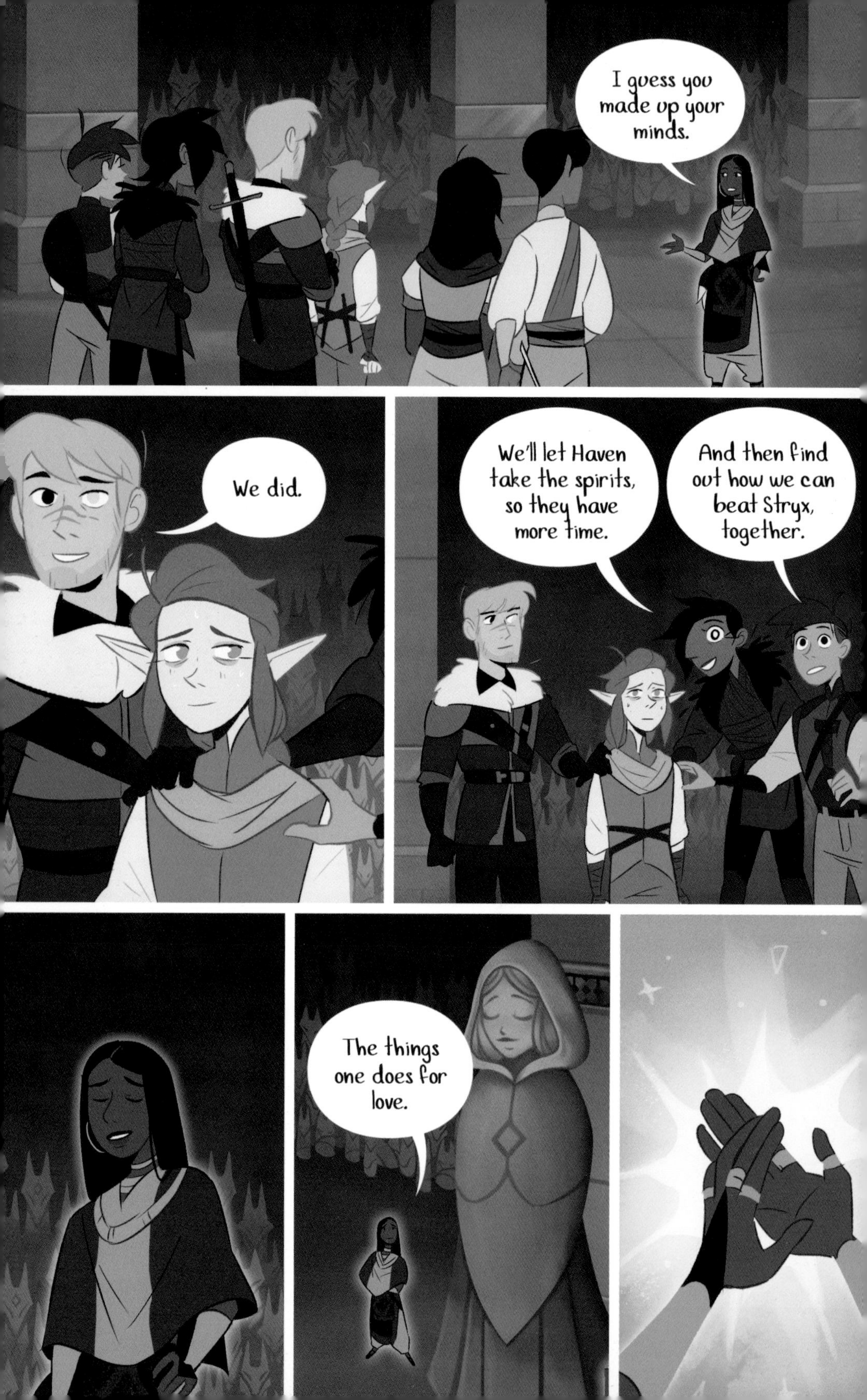
I guess you made up your minds.
We did.
We'll let Haven take the spirits, so they have more time.
And then find out how we can beat Stryx, together.
The things one does for love.

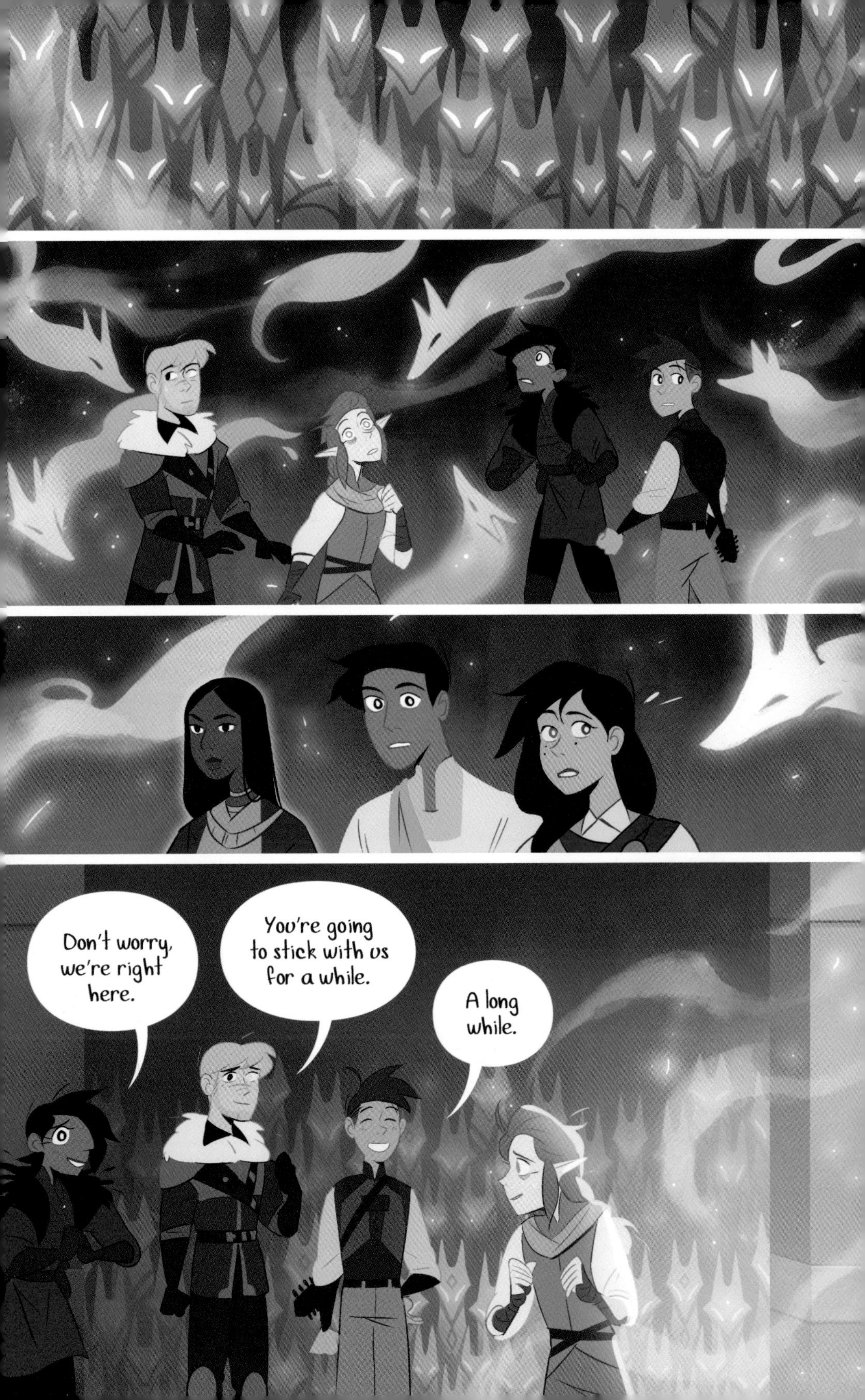
Don't worry, we're right here.
You're going to stick with us for a while.
A long while.

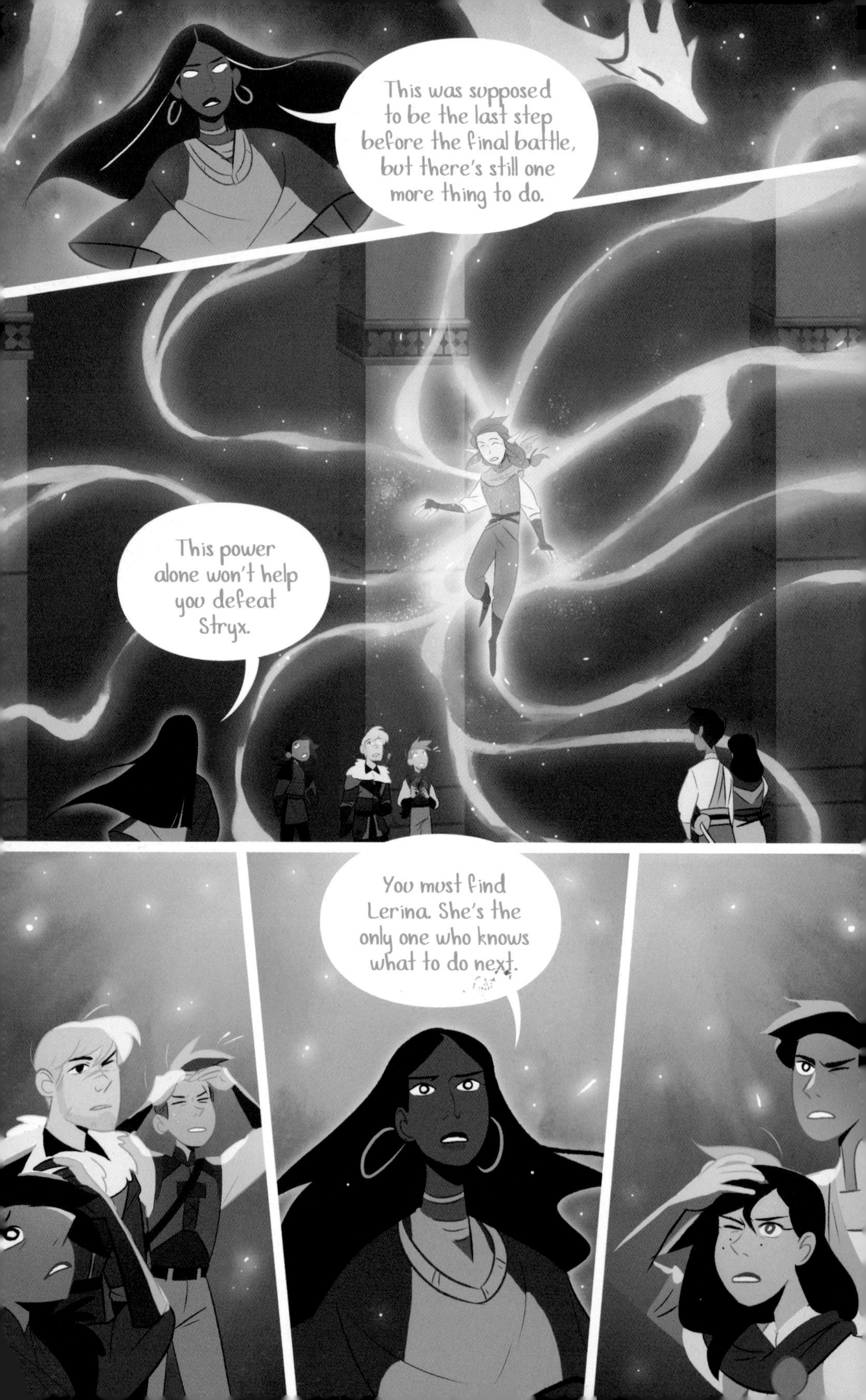
This was supposed to be the last step before the final battle, but there's still one more thing to do.
This power alone won't help you defeat Stryx.
You must find Lerina. She's the only one who knows what to do next.

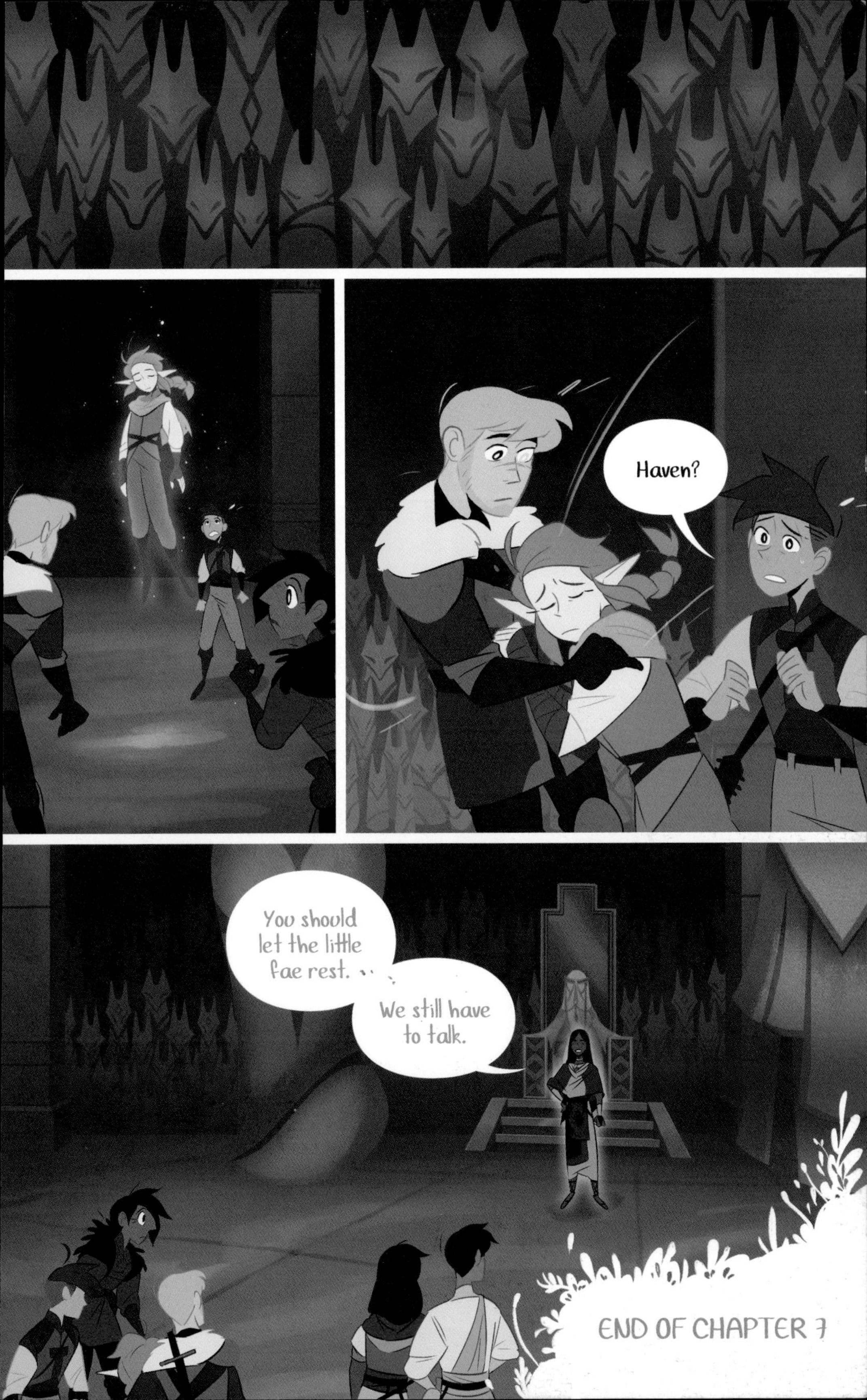
Haven?
You should let the little fae rest.
We still have to talk.
END OF CHAPTER 7

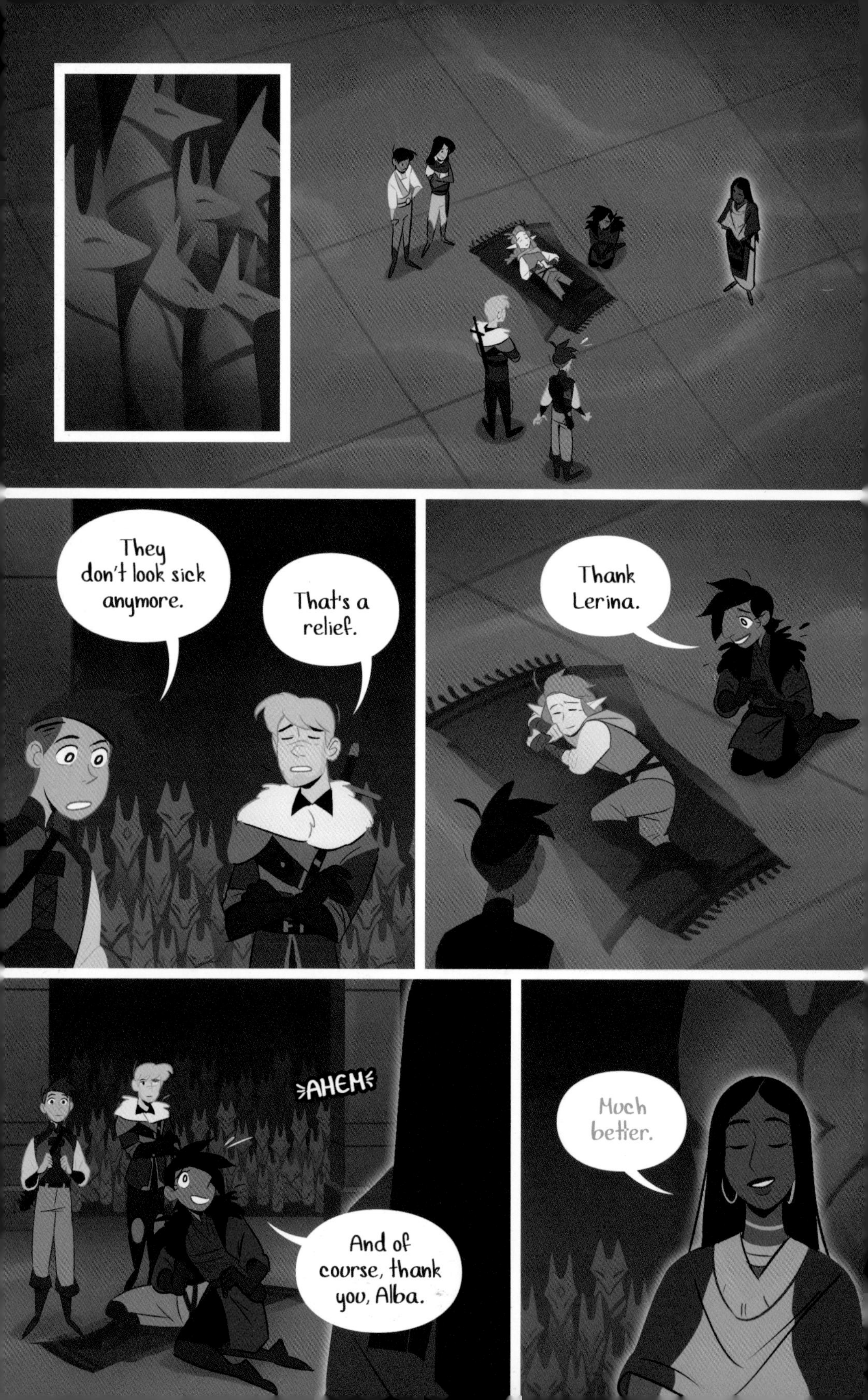

They don't look sick anymore.
That's a relief.
Thank Lerina.
AHEM
And of course, thank you, Alba.
Much better.

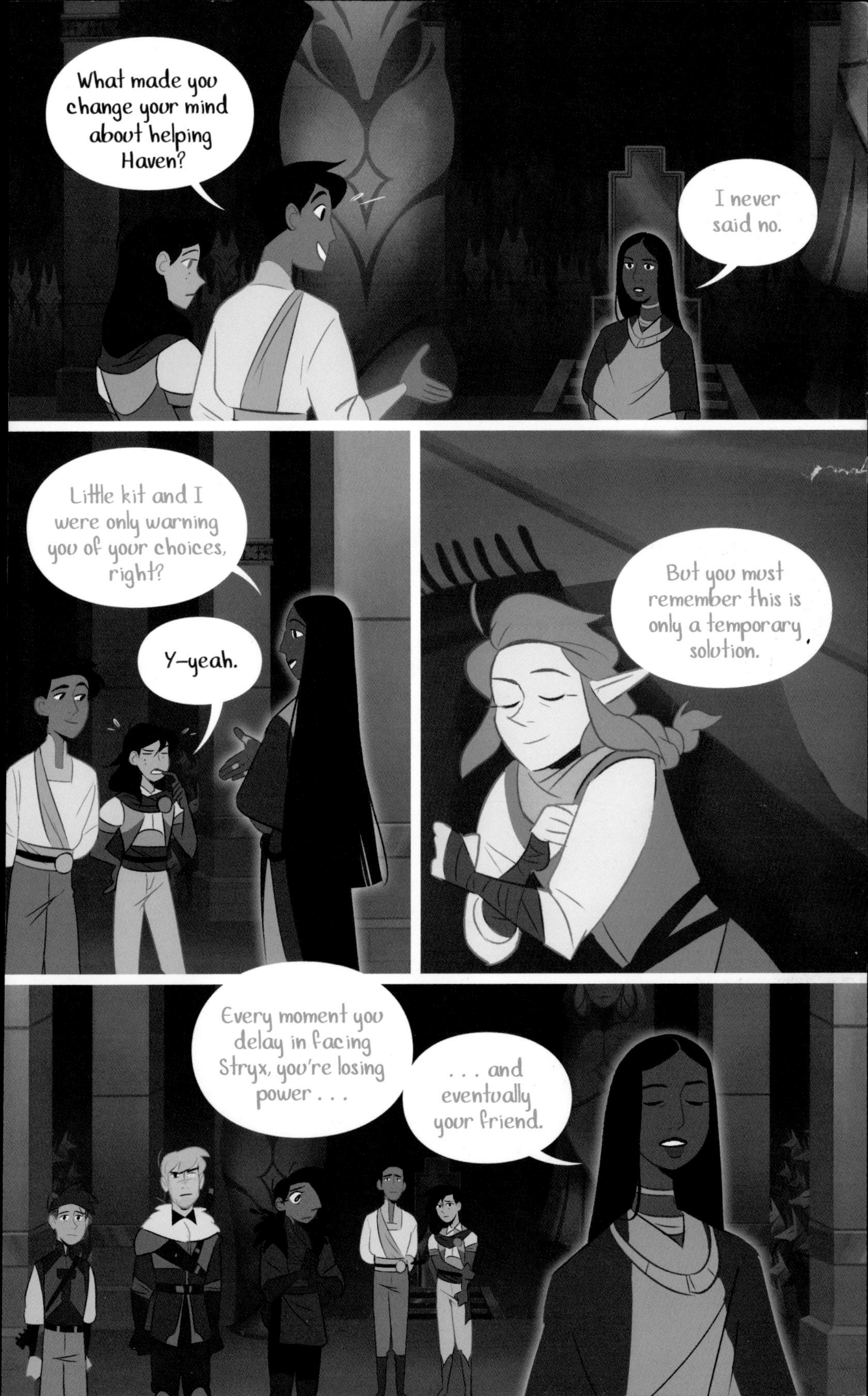
What made you change your mind about helping Haven?
I never said no.
Little kit and I were only warning you of your choices, right?
Y-yeah.
But you must remember this is only a temporary solution.
Every moment you delay in facing Stryx, you're losing power . . .
. . . and eventually your friend.

## Chapter 8
# The Fox-gotten

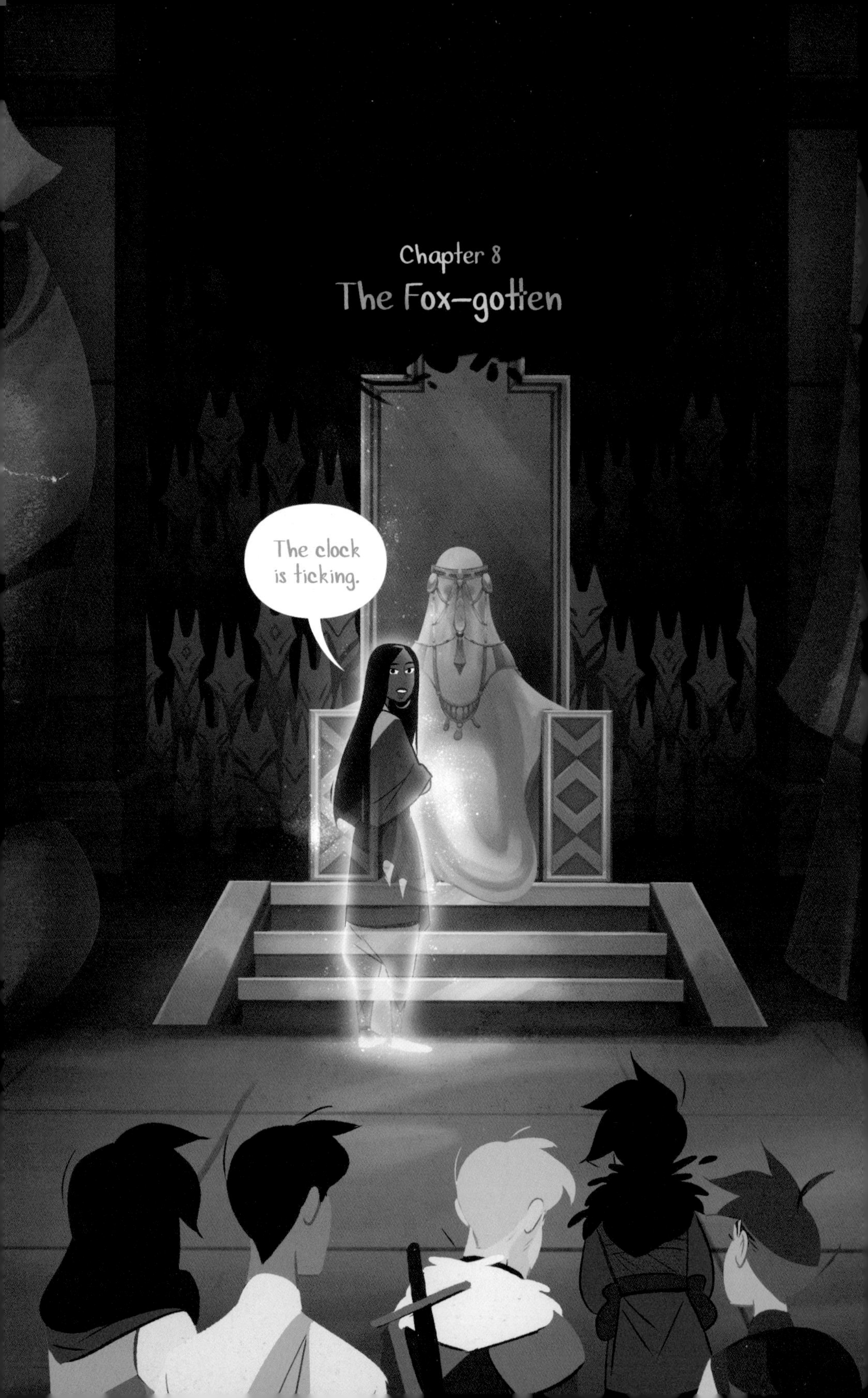
The clock is ticking.

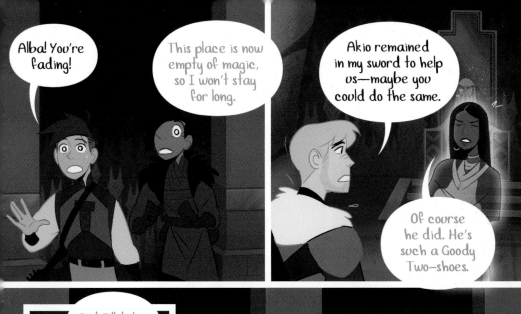

Alba! You're fading!

This place is now empty of magic, so I won't stay for long.

Akio remained in my sword to help us—maybe you could do the same.

Of course he did. He's such a Goody Two-shoes.

But I'll take your advice.

There's no way I can let him be the only one who gets to see Lerina again.

HA HA HA HA HA HA HA

Okay, so! You said we need to find Lerina.

That's right, you should go to That City.

What cit—

Don't!

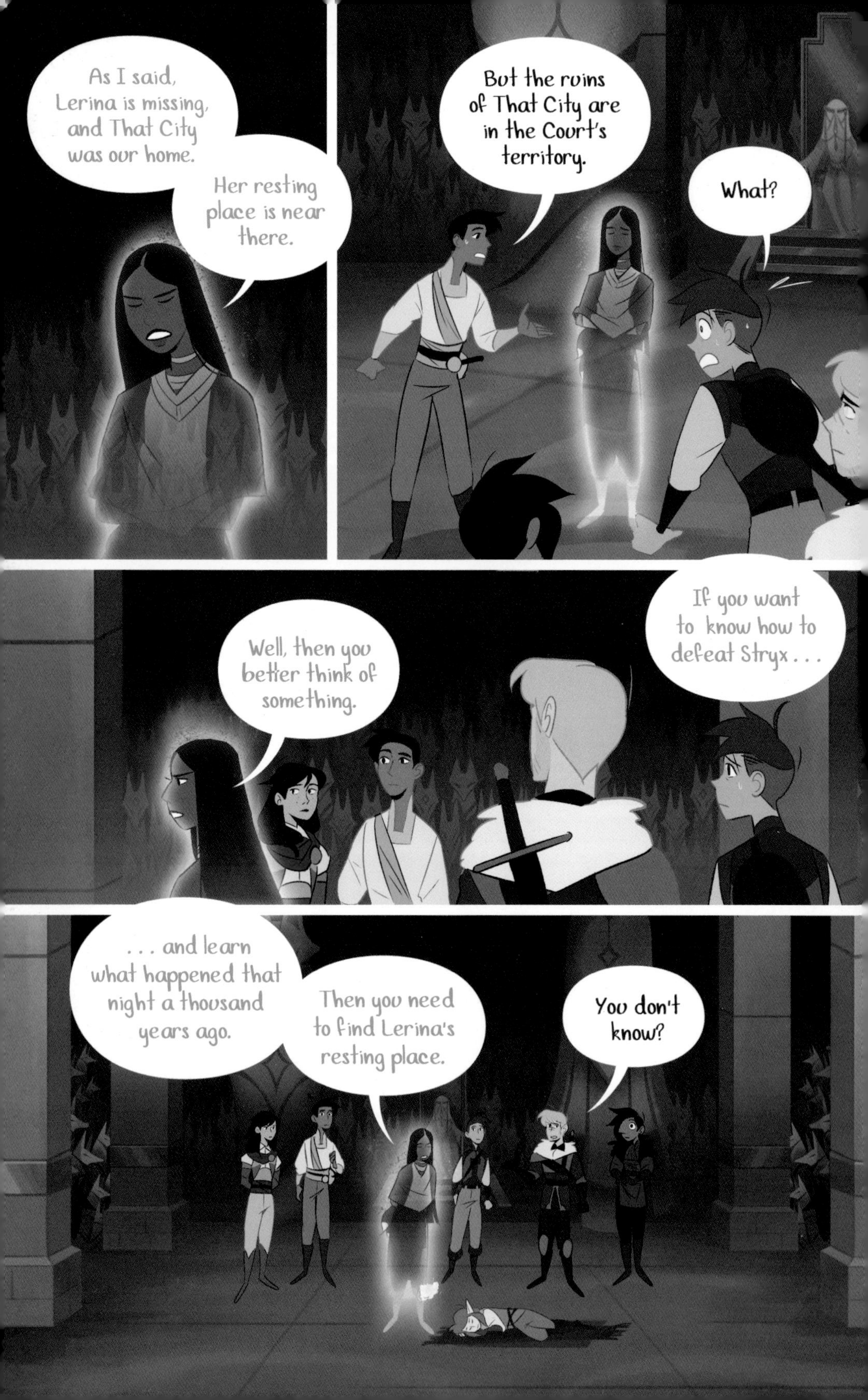
As I said, Lerina is missing, and That City was our home.
Her resting place is near there.
But the ruins of That City are in the Court's territory.
What?
Well, then you better think of something.
If you want to know how to defeat Stryx . . .
. . . and learn what happened that night a thousand years ago.
Then you need to find Lerina's resting place.
You don't know?

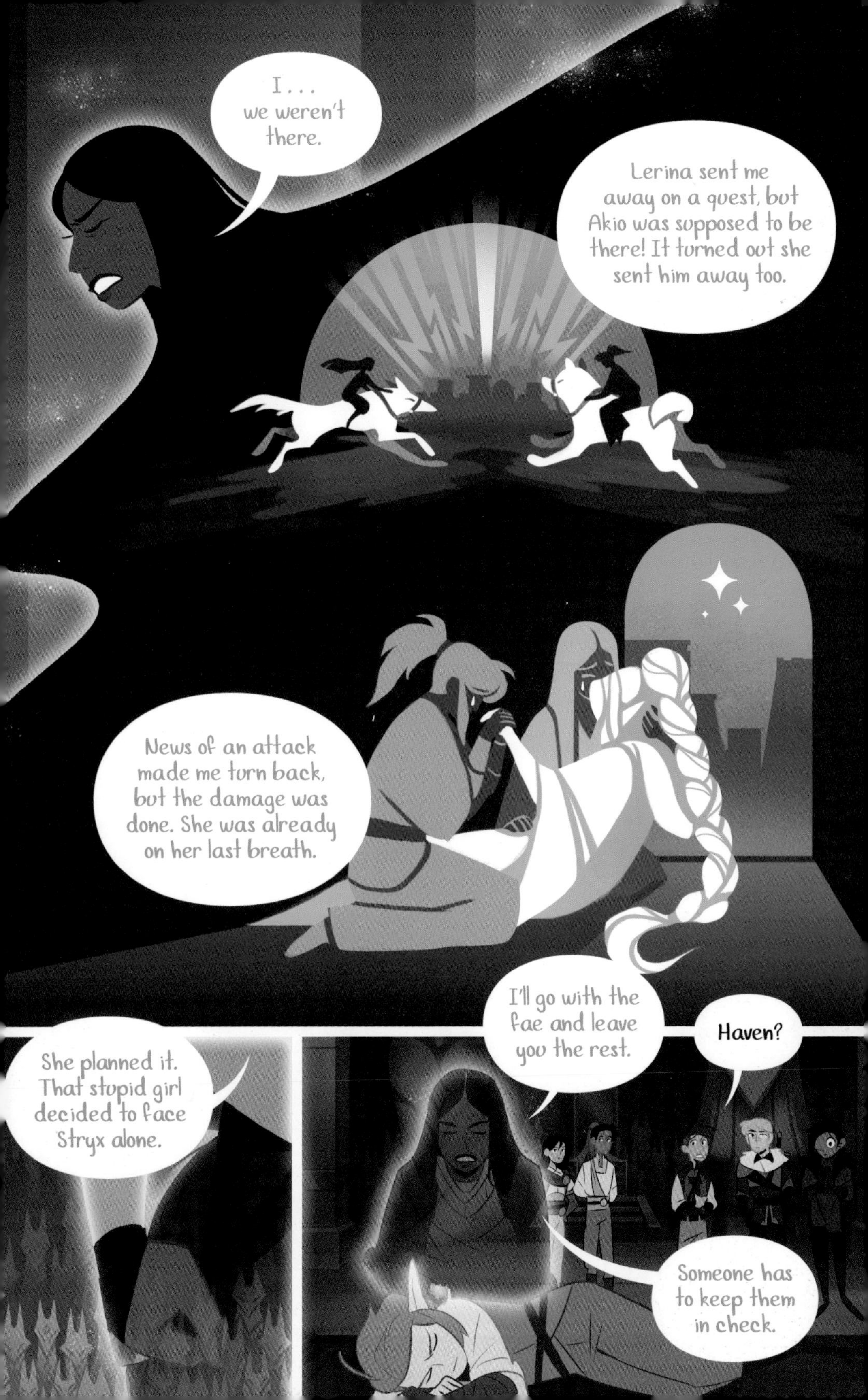
I . . .
we weren't
there.
Lerina sent me away on a quest, but Akio was supposed to be there! It turned out she sent him away too.
News of an attack made me turn back, but the damage was done. She was already on her last breath.
She planned it. That stupid girl decided to face Stryx alone.
I'll go with the fae and leave you the rest.
Haven?
Someone has to keep them in check.

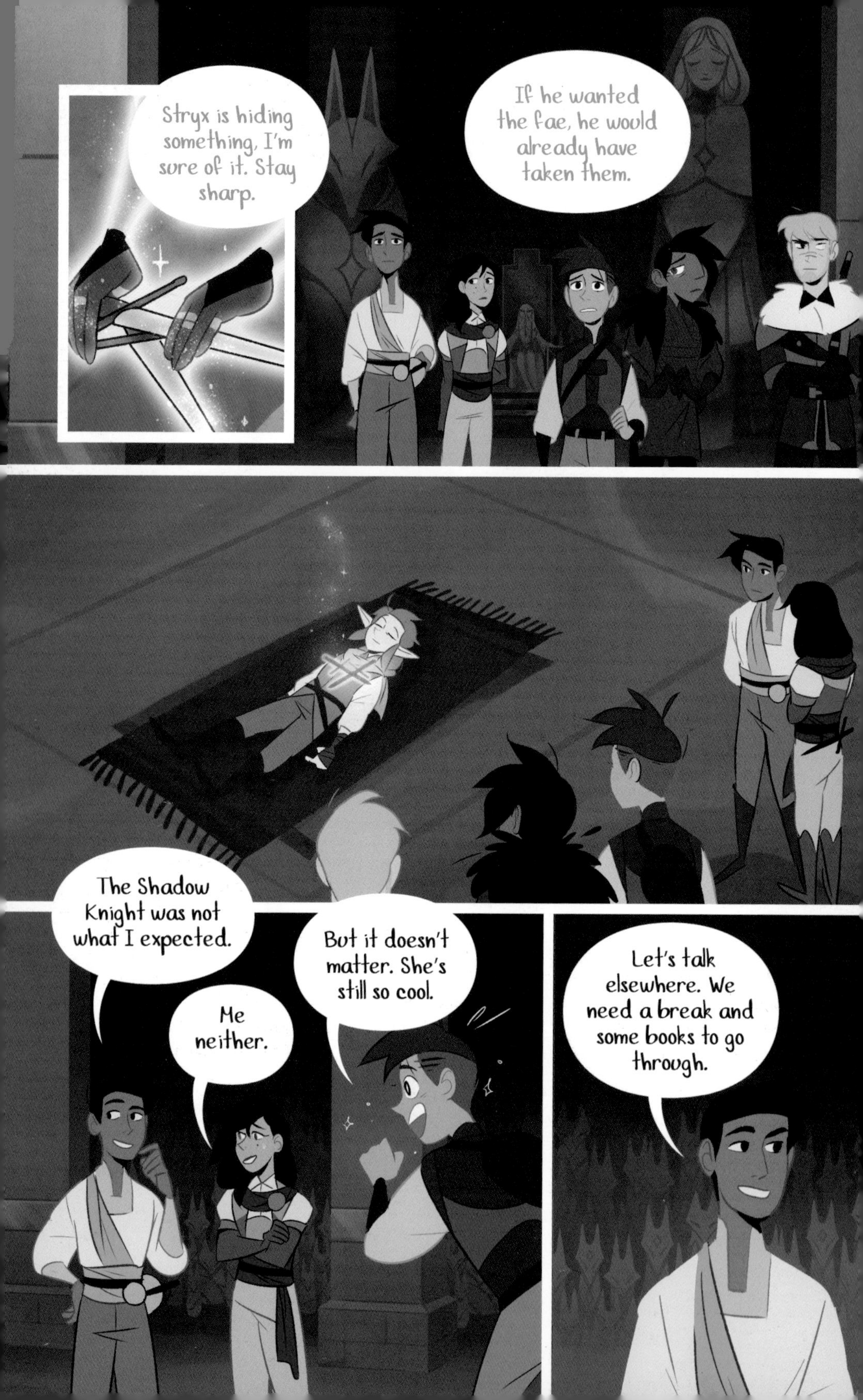
Stryx is hiding something, I'm sure of it. Stay sharp.
If he wanted the fae, he would already have taken them.
The Shadow Knight was not what I expected.
Me neither.
But it doesn't matter. She's still so cool.
Let's talk elsewhere. We need a break and some books to go through.

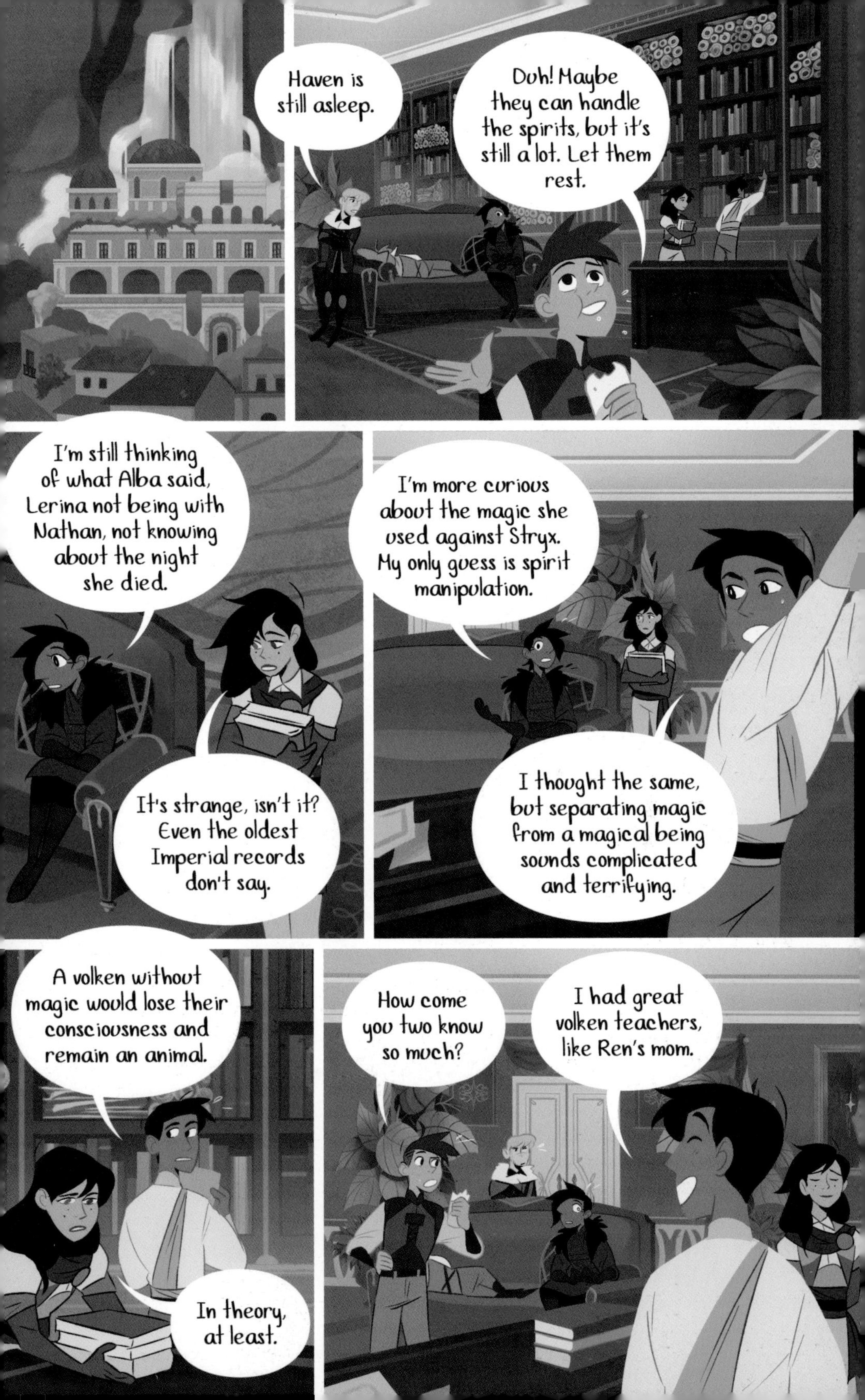
Haven is still asleep.
Duh! Maybe they can handle the spirits, but it's still a lot. Let them rest.
I'm still thinking of what Alba said, Lerina not being with Nathan, not knowing about the night she died.
It's strange, isn't it? Even the oldest Imperial records don't say.
I'm more curious about the magic she used against Stryx. My only guess is spirit manipulation.
I thought the same, but separating magic from a magical being sounds complicated and terrifying.
A volken without magic would lose their consciousness and remain an animal.
In theory, at least.
How come you two know so much?
I had great volken teachers, like Ren's mom.

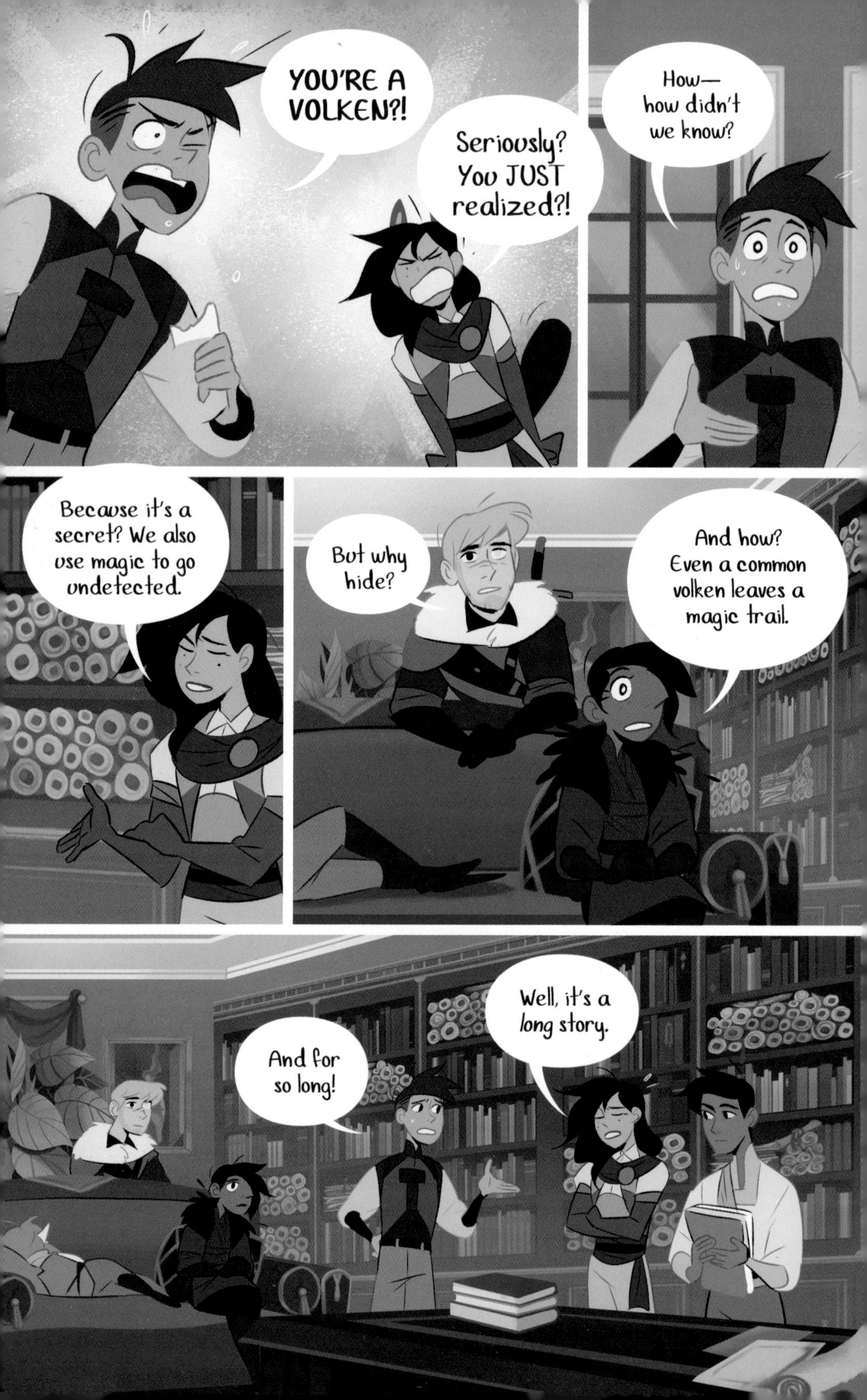
YOU'RE A VOLKEN?!
Seriously? You JUST realized?!
How— how didn't we know?
Because it's a secret? We also use magic to go undetected.
But why hide?
And how? Even a common volken leaves a magic trail.
And for so long!
Well, it's a long story.

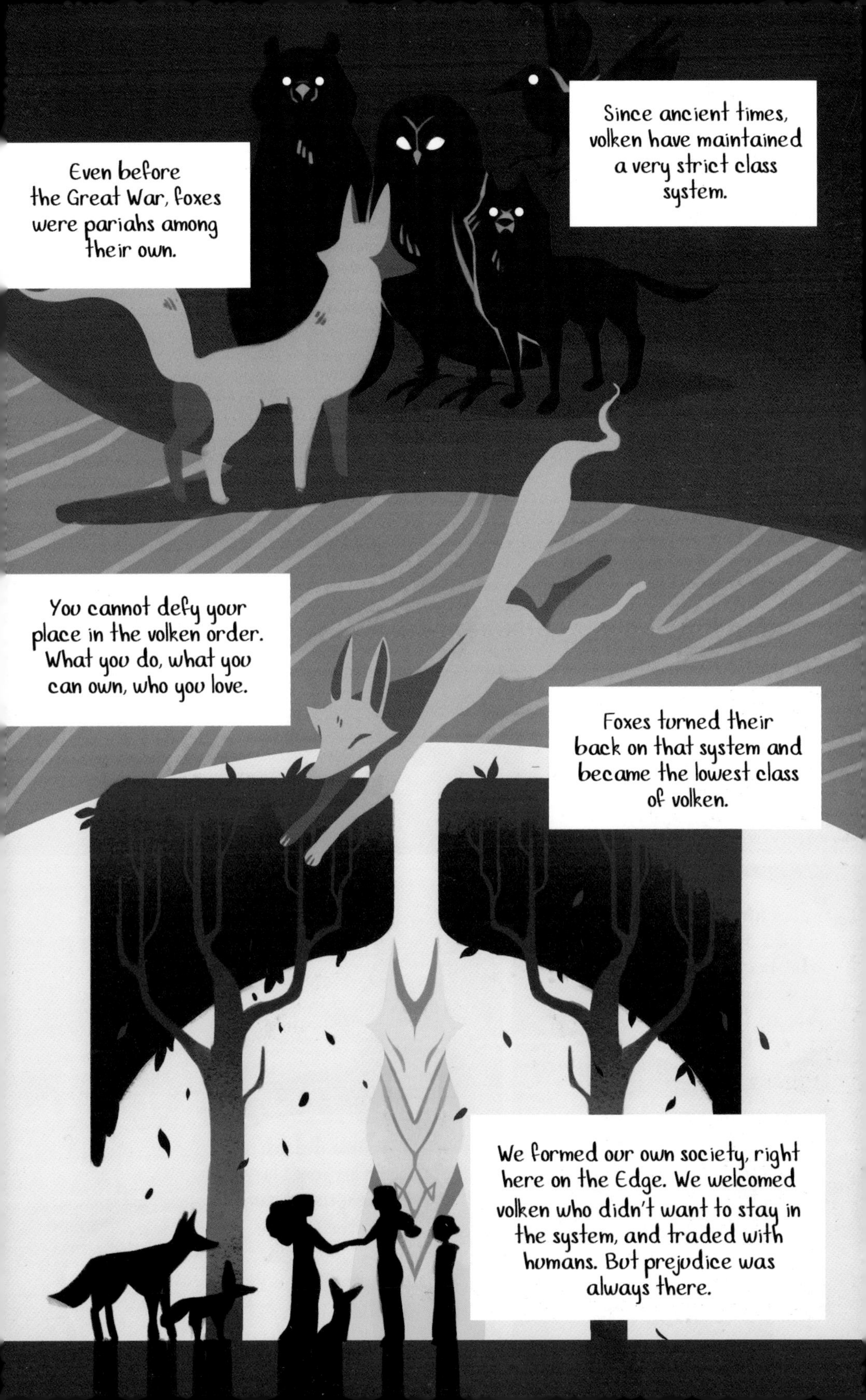
Even before the Great War, foxes were pariahs among their own.
Since ancient times, volken have maintained a very strict class system.
You cannot defy your place in the volken order. What you do, what you can own, who you love.
Foxes turned their back on that system and became the lowest class of volken.
We formed our own society, right here on the Edge. We welcomed volken who didn't want to stay in the system, and traded with humans. But prejudice was always there.

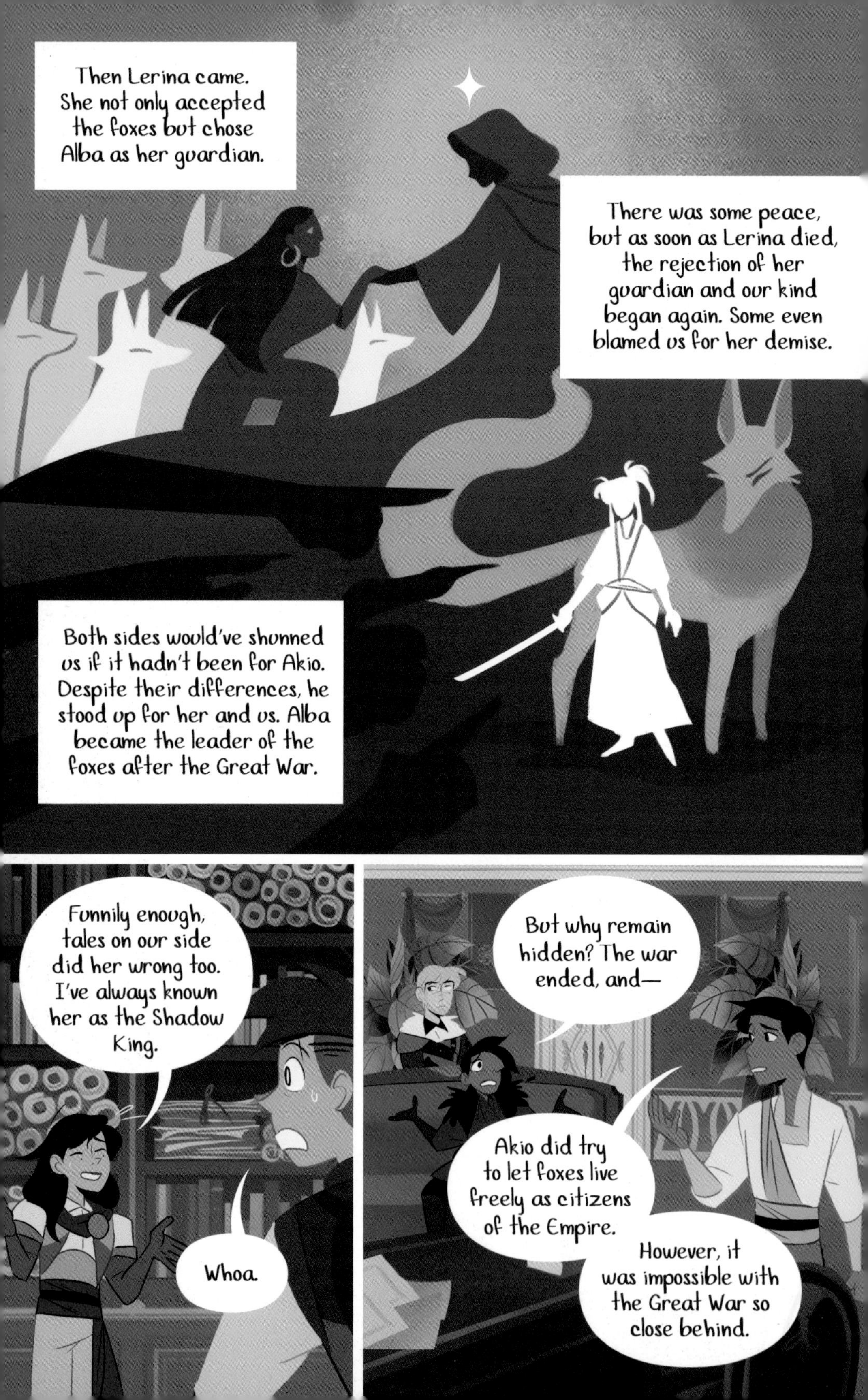
Then Lerina came. She not only accepted the foxes but chose Alba as her guardian.
There was some peace, but as soon as Lerina died, the rejection of her guardian and our kind began again. Some even blamed us for her demise.
Both sides would've shunned us if it hadn't been for Akio. Despite their differences, he stood up for her and us. Alba became the leader of the foxes after the Great War.
Funnily enough, tales on our side did her wrong too. I've always known her as the Shadow King.
Whoa.
But why remain hidden? The war ended, and—
Akio did try to let foxes live freely as citizens of the Empire.
However, it was impossible with the Great War so close behind.

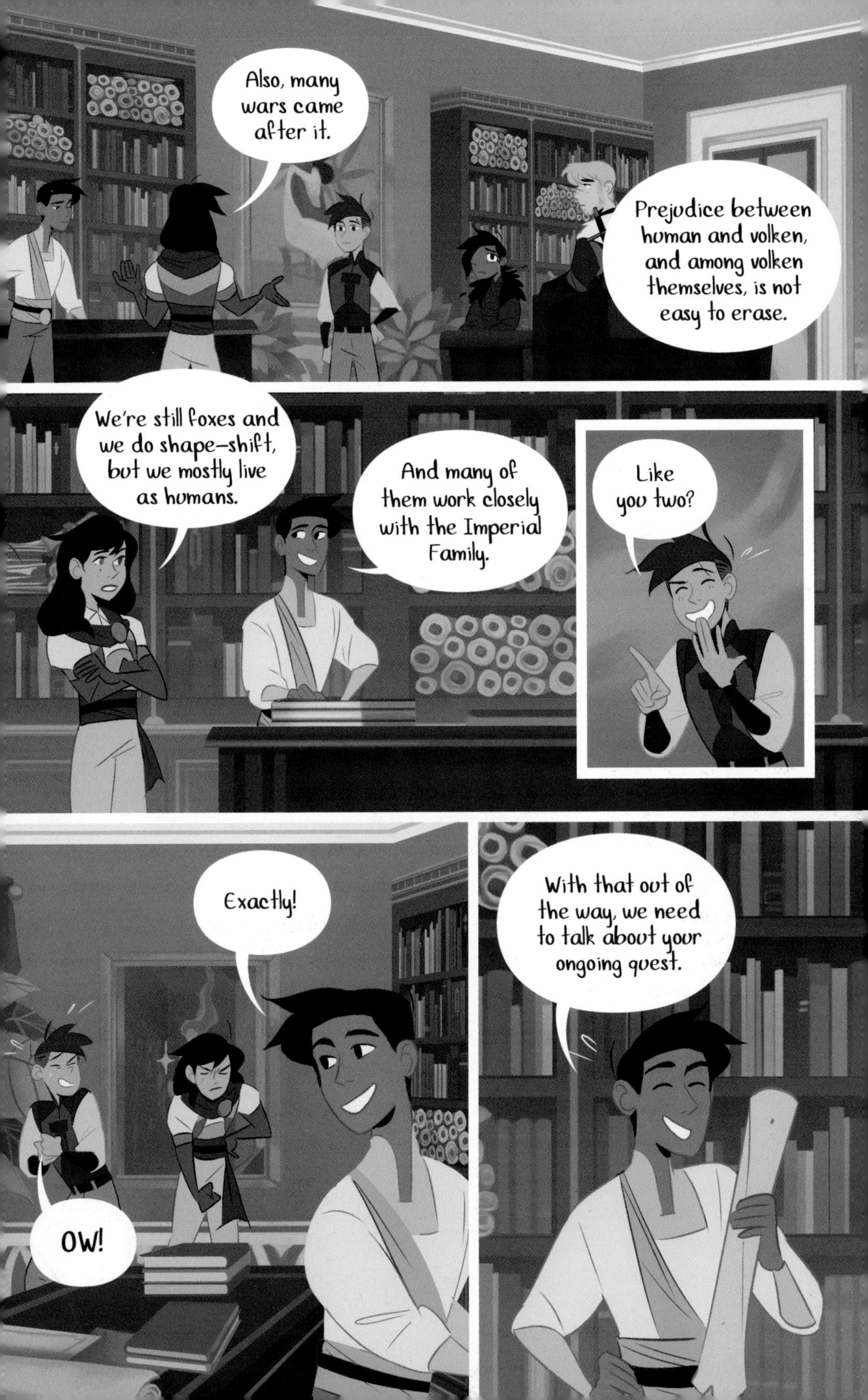
Also, many wars came after it.
Prejudice between human and volken, and among volken themselves, is not easy to erase.
We're still foxes and we do shape-shift, but we mostly live as humans.
And many of them work closely with the Imperial Family.
Like you two?
Exactly!
OW!
With that out of the way, we need to talk about your ongoing quest.

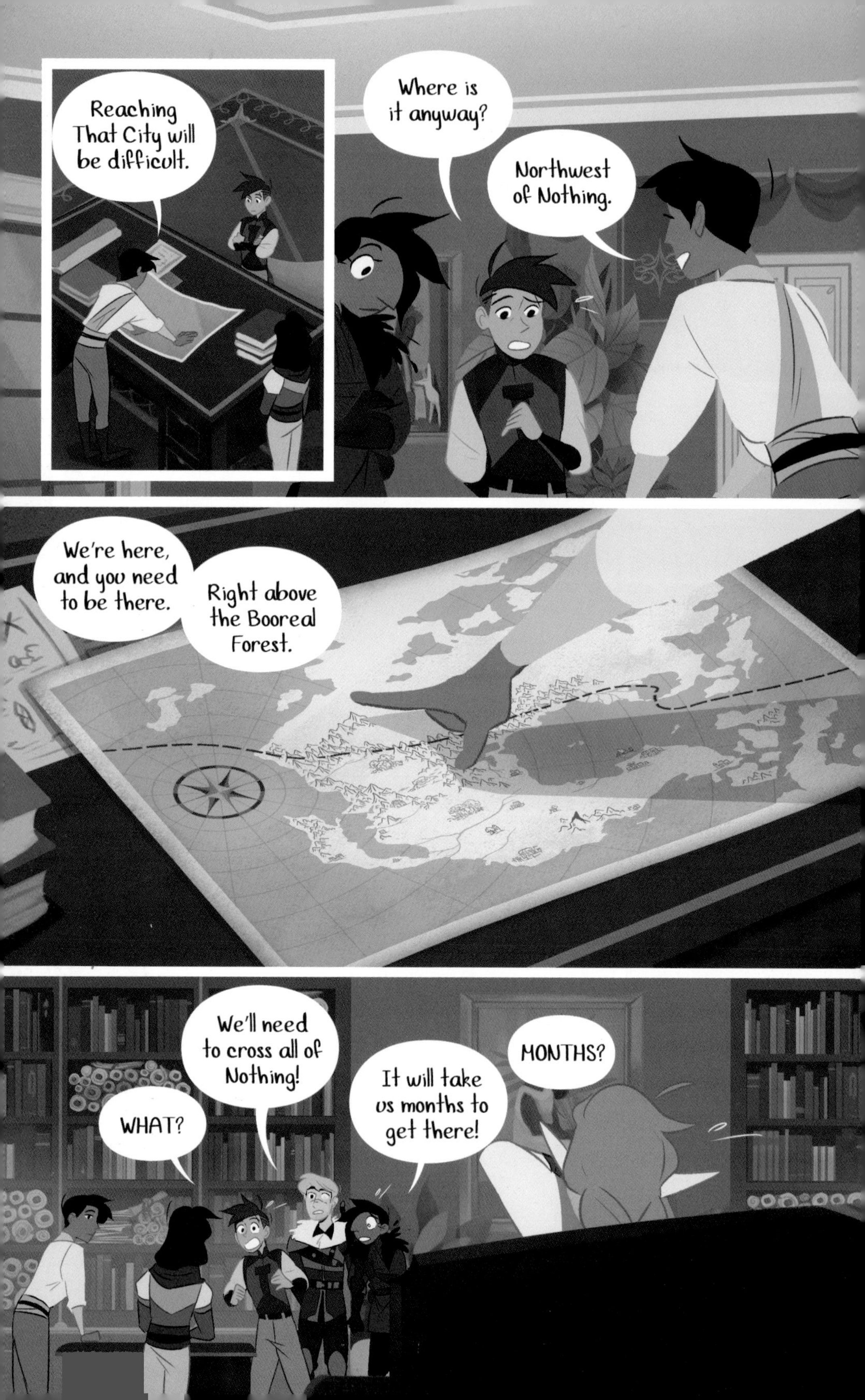
Reaching That City will be difficult.
Where is it anyway?
Northwest of Nothing.
We're here, and you need to be there.
Right above the Booreal Forest.
WHAT?
We'll need to cross all of Nothing!
It will take us months to get there!
MONTHS?

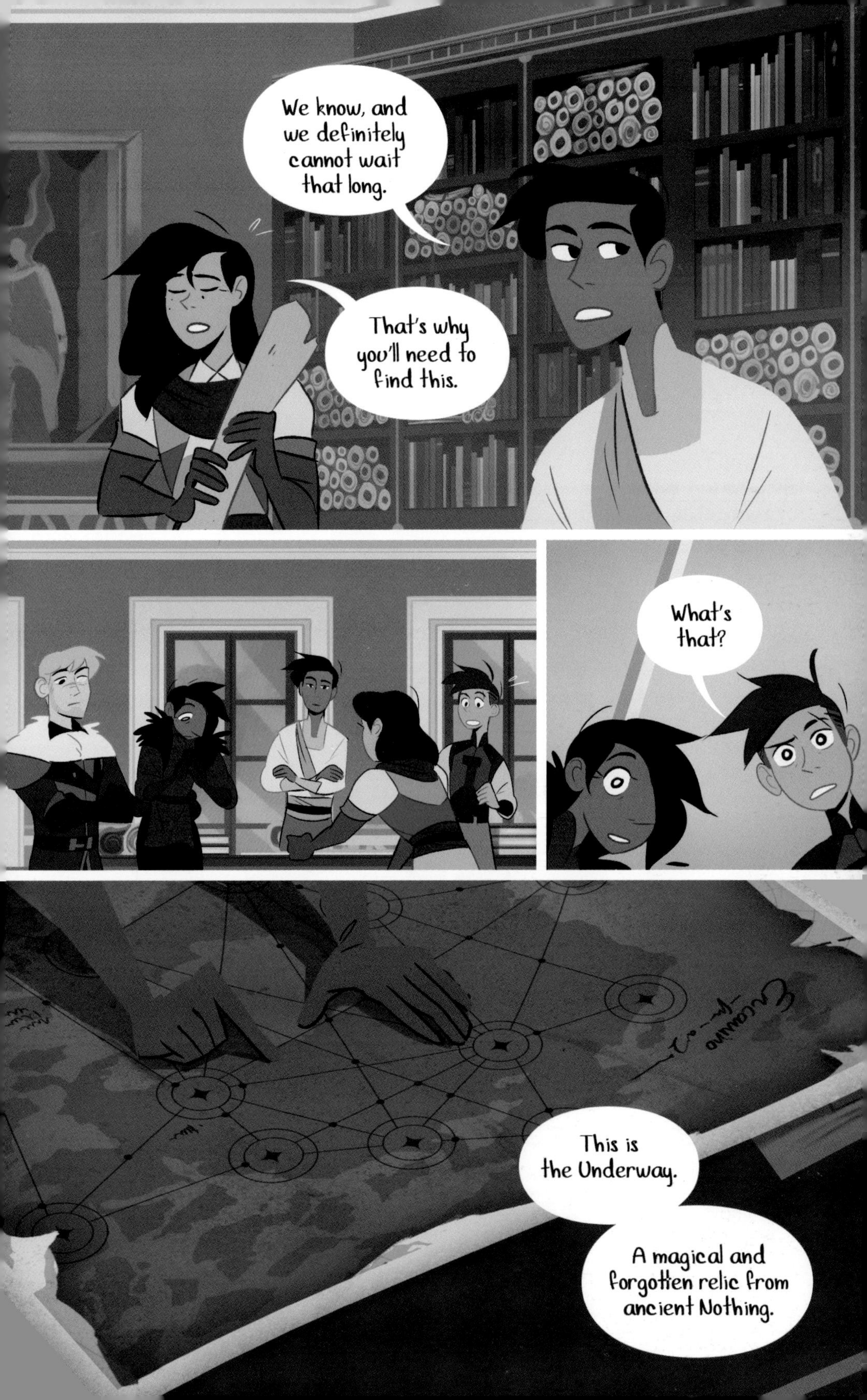
We know, and we definitely cannot wait that long.
That's why you'll need to find this.
What's that?
This is the Underway.
A magical and forgotten relic from ancient Nothing.

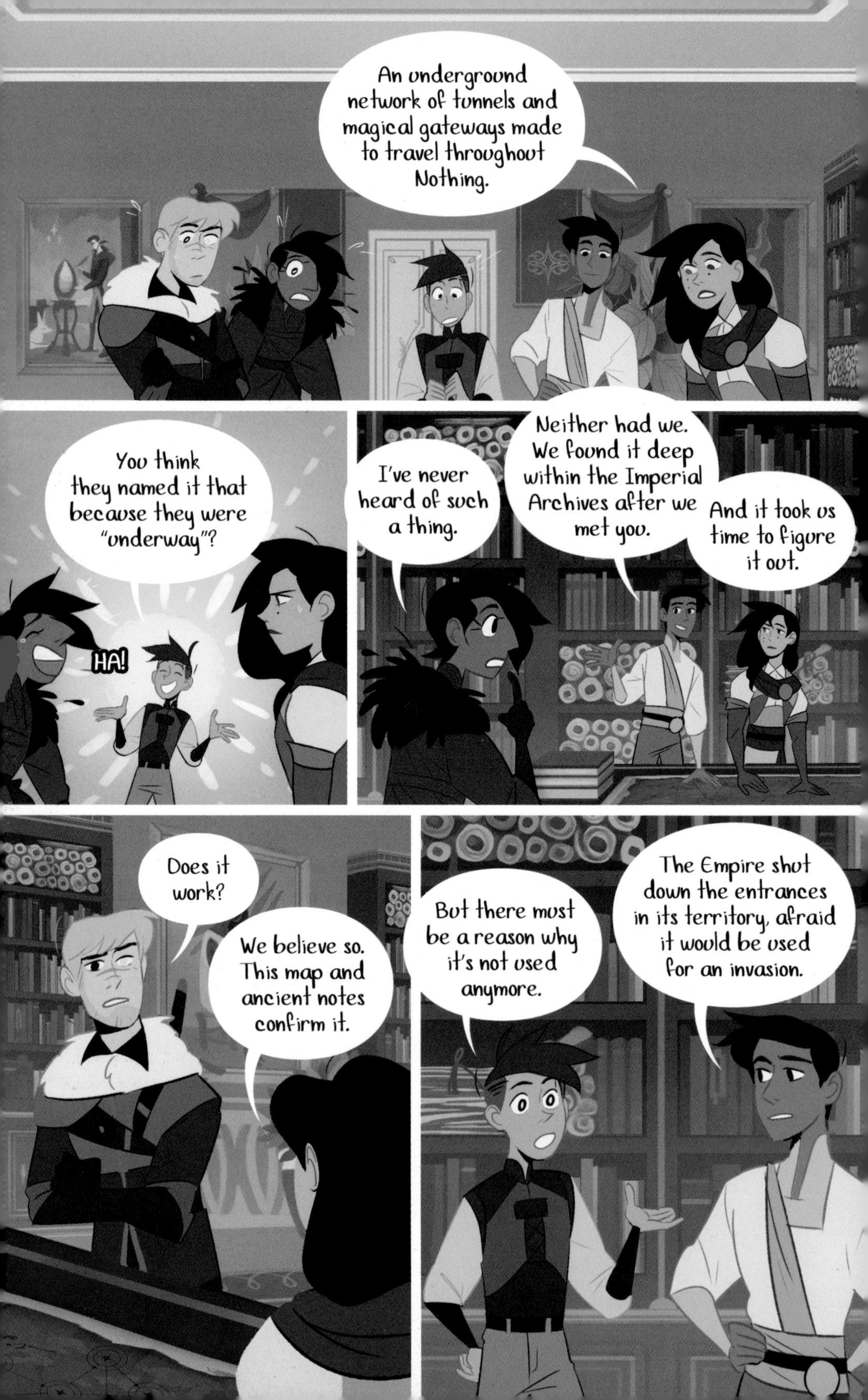
An underground network of tunnels and magical gateways made to travel throughout Nothing.
You think they named it that because they were "underway"?
HA!
I've never heard of such a thing.
Neither had we. We found it deep within the Imperial Archives after we met you.
And it took us time to figure it out.
Does it work?
We believe so. This map and ancient notes confirm it.
But there must be a reason why it's not used anymore.
The Empire shut down the entrances in its territory, afraid it would be used for an invasion.

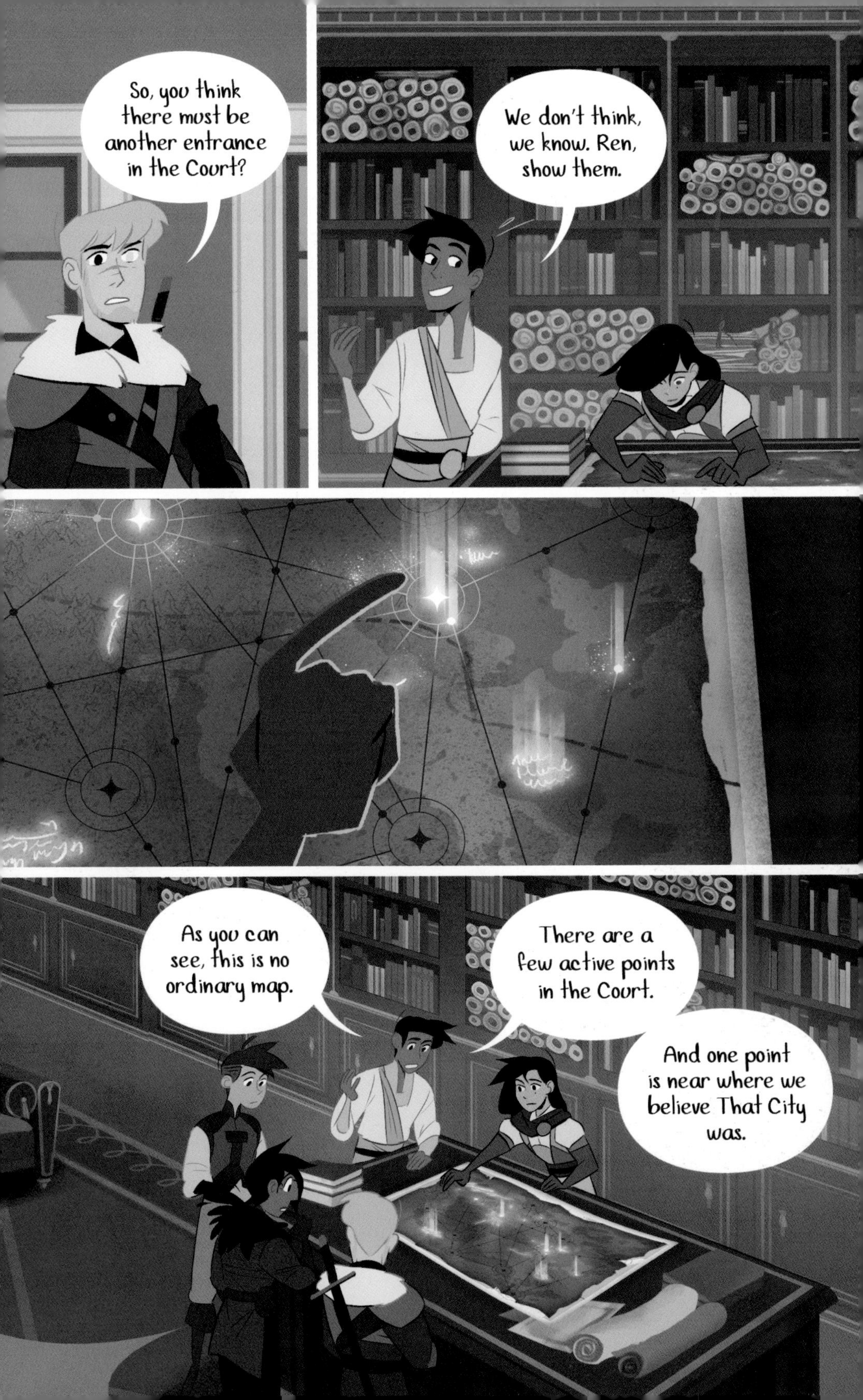
So, you think there must be another entrance in the Court?
We don't think, we know. Ren, show them.
As you can see, this is no ordinary map.
There are a few active points in the Court.
And one point is near where we believe That City was.

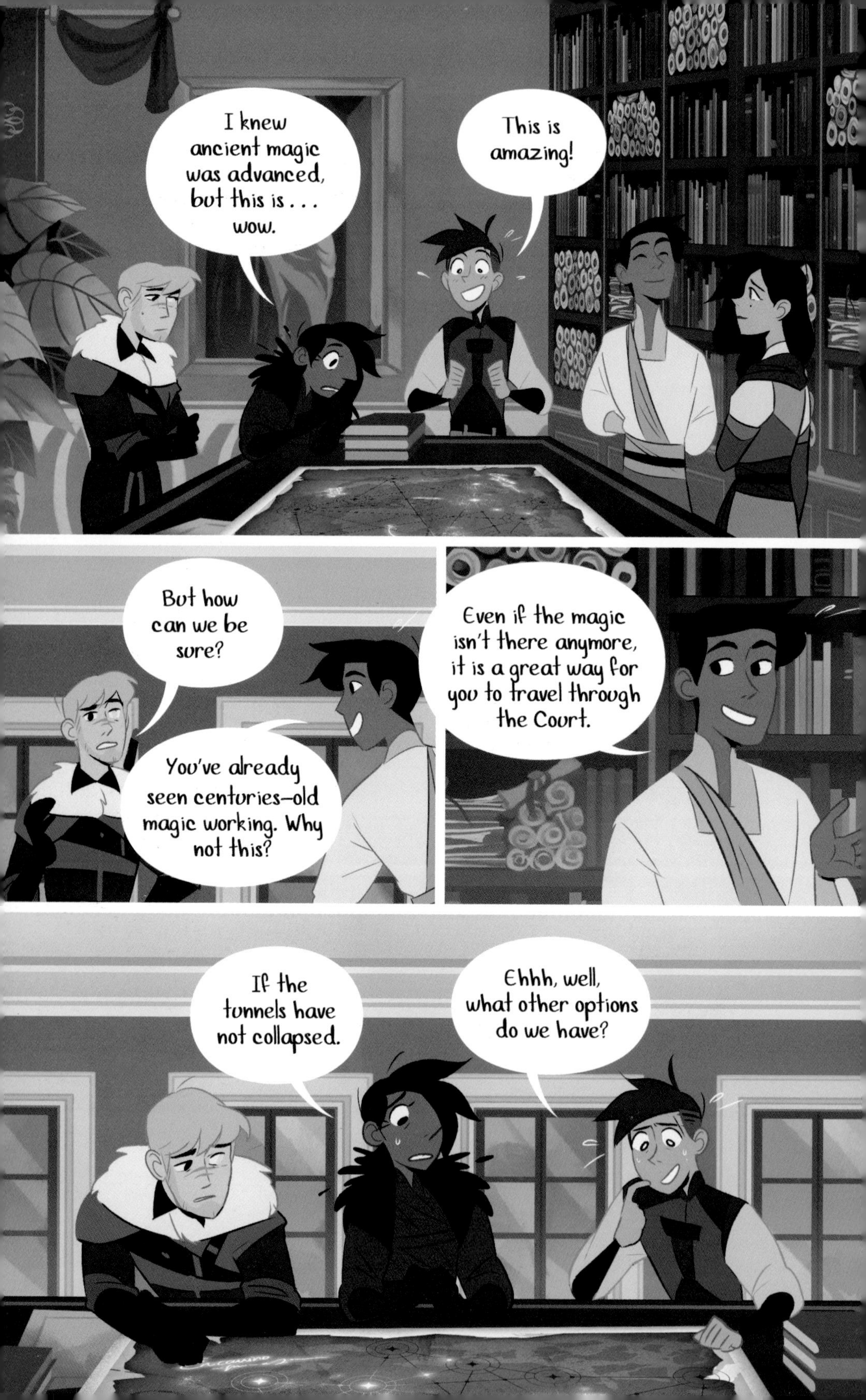
I knew ancient magic was advanced, but this is . . . wow.
This is amazing!
But how can we be sure?
You've already seen centuries-old magic working. Why not this?
Even if the magic isn't there anymore, it is a great way for you to travel through the Court.
If the tunnels have not collapsed.
Ehhh, well, what other options do we have?

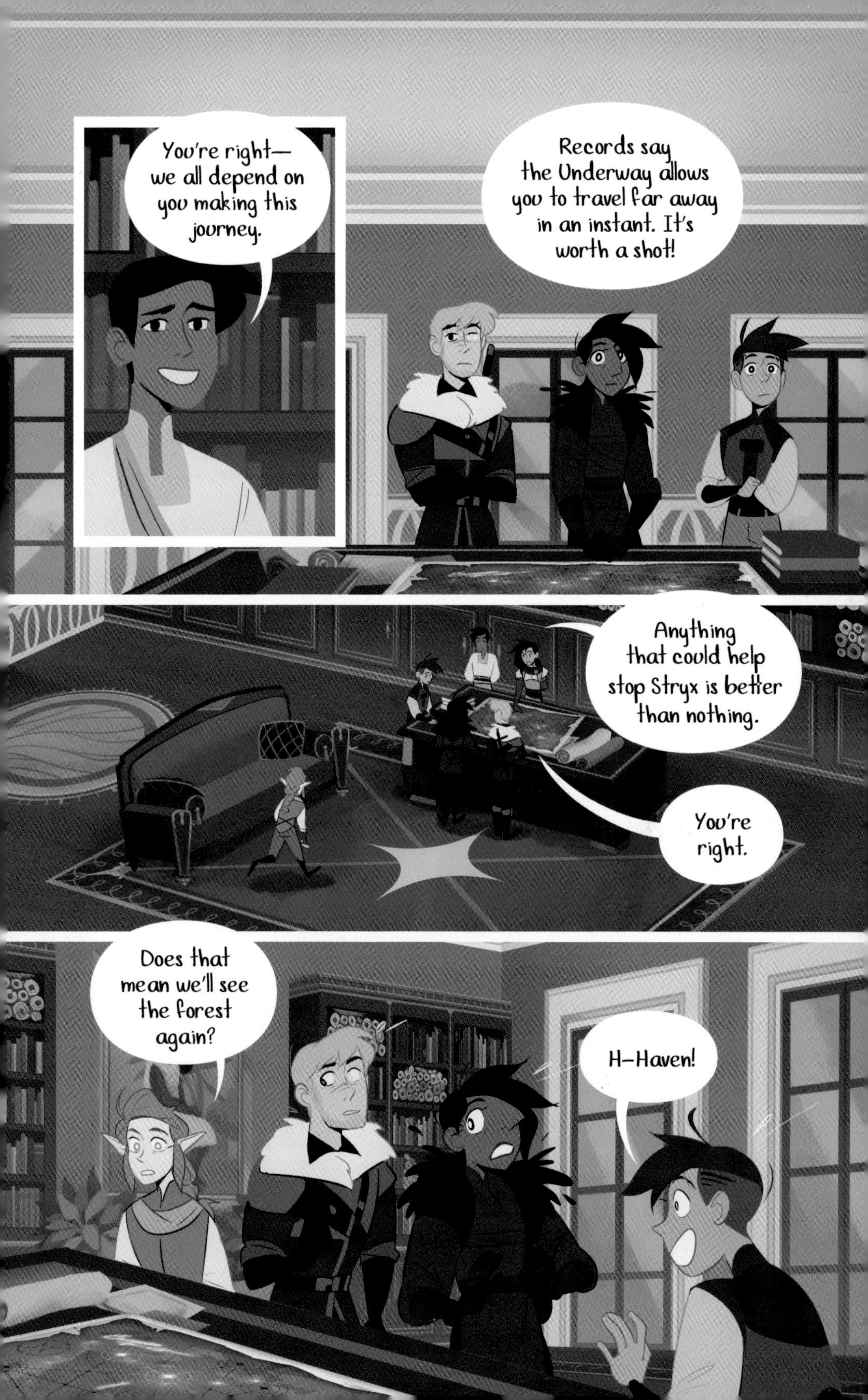
You're right—we all depend on you making this journey.
Records say the Underway allows you to travel far away in an instant. It's worth a shot!
Anything that could help stop Stryx is better than nothing.
You're right.
Does that mean we'll see the forest again?
H–Haven!

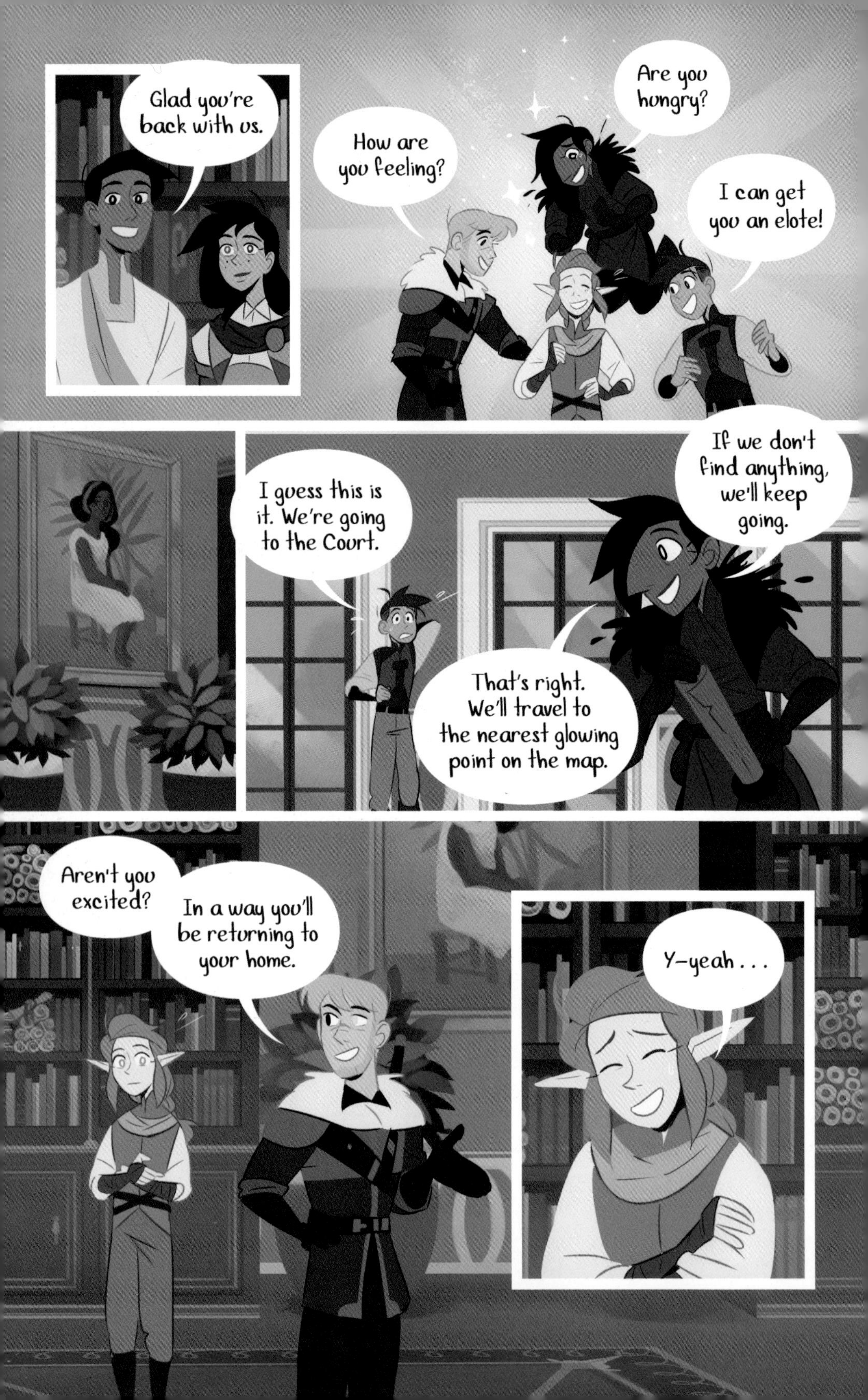
Glad you're back with us.
How are you feeling?
Are you hungry?
I can get you an elote!
I guess this is it. We're going to the Court.
If we don't find anything, we'll keep going.
That's right. We'll travel to the nearest glowing point on the map.
Aren't you excited?
In a way you'll be returning to your home.
Y-yeah . . .

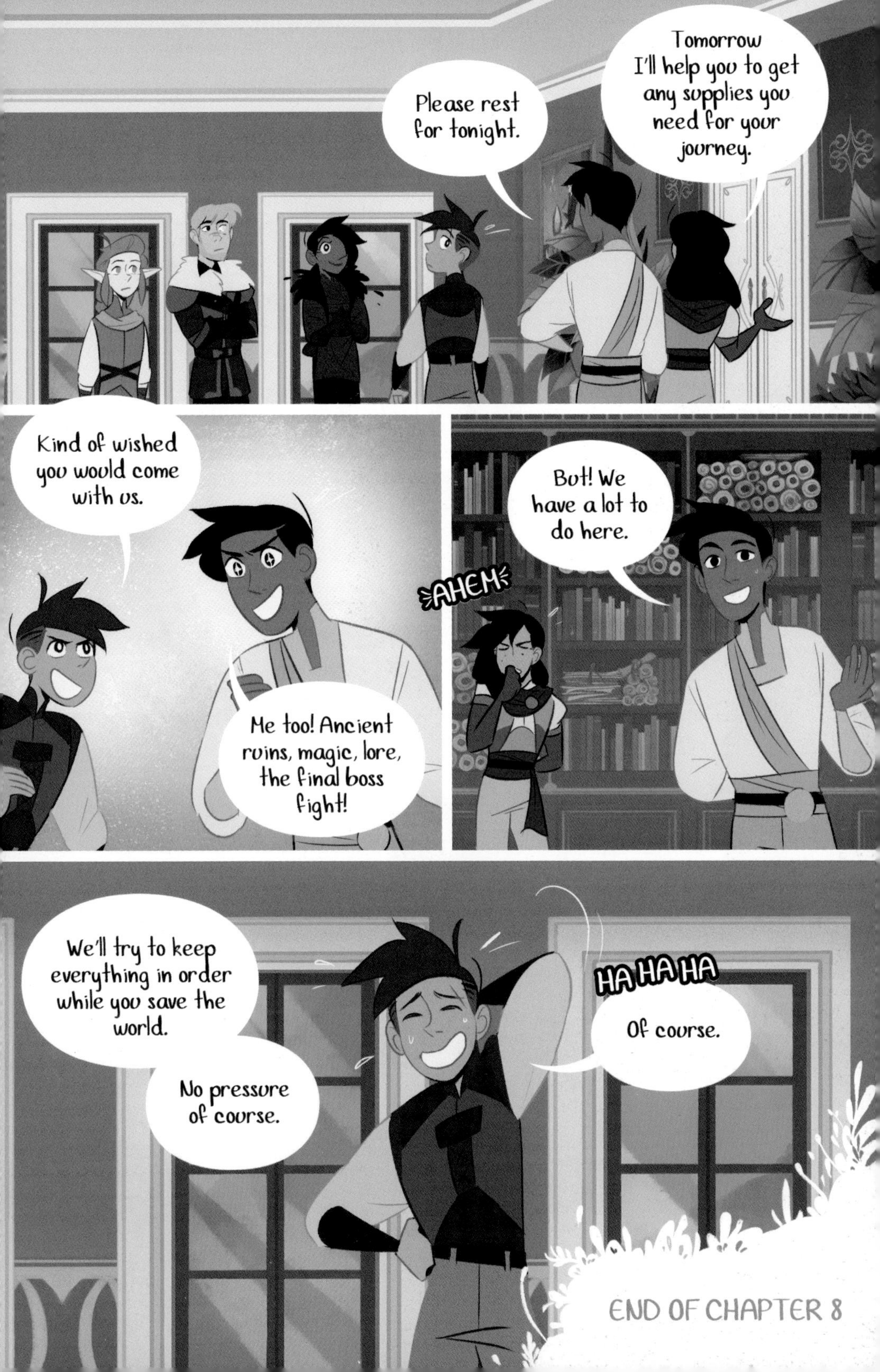
Please rest for tonight.
Tomorrow I'll help you to get any supplies you need for your journey.
Kind of wished you would come with us.
Me too! Ancient ruins, magic, lore, the final boss fight!
AHEM
But! We have a lot to do here.
We'll try to keep everything in order while you save the world.
No pressure of course.
HA HA HA
Of course.
END OF CHAPTER 8

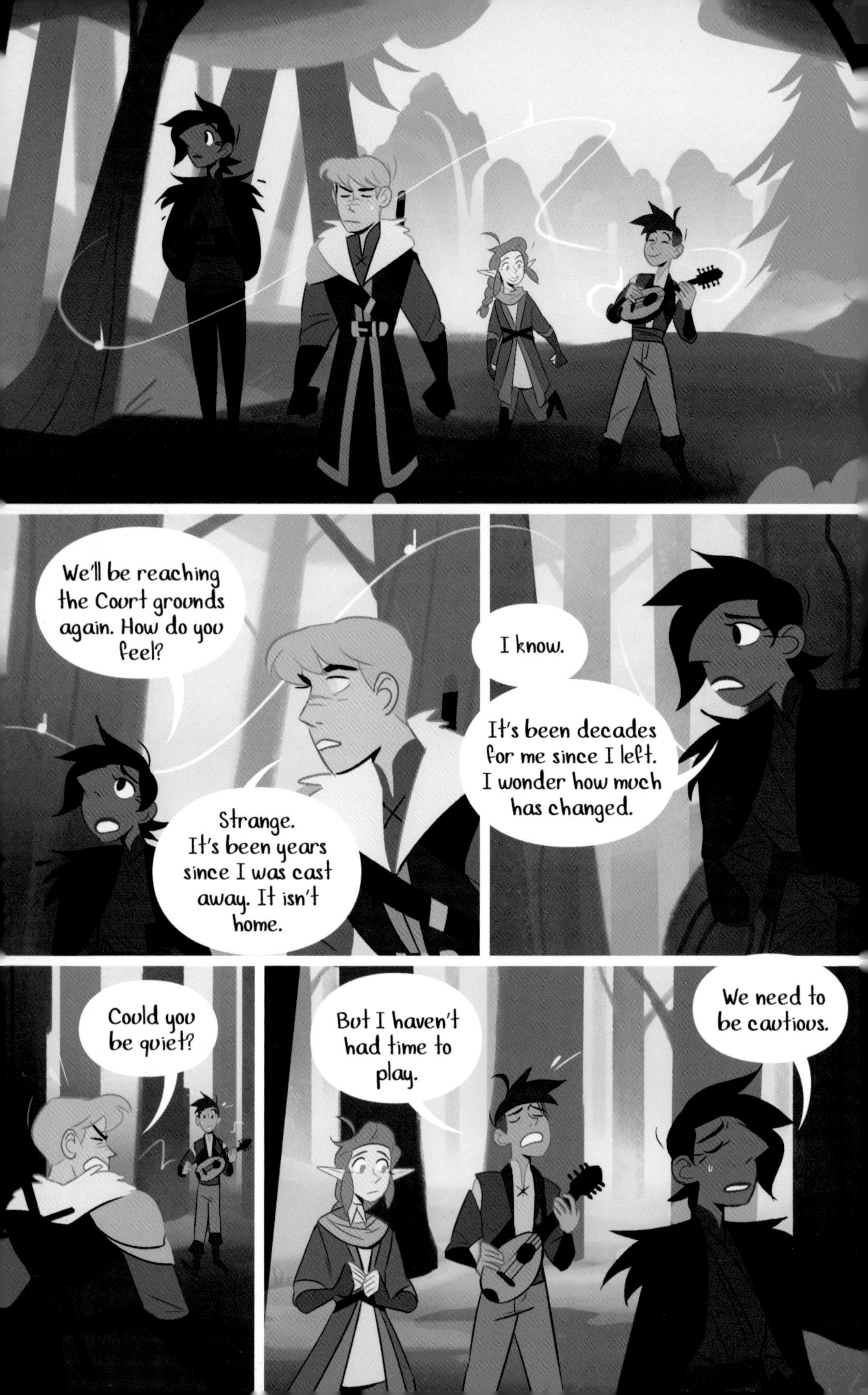
We'll be reaching the Court grounds again. How do you feel?
Strange. It's been years since I was cast away. It isn't home.
I know.
It's been decades for me since I left. I wonder how much has changed.
Could you be quiet?
But I haven't had time to play.
We need to be cautious.

We don't know if Court soldiers will be near.

*Sigh* Fine.

Haven?

Do you hear that?

Haven, wait!

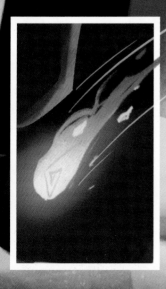

Chapter 9
Crowsroads
What are you lot doing here?
We could ask you the same thing!

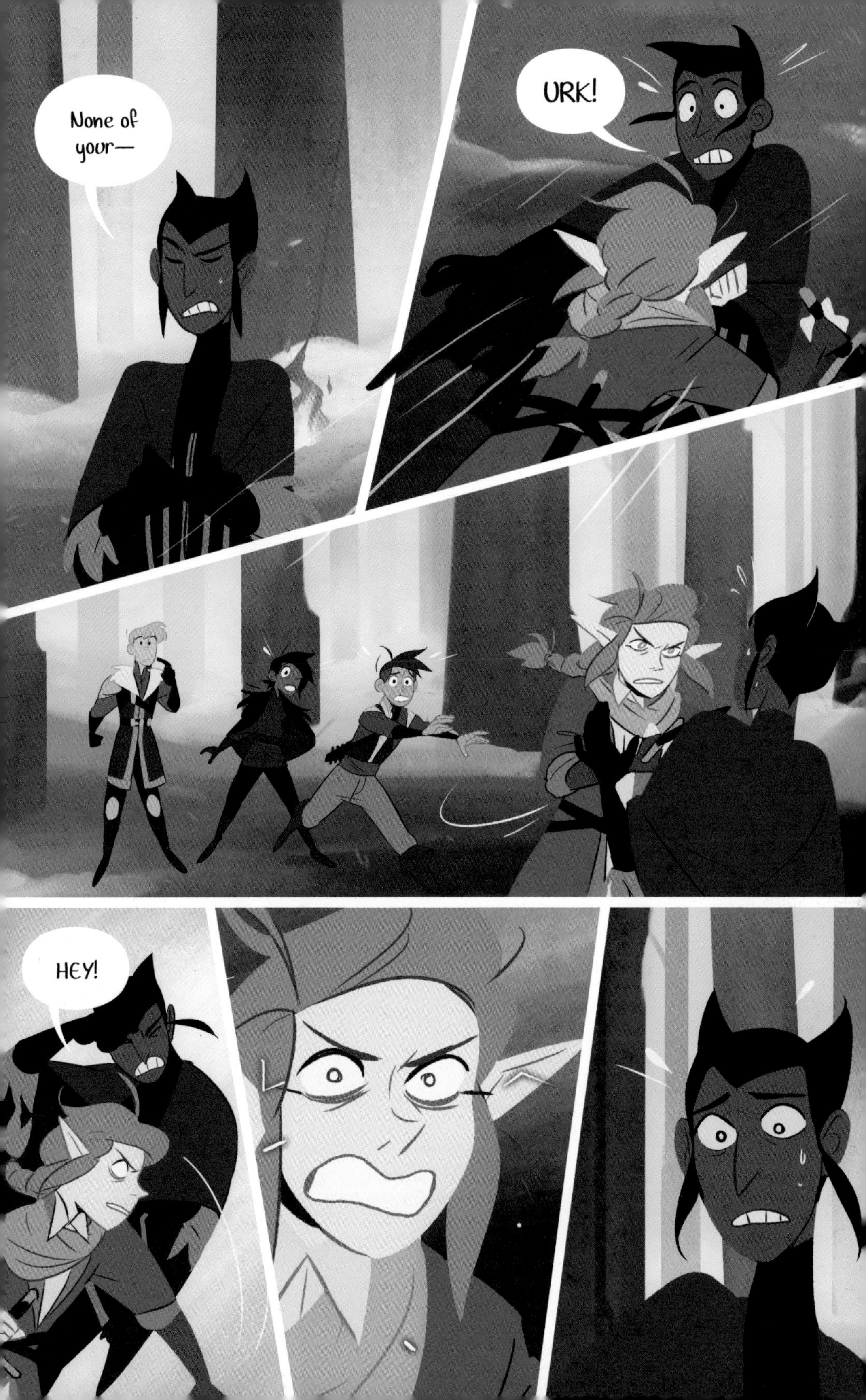
None of your—
URK!
HEY!

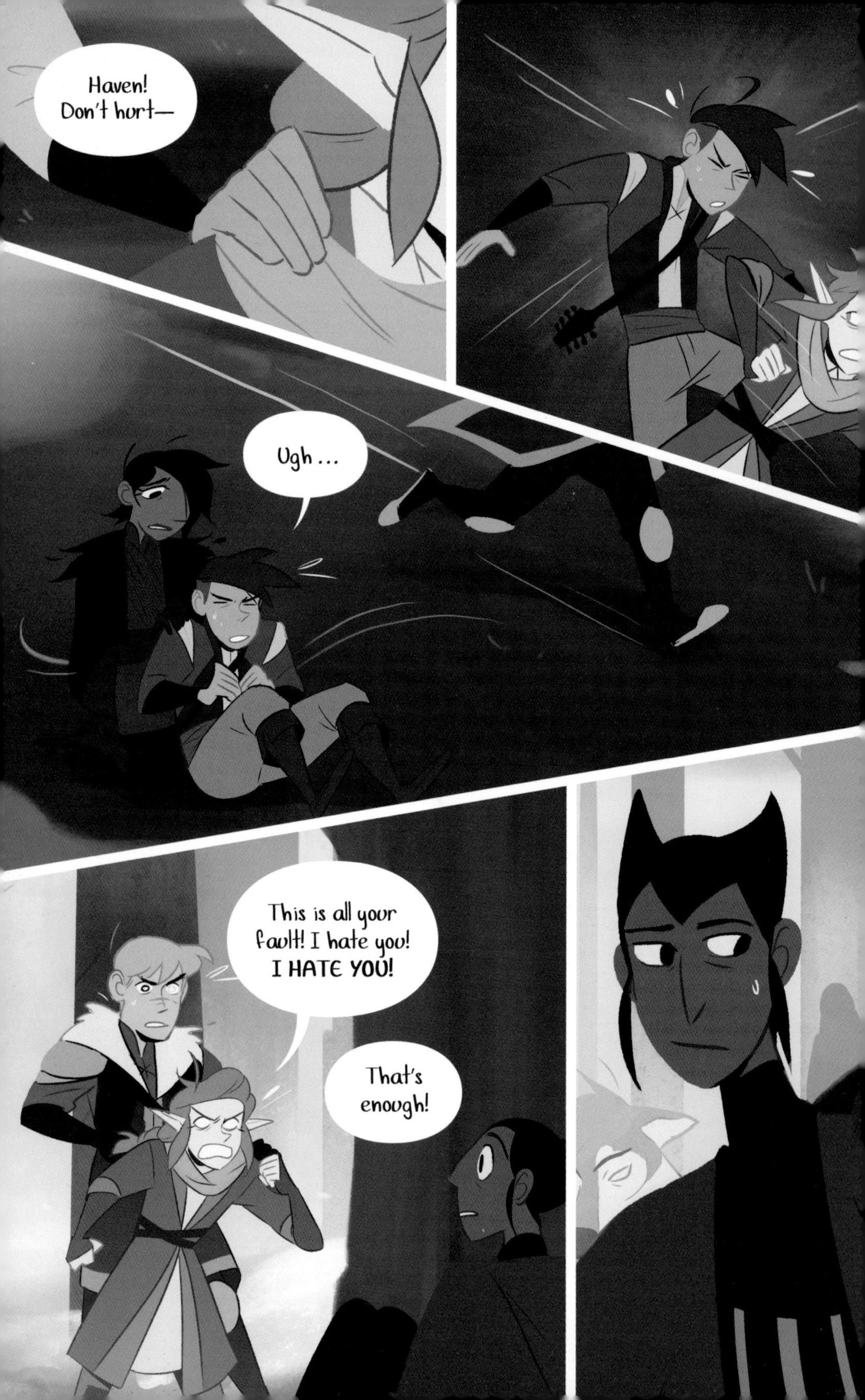
Haven!
Don't hurt—
Ugh . . .
This is all your fault! I hate you! I HATE YOU!
That's enough!

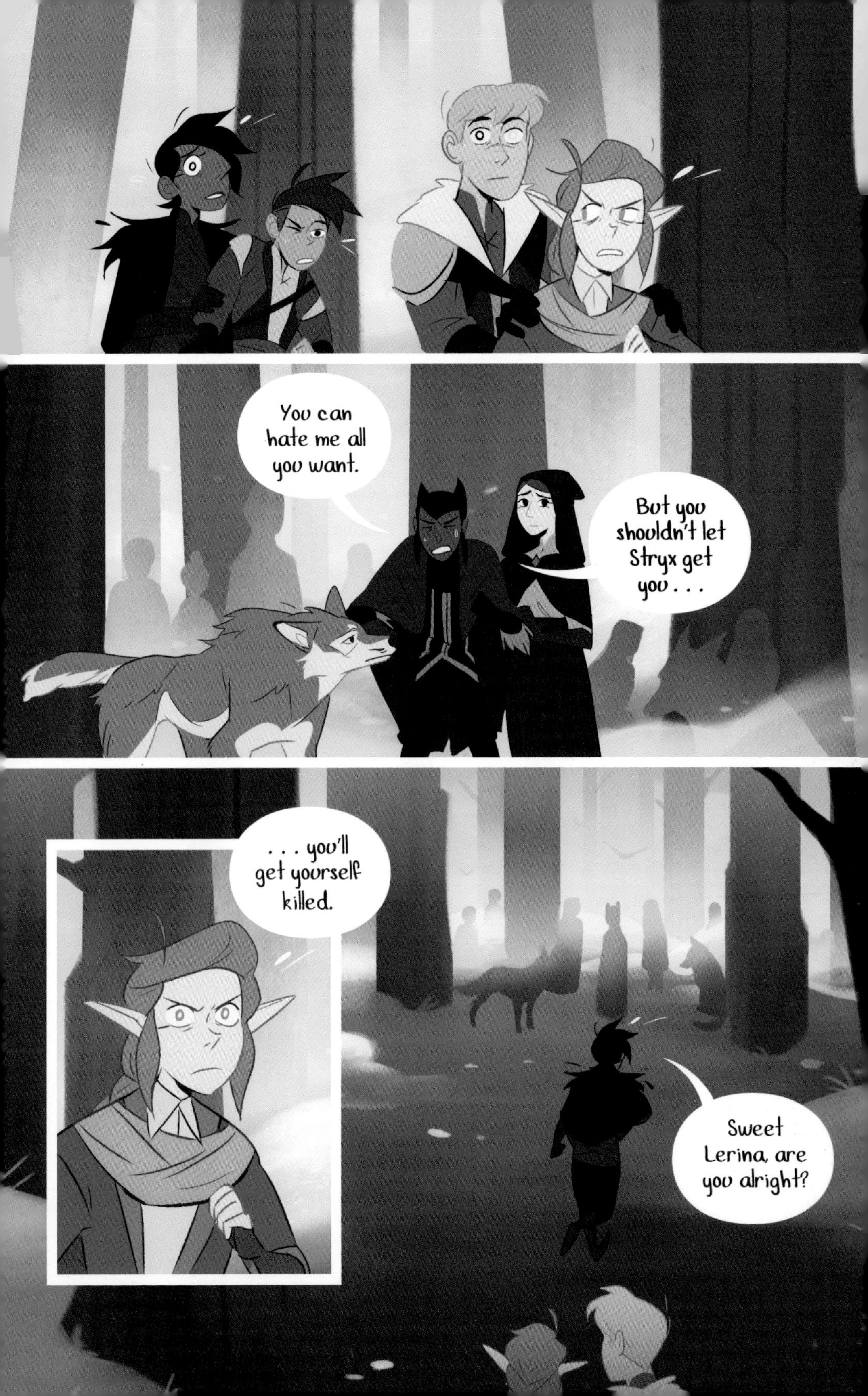
You can hate me all you want.
But you shouldn't let Stryx get you . . .
. . . you'll get yourself killed.
Sweet Lerina, are you alright?

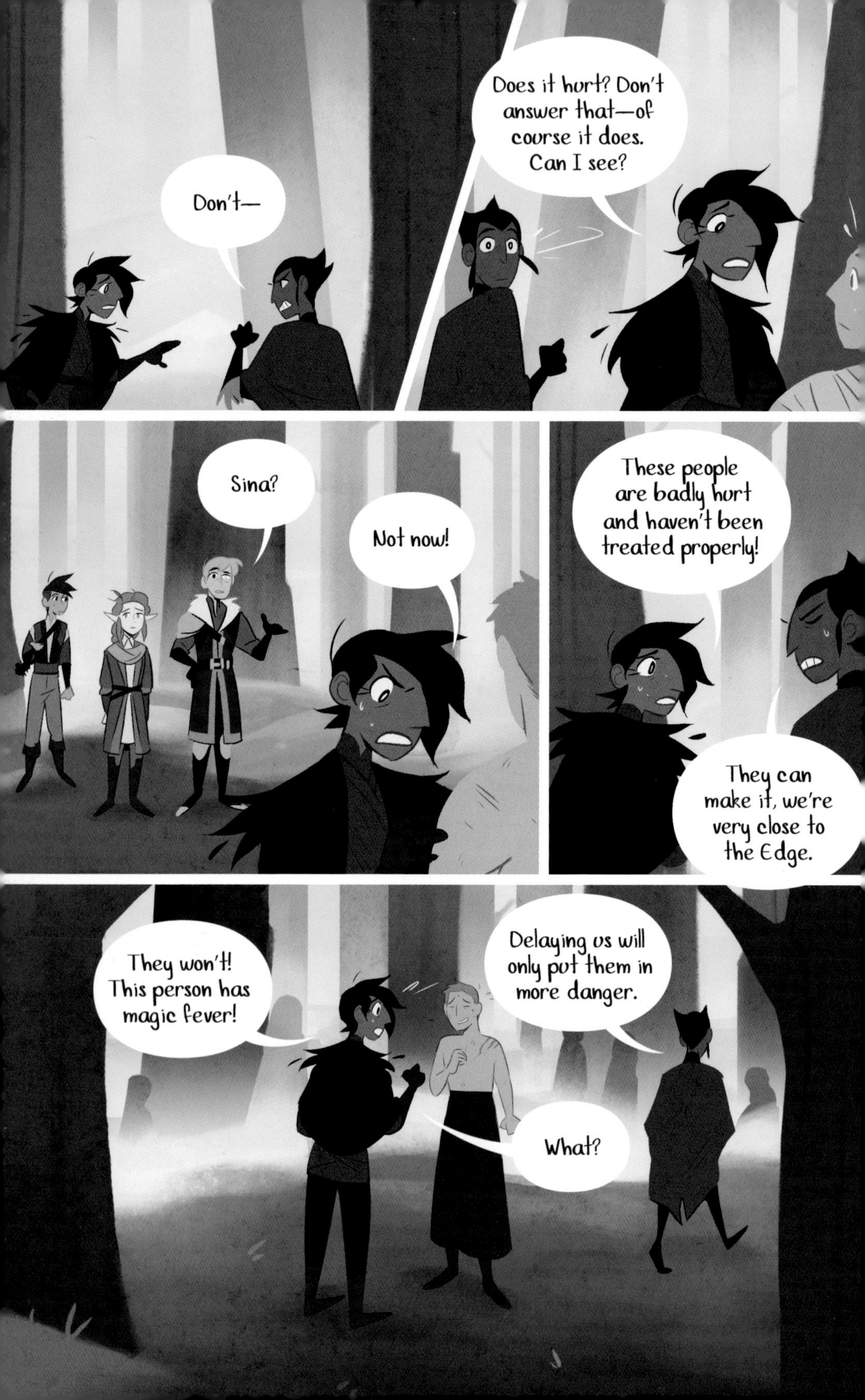
Don't—
Does it hurt? Don't answer that—of course it does. Can I see?
Sina?
Not now!
These people are badly hurt and haven't been treated properly!
They can make it, we're very close to the Edge.
They won't! This person has magic fever!
Delaying us will only put them in more danger.
What?

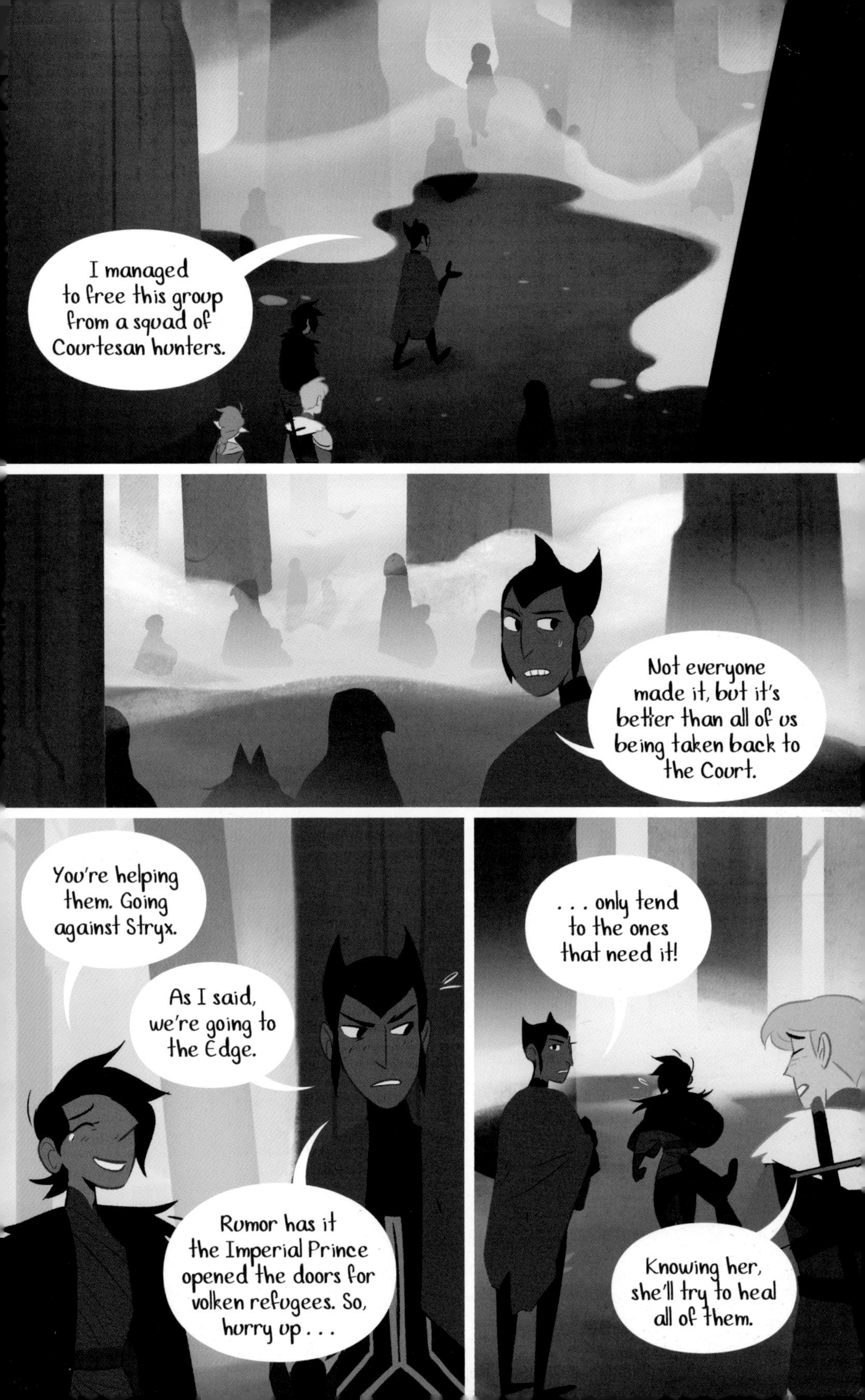
I managed to free this group from a squad of Courtesan hunters.
Not everyone made it, but it's better than all of us being taken back to the Court.
You're helping them. Going against Stryx.
As I said, we're going to the Edge.
Rumor has it the Imperial Prince opened the doors for volken refugees. So, hurry up . . .
. . . only tend to the ones that need it!
Knowing her, she'll try to heal all of them.

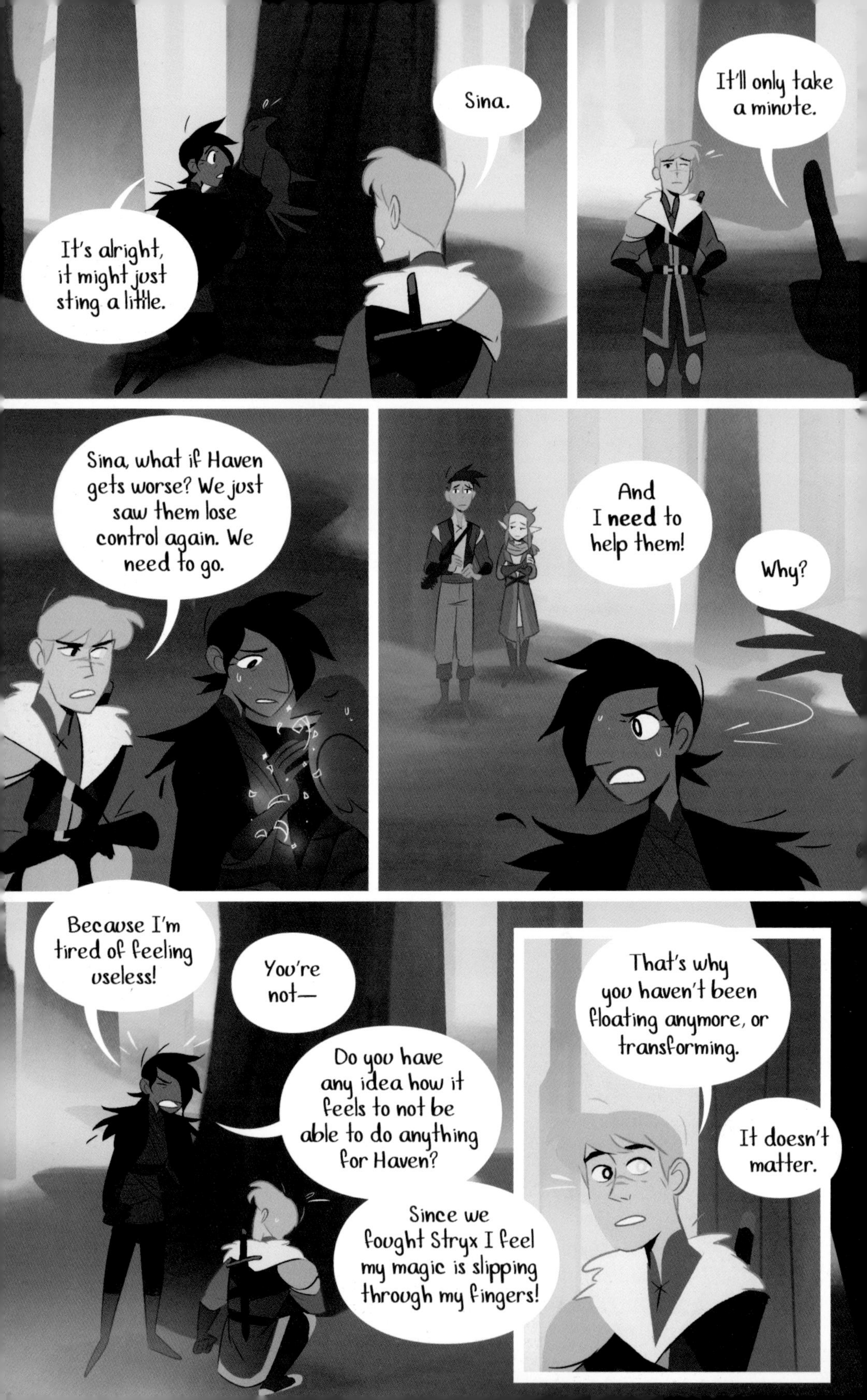
It's alright, it might just sting a little.
Sina.
It'll only take a minute.
Sina, what if Haven gets worse? We just saw them lose control again. We need to go.
And I **need** to help them!
Why?
Because I'm tired of feeling useless!
You're not—
Do you have any idea how it feels to not be able to do anything for Haven?
Since we fought Stryx I feel my magic is slipping through my fingers!
That's why you haven't been floating anymore, or transforming.
It doesn't matter.

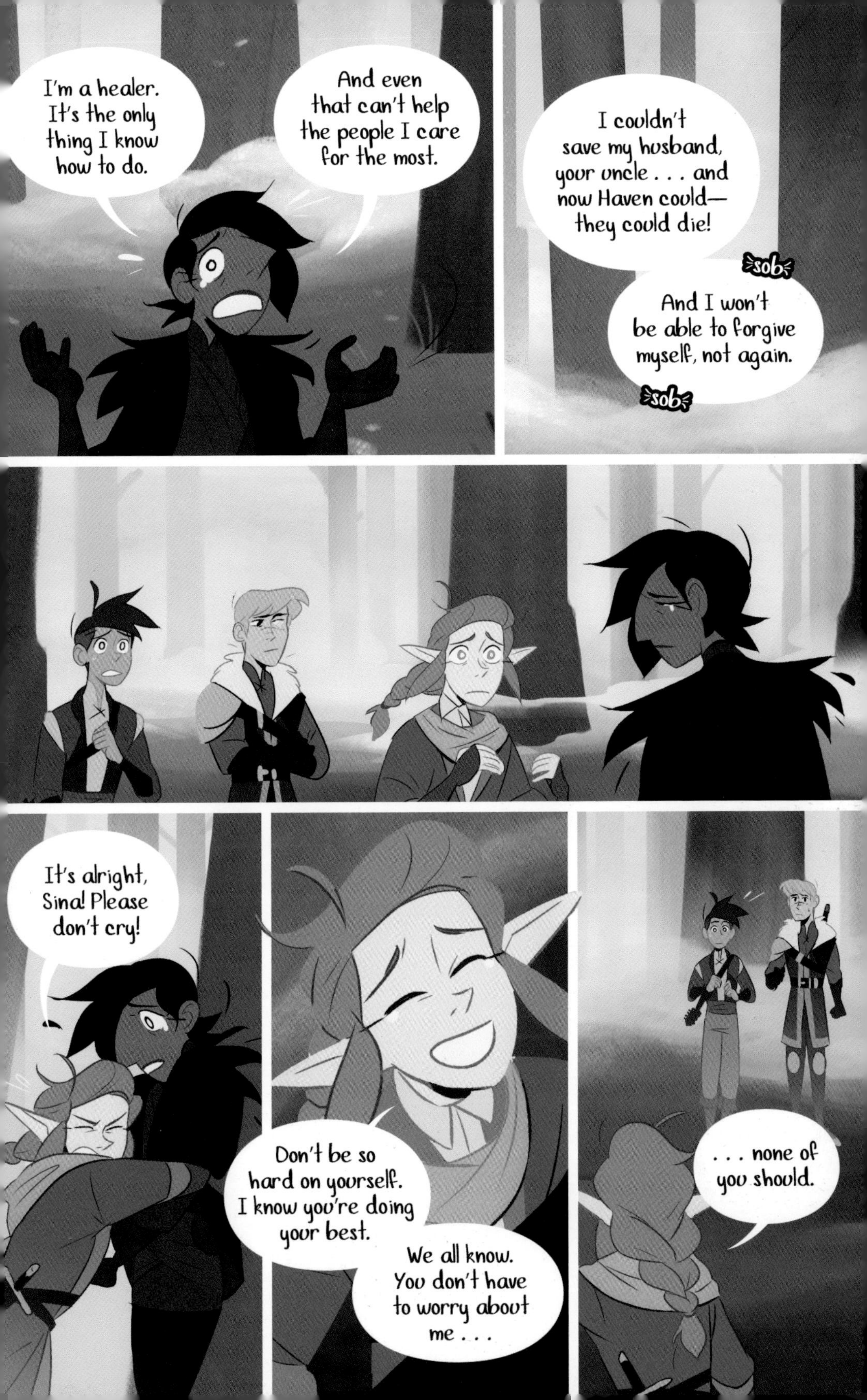
I'm a healer. It's the only thing I know how to do.
And even that can't help the people I care for the most.
I couldn't save my husband, your uncle . . . and now Haven could— they could die!
sob
And I won't be able to forgive myself, not again.
sob
It's alright, Sina! Please don't cry!
Don't be so hard on yourself. I know you're doing your best.
We all know. You don't have to worry about me . . .
. . . none of you should.

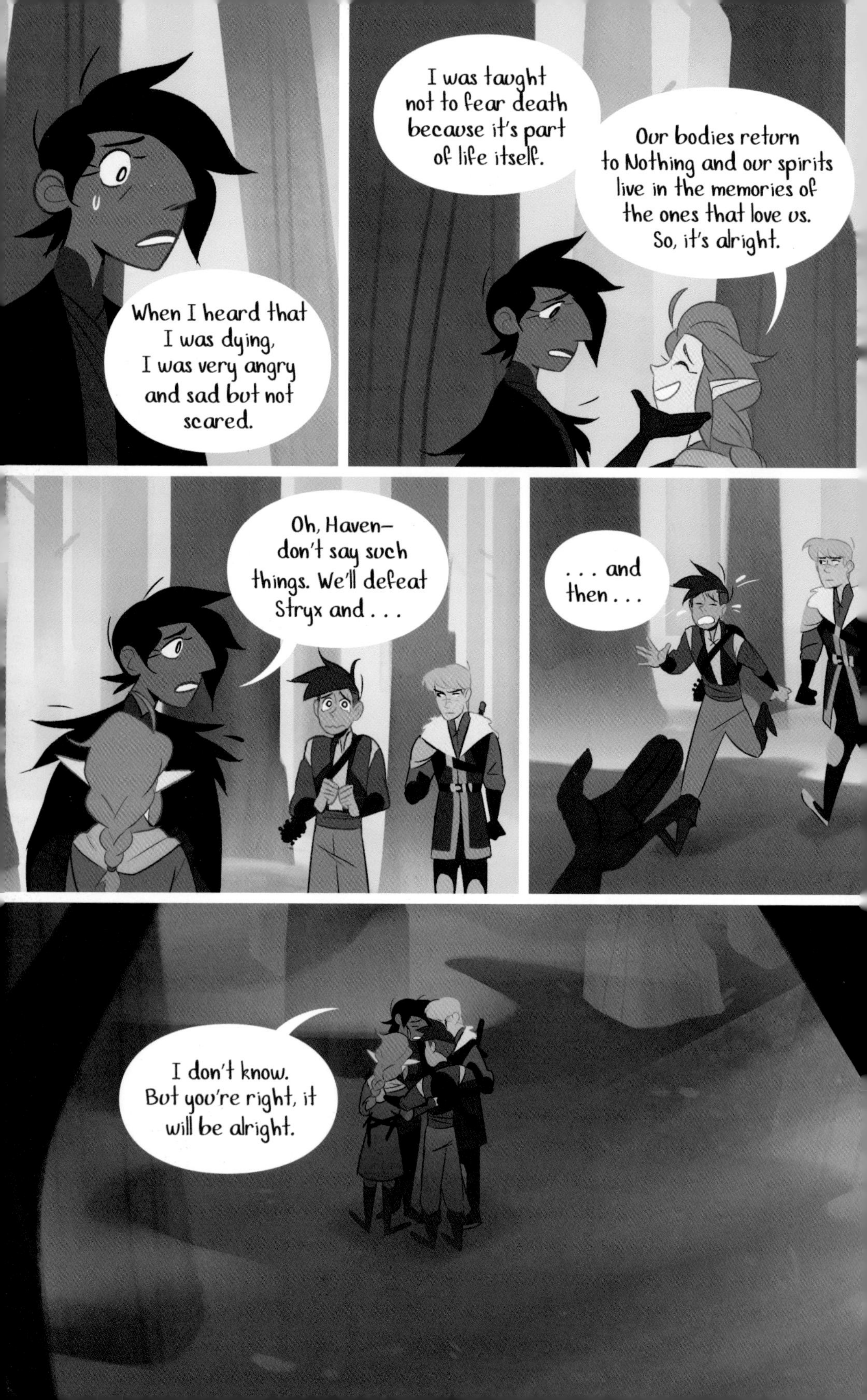
When I heard that I was dying, I was very angry and sad but not scared.
I was taught not to fear death because it's part of life itself.
Our bodies return to Nothing and our spirits live in the memories of the ones that love us. So, it's alright.
Oh, Haven– don't say such things. We'll defeat Stryx and . . .
. . . and then . . .
I don't know. But you're right, it will be alright.

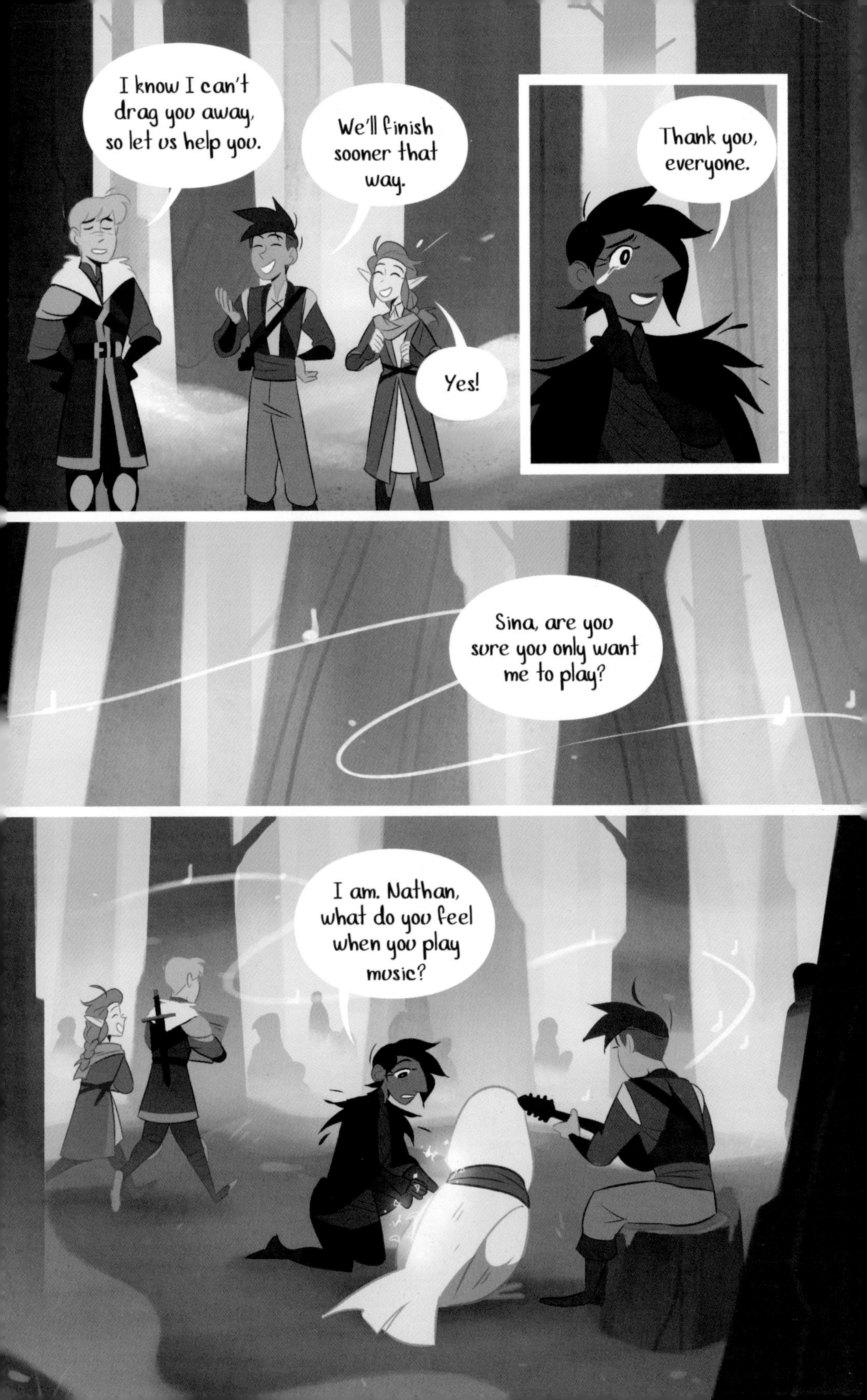
I know I can't drag you away, so let us help you.
We'll finish sooner that way.
Yes!
Thank you, everyone.
Sina, are you sure you only want me to play?
I am. Nathan, what do you feel when you play music?

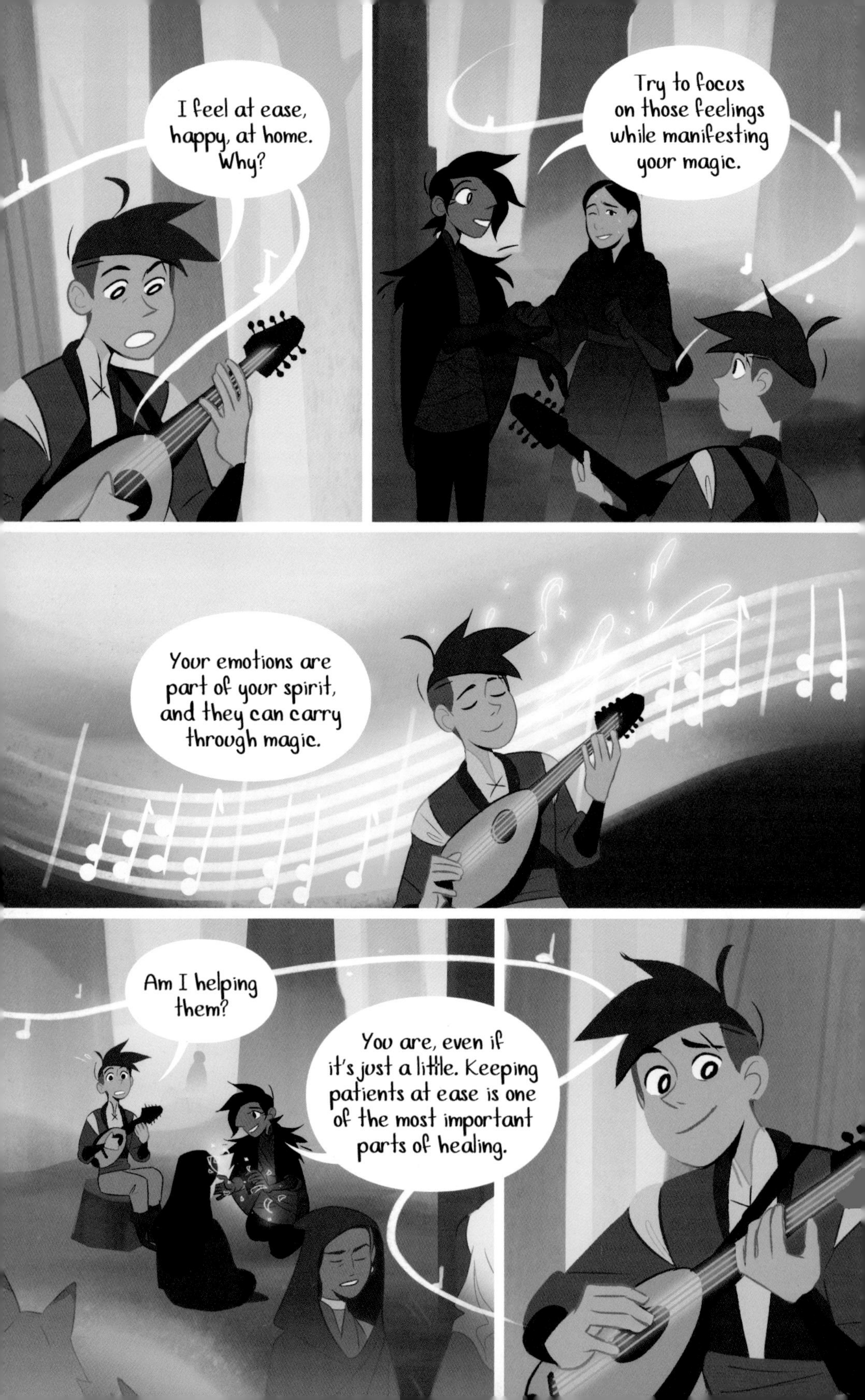
I feel at ease, happy, at home. Why?
Try to focus on those feelings while manifesting your magic.
Your emotions are part of your spirit, and they can carry through magic.
Am I helping them?
You are, even if it's just a little. Keeping patients at ease is one of the most important parts of healing.

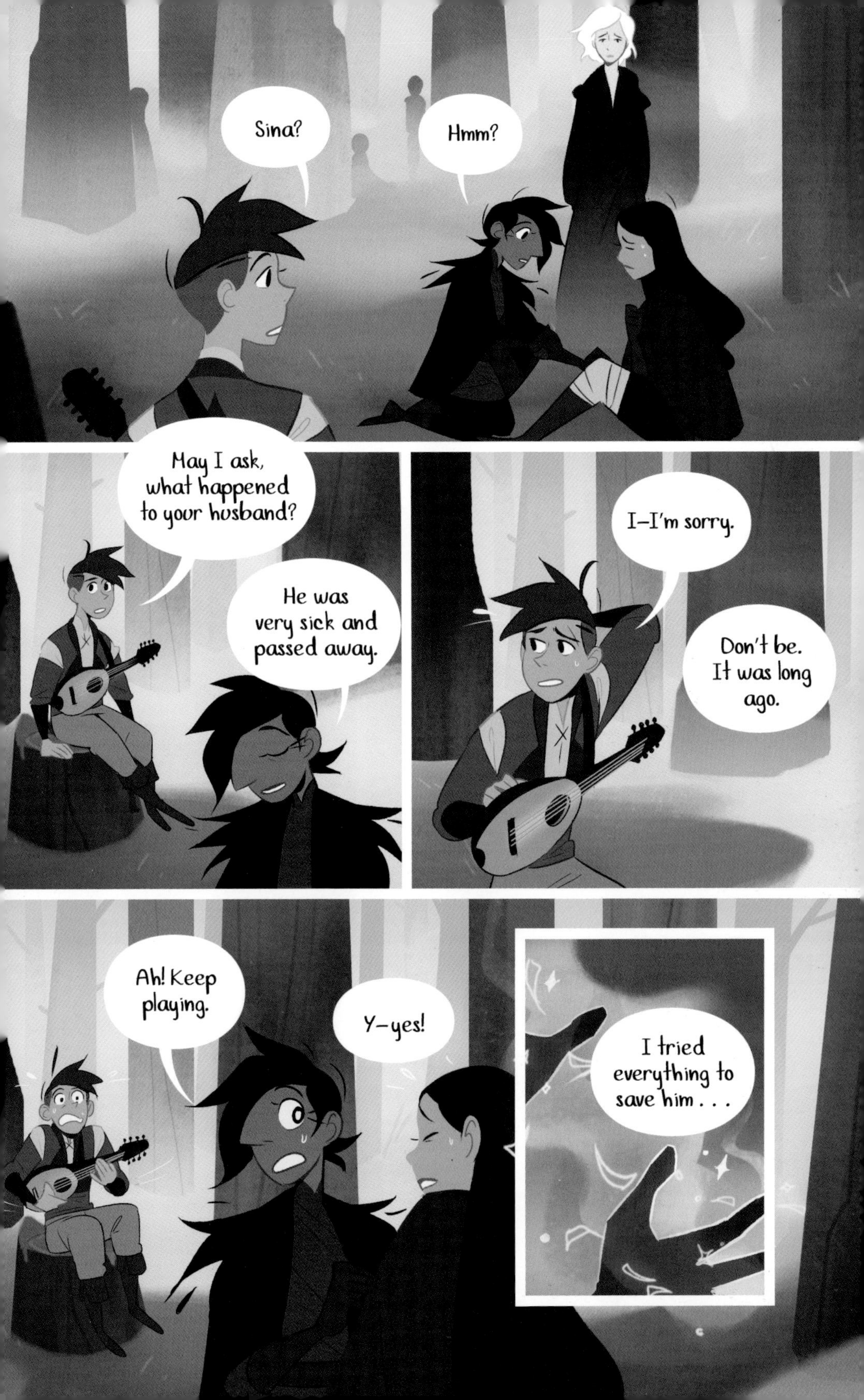
Sina?
Hmm?
May I ask, what happened to your husband?
He was very sick and passed away.
I–I'm sorry.
Don't be. It was long ago.
Ah! Keep playing.
Y–yes!
I tried everything to save him . . .

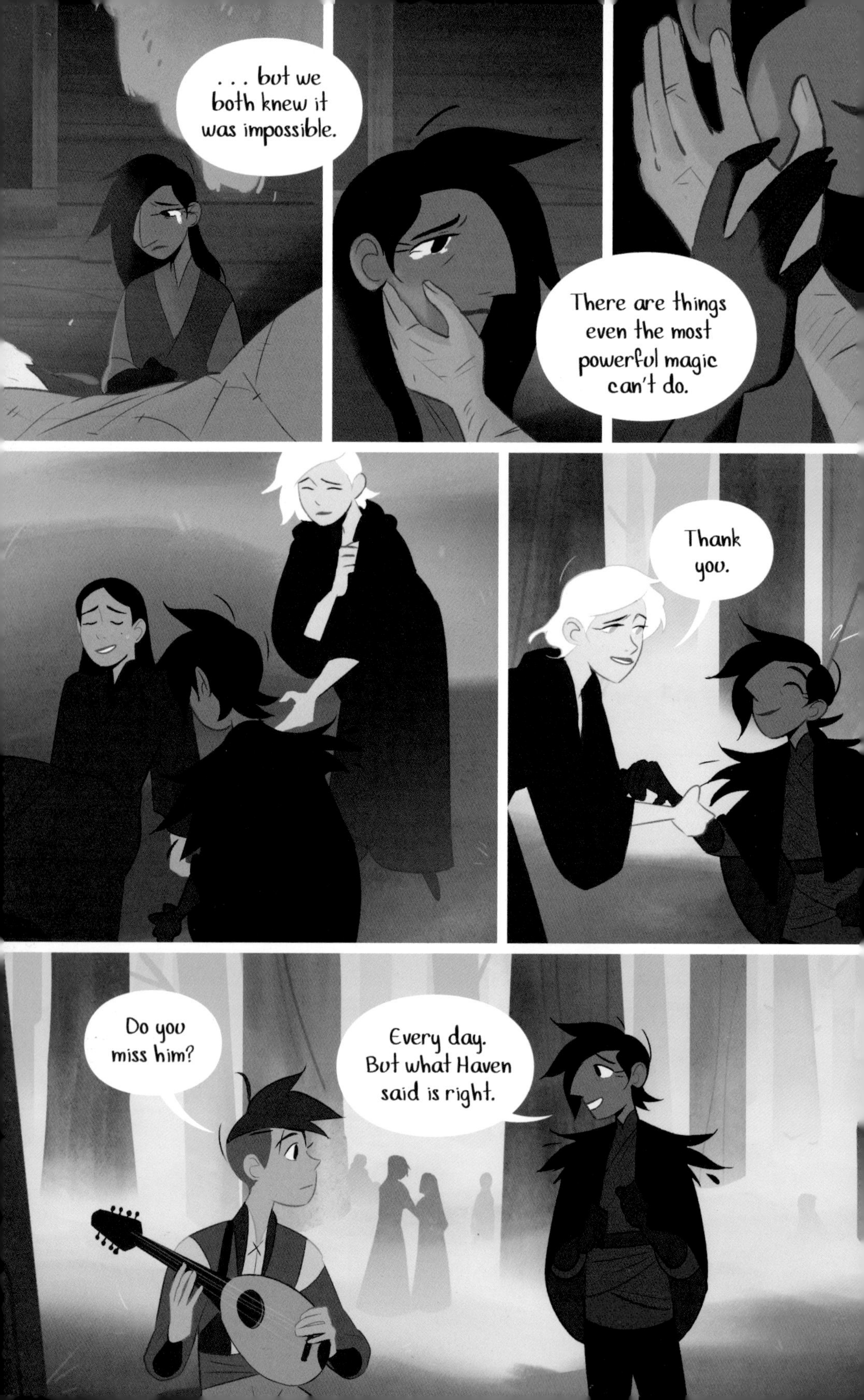
. . . but we both knew it was impossible.
There are things even the most powerful magic can't do.
Thank you.
Do you miss him?
Every day. But what Haven said is right.

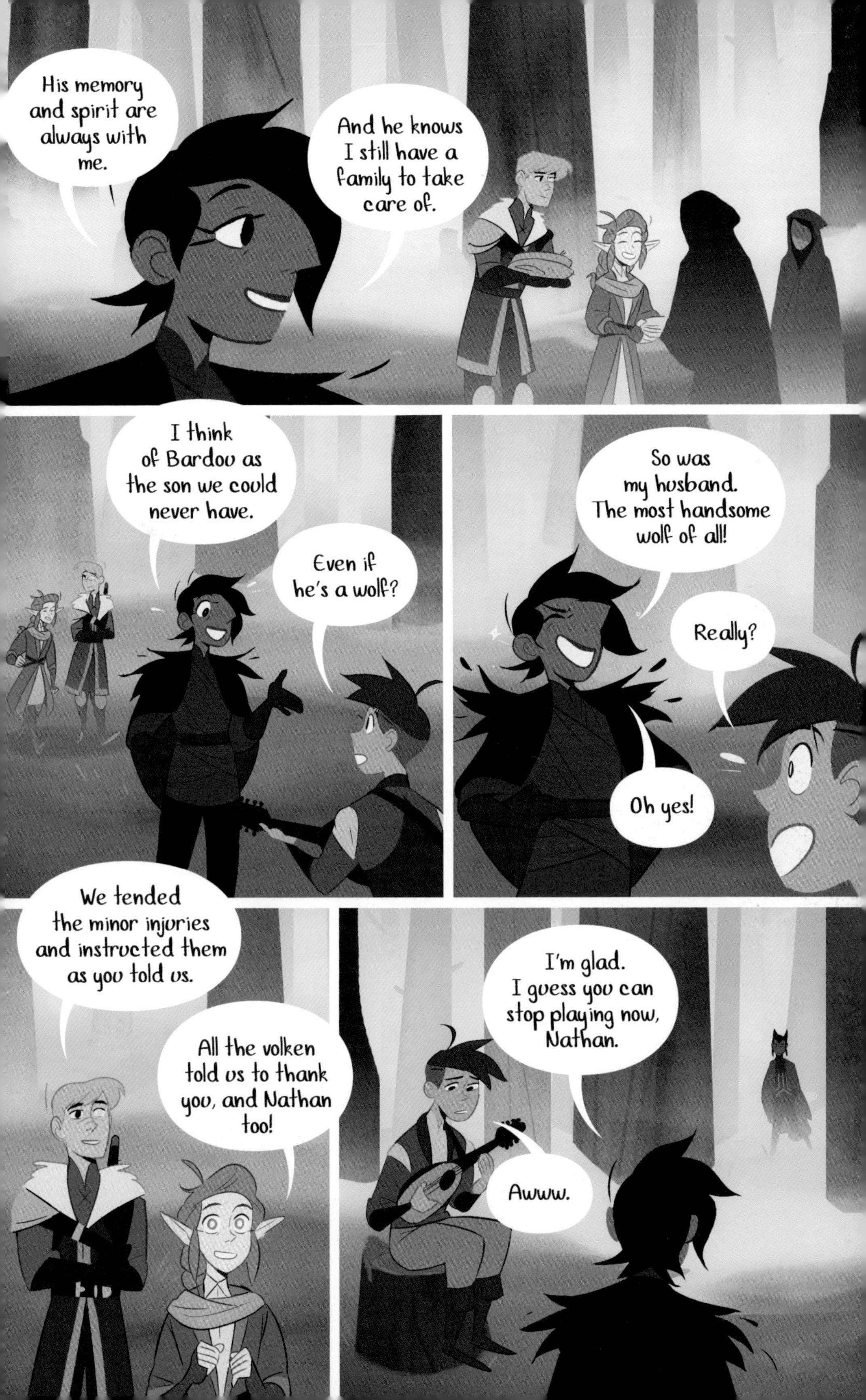
His memory and spirit are always with me.
And he knows I still have a family to take care of.
I think of Bardou as the son we could never have.
Even if he's a wolf?
So was my husband. The most handsome wolf of all!
Really?
Oh yes!
We tended the minor injuries and instructed them as you told us.
All the volken told us to thank you, and Nathan too!
I'm glad. I guess you can stop playing now, Nathan.
Awww.

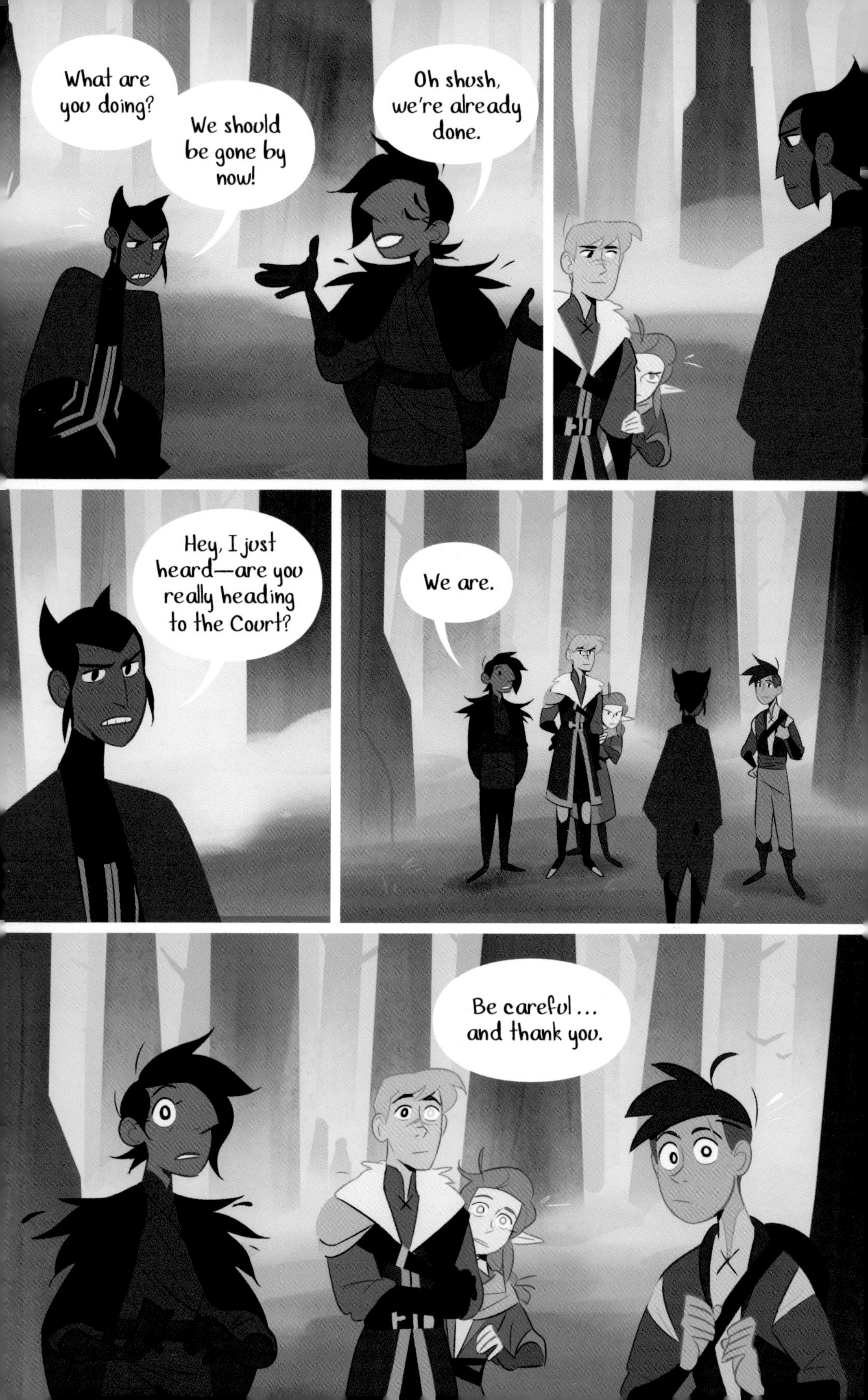
What are you doing?
We should be gone by now!
Oh shush, we're already done.
Hey, I just heard—are you really heading to the Court?
We are.
Be careful ... and thank you.

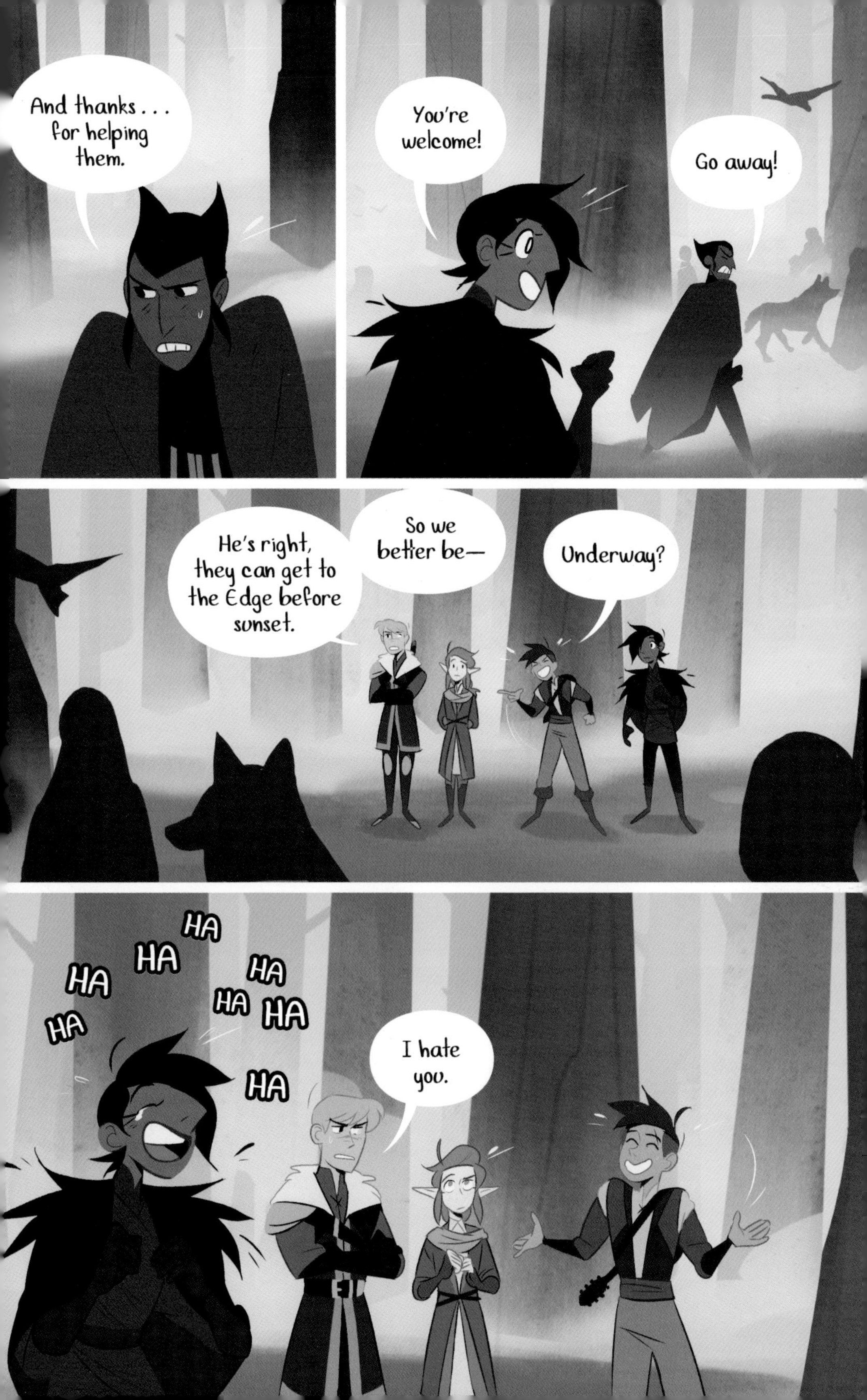
And thanks . . . for helping them.
You're welcome!
Go away!
He's right, they can get to the Edge before sunset.
So we better be—
Underway?
HA
HA
HA
HA
HA
HA HA
HA
I hate you.

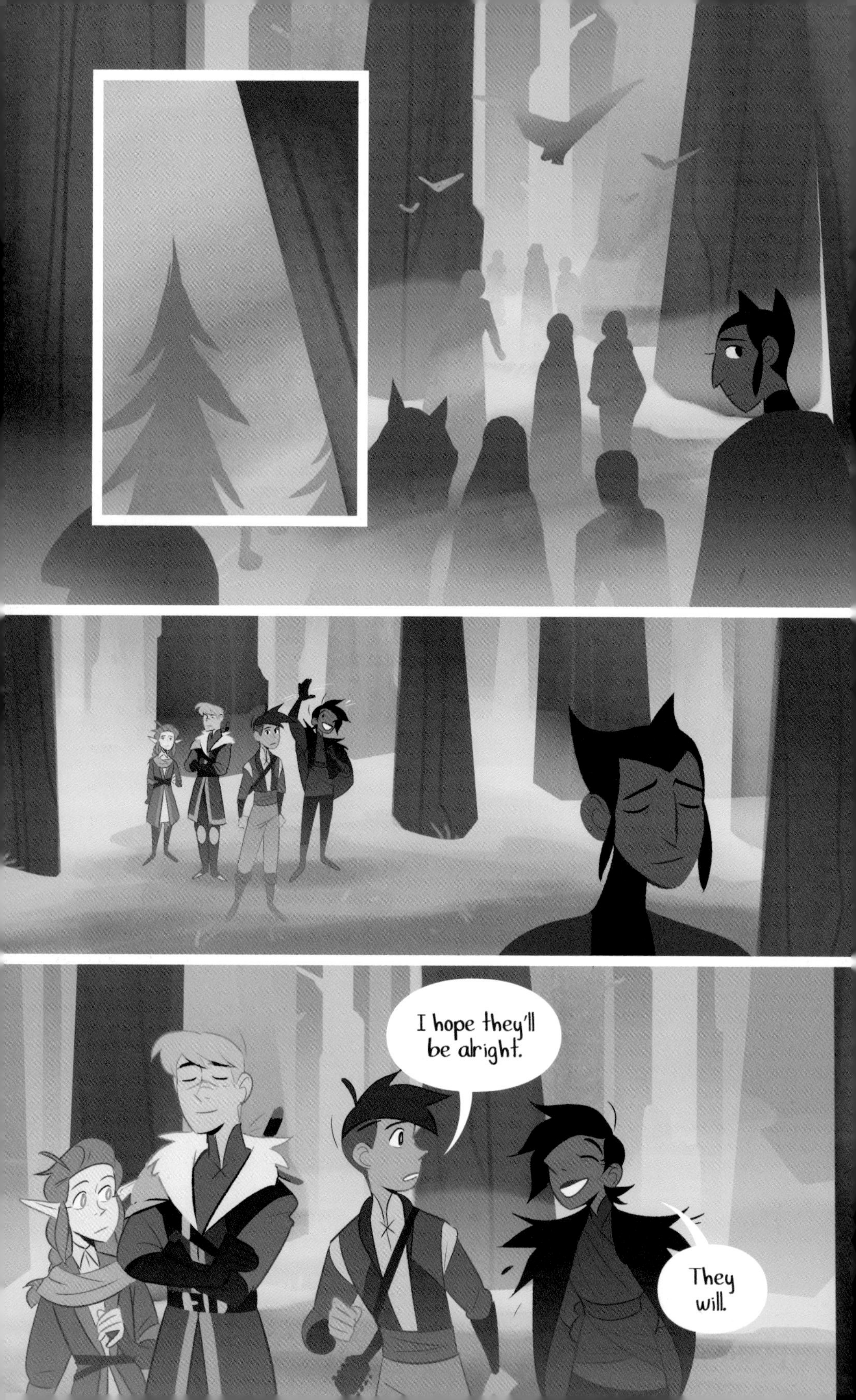
I hope they'll be alright.
They will.

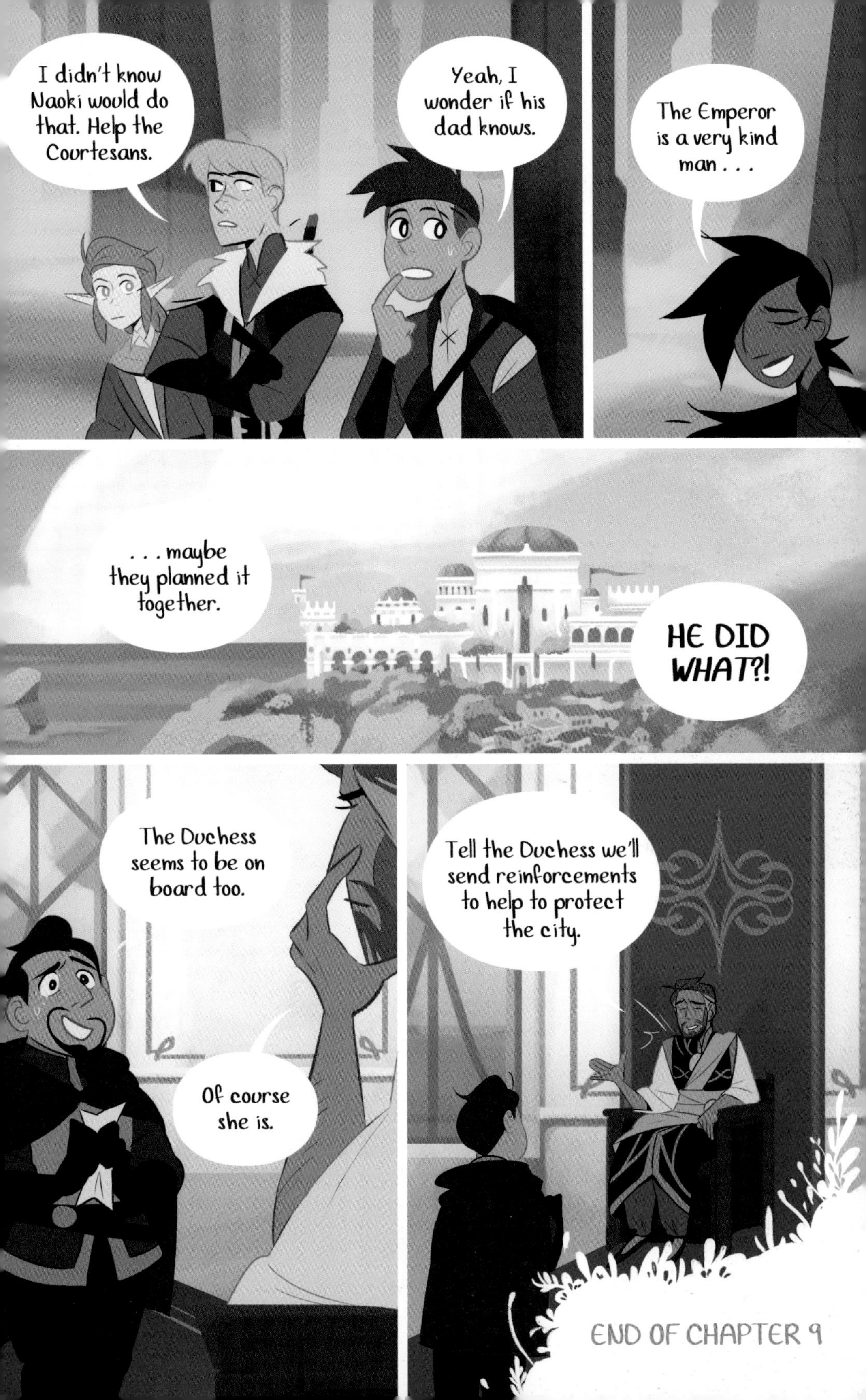
I didn't know Naoki would do that. Help the Courtesans.
Yeah, I wonder if his dad knows.
The Emperor is a very kind man . . .
. . . maybe they planned it together.
HE DID WHAT?!
The Duchess seems to be on board too.
Of course she is.
Tell the Duchess we'll send reinforcements to help to protect the city.
END OF CHAPTER 9

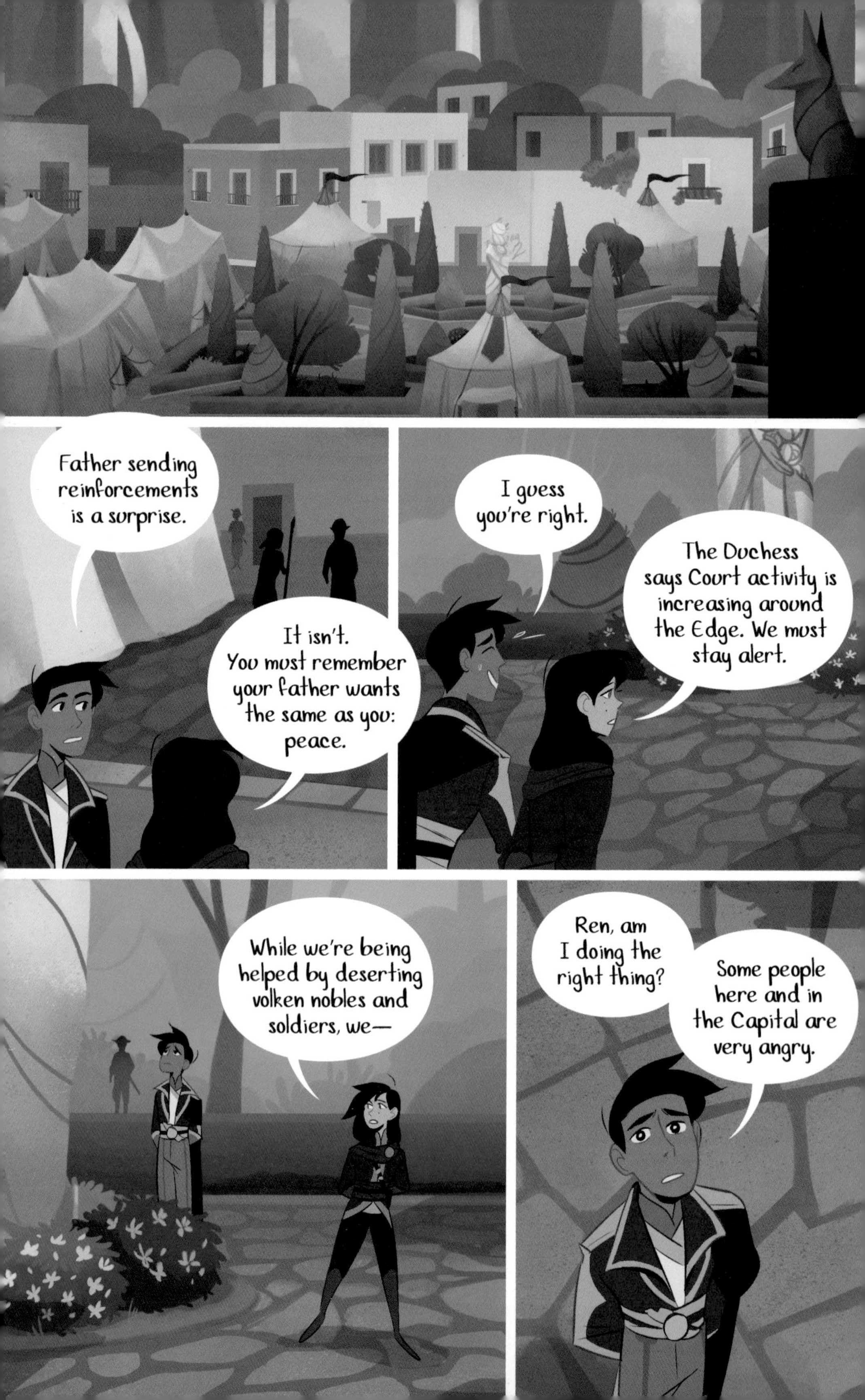
Father sending reinforcements is a surprise.
It isn't. You must remember your father wants the same as you: peace.
I guess you're right.
The Duchess says Court activity is increasing around the Edge. We must stay alert.
While we're being helped by deserting volken nobles and soldiers, we—
Ren, am I doing the right thing?
Some people here and in the Capital are very angry.

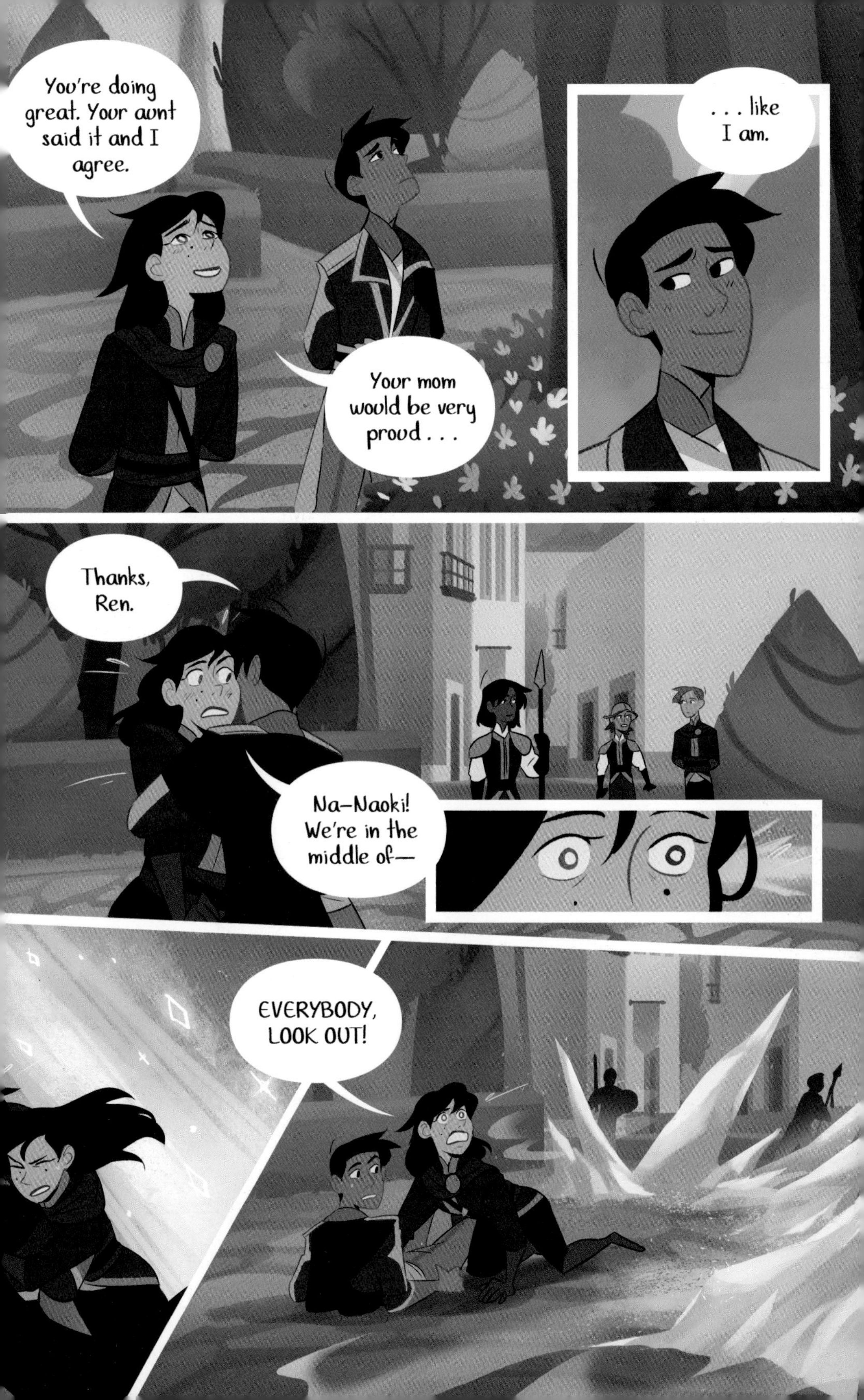
You're doing great. Your aunt said it and I agree.
Your mom would be very proud . . .
. . . like I am.
Thanks, Ren.
Na–Naoki! We're in the middle of—
EVERYBODY, LOOK OUT!

Chapter 10
Prepare for Trouble
Aww, aren't you adorable? The weirdo and his pet.
I should've known you'd come back . . .

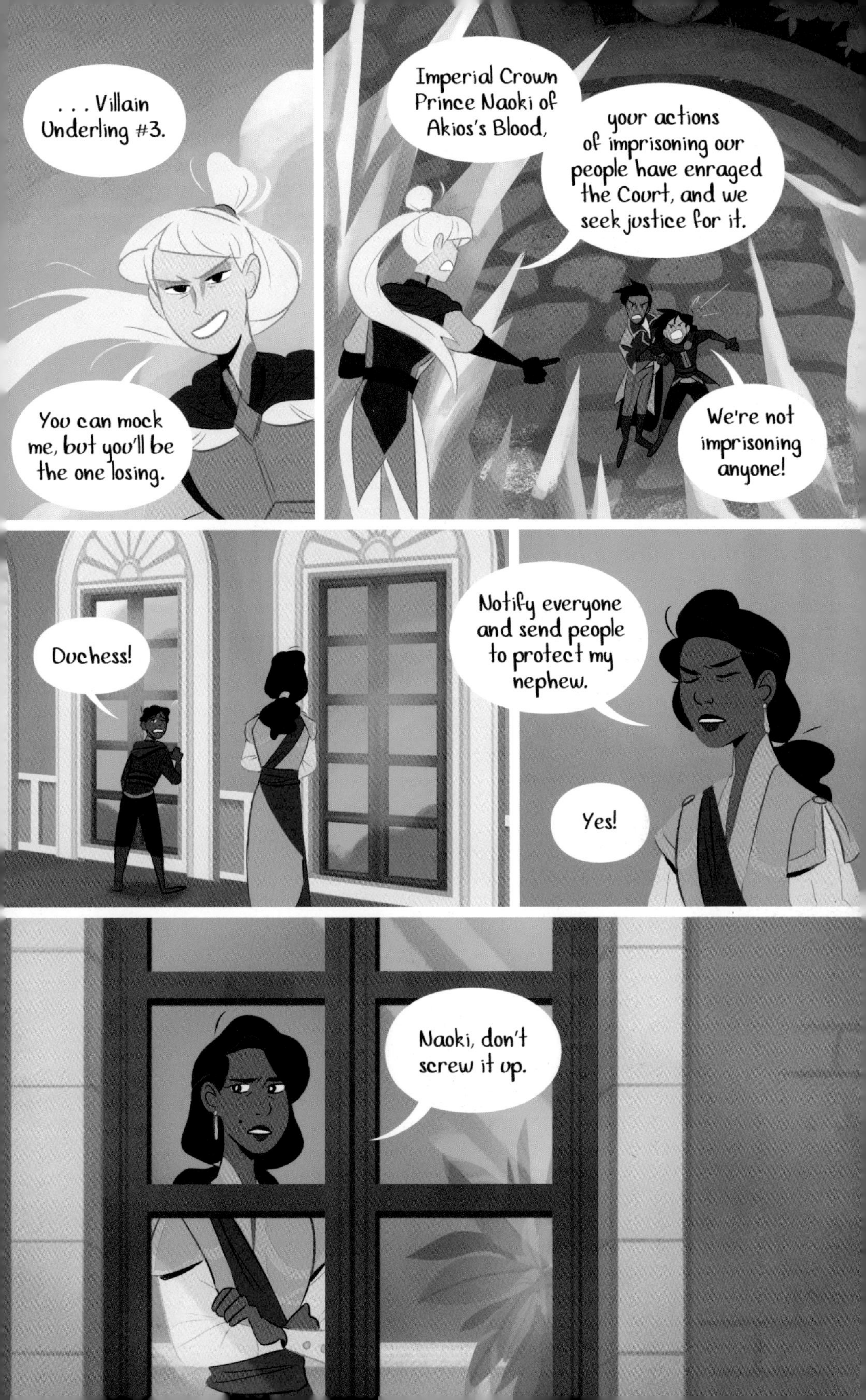
. . . Villain Underling #3.
You can mock me, but you'll be the one losing.
Imperial Crown Prince Naoki of Akios's Blood,
your actions of imprisoning our people have enraged the Court, and we seek justice for it.
We're not imprisoning anyone!
Duchess!
Notify everyone and send people to protect my nephew.
Yes!
Naoki, don't screw it up.

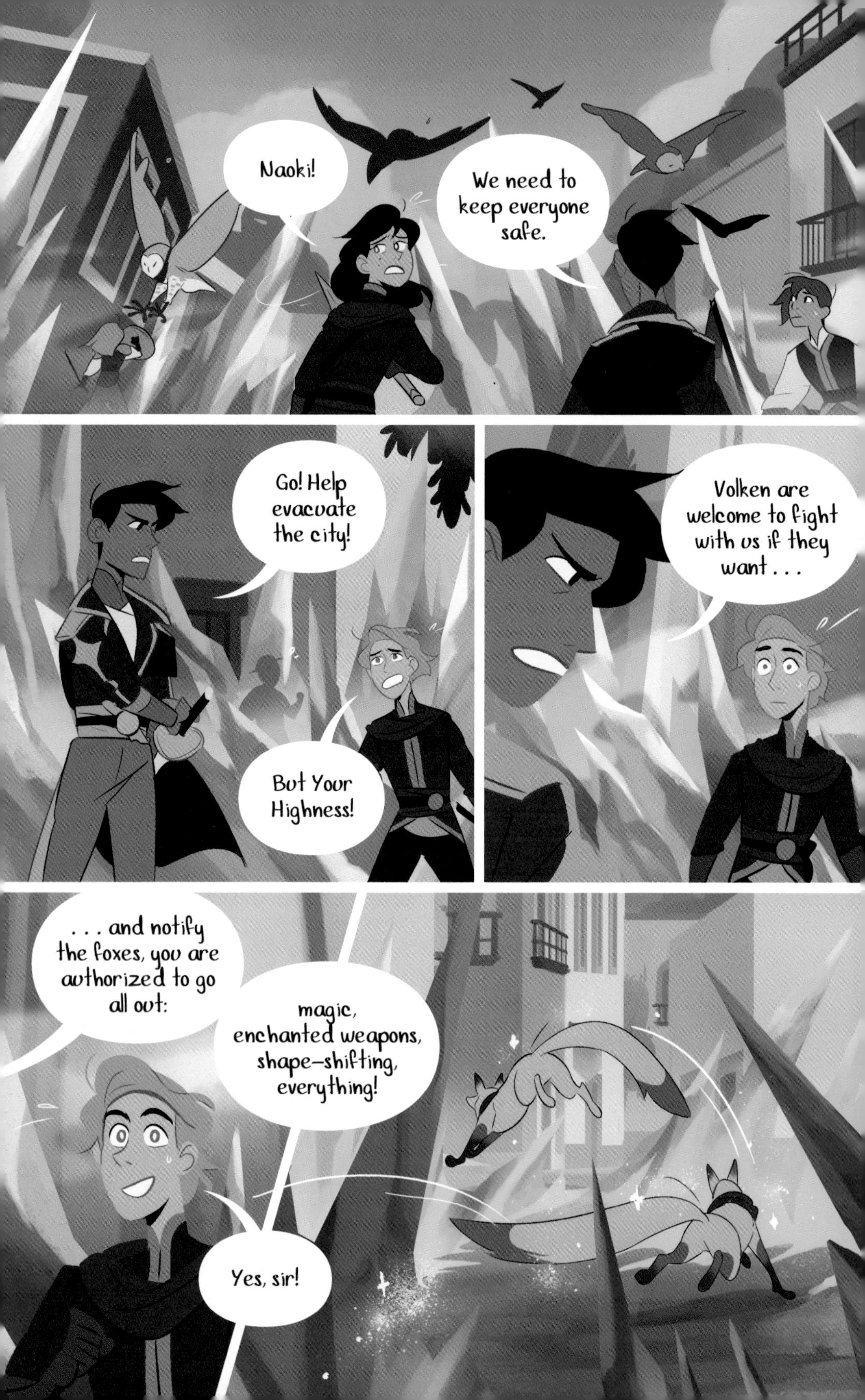
Naoki!
We need to keep everyone safe.
Go! Help evacuate the city!
But Your Highness!
Volken are welcome to fight with us if they want . . .
. . . and notify the foxes, you are authorized to go all out:
magic, enchanted weapons, shape-shifting, everything!
Yes, sir!

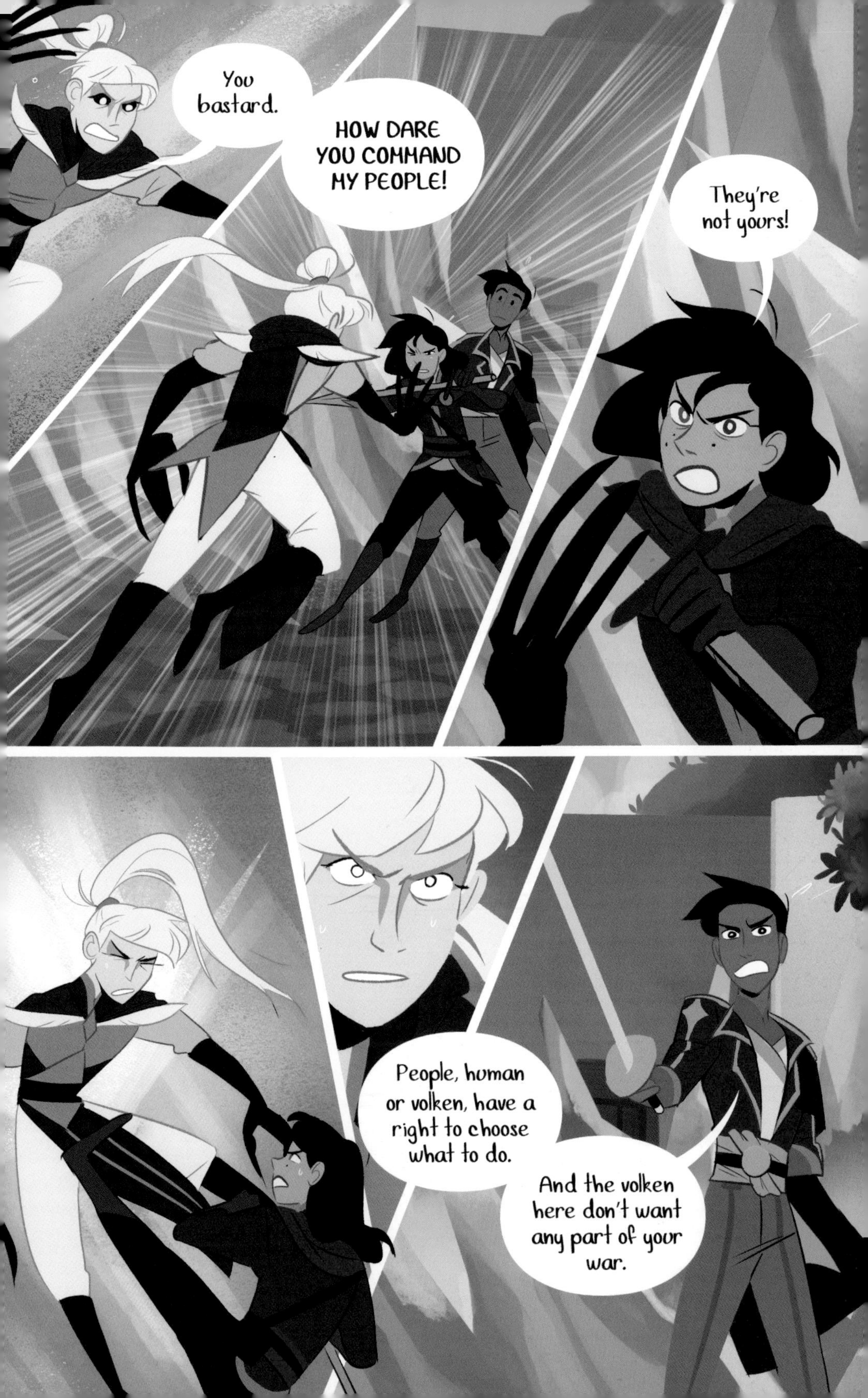
You bastard.
HOW DARE YOU COMMAND MY PEOPLE!
They're not yours!
People, human or volken, have a right to choose what to do.
And the volken here don't want any part of your war.

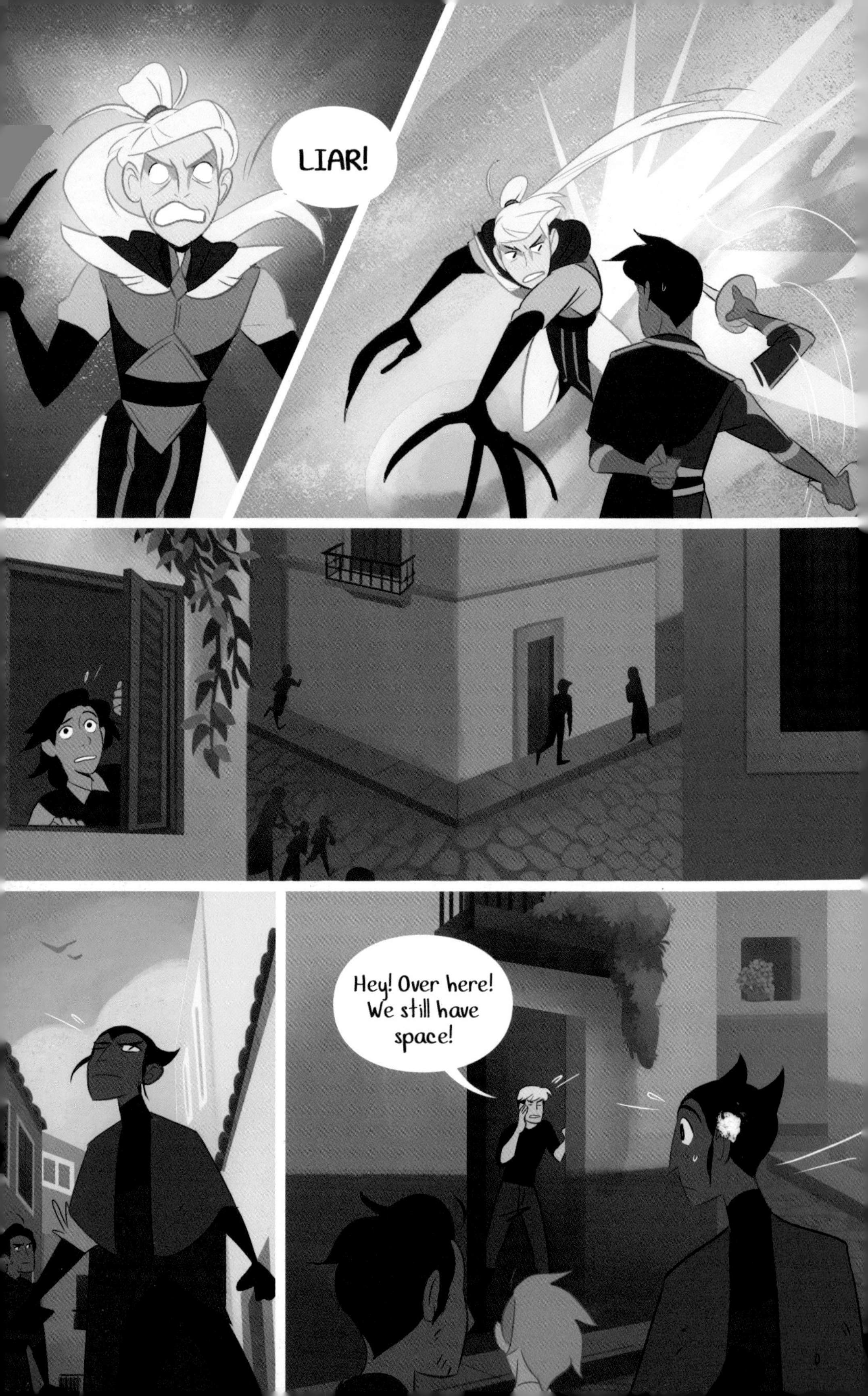
LIAR!
Hey! Over here! We still have space!

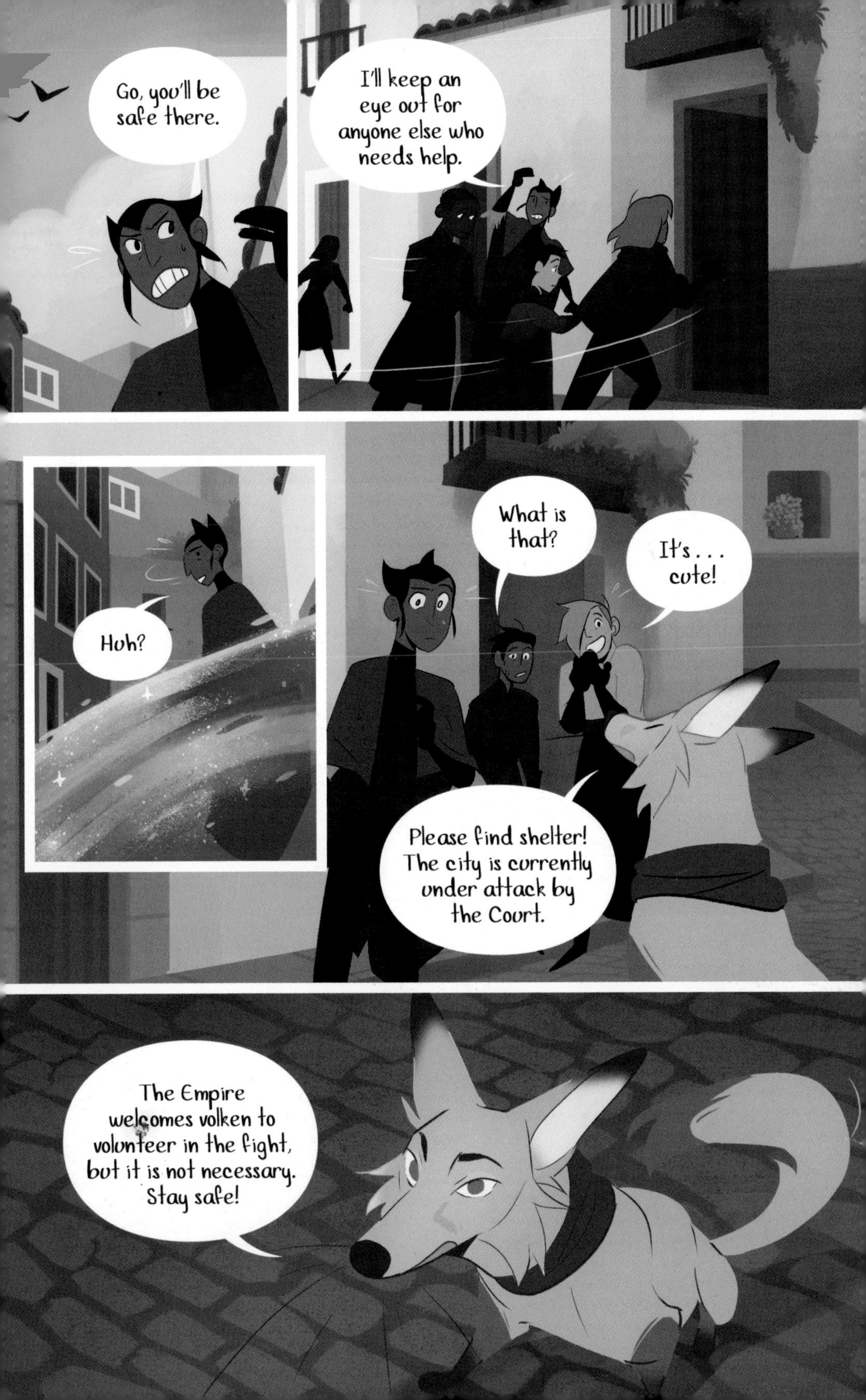
Go, you'll be safe there.
I'll keep an eye out for anyone else who needs help.
Huh?
What is that?
It's . . . cute!
Please find shelter! The city is currently under attack by the Court.
The Empire welcomes volken to volunteer in the fight, but it is not necessary. Stay safe!

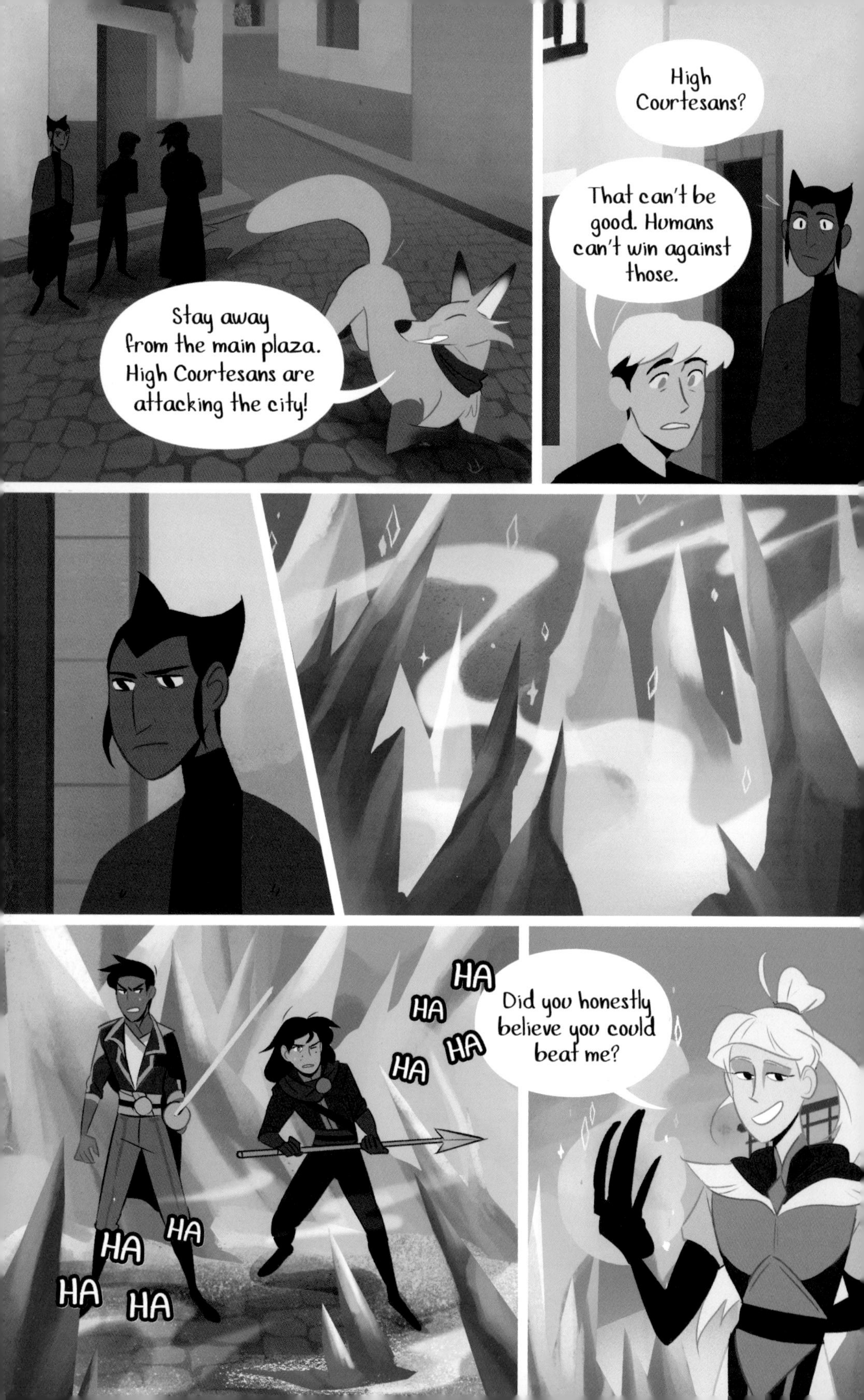
Stay away from the main plaza. High Courtesans are attacking the city!
High Courtesans?
That can't be good. Humans can't win against those.
HA
HA
HA
HA
HA
HA
HA
HA
Did you honestly believe you could beat me?

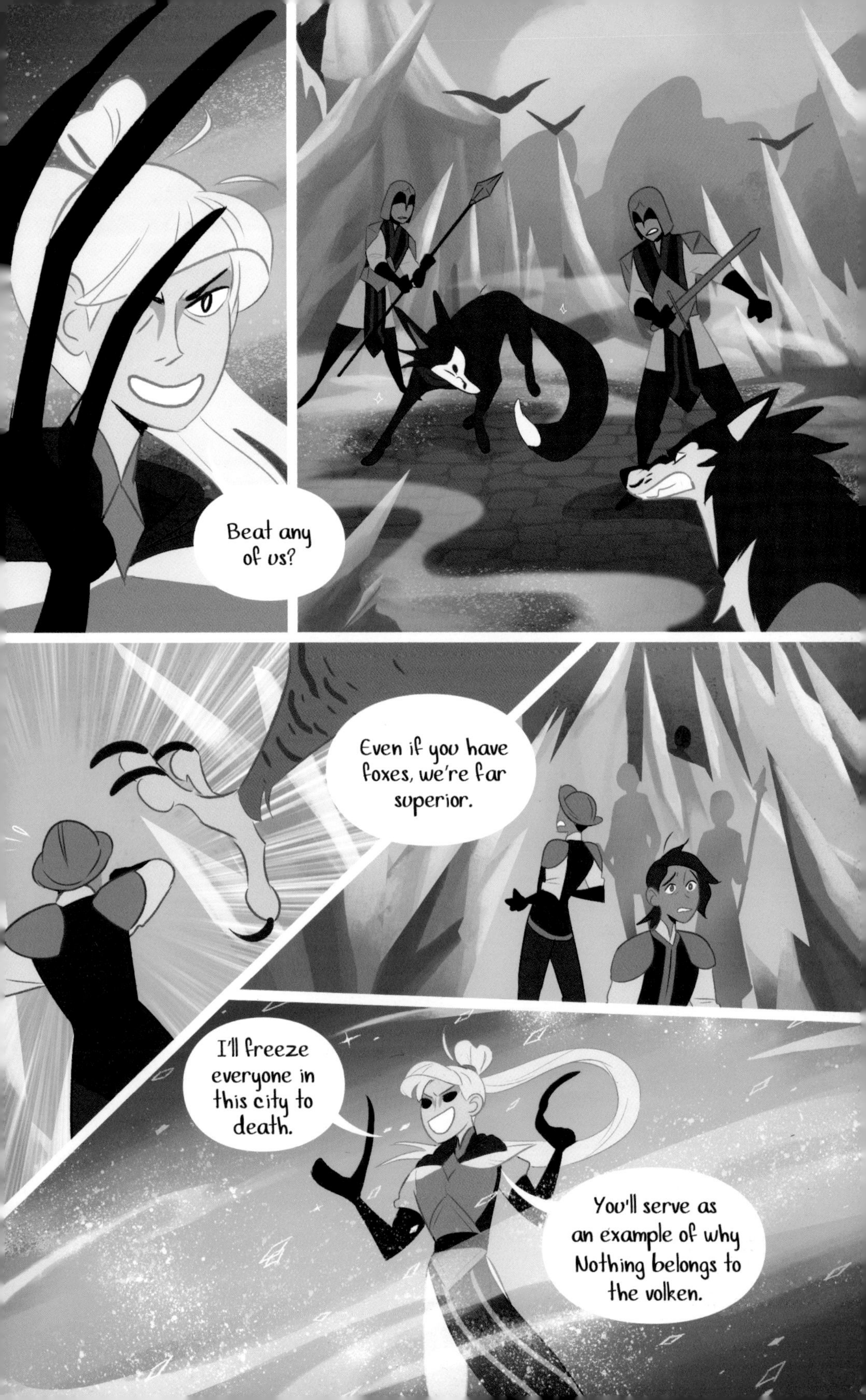
Beat any of us?
Even if you have foxes, we're far superior.
I'll freeze everyone in this city to death.
You'll serve as an example of why Nothing belongs to the volken.

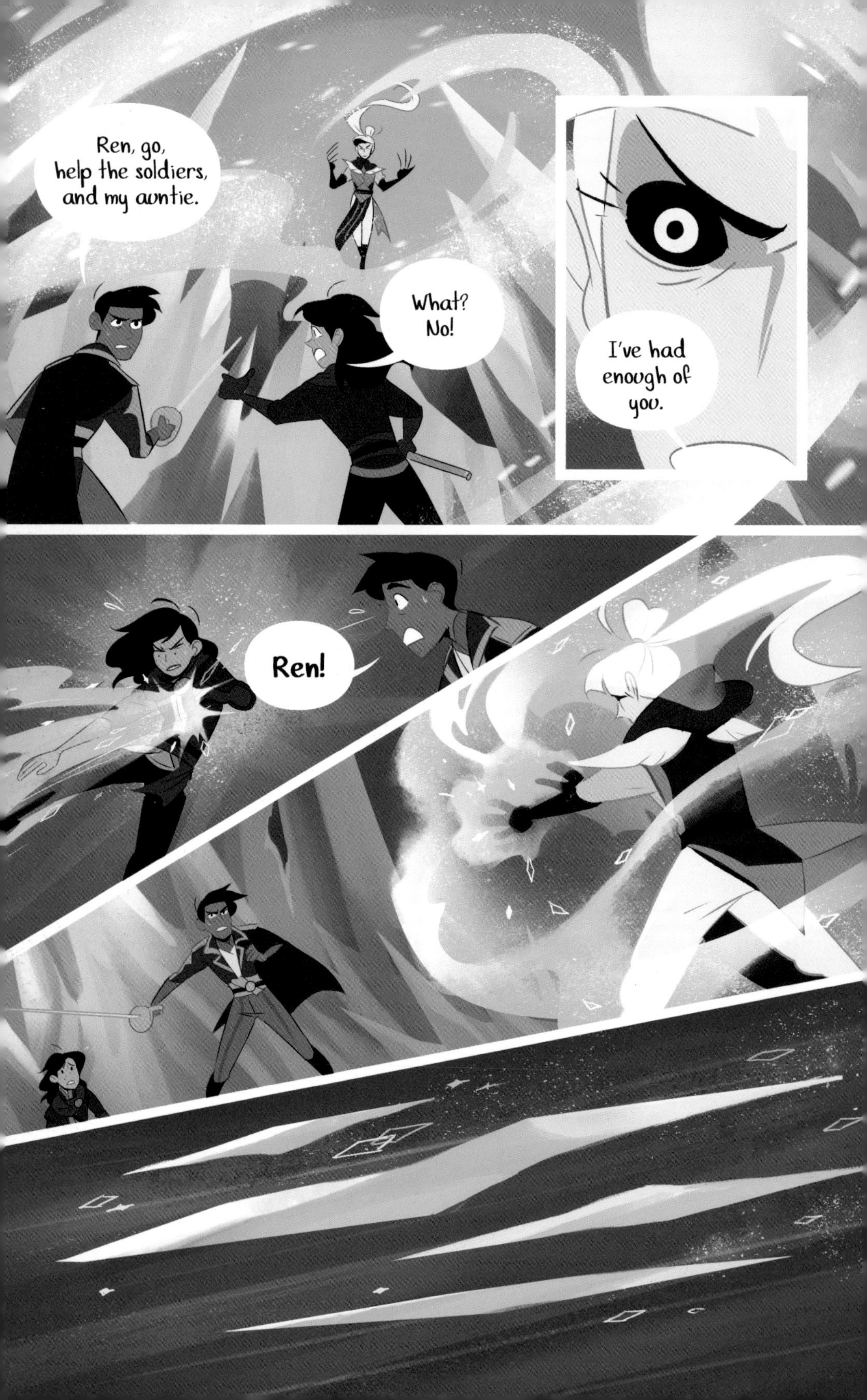
Ren, go, help the soldiers, and my auntie.
What? No!
I've had enough of you.
Ren!

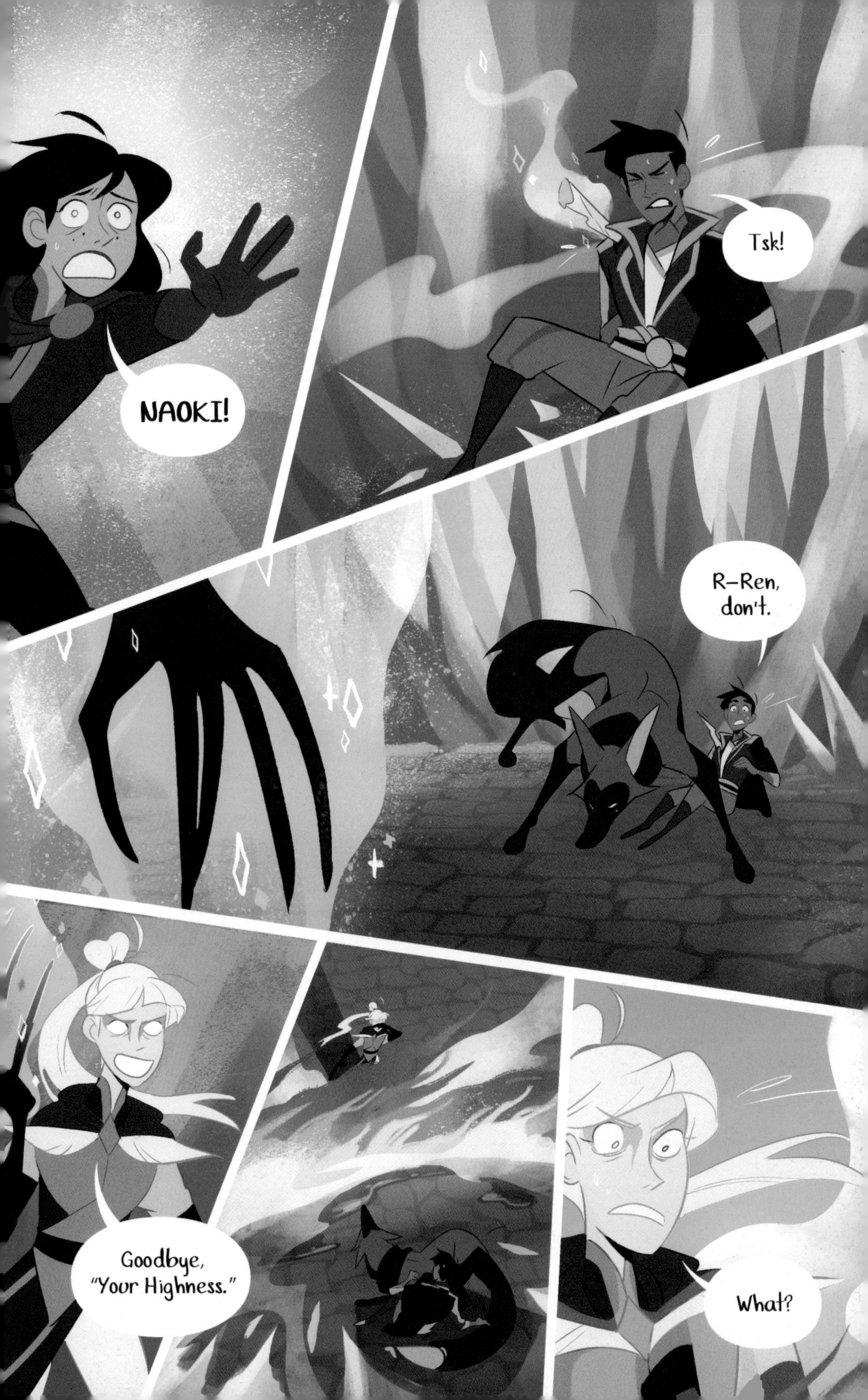
NAOKI!
Tsk!
R-Ren, don't.
Goodbye, "Your Highness."
What?

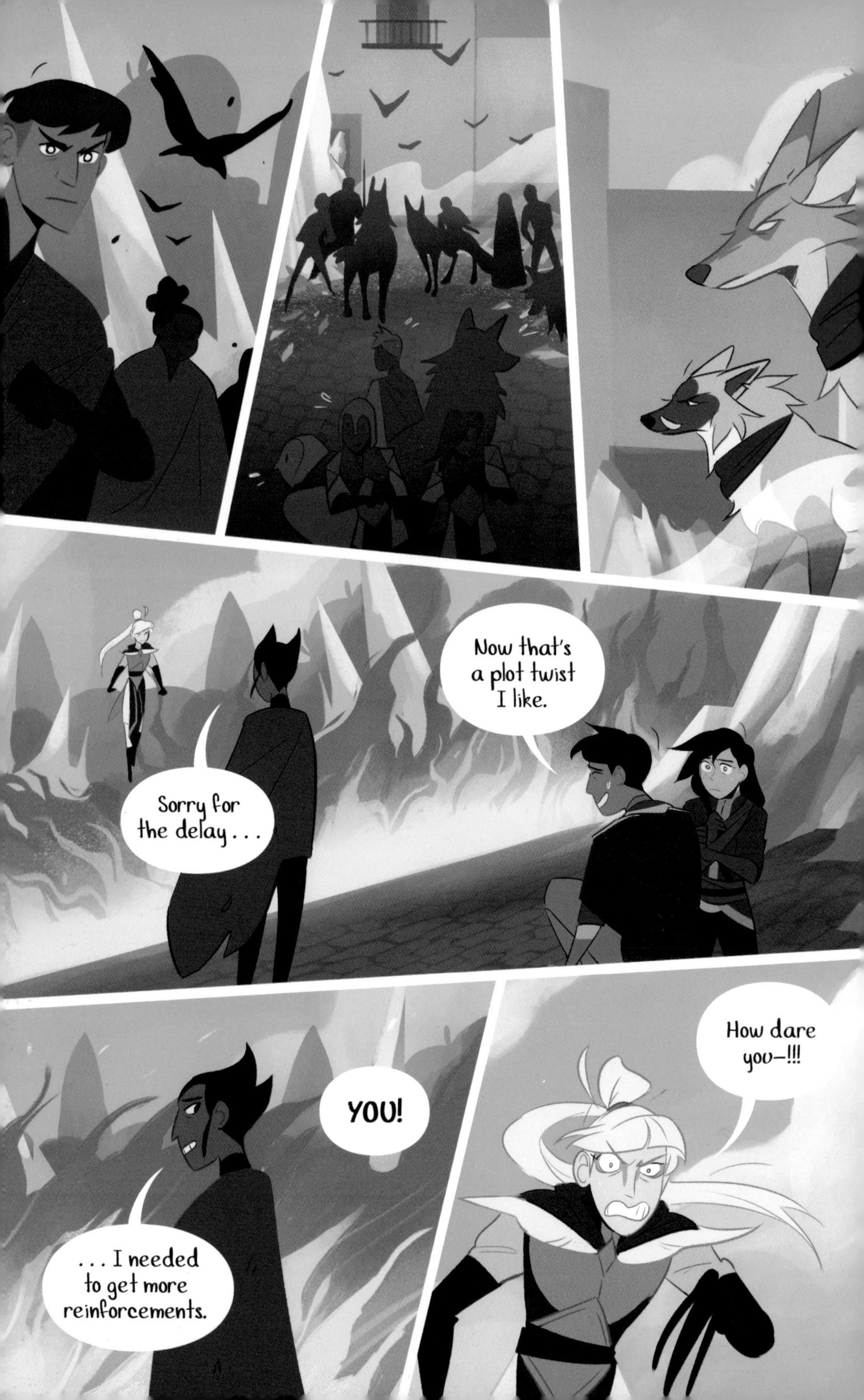
Now that's a plot twist I like.
Sorry for the delay . . .
. . . I needed to get more reinforcements.
YOU!
How dare you—!!!

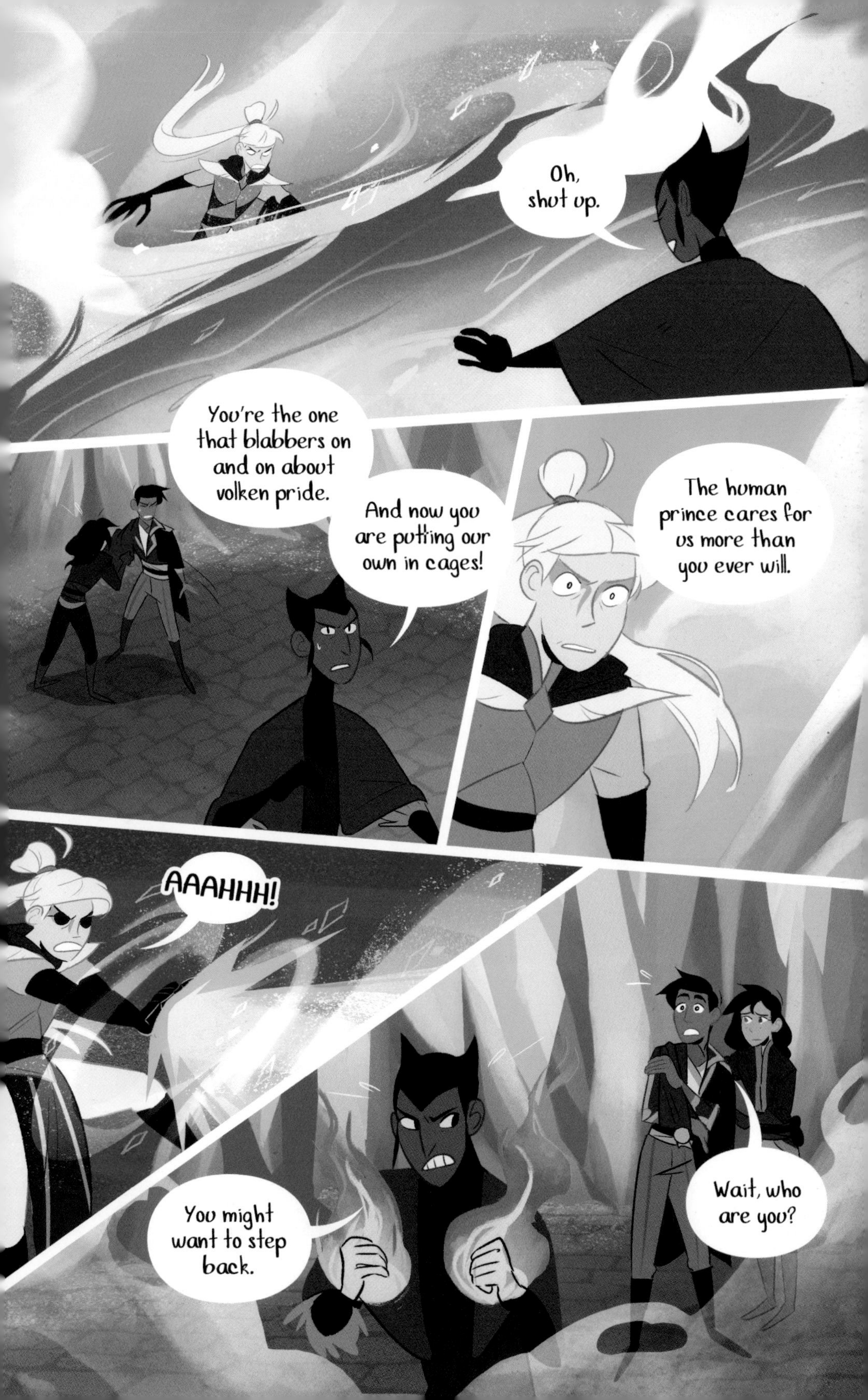
Oh, shut up.
You're the one that blabbers on and on about volken pride.
And now you are putting our own in cages!
The human prince cares for us more than you ever will.
AAAHHH!
Wait, who are you?
You might want to step back.

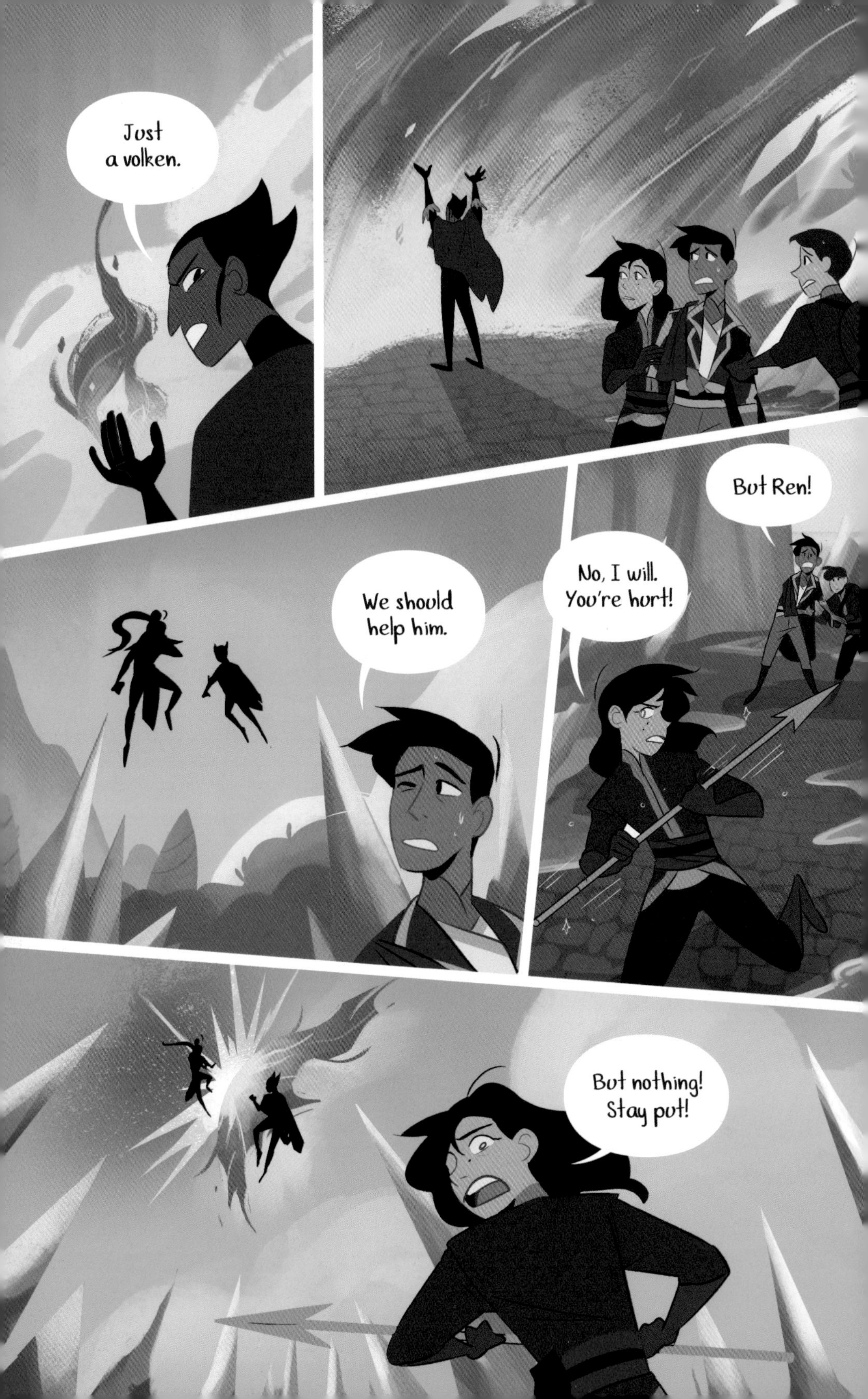
Just a volken.
We should help him.
No, I will. You're hurt!
But Ren!
But nothing! Stay put!

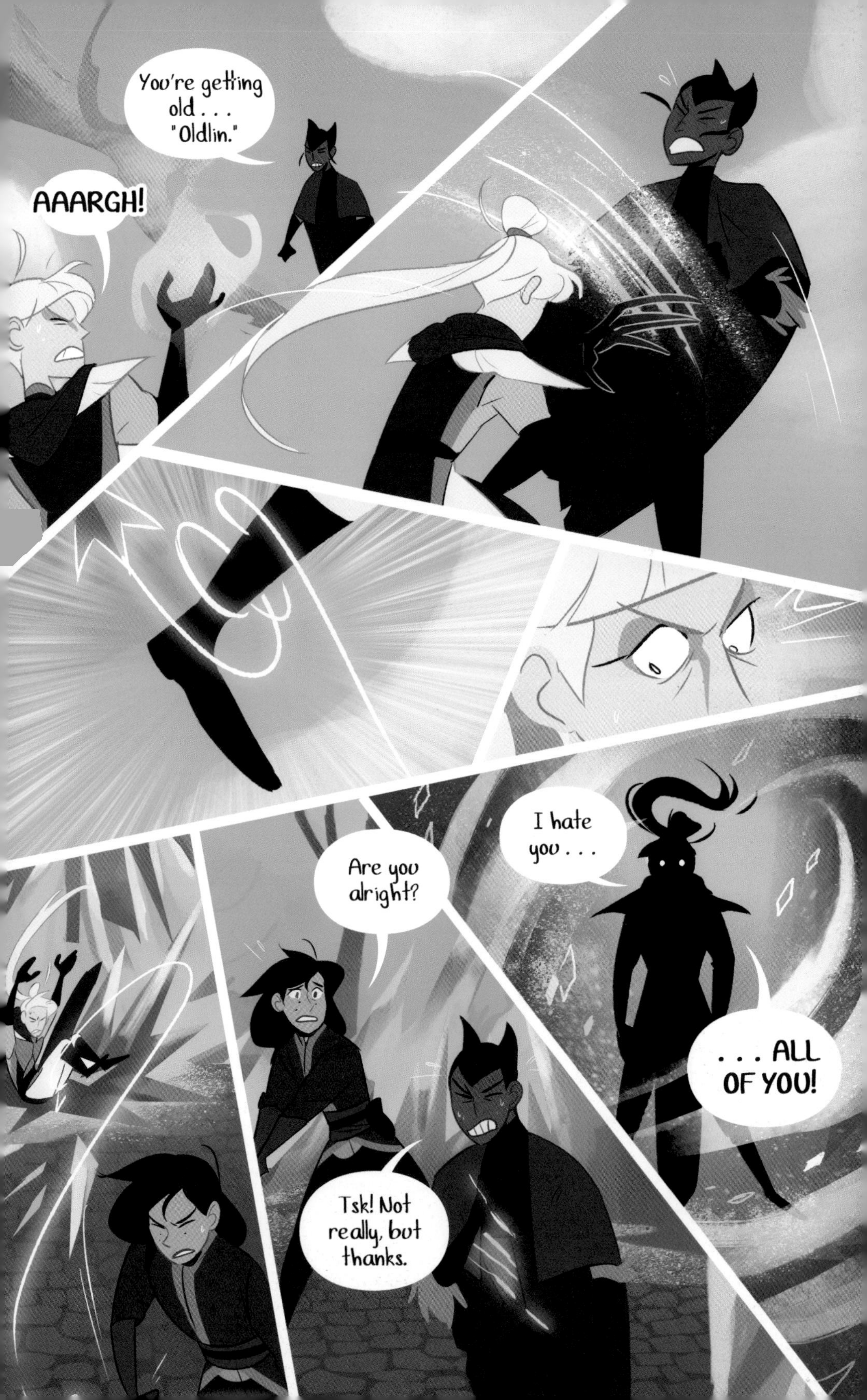
You're getting old . . . "Oldlin."
AAARGH!
Are you alright?
Tsk! Not really, but thanks.
I hate you . . .
. . . ALL OF YOU!

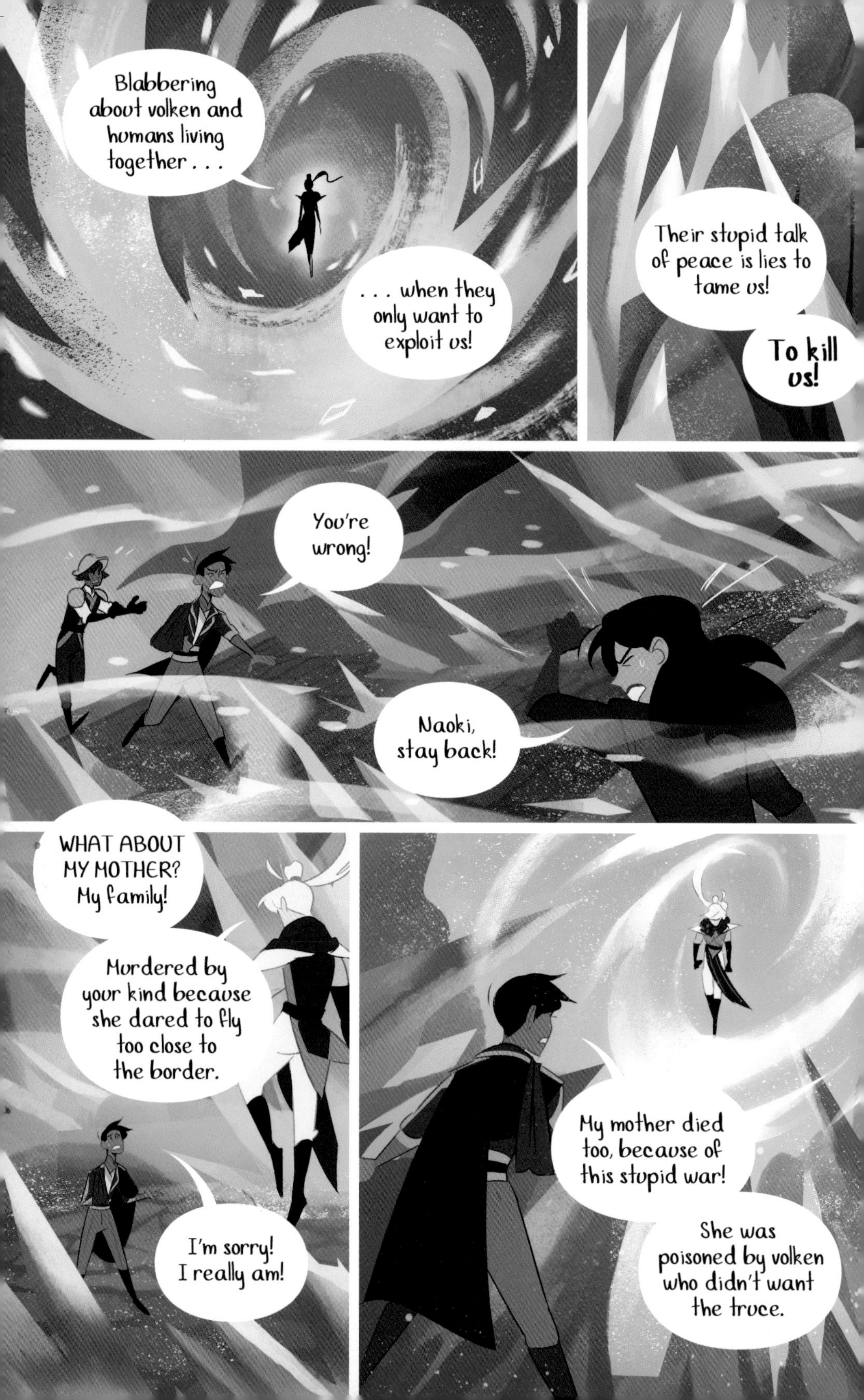
Blabbering about volken and humans living together . . .
. . . when they only want to exploit us!
Their stupid talk of peace is lies to tame us!
To kill us!
You're wrong!
Naoki, stay back!
WHAT ABOUT MY MOTHER? My family!
Murdered by your kind because she dared to fly too close to the border.
I'm sorry! I really am!
My mother died too, because of this stupid war!
She was poisoned by volken who didn't want the truce.

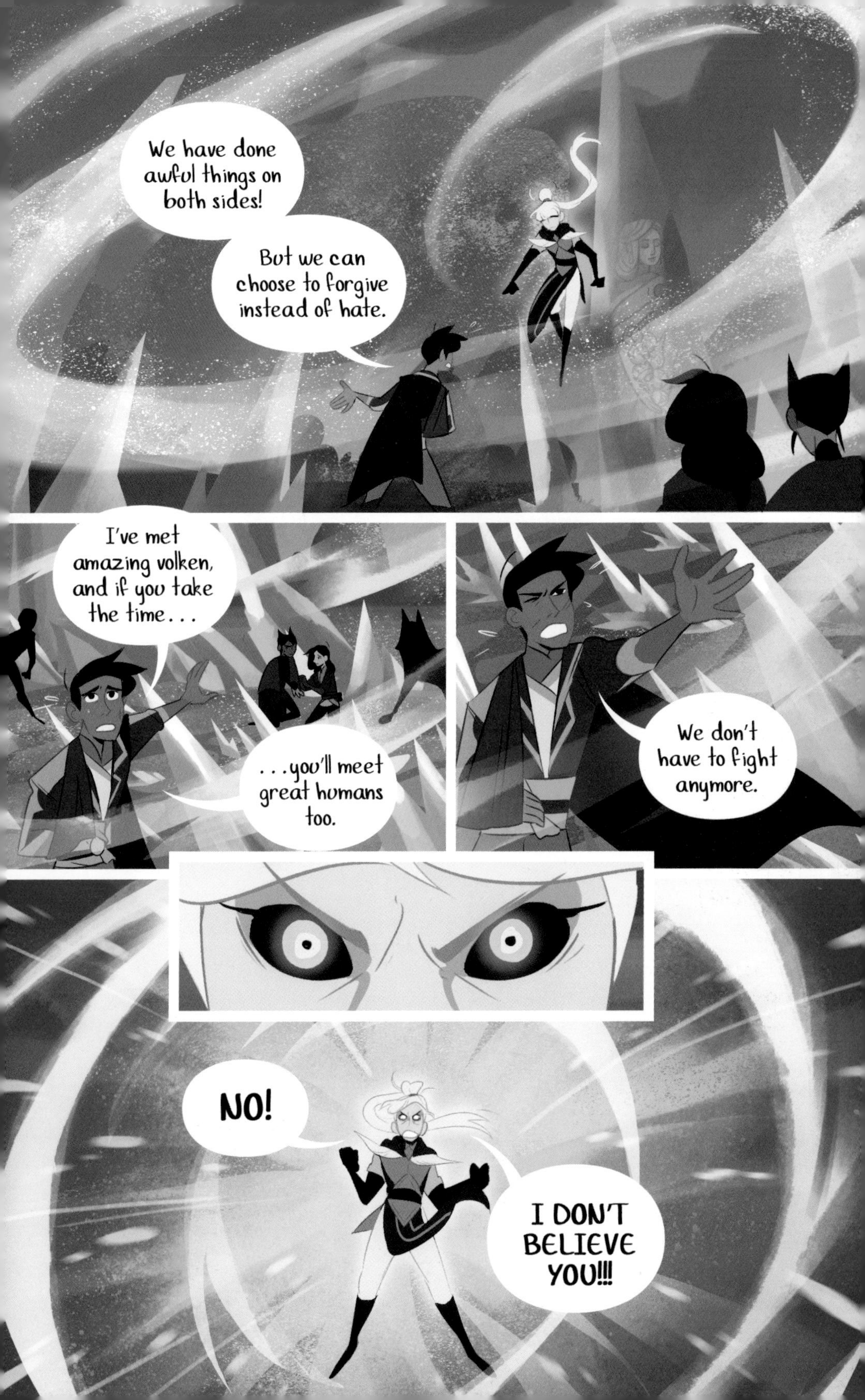
We have done awful things on both sides!
But we can choose to forgive instead of hate.
I've met amazing volken, and if you take the time...
...you'll meet great humans too.
We don't have to fight anymore.
NO!
I DON'T BELIEVE YOU!!!

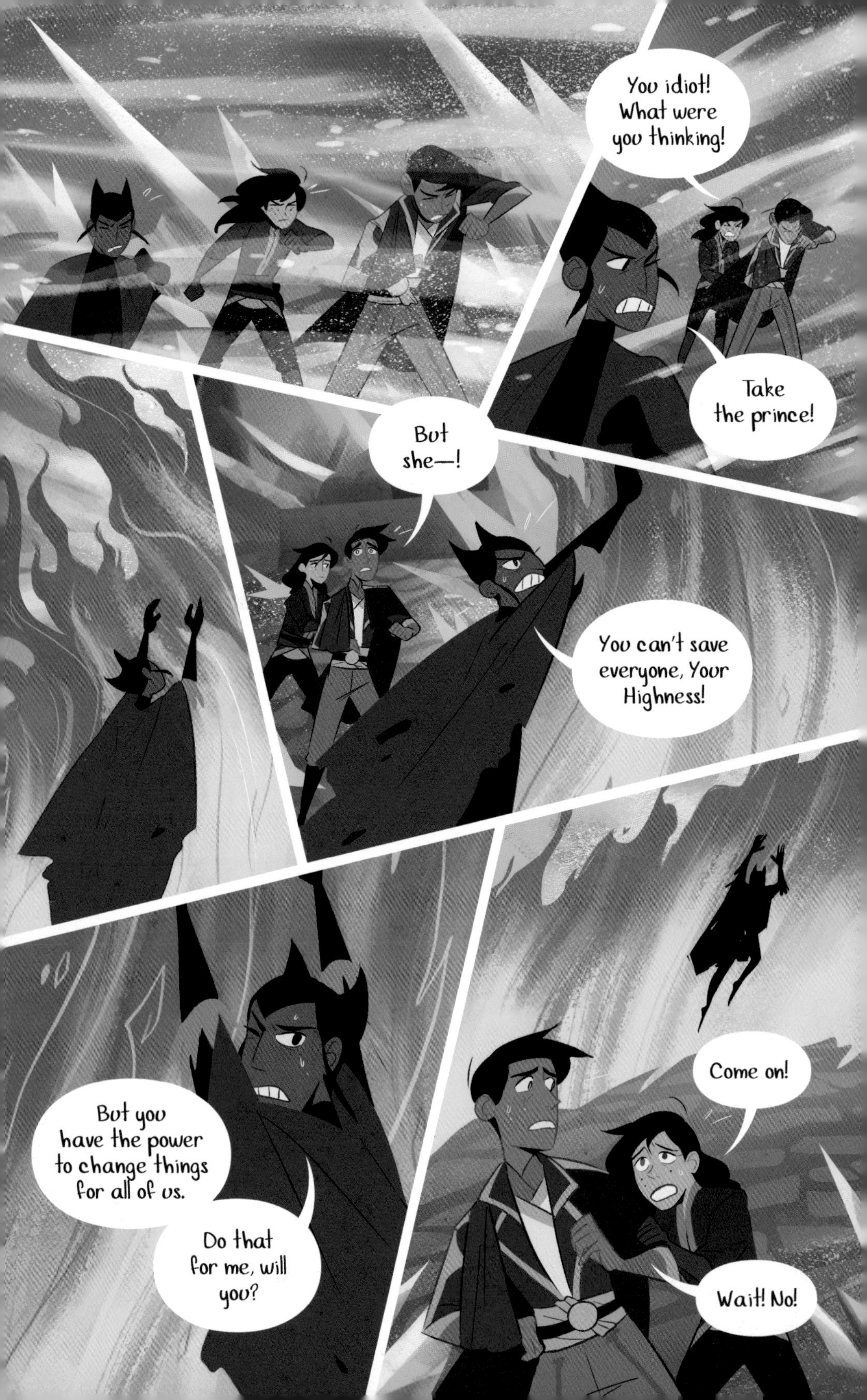
You idiot! What were you thinking!
Take the prince!
But she—!
You can't save everyone, Your Highness!
But you have the power to change things for all of us.
Do that for me, will you?
Come on!
Wait! No!

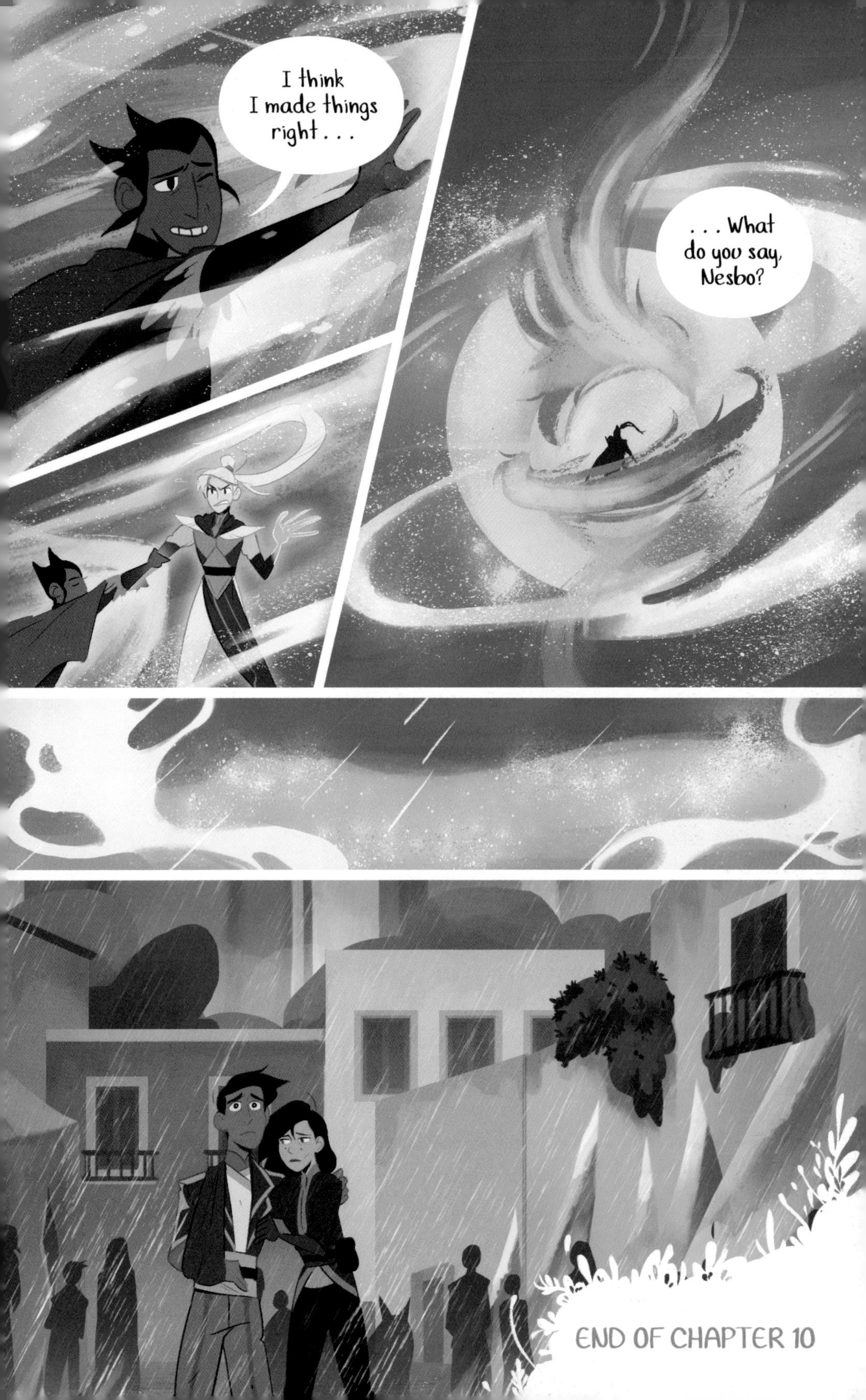
I think I made things right . . .
. . . What do you say, Nesbo?
END OF CHAPTER 10

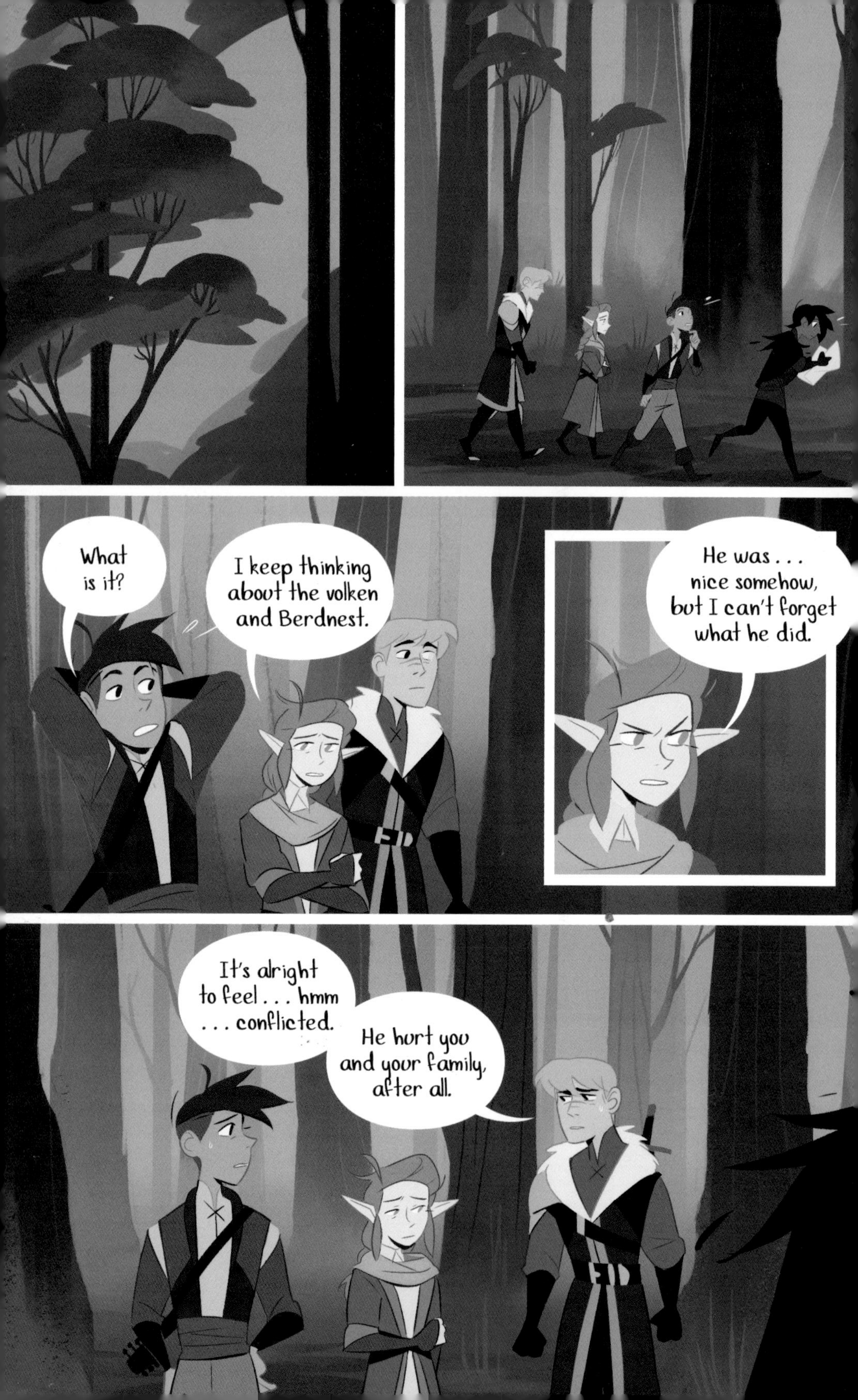
What is it?
I keep thinking about the volken and Berdnest.
He was . . . nice somehow, but I can't forget what he did.
It's alright to feel . . . hmm . . . conflicted.
He hurt you and your family, after all.

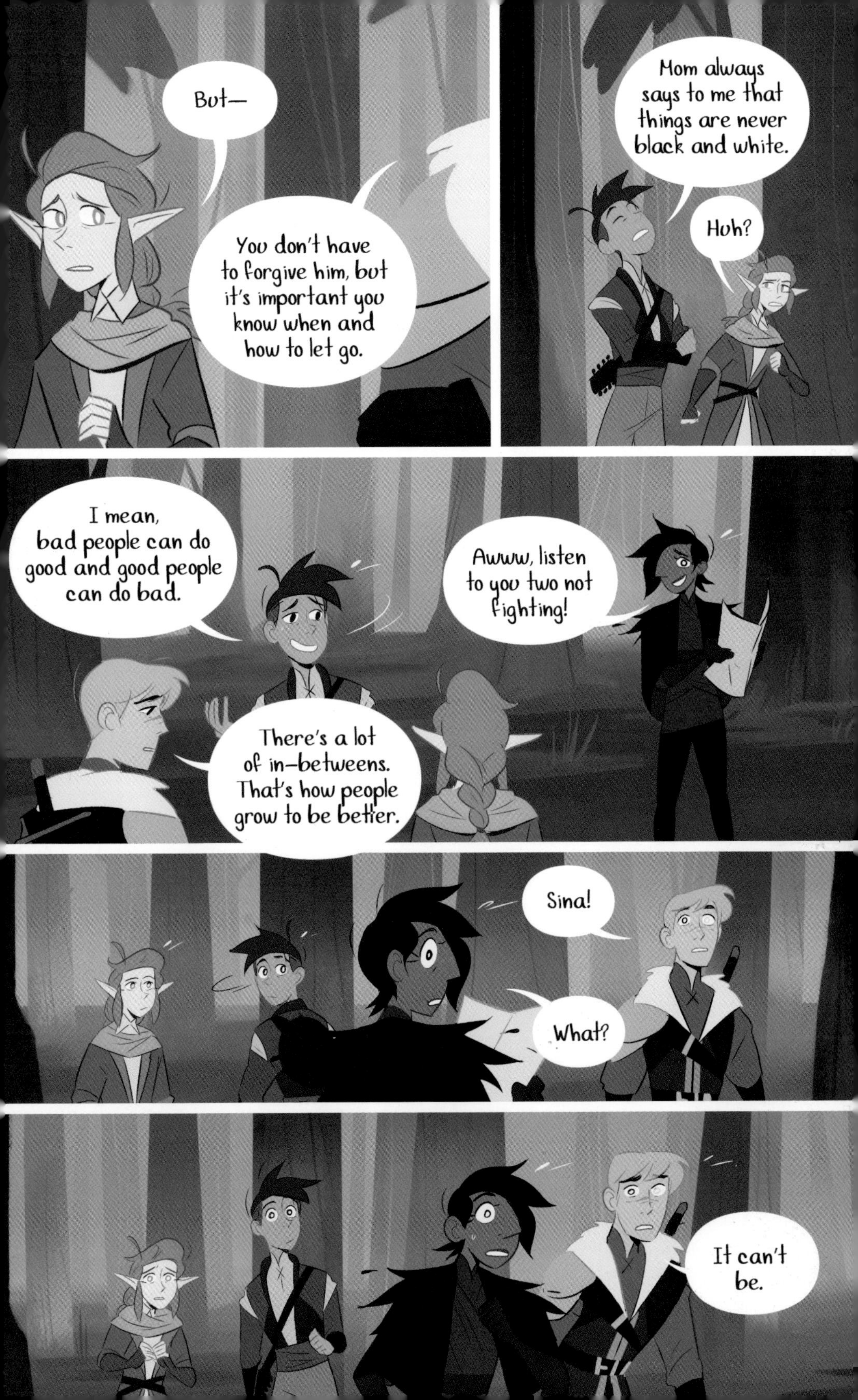
But—
You don't have to forgive him, but it's important you know when and how to let go.
Mom always says to me that things are never black and white.
Huh?
I mean, bad people can do good and good people can do bad.
There's a lot of in-betweens. That's how people grow to be better.
Awww, listen to you two not fighting!
Sina!
What?
It can't be.

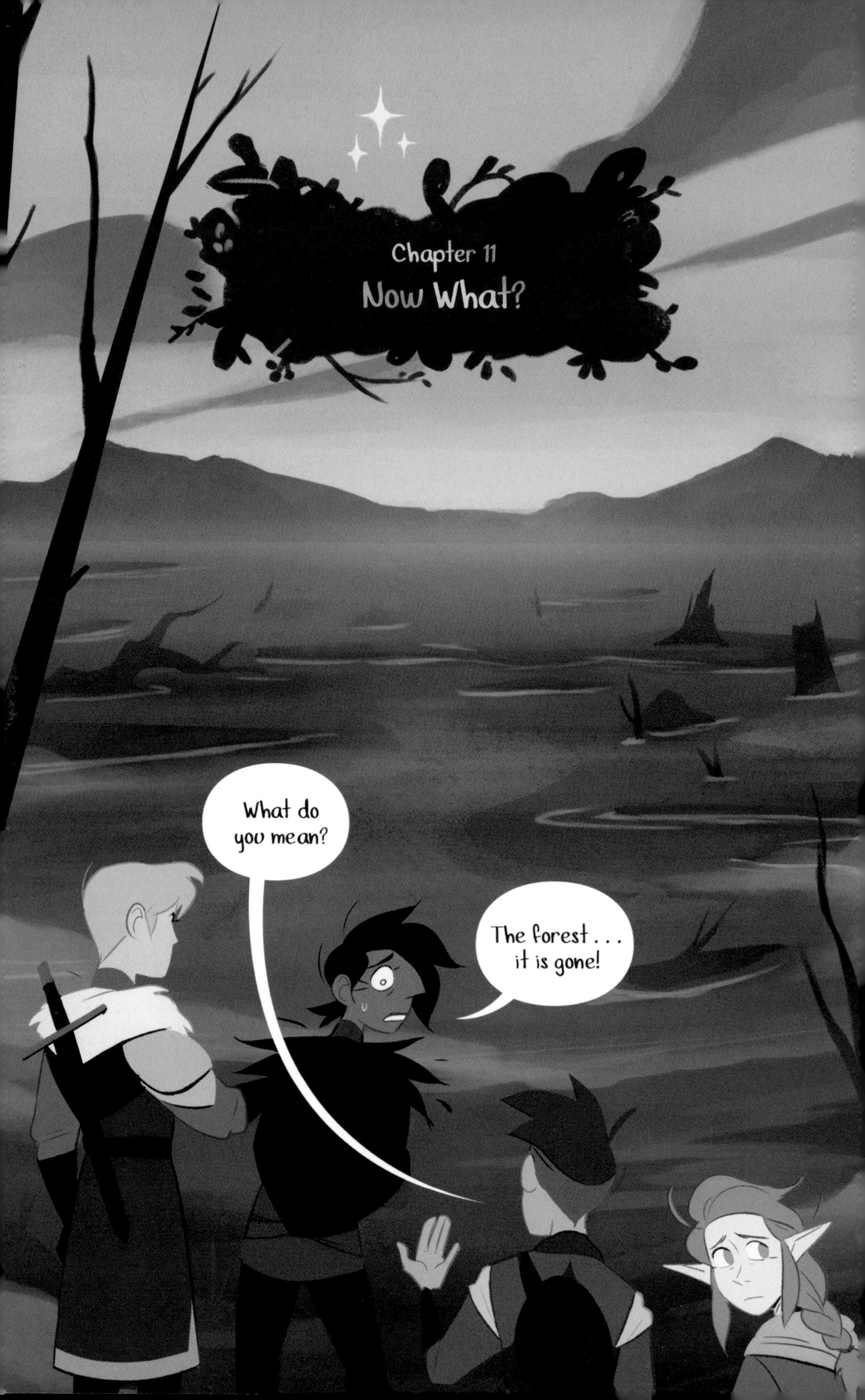
Chapter 11
Now What?
The forest . . . it is gone!
What do you mean?

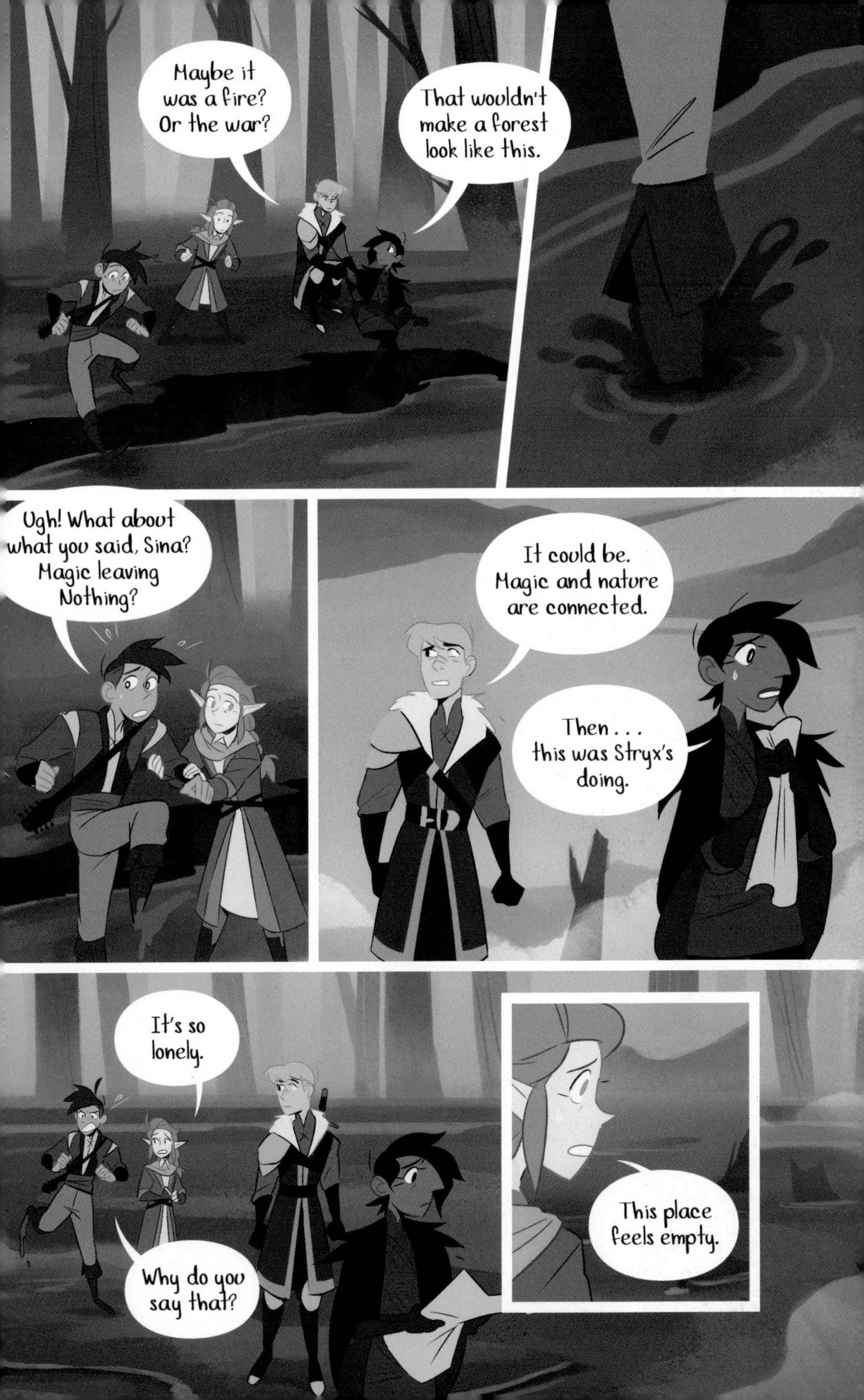
Maybe it was a fire? Or the war?
That wouldn't make a forest look like this.
Ugh! What about what you said, Sina? Magic leaving Nothing?
It could be. Magic and nature are connected.
Then . . . this was Stryx's doing.
It's so lonely.
Why do you say that?
This place feels empty.

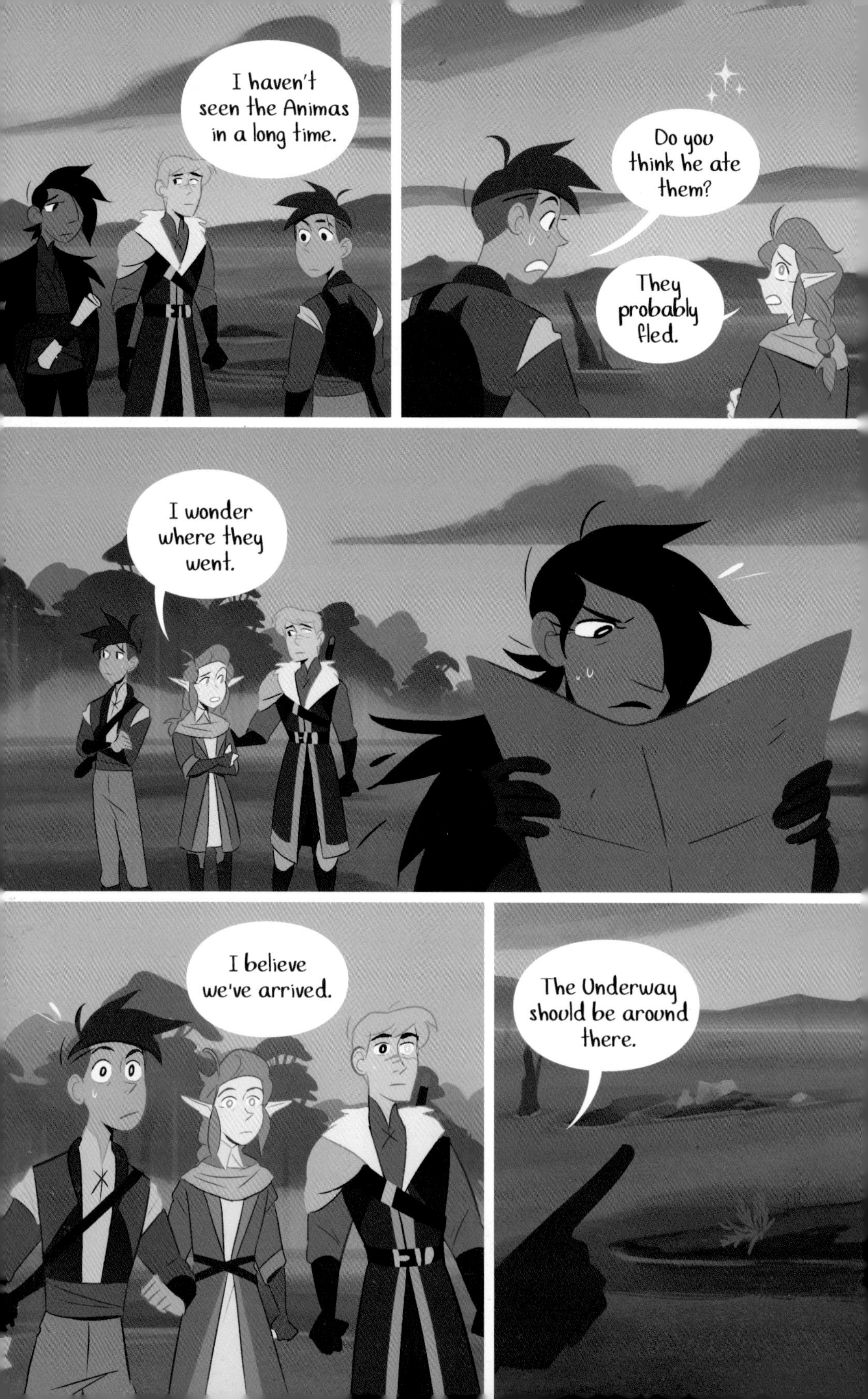
I haven't seen the Animas in a long time.
Do you think he ate them?
They probably fled.
I wonder where they went.
I believe we've arrived.
The Underway should be around there.

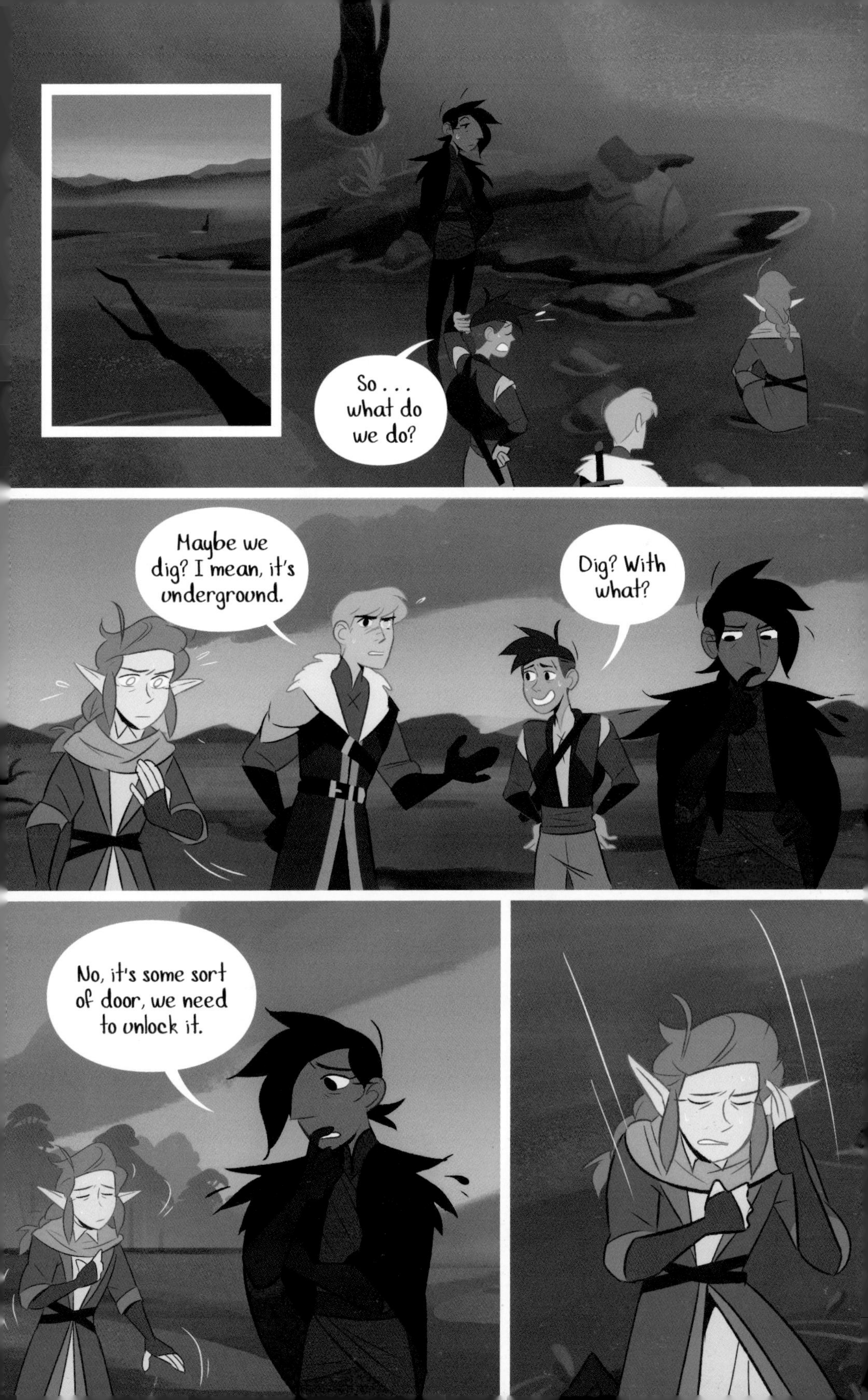
So . . . what do we do?
Maybe we dig? I mean, it's underground.
Dig? With what?
No, it's some sort of door, we need to unlock it.

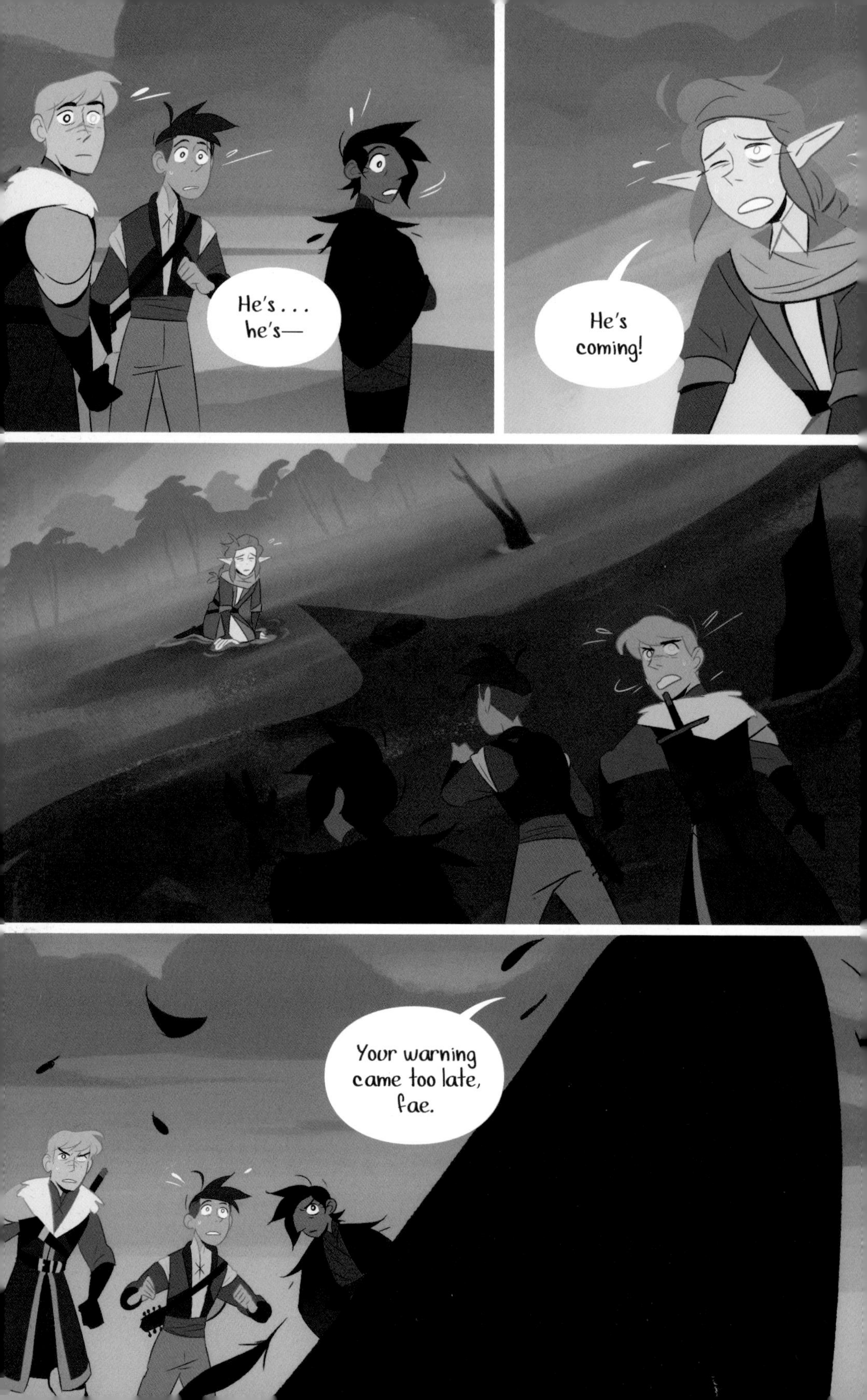
He's . . .
he's—
He's coming!
Your warning came too late, fae.

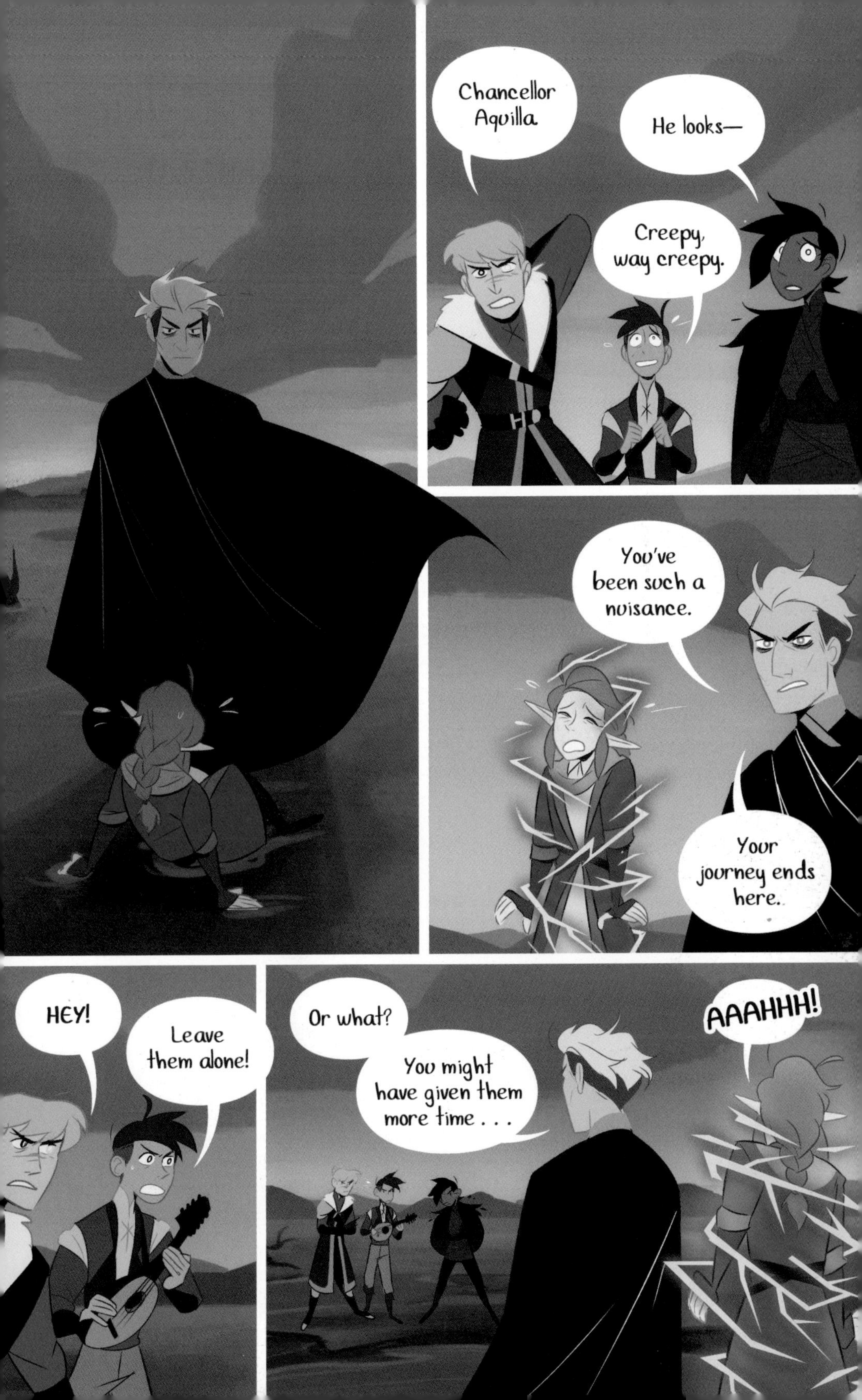
Chancellor Aquilla
He looks—
Creepy, way creepy.
You've been such a nuisance.
Your journey ends here.
HEY!
Leave them alone!
Or what?
You might have given them more time . . .
AAAHHH!

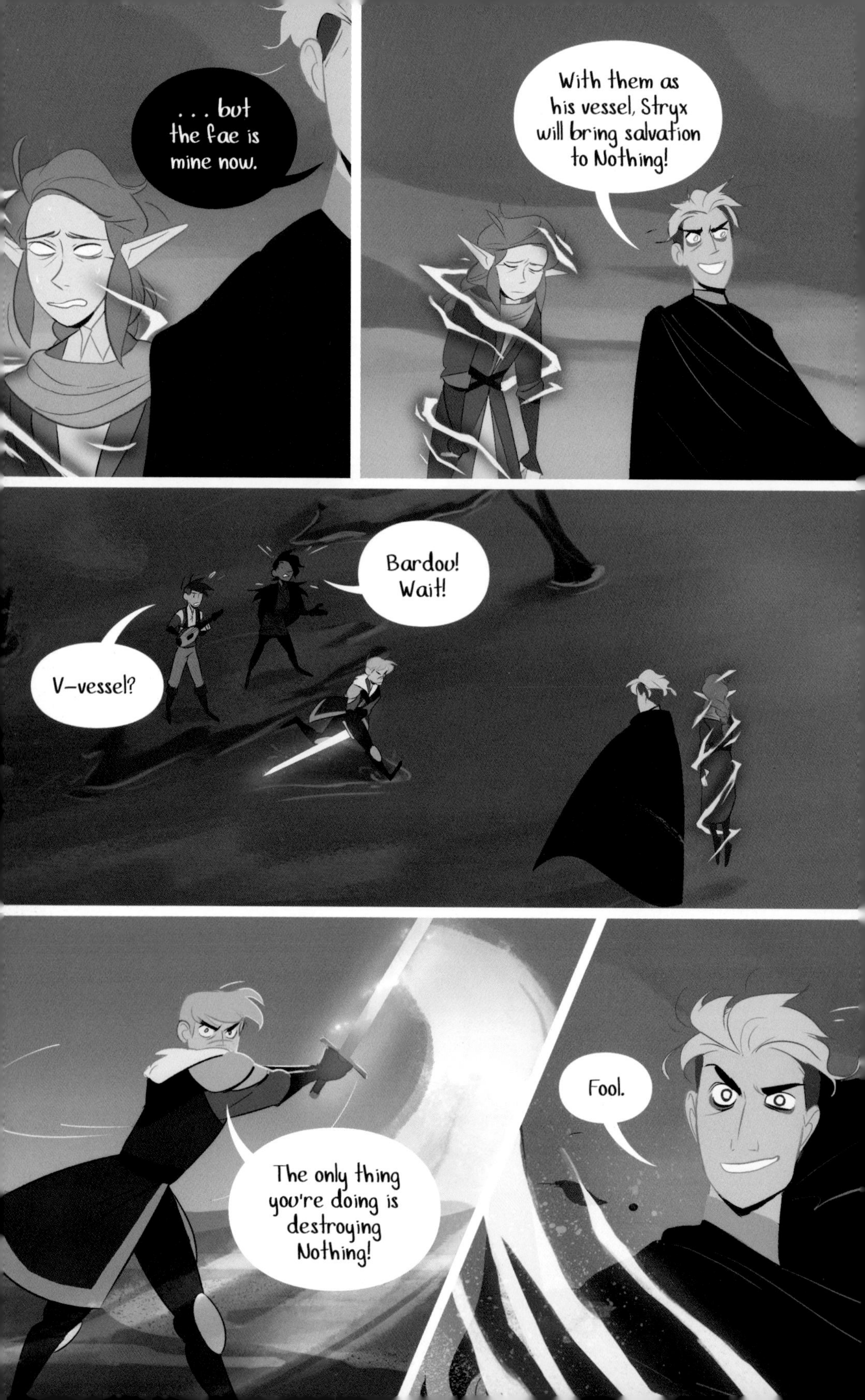
. . . but the fae is mine now.
With them as his vessel, Stryx will bring salvation to Nothing!
Bardou! Wait!
V-vessel?
The only thing you're doing is destroying Nothing!
Fool.

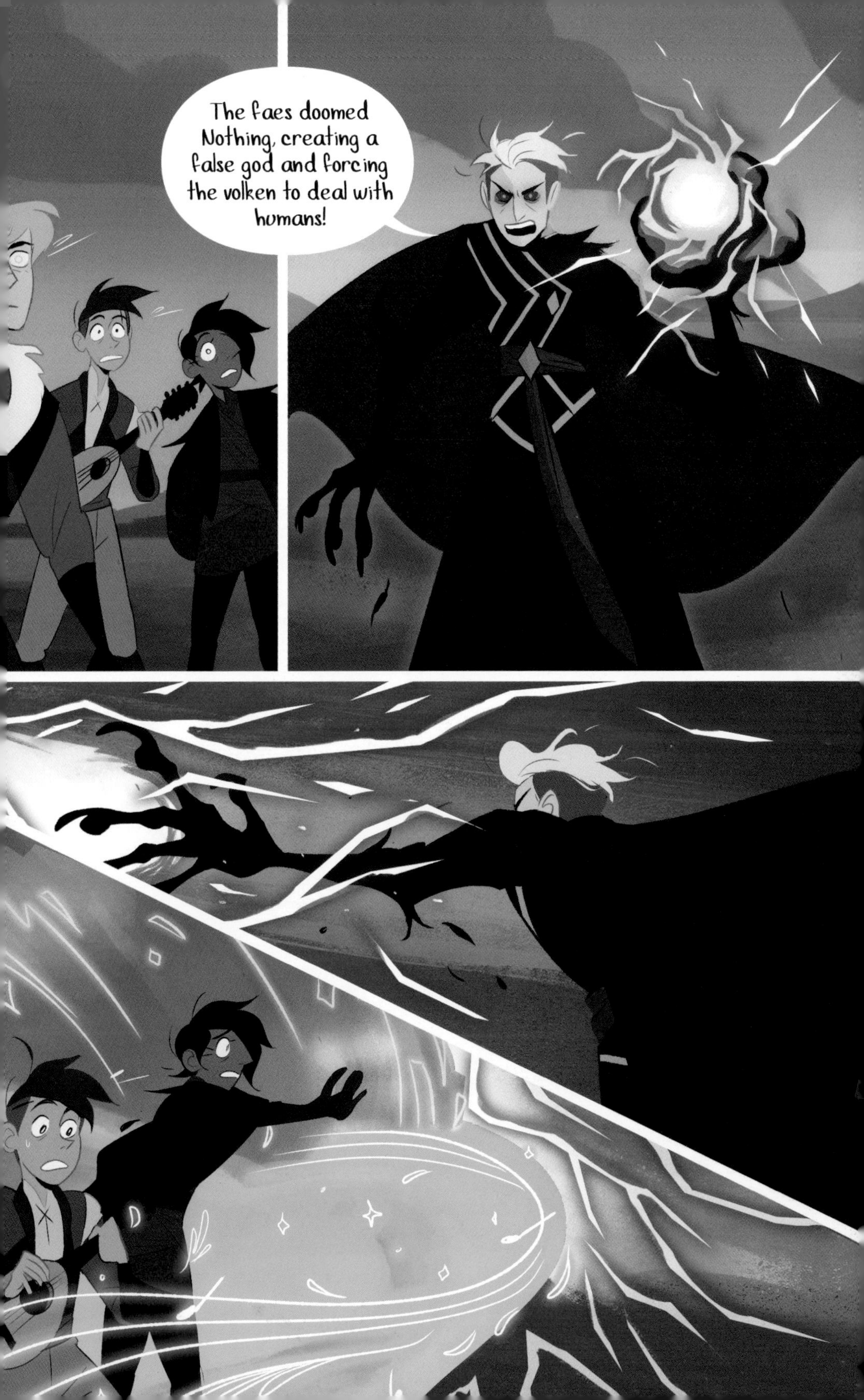
The faes doomed Nothing, creating a false god and forcing the volken to deal with humans!

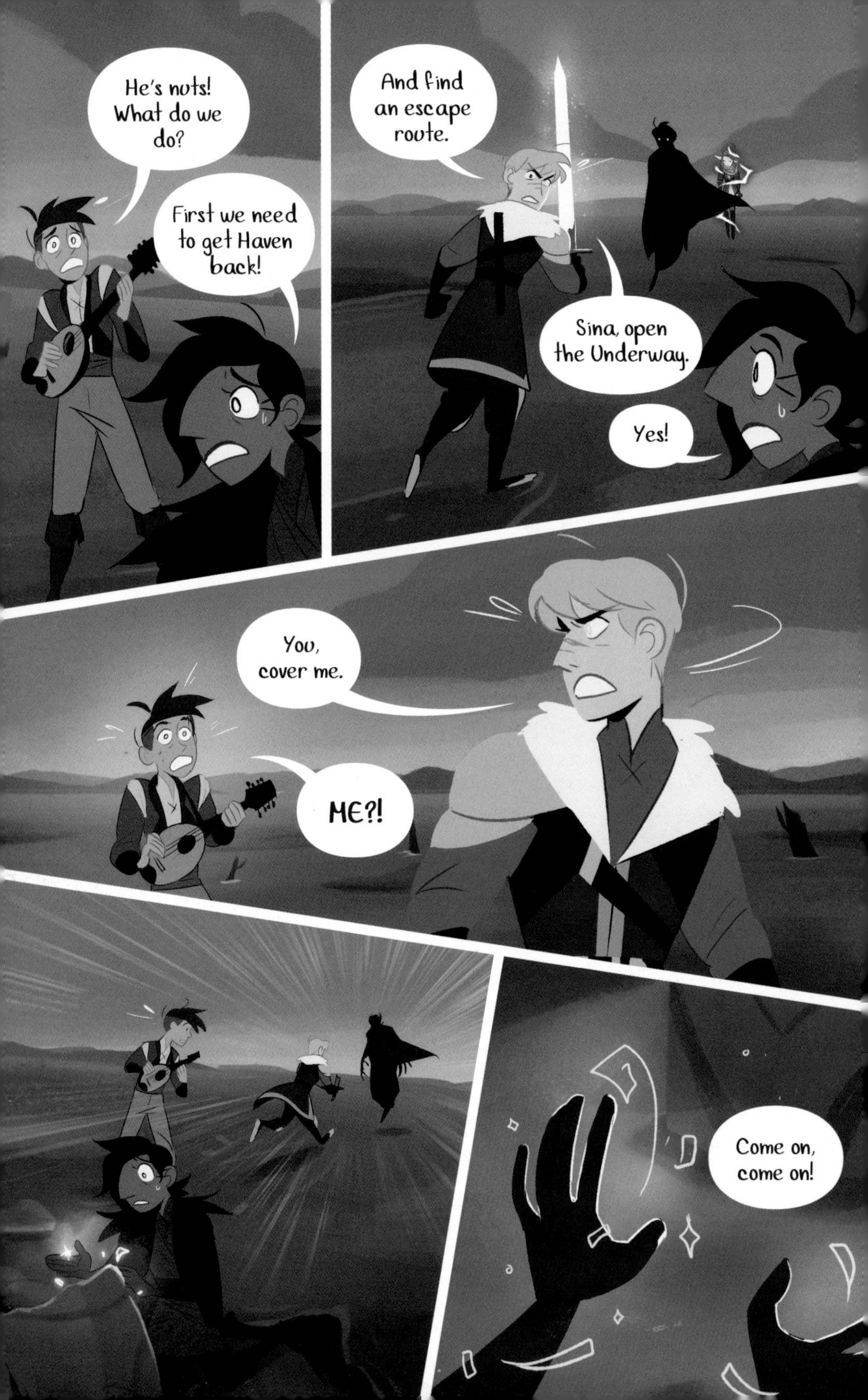
He's nuts! What do we do?
First we need to get Haven back!
And find an escape route.
Sina, open the Underway.
Yes!
You, cover me.
ME?!
Come on, come on!

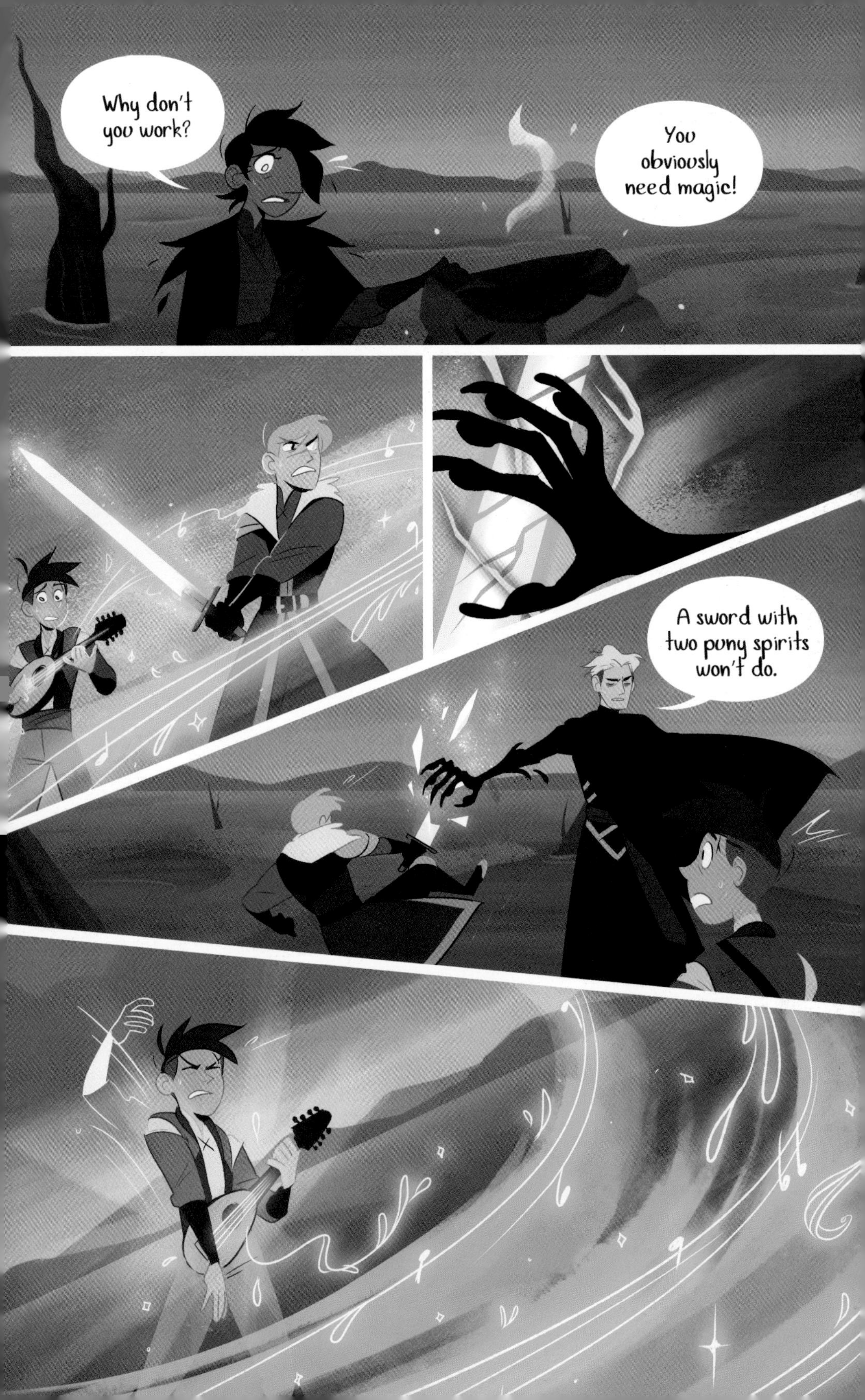
Why don't you work?
You obviously need magic!
A sword with two puny spirits won't do.

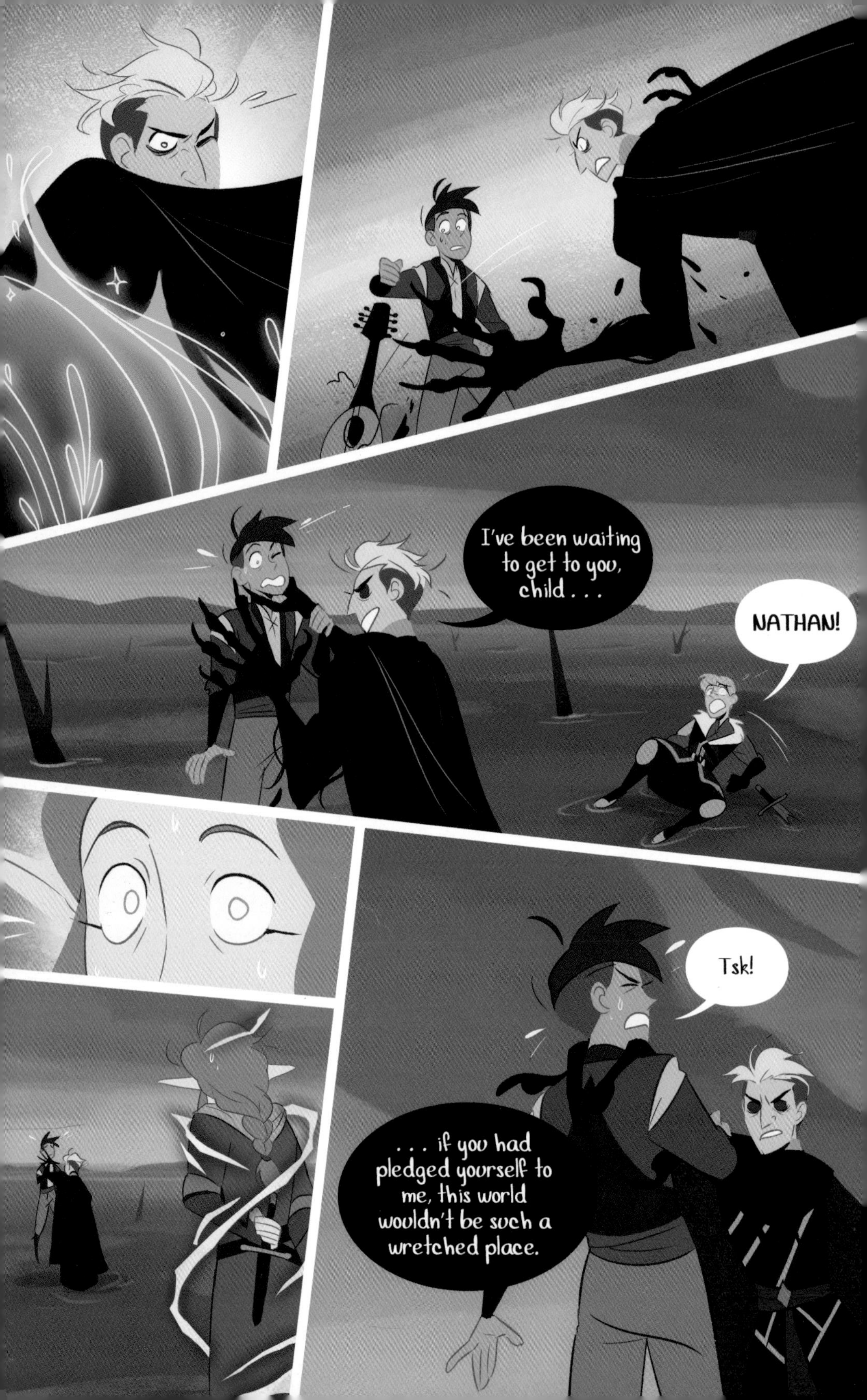
I've been waiting to get to you, child . . .
NATHAN!
Tsk!
. . . if you had pledged yourself to me, this world wouldn't be such a wretched place.

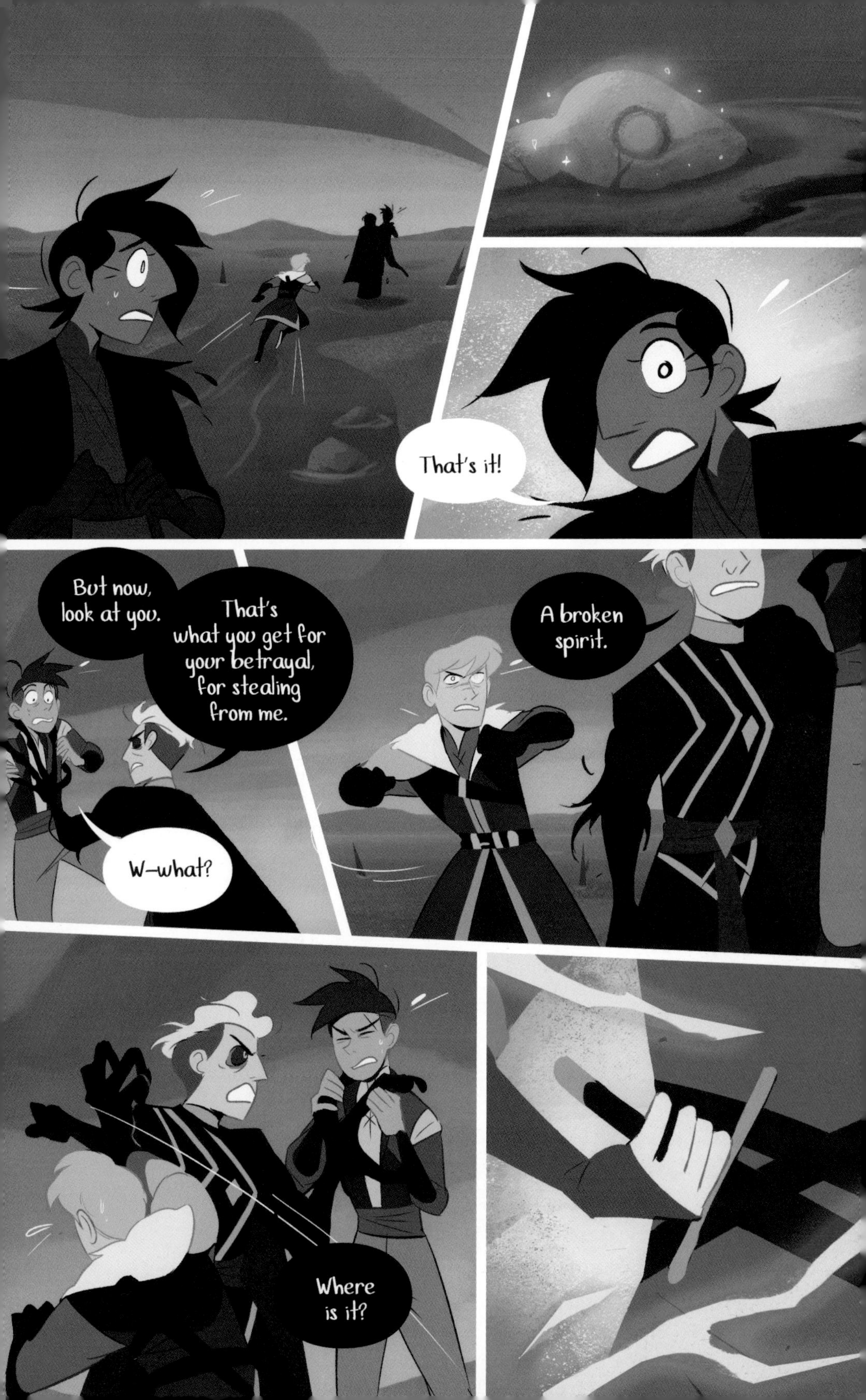
That's it!
But now, look at you.
That's what you get for your betrayal, for stealing from me.
W—what?
A broken spirit.
Where is it?

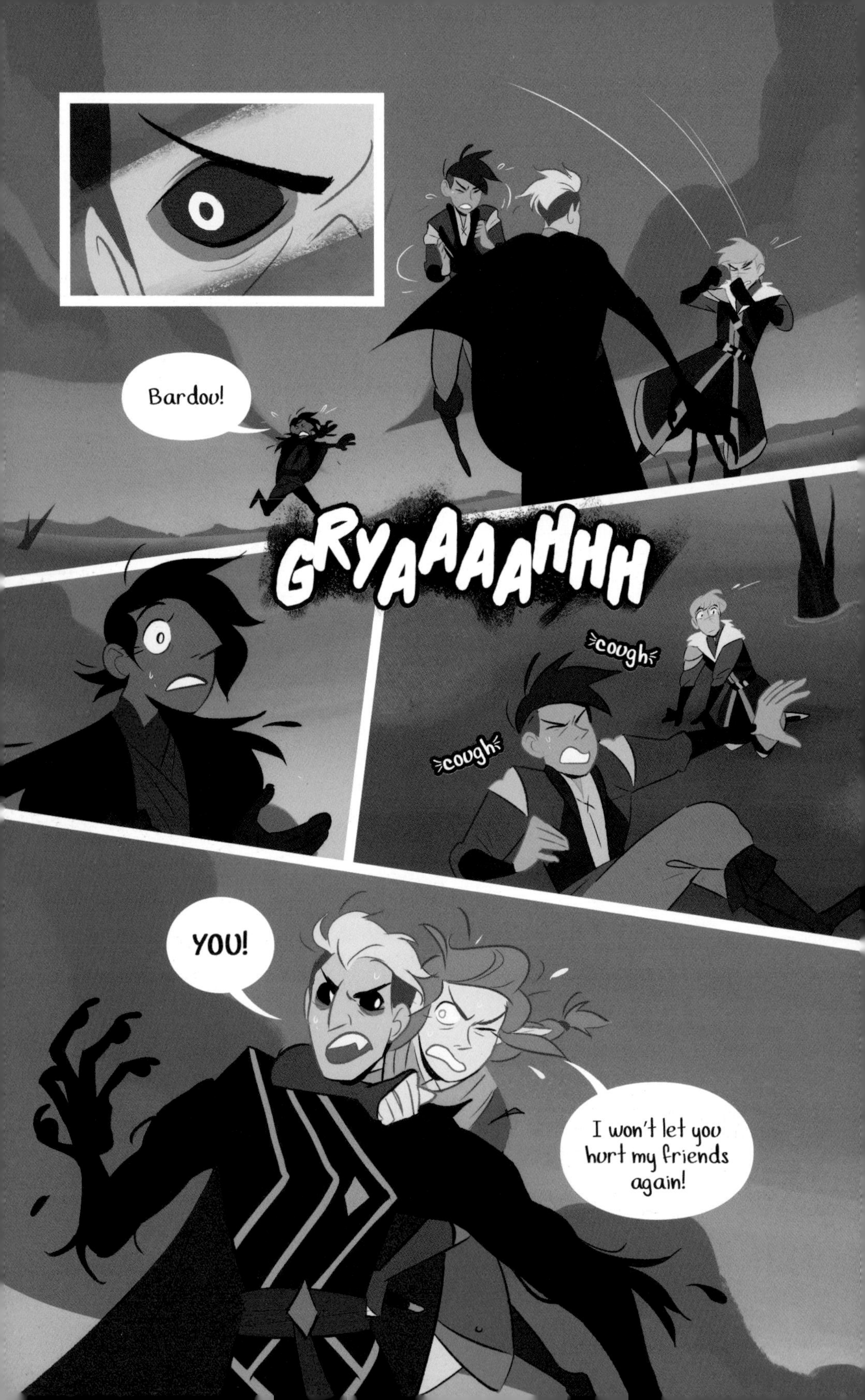
Bardou!
GRYAAAAHHH
cough
cough
YOU!
I won't let you hurt my friends again!

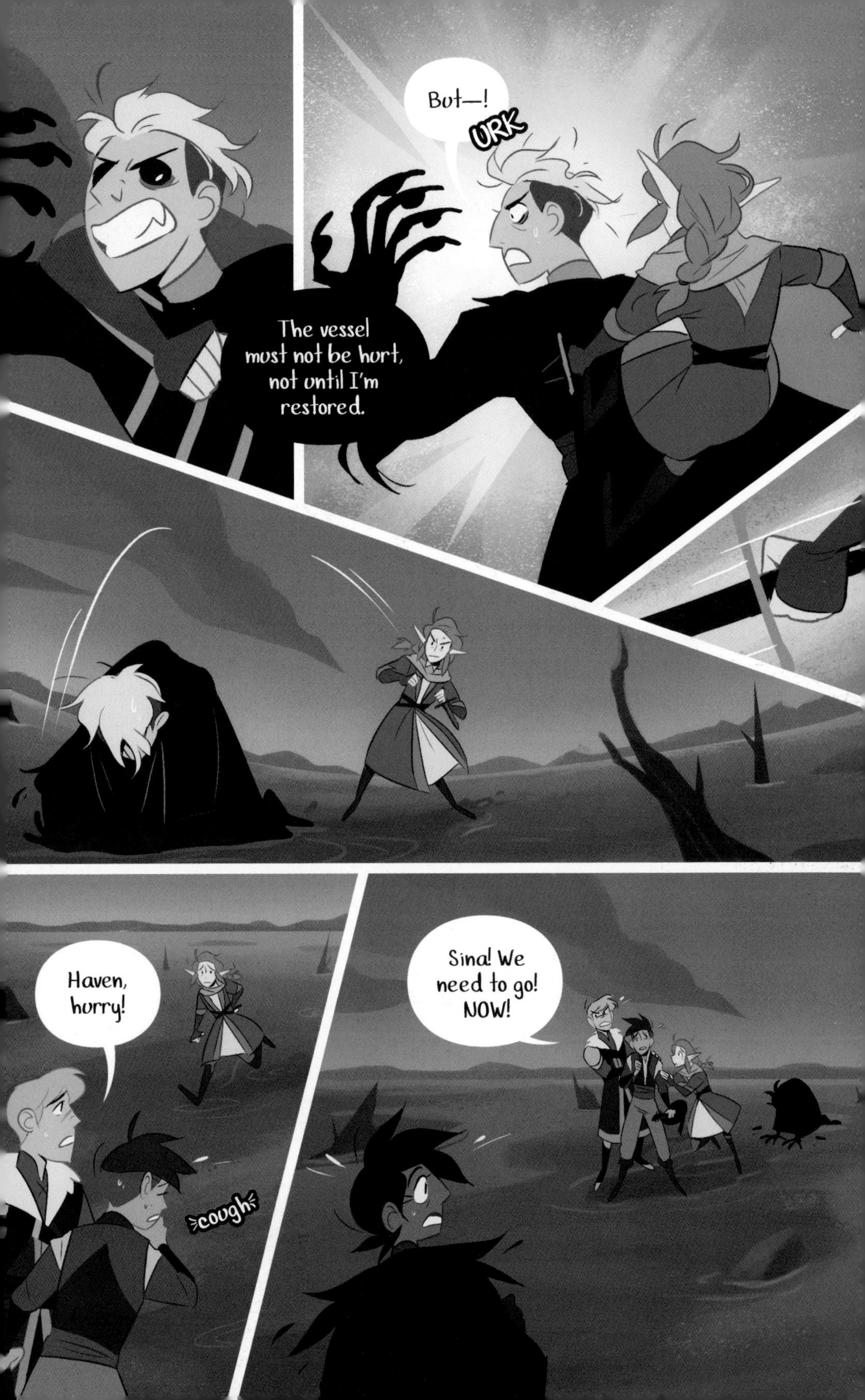
But—!
URK
The vessel must not be hurt, not until I'm restored.
Haven, hurry!
cough
Sina! We need to go! NOW!

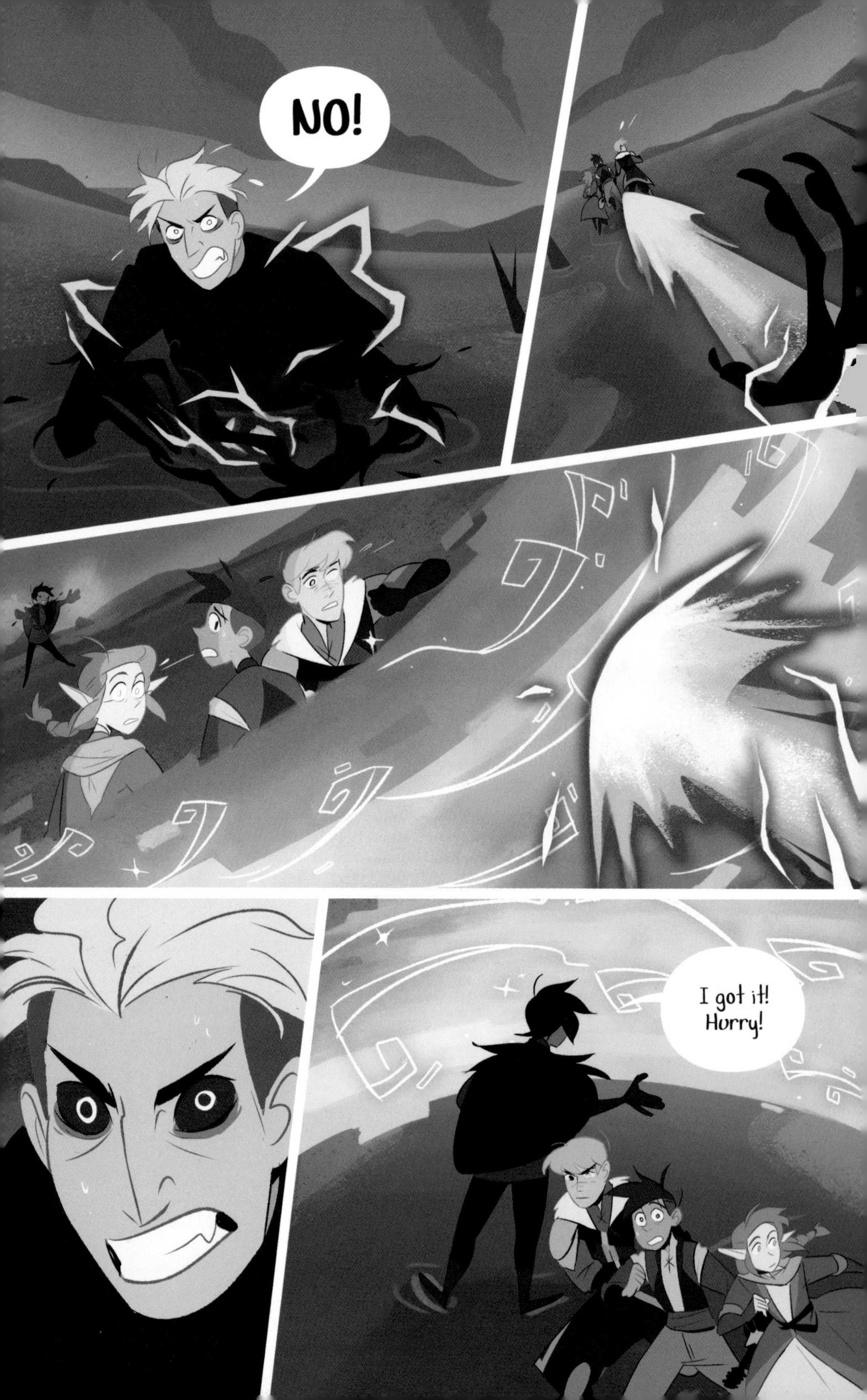
NO!
I got it! Hurry!

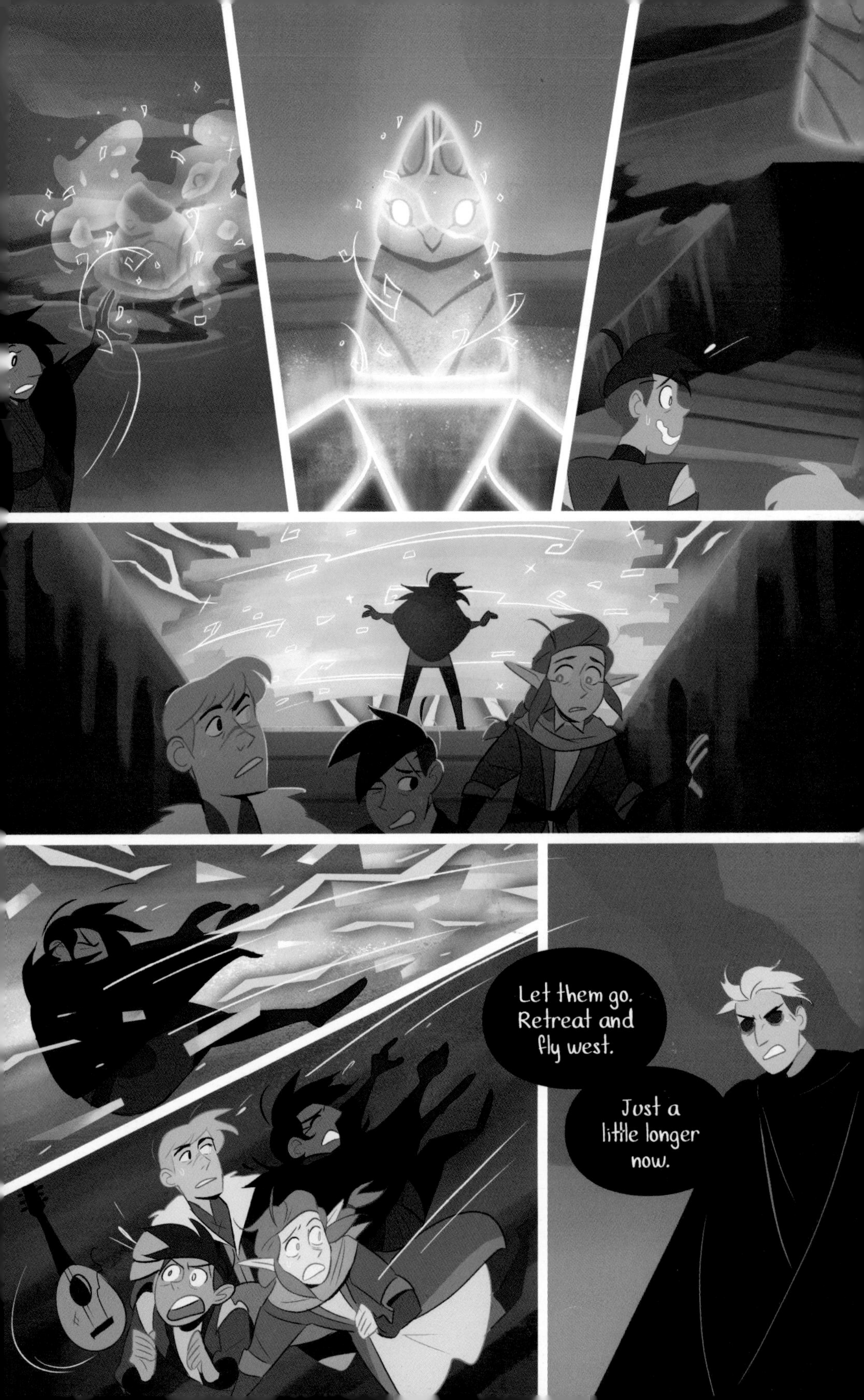

Let them go. Retreat and fly west.
Just a little longer now.

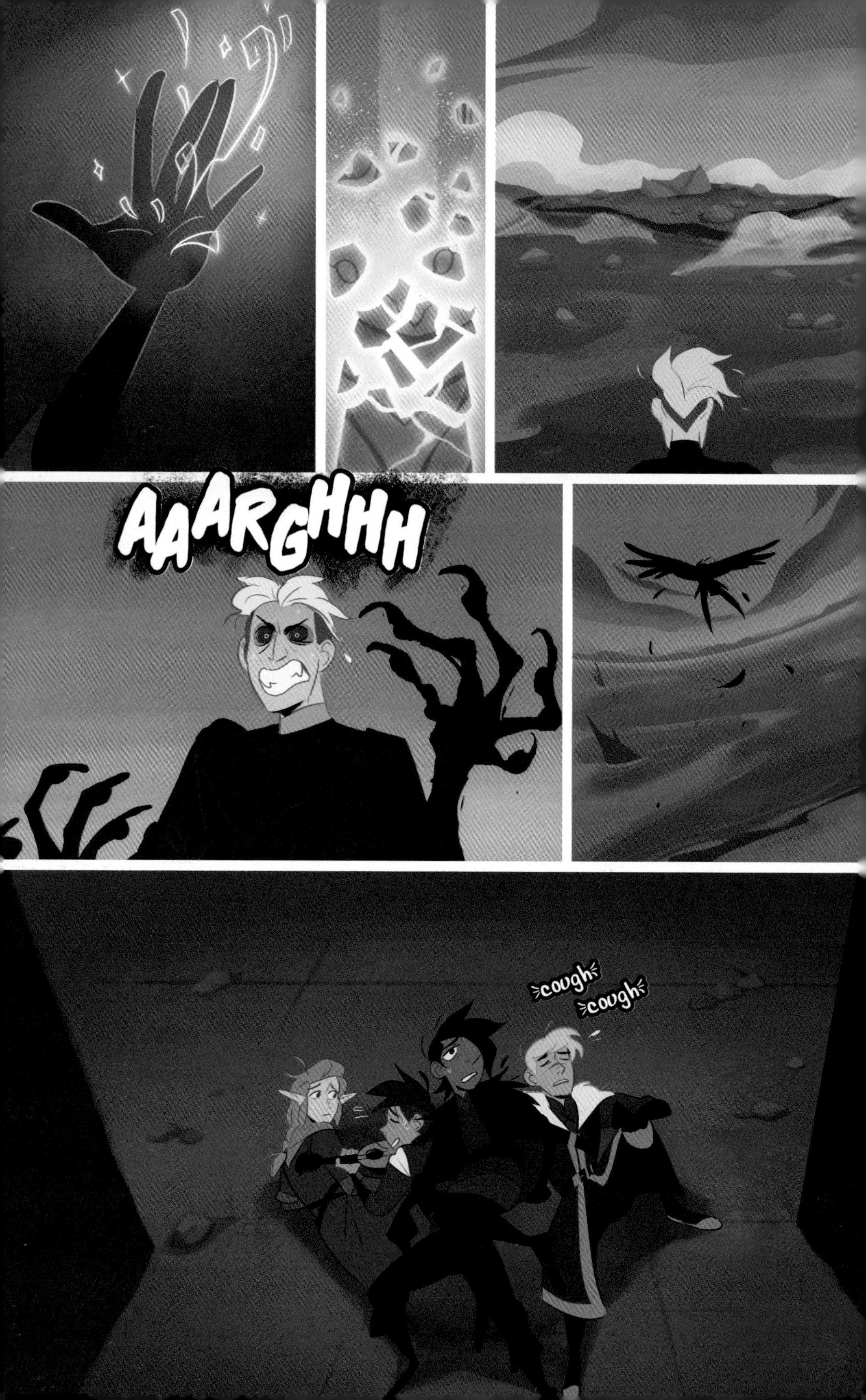
AAARGHHHH
cough
cough

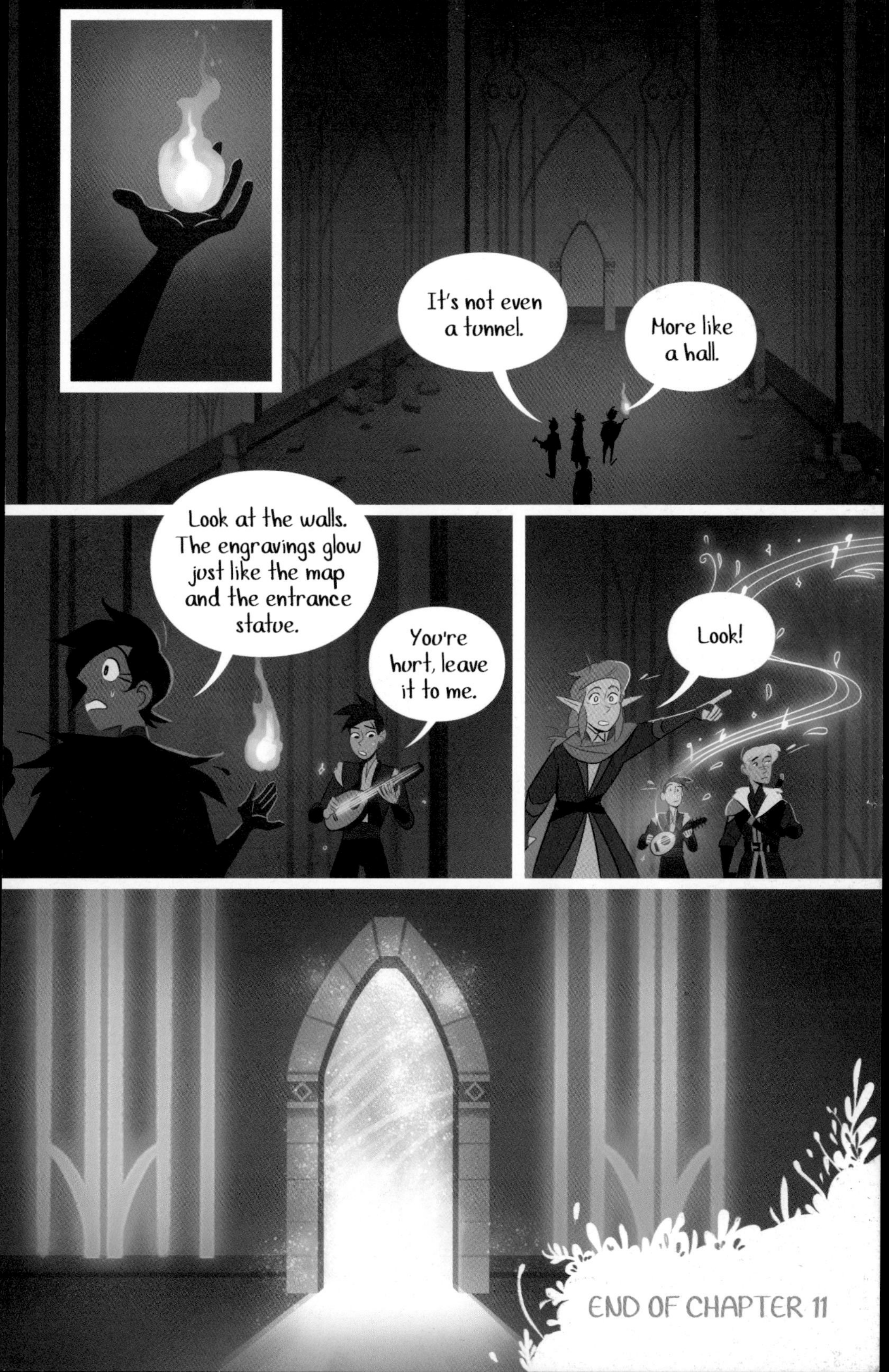
It's not even a tunnel.
More like a hall.
Look at the walls. The engravings glow just like the map and the entrance statue.
You're hurt, leave it to me.
Look!
END OF CHAPTER 11

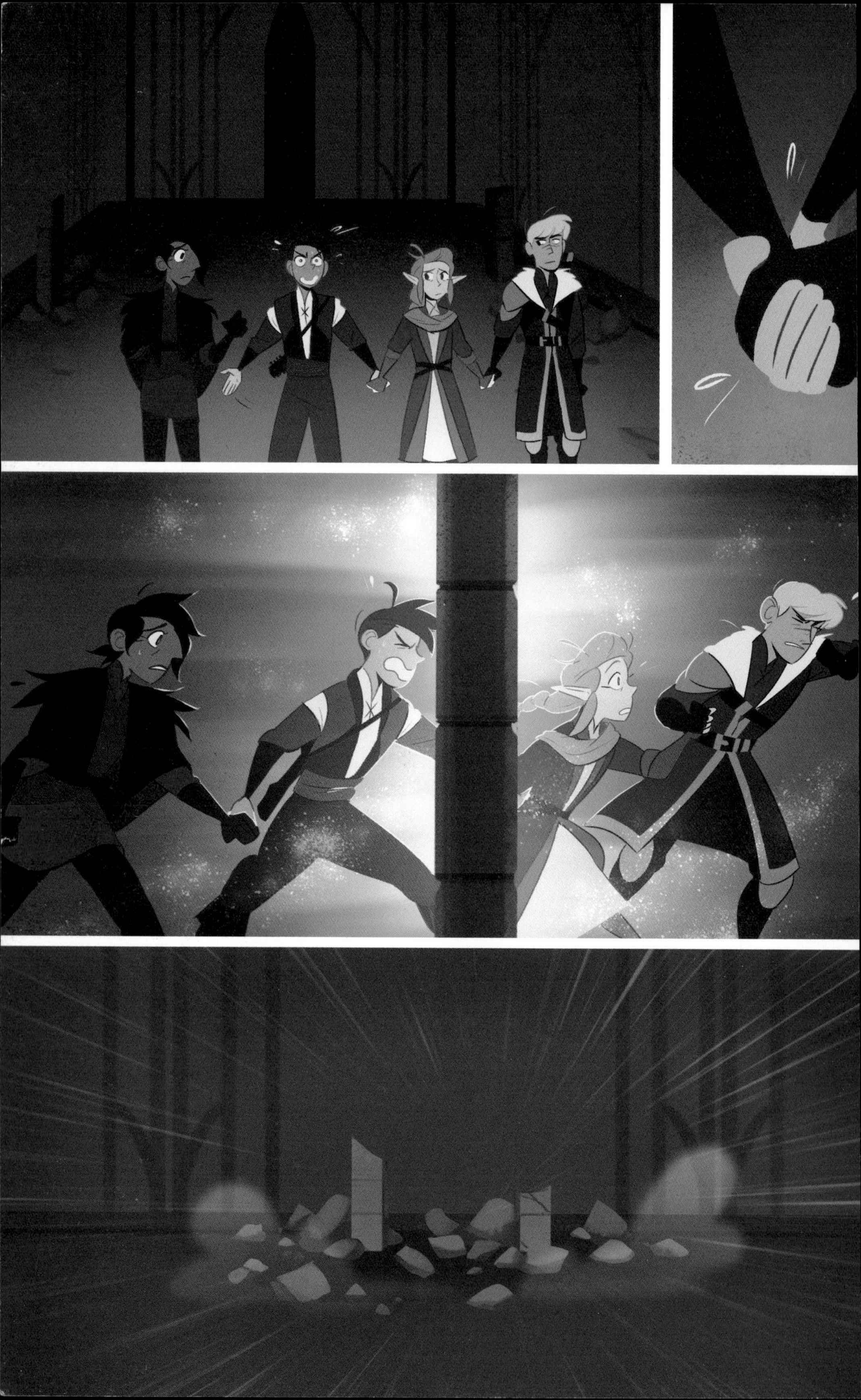

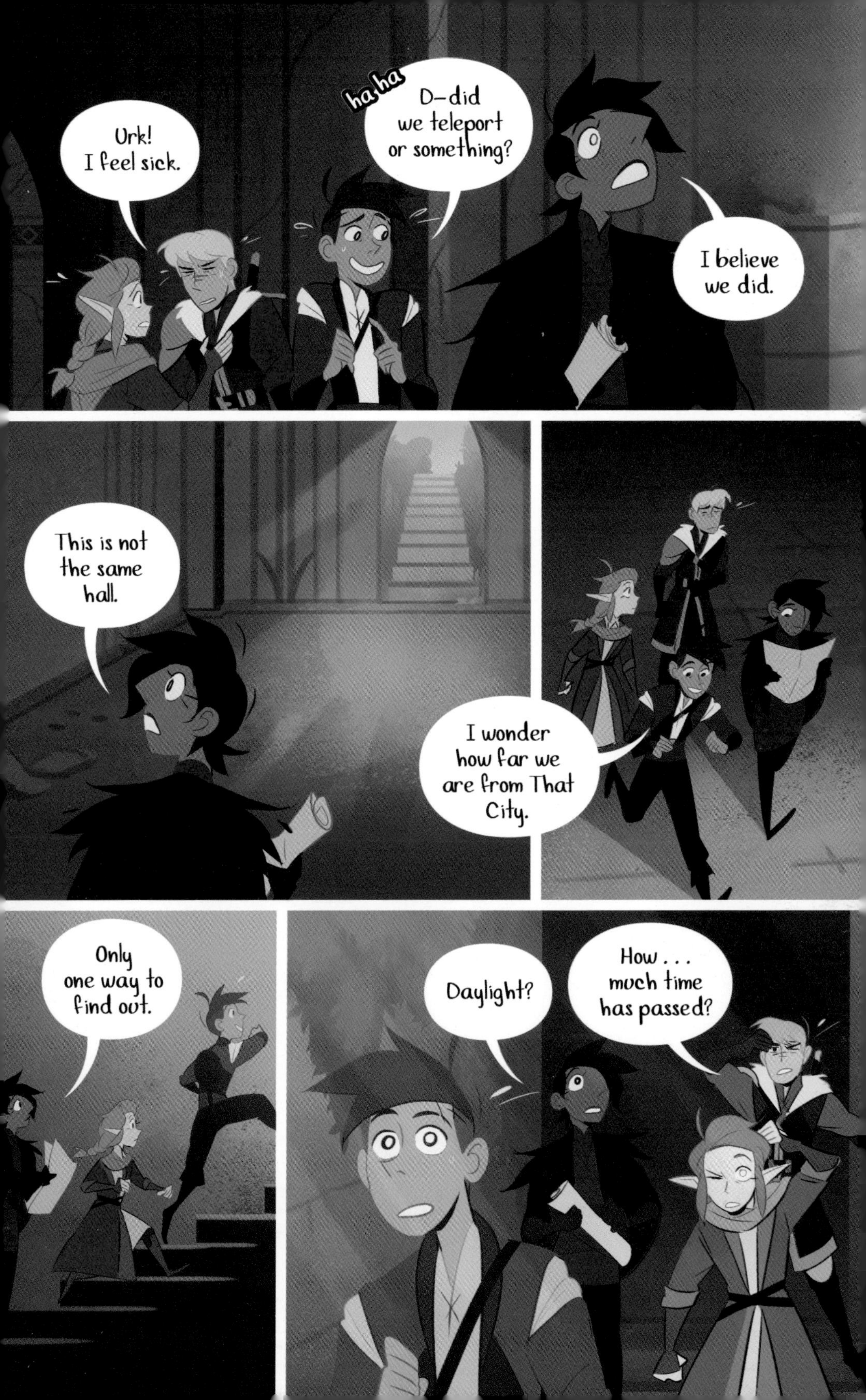
Urk! I feel sick.
ha ha
D—did we teleport or something?
I believe we did.
This is not the same hall.
I wonder how far we are from That City.
Only one way to find out.
Daylight?
How . . . much time has passed?

# Chapter 12

## That Place and Time

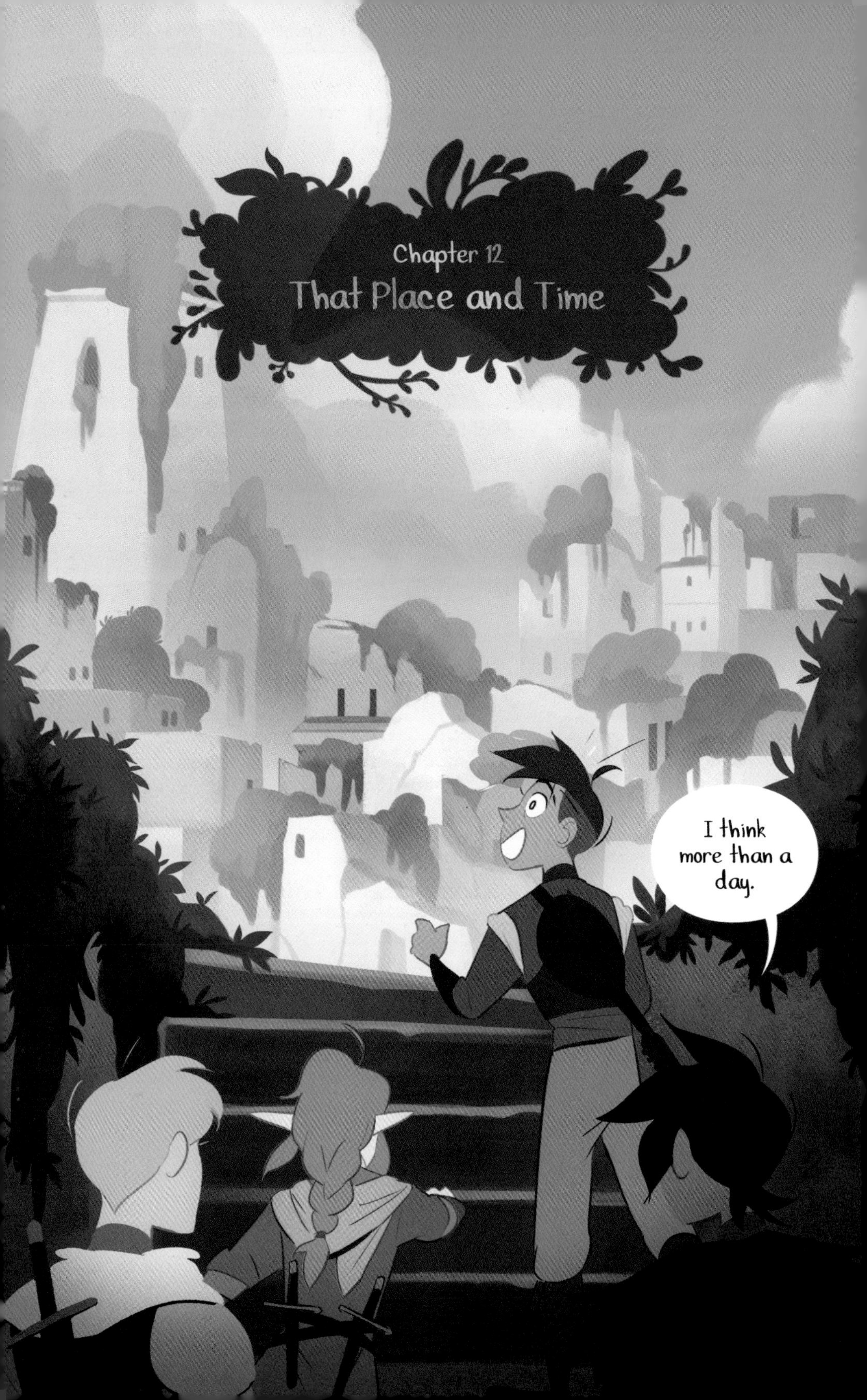
I think more than a day.

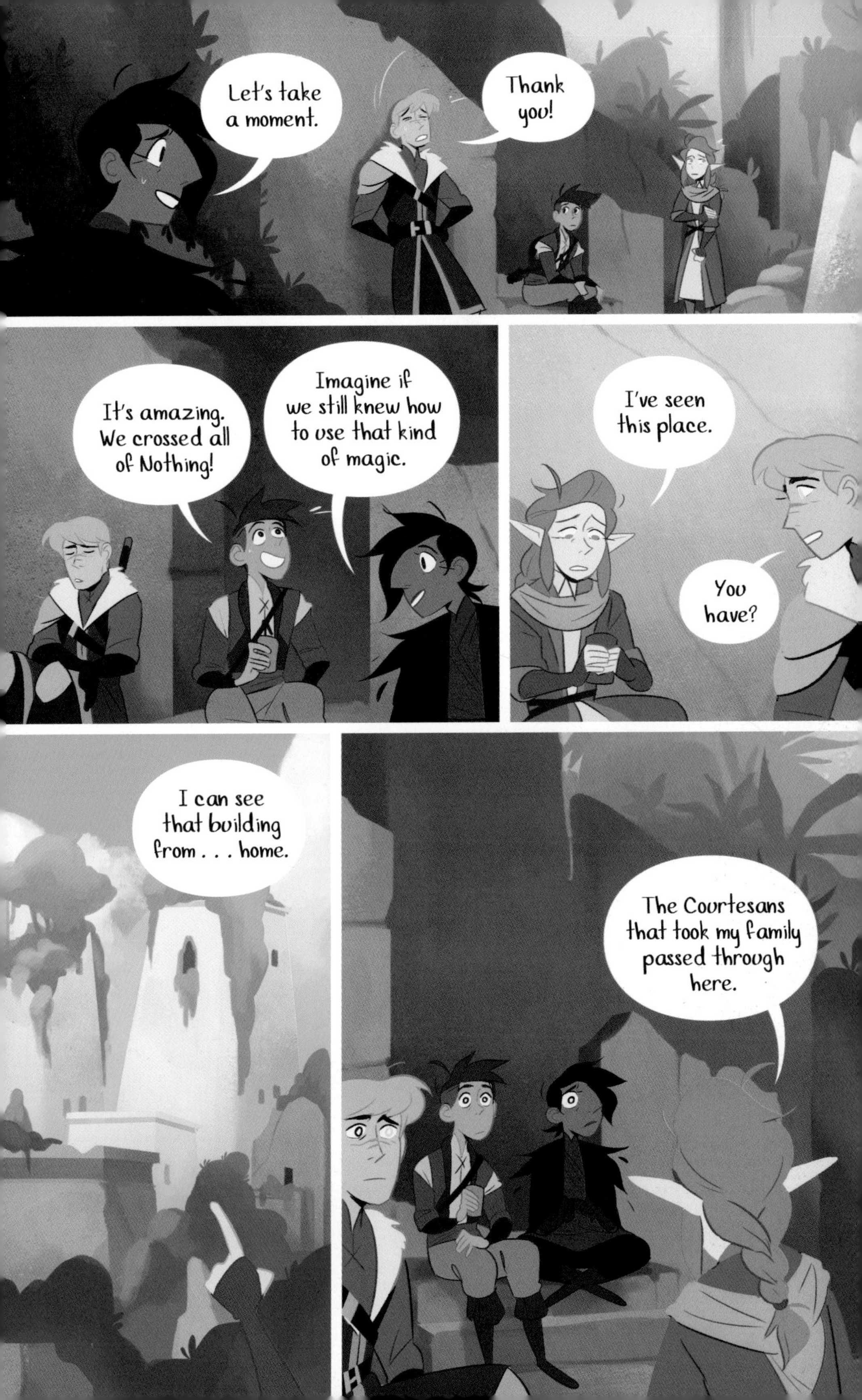
Let's take a moment.
Thank you!
It's amazing. We crossed all of Nothing!
Imagine if we still knew how to use that kind of magic.
I've seen this place.
You have?
I can see that building from . . . home.
The Courtesans that took my family passed through here.

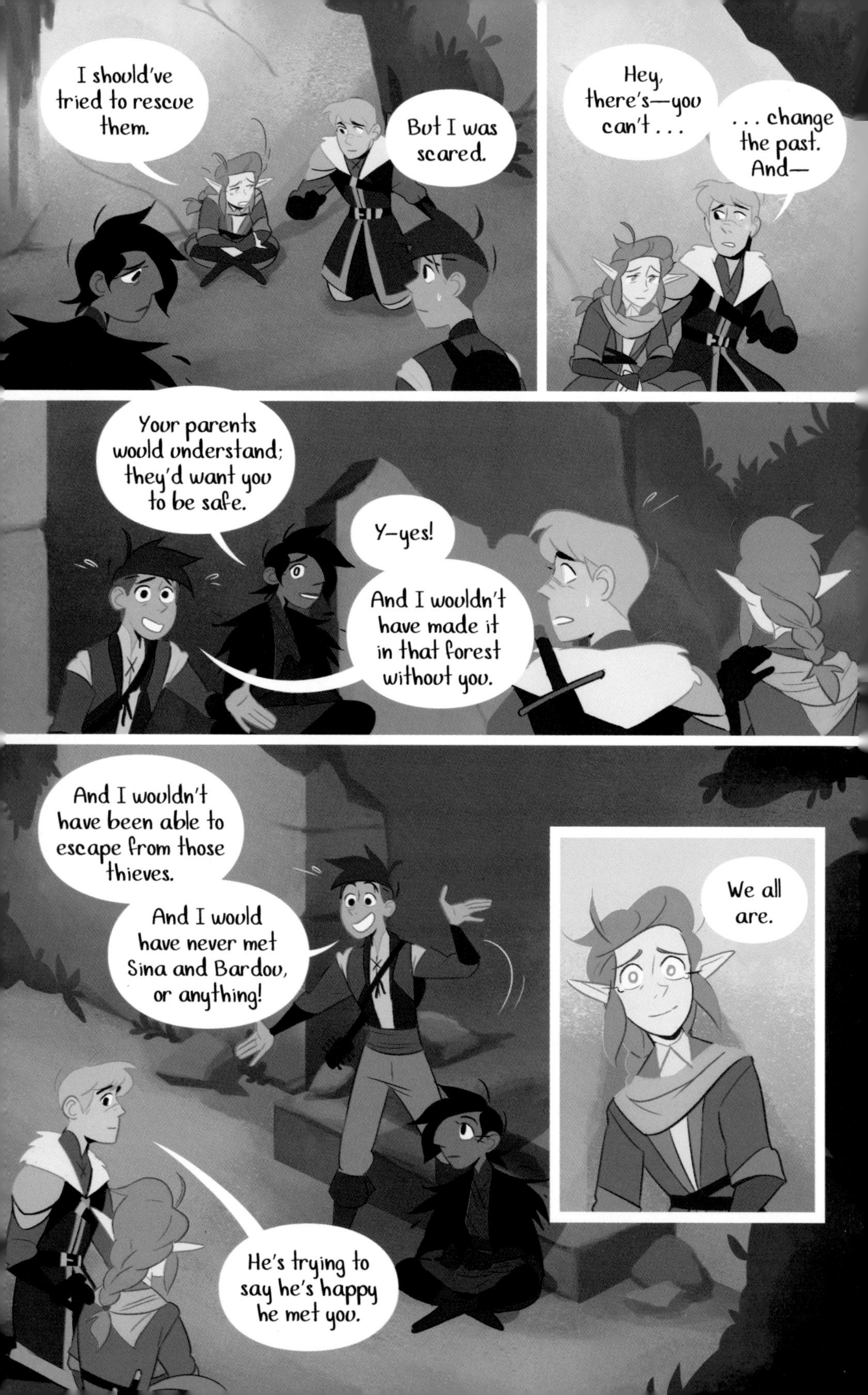
I should've tried to rescue them.
But I was scared.
Hey, there's—you can't . . .
. . . change the past. And—
Your parents would understand; they'd want you to be safe.
Y—yes!
And I wouldn't have made it in that forest without you.
And I wouldn't have been able to escape from those thieves.
And I would have never met Sina and Bardou, or anything!
We all are.
He's trying to say he's happy he met you.

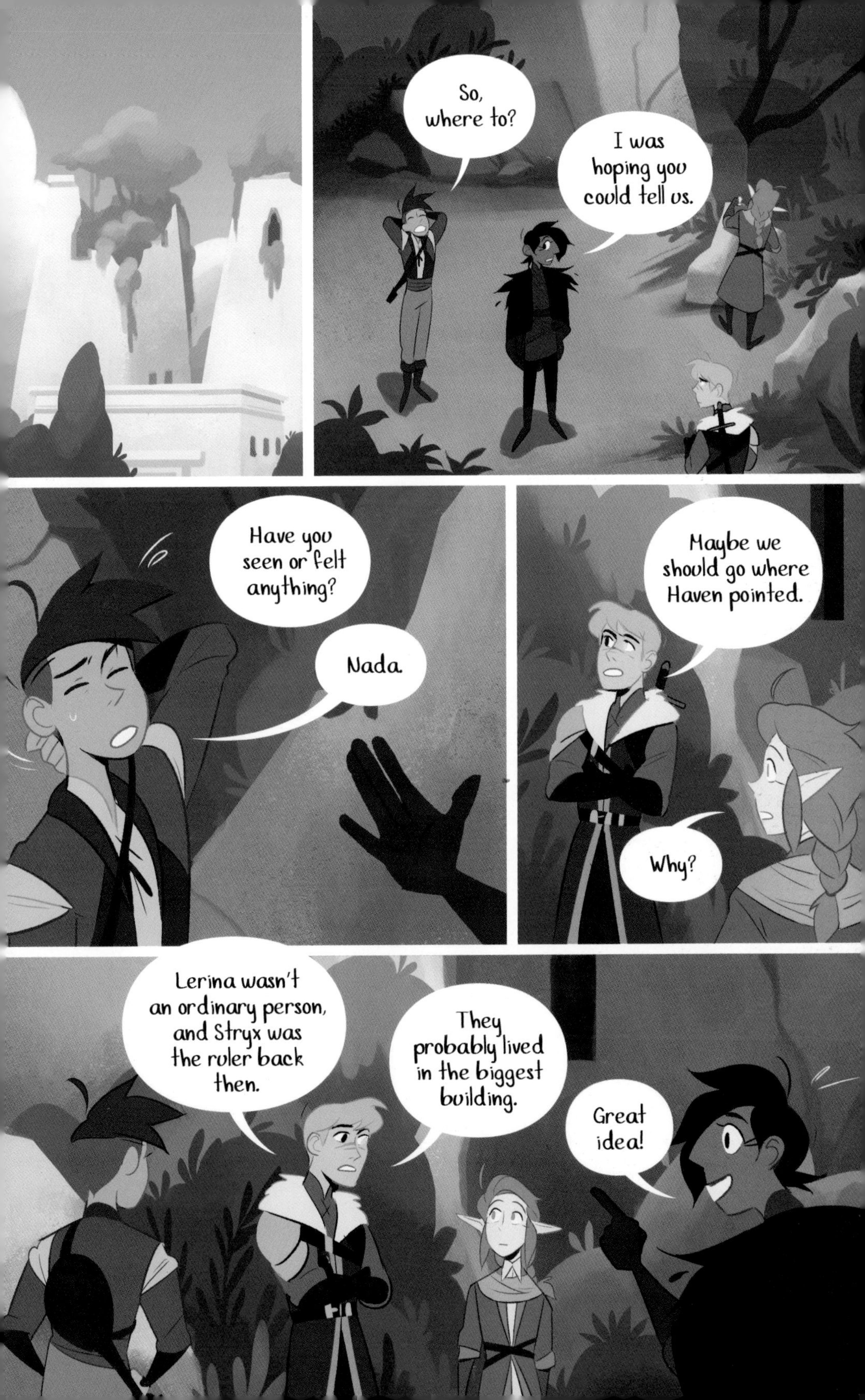
So, where to?
I was hoping you could tell us.
Have you seen or felt anything?
Nada.
Maybe we should go where Haven pointed.
Why?
Lerina wasn't an ordinary person, and Stryx was the ruler back then.
They probably lived in the biggest building.
Great idea!

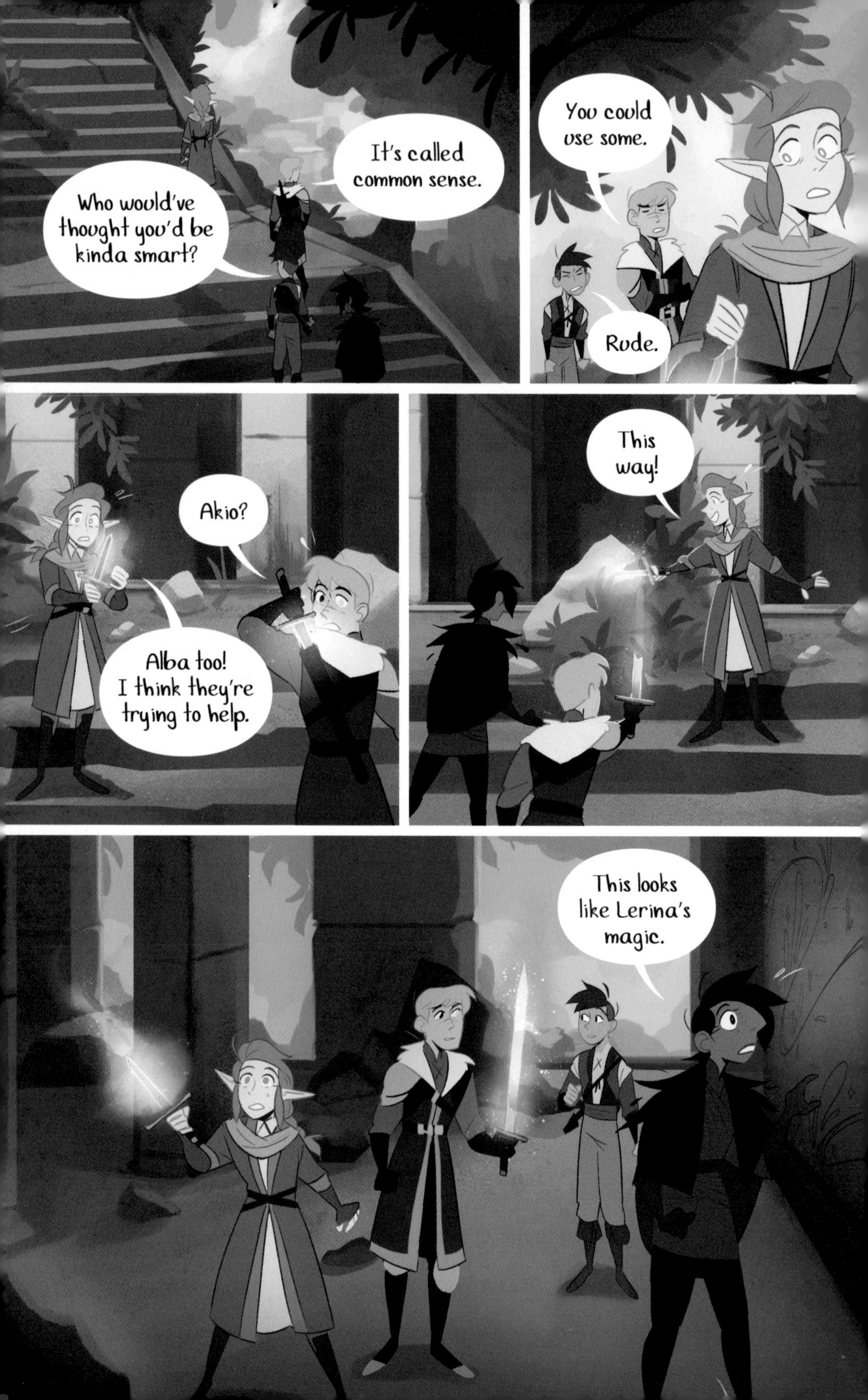

Who would've thought you'd be kinda smart?
It's called common sense.
You could use some.
Rude.
Akio?
Alba too! I think they're trying to help.
This way!
This looks like Lerina's magic.

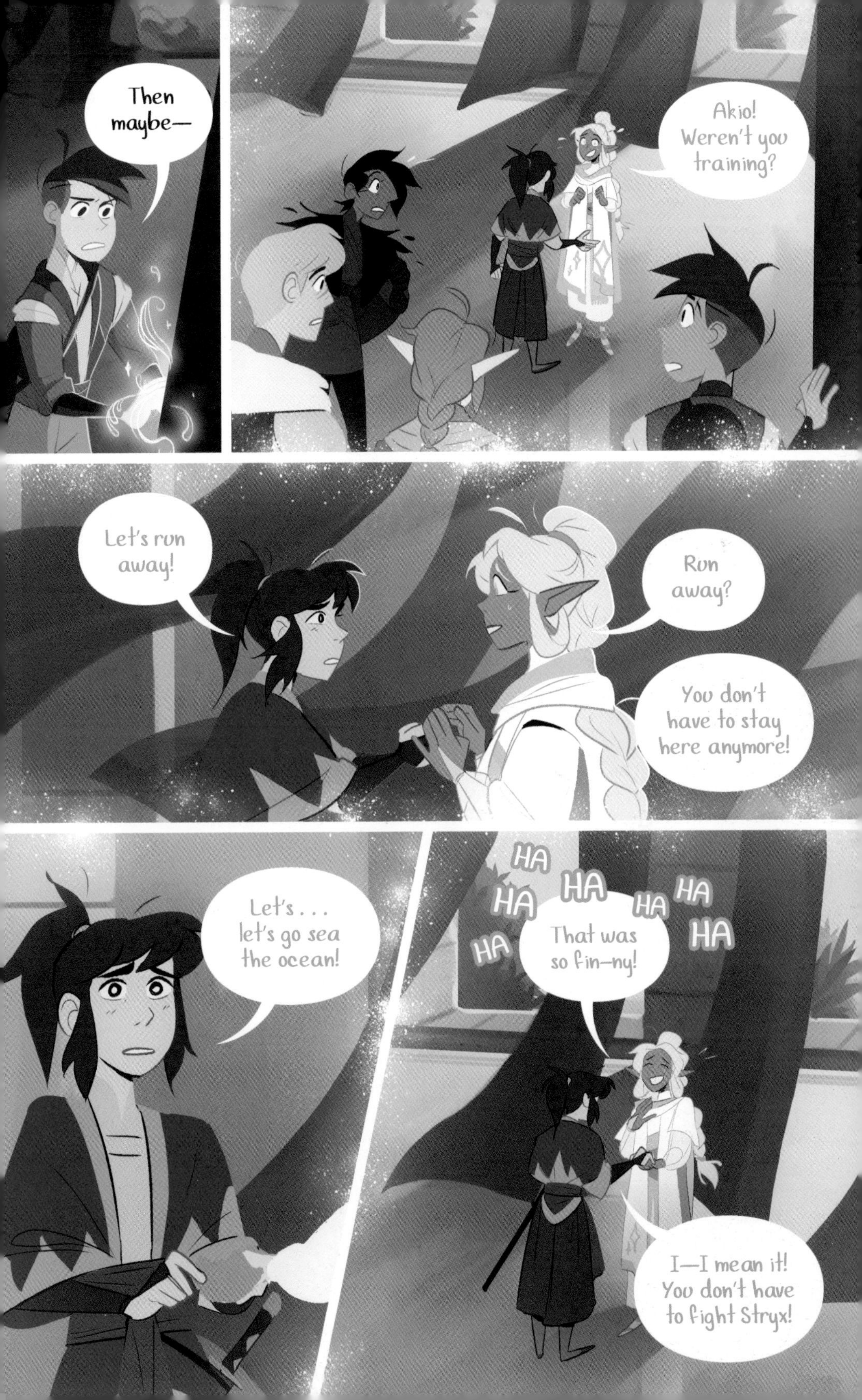
Then maybe—
Akio! Weren't you training?
Let's run away!
Run away?
You don't have to stay here anymore!
Let's . . . let's go sea the ocean!
HA HA HA HA HA HA HA
That was so fin-ny!
I—I mean it! You don't have to fight Stryx!

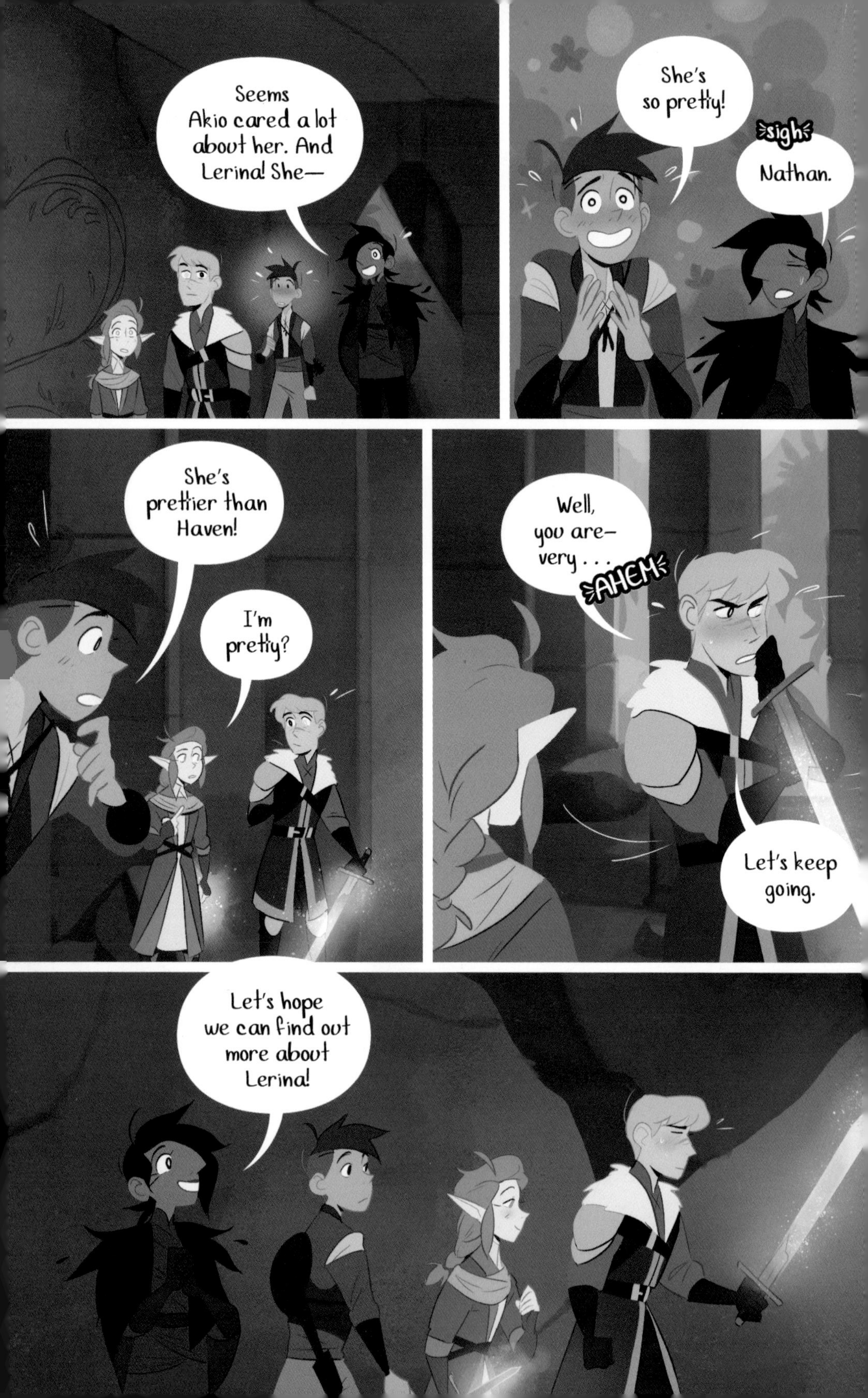
Seems Akio cared a lot about her. And Lerina! She—
She's so pretty!
sigh
Nathan.
She's prettier than Haven!
I'm pretty?
Well, you are— very . . .
AHEM
Let's keep going.
Let's hope we can find out more about Lerina!

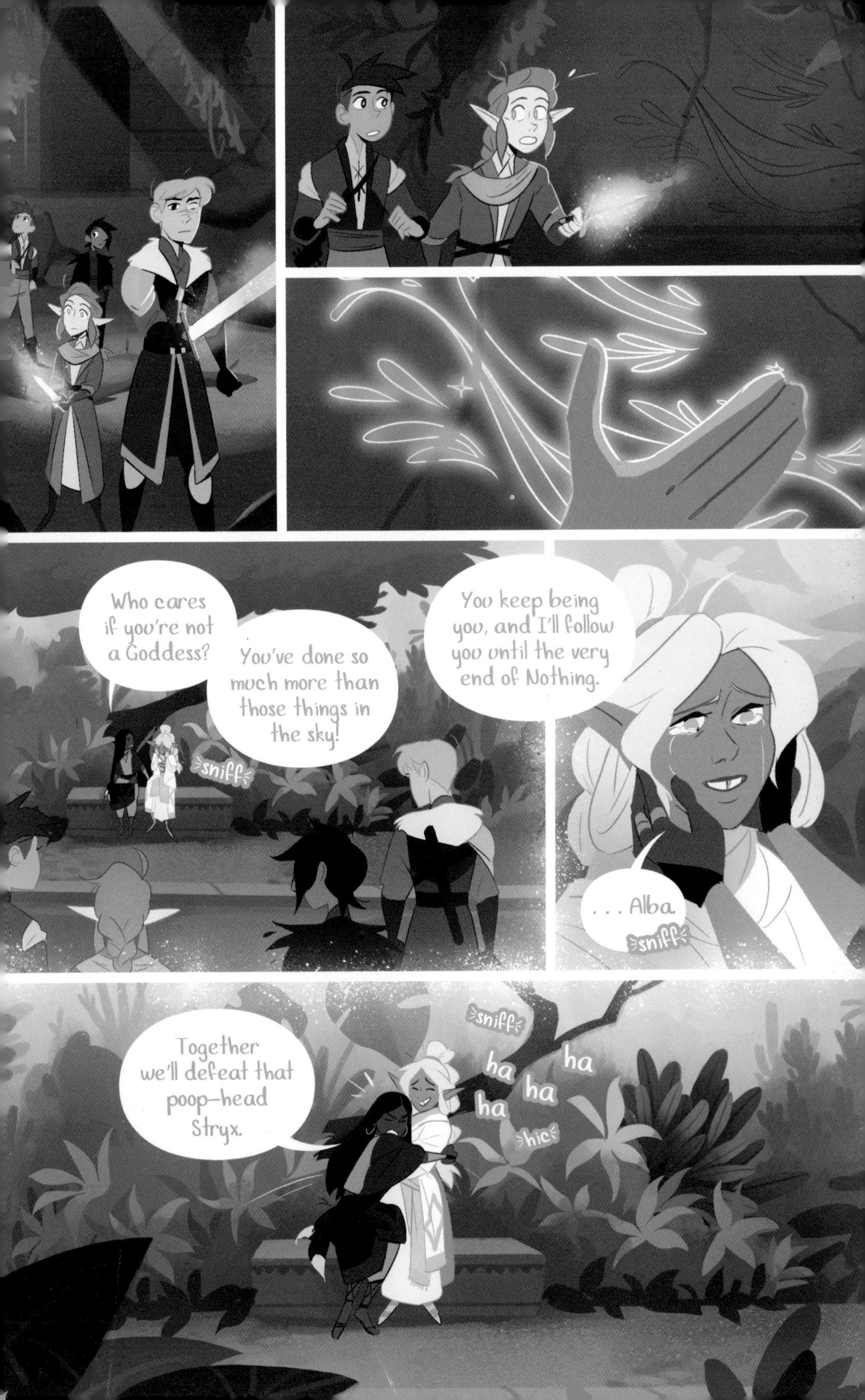
Who cares if you're not a Goddess?
You've done so much more than those things in the sky!
You keep being you, and I'll follow you until the very end of Nothing.
sniff
. . . Alba.
sniff
sniff
Together we'll defeat that poop-head Stryx.
ha
ha
ha
ha
hic

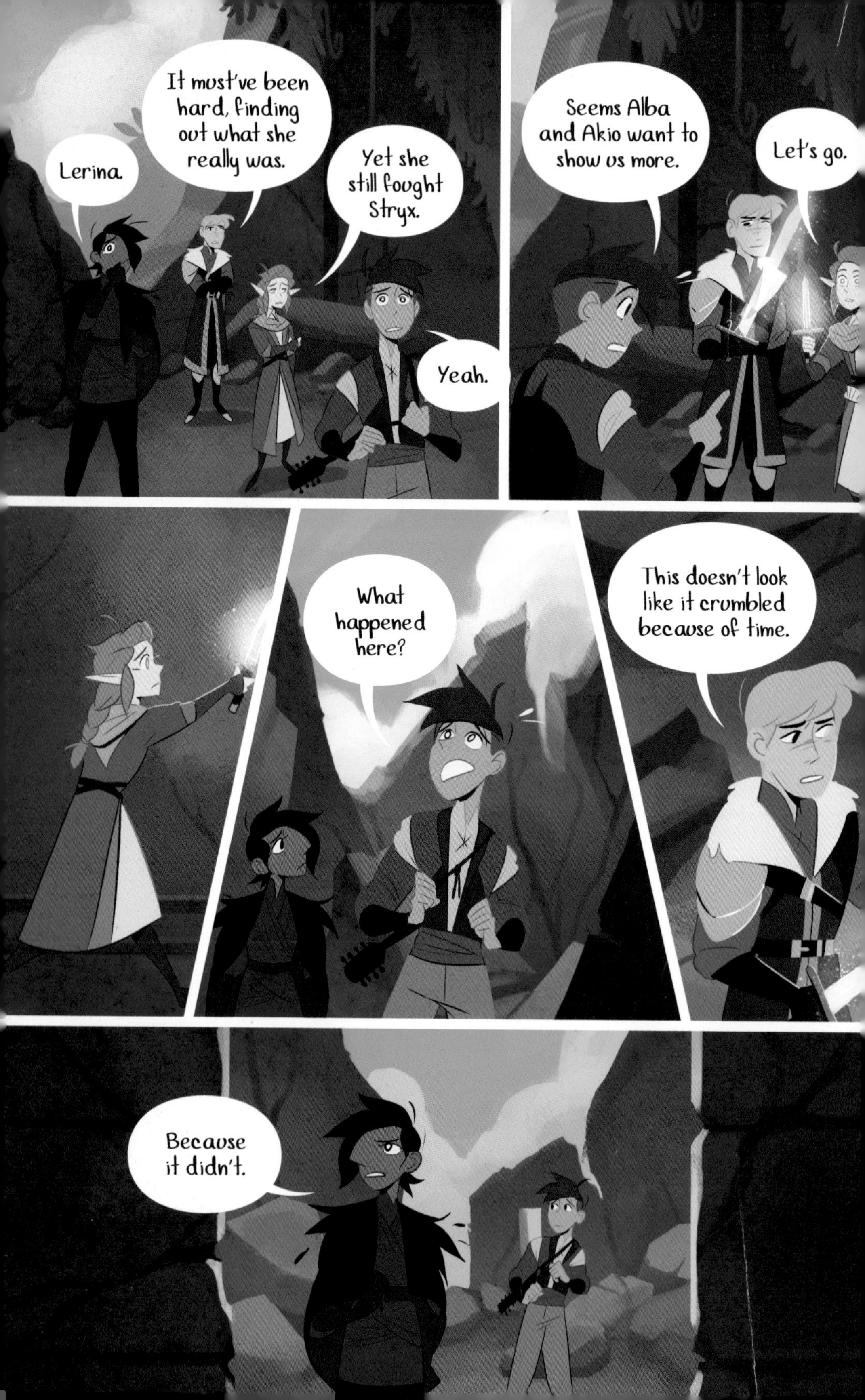
Lerina.
It must've been hard, finding out what she really was.
Yet she still fought Stryx.
Yeah.
Seems Alba and Akio want to show us more.
Let's go.
What happened here?
This doesn't look like it crumbled because of time.
Because it didn't.

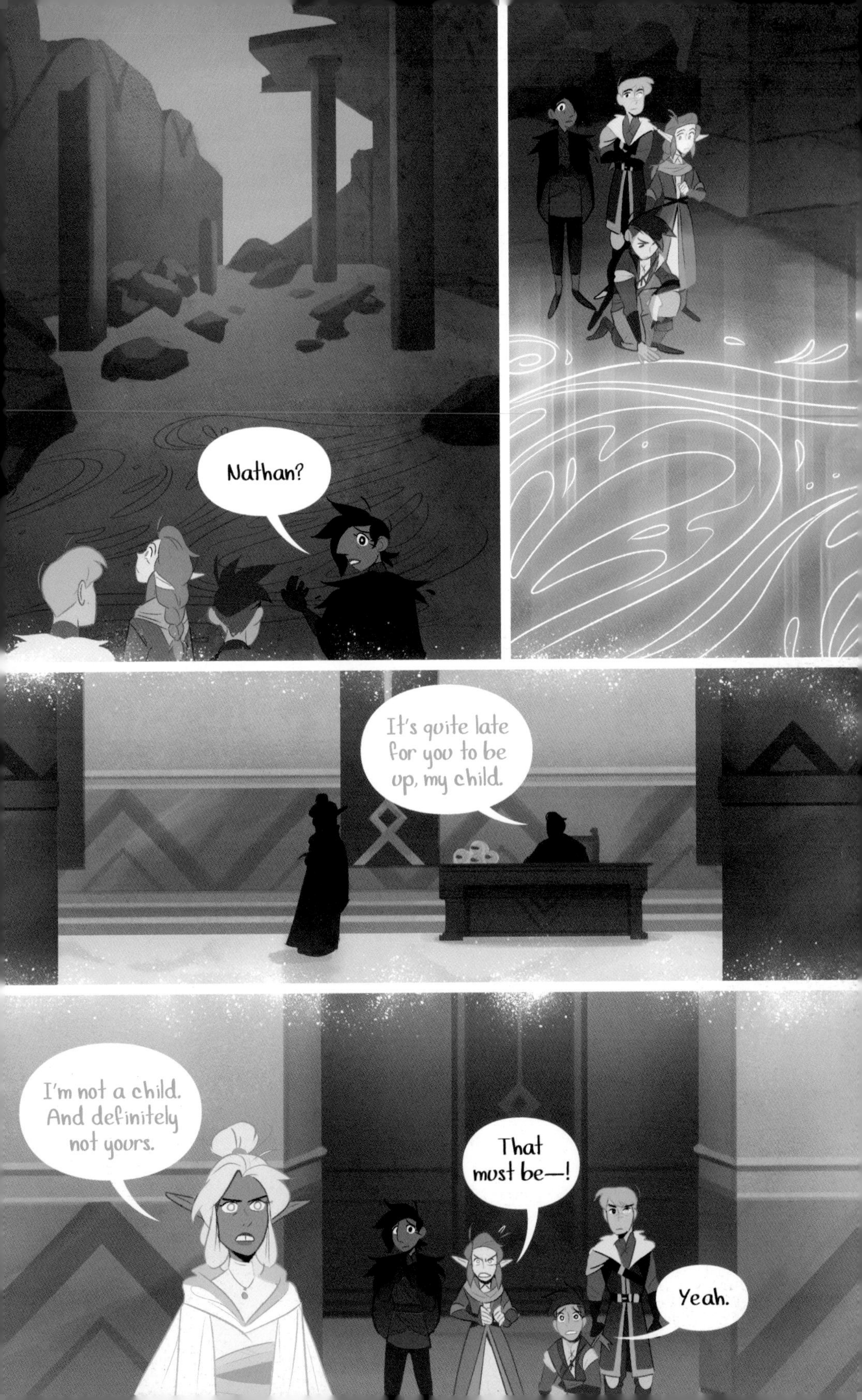
Nathan?
It's quite late for you to be up, my child.
I'm not a child. And definitely not yours.
That must be—!
Yeah.

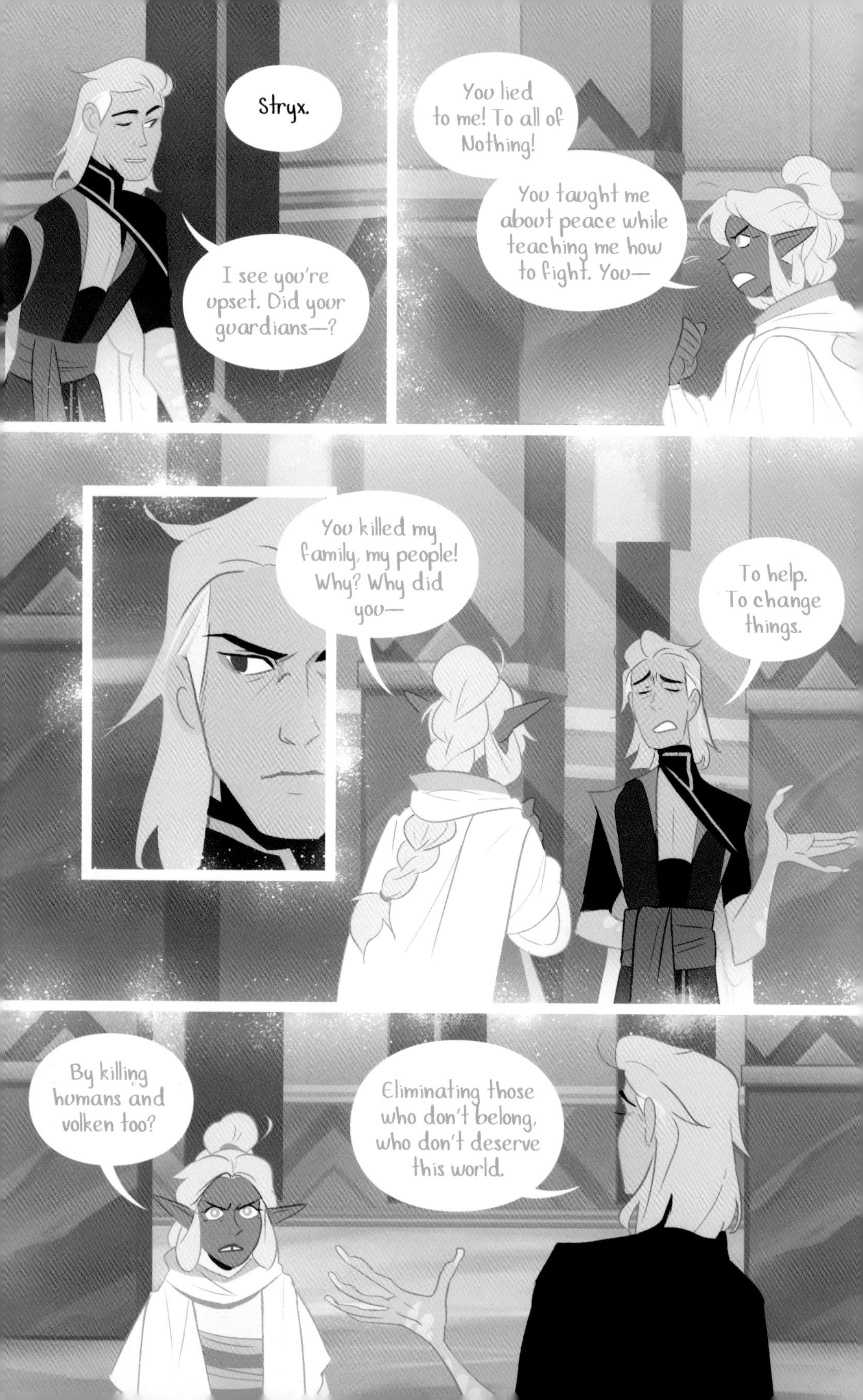
Stryx.
I see you're upset. Did your guardians—?
You lied to me! To all of Nothing!
You taught me about peace while teaching me how to fight. You—
You killed my family, my people! Why? Why did you—
To help. To change things.
By killing humans and volken too?
Eliminating those who don't belong, who don't deserve this world.

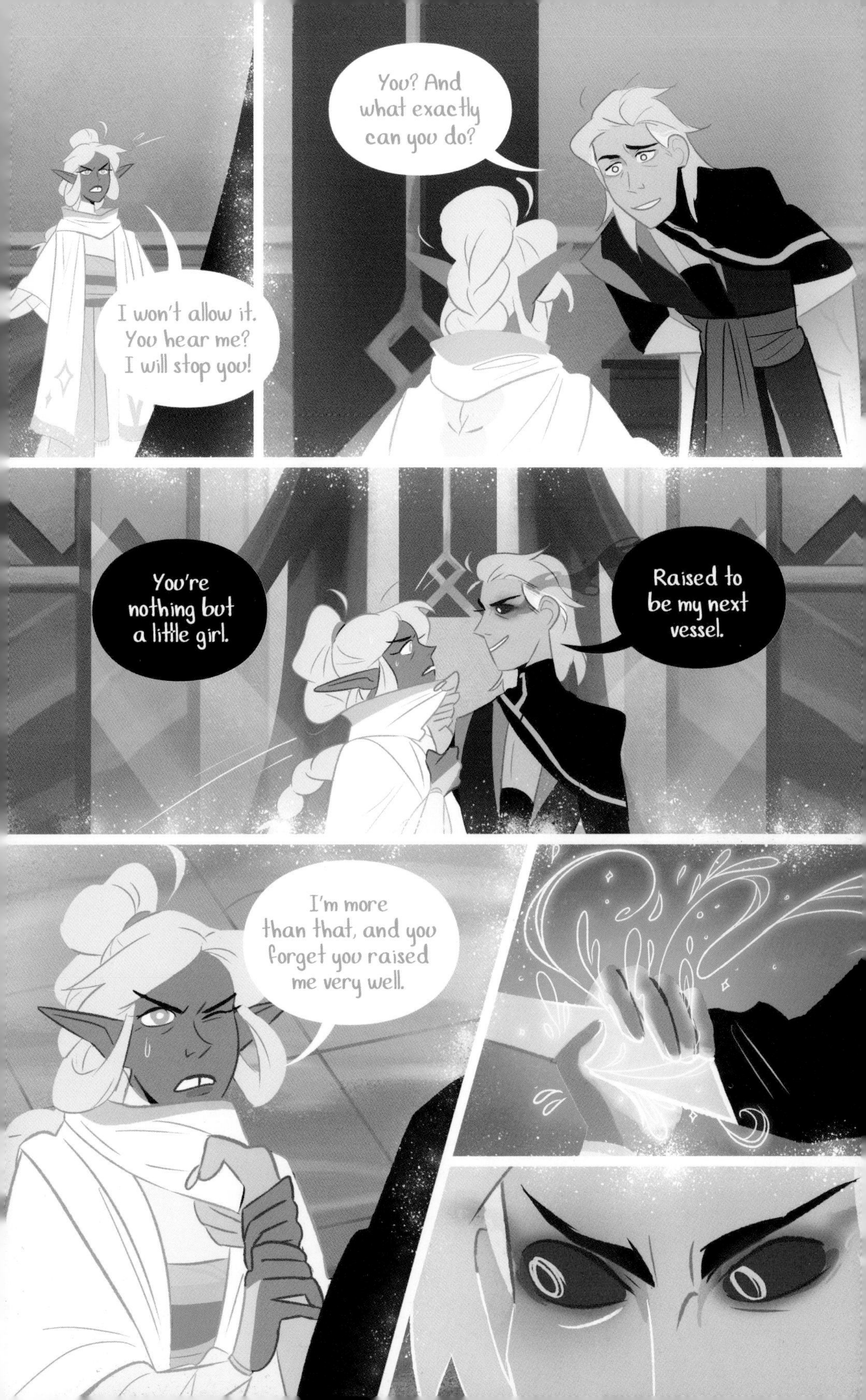
I won't allow it. You hear me? I will stop you!
You? And what exactly can you do?
You're nothing but a little girl.
Raised to be my next vessel.
I'm more than that, and you forget you raised me very well.

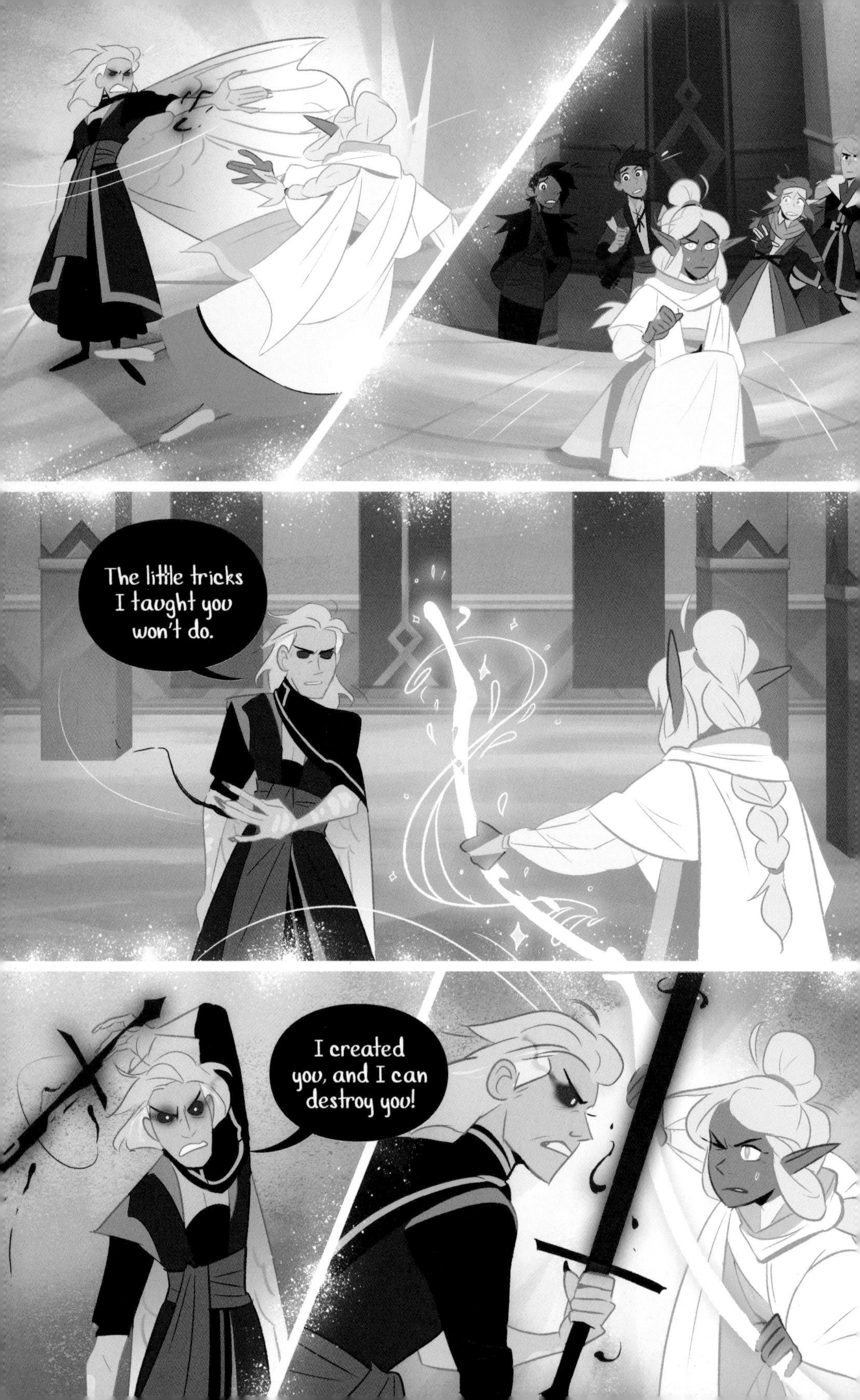
The little tricks I taught you won't do.
I created you, and I can destroy you!

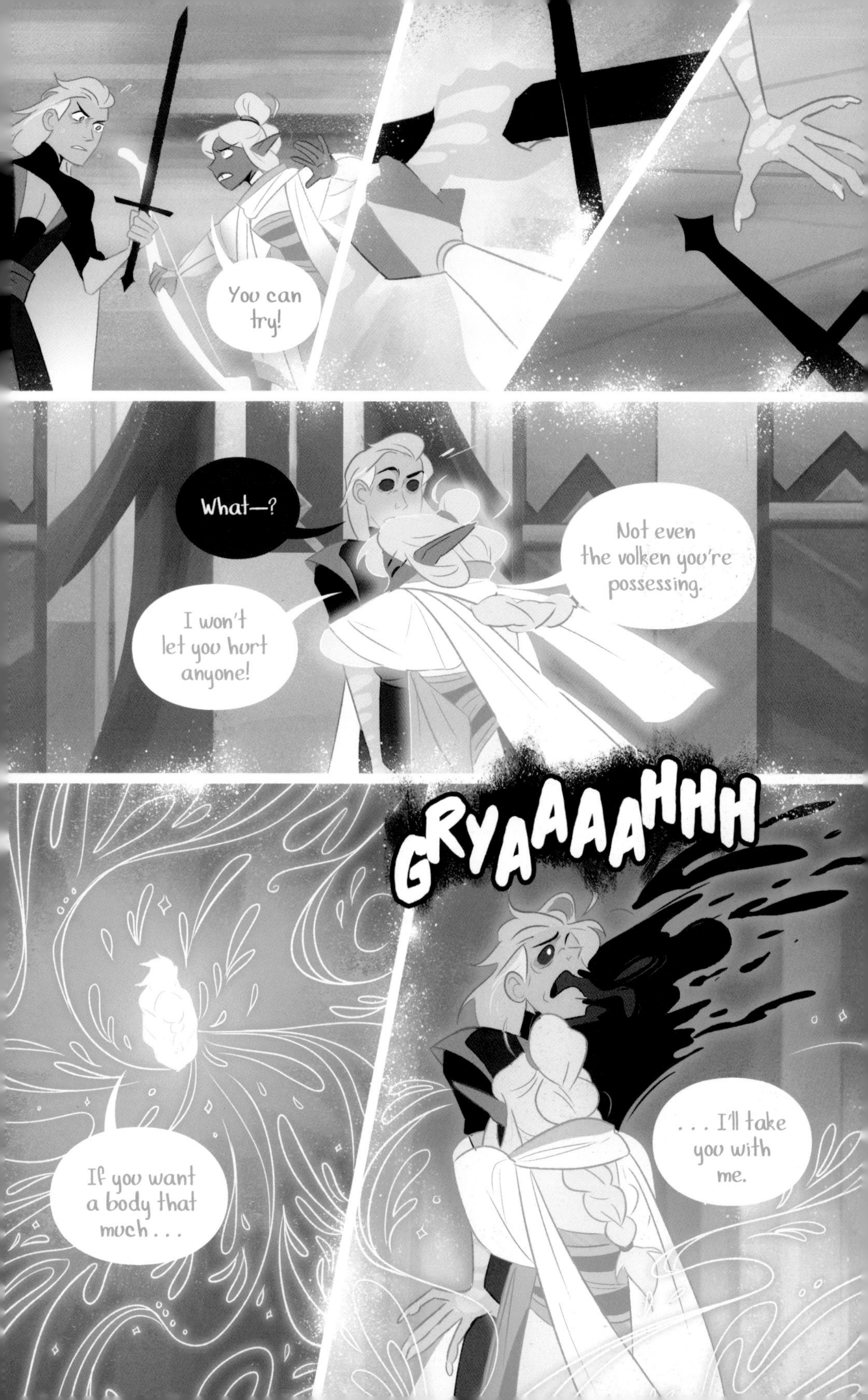
You can try!
What—?
I won't let you hurt anyone!
Not even the volken you're possessing.
GRYAAAAHHH
If you want a body that much . . .
. . . I'll take you with me.

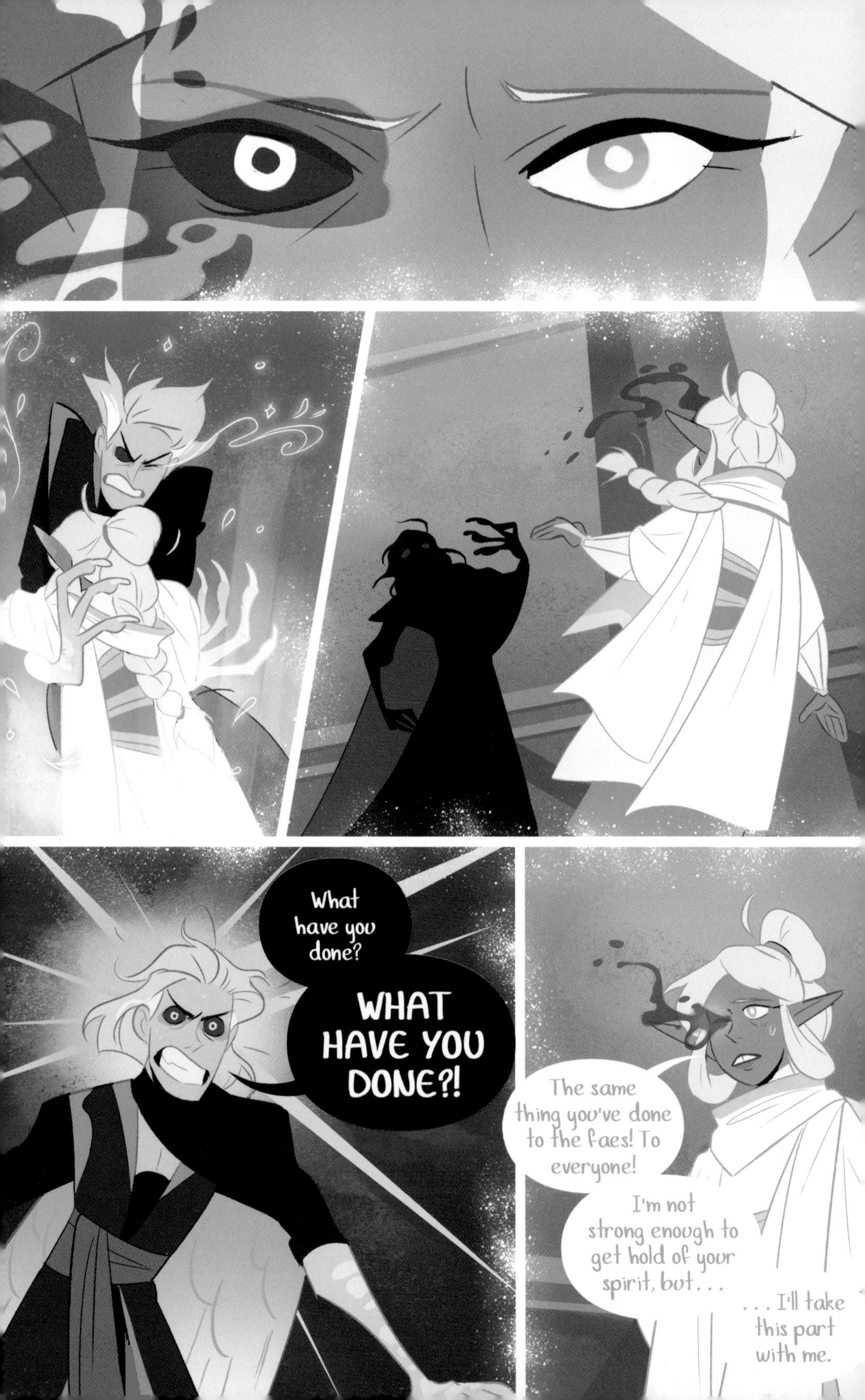
What have you done?
WHAT HAVE YOU DONE?!
The same thing you've done to the faes! To everyone!
I'm not strong enough to get hold of your spirit, but. . .
. . . I'll take this part with me.

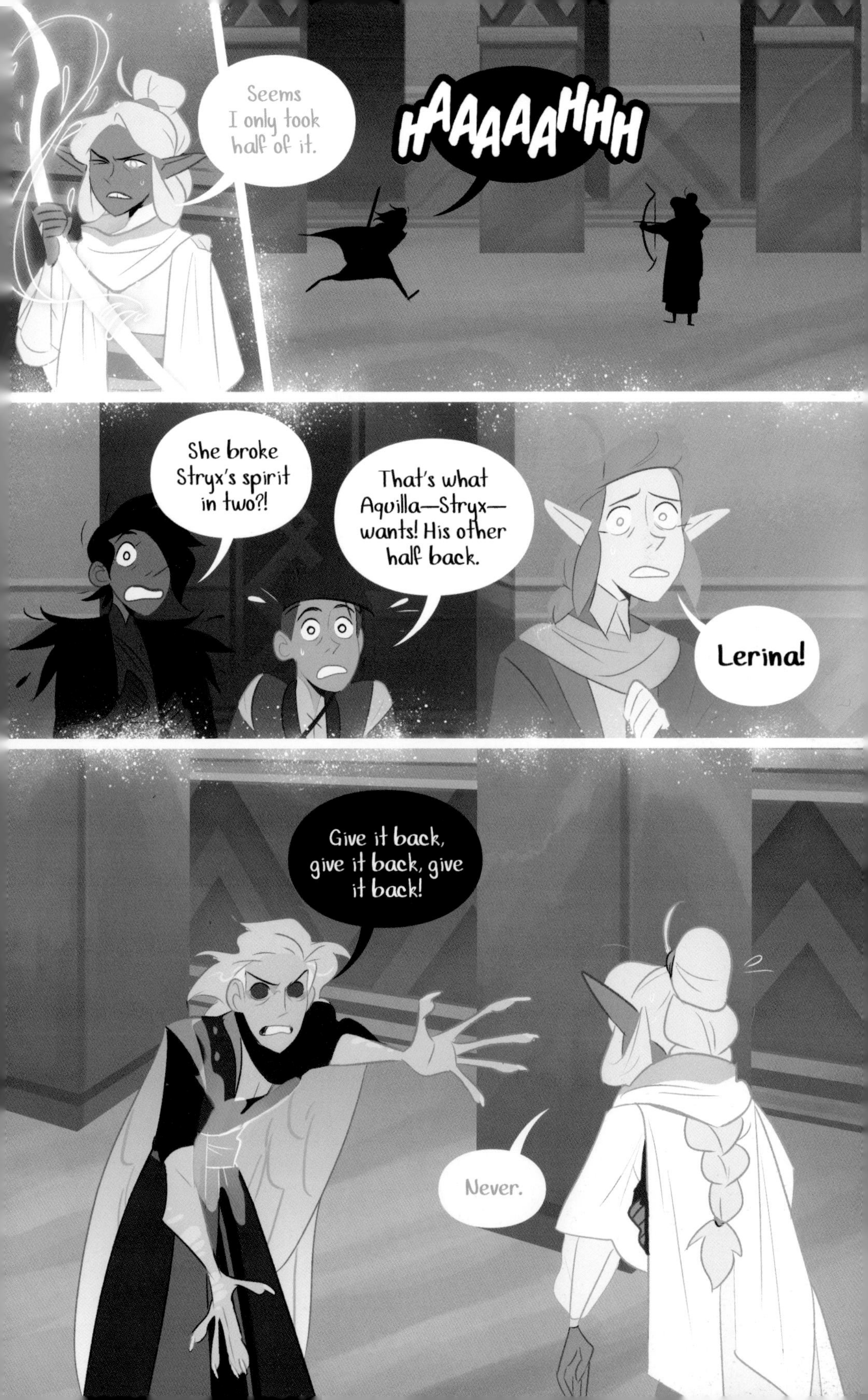
Seems I only took half of it.
HAAAAAHHH
She broke Stryx's spirit in two?!
That's what Aquilla—Stryx—wants! His other half back.
Lerina!
Give it back, give it back, give it back!
Never.

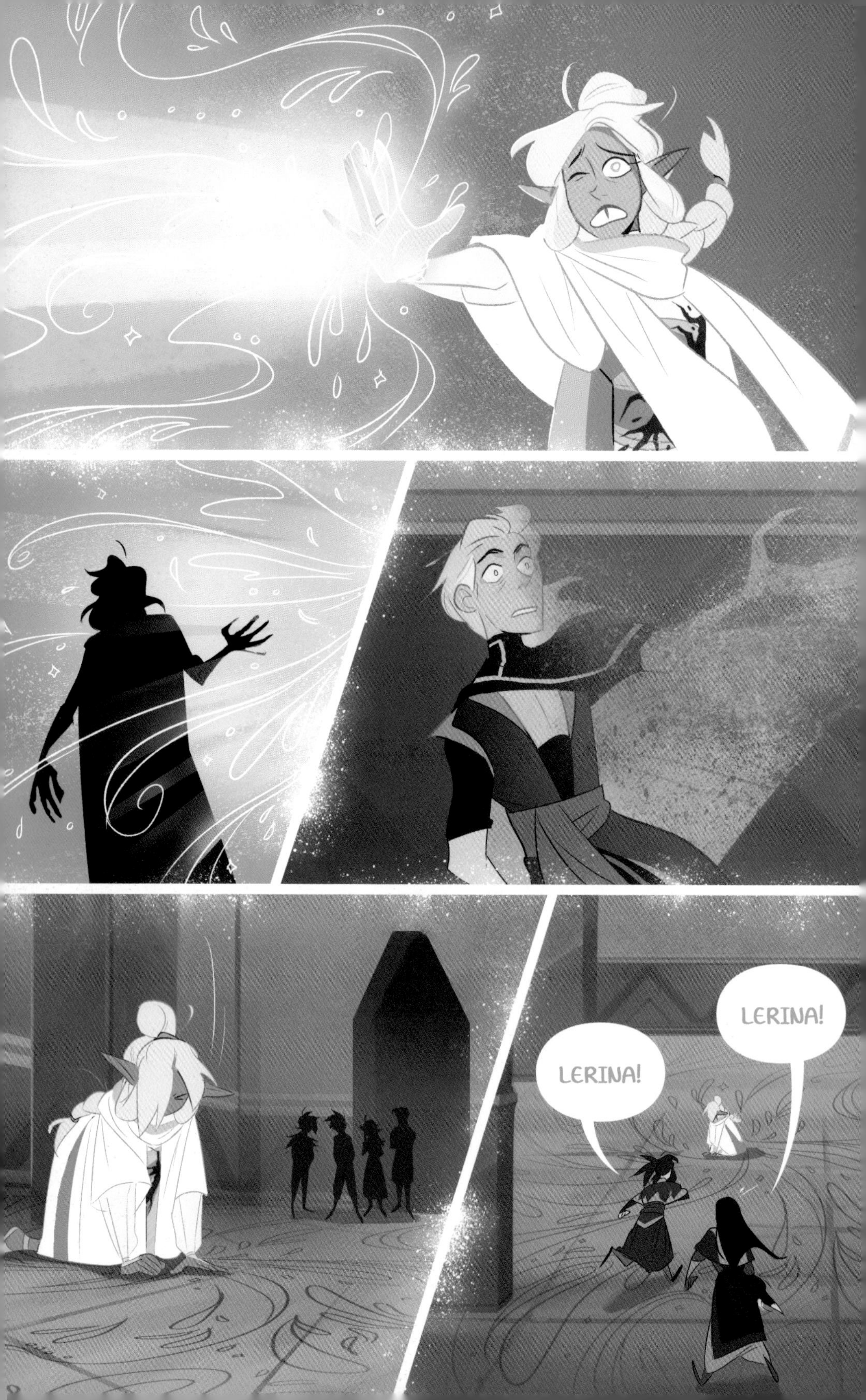
LERINA!
LERINA!

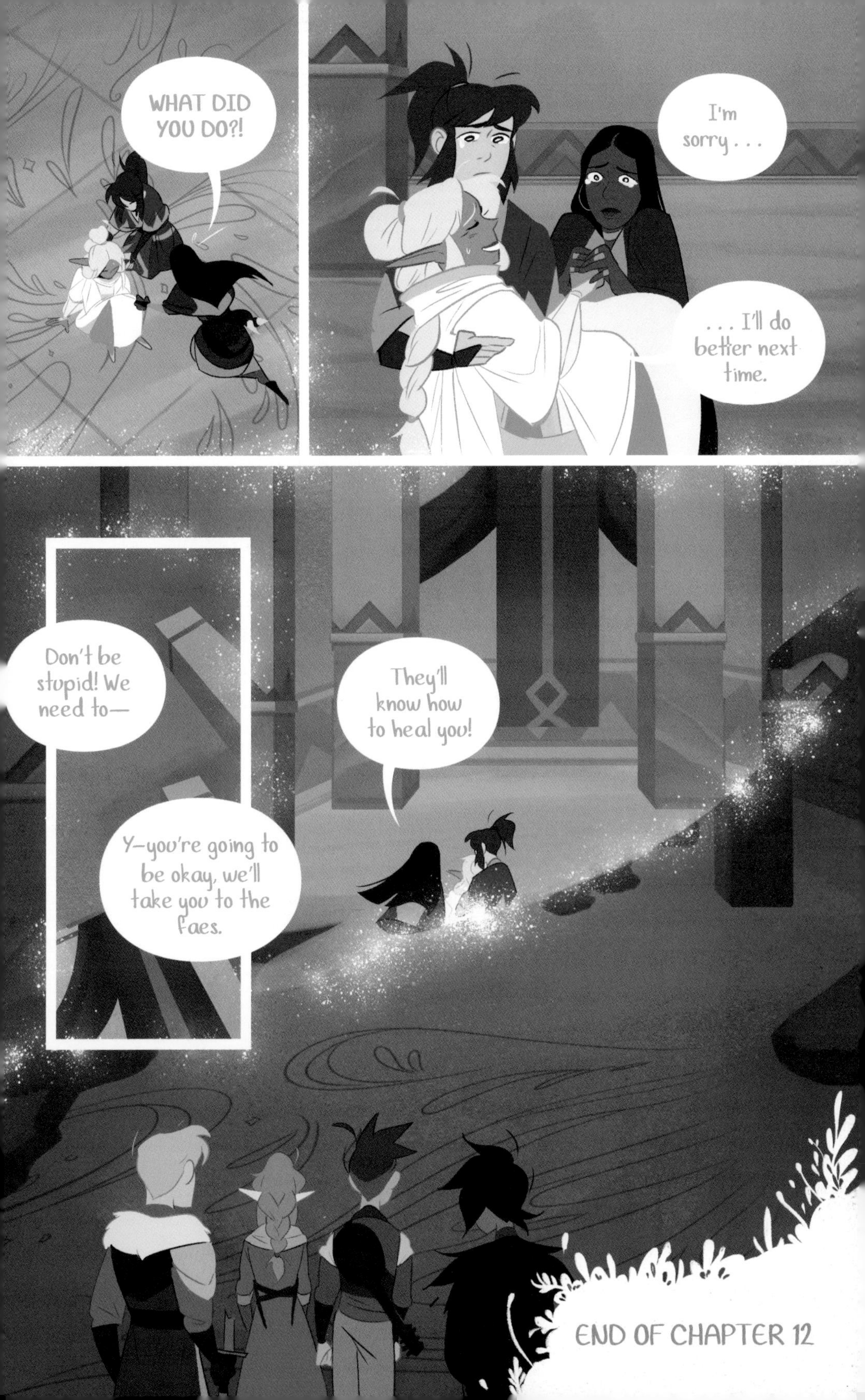
WHAT DID YOU DO?!
I'm sorry . . .
. . . I'll do better next time.
Don't be stupid! We need to—
They'll know how to heal you!
Y—you're going to be okay, we'll take you to the faes.
END OF CHAPTER 12

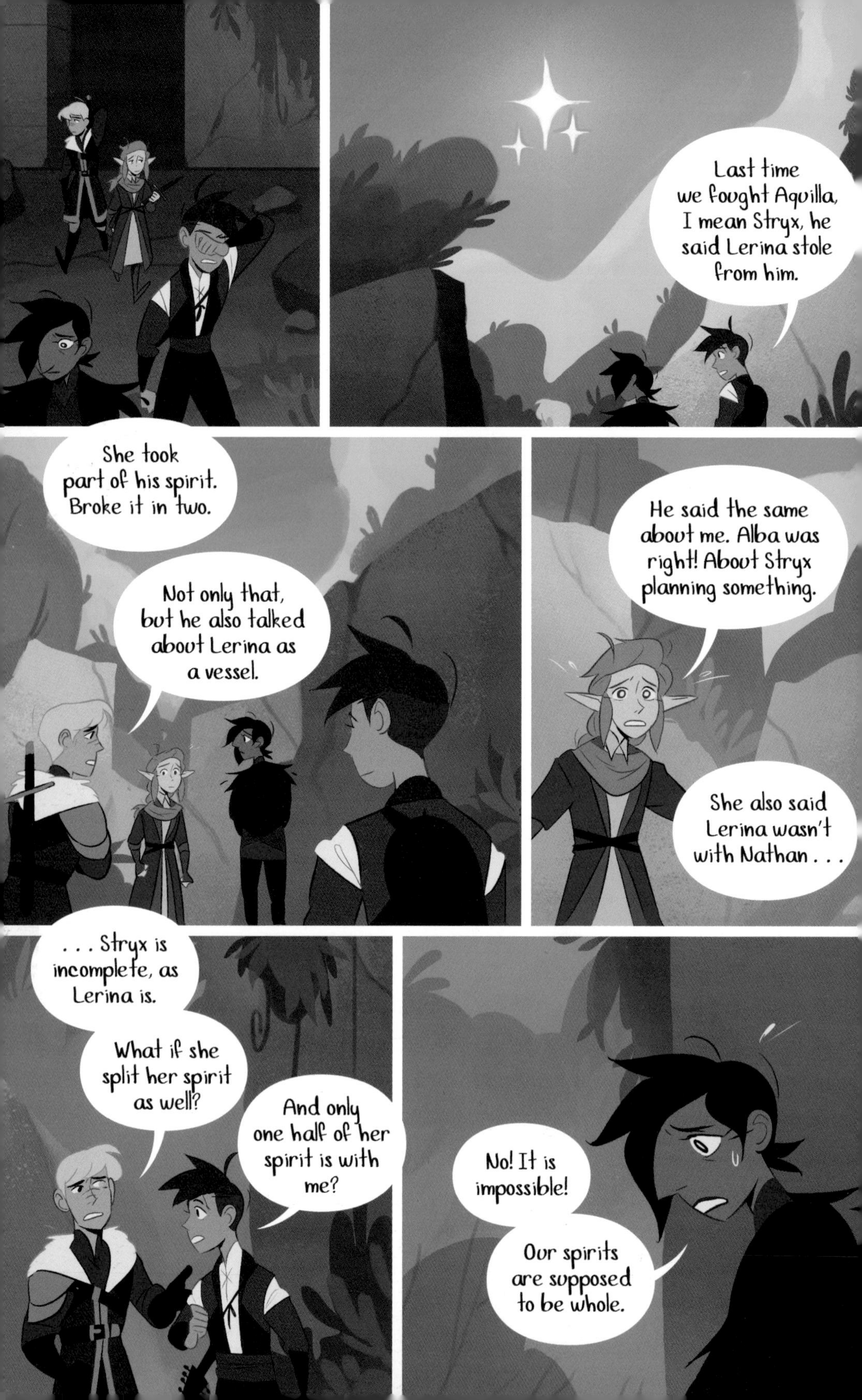
Last time we fought Aquilla, I mean Stryx, he said Lerina stole from him.
She took part of his spirit. Broke it in two.
Not only that, but he also talked about Lerina as a vessel.
He said the same about me. Alba was right! About Stryx planning something.
She also said Lerina wasn't with Nathan . . .
. . . Stryx is incomplete, as Lerina is.
What if she split her spirit as well?
And only one half of her spirit is with me?
No! It is impossible!
Our spirits are supposed to be whole.

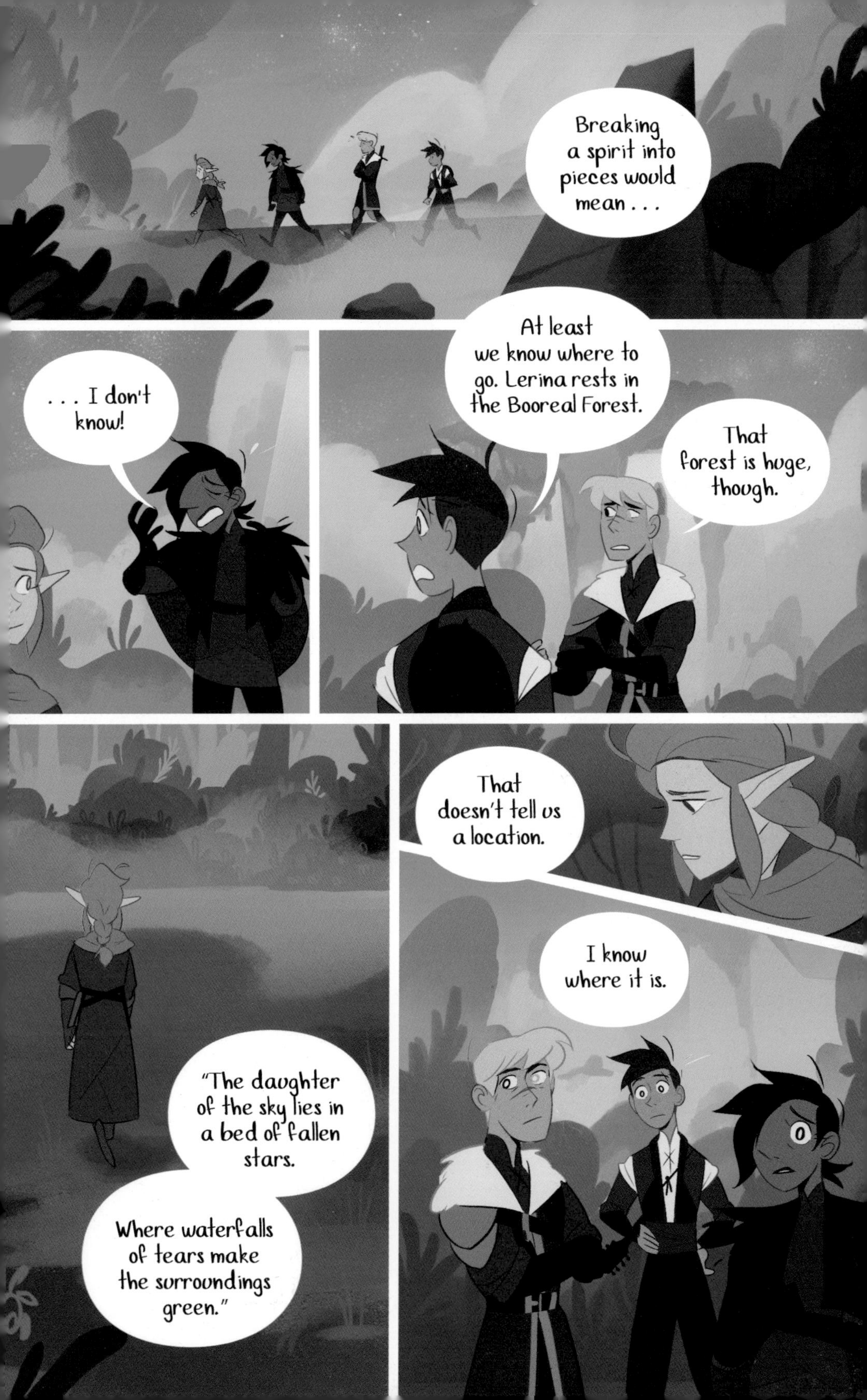

Breaking a spirit into pieces would mean . . .
. . . I don't know!
At least we know where to go. Lerina rests in the Booreal Forest.
That forest is huge, though.
"The daughter of the sky lies in a bed of fallen stars.
Where waterfalls of tears make the surroundings green."
That doesn't tell us a location.
I know where it is.

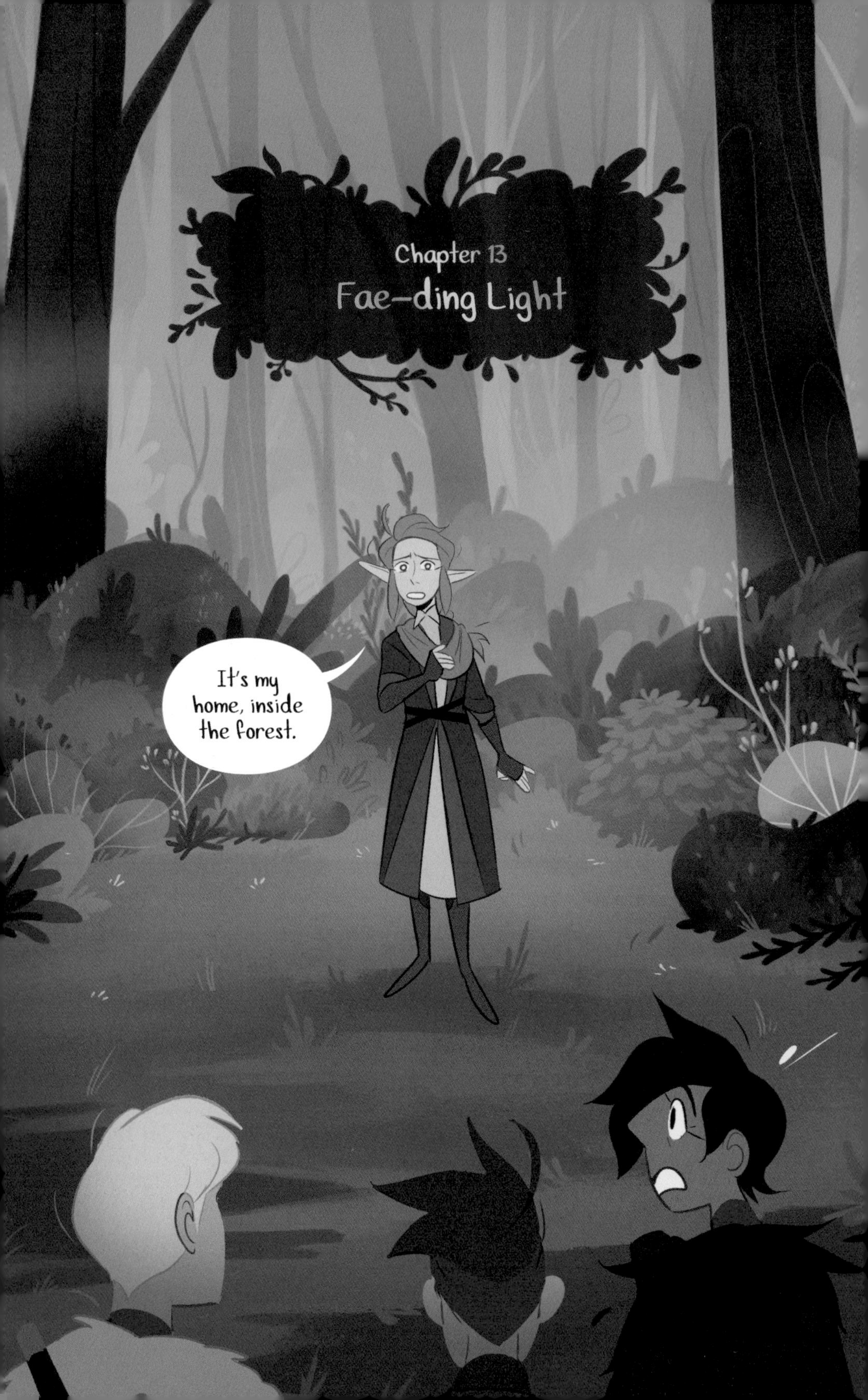
Chapter 13
Fae-ding Light
It's my home, inside the forest.

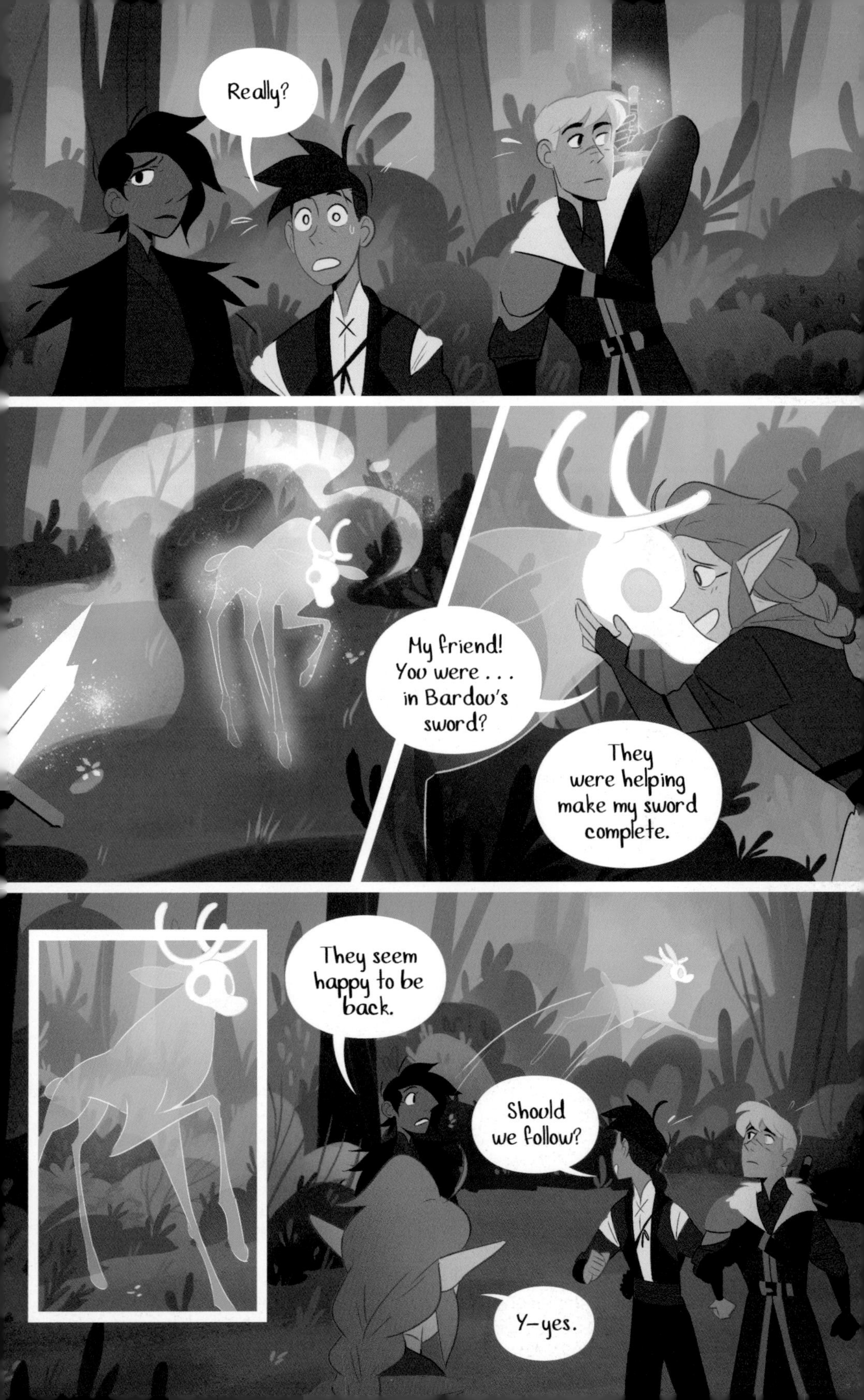
Really?
My friend! You were . . . in Bardou's sword?
They were helping make my sword complete.
They seem happy to be back.
Should we follow?
Y-yes.

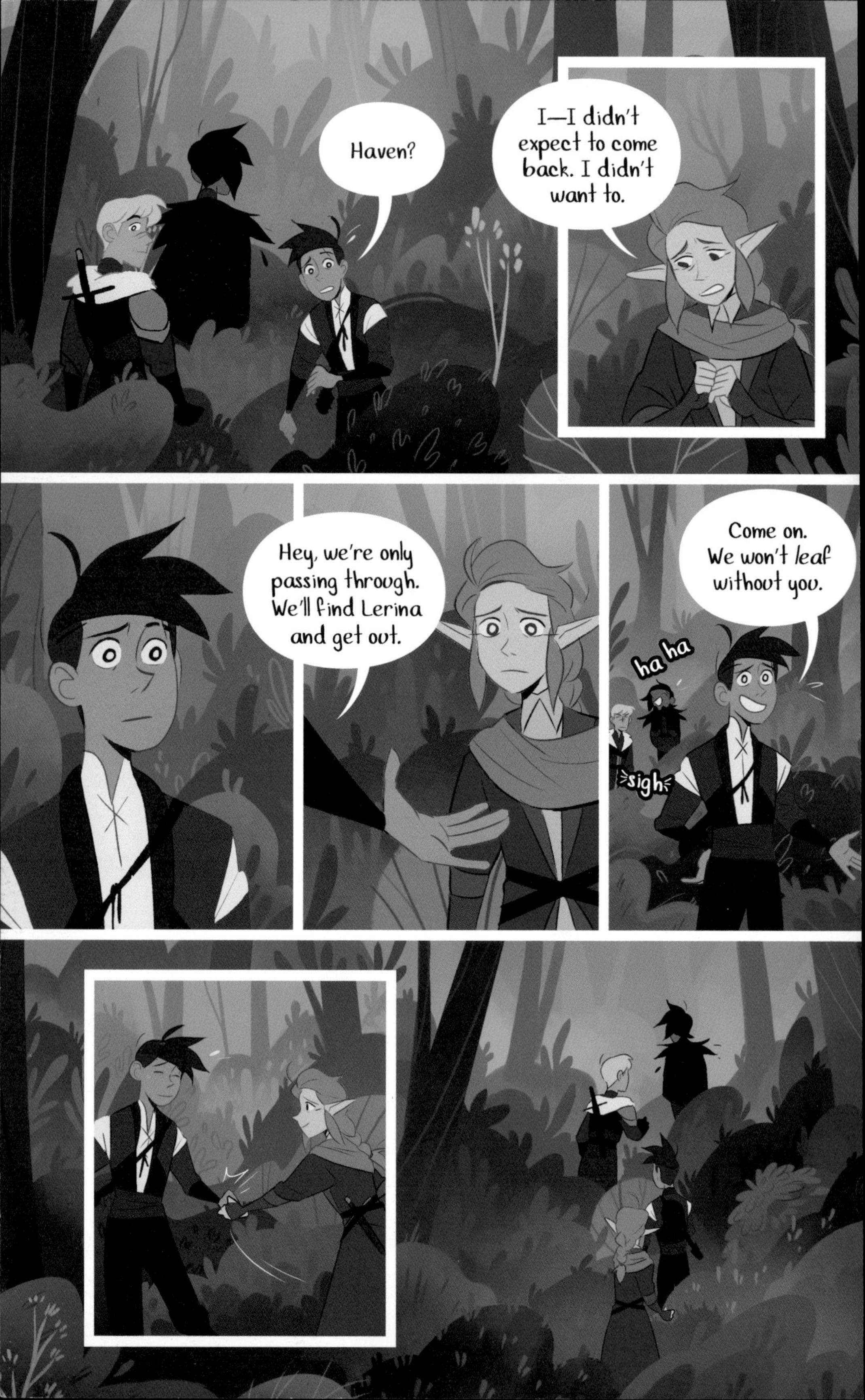
Haven?
I—I didn't expect to come back. I didn't want to.
Hey, we're only passing through. We'll find Lerina and get out.
Come on. We won't leaf without you.
ha ha
sigh

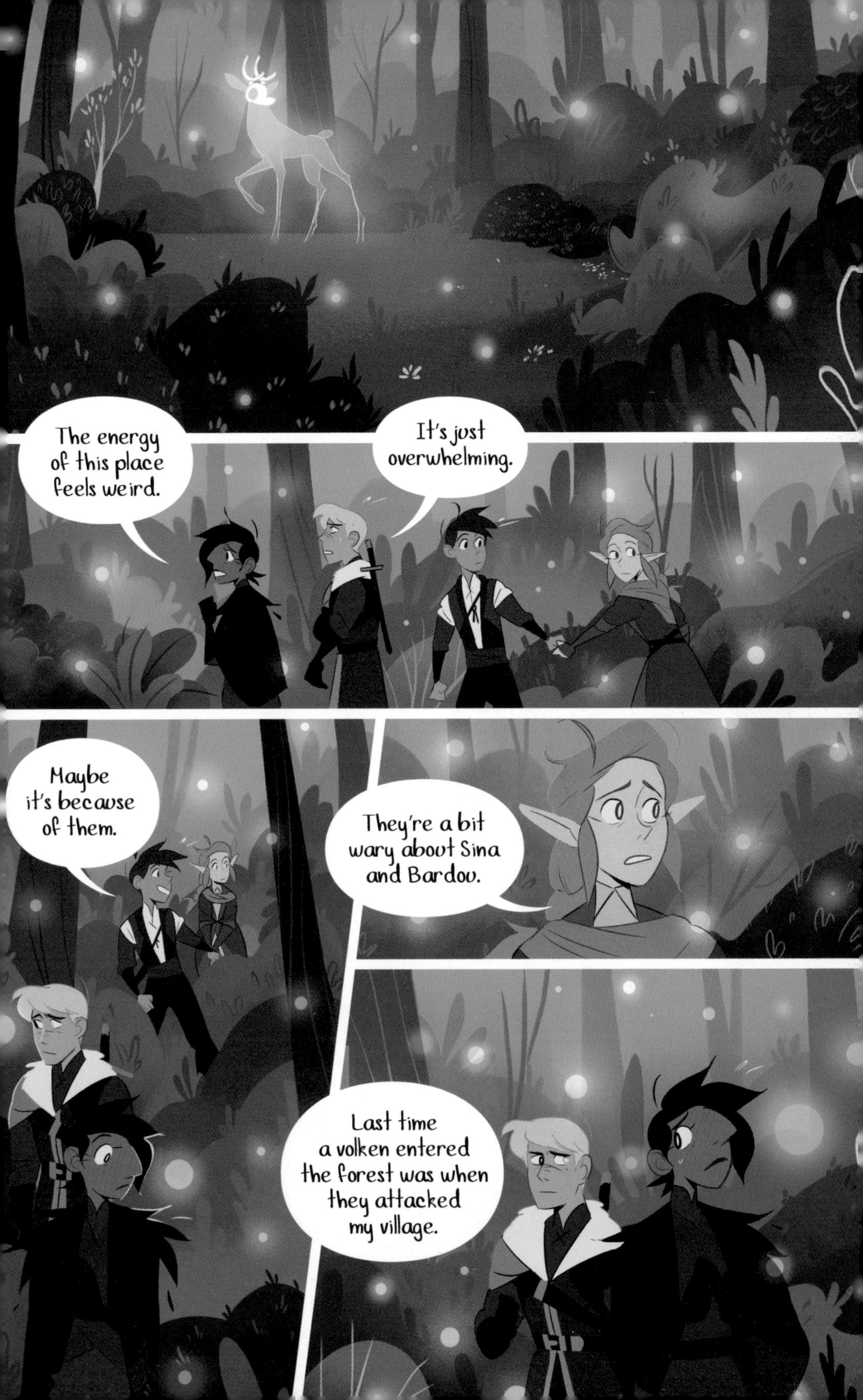
The energy of this place feels weird.
It's just overwhelming.
Maybe it's because of them.
They're a bit wary about Sina and Bardou.
Last time a volken entered the forest was when they attacked my village.

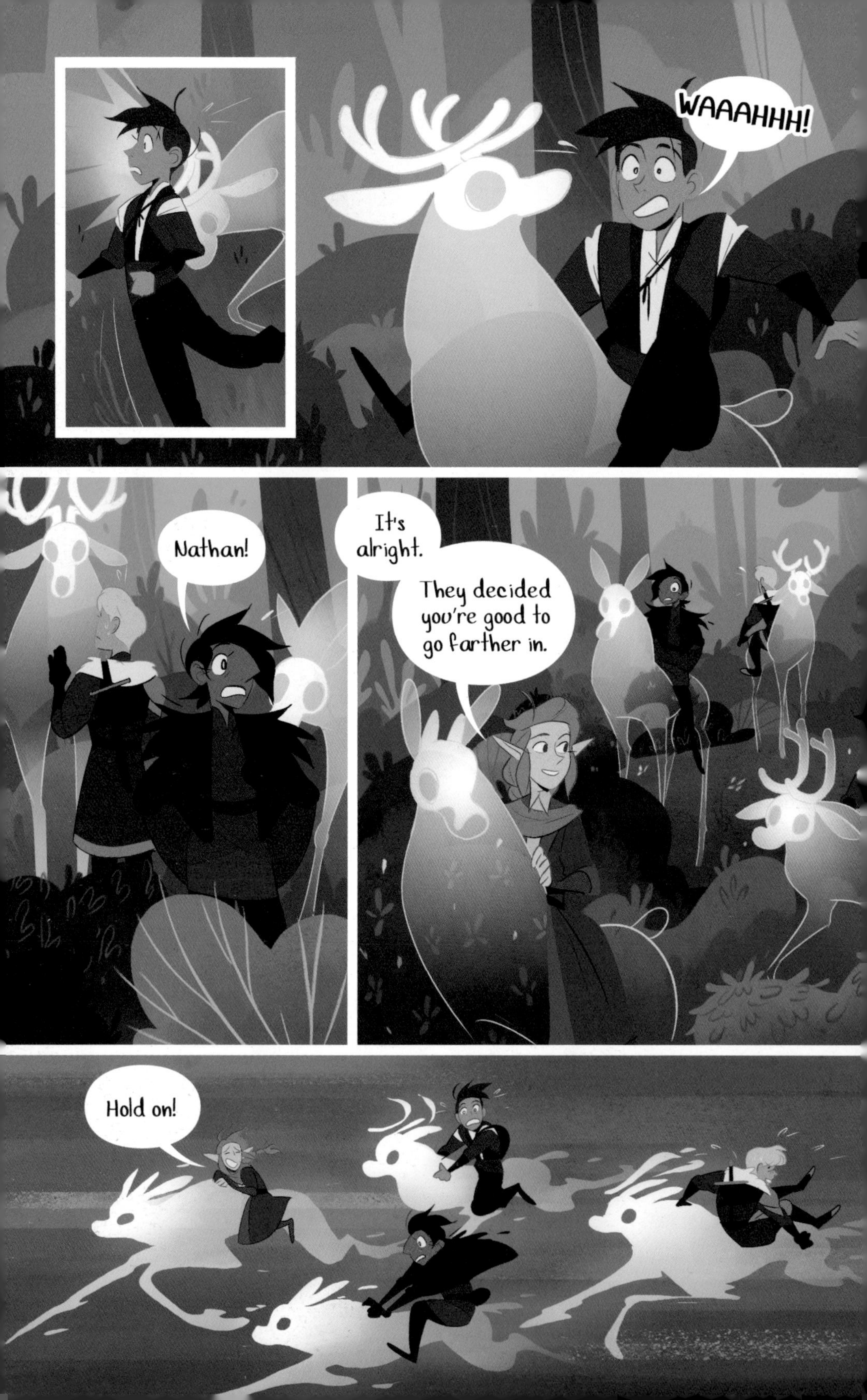

WAAAHHH!
Nathan!
It's alright.
They decided you're good to go farther in.
Hold on!

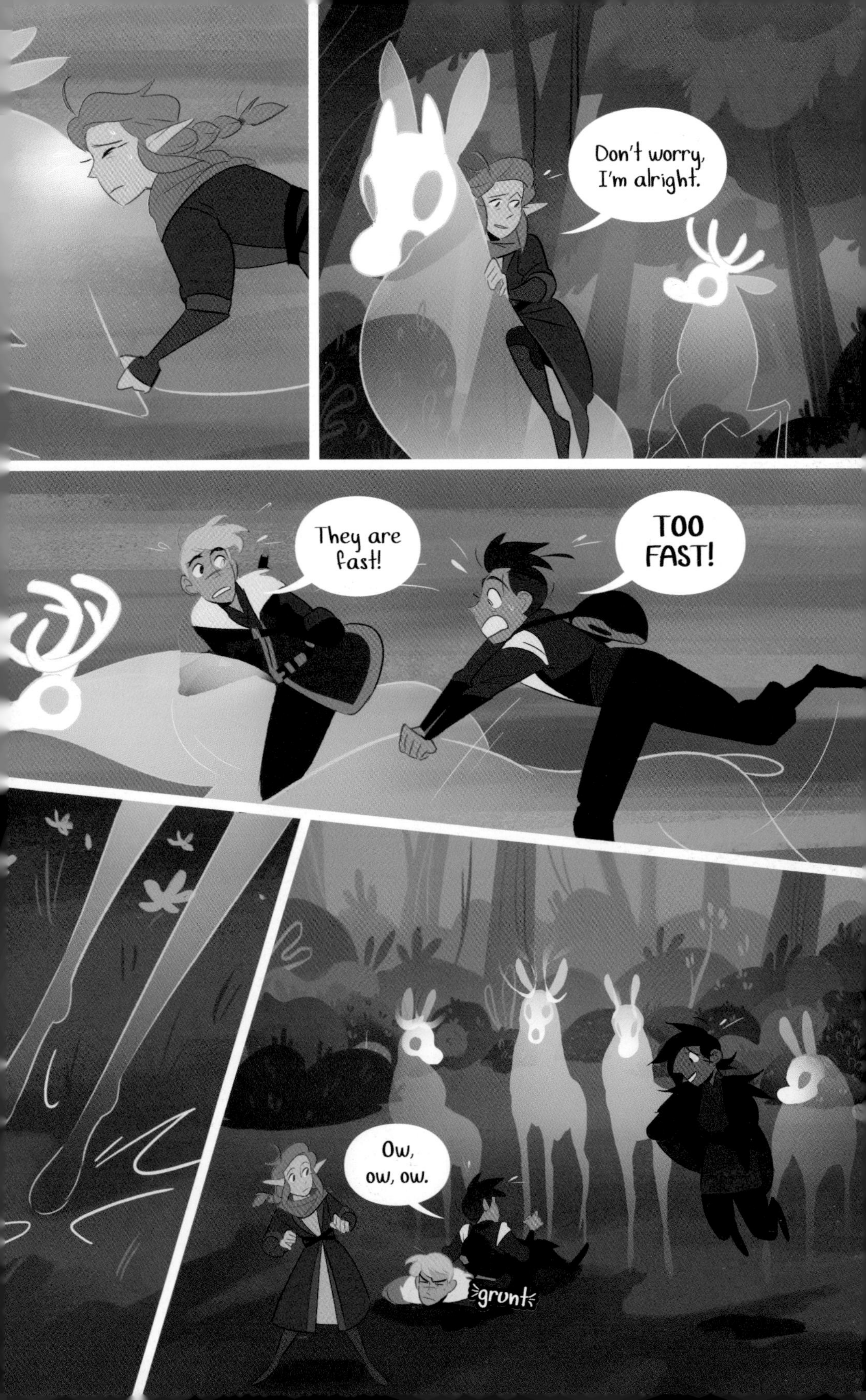
Don't worry, I'm alright.
They are fast!
TOO FAST!
Ow, ow, ow.
grunt

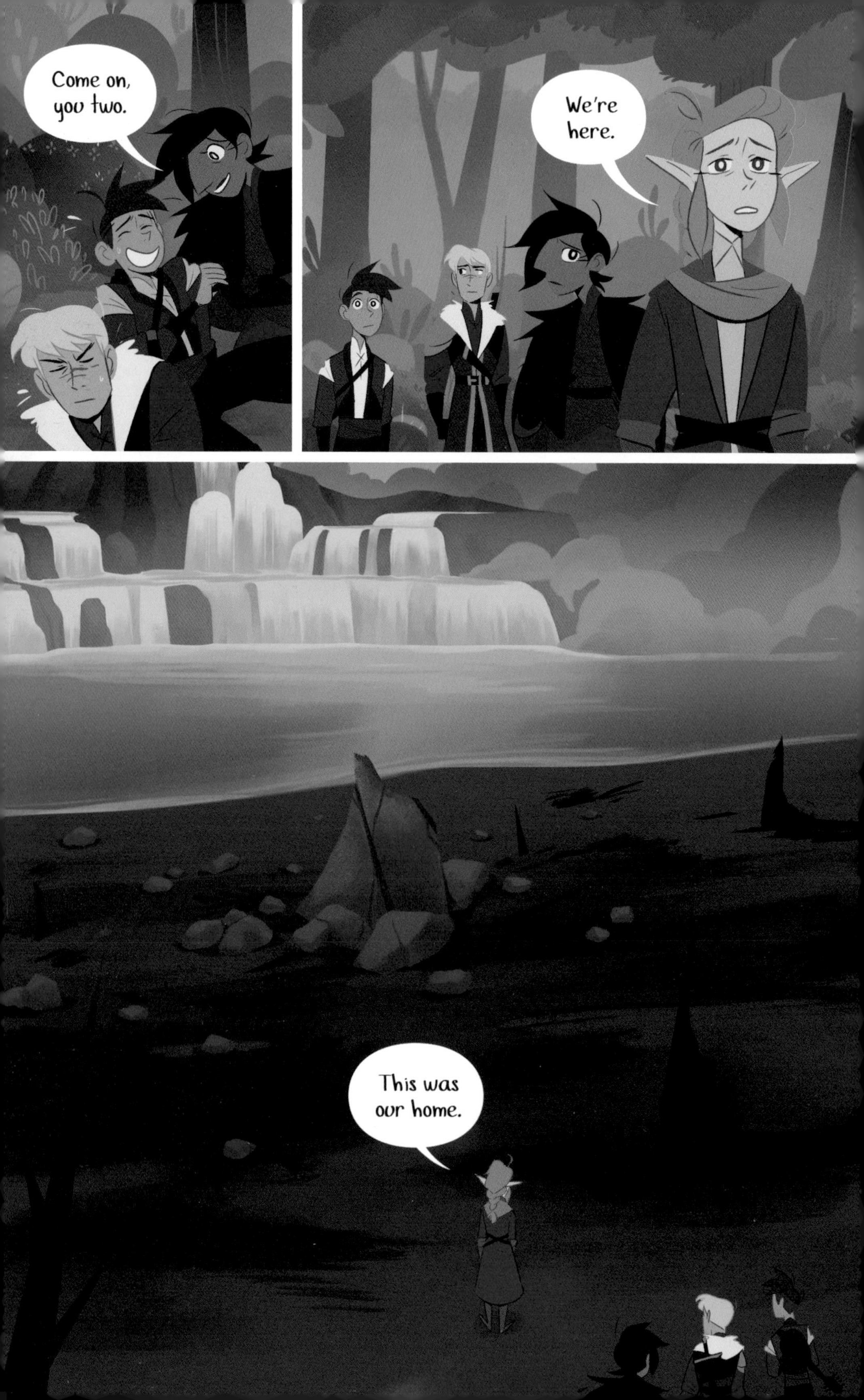
Come on, you two.
We're here.
This was our home.

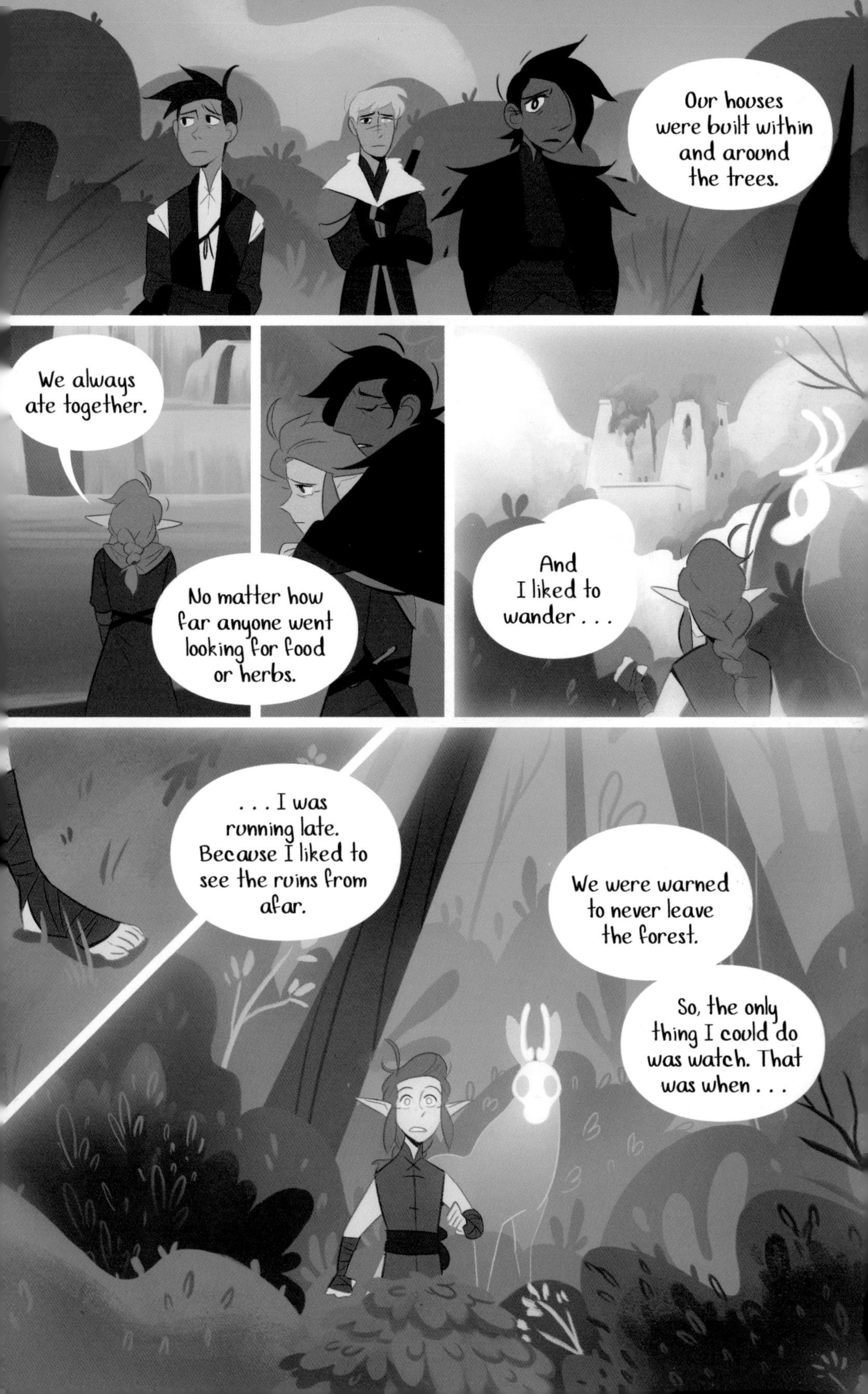
Our houses were built within and around the trees.
We always ate together.
No matter how far anyone went looking for food or herbs.
And I liked to wander . . .
. . . I was running late. Because I liked to see the ruins from afar.
We were warned to never leave the forest.
So, the only thing I could do was watch. That was when . . .

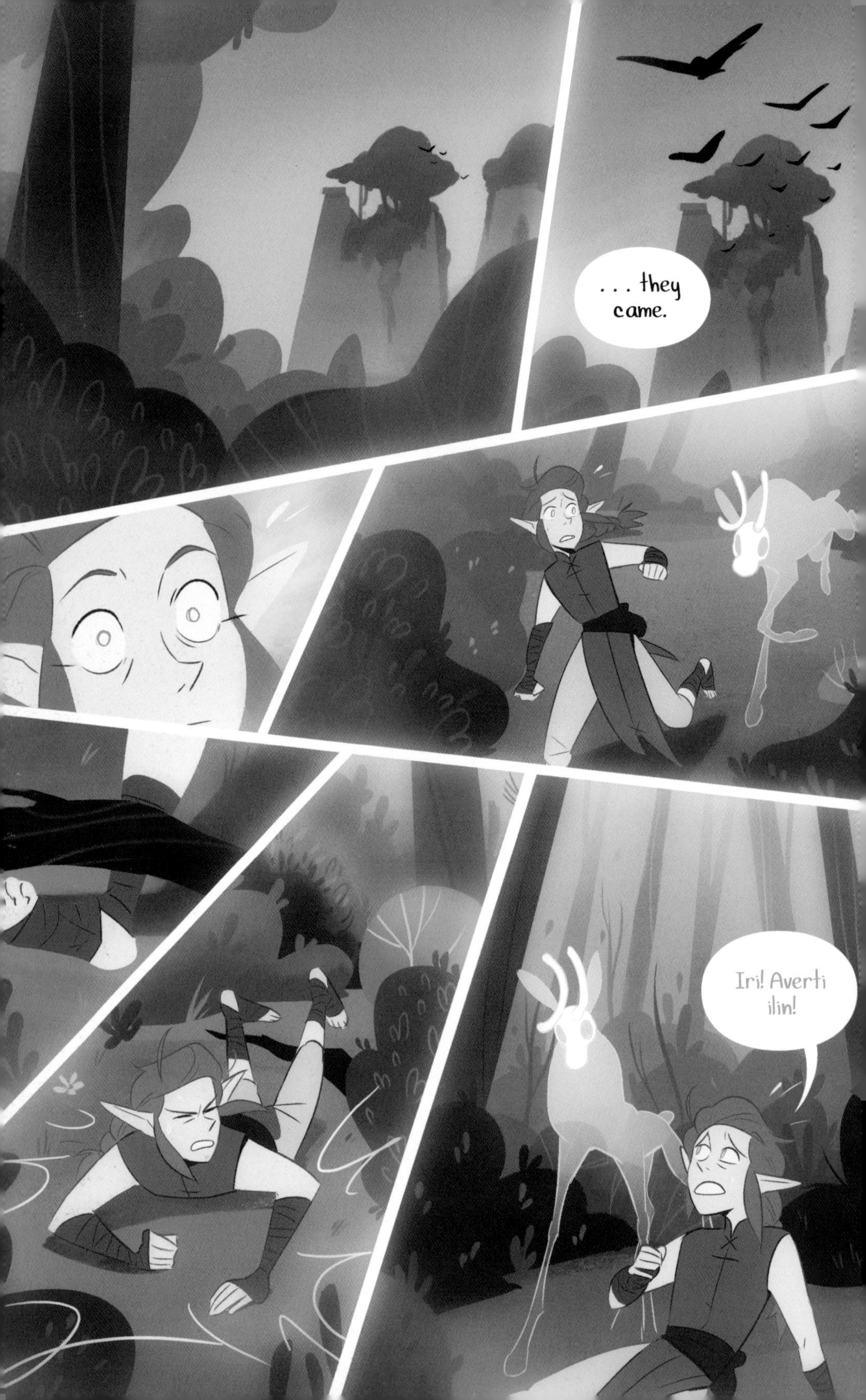
. . . they came.
Iri! Averti ilin!

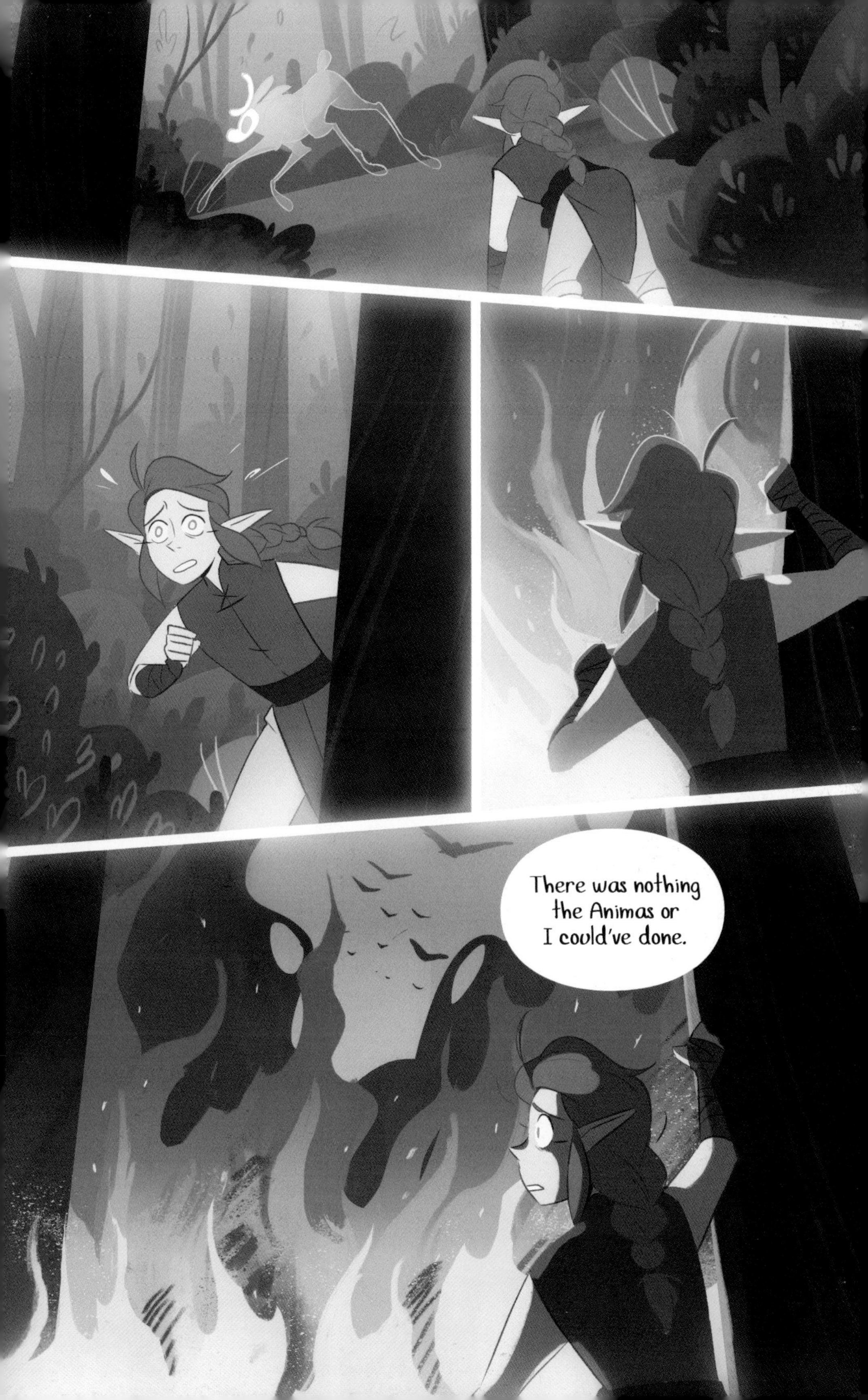
There was nothing the Animas or I could've done.

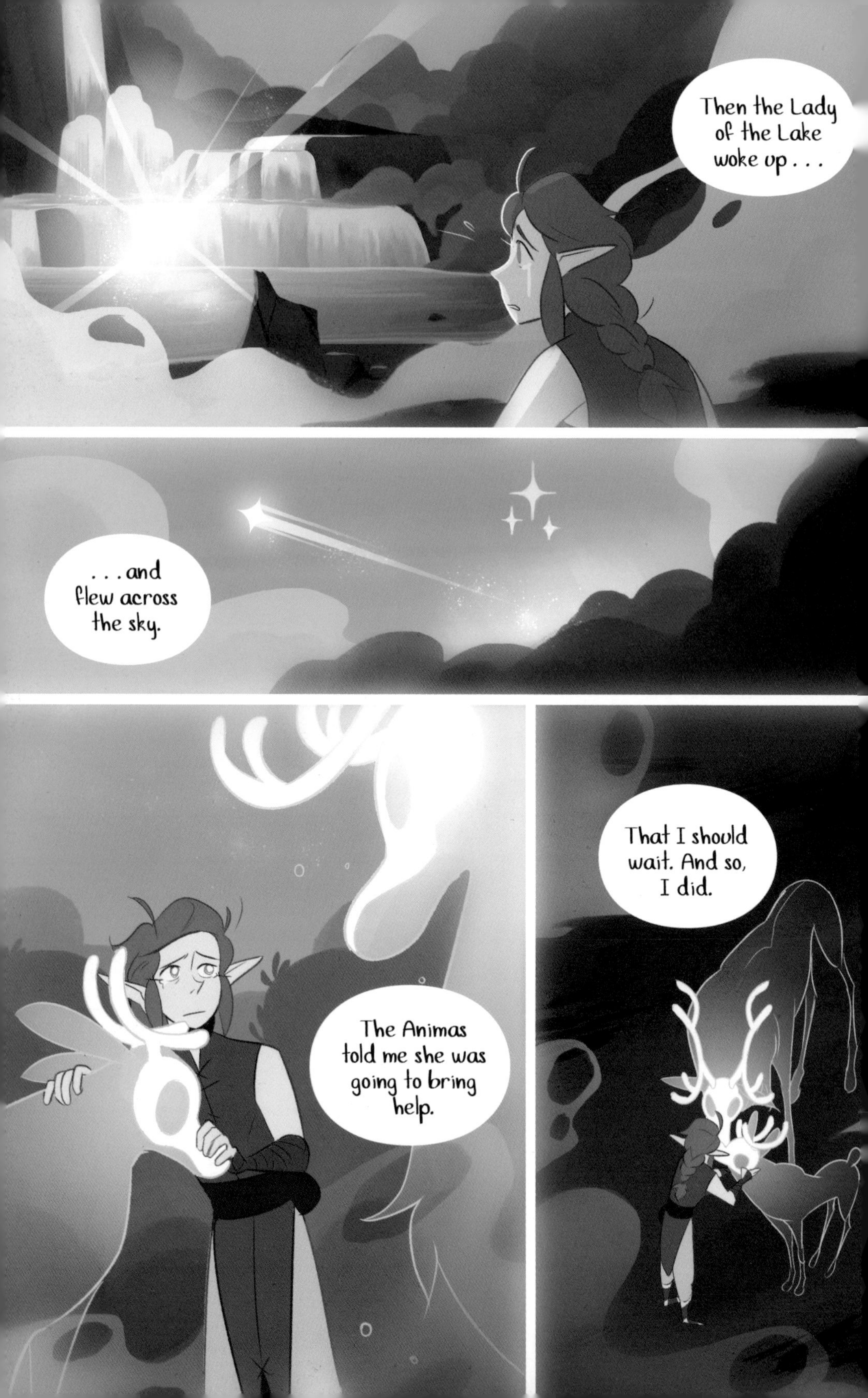
Then the Lady of the Lake woke up . . .
. . . and flew across the sky.
The Animas told me she was going to bring help.
That I should wait. And so, I did.

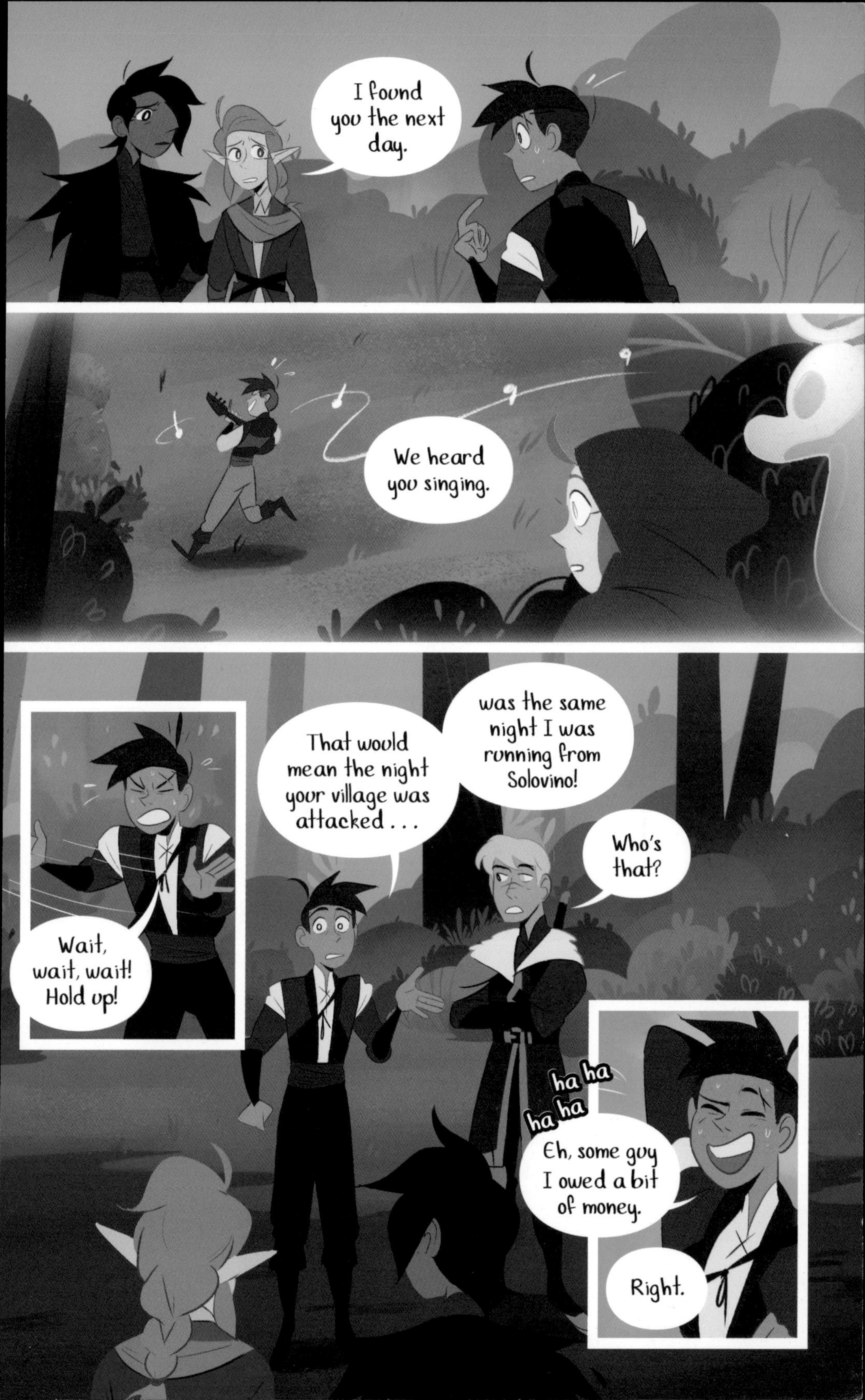

I found you the next day.
We heard you singing.
That would mean the night your village was attacked . . .
was the same night I was running from Solovino!
Wait, wait, wait! Hold up!
Who's that?
ha ha ha ha
Eh, some guy I owed a bit of money.
Right.

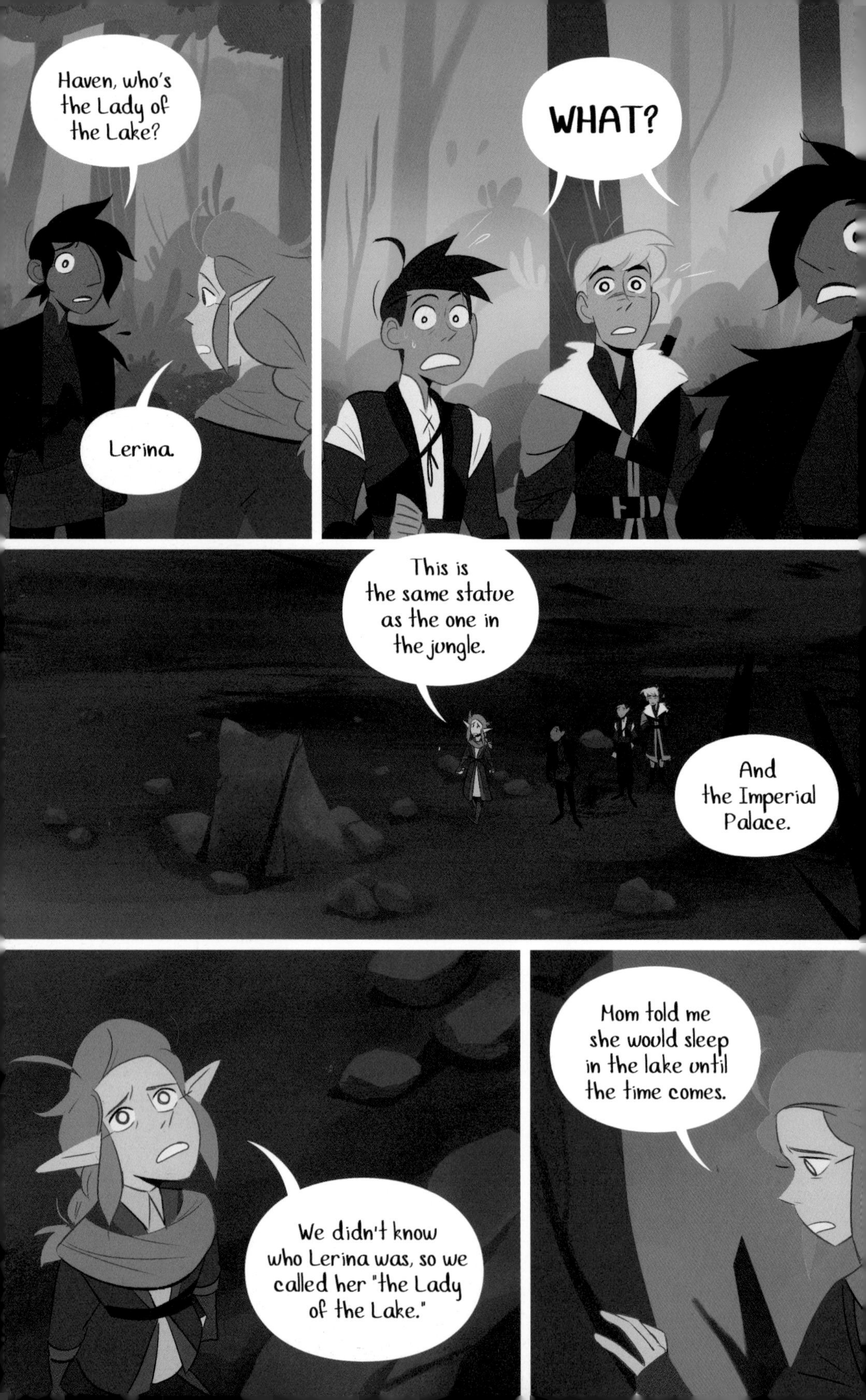
Haven, who's the Lady of the Lake?
Lerina.
WHAT?
This is the same statue as the one in the jungle.
And the Imperial Palace.
We didn't know who Lerina was, so we called her "the Lady of the Lake."
Mom told me she would sleep in the lake until the time comes.

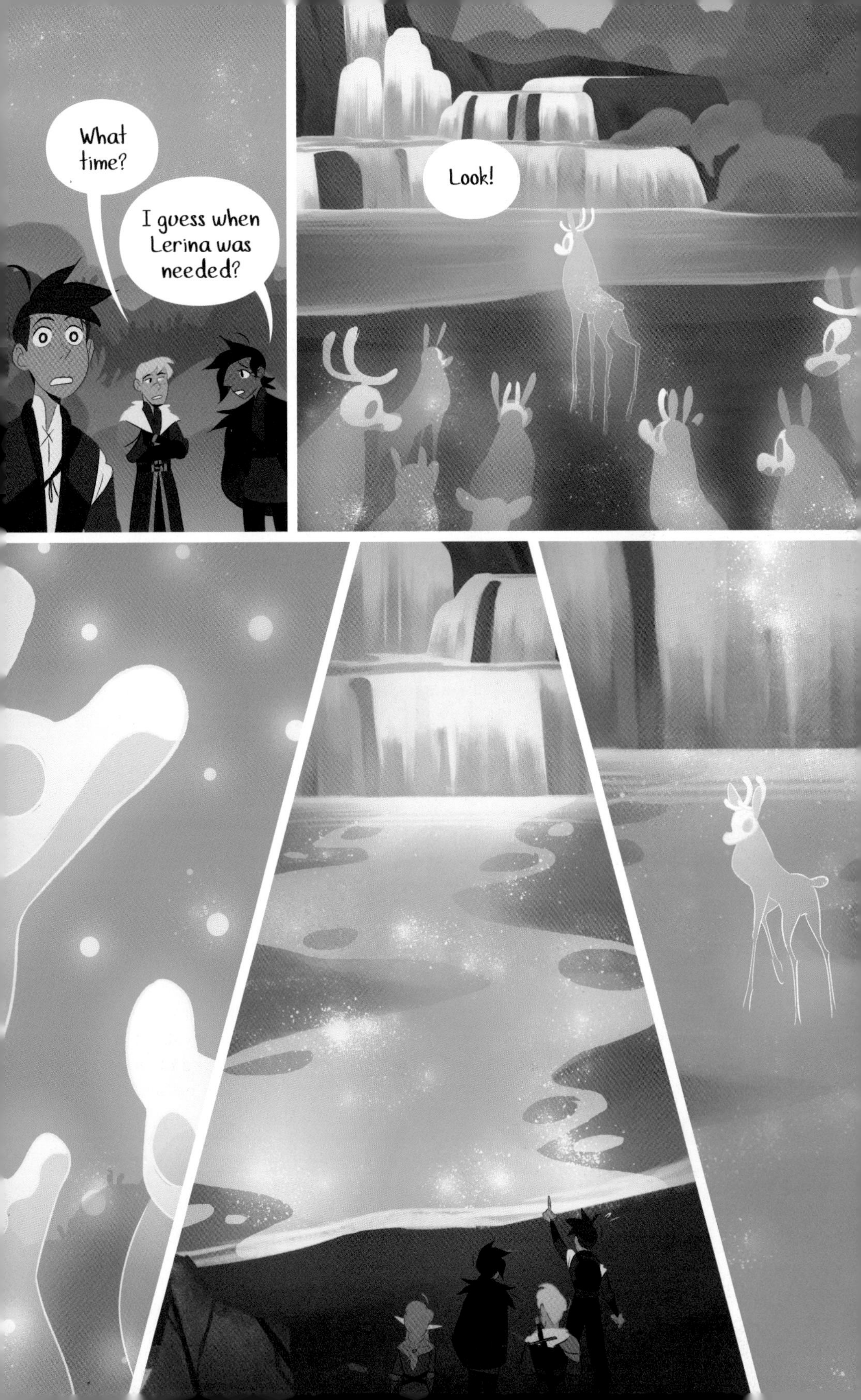
What time?
I guess when Lerina was needed?
Look!

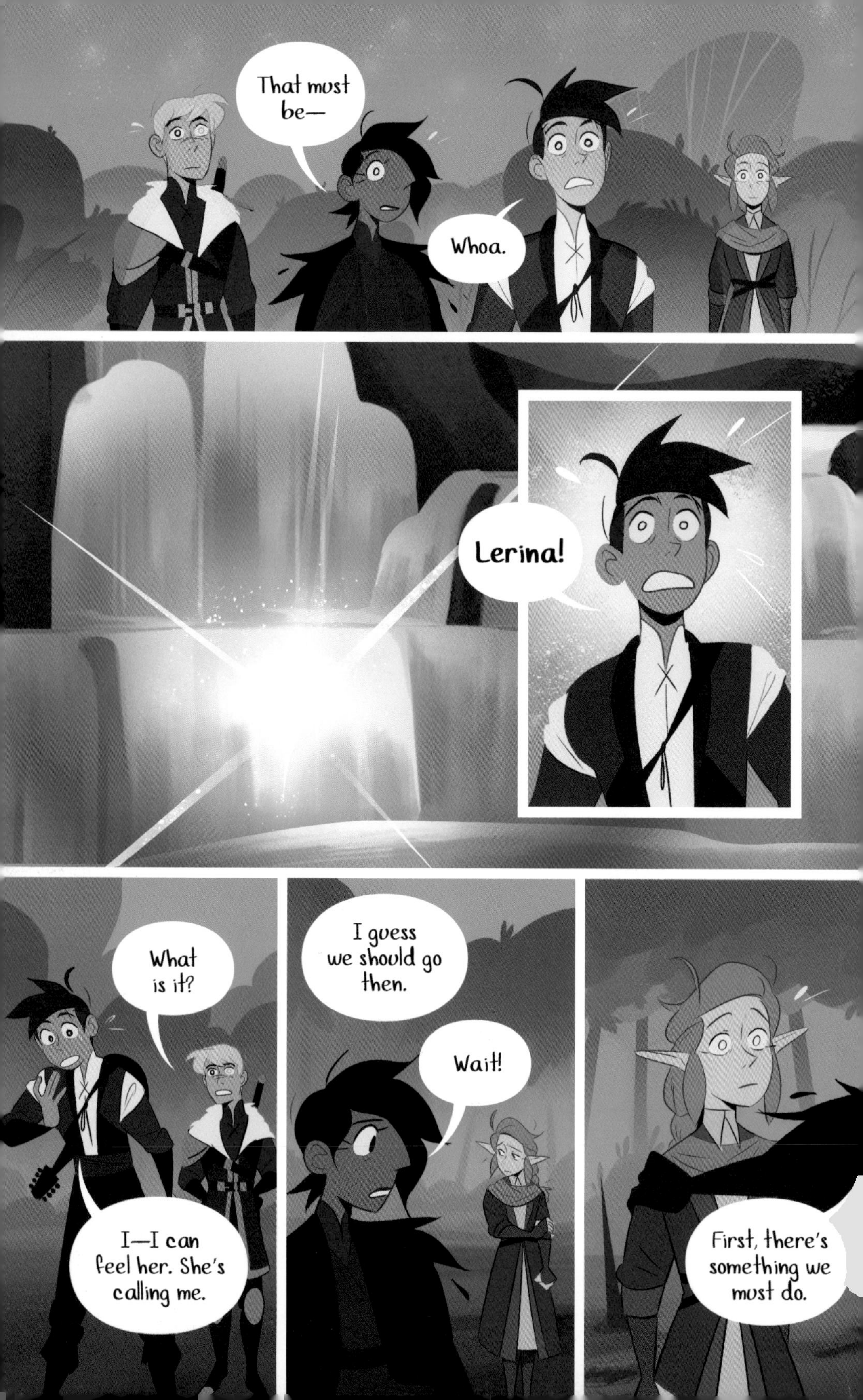
That must be—
Whoa.
Lerina!
What is it?
I—I can feel her. She's calling me.
I guess we should go then.
Wait!
First, there's something we must do.

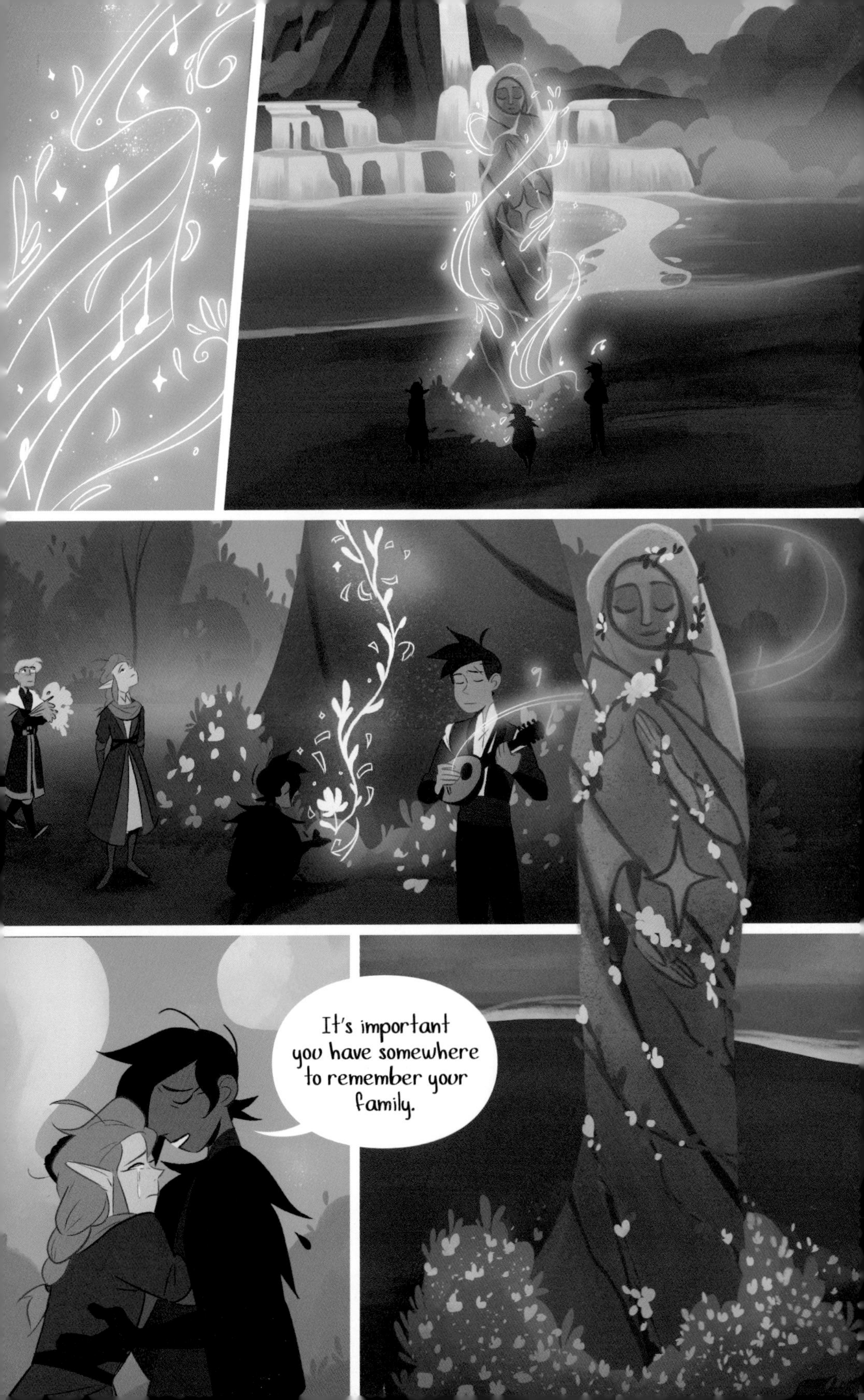
It's important you have somewhere to remember your family.

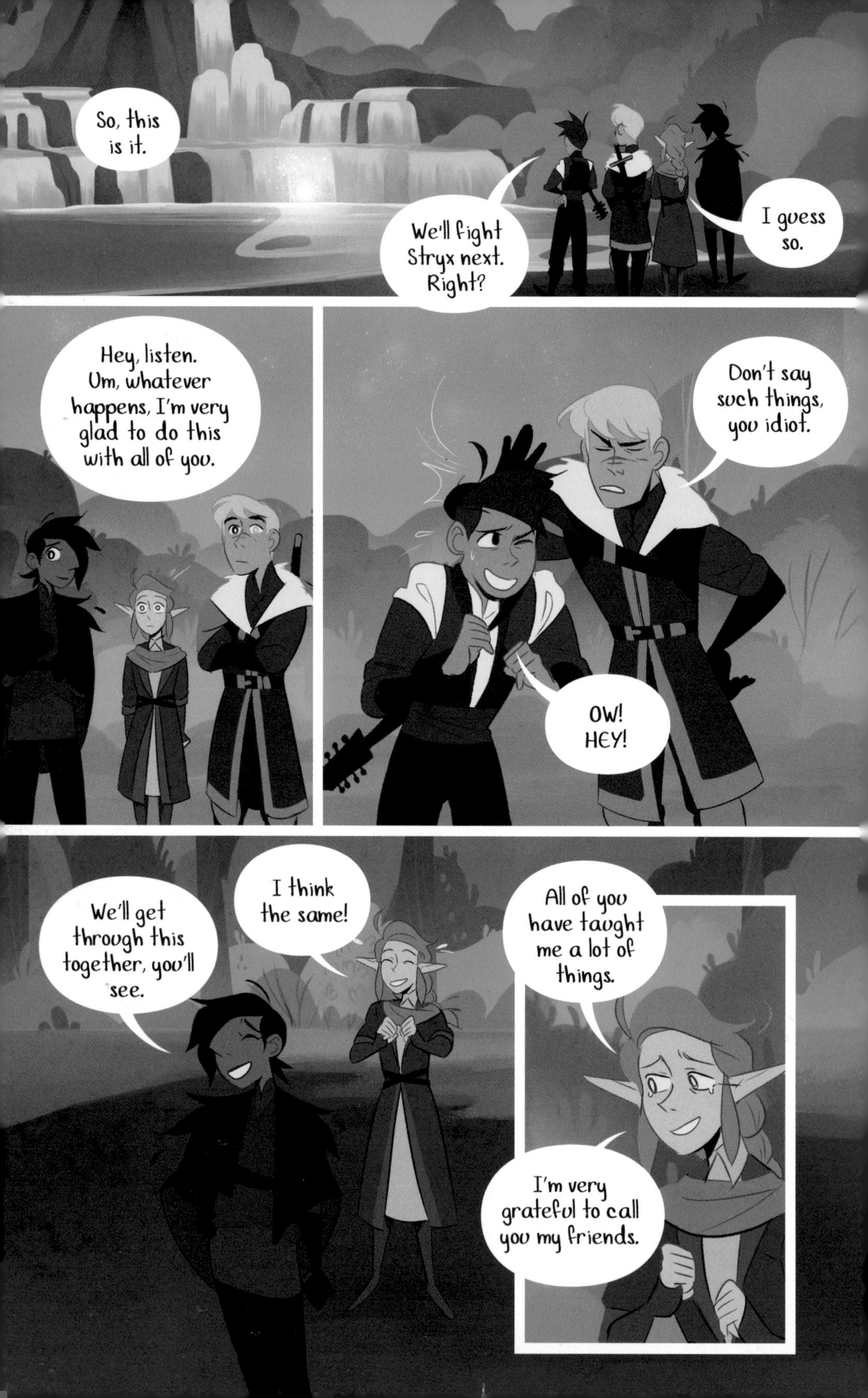
So, this is it.
We'll fight Stryx next. Right?
I guess so.
Hey, listen. Um, whatever happens, I'm very glad to do this with all of you.
Don't say such things, you idiot.
OW! HEY!
We'll get through this together, you'll see.
I think the same!
All of you have taught me a lot of things.
I'm very grateful to call you my friends.

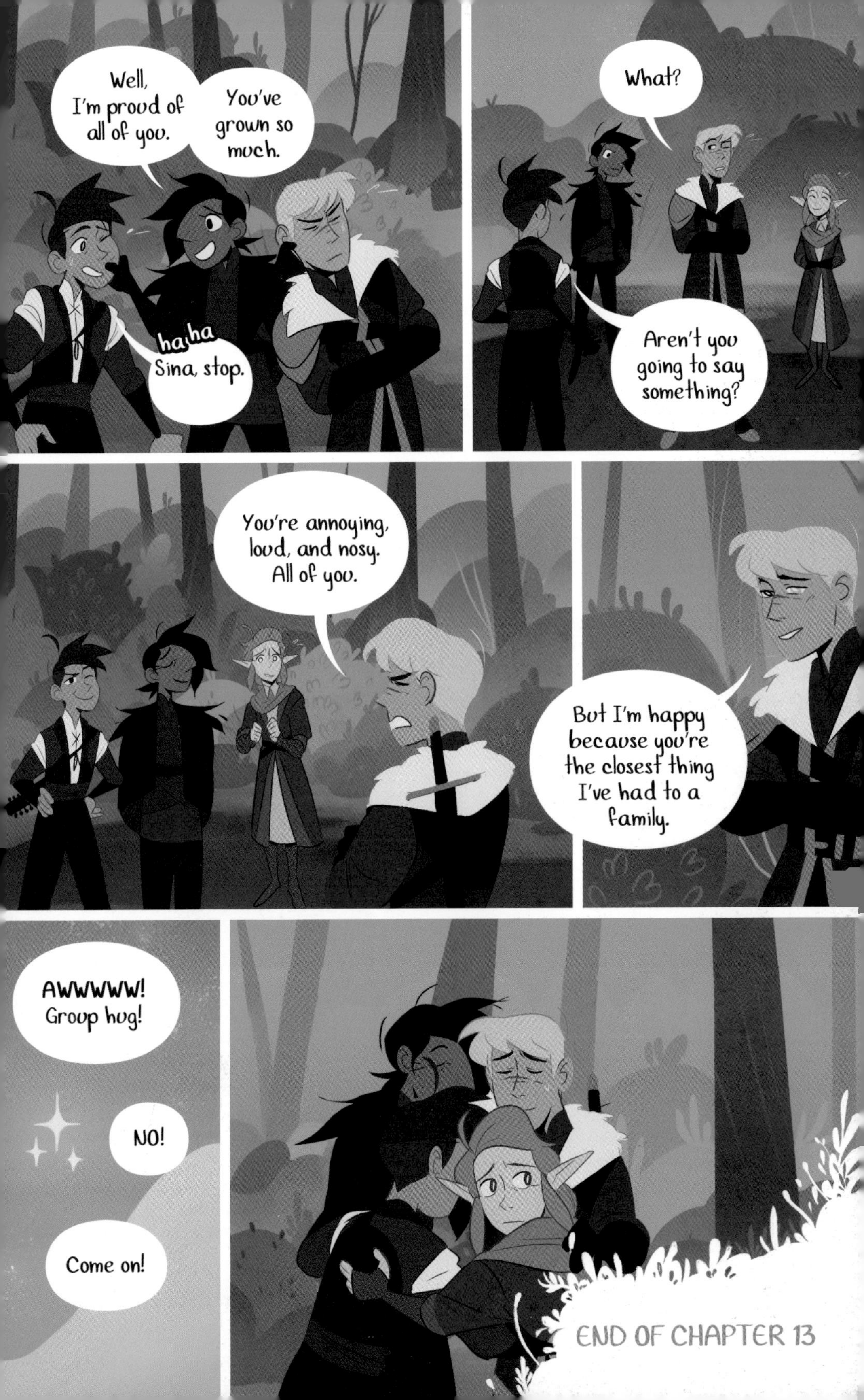
Well,
I'm proud of all of you.
You've grown so much.
ha ha
Sina, stop.
What?
Aren't you going to say something?
You're annoying, loud, and nosy. All of you.
But I'm happy because you're the closest thing I've had to a family.
AWWWWW! Group hug!
NO!
Come on!
END OF CHAPTER 13

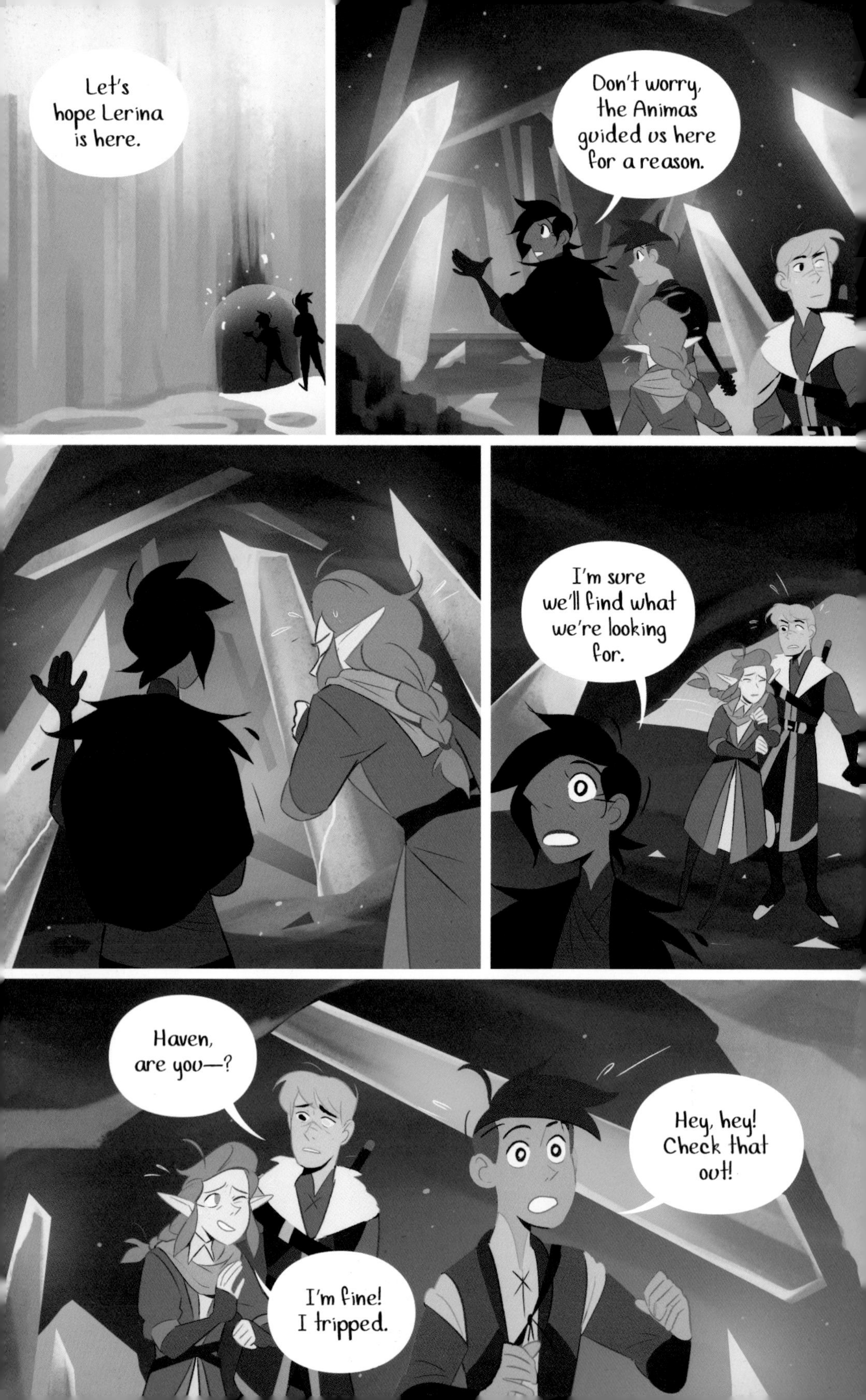
Let's hope Lerina is here.
Don't worry, the Animas guided us here for a reason.
I'm sure we'll find what we're looking for.
Haven, are you—?
I'm fine! I tripped.
Hey, hey! Check that out!

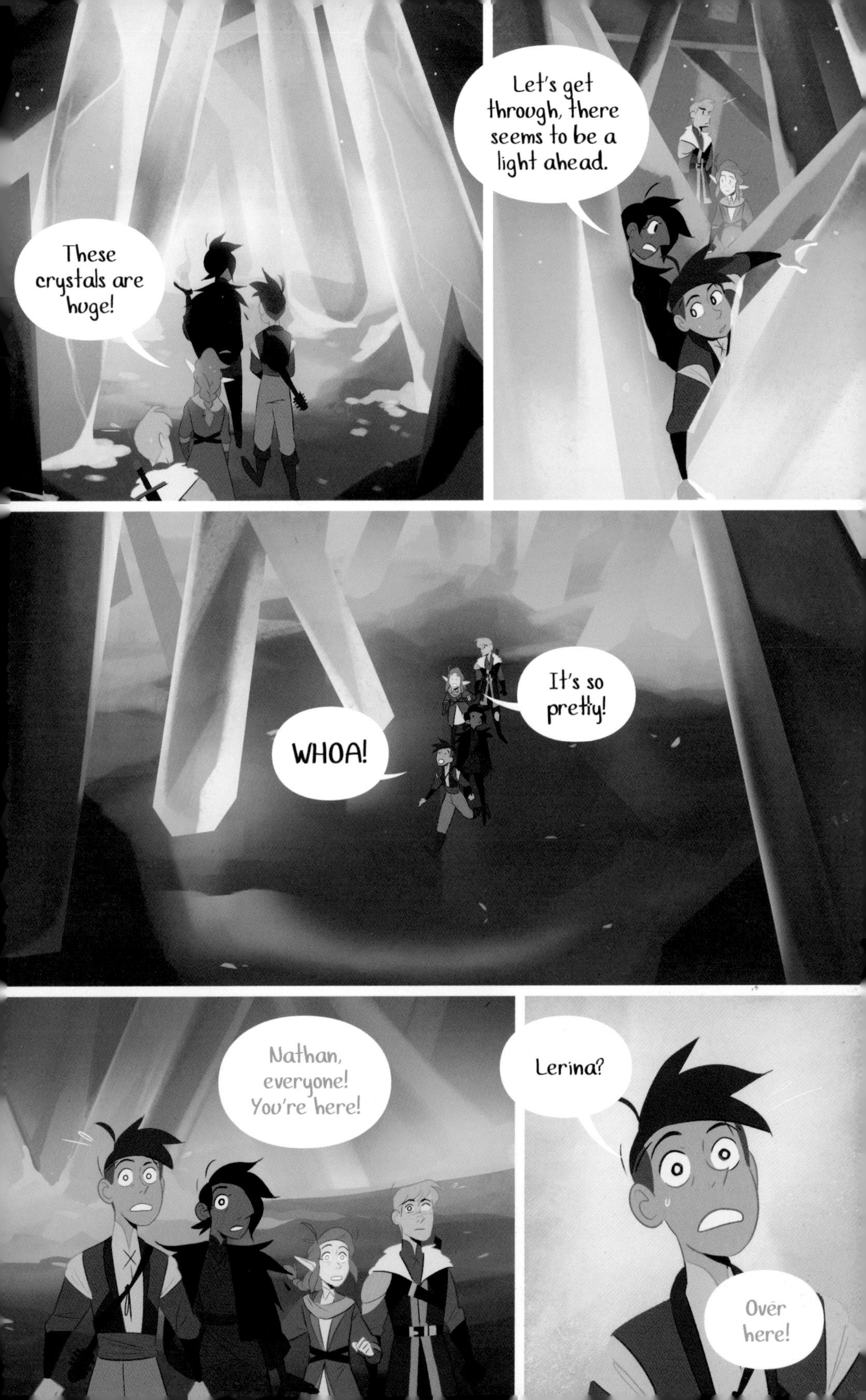
These crystals are huge!
Let's get through, there seems to be a light ahead.
WHOA!
It's so pretty!
Nathan, everyone! You're here!
Lerina?
Over here!

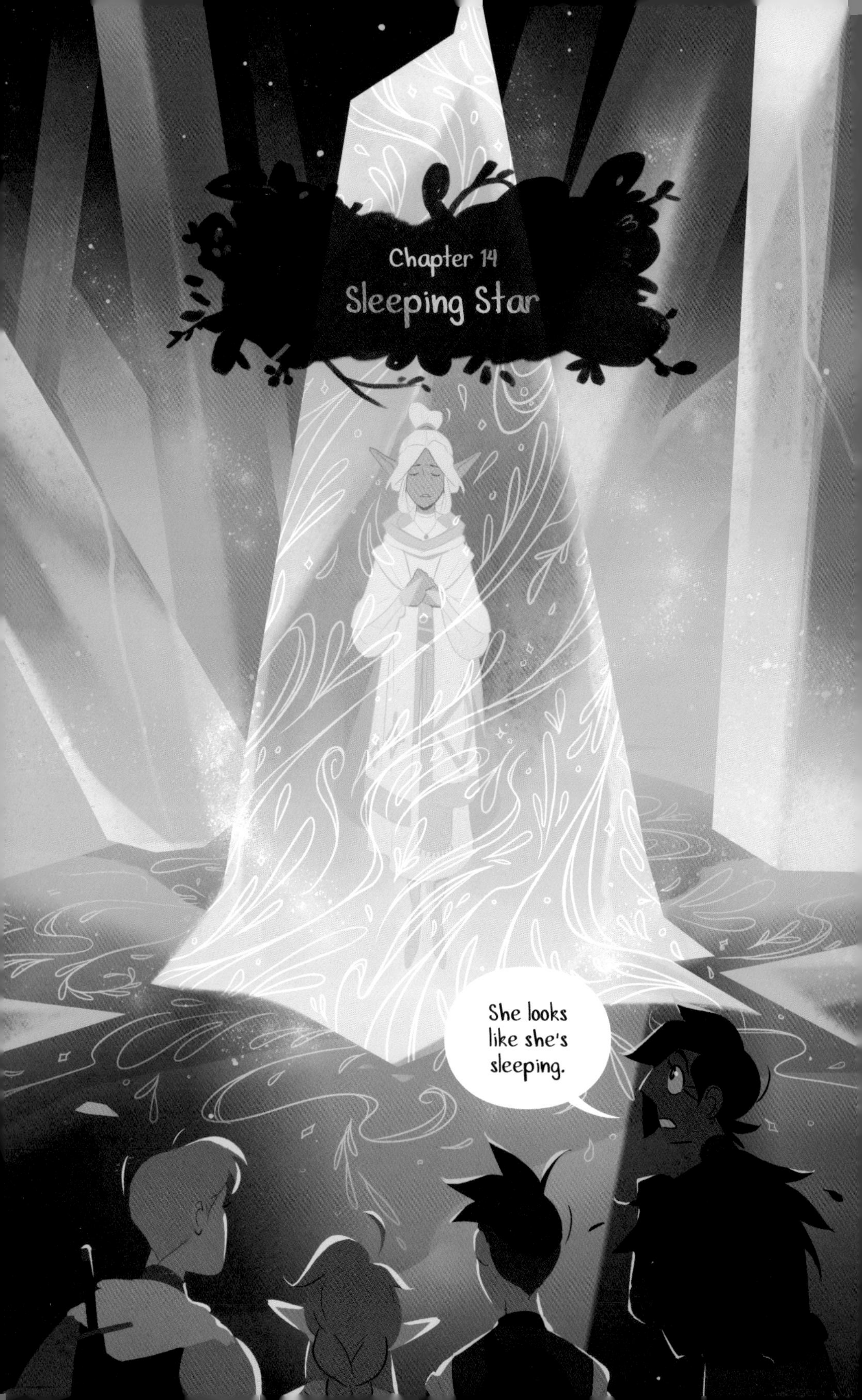
Chapter 14
Sleeping Star
She looks like she's sleeping.

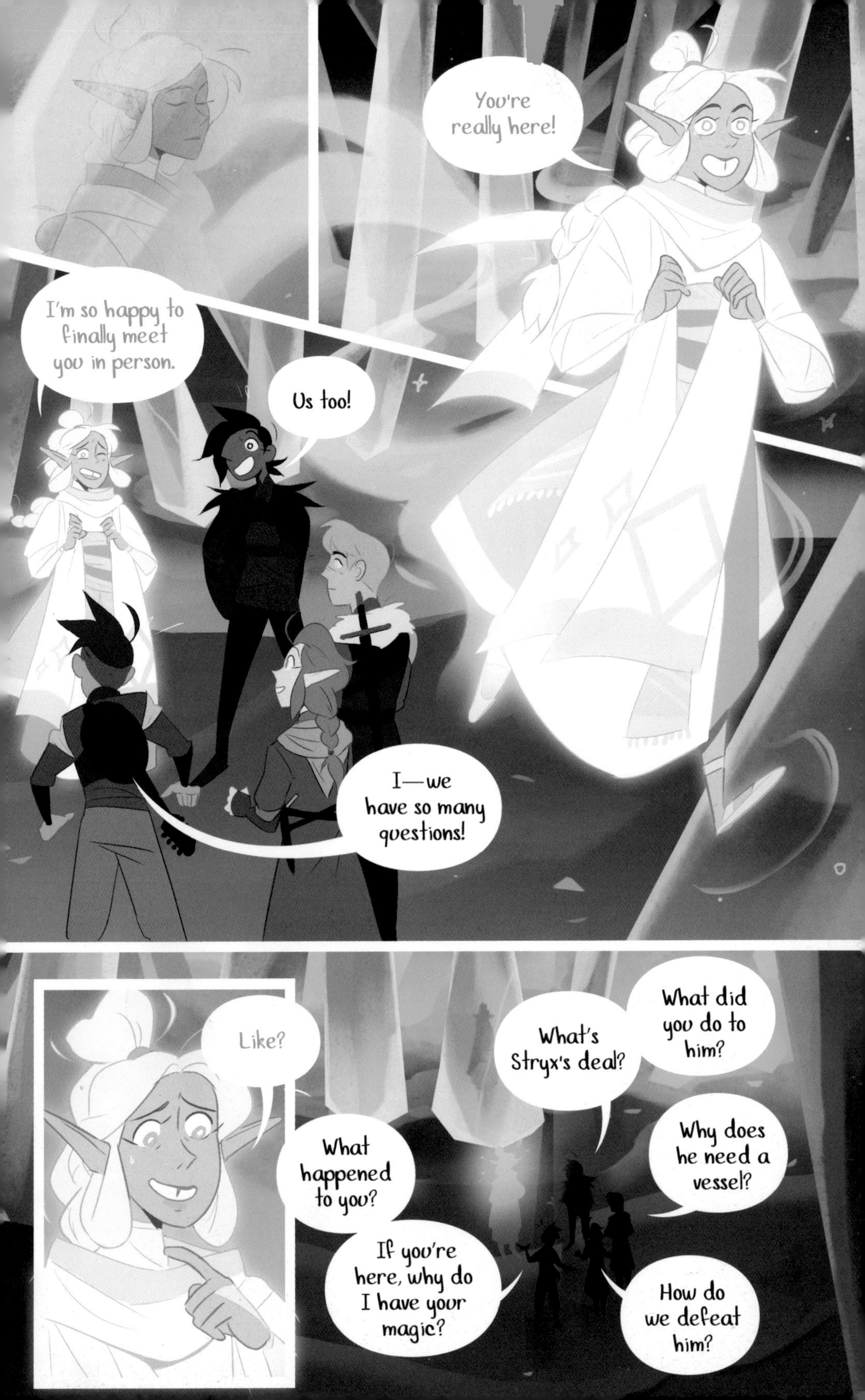
You're really here!
I'm so happy to finally meet you in person.
Us too!
I—we have so many questions!
Like?
What's Stryx's deal?
What did you do to him?
What happened to you?
Why does he need a vessel?
If you're here, why do I have your magic?
How do we defeat him?

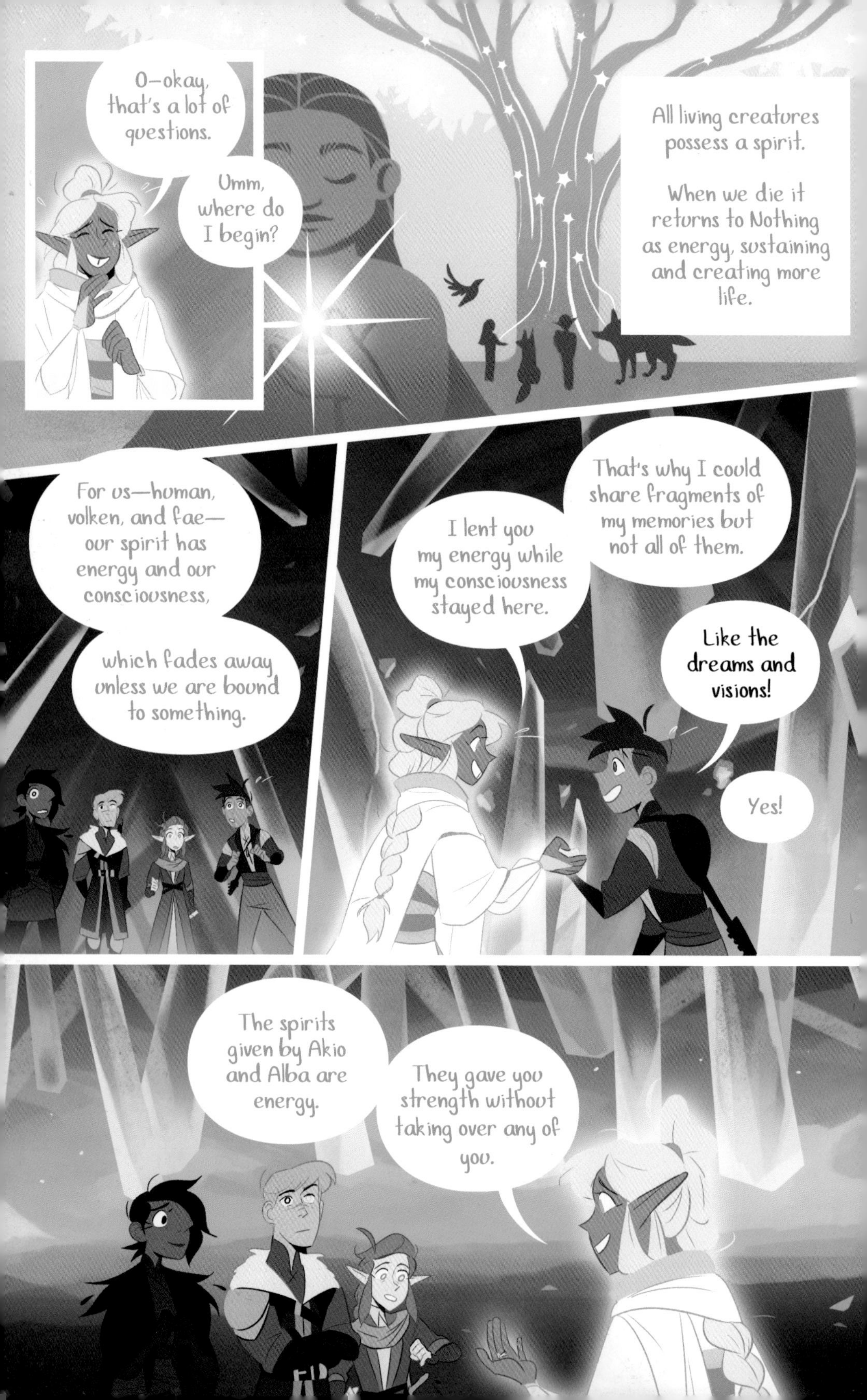
O—okay, that's a lot of questions.
Umm, where do I begin?
All living creatures possess a spirit.
When we die it returns to Nothing as energy, sustaining and creating more life.
For us—human, volken, and fae—our spirit has energy and our consciousness,
which fades away unless we are bound to something.
I lent you my energy while my consciousness stayed here.
That's why I could share fragments of my memories but not all of them.
Like the dreams and visions!
Yes!
The spirits given by Akio and Alba are energy.
They gave you strength without taking over any of you.

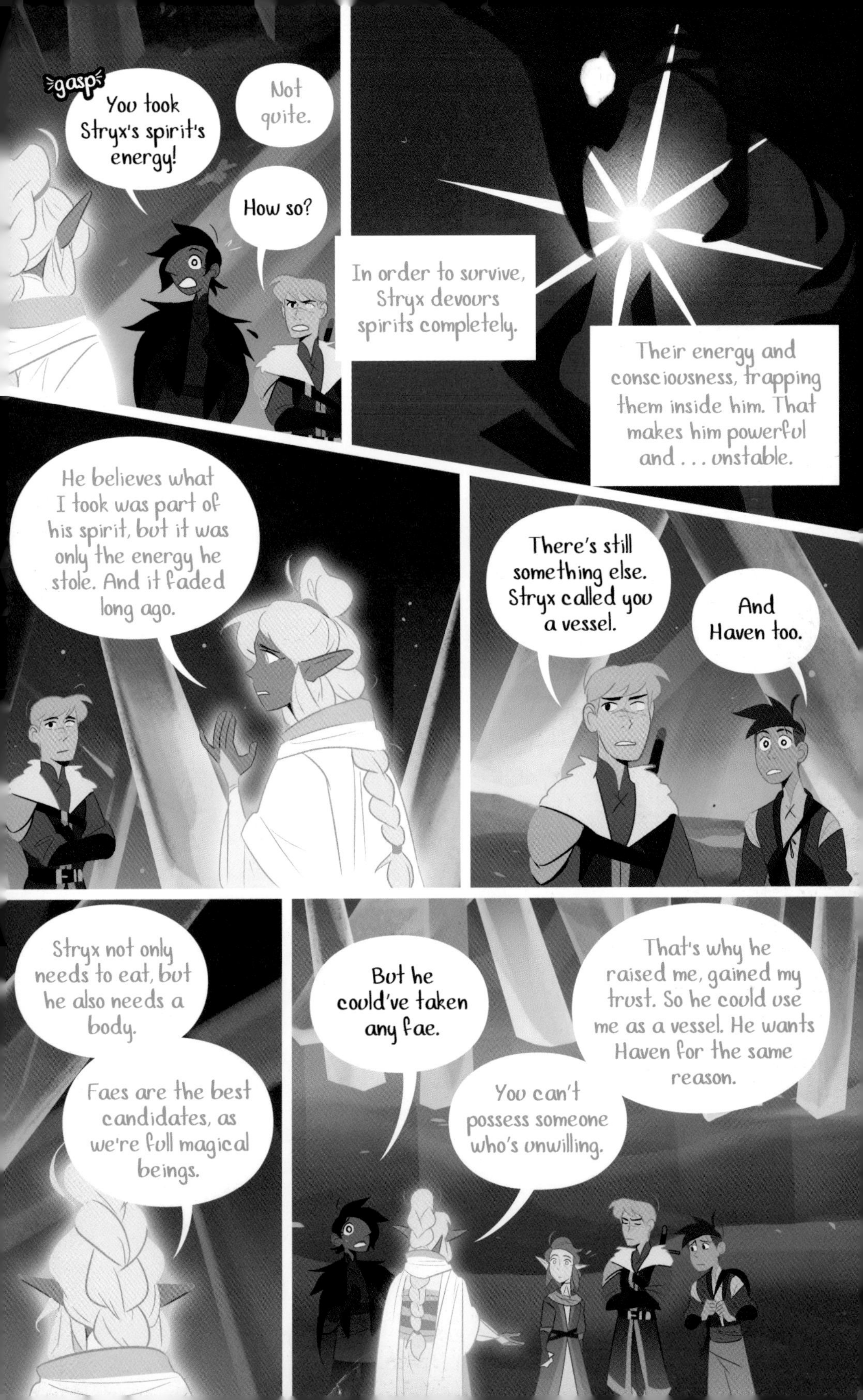
gasp
You took Stryx's spirit's energy!
Not quite.
How so?
In order to survive, Stryx devours spirits completely.
Their energy and consciousness, trapping them inside him. That makes him powerful and . . . unstable.
He believes what I took was part of his spirit, but it was only the energy he stole. And it faded long ago.
There's still something else. Stryx called you a vessel.
And Haven too.
Stryx not only needs to eat, but he also needs a body.
Faes are the best candidates, as we're full magical beings.
But he could've taken any fae.
That's why he raised me, gained my trust. So he could use me as a vessel. He wants Haven for the same reason.
You can't possess someone who's unwilling.

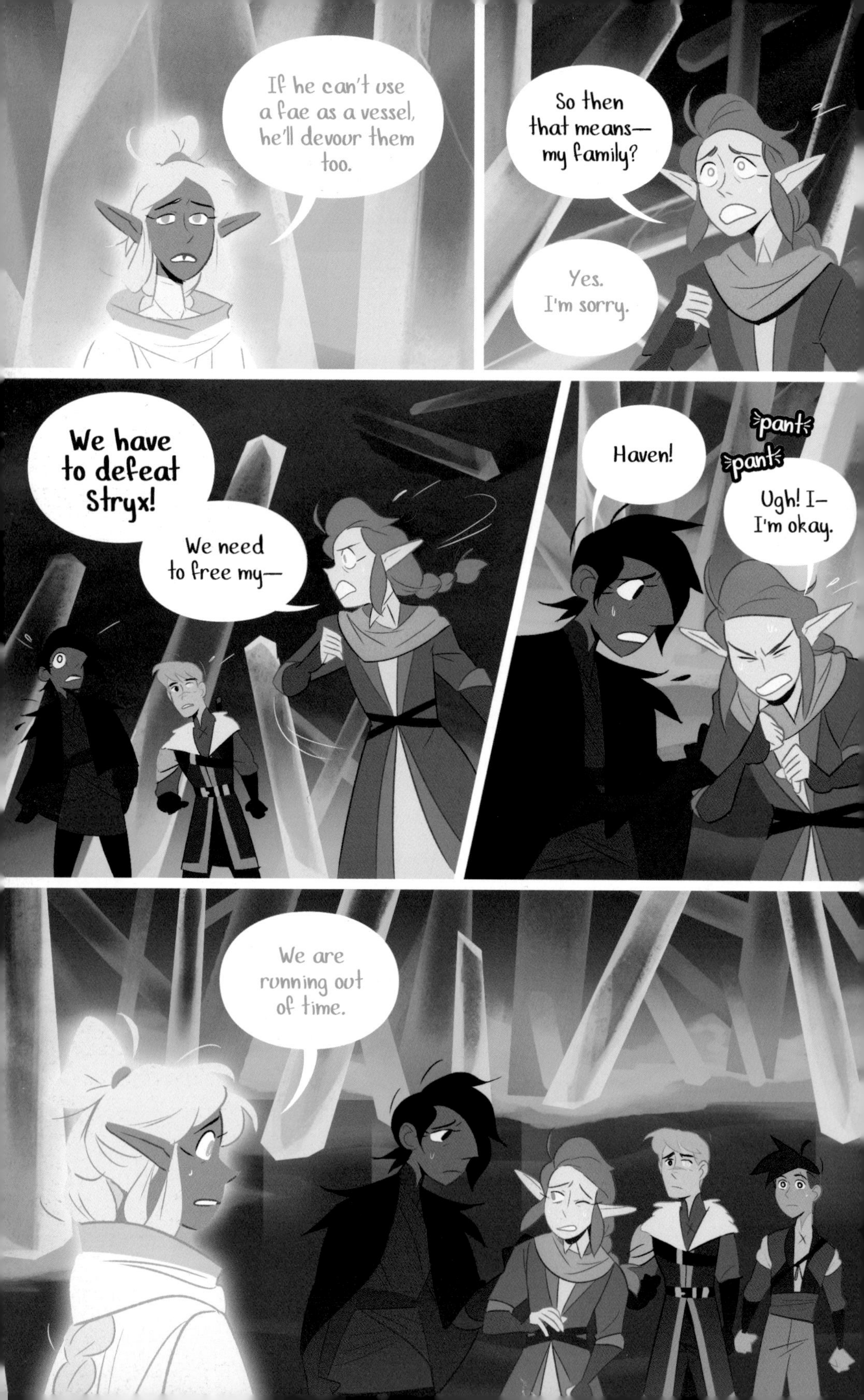
If he can't use a fae as a vessel, he'll devour them too.
So then that means— my family?
Yes. I'm sorry.
We have to defeat Stryx!
We need to free my—
Haven!
pant
pant
Ugh! I— I'm okay.
We are running out of time.

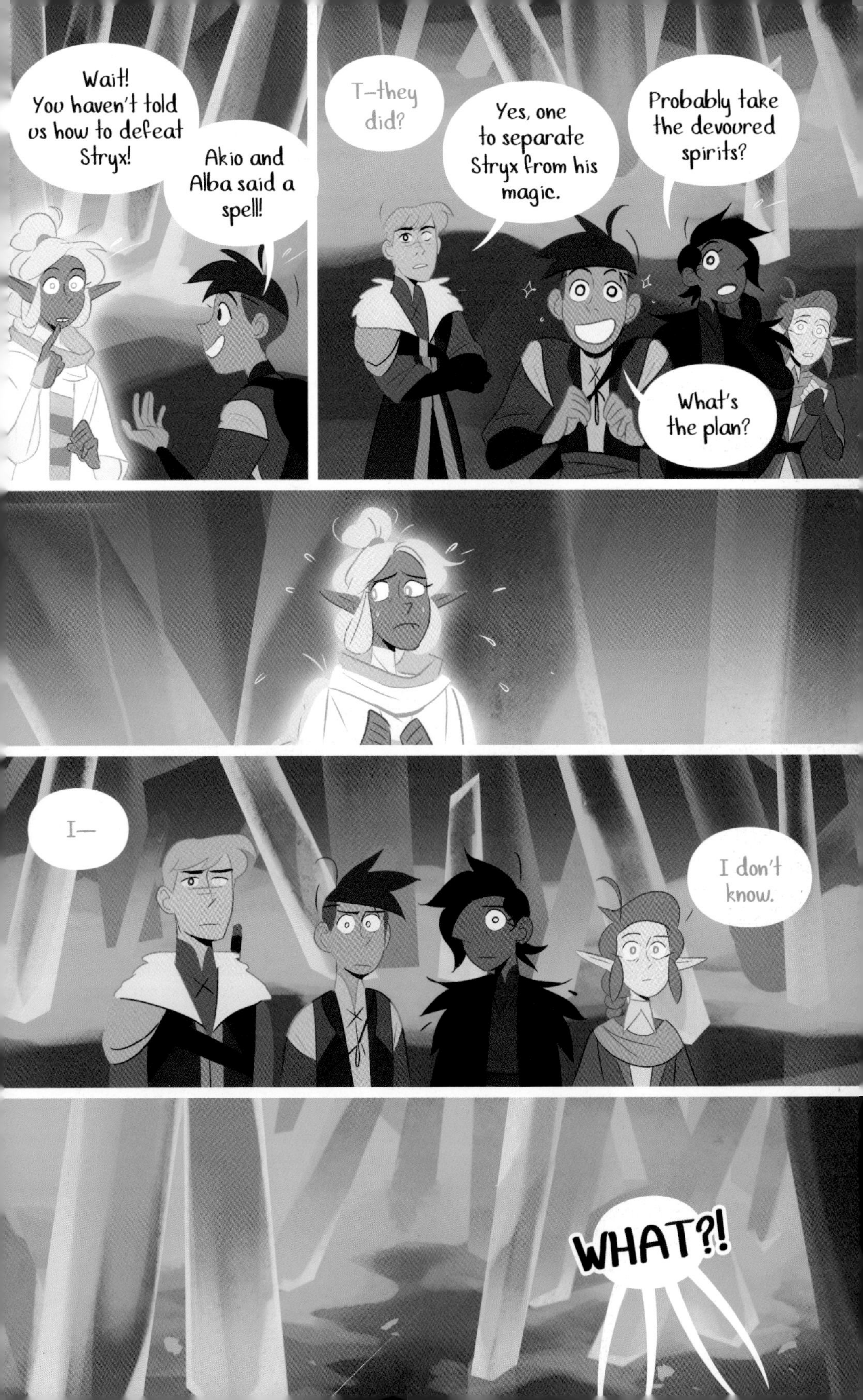
Wait! You haven't told us how to defeat Stryx!
Akio and Alba said a spell!
T—they did?
Yes, one to separate Stryx from his magic.
Probably take the devoured spirits?
What's the plan?
I—
I don't know.
WHAT?!

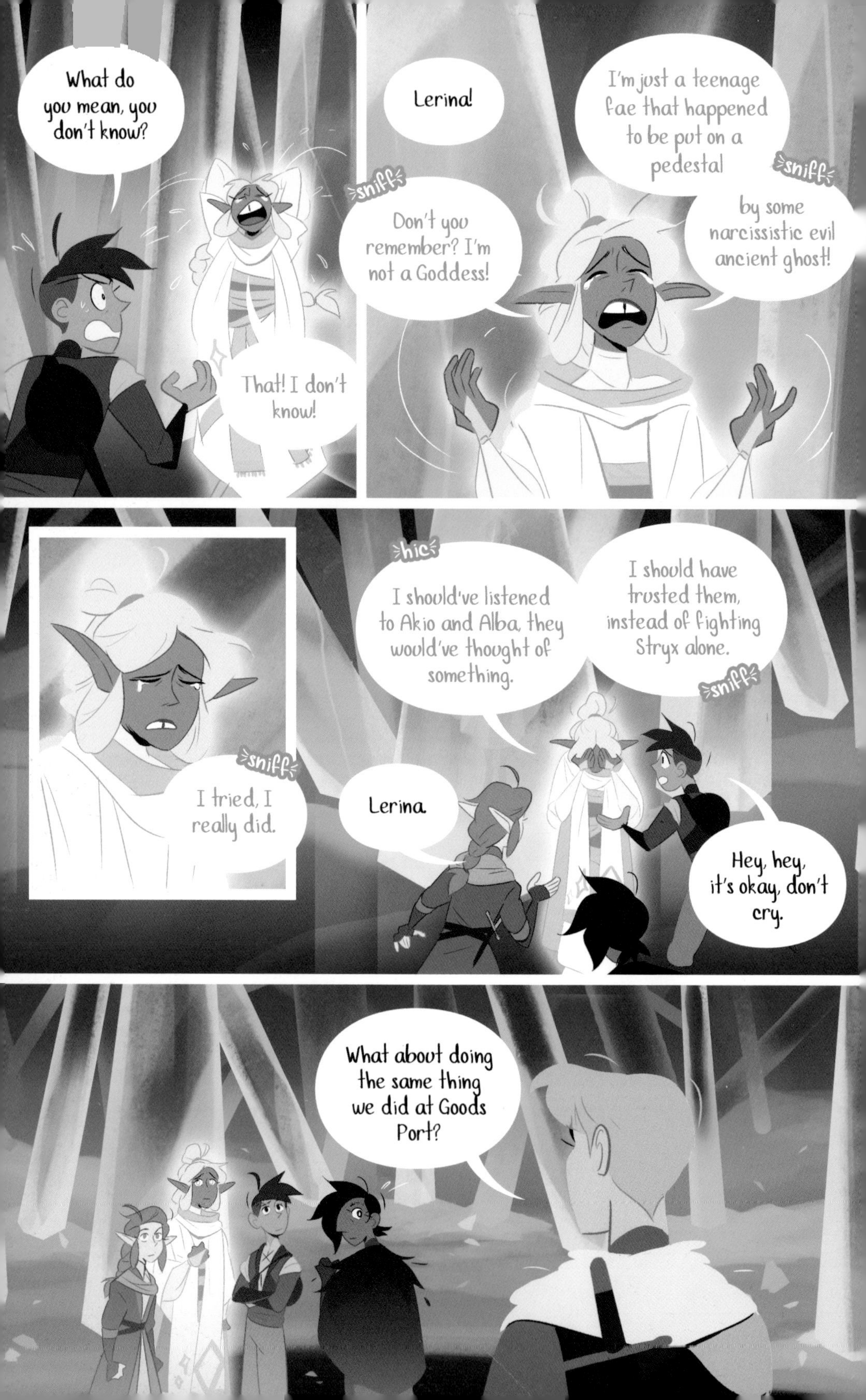
What do you mean, you don't know?
That! I don't know!
sniff
Don't you remember? I'm not a Goddess!
Lerina!
I'm just a teenage fae that happened to be put on a pedestal
sniff
by some narcissistic evil ancient ghost!
sniff
I tried, I really did.
hic
I should've listened to Akio and Alba, they would've thought of something.
I should have trusted them, instead of fighting Stryx alone.
sniff
Lerina.
Hey, hey, it's okay, don't cry.
What about doing the same thing we did at Goods Port?

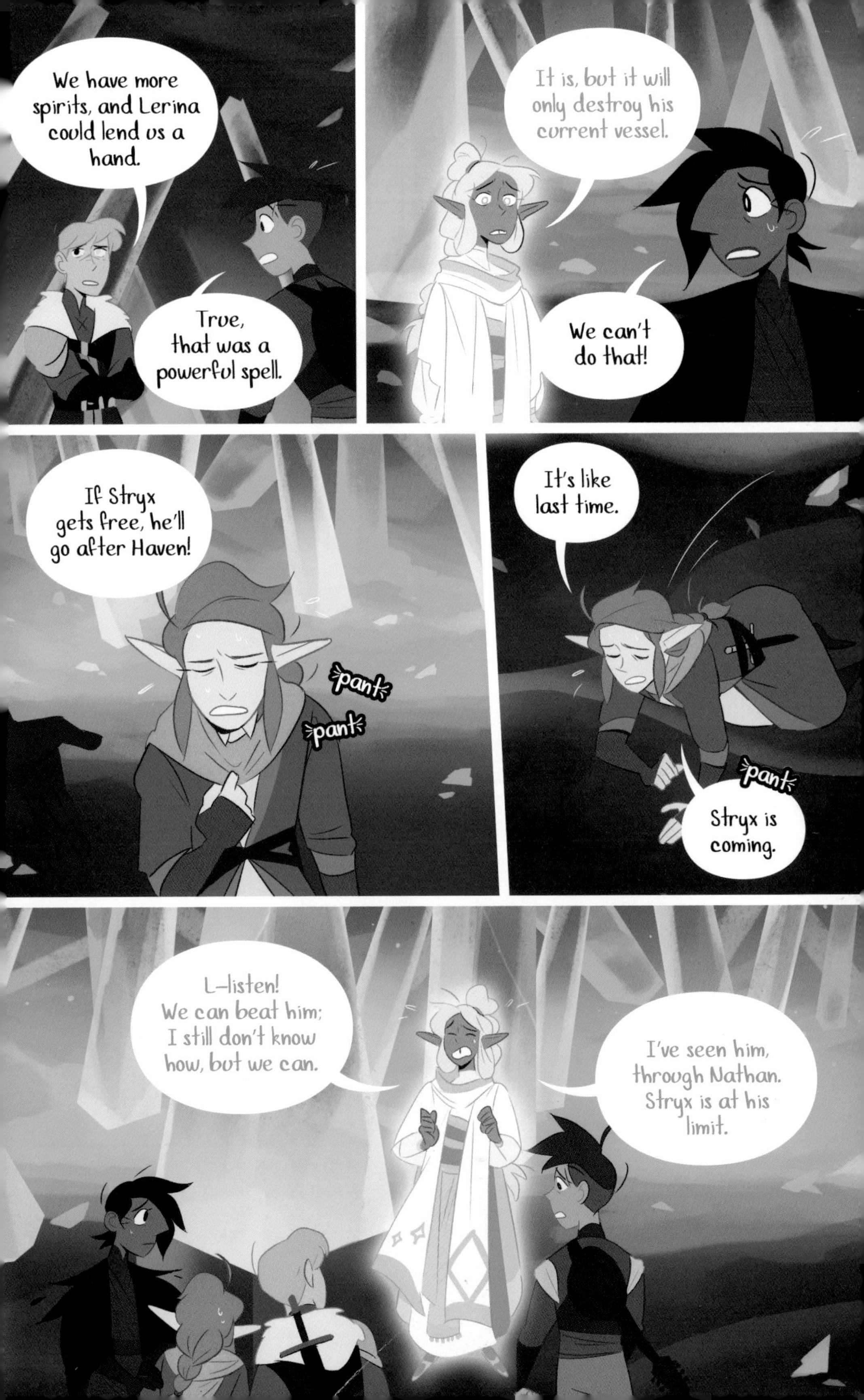
We have more spirits, and Lerina could lend us a hand.
True, that was a powerful spell.
It is, but it will only destroy his current vessel.
We can't do that!
If Stryx gets free, he'll go after Haven!
pant
pant
It's like last time.
pant
Stryx is coming.
L–listen! We can beat him; I still don't know how, but we can.
I've seen him, through Nathan. Stryx is at his limit.

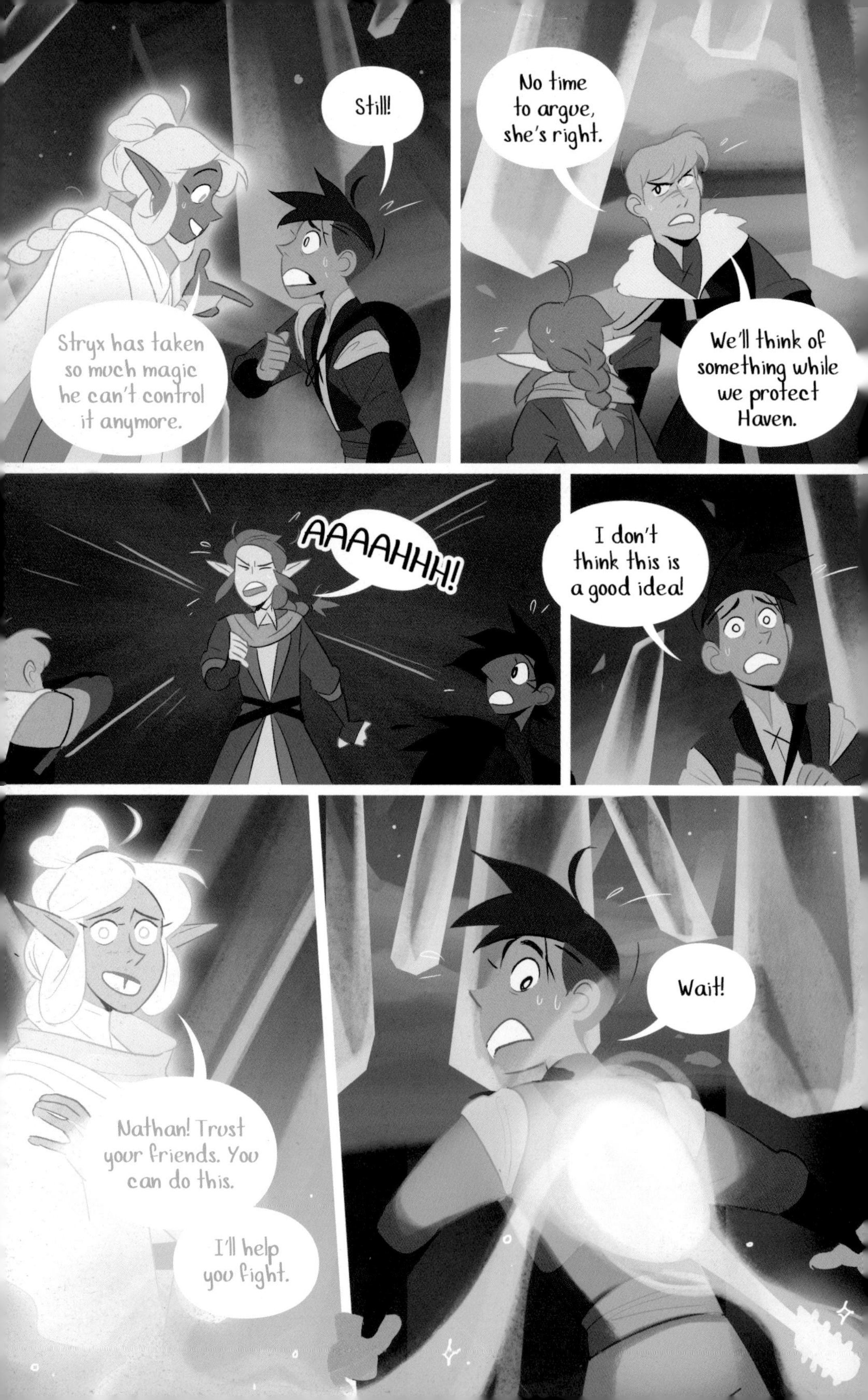
Still!
Stryx has taken so much magic he can't control it anymore.
No time to argue, she's right.
We'll think of something while we protect Haven.
AAAAHHH!
I don't think this is a good idea!
Nathan! Trust your friends. You can do this.
I'll help you fight.
Wait!

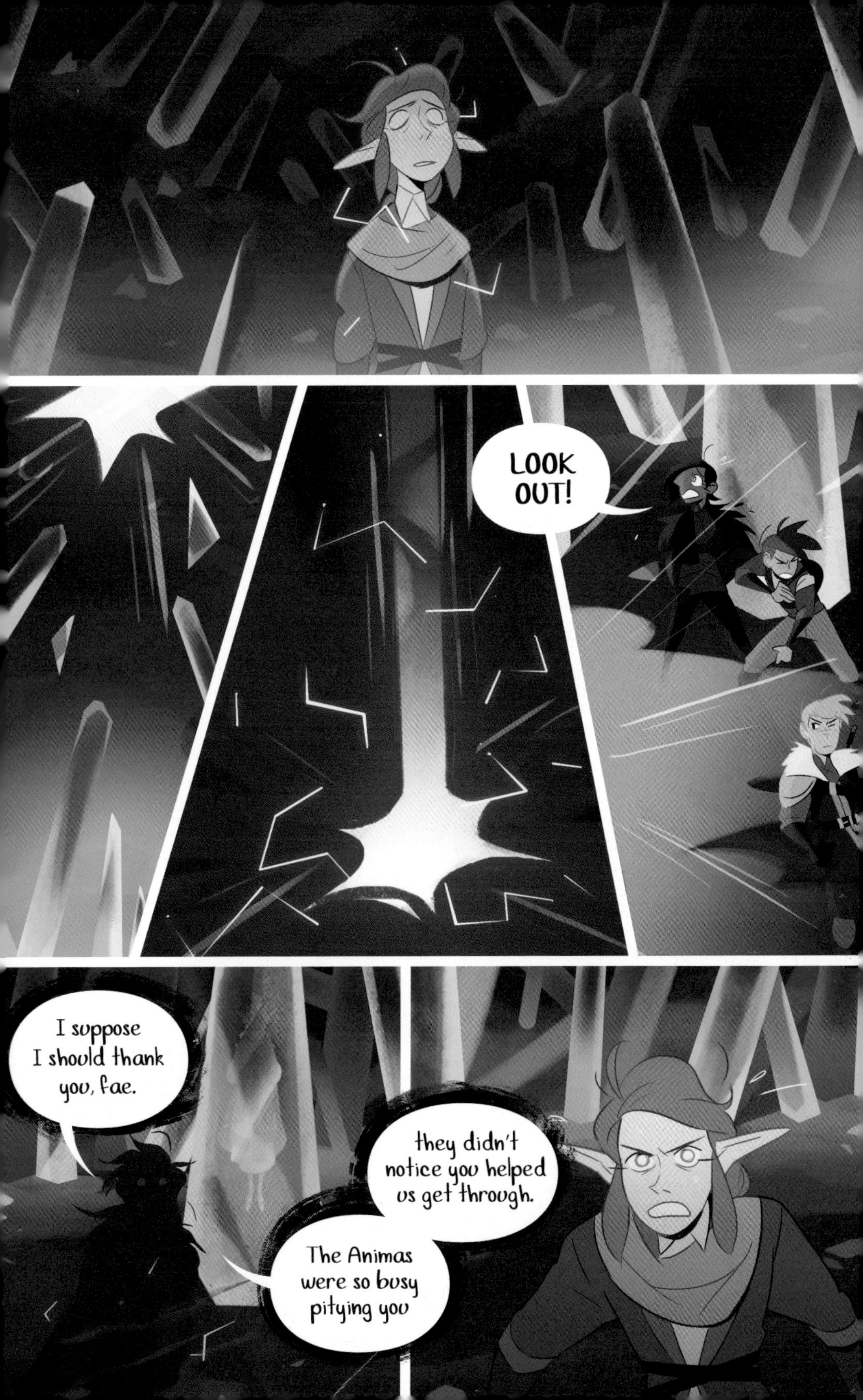
LOOK OUT!
I suppose I should thank you, fae.
The Animas were so busy pitying you
they didn't notice you helped us get through.

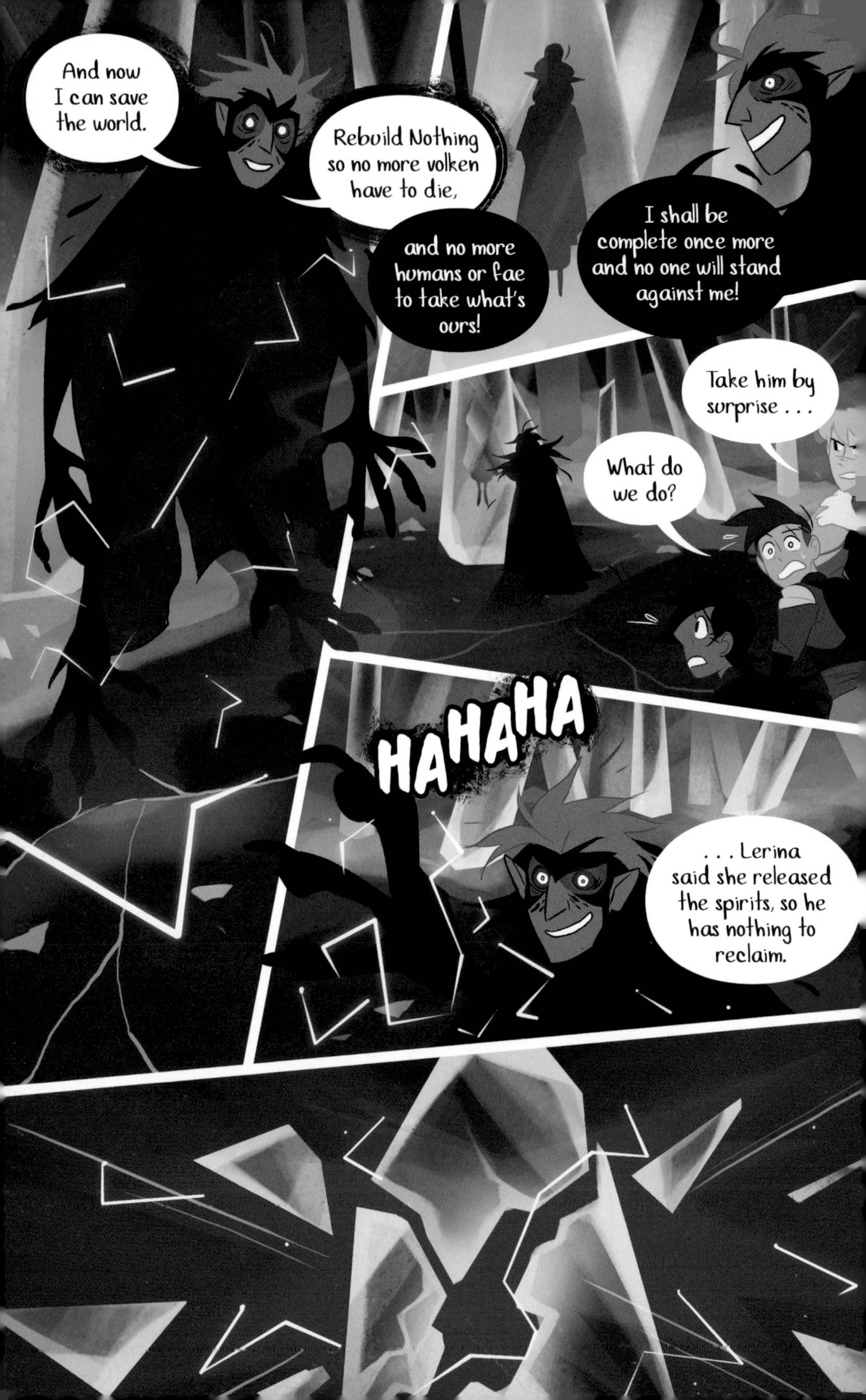
And now I can save the world.
Rebuild Nothing so no more volken have to die,
and no more humans or fae to take what's ours!
I shall be complete once more and no one will stand against me!
Take him by surprise . . .
What do we do?
HAHAHA
. . . Lerina said she released the spirits, so he has nothing to reclaim.

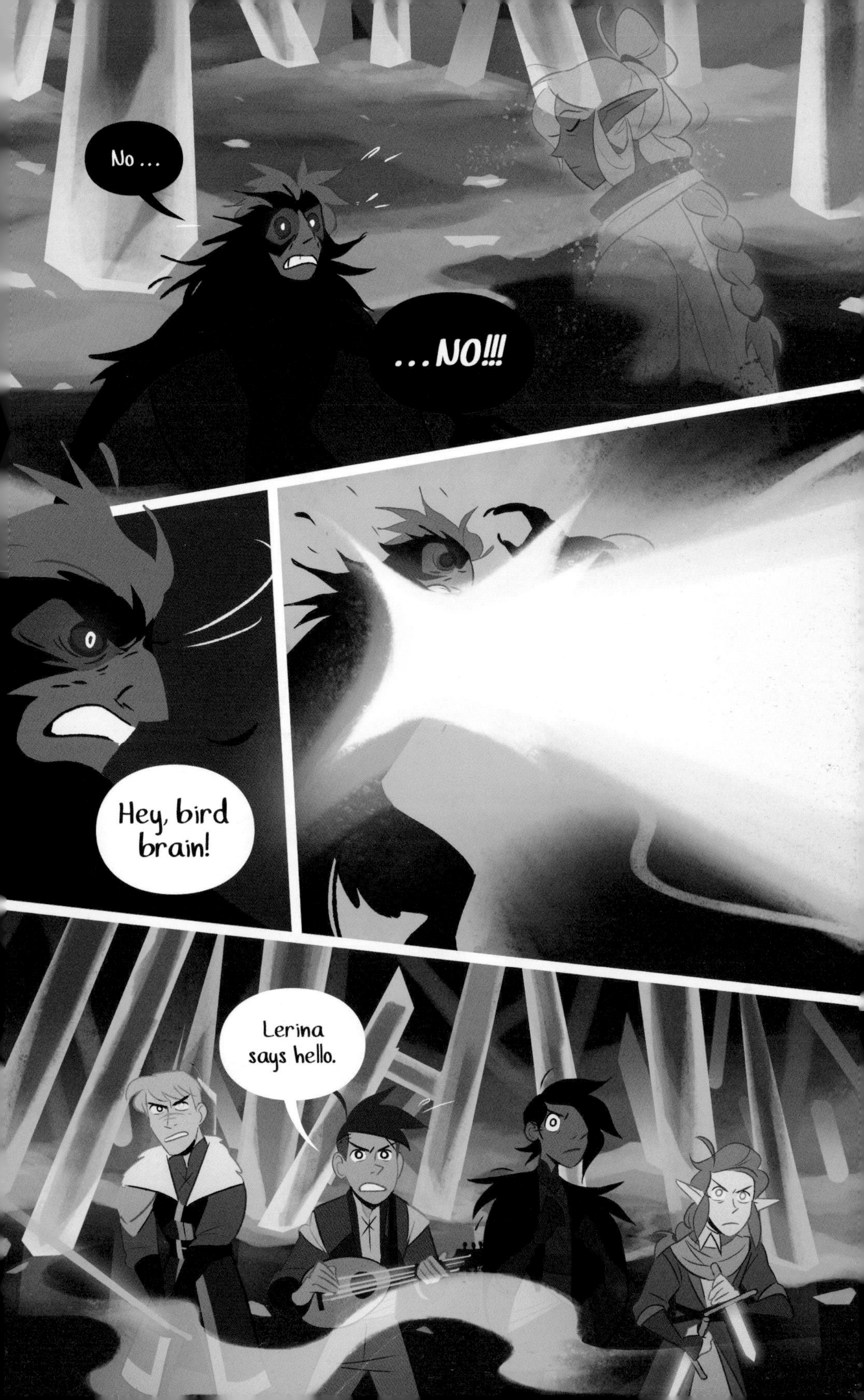
No . . .
. . . NO!!!
Hey, bird brain!
Lerina says hello.

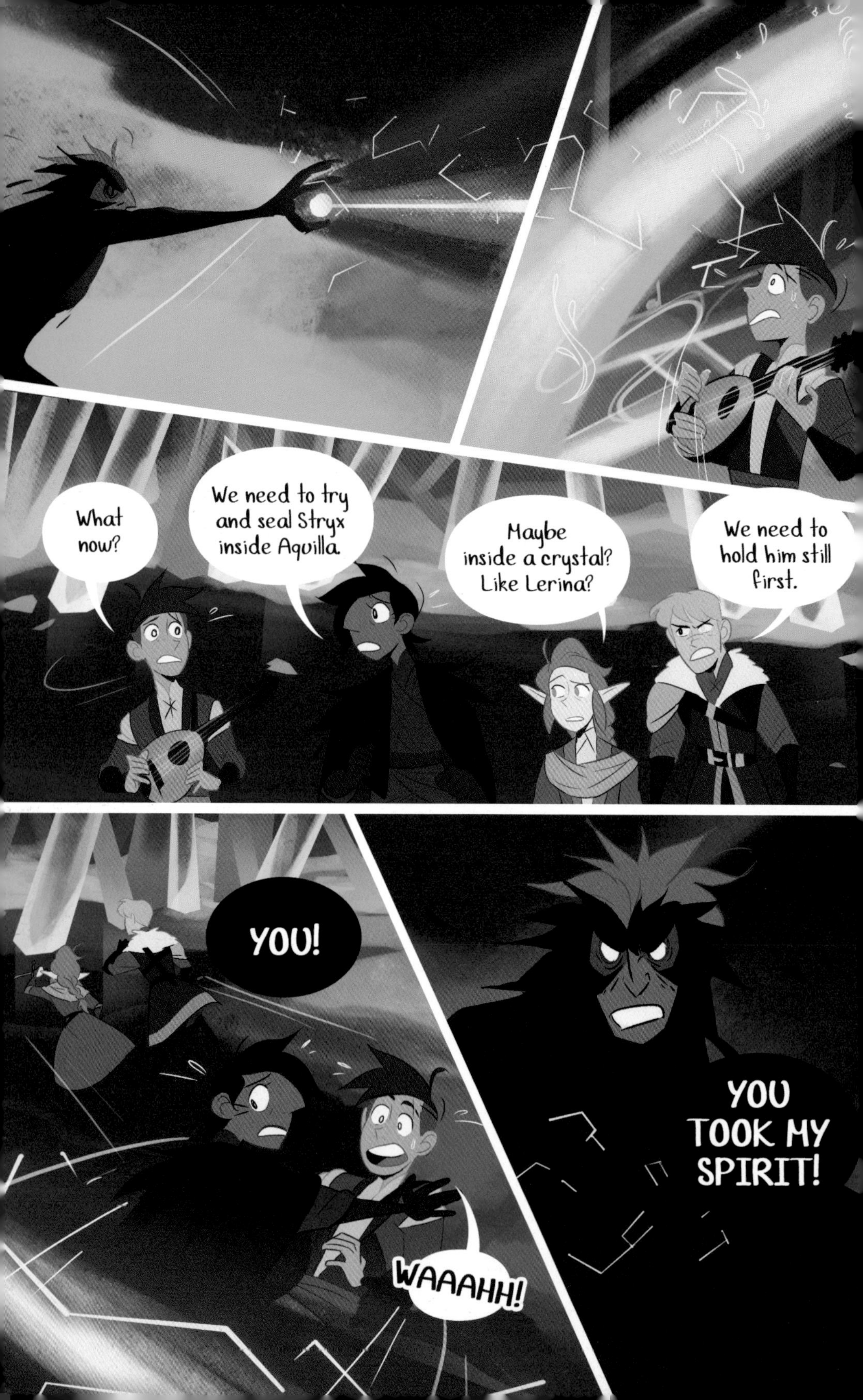
What now?
We need to try and seal Stryx inside Aquilla.
Maybe inside a crystal? Like Lerina?
We need to hold him still first.
YOU!
WAAAHH!
YOU TOOK MY SPIRIT!

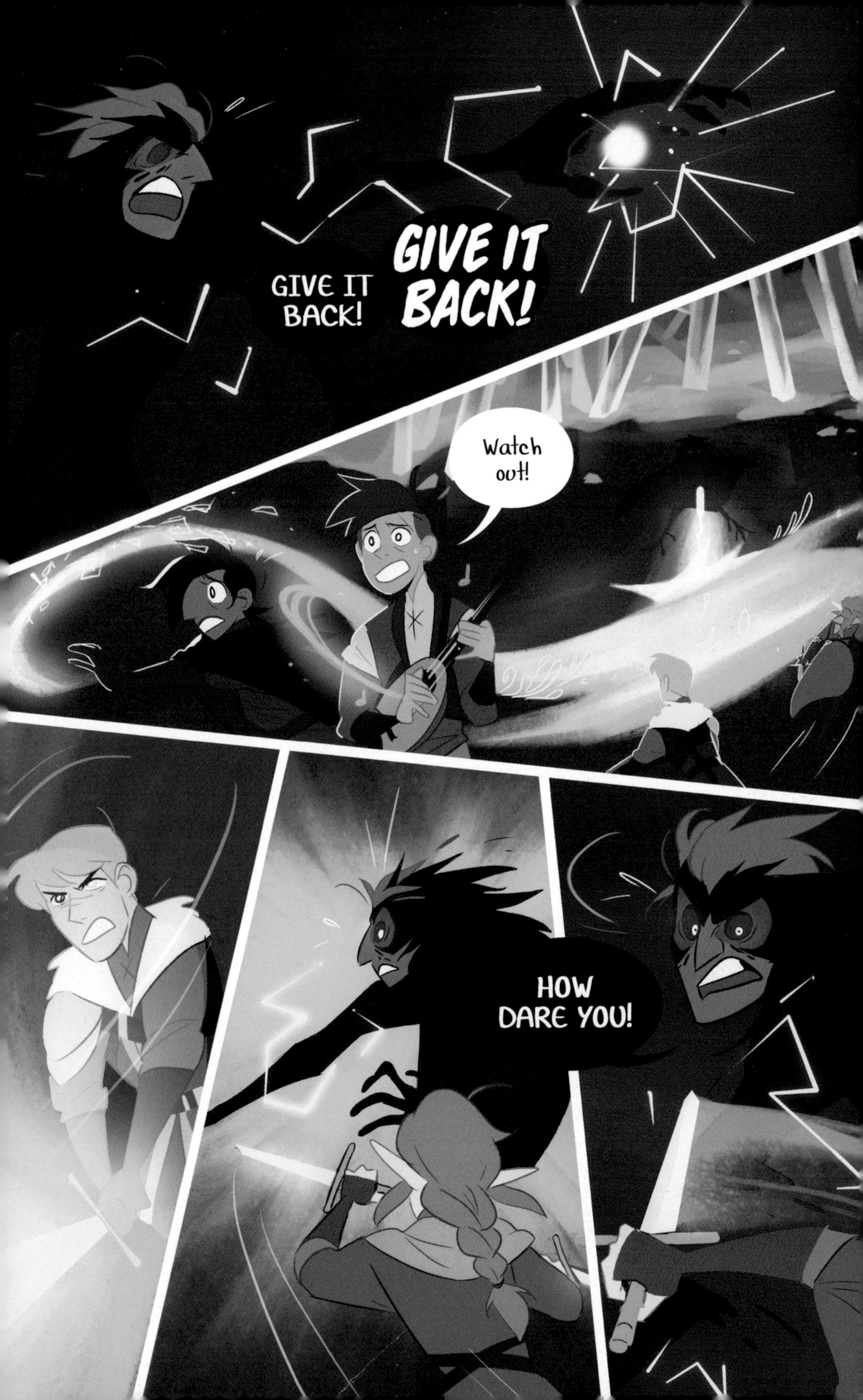
GIVE IT BACK!
GIVE IT BACK!
Watch out!
HOW DARE YOU!

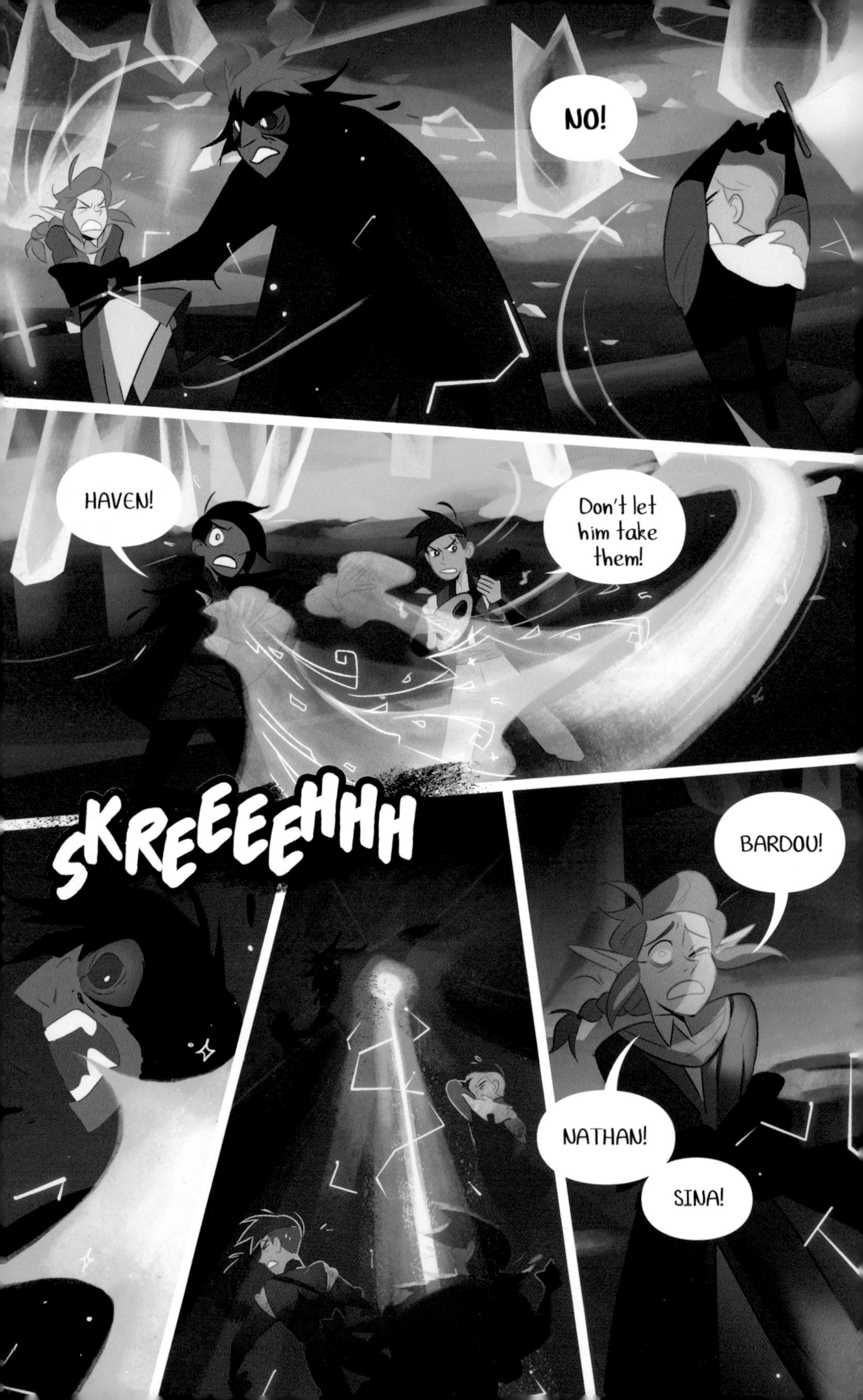
NO!
HAVEN!
Don't let him take them!
SKREEEEHHH
BARDOU!
NATHAN!
SINA!

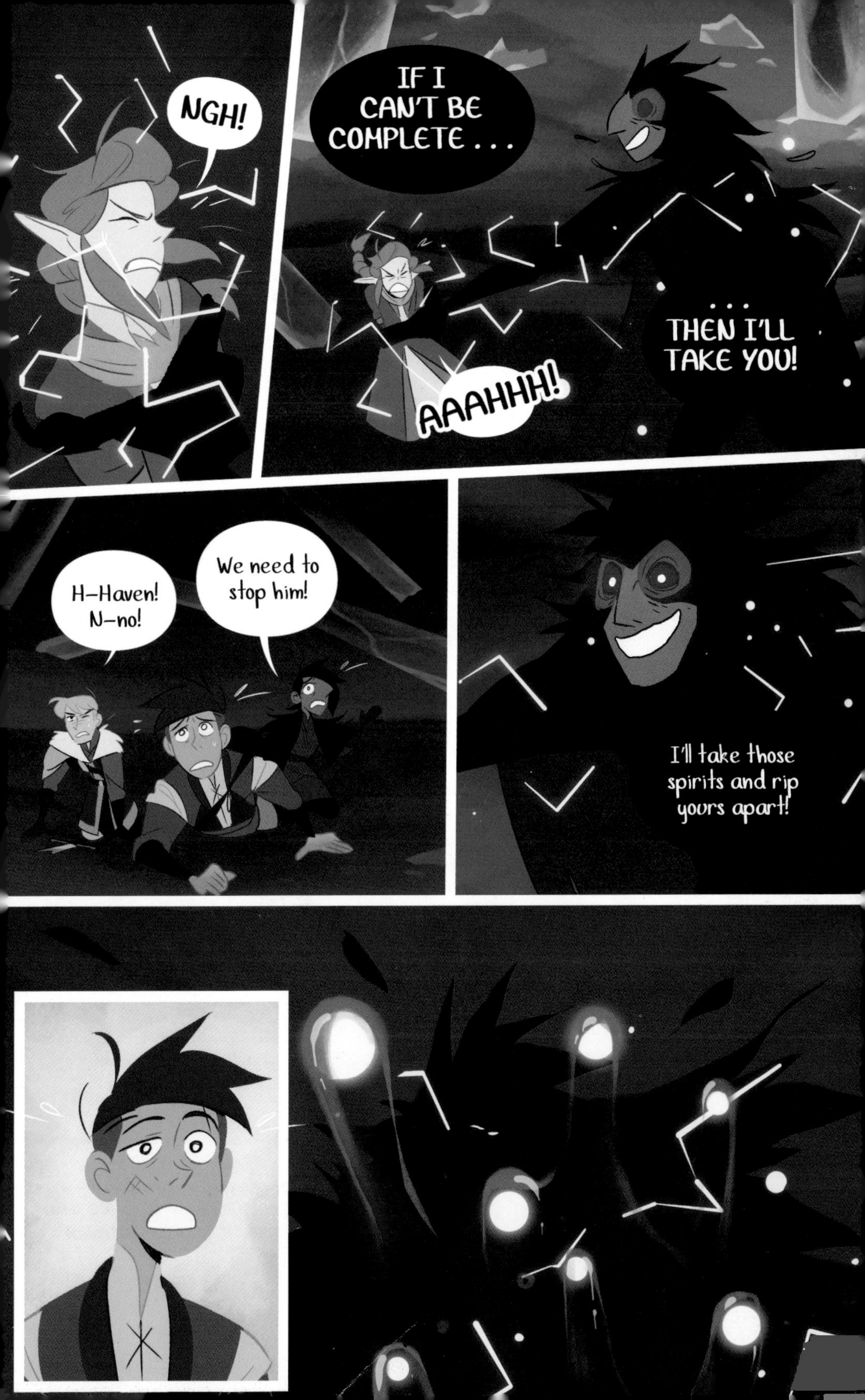
NGH!
IF I CAN'T BE COMPLETE . . .
. . . THEN I'LL TAKE YOU!
AAAHHH!
H–Haven! N–no!
We need to stop him!
I'll take those spirits and rip yours apart!

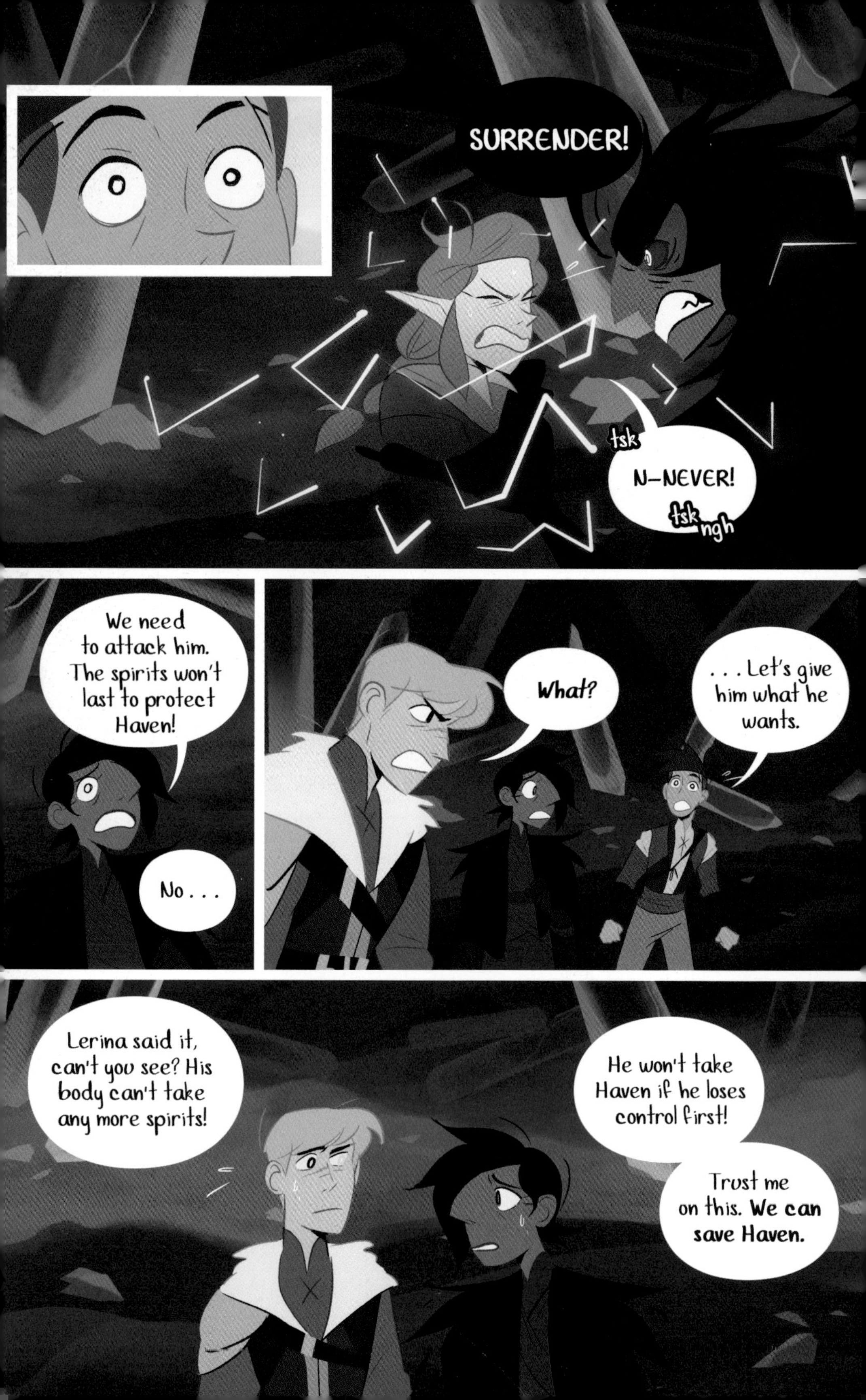
SURRENDER!
tsk
N-NEVER!
tsk ngh
We need to attack him. The spirits won't last to protect Haven!
No . . .
What?
. . . Let's give him what he wants.
Lerina said it, can't you see? His body can't take any more spirits!
He won't take Haven if he loses control first!
Trust me on this. We can save Haven.

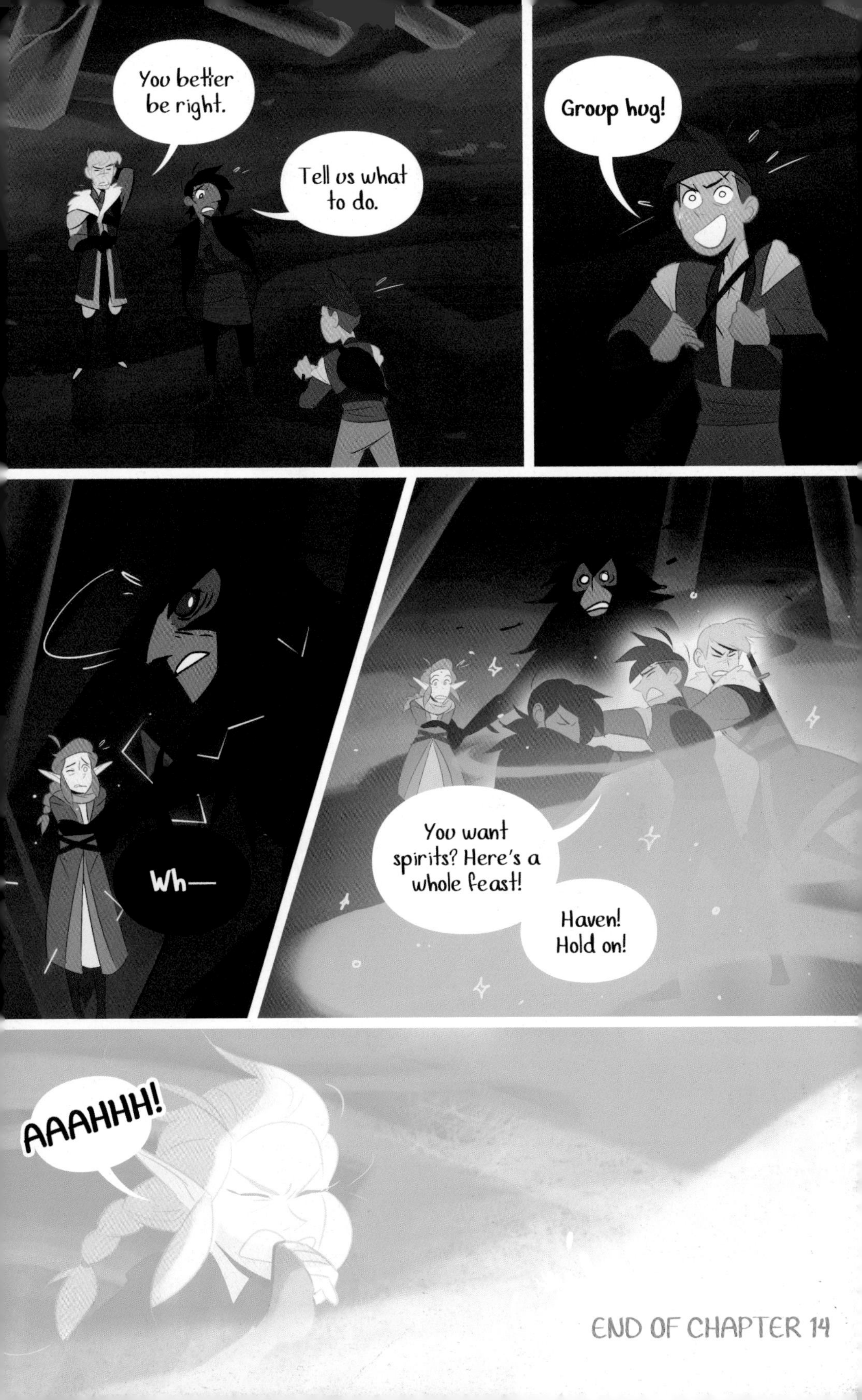
You better be right.
Tell us what to do.
Group hug!
Wh—
You want spirits? Here's a whole feast!
Haven! Hold on!
AAAHHH!
END OF CHAPTER 14

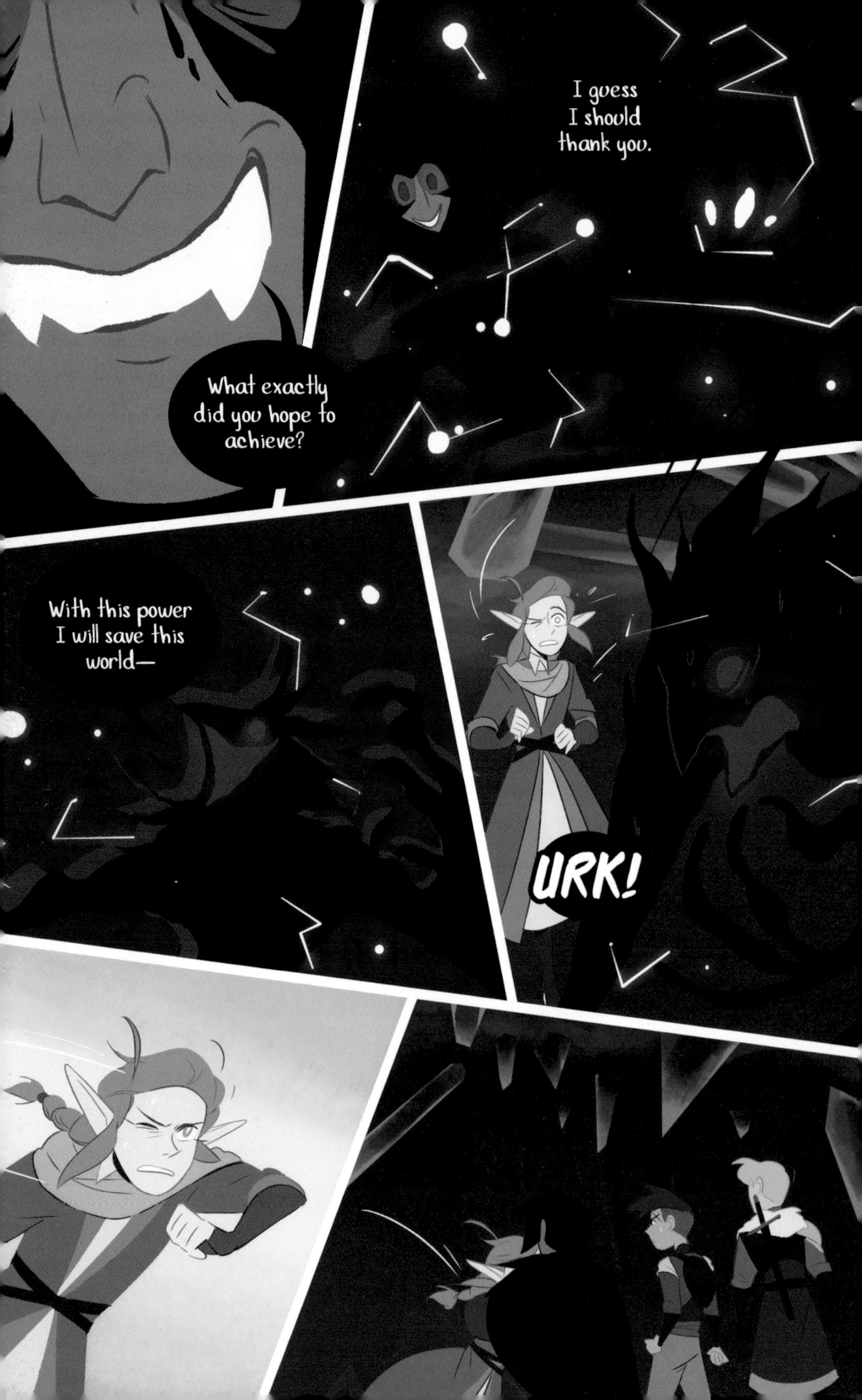
I guess
I should
thank you.
What exactly
did you hope to
achieve?
With this power
I will save this
world—
URK!

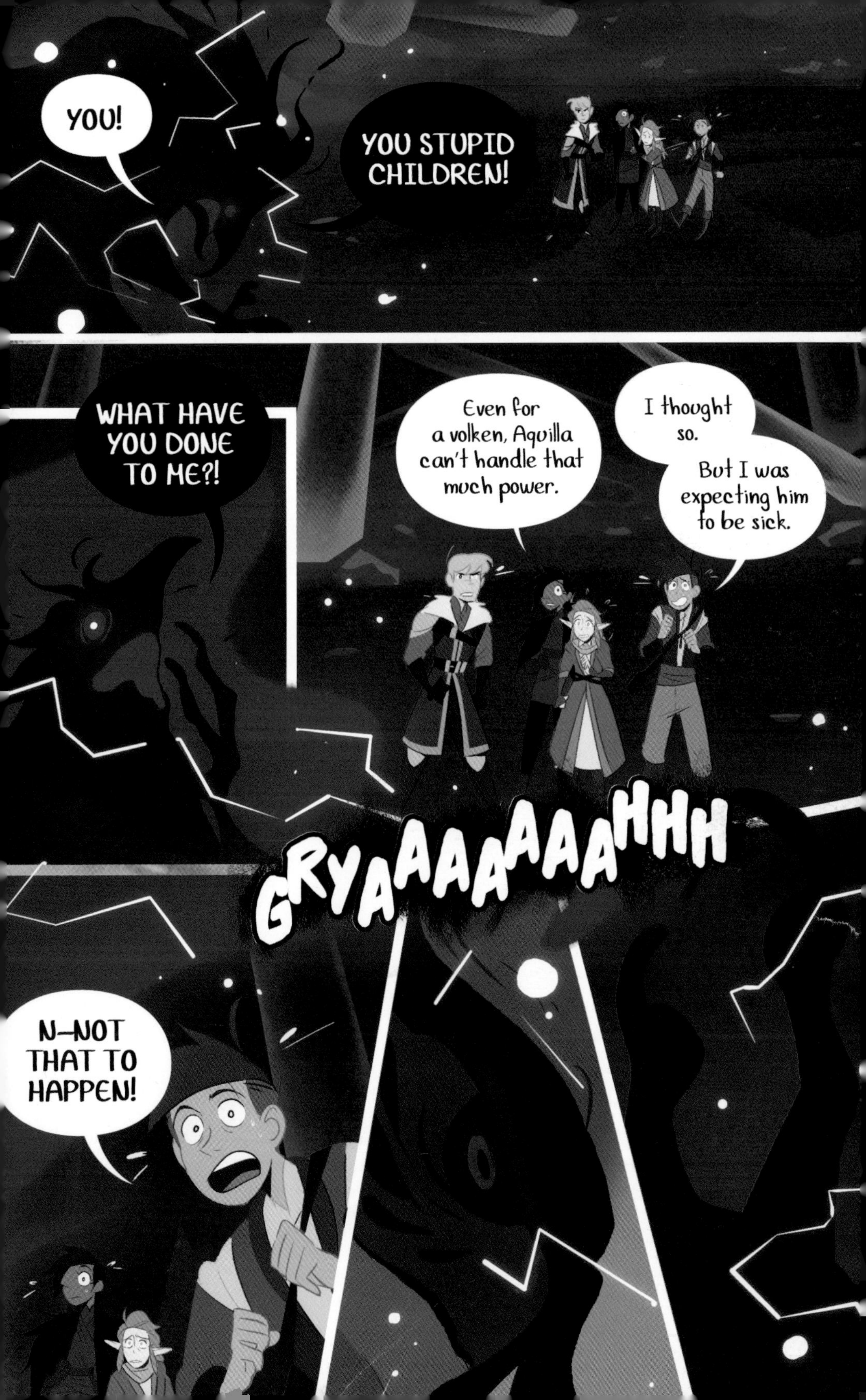
YOU!
YOU STUPID CHILDREN!
WHAT HAVE YOU DONE TO ME?!
Even for a volken, Aquilla can't handle that much power.
I thought so.
But I was expecting him to be sick.
GRYAAAAAAAHHHH
N—NOT THAT TO HAPPEN!

## Chapter 15

# The Final Countdown

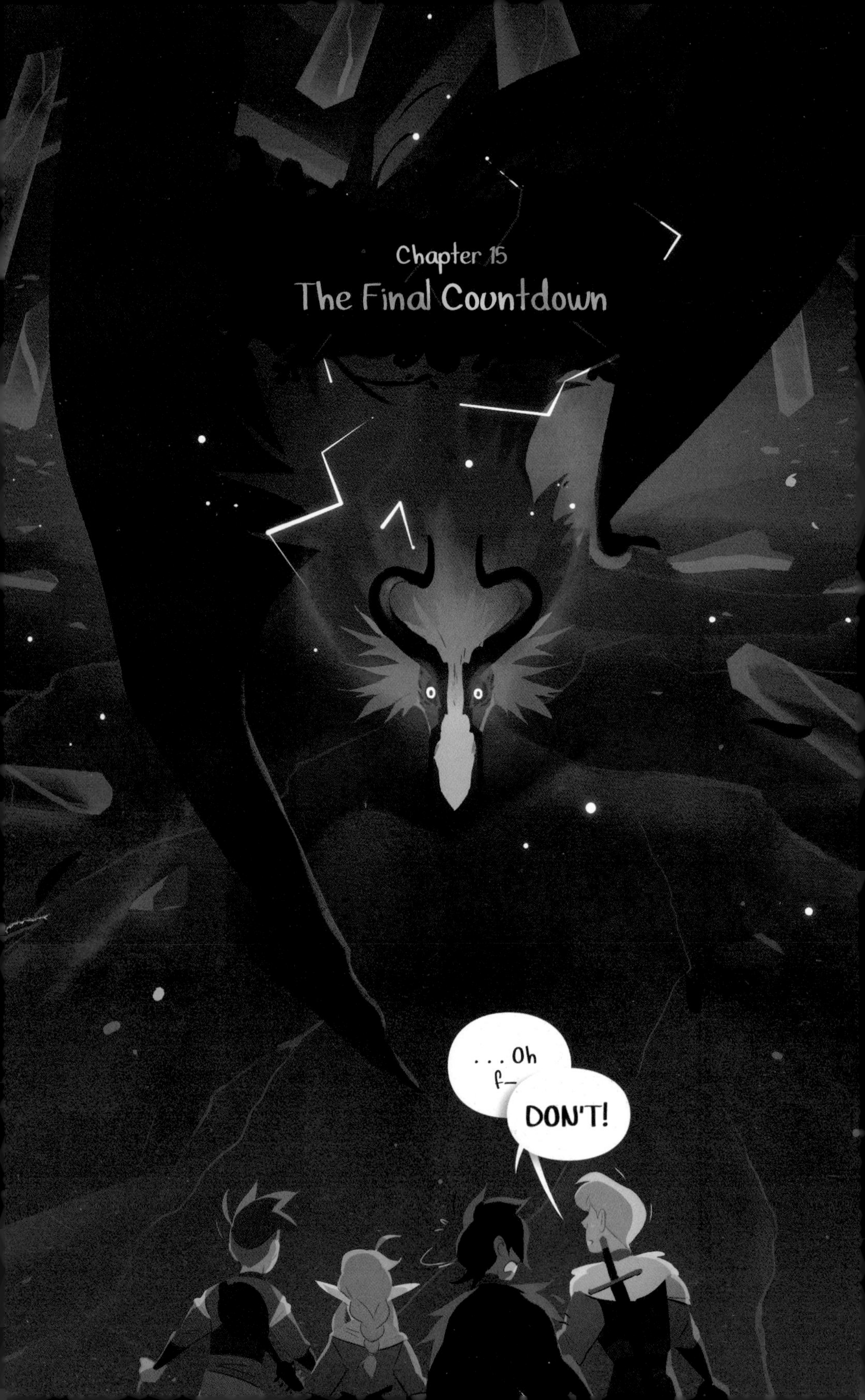

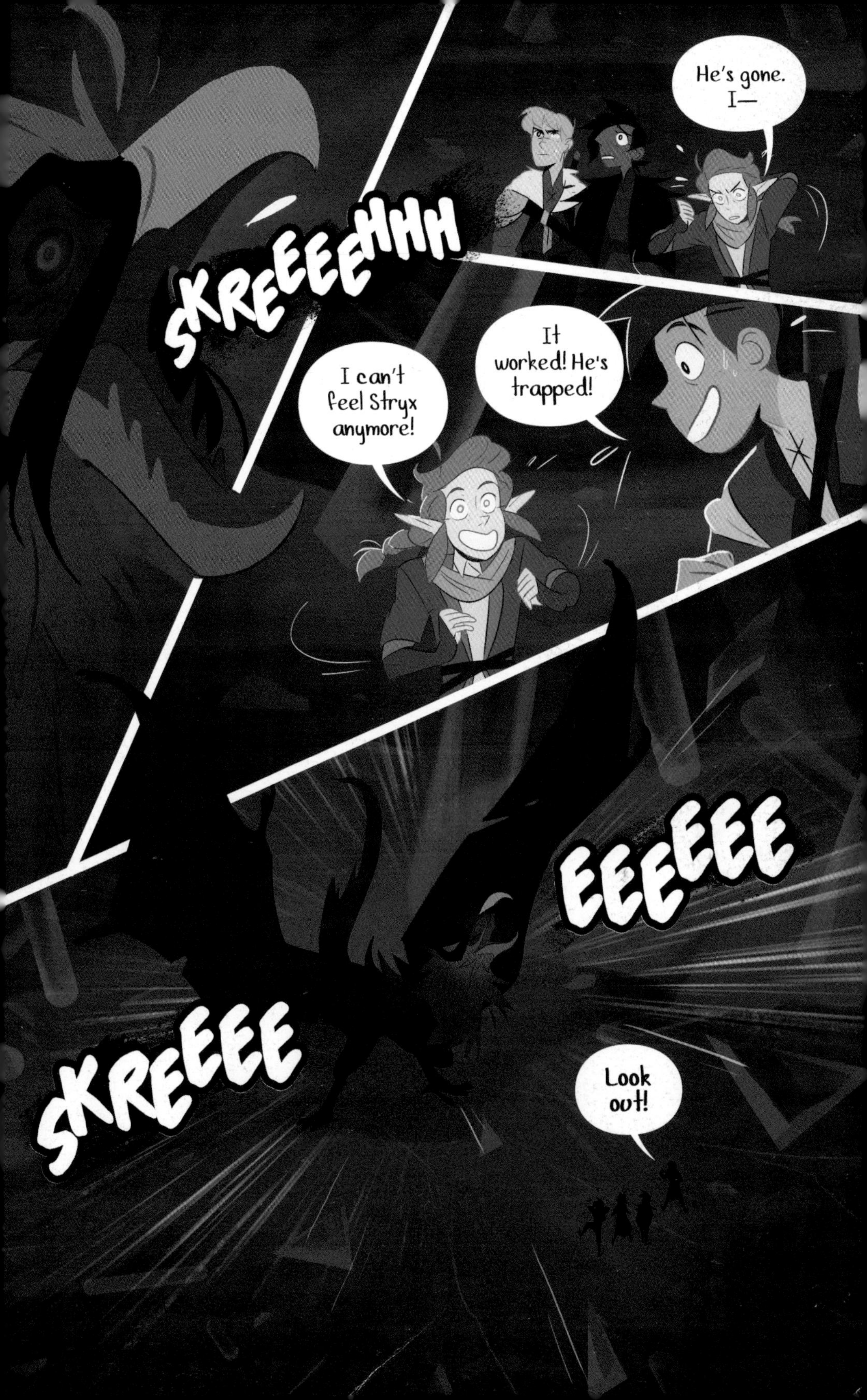
SKREEEEEHHH
He's gone. I—
It worked! He's trapped!
I can't feel Stryx anymore!
EEEEEE
SKREEEE
Look out!

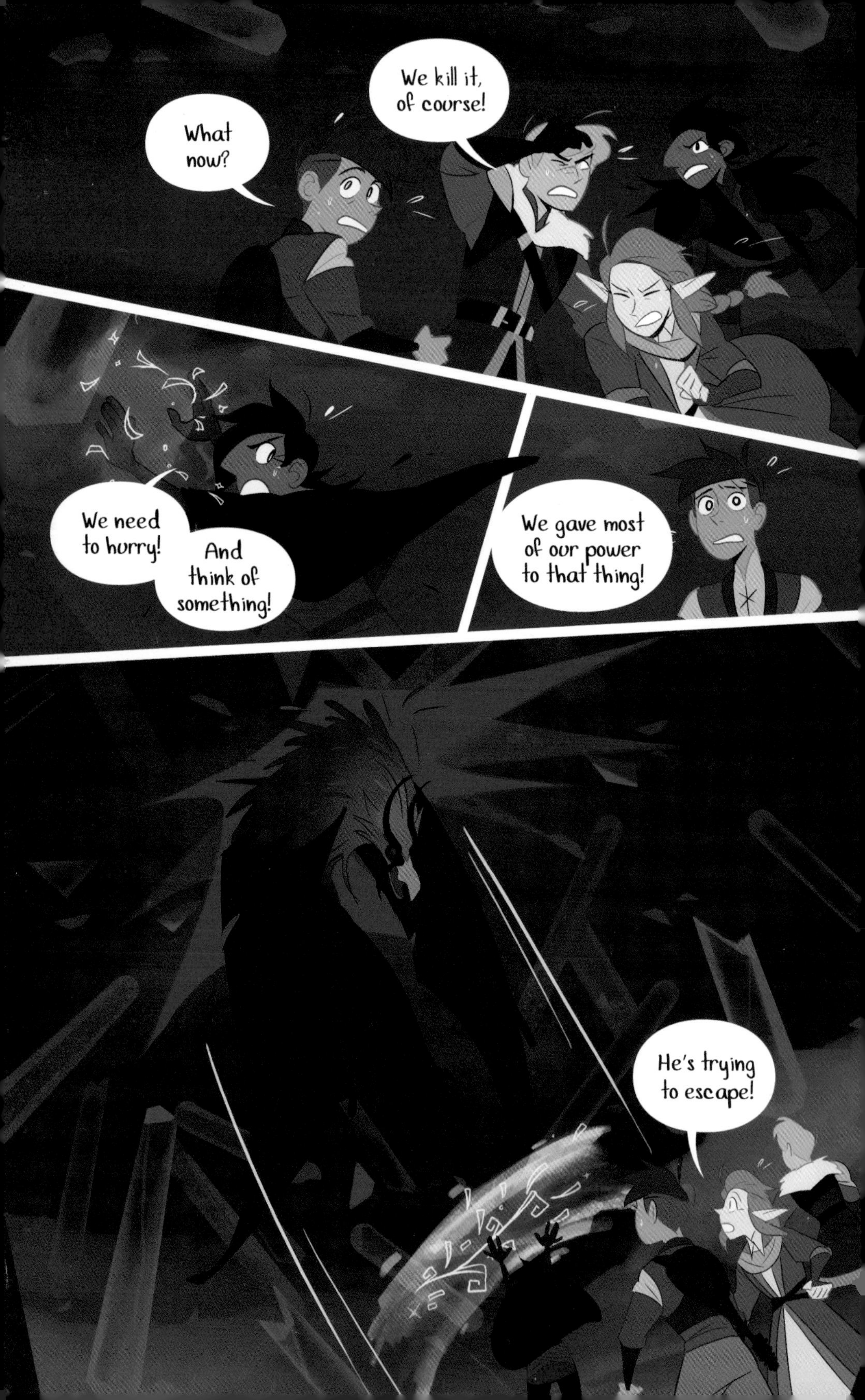
What now?
We kill it, of course!
We need to hurry!
And think of something!
We gave most of our power to that thing!
He's trying to escape!

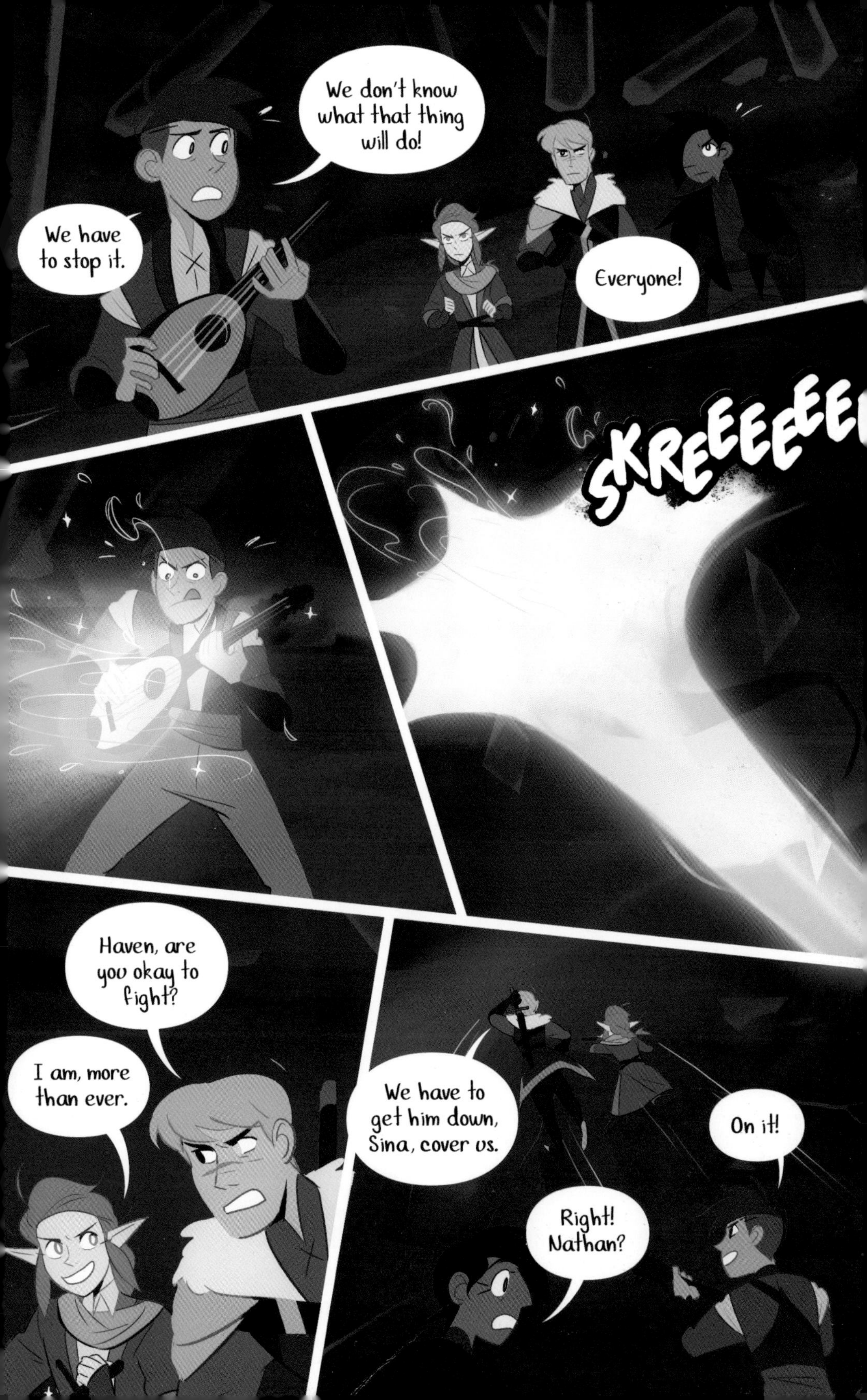
We have to stop it.
We don't know what that thing will do!
Everyone!
SKREEEEEEE
Haven, are you okay to fight?
I am, more than ever.
We have to get him down, Sina, cover us.
On it!
Right! Nathan?

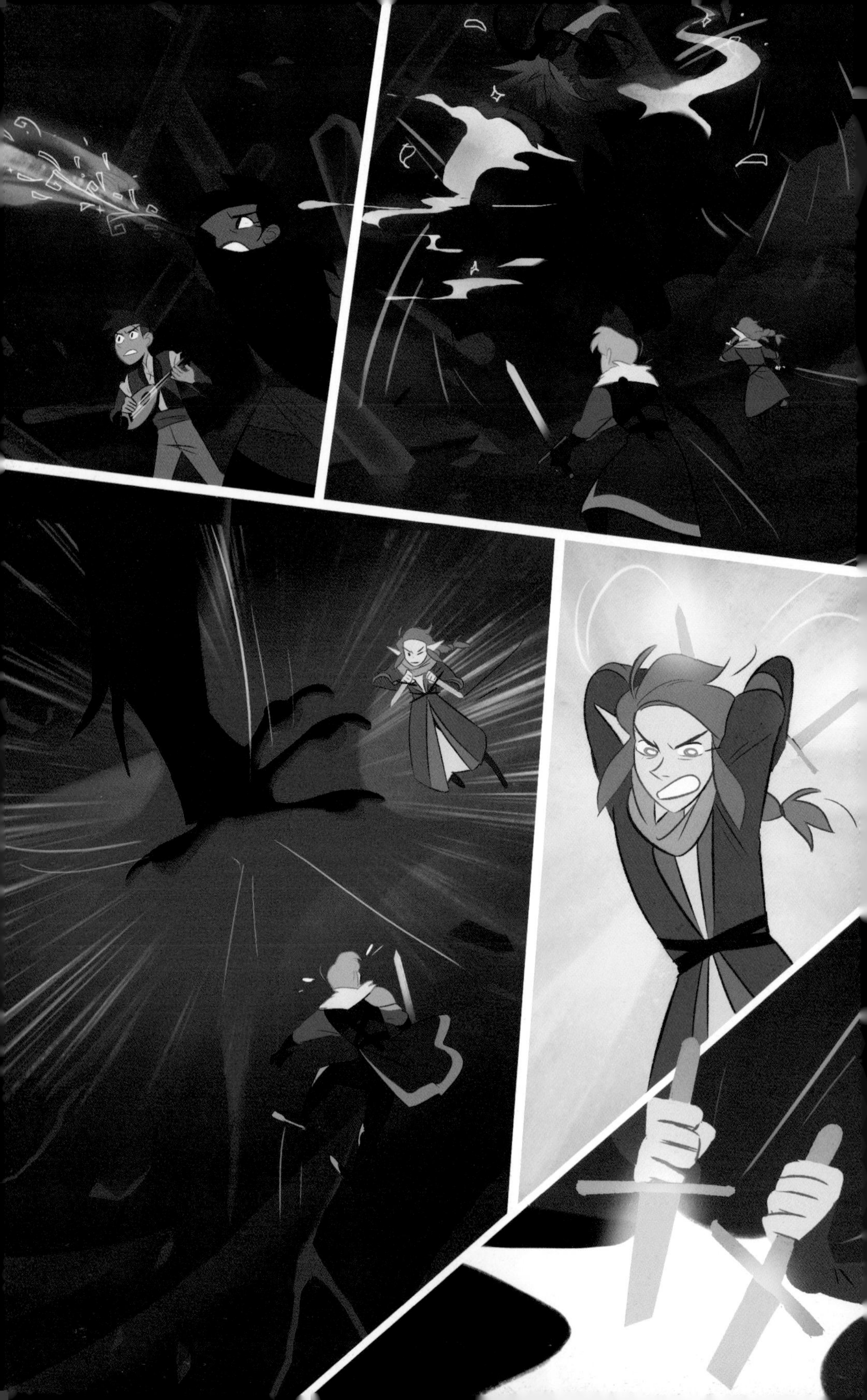

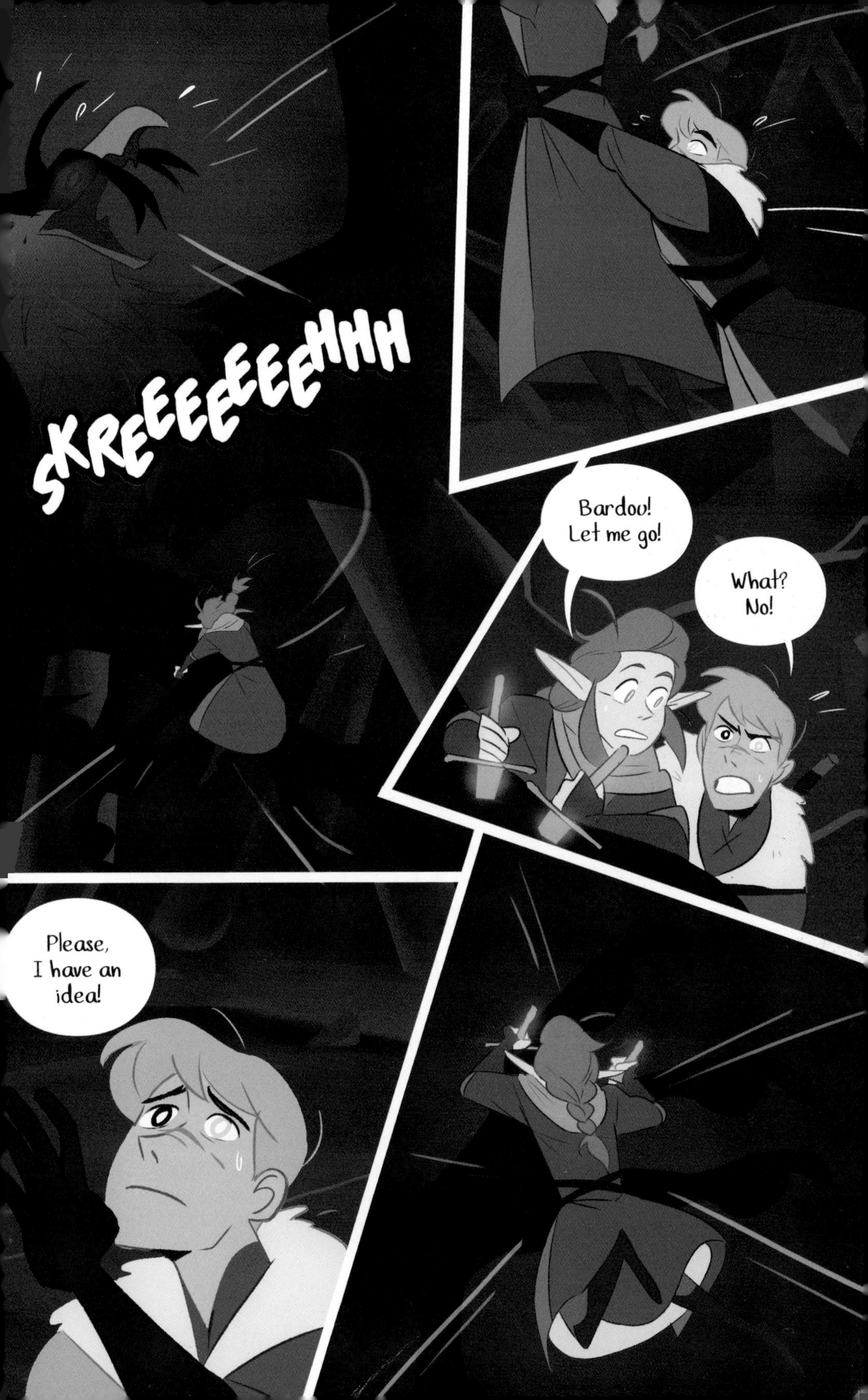
SKREEEEEEEHHH
Bardou! Let me go!
What? No!
Please, I have an idea!

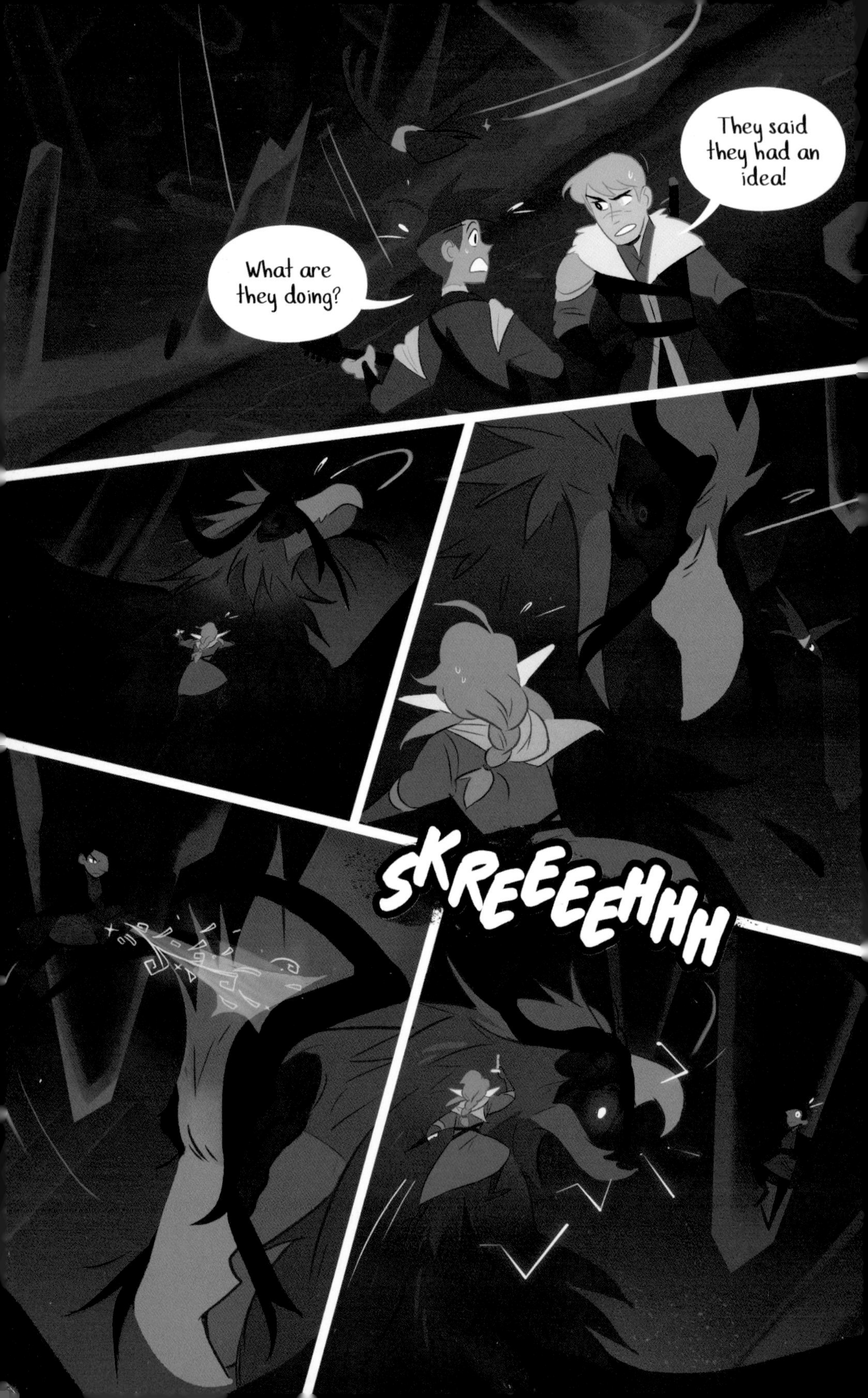
What are they doing?
They said they had an idea!
SKREEEEHHH

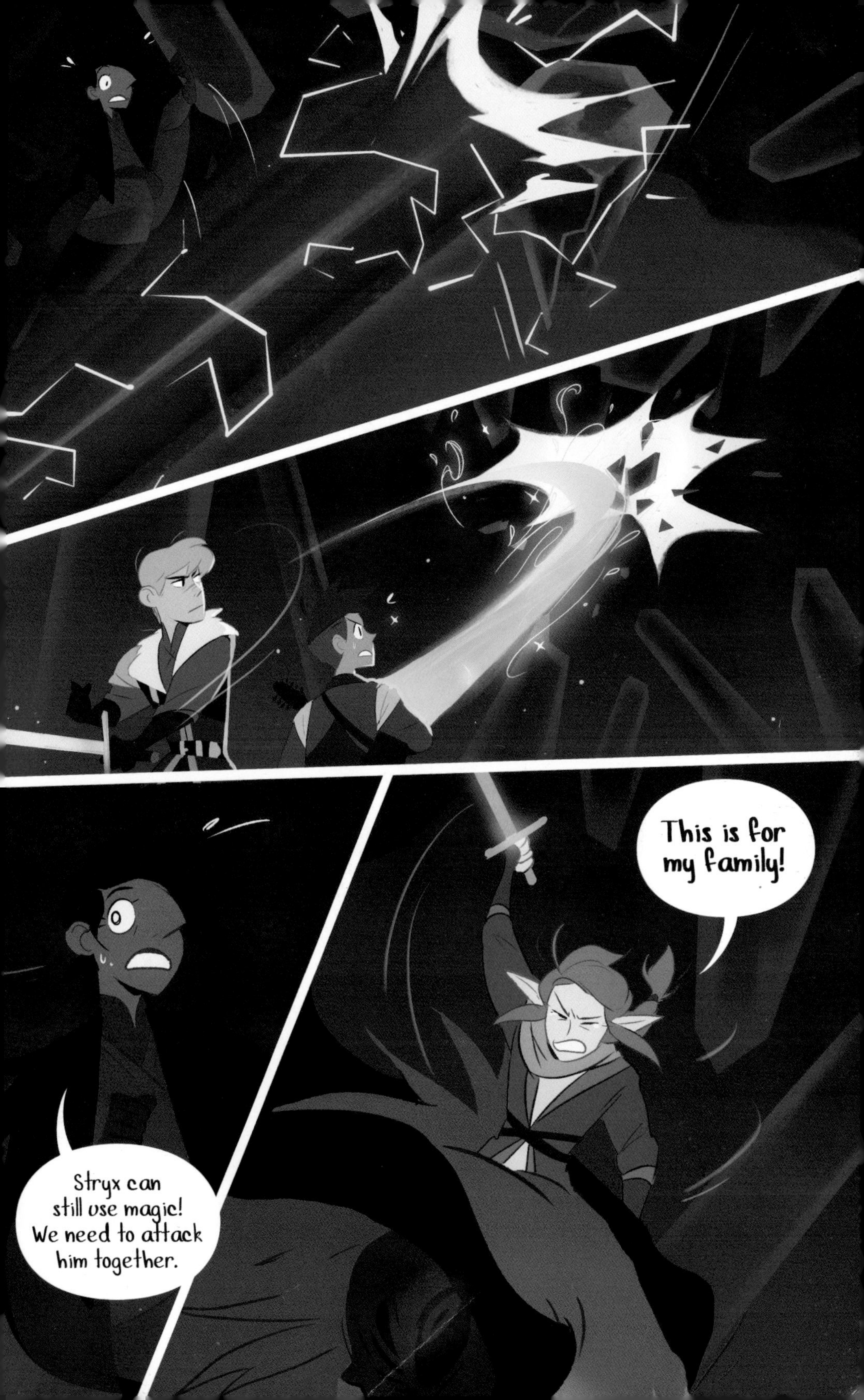
Stryx can still use magic! We need to attack him together.
This is for my family!

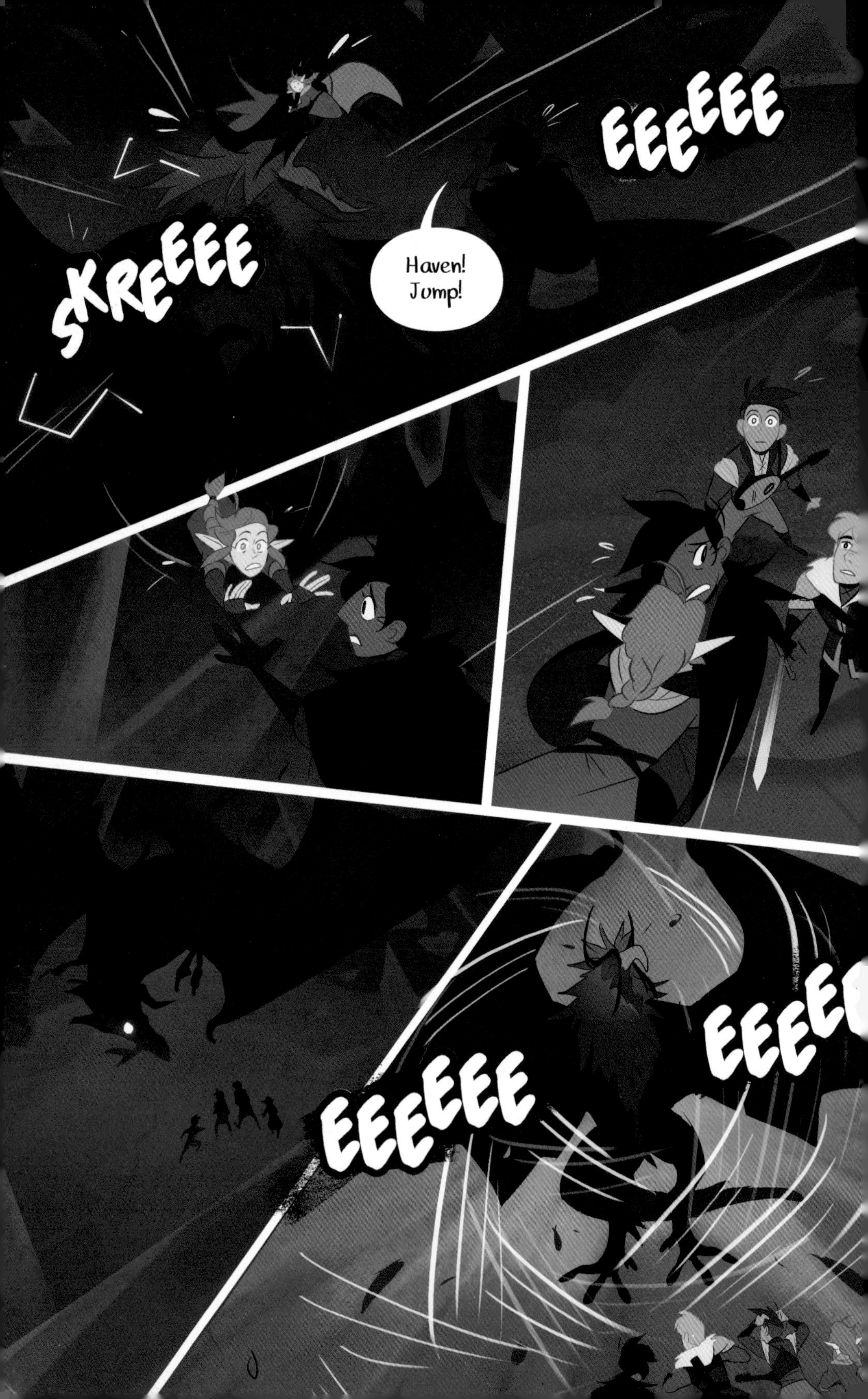
EEEEEE
SKREEEE
Haven! Jump!
EEEEEE
EEEEE

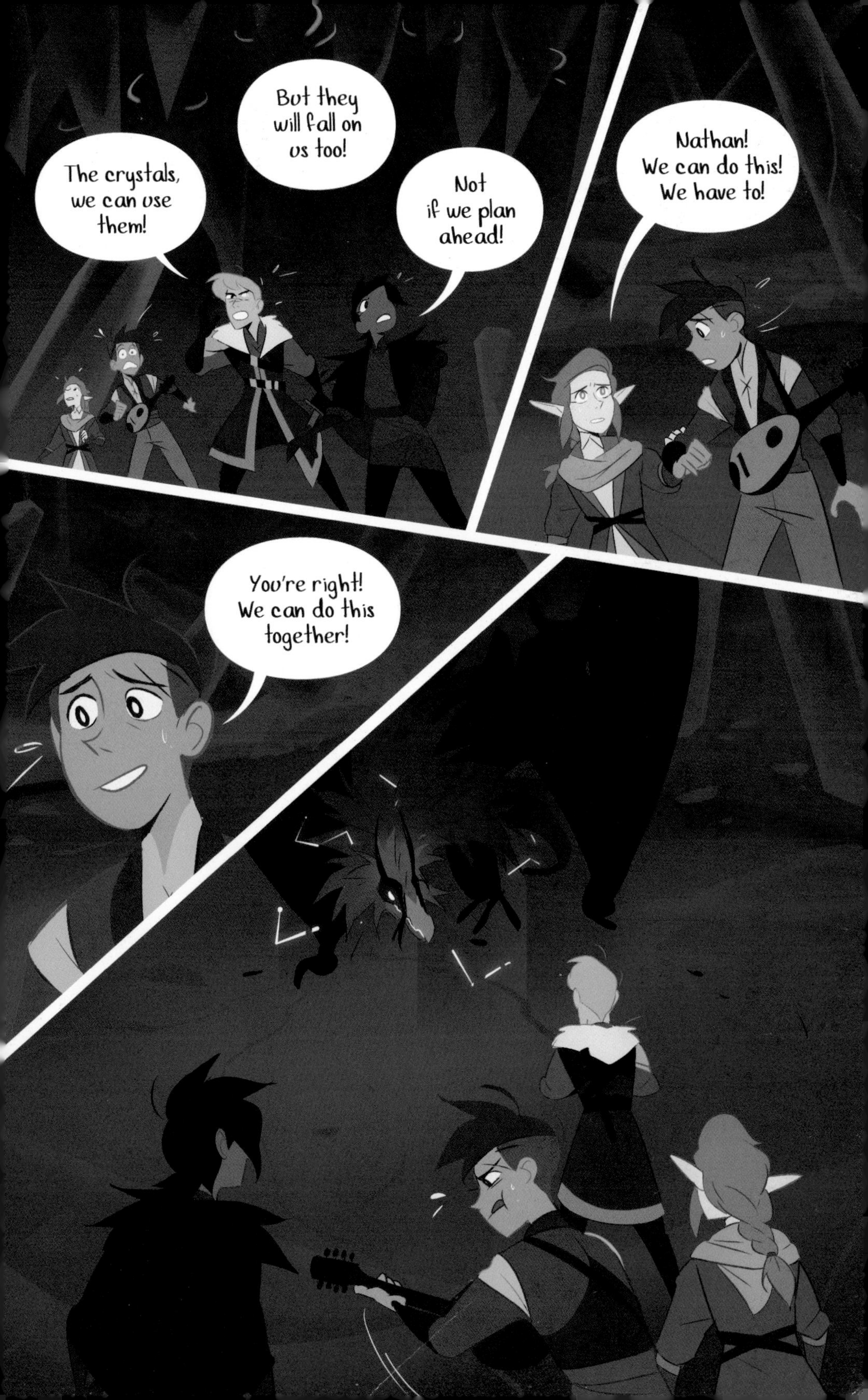
The crystals, we can use them!
But they will fall on us too!
Not if we plan ahead!
Nathan! We can do this! We have to!
You're right! We can do this together!

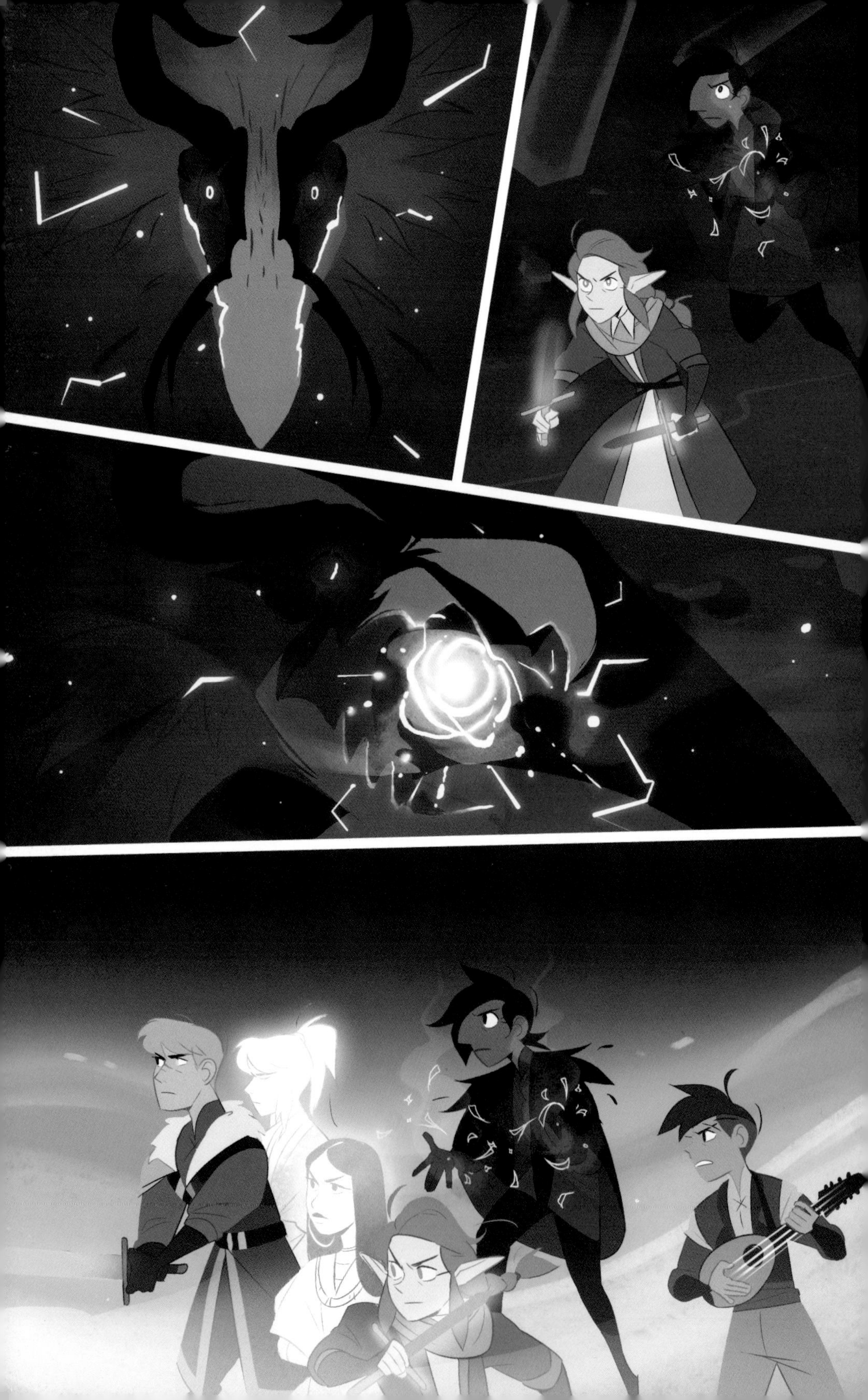

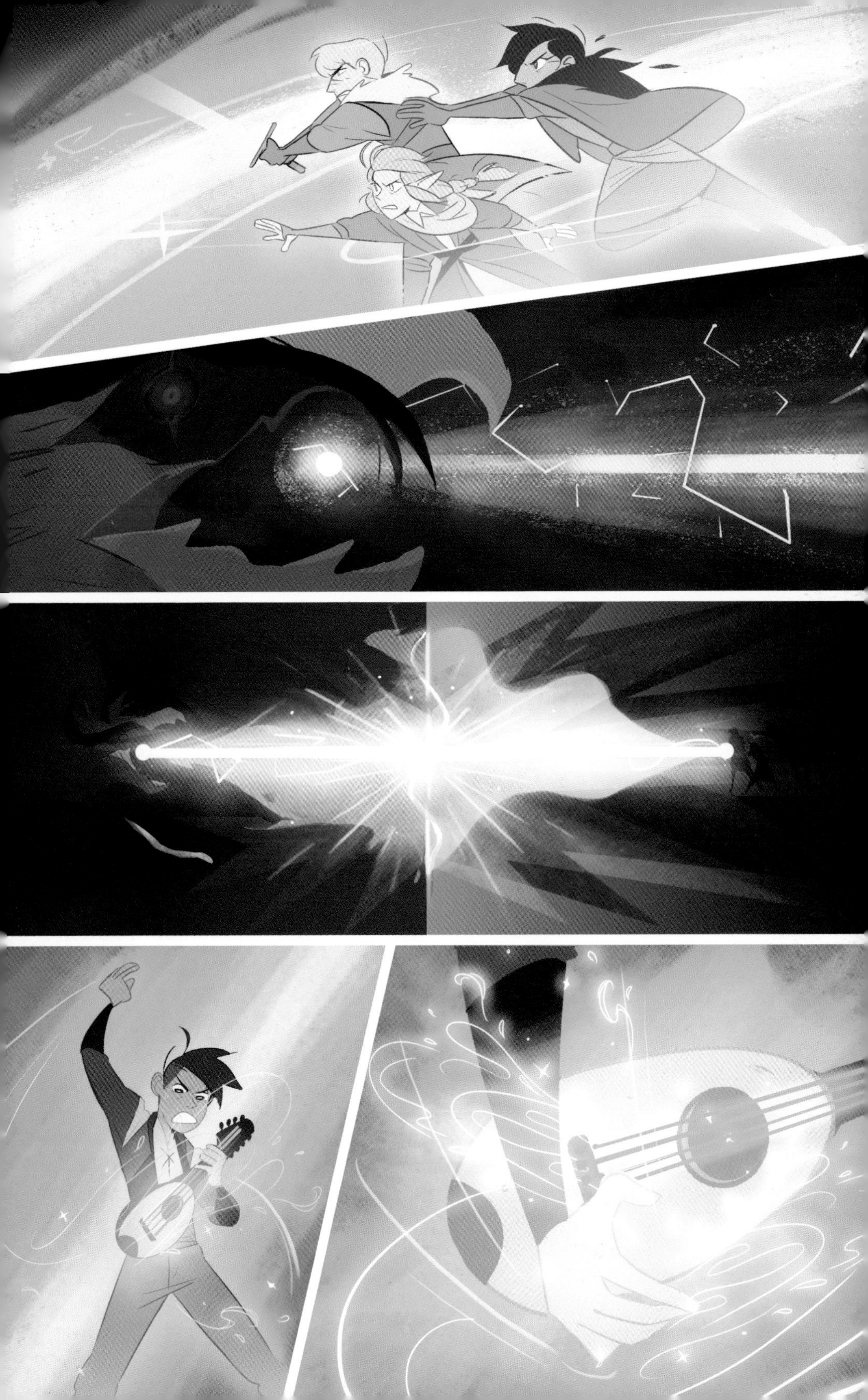

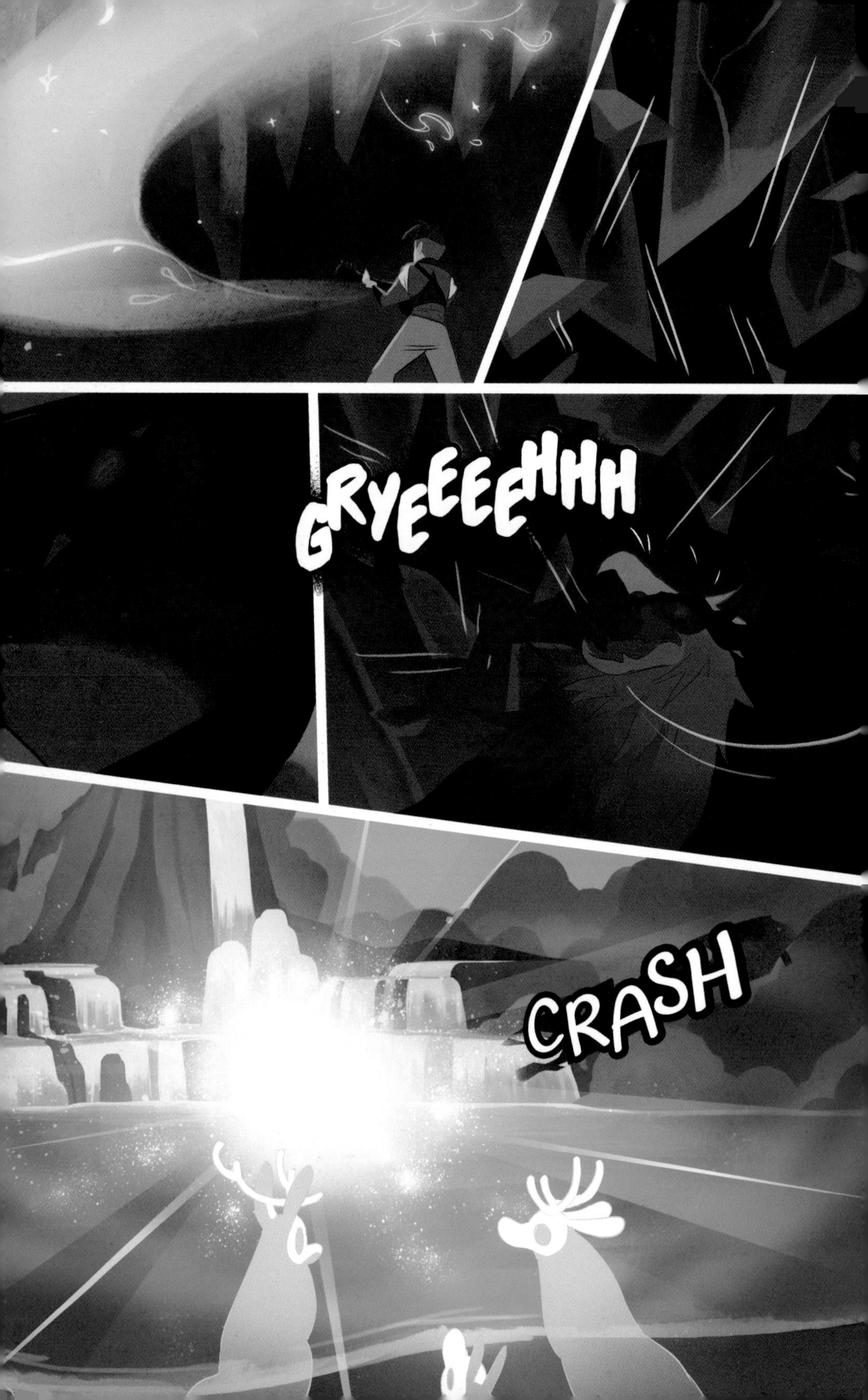
GRYEEEEHHH
CRASH

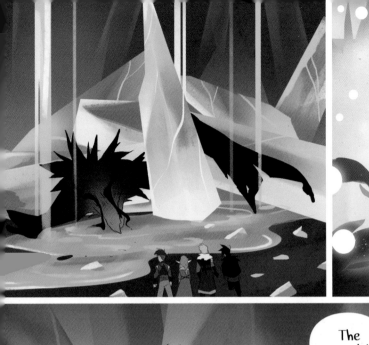

The spirits!

Now that they are free . . .

. . . they can finally return to Nothing.

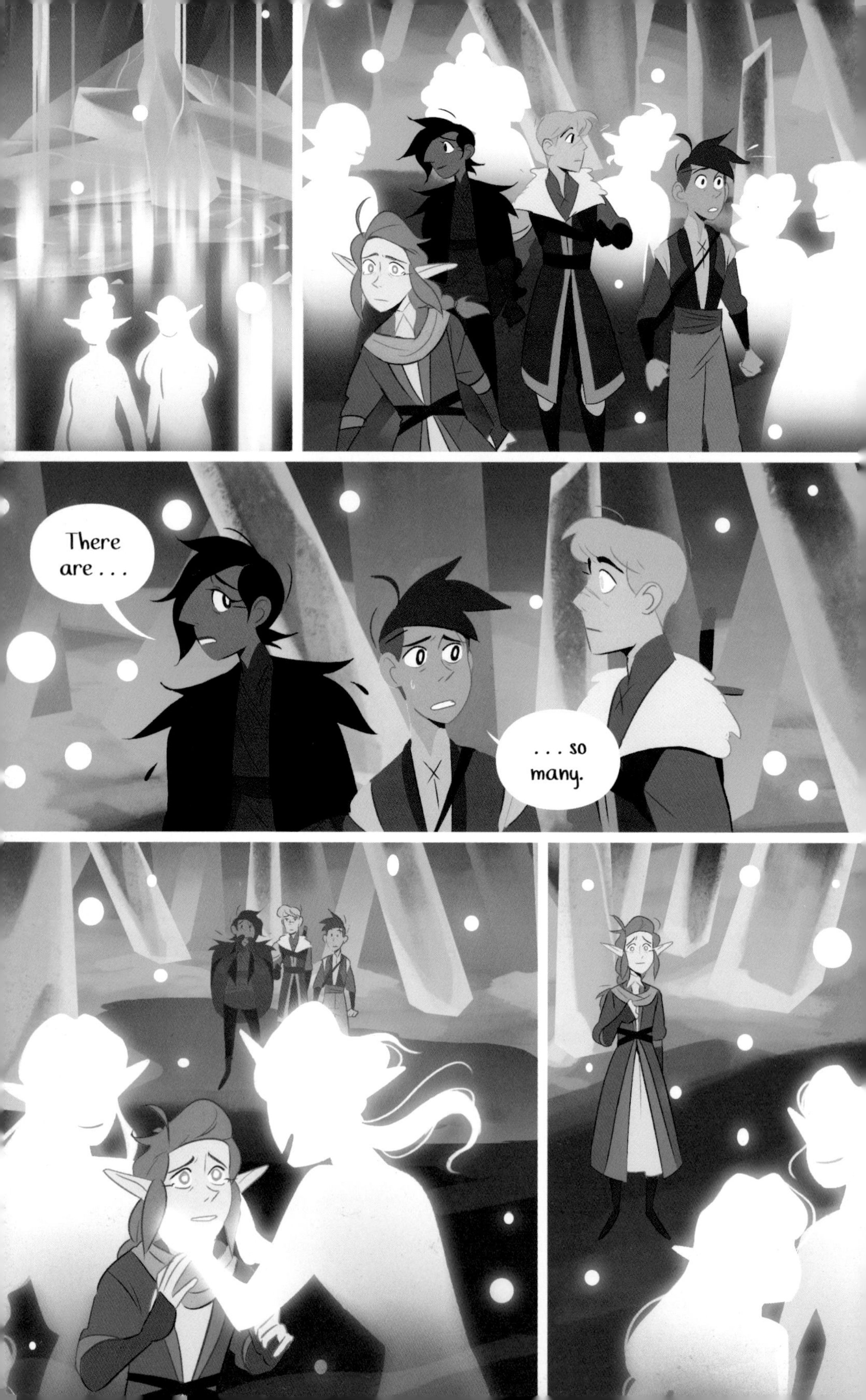
There are . . .
. . . so many.

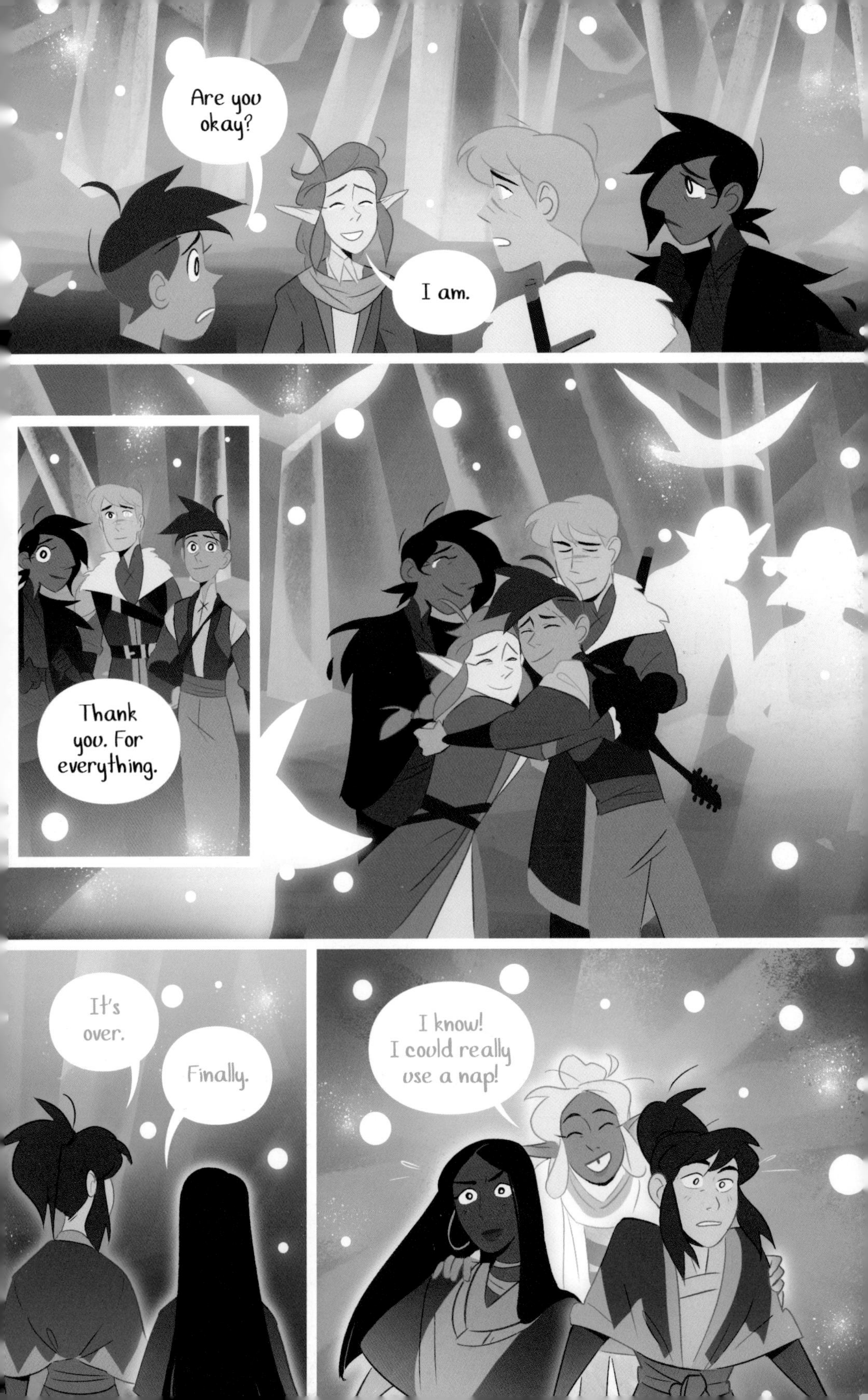
Are you okay?
I am.
Thank you. For everything.
It's over.
Finally.
I know! I could really use a nap!

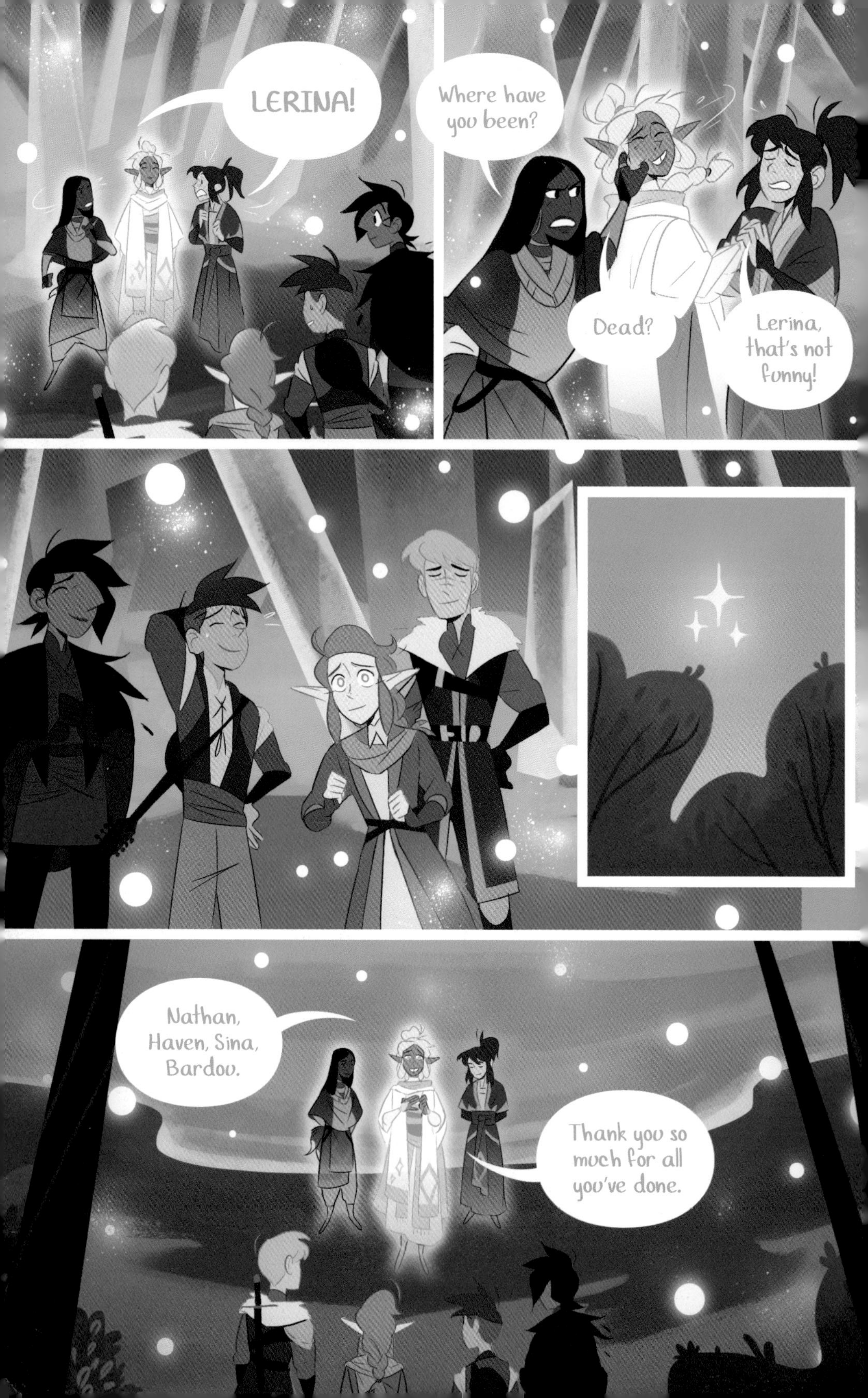
LERINA!
Where have you been?
Dead?
Lerina, that's not funny!
Nathan, Haven, Sina, Bardou.
Thank you so much for all you've done.

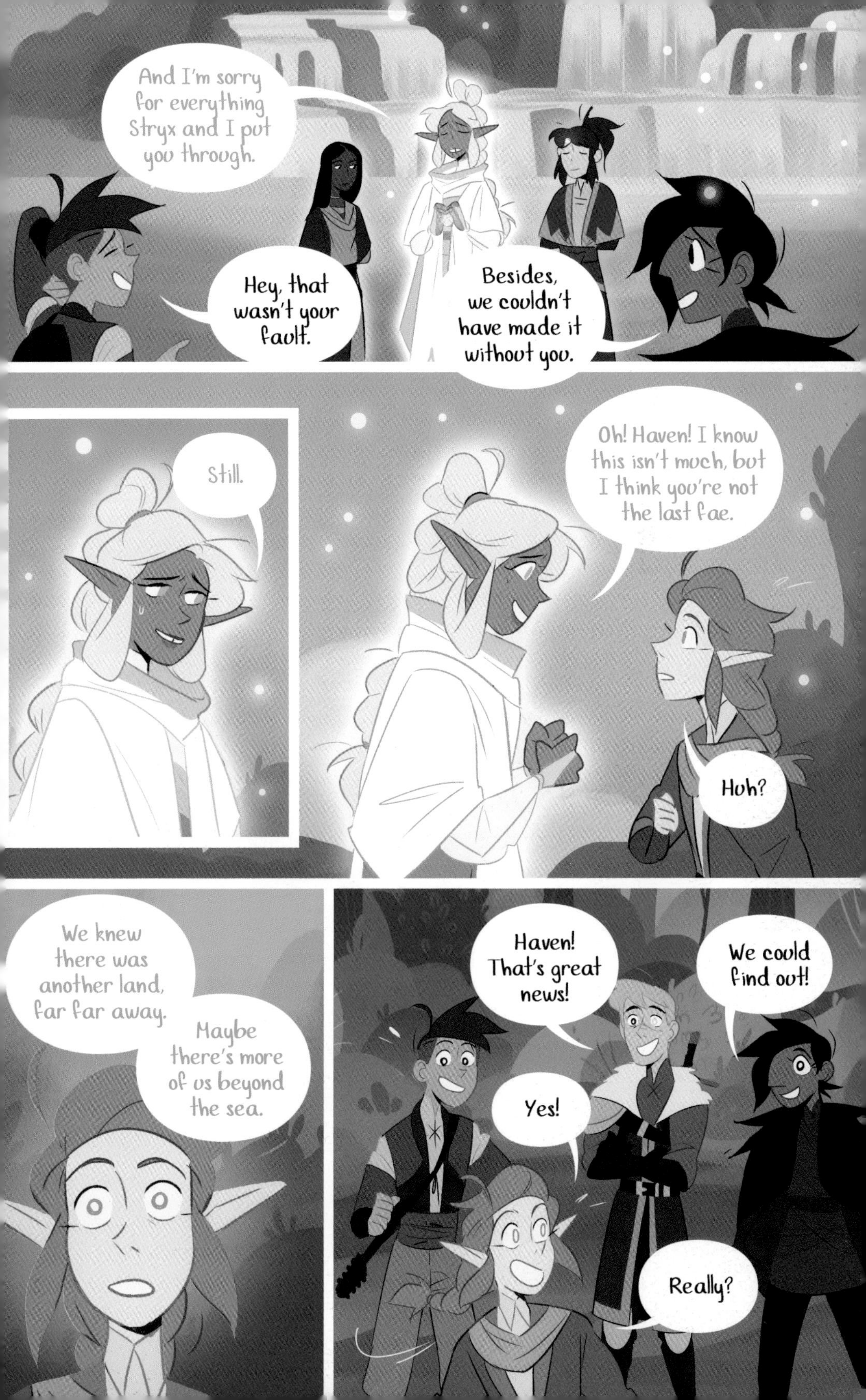
And I'm sorry for everything Stryx and I put you through.
Hey, that wasn't your fault.
Besides, we couldn't have made it without you.
Still.
Oh! Haven! I know this isn't much, but I think you're not the last fae.
Huh?
We knew there was another land, far far away.
Maybe there's more of us beyond the sea.
Haven! That's great news!
We could find out!
Yes!
Really?

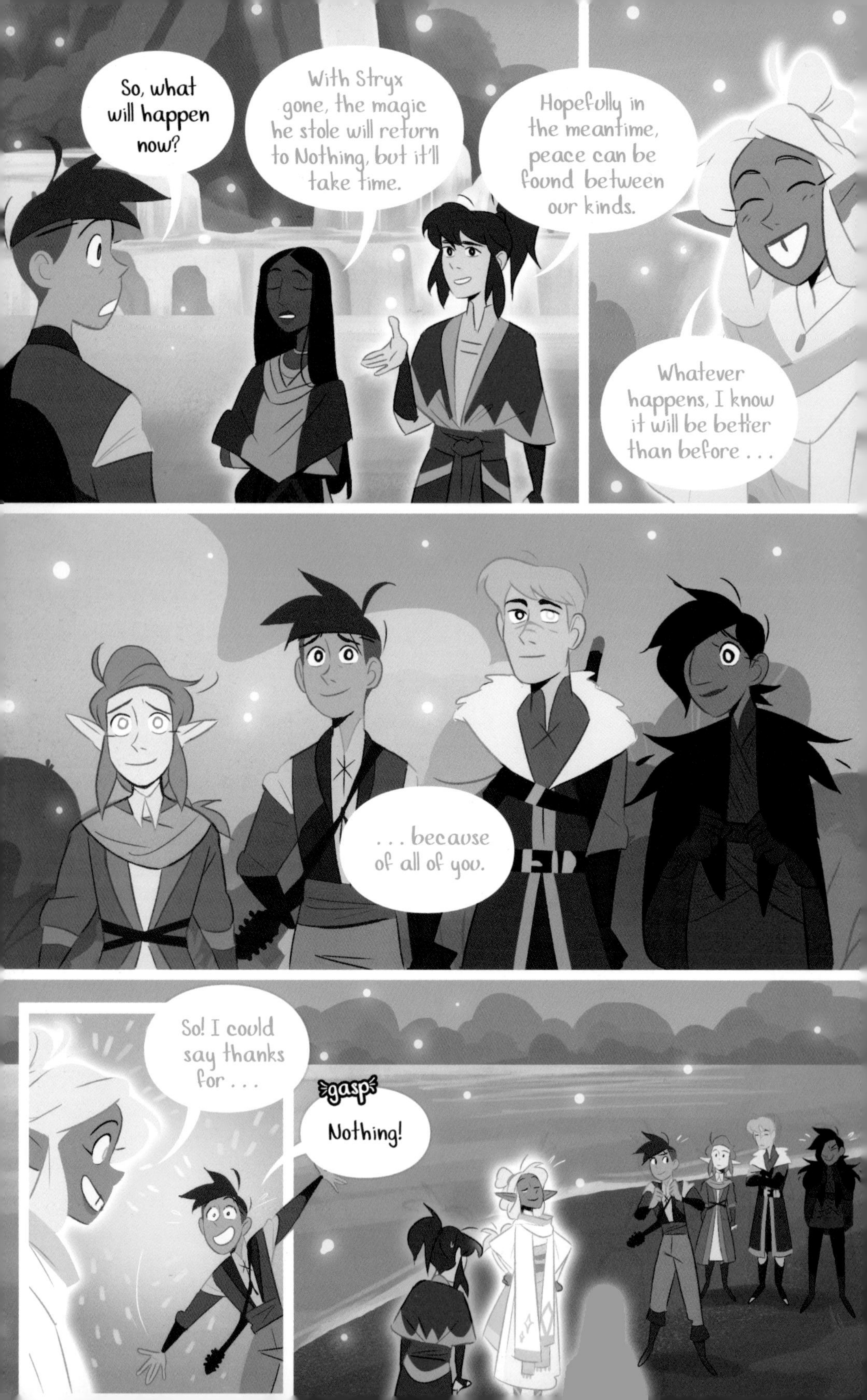
So, what will happen now?
With Stryx gone, the magic he stole will return to Nothing, but it'll take time.
Hopefully in the meantime, peace can be found between our kinds.
Whatever happens, I know it will be better than before . . .
. . . because of all of you.
So! I could say thanks for . . .
gasp
Nothing!

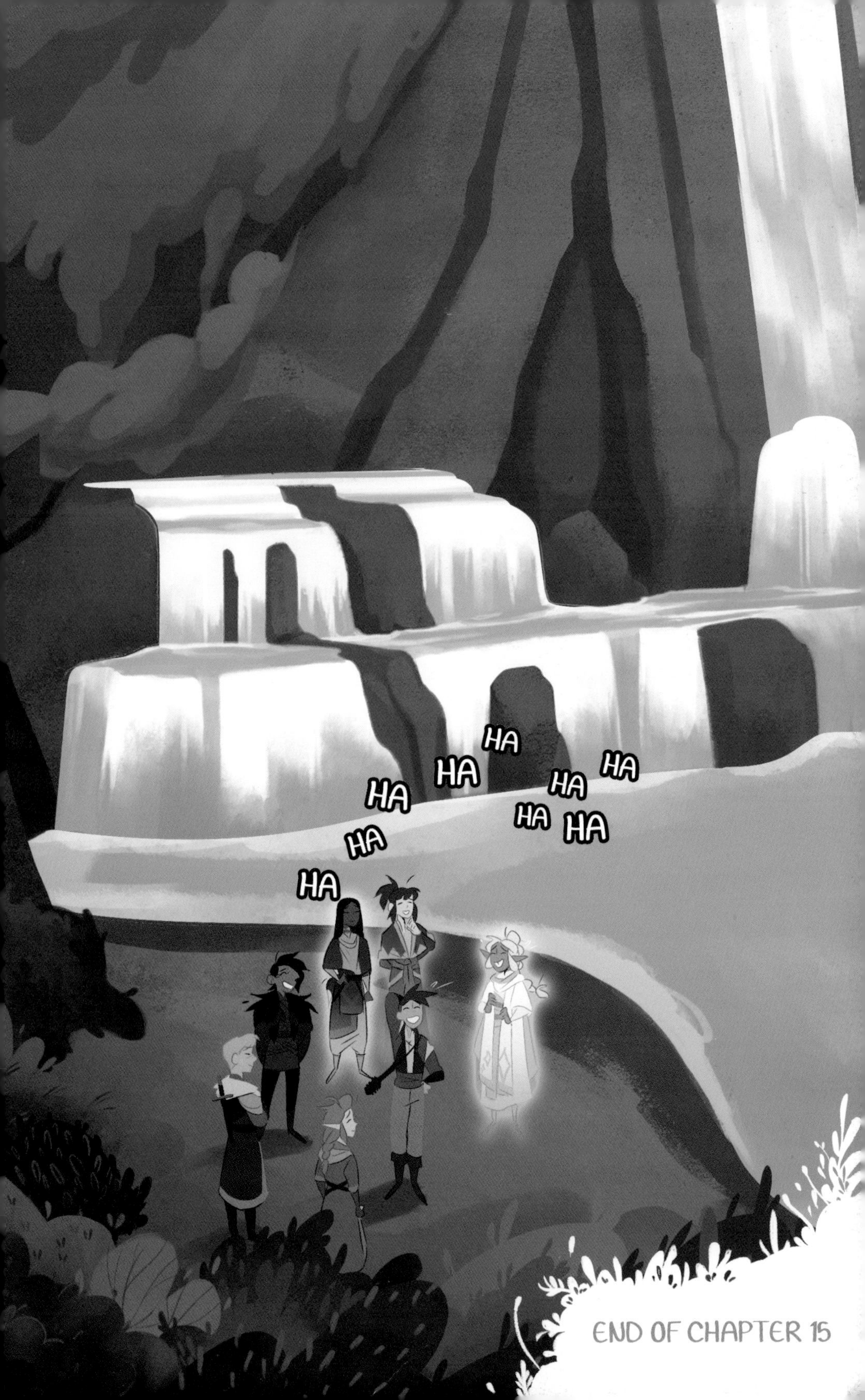
HA
HA
HA
HA
HA
HA
HA
HA
HA
END OF CHAPTER 15

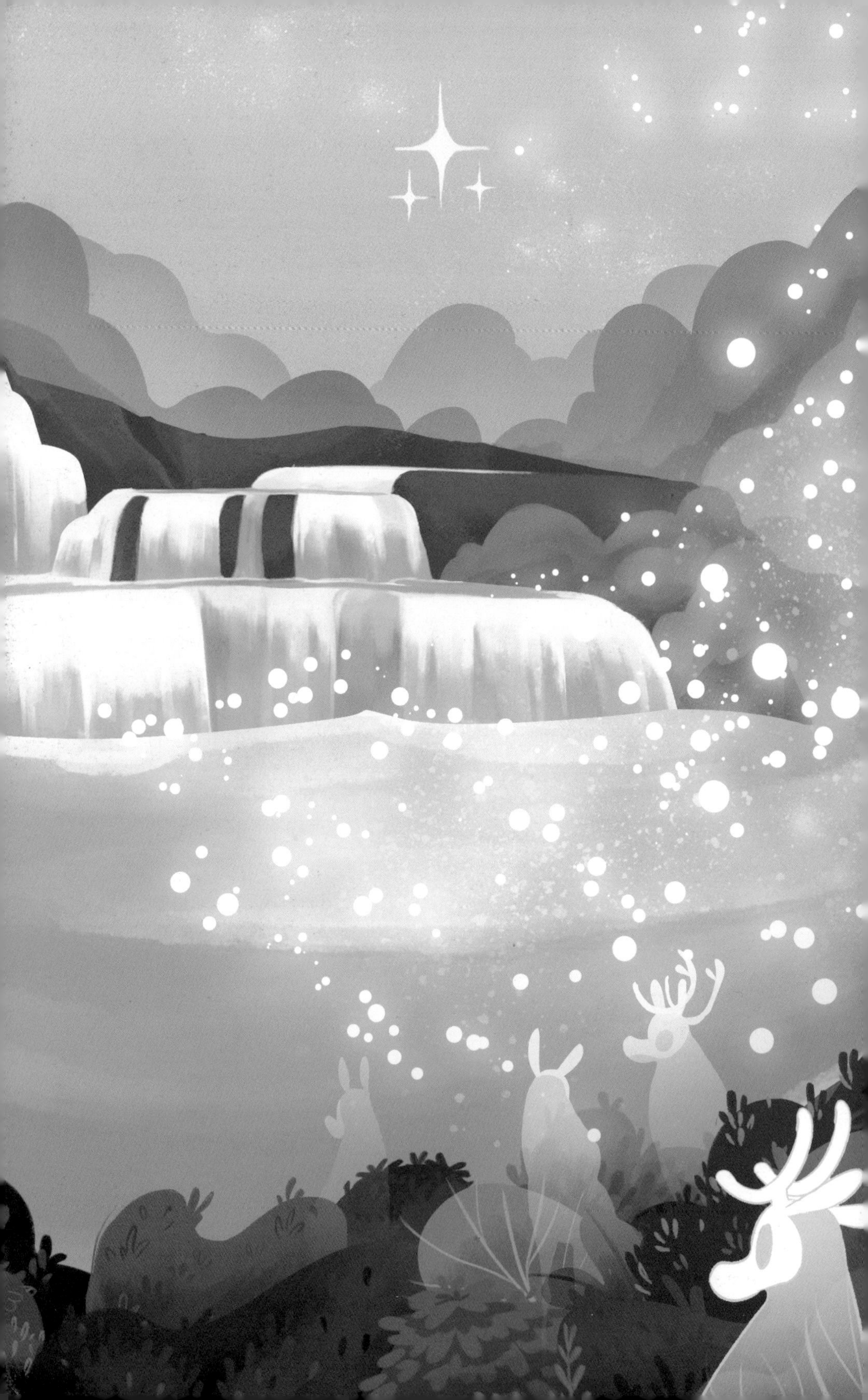

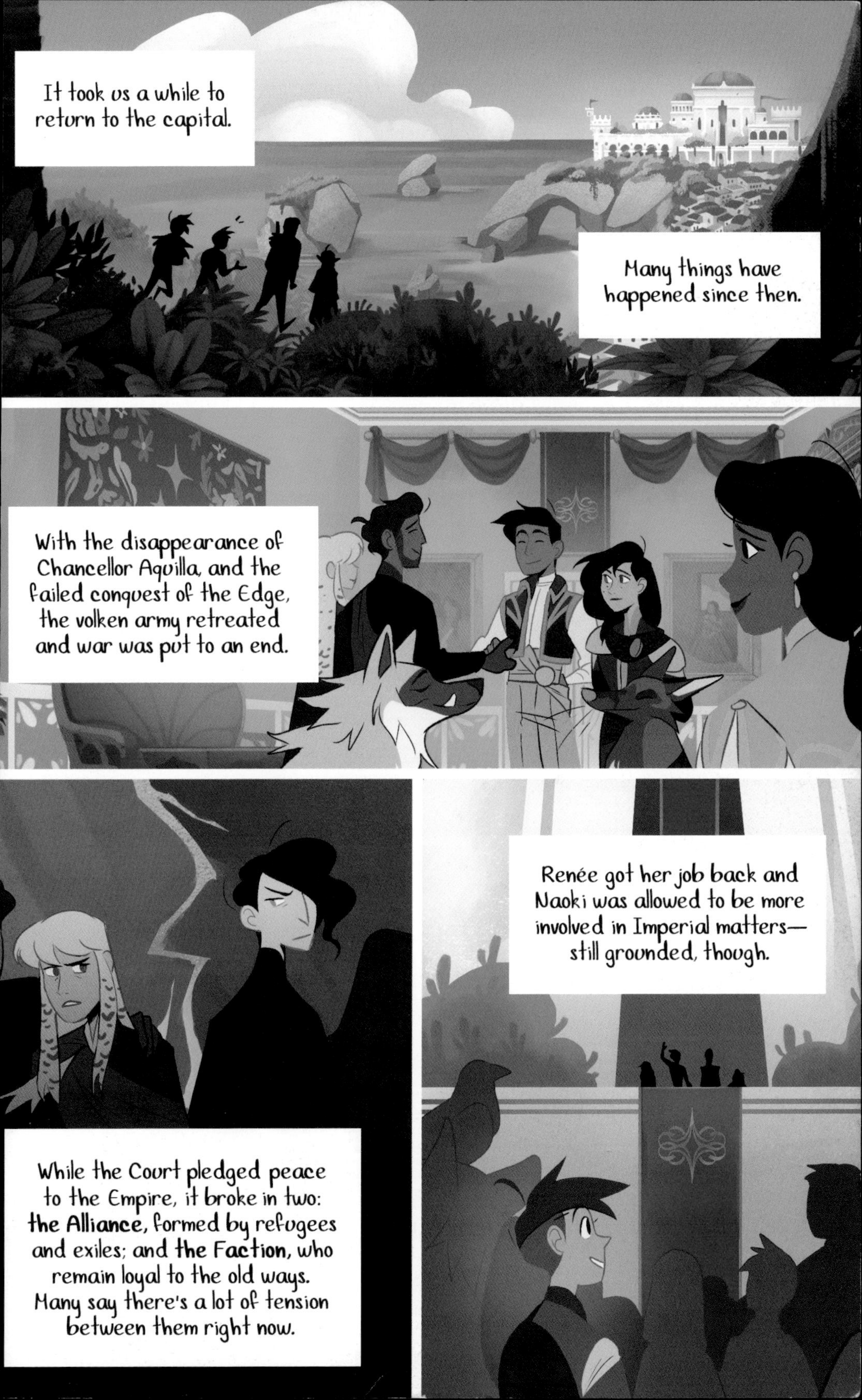
It took us a while to return to the capital.
Many things have happened since then.
With the disappearance of Chancellor Aquilla, and the failed conquest of the Edge, the volken army retreated and war was put to an end.
While the Court pledged peace to the Empire, it broke in two: **the Alliance**, formed by refugees and exiles; and **the Faction**, who remain loyal to the old ways. Many say there's a lot of tension between them right now.
Renée got her job back and Naoki was allowed to be more involved in Imperial matters—still grounded, though.

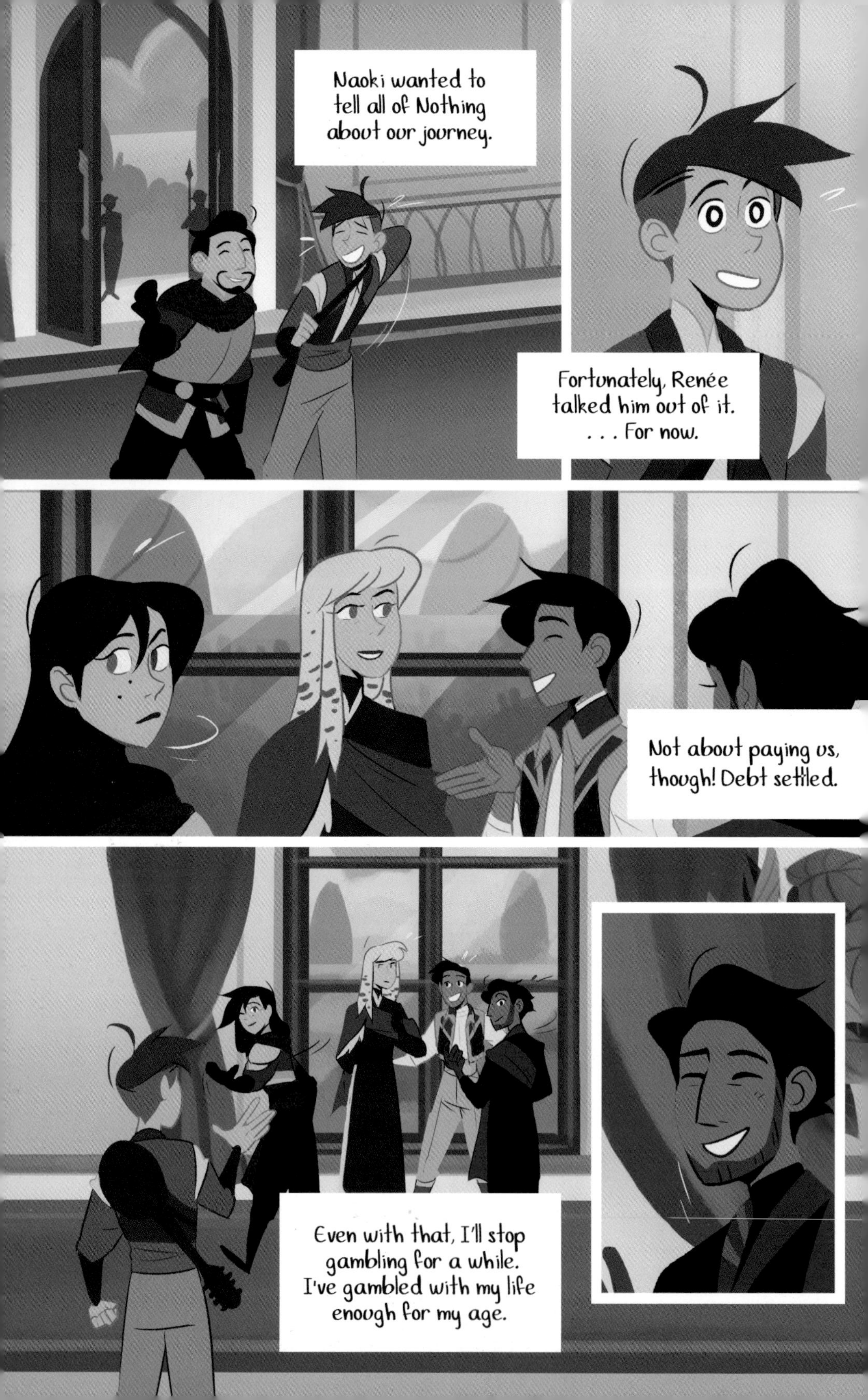
Naoki wanted to tell all of Nothing about our journey.
Fortunately, Renée talked him out of it. . . . For now.
Not about paying us, though! Debt settled.
Even with that, I'll stop gambling for a while. I've gambled with my life enough for my age.

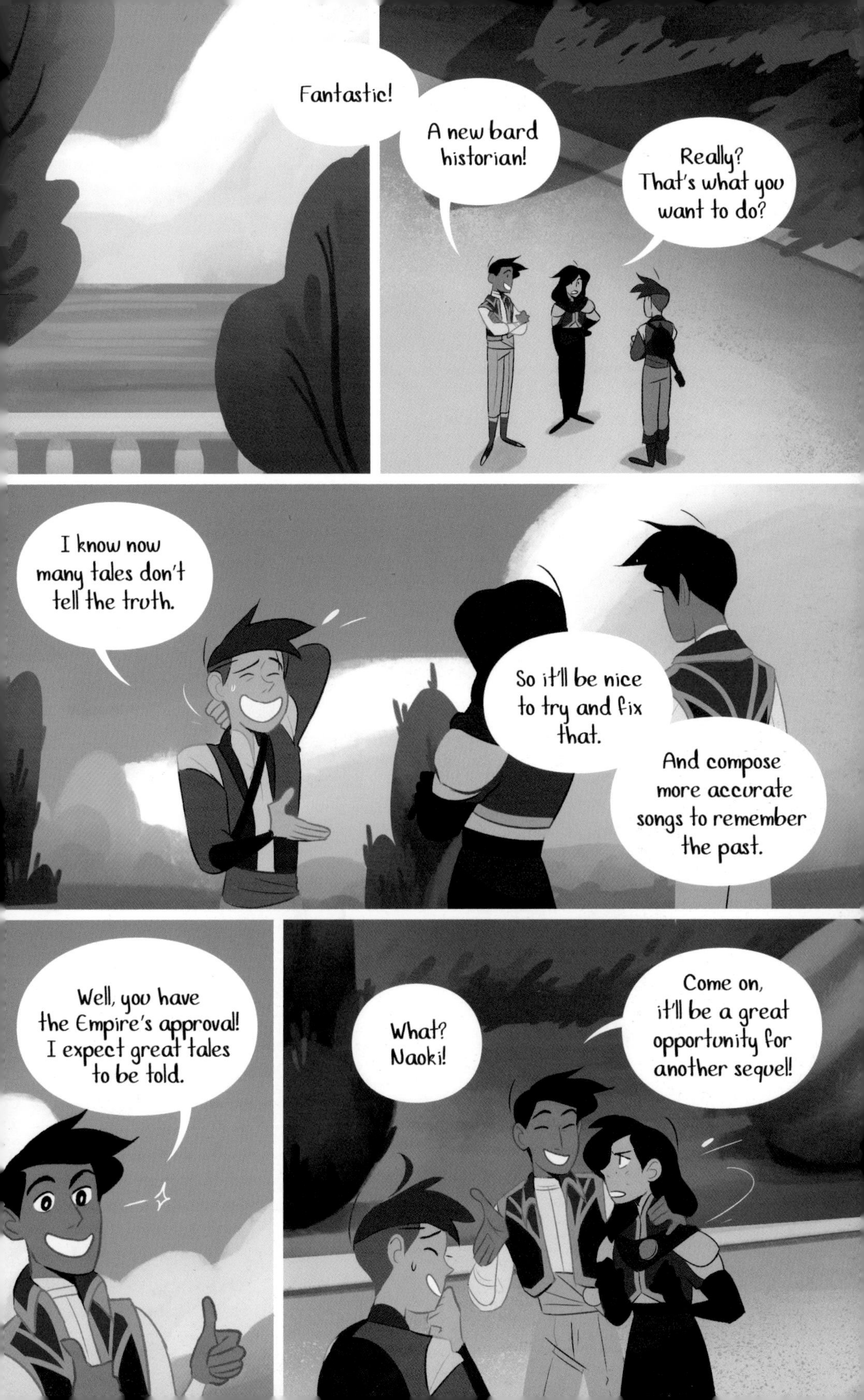
Fantastic!
A new bard historian!
Really? That's what you want to do?
I know now many tales don't tell the truth.
So it'll be nice to try and fix that.
And compose more accurate songs to remember the past.
Well, you have the Empire's approval! I expect great tales to be told.
What? Naoki!
Come on, it'll be a great opportunity for another sequel!

Naoki!

Coming!

What about the trip? Will the others join you?

Of course, they're all for it. Even Bardou.

I'm glad. It's a shame you don't have magic anymore.

Please take care.

ha ha ha
Yeah, yeah.

I've got to go. Write once in a while, will you?

Of course...
Your Future Highness.

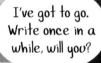

Seems that despite being an official couple now, Ren remains the same.

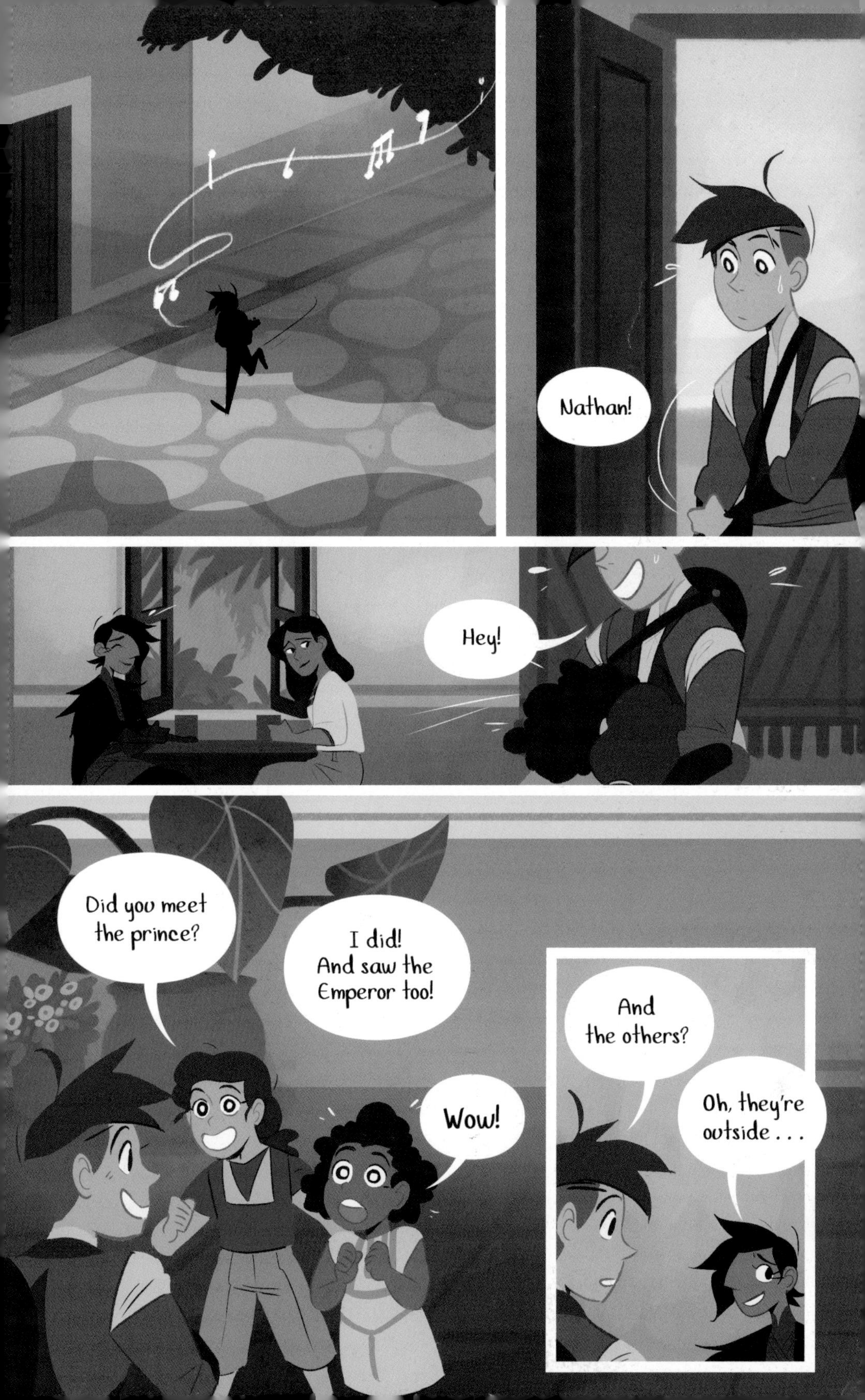
Nathan!
Hey!
Did you meet the prince?
I did! And saw the Emperor too!
Wow!
And the others?
Oh, they're outside . . .

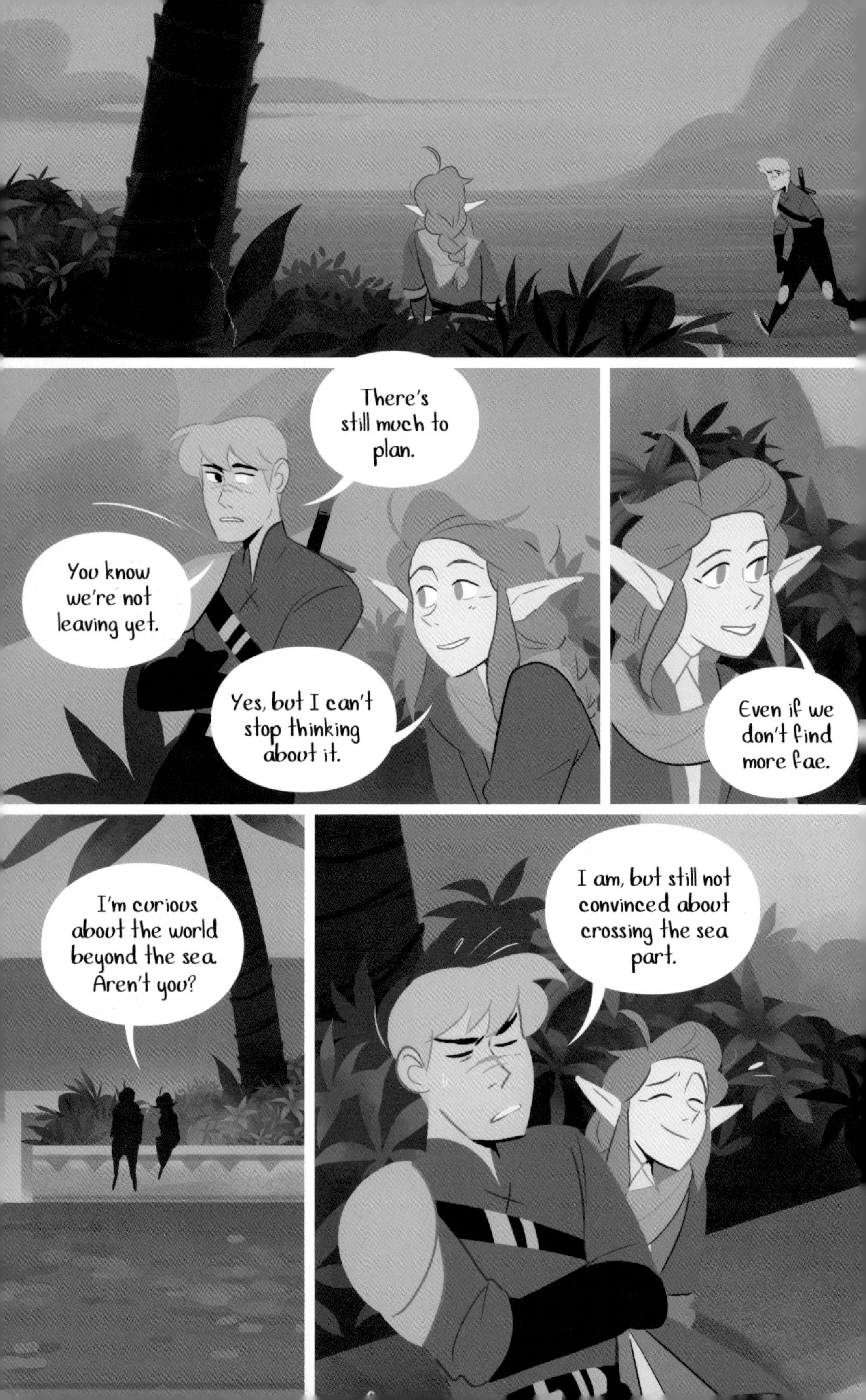
There's still much to plan.
You know we're not leaving yet.
Yes, but I can't stop thinking about it.
Even if we don't find more fae.
I'm curious about the world beyond the sea. Aren't you?
I am, but still not convinced about crossing the sea part.

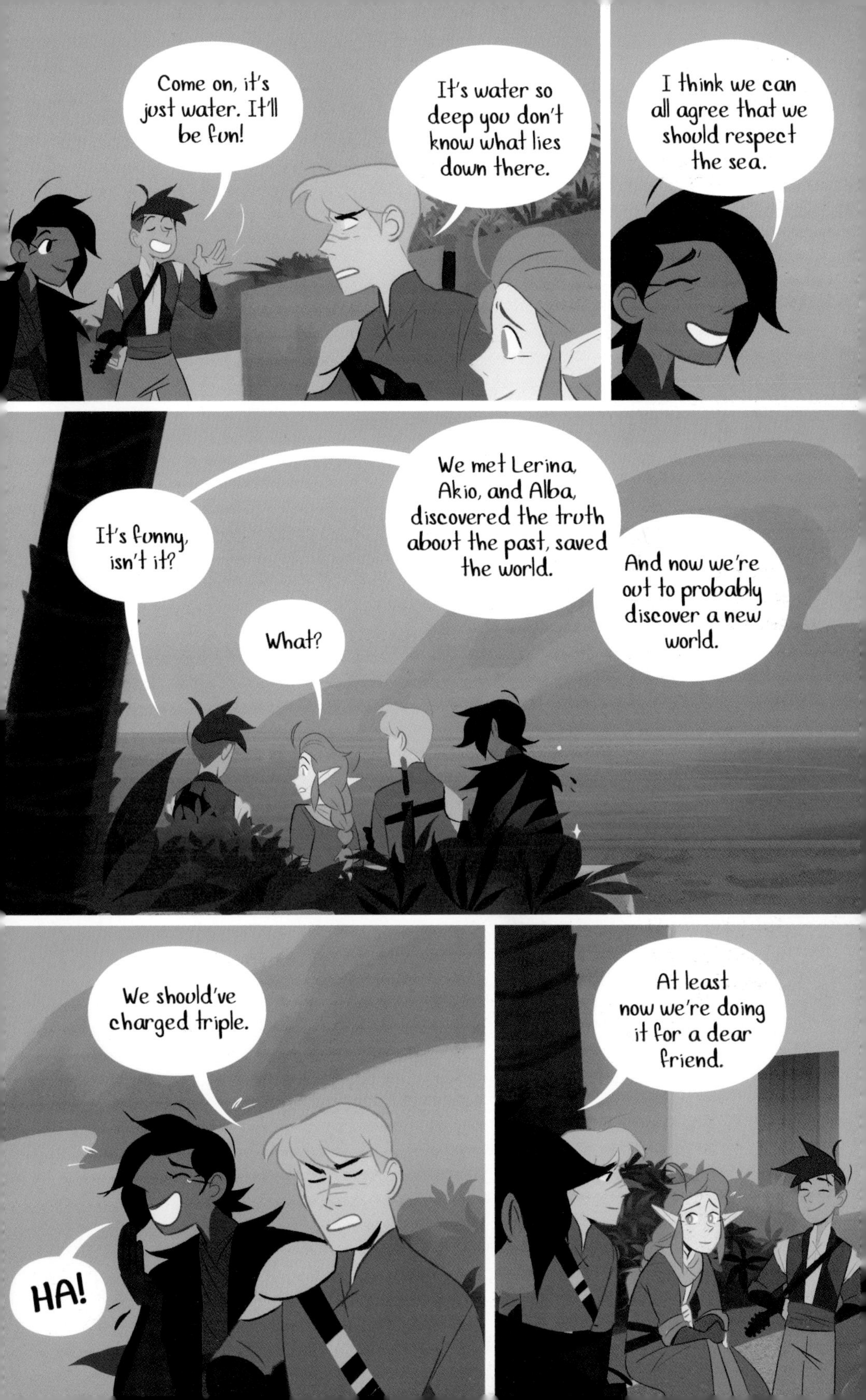
Come on, it's just water. It'll be fun!
It's water so deep you don't know what lies down there.
I think we can all agree that we should respect the sea.
It's funny, isn't it?
What?
We met Lerina, Akio, and Alba, discovered the truth about the past, saved the world.
And now we're out to probably discover a new world.
We should've charged triple.
HA!
At least now we're doing it for a dear friend.

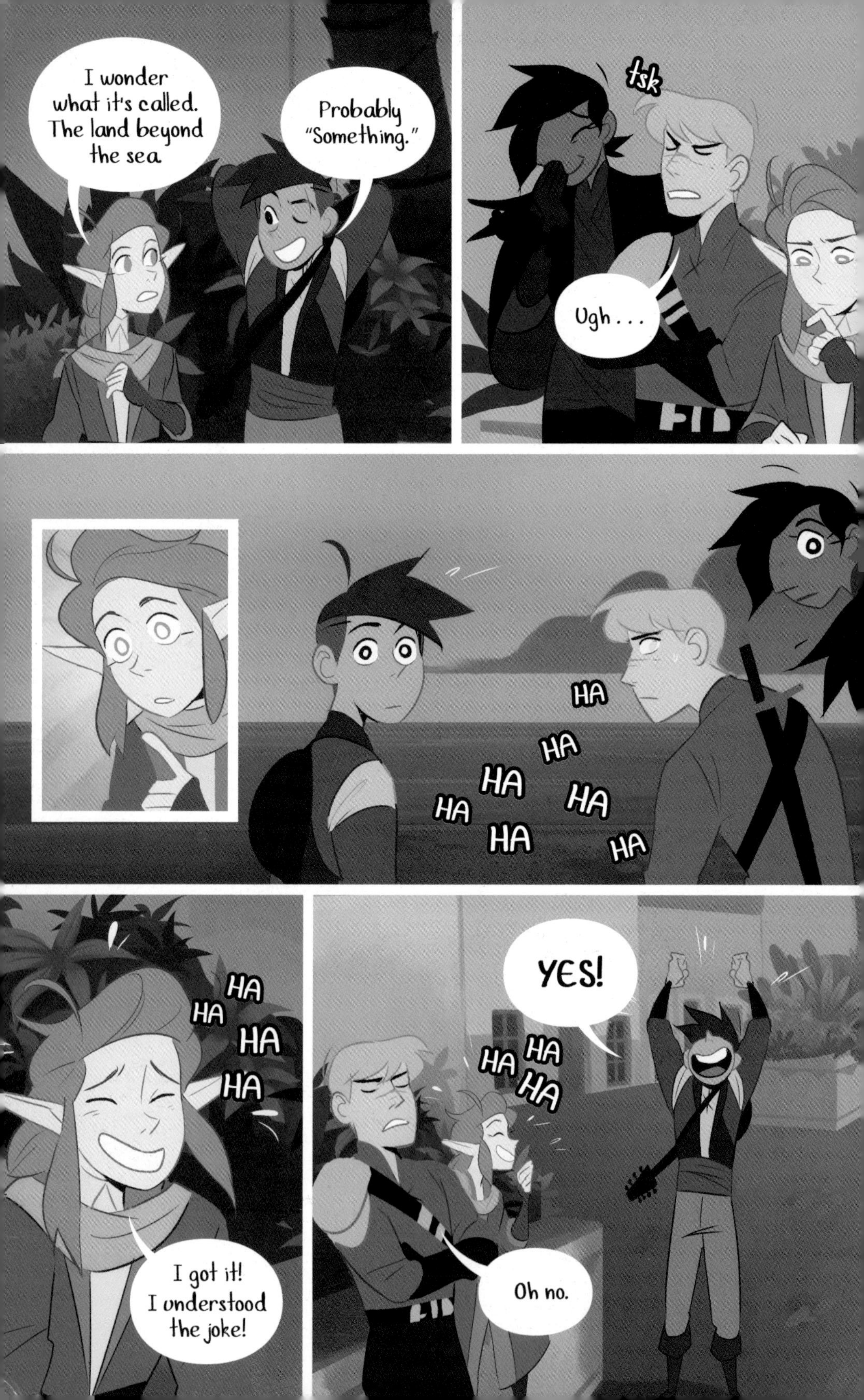
I wonder what it's called. The land beyond the sea
Probably "Something."
tsk
Ugh . . .
HA
HA
HA
HA
HA
HA
HA
HA
HA
HA
HA
I got it! I understood the joke!
YES!
HA
HA
HA
Oh no.

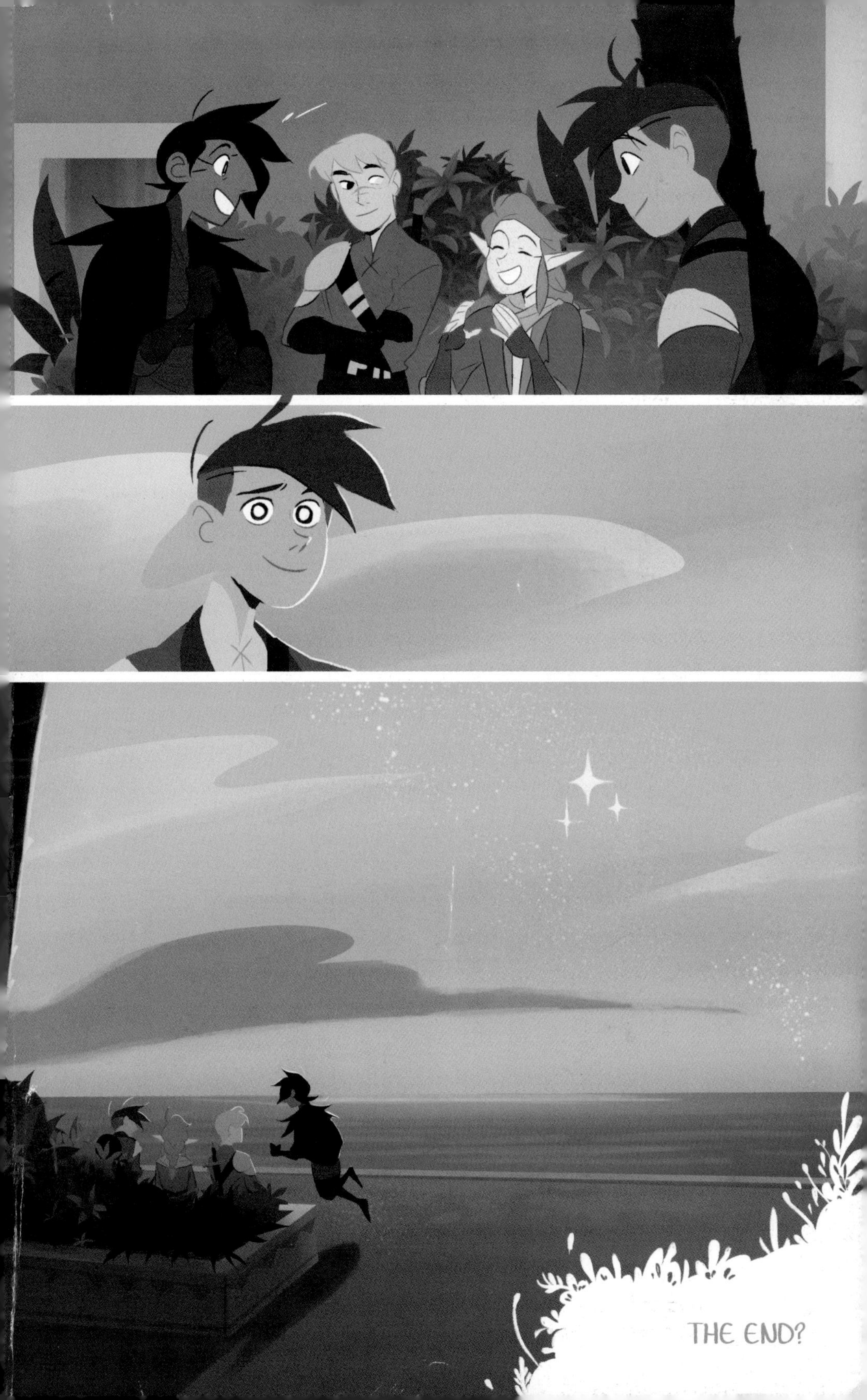
THE END?

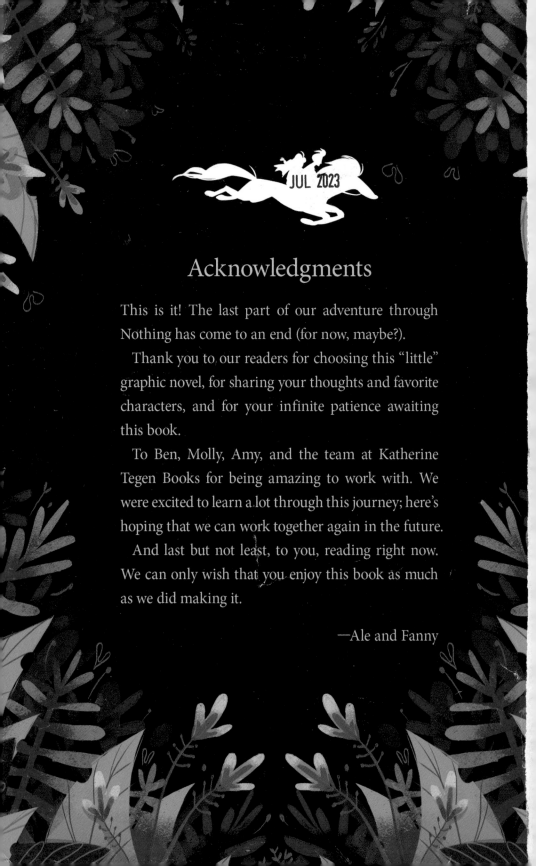

JUL 2023

# Acknowledgments

This is it! The last part of our adventure through Nothing has come to an end (for now, maybe?).

Thank you to our readers for choosing this "little" graphic novel, for sharing your thoughts and favorite characters, and for your infinite patience awaiting this book.

To Ben, Molly, Amy, and the team at Katherine Tegen Books for being amazing to work with. We were excited to learn a lot through this journey; here's hoping that we can work together again in the future.

And last but not least, to you, reading right now. We can only wish that you enjoy this book as much as we did making it.

—Ale and Fanny